M000101267

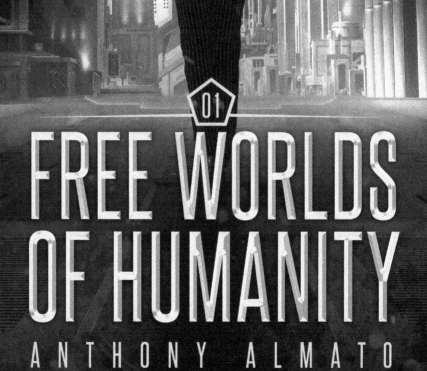

FREE WORLDS
OF HUMANITY

ANTHONY ALMATO

Published by Bearfort Roundtop

ISBN: 978-1-7374580-2-9

Editor: Lesley Jones
Cover design: Jeff Brown Graphics / www.jeffbrowngraphics.com
Map design: Alec McKinley
Interior design & typesetting: Mark Thomas / Coverness.com

Thank you to the people who helped show me the way by assisting
with advice, teaching, and corrections to my writing style:
KJ Kennedy
E.E. Hornburg
Marion Mavis
Eileen Gormley

And a special thanks to Mercedes Lackey, an author who convinced me
to write this book myself instead of handing it off to another.

Keep being you, Mercedes.

We all have a dark side. Inner demons of jealousy, greed, envy, desire, or hate, trying to manifest themselves into physical form. With the right motivation or push to steer personal feelings into actions, we're capable of such terrible things. Some of us have the fortitude to hold our darkest desires at bay, while others lack the willpower to resist temptations.
We all have them, each one of us. I channel mine by writing.

How do you control yours?

Anthony Almato

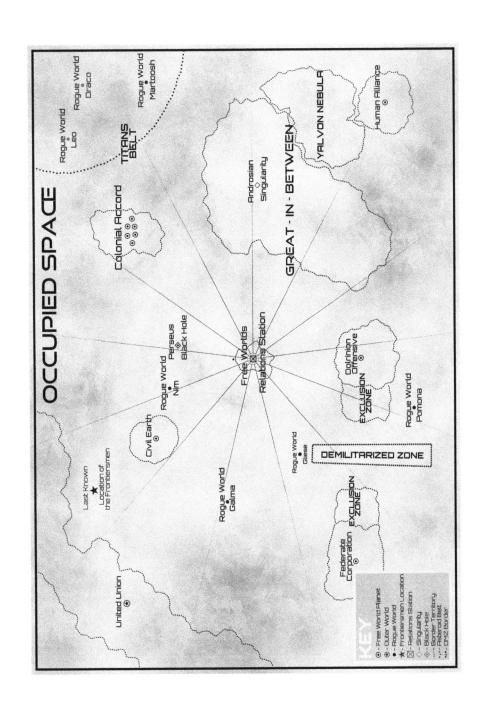

Map of Occupied Space (rotate to view)

CHAPTER 1

Invasion on the Rogue World Gliese

A Dolrinion Offensive Sentinel of the Red Legion

War.

At the thought of that word, my heart raced. Ever since we had left the Great Darkness and saw our future success while touching the memory stone, conquest had been our primary focus. We tried not to interfere with that relations station, but our invasion was unavoidable. Conquer, attack, and expand our Offensive was all that mattered in a sentinel's mind. Duty, valor, and glory to the Offensive.

Around our drop capsule were faces, the hard faces of my brothers and sisters of Force Command Red Legion. We had always been the thick spine that held up our glorious Offensive, tall and proud. Our Legion brigades were at the vanguard, first in and last out of every major engagement since the creation of our command, founded by Supreme General Constantine, the First Champion. I pictured him conquering some of the first worlds for our Offensive, long before the Federates existed.

The Corporation was our greatest adversary for countless years. They had chosen that rogue world to create a new battlefront. They were weak of body but strong of mind with transgressions against our honor that we couldn't ignore. The Legion had received great intelligence on the Federate invasion from Force Command Overwatch, and we would win that day.

My focus returned; we were coming in hard for a landing, and Gliese would feel the power of our Force Command. Our husk commander was sitting across from me, and she made me proud to be a sentinel. The crossbones lining her thick armor chest plate, showing her kills, were a marvel to see. She had one hundred of them, at least. Lieutenant Ballo is a true warrior, and I'd show her my worth and earn a place on the memory stone so that my soul would live forever on Kora, our homeworld.

Flak-cannon fire: the noise was loud outside with crackles and booms exploding so nearby, the percussion through the thick walls of the capsule felt intense. That weapons fire wasn't from the Federates. No, those explosions were coming from the local population of that rogue world, trying to prevent us from landing. A broad smile formed on my face at that thought. A puny world that had only left the Great Darkness within the last few hundred years, and only recently started exploring their stellar system with satellites and landing exploratory ships on their moon. Weak, all of them.

Sentinel Huttner, sitting next to me, nudged my arm and said, "A great landing, my brother. My blood's boiling with anticipation. I want to jump from this pod and kill them all."

The sentinels around our capsule who could hear over the loud noise of landing, shouted with me, echoing, "Duty, valor, and glory to the Offensive!"

Lieutenant Ballo spoke, her voice deep and proud. "These Federate scum think they can invade here to gain an advantage over us. That relations station will sit on their hands while this world falls to us, I swear it to you all."

Another cheer of approval rang out through the capsule. The demilitarized zone, which spanned several light-years across space, contained five uninhabited rogue worlds. They'd already been through what this planet was experiencing at that moment. Those worlds were withering away in complete ruin.

Before the establishment of the DMZ was voted for on the relations station, we invaded those planets, too. Now, Gliese would feel our power, and the Federates trying to gain an advantage over us would regret the day they decided to come here. The planet's native population trying to defend themselves must have known that eventually our fighting would spill onto their world. Gliese was only a few hours' faster-than-light travel outside the demilitarized zone.

I replied to Huttner with approval. "Glorious landing, indeed, sentinel. Another row of crossbones to my battle armor should suit me well."

On my chest plate were confirmed kills from previous battles. There were twenty-two, in rows of ten each, and that made me happy. Another completed row would bring pride to my family.

Lieutenant Ballo called out loudly, "One minute. Be ready." As she spoke, red lights inside the capsule flashed, letting us know we'd land soon. Everything in the capsule shone red from the blinking lights.

The shoulder locks that kept us in our seats released slightly so we could stretch and prepare ourselves. I pulled hard on my neck cover, feeling sweat under the battle armor and inside my helmet. The temperature regulator had not activated yet; it was conserving power for the long fight ahead without the need to recharge my armor. The native population's anti-air fire was increasing, and on the display screen a few of the drop capsules disappeared. Those sentinels died wonderfully, the way all sentinels should die serving the Offensive. The destruction of those husks infuriated me. That the locals thought they could defy us was outrageous. They would pay for that treachery.

A gunnery sergeant who was sitting at the other end of the pod raised his voice to us all. "Sentinels of the Legion. You are the Red Death that puts fear into the hearts of all humanity. Free, outer, and rogue worlds combined know your name and fear you. This day is yours, a red day of death for our enemies. Fight strong, fight hard, and know that you will earn the right to have your name carved onto the memory stone for your celebrated deeds. Duty, valor, and glory to the Offensive!"

We all echoed his call. "Duty, valor, and glory!" The red lights flashed faster, and the pressure of a hard combat landing was upon us. Our husk medium-range spinners fired rapidly, hundreds of rounds at high speed. A rapid clinking behind me came from the wall of empty shells rolling down the side of the capsule, and my heart beat faster.

"We are in it now, my brother and sister sentinels," I said, and my fellow sentinels answered with shouts. There was such adrenaline and excitement in my bones.

The light turned green, and my shoulder locks released. It was time for battle. All sentinels jumped from their seats and stacked up on the door. I was in the middle, with at least a hundred to my front and another hundred to the rear. The huge thick-plated doors opened, and our screams were so loud, supreme generals might have heard them on Kora.

Lieutenant Ballo charged, holding her rifle out in front of her. "The Red Death has come for you all."

We sentinels could perform those duties in our sleep. Whether through drill or combat, a battle charge came instinctively to us and our muscle memory from years of training. I cleared the airlock door and stepped out onto the grass, feeling light on my feet. All other air-breathing worlds of Humanity had lighter gravity compared to Kora. Our gravity was three times stronger, and there on that rogue world, feeling so buoyant, was invigorating. To the left and right in the surrounding area, other capsules had landed successfully, their defenses firing thousands of rounds in different directions. Medium-range spinners, missiles, and mortars fired in succession. It was more intense than any meteor shower in Titans' Belt. More than likely, from the number of projectiles in the air, the husks had already killed hundreds.

There was a hill in front of us so high we couldn't see over the other side—at least forty-five meters. Our Force Command flag carriers charged the hill in a line together, followed by warrior sentinels and commanding officers. The flags blowing in the wind next to each other looked like a red tidal wave of destruction. Bright green-grass hills surrounded us. Trees were in the distance, but around the pods, nothing but grass. The sky was gray, a bleak color, and nothing like the orange and red sky of Kora.

Huttner hit my pauldron and said, "Sentinel, let's move."

We ran up the hill with all the rest. That charging wave of Red Death made me scream out as loud as ever before. The flags danced to beats of the wind, and the mortar rounds fired in succession.

"I am a Red Reaper, bringing death to all."

We cleared the hill; looking through my helmet cover's live-emitting-nano-surveillance I observed Federate Corporation hoppers landing a half-kilometer away. Their operators and enormous battle bots charged in our direction. Those pathetic Federates used robots to fight at their sides during a war. Only people with a fear of facing their enemy would do something so shameful. Through the LENS, a different defensive encampment altogether came into focus about a hundred and eighty meters away: trenches dug in, with machine-gun nests and primitive tanks. We had tanks just like those two thousand years ago. The thought made me laugh out loud. The land surrounding the enemy forces was waterlogged like the outskirts of a swamp as if it had been worked over several times by tanks, troops, and transports moving to and from that area.

Gliese's military forces were puny compared to ours. They shot down some of our drop capsules and would feel our wrath. Their artillery rounds fired. My LENS tracked the incoming ordnance, and fellow sentinels saw them, too. Our automated shoulder weapons would deal with those children's toys. We continued our advance as shoulder rockets at the front of the battle line fired to take out the explosive landing projectiles from the native military.

Our Force Command and regiment flags were still flying high, heading towards the enemy encampment. The natives would drown in red soon. Some of the mortar rounds got past our defenses, and massive explosions thundered around us. Sentinels were dying. Dirt, blood, and ash flew through the air while I continued my charge. We were finally close enough, and I fired my rifle.

Our battle rifles were far superior to the ones held by these pests. Even hiding behind their concrete fortifications and sandbag trenches, they didn't stand a chance against us. I ran faster and got myself to the front line, joining the vanguard of the assault, which made me proud.

Contact.

Launching my body into the air was easy, and because of the low gravity and the power from my battle armor, I leaped at least three meters off the ground. I saw fear in the eyes of the weaklings I looked down on. They wore primitive protective vests and helmets that wouldn't work in space.

I yelled while still in the air, "Now you die, maggots! Red will be the last thing you see on this day."

Bullets came from my weapon with a trigger pull as I landed and crushed one of the enemy soldiers under my battle armor, his bones splitting as my weight came down onto him. The sound of the breaking body and his screams of terror were marvelous to hear. Enemy soldiers stood to my left and right, but their weapons couldn't penetrate legion armor.

"Pathetic," I said, shooting to the left, killing four. The LENS was keeping track of kills so that when the battle ended, the total could be added to my chest-plate crossbones.

Huttner landed to my right, using his armored fists to kill two soldiers. His natural strength caused his punch to go through the soldier's head and out of the back of his skull. We Dolrinions had to look up at most other races in occupied space because of our short stature, under a meter and a half, but our strength was far greater than theirs. Our homeworld's gravity had stunted our height after thousands of years living there, but that same gravity made us physically stronger than others.

"Splendid entry into the fight."

Huttner bellowed, laughing, and turned toward a loud explosion.

A massive anti-personnel drummer fired round after round in the direction of our main battle line. The smell of gunpowder surrounded us and the dirt beneath me rattled with each bright flash. The percussion was so intense, the air rippled around the weapon; the spring-action release lifted on both sides while the empty shells fell to the ground. Red legionnaires were dying because of that weapon; it was a Free Worlds' military weapon platform, not the primitive armaments we had seen so far. They must have acquired it somehow, gearing up for a fight. At least two flag carriers were blown to bits and dropped their standards along with other frontline sentinels, whose bodies littered the ground like winter's first snowfall.

Huttner and I ran through this trench, firing our weapons at the local defending primitives. Our wide bodies made moving through the trench difficult—these people were not as broad as us—especially while wearing battle armor. When we could go no farther, we leaped out of the trench, moving in the direction of the mounted anti-personnel drummer still shooting. The spent shell casings falling from the release springs were at least sixty centimeters long, and the explosions dealt great devastation to our battle line.

We were finally close enough; I racked a round into my grenade launcher and fired it at the drummer, Huttner's shoulder rockets engaging too. Within a blink of an eye, the weapon and its shooters were eviscerated. It erupted like a volcano.

"Magnificent death," I said gleefully as the stacked drummer rounds nearby exploded. Native forces died in high numbers from those explosions. My LENS would have trouble keeping count.

Huttner raised his voice. "Death by their own weapon."

We had to pick up the two flags on the ground to continue the charge. Only the Red Legion Force Command charge in battle; our fellow Dolrinions from other commands didn't perform that act of bravery on a battlefield. It was the red blitz, and typically overwhelmed enemies before a defensive setup or counterattack occurred. Our regiment battle flags were critical to a charge. Good: both flags were in the hands of sentinels, and those carrying them charged to the front of the battle line.

Over my shoulder, the Corporation filth were landing in their hopper ships.

"Sentinel, look, they're already here," I said to Huttner.

He smiled. "Great. They're in a hurry to die, I see."

Our vanguard blitz line advanced far past us, charging straight at the Corporation operators and their disgraceful battle bots.

My LENS tracked ten primitive combustion-engine military jets flying right at the front line. They were going to try to attack both sides as they met. The LENS recorded data and sent it to the command-and-control ships above in orbit over the planet. Before those simple jets could reach us, intensely bright flashes like lightning in the upper atmosphere fired high-caliber rounds at the aircraft and struck down at least half of them. It was illegal, per the relations station, for any Free World to use orbital bombardment on another Free Worlds soul. Rogue worlds didn't count in that law, which was why we were able to take them out. Our primary battle groups were too busy engaging the Federate fleets to worry about firing on their ground forces anyway.

We'd deal with the ground forces with ease. The front line fired their rifles; grenades, rockets, and high-powered railguns opened up from the first hill we charged. The Federates fired back and, to my surprise, continued coming right at us. They still hadn't learned, after all these years, that they couldn't hope to survive a charge from the Red Death.

Both lines met, and the sound of metal-on-metal echoing through the entire field of battle was deafening. Federate operators fired rifles, swung bladed weapons, and some even used their fists. They were pitiful. Enormous battle bots shot various armaments, also using their considerable physical strength to crush some of my fellow sentinels.

We sprinted to join the fighting already in progress. Lieutenant Ballo joined us, screaming with delight as she charged with our regimental battle flag carried next to her by another sentinel.

"Bayonets," she yelled to all running with her.

Heavy thirty-centimeter-long blades extended from the bottoms of our rifles. Lieutenant Ballo's screams encouraged me to run even faster.

She shouted while firing her shoulder rockets at the enemy soldiers. "I'm the harbinger of death, come to claim my reward. Die now, die now, you Federate filth!"

Her valor and screams were astonishing to witness as she ran right at Federate operators without hesitation. As a true warrior, I planned to make her proud of my performance. I charged ahead, faster than her and Huttner.

A battle bot was before me, smashing sentinels under its motorized legs as thick as tree trunks. It turned to me and raised a massive limb.

From a slide release on my armor, I activated a reverse-gravity grenade. That technology was rare among the Free Worlds, utilizing Old World knowledge, hard to duplicate. A large bubble formed, shielding my body from incoming bullets and the metal leg.

The battle bot tried to step on me, but the clear rounded bubble pushed all incoming force away. It lasted only for a few seconds and then disappeared. The bot stumbled and that was the time to scale its leg. At the top, its cover platform housing most of the weapons systems was vulnerable. Sentinels attempted to shoot the bot from underneath, with little success. Bot armor was too strong for our rifles. My fingers dug into the top cover; I pulled with all my might. It was difficult to remove and required much strength. My arms shook, and my armor strained audibly. Finally, the sealed cover came off; beneath, internal systems glittered with small pulsing lights and wires. I pulled an explosive grenade and dropped it inside.

Raising my arms high, I screamed, "Sentinels, witness me and behold my victory," then leaped as far away as possible while the upper part of the Federate battle bot exploded into countless shards.

Cheers erupted, but the landscape littered with dead bodies from both sides on the muddied ground overshadowed the excitement. The flag carrier for our regiment had fallen again, and this time I took the flag in my hands. The rubble from the bot just destroyed was before me, and I felt even more boldness than before.

Gears from my battle armor rolled with each step up the pile of debris and a smile took hold of me. I stood at least three meters above the ground with the battle flag waving in the wind. That would rally our sentinels. The flag towered over me by another meter and a half, at least. Fellow sentinels, including commanding officers, screamed proudly, seeing me standing there. A few bullets from Federate weapons struck, and there was pain from rounds that penetrated the armor.

"Bug bites," I said, leaping to the ground and continuing the charge with my battle regiment flag held high.

Blood, mud, and soot had darkened the flag, which was good. Those standards should always appear that way. My heart raced to see such numbers of sentinels following the flag in my hands.

The LENS on my helmet display alerted me to the hill about three hundred sixty meters to the right. The native military came over the top in large numbers and fired rounds at both sides of the battle. Dozens upon dozens of primitive tanks shot nearly simultaneously, and the Federate battle bots returned fire at the hill, destroying most of the forces there. Tank rounds landed, striking without prejudice, killing Federate Corporation and Dolrinions alike. Those archaic rounds wouldn't prevent our victory on that day.

Out of nowhere, there was a flash, and I was down. Gazing at the surroundings made me realize I had moved at least nine meters from my previous location. My regiment battle flag was no longer in my hands. I tried to stand but couldn't. What had happened to me?

The battle flag was to my left on the ground. A fellow sentinel picked up the standard and charged on. Huttner was gone. Where did he go? After peering around in confusion, I looked along my body. From just above my knees down, there was nothing. There was an overwhelming metallic taste in my mouth. A deep cough took hold of me and I tasted blood—there had to be internal damage to my organs. That explosion took my legs. The battle armor administered pain suppression and antibiotics automatically, but that didn't matter. It was too late.

Lieutenant Ballo appeared above me. She leaned down and grabbed my hand, saying, "A glorious death, sentinel. I witnessed your duty, and because of your valor in the battle, you shall receive the glory that all Dolrinions yearn for. Rest easy and know that I will personally see to it that your name is etched onto the memory stone so that your soul may live forever."

I took a deep breath in and said, "Duty, valor, and glory to the Offensive." Those would be the last words ever spoken out loud from me, and I spoke them proudly.

On that rogue world of Gliese, I would die, but that death would be superb and it gave me satisfaction to know that I'd go to the memory stone with the most renowned sentinels of our past. Civil Earth, Colonial Accord, Human Alliance, and this Federate Corporation would tremble when they heard my story. All five recognized Free Worlds governments and that relations station will know my name from the day's deeds. I will be remembered …

CHAPTER 2

A Free Worlds representative
of the relations station

Statements given six months prior during private donor
fundraising event in Warwick on Uropa.

"*H*umanity.

    A simple word with such complexity in its meaning for our species and history throughout all occupied space. For the Free Worlds, the name is more than a simple word of eight letters. Each character should carry a thousand phrases within that would better explain what it means to be one of us. From every free, outer, and rogue world combined across all occupied space, our story is long, full of hardship and depth, because it took us so long to leave the Great Darkness.

    If I asked each of the five Free Worlds' governing societies what humanity meant to them, the answers would garner such different responses.

    Civil Earth, Colonial Accord, Dolrinion Offensive, Human Alliance, and the Federate Corporation all represent our governing Free Worlds of Humanity on the relations station, and all still try to do everything in their power to gain an advantage over one another inside the five walls of the Capitol Forum. Each wall representing one of the governing bodies is like a massive domino thousands of kilometers high, leaning slightly one way or the other from changing events. In the shadows below each piece are billions of people. Should one end of the domino or the other collapse, all beneath will perish under the crushing weight and affect each other piece in turn.

We need each other more than any of the fourteen other representatives inside the Capitol Forum realize, and it is we who control which way the domino leans. Our humanity spans hundreds of natural and artificial planets with all their inhabitants living in the shadows of the Free Worlds' authority. All of it is within my control. With your donation funds, I can continue to ensure our union, the Twenty-Third Entente, controls everything. Besides, I prefer chess over dominos anyway."

Representative Henry McWright
Labor Party leader
Union wielder of the Hammer of Labor

The start of a historic day (Henry)

Aly kissed me and put her head against my thigh in all her nakedness. She was younger than me by twenty-four years. The unions and political rivals across the Accord had given me grief about our age difference over the years. Obviously, they were wrong. I smiled down at her.

She lowered her eyebrows. "What?"

"The Hammer of Labor doesn't work without a handle."

Alyssa laughed. "Come again?"

"I was thinking how lucky I am to have you. Labor Party leadership told me before we met that 'The wielder of our Hammer of Labor doesn't work without a handle', and that I needed to remarry to ensure I came across the right way with the Party."

She curled her lip up to a half-smile. "They were right. Besides, the handle is always stronger than the hammer, or it would break."

"Hah—is that you, my love? Are you the handle?"

"That I am, Henry."

Alyssa turned the TV on. The Free Worlds' twenty-four-hour news showed a newscaster talking about my speech tonight for open session. It happened every week; however, the live broadcasts were always localized and didn't display on prime networks. My statements for that night would be the first live cast in nearly two years.

"Colonial Accord Representative McWright will speak tonight live with dignitaries present from all Free Worlds, and even members of the United Union Royal Family are here."

A video clip showing Alyssa and me at a fundraising event months past, on my homeworld Uropa, was on the screen.

"Tonight's speech doesn't come without controversy. Inside sources claim McWright pushed himself to the top choice through aggressive persuasion and strong-arming other representatives. Right Seat Representative JJ Richmond from the Accord, who represents Rose Party of Ardum's interests, said, 'Anyone who hasn't lived on his homeworld for twenty-two years shouldn't be representing its constituents.'"

Richmond was talking to reporters while walking down the golden road from the Capitol Forum under the dome.

"It's time for McWright to give up the Hammer of Labor for someone else to lead. He's been in public office for thirty-four years with a distinguished career, but the time has come."

He turned and looked into the camera as if he were speaking directly to me. "Henry, it's time. Enjoy your golden years. You can stay up here on the station you love so much for all I care."

Interesting that he chose to walk the golden road through the busy streets when we had private entryways in and out of the forum. All for theater.

Alyssa frowned and tightened her shoulders as if she was preparing to fight someone. "It sounds like he's threatening you."

She was the most beautiful woman in our Colonial bubble, maybe the main cylinder too, and fit my personality better than my last wife. Alyssa was confident and knew that her last name brought a level of authority on the station, but that didn't take away from her naturally outgoing and commanding personality.

Aly glanced at me from the bed with her lip pulled back as we made eye contact. It made my heart race, and I wanted to go again, but we couldn't. Maybe my age was getting the best of me. In my youth, I could have done that all morning, gone to political rallies, donated camera time with the less fortunate, and given a crucial speech without a second thought.

The segment continued. "Representative McWright's speech focuses on Free Worlds union issues. Given his experience with his homeworld's unions, his bill concentrates on increased workers' rights. However, our specialists and even some representatives believe those concerns ignore the renewed fighting between the Dolrinion Offensive and Federate Corporation on Gliese, a rogue world near the DMZ."

On my end table was the speech written on numerous pages with corrections and crossed-out words. I'd revised it countless times, and it was now unreadable hieroglyphs from the Old World. My ears warmed with growing anger.

The voice gained my attention again. "Officials with the provisional government of our main cylinder are siding with Representative McWright because of last month's explosion inside the lower dock. Inspectors from station command found dozens of violations of safety protocols. Union leaders reached out for assistance to the Labor Party and, although their jurisdiction doesn't stretch this far, resources and time went into bringing these concerns to light."

I exhaled loudly and chuckled. Alyssa raised an eyebrow in my direction. She tilted her head and narrowed both eyes, so I spoke.

"The other Free Worlds unions worship the ground our Labor Party walks on. I laughed because they have no real political power or ability to control society as our Labor Unions do."

"Well, of course they don't. We were the only Free World to see the power of unions and use them as a political weapon. But ..." She paused, contemplating her next sentence. "The Roses also control nearly as much political power in the Accord."

Aly knew my feelings towards Ardum and their Rose. Even hearing their name irritated me. I turned back to the television.

She pulled her hand away and asked, "What are you going to do about JJ?"

I sighed. "He challenged me openly." I spoke louder. "Me, the center seat representative of our Colonial wall. It makes us look weak. If the other representatives smelled blood, it would be like a fox in the henhouse."

Alyssa hesitated and frowned. "Things are more sensitive because of Gliese." Her next word came as a jape. "Dolrinions."

"Yes. The fifteen inside the pentagon are paranoid enough without anything adding fuel to the fire. JJ Richmond's been a representative for seven years, and there's no way I could ever get along with him. Rose Party elitist hothead. The Thorns of Ardum and its supporters are all the same."

"The Roses have been our rivals for thousands of years, love."

"Everyone is at each other's throats. The dominos are swaying."

"Dominos?" Alyssa asked.

"Never mind."

Fellow representatives constantly pointed fingers, blaming others for the things wrong in occupied space, more kindling for the fire. We could rant all day about those issues, but I'd miss my speech tonight. Station command did its best to keep the peace in the main cylinder when citizens from Free Worlds brought their problems with them like traveling baggage. I was irritated.

"Change channel, one up."

I stood, grabbed my wrinkled chicken-scratch pieces of paper from the end table, and walked into the bathroom while sporting highlights of the latest power-ball games echoed through the room. Goose bumps formed in the chill of my nakedness.

"You've revised that speech so many times. I'm sure it's great, Henry."

Alyssa was still on the bed. Seeing her there naked made my heart pump faster again.

"Benjamin will be here soon. Put some clothes on."

She always had a flirtatious and outgoing personality, but compared to other attractive women, Alyssa sometimes gave the wrong impression. She puffed her lips up in a face of sarcastic mockery, and I returned a silly grin. Our bedroom was the only safe place to act in the same way.

My closet was full of suits. They were the best money could buy, blended fabrics and skins from across occupied space. Slim-cut suits fitted my shape well, and I always had a vest with my hanging chain, our Hammer of Labor ornament, swinging on the inner lining.

Alyssa stood, came to me, and straightened my Twenty-Third Entente pin, strongest of all Labor Party unions, followed by the pentagon golden pin above.

"Do you ever grow tired of wearing those suits, love? Even on your days off, you always dress to impress."

I held my chin high, and replied, "Always dress in your suit of armor before stepping into the battlefield of station politics."

Our bedroom had several entrances, and a high open ceiling with an upper catwalk to my office that overlooked the room. At one end, near my closet, was a spiral staircase down to the kitchen and lounge. By tradition, I should have left that apartment after being elected as a representative since it was the ambassador's official housing. I didn't give it up, and the new bubble head, who was timid, had another apartment built.

At the bottom of the spiral stairs, my Capitol Security lead officer stood guard.

"Good morning, Oliver."

How much of Alyssa and me did he hear? Fast thrumming bass music was blaring from upstairs, and she started singing as Ollie nodded. Josue was beyond the kitchen down the hall, standing near the foyer lift door. My trust for them came from years of loyal service. Zoey was out on the terrace, and she did well keeping Alyssa safe.

"Good morning, Josue."

The easiest part of that day would be breakfast. It was the real stuff most days, but there was no time to waste, so bland tasting sustenance would do. I swiped left through the artificial dispenser and picked raspberry tacks and blended eggs, a fancy name for fake eggs of the wrong color.

After a few bites of food, I cleared my throat and read part of the speech out loud. "We of the Free Worlds are free. Free to make our own choices, whether they're for the betterment of all humanity or they plunge us back into the Great Darkness. I believe with every fiber of my being that with these small revisions to union labor laws under article nine of the Free Worlds' Relations Policy, all middle-class citizens of the Free Worlds would have more protection and added income for the betterment of their family and lifestyle."

Below that sentence were my listed revisions to the laws. Of course, the Dolrinions didn't have unions, so I didn't think they'd be hard to convince. I tapped on the table, crossed out more words, and revised sentences to make my hieroglyph scrabble even more illegible.

Oliver touched his earpiece and spoke, "The lobby officer notified that Benjamin's on his way up, sir."

"Great. Thank you, Ollie."

Oliver hesitated. "Your speech sounds great."

I smiled. "I will never forget where I come from, Ollie. My father taught me that when I was young, and it stuck with me."

That man taught me things that I couldn't discuss unless behind a closed door, and the most important of all was keeping certain things buried in the recesses of my mind.

"I know the hardships of working-class people. That's why I made you my primary focus in politics."

Oliver seemed satisfied with my comments. He'd never smile, but body language gave him away. He returned to a position of attention. Benjamin arrived with a smile full of energy. He was a tall lad, light skin and dark hair, attractive, confident, and loyal. Ben had spent the last five years with me and would have a successful political union career in Warwick one day.

"Good morning, sir." His tone was one of eager youthfulness. He was under thirty. I was sure of that.

"You don't need to *sir* me when no one's around. I must remind you every week."

"Sorry, sir, I mean, sorry. Old habits, you know."

He looked at the crumpled papers. "The speechwriters completed a draft for you. Do you want to review it?"

That was the third or fourth time he'd suggested using a prewritten speech.

"I'm a politician from a different time. Something this important should come from my hands."

"The first part of today should be easy enough. Malcolm thinks it will boost public morale, seeing you with schoolchildren."

Benjamin was jealous of my chief of staff. He'd been with me for twenty years and did things behind the curtain to achieve my goals.

"How's your father doing?"

"He's good. A few nights ago, I talked to him, and he told me to say, 'Tell Knuckles I said hi.' Dad laughed when he said it."

I grinned. "Your dad gave me that nickname when we were young. I fought often, won most, but not always."

Ben should only have had one year left with me before he needed to return to Warwick on Uropa. That was the deal worked out with Chip. Everything was going fine until last year. For whatever reason, he decided to stay with me permanently. Maybe he wanted Malcolm's job. That would never happen.

"Is everything prepared for after the school visit?"

Ben pulled his lips in tight. "All the union leaders will be there for you with nearly two hundred workers. There's still blast burns in that dock from the explosion."

"Good, that will add more drama to our rally. Those weaker Free Worlds unions look up to our Labor Party. We need to appear as they expect us to."

"It's all in disarray," Benjamin said, "because of the union's dispute with management over those deaths."

"The lower docks are a dangerous place to work. Those two substances shouldn't have been in the same container together. It was the damn rock smackers in the belt. They couldn't care less and didn't pay attention."

The dock was on the opposite side of the station, and using regular interior tubes would be a full day's travel. My transport ship was in for maintenance, so I'd have to use one of our capital ships, for which my fellow representatives would give me grief.

"Representative Stavish's aide sent me a location for your minutes meeting. Eatontown Avenue Café, near the cathedral."

Mia Stavish had been a Civil Earth representative for the last eleven years and was a total goliath inside the Capitol Forum. She could be my closest ally or second-most bitter enemy depending on that month's session discussions. Her support was critical for my proposed bill, and she was the reason for those infinite changes.

The newscaster on the television earlier wasn't wrong. It had taken lots of coaxing to get the votes for my speech. She didn't talk about the bribes to some, threats to others, and favors called in. Without Mia's help, carefully moving the chess pieces, tonight's speech wouldn't have been possible. She asked for revisions, and I obliged, to a degree. Paying to play was the normal way under the dome. To public eyes, it was nothing but smiles and handshaking, while behind the curtain, we were slitting each other's throats for desired results. Mia was playing games; she knew I ate at Eatontown's main avenue last month, and none of her actions was without purpose.

"Are we still on for my meeting with Ficco?" The senior agent would probably complain about Nicolas Nomikos who would be sitting in to represent station command at the next Guild council meeting.

Ben scrolled through his personal display device before replying, "Yes, Malcolm confirmed and said he would meet us at the cathedral. The senior agent will be at Academy Hall all day."

I'd spent years grooming Ficco for command and nodded my head. "Did Chief Ashton retire today?"

Benjamin laughed, understanding my sarcasm. "No, sorry, not today.

She's still the most senior of the five chiefs of the cathedral."

"Ficco will be her replacement. I'll see to that. She doesn't want Ficco to replace her and knows he's my candidate for the position. The woman is delaying her retirement, holding out with hopes I'll get voted out of office. I didn't spend the last seventeen years grooming him to fail." We accomplished too much behind the curtain together. "I won't allow a bitter old badge to defeat us. We're at the end of the month. Who am I missing for minutes meetings?"

Benjamin frowned, and I already knew the answer to my question. "When we get back to the dome, you'll have some time for yourself, but ..." He paused. "You and Representative Richmond aren't caught up for the month." Ben glanced at his PDD again. "He's not available until after six o'clock, an hour before your speech. I can't bump it—"

"Nor should you, lad. How would it look if the Accord's center seat missed required monthly minutes with his right seat of the same wall? I'll meet with him and let his antagonistic words go in one ear and out the other. JJ will try to shake me up like he always does. It's a packed day, just the way I like it."

Alyssa came down the spiral staircase singing away for all to hear with wet hair from a shower—and, of course, she hadn't listened; she was wearing a loose-fitting silk robe. It wasn't long enough for my liking. Not with Benjamin and Oliver standing there. She shuffled across the kitchen floor, still singing.

Oliver and Benjamin tried averting their eyes, and I hoped it was with modesty as both said good morning. Benjamin might have side-eyed her longer than appreciated, but I wouldn't hold it against him. She did these things on purpose and enjoyed the attention. As a younger man, it would've enraged me, but I'd learned much through the years. Aly leaned on the center island across from me, shimmying from side to side to her own music so her robe waved back and forth. She wore her flirtatious smile of confidence.

"What are your plans today, love?" I attempted to keep my tone level without giving any hint of frustration. I was angrier with JJ, but her short robe bothered me.

21

She sang a few more lines to the loud music still playing upstairs before answering. "Breakfast with the girls, class at the gym, and later, I'm going to buy a new dress for tonight."

The girls were women of varying ages in the upper class of our Colonial bubble, one of whom was the current ambassador's wife, a mildly attractive woman. The girls got together several times a week socially and formally, depending on the month. Alyssa was the youngest but commanded the most respect.

I was agitated. "You didn't dress as I asked you to."

Alyssa raised an eyebrow and pursed her lips. "It's my house too, Henry. Don't worry, love. These strapping men have more respect than to stare at me in my kitchen."

I rubbed my temple; a headache was forming. "It is your house too. The day's politics are to blame."

She leaned in and kissed my cheek gently. Ben was across the kitchen, scrolling through his PDD, and he glanced up in our direction quickly before burying his eyes back to the screen. He could probably see her rear under the short-fitting robe.

After pulling away and clearing my throat, I said, "It's time, Benjamin, let's get this day started."

Ben looked away from Alyssa and moved to the foyer. "Yes, sir."

Aly chuckled under her breath, poured a cup of tea, and started up the staircase. Zoey, with her ever-solid somber glare—she rarely changed her expression—came from the back terrace and took a position in the kitchen. She was an overachiever with Capitol Security and never left Alyssa's side. Another security officer would join us in the lobby, but he was new. What was his name again?

We walked to the lift and my mind trailed off into numerous thoughts. My endless preparation for that speech including every written version was seared into my brain. It took such an effort to get through closed session, but there was still no guarantee that I'd get it passed on the floor of open session. Nothing inside the forum or the station was ever guaranteed. Although the speech was less than half a day away, things could go drastically wrong in an instant, and all my efforts would be for nothing.

I had no choice but to hold firm on my battle line and do everything I could to ensure victory. JJ wasn't strong enough …

Strange, was I questioning myself or making a statement? I couldn't be entirely sure.

CHAPTER 3

Civil Earth
Surviving on the Surface

There is no caste system on the surface (Kathryn)

D eath.
That was the most common word on the surface of Civil Earth, and it happened so frequently. Breathing the yellow haze was the worst part.

I felt a headache forming. The sharp pain made me squeeze my eyes tight. I heard power tools outside in the distance—engineers doing whatever it was they did. Probably another failed exterior air vent. They woke me most mornings that way. The workers did it on purpose. I knew it.

Peeking through a crack in the wall, I saw that the haze was extra potent as my stomach growled. I was so hungry and looked at my wrist. A memory came to me of my first day outside all those years ago when the tin suits threw me through the airlock.

"Hey, girl! Come here."

"No," I replied, cowering away in fear.

He grabbed my wrist and yanked it closer to him. Seeing my watch, he narrowed his eyes with a grin. "Give it here, bitch!"

I cried. Why wouldn't I? What ten-year-old wouldn't? He punched me and took the watch. Seven years later, I was grateful. If it had been one of the gangs, they would have killed me.

Sadness found me a few days later.

I was alone, crying in the thick yellow haze. He came from behind. Sadness was so quiet I didn't hear him sneak up on me over my tears. I realized he was there when his looming shadow blanketed over me. What did I know about living in the most hostile areas of Civil Earth, outside on the surface?

He stared at me for some time with pure focus before breaking his silence. I didn't realize how dangerous it was at that time to be face to face with a stranger on the surface.

"Are you alone, child?"

I remember rubbing the tears and dirt from my face before nodding my head. I was too scared at ten years old to speak to him. It would have been overwhelming for anyone.

He peered into the distant streets of the megastructures and endless red mud and yellow haze. When his eyes came back to mine, he spoke. "You have two choices. You can turn back and go in that direction on your own." He paused as I looked into the distance. "Or you can come with me and learn how to survive these unforgiving streets."

I glanced at him and down the street several times then slowly reached my hand to his. The two years I spent with Sadness were my earliest memories, and I tried to keep them fresh in my mind. Without him, I would've died.

My attention came back to a tight neck from sleeping on sandbags from the old collapsed dam. Sadness had told me that the year after the flood was the hardest year of surface life in our megacity's history.

I groaned as I stood and took a few moments to stretch my back and legs. They were so stiff. My daily wake-up coughing fit started. The haze poisoned our lungs over time, and the phlegm, blood, and soreness in my throat was a reminder of that. I couldn't do anything about it. The tin suits wouldn't let me back inside.

It was time to find some food. I pulled out a small rusted pocketknife

I had found embedded in a teen girl's wrist not long ago. She was alone and still had her belongings, which indicated that she had killed herself. If another had taken her life, they wouldn't have left her with things. That was how I knew. I did what Sadness taught me and took it all. There wasn't a point in abandoning it. The dead needed nothing.

My stomach growled again, that time so loud, I cradled my belly with both hands. It was time to hunt some sewer moles. My fierce protector had taught me how to find them.

I sat on the wet muddy ground and fastened the knife to the end of a metal utility rod stolen from a city worksite last year.

A noise outside my broken-down shed. I froze. What was that? It sounded like voices. I heard their cough. It couldn't be Johnathan. He was collecting water from an air handler at the eastern square. Those voices weren't his.

My grip tightened on the pole and I glanced at the knife. Why did I have to be seventeen? My age made me more cautious. The gangs looked at me like a wild animal that needed to be put down, and others had tried before, thinking I was nothing more than a victim. They always tried and always failed.

Sadness taught me how to fight.

He always said, "No one will match you with this training. I promise you that, child. The key is to practice every day."

I loved seeing Johnathan's face as I trained. He would watch me and smile.

The sounds were louder. Whoever was outside my shed was closer. I quickly gathered my things and climbed the rafters, hiding behind some plywood. Their coughing echoed through the shed from outside. Quiet, Kat. Breathe slow, and don't cough. My hands were sweating as I squeezed the spear. The door scraped open. Stepping feet soaked in wet mud made squishing sounds. There were two, maybe three. I couldn't be sure.

"We're wasting time, man. There's nothing here. Let's get to the eastern square before that handler turns off for the day. It leaks more than the other ones, and I'm thirsty."

He sounded around my age, and that helped my odds.

"Shut your mouth if you know what's good for you, or I'll shut it when I break your jaw."

The second voice was deeper, snapping with authority, and pierced through the shed so I knew he was a large man.

"Look, here, some sandbags. We can use these for something. Grab 'em, boys, and let's go."

Shit. They took the sandbags and left. It was more comfortable sleeping on those than the wet ground or this plywood. Damn it. Those sacks were mine. A few minutes passed, and I climbed down. Alone again, the way I liked it.

My cough returned with a thick glob of mucus in my throat. After spitting it out, I opened my eyes wide. Wait! They said they were going to the eastern air handler. He was there, all alone. He wasn't good at defending himself, and the noise of that machinery would make it harder to hear them coming. Without me there to help him, they would kill Johnathan.

I felt the thumping in my chest. He was the only person I had talked to since Sadness died. It was hard admitting it, but I cared deeply for Johnathan.

A loud creak came as I slowly opened the door, looking left and right to ensure no one was nearby. After a moment of staring through the haze and listening, I broke free of the shed and ran east, towards the sun. They'd be slow, carrying the heavy bags. My chest burned slightly as I took a deep breath and exhaled, running faster.

It was so dangerous to travel through the streets of our city line like this. I knew it but didn't have a choice. Getting stuck between two megastructures was like being trapped in a room with no exit. I looked over my shoulder as building thirty-three disappeared into the haze as if it had stepped behind a hanging sheet.

At the next corner, three outlined shadows appeared. They were talking; from the voices, it was them, out in the open, between buildings and still headed for the eastern square, but traveling slow.

I followed a street, moving parallel with the thieves. Eventually, sharp jagged rocks pushed through the yellow. It was the eastern square, named for the Old World ruins of crumbling stone walls.

Even with time against me, I couldn't help but wonder what that place looked like all those thousands of years ago, before the megacities. Before the caste system, and before Civil Earth became civil under the Cloud Walkers.

Sadness told me people from before the Great Darkness were superior to us and that they looked up to giants called Titans standing two point seven meters tall, who taught us how to use advanced technology, but how would we know? There wasn't anything left to prove what Sadness had told me besides those old decaying ruins. One of the ancient walls had a doorway that was taller than any I'd seen before; that part was true.

Johnathan believed in flying cities, disappearing stars, and giant space whales that lived in some nebula at the other side of occupied space. For me, belief in things only came from what I could see.

I heard the rumbling of a megastructure's broken air handler, the one Johnathan was coming to get water from. A beam of sunlight punched through the thick yellow and lit the area better than I'd seen in years. After an instant, the light was gone. I cautiously followed one crumbling pile of stone to the next as the air-handler buzzing grew louder and overwhelmed my ears.

I didn't see Johnathan. There was dried blood on a piece of stone that pushed up like a jagged knife through the soggy mud, and I gasped. The bloodstain was shaped like a handprint.

Was that Johnathan?

There were specks of blood like a trail of breadcrumbs leading from one stone ridge lining to the next. At last, I saw a body and rolled it over. Johnathan! He was breathing.

"Wake up, Johnathan. Wake up now," I shouted.

He moved his head to the left and groaned. The ones who stole from me would be here soon. I pulled on Johnathan's shirt and slapped his face. "Wake up!"

He opened his eyes and looked at me, tears overwhelming him. When he focused, a slight smile arched from one side of his face.

"What took you so long, Kathryn?"

I felt warmth on my face and butterflies in my stomach.

"You know I prefer you calling me Kat."

"Yeah, but your full name is better."

He carefully sat up with my help and leaned against the rough decaying stone.

"What happened to you?" I asked. "Why are you bleeding?"

He held his blood-soaked head and grumbled again, showing signs of extreme pain with a frown.

"I was gathering water ... Rockland gang members came at me from behind the wall. They beat me up and thought I'd die from the hit to my head. I lost all my stuff. When I woke up, you were here."

Johnathan raised his eyes to mine and smiled. It made my heart flutter.

"We have to go. Others are coming, and they already stole from me at the shed. Let's go."

I helped him stand by supporting his weight and he groaned louder and held his head. They hit him hard. We took a few steps, the wet mud sucking at our feet. It was hard moving like that, and we only made it a few meters before Johnathan collapsed and passed out again. I heard faint voices in the distance. It was them. Johnathan was unconscious and too heavy to move alone. There was no choice but to fight. I thought again of Sadness.

Sadness said, "Surprising stronger enemies is a powerful tool. There's always a way to win with the element of surprise."

My focus returned; nearby was a nine-meter stone wall to hide behind so they wouldn't see me. I had fought like that numerous times throughout the years. Experience was a powerful weapon in itself, and I had to move with precision. I walked along the wall to the far side, where missing bricks allowed me to see the three thieves for the first time as they came through the haze.

They had cut armbands made from tube socks on their left arms, which meant only one thing. BreakNeck Boys, the misfits who were either never allowed into or were thrown out of the more common surface gangs within the city line. BreakNeck Boys were the lowest of the low, and I had seen them do terrible things to people.

The youngest-looking one ran up to the dripping water from the air handler and pulled a bucket from his pack to collect the steady drops.

"I'll get the water," he said excitedly.

The biggest of the three spoke fast. "Get it already, we don't have all day. Rockland comes here often, and if they catch us, we will have one hell of a fight on our hands."

As the youngest one filled his cracked bucket with water, the other two scurried about scavenging for anything they could use. That was something we all did out here. Utilize everything at your disposal, no matter what it was. They hadn't found Johnathan yet, and hopefully, they'd collect their water and leave.

A third voice spoke, wheezing for air. "My arms feel like jello, man."

"Shut your trap and look over here. It's a dead one, probably taken out by them Rockland punks."

They'd found Johnathan. My heart was racing. It was time to make a move.

The tired boy said, "He's breathing."

At the crumbling wall end, I peeked my head around where the younger BreakNeck Boy held his bucket up, collecting the drips of water. He didn't see me because all three were facing Johnathan.

The bucket holder yelled over the air-handler noise. "Just kill him already. I want his shirt."

Hearing those words made me clench my hands and tighten my jaw. The tired feeling in my legs was gone; the hunger in my stomach had vanished. There was nothing but strength through my body to do what was necessary. The older man pulled a long shiny knife from his waistband. It had a brown handle and wasn't as rusted as the blade fastened to my spear.

There wasn't time to waste. It had to end before they killed Johnathan. The air handler rumbling would cover my approach. Each swift step towards the young one holding the bucket came with nerves, wondering if he'd turn and see me. That didn't happen. The rusted blade found its mark. I lunged forward, thrusting accurately. It took more force than usual to penetrate his skin and bone because the knife was dull. I pulled the blade back from the dead center of his neck just under the head, and he let out a soft screech before falling instantly lifeless. His body soaked into the reddish-brown mud like a leaf slowly sinking into water. The bucket landed face up with the drips of water tumbling inside—one down, two to go. The odds were improving.

Sadness's voice was in my head. "Make sure they're dead before moving on."

I glared at his body beneath my feet. His face was already being swallowed into the mud. I looked back up and got the chills; the hair on my neck raised. The other two standing near Johnathan were staring at me.

The one with heavier eyes from exhaustion said, "She's alone and not wearing Rockland gang colors."

Jonathan's chest was rising and falling. He was still alive.

The older, larger man pointed his knife to Johnathan. "I think she's here for him."

He handed his big knife to the tired one and said, "Finish this already. We'll take their stuff and go."

I gripped the spear tighter. My hands were clammy, but my hold was firm. The one with the knife leaped towards me with his blade up high, but the strike was sloppy and slow. He was still sweating and breathing hard. His form was terrible, and I slapped away the blade as he advanced. I jumped back and knocked it from his hands and he screamed in pain. He didn't waste time and grabbed my spear pole with both hands. We were struggling for control. With all my might, I pulled it down and snapped it back up towards his face. The metal connected to his nose; he gave up and let go, falling to the mud. Our struggle had led us back to the crumbled stone wall, further away from Johnathan. Blood leaked from my opponent's nose and he cried out in agony. I spun the spear so the point faced him and, without hesitation, struck his chest on the right side. Those motions were natural to me from Sadness's training. The BreakNeck Boy tried grabbing the knife portion of my spear, gripping it tightly; we locked eyes until I twisted the blade and pulled back to gain control.

A tremendous blow bashed my head. It was so severe, everything within sight lit up like the sun was shining down on us. Was that a camera flash? No, it couldn't be, not out there in the haze. A loud ringing filled my ears, and I fell. Where'd my spear go? It was gone, and next to me was the dying one who lost our struggle seconds earlier.

Gritty wet mud was on my face. Chunks of saturated red clay covered my shirt and pants. He was above me, smiling and peering down. He picked up the spear and leaned on it like a walking stick. A gurgling sound drew my attention to the dying teen next to me, holding his chest as massive amounts of blood poured from the wound and his mouth. Maybe that was the reason for the red mud beneath us. Was it from endless blood that stained everything? There was only another minute or so of life left for that one.

"Well, damn it, girl, you have some fight in you." The powerful man looked at his dying underling next to me and squinted. "I was only going to kill you and take your stuff, like any normal surface rat out here would. But now, I want more. You got me in the mood."

My heart raced. I knew what he was planning, and the mud put me at a huge disadvantage. I couldn't sweep his legs out or move with speed. There had to be something to use. Behind him, the brown handle of the knife stuck out of the mud. It was too far away and out of my reach. Nothing but reddish-brown gunk and a dying teen. He unbuckled his belt with an eerie smile, glaring down like I was cooked meat he was preparing to devour. The pants fell into the mud, not making much of a sound at all; his legs were hairy.

"If you resist this in any way, I'll beat your face into a pile of mush. Do you understand, girl? I'm going to take what I want anyway."

Even with my years of training and the uncountable odds against me, his words made me cross my legs and lock them together with fear. I felt powerless to act. A strange clamminess instantly formed on my skin, and I bit my lip. My arms became weak, and my legs were paralyzed with pins and needles. I peered at his horrible smiling face one last time, but something changed in an instant. His smile turned to shock, and his eyes opened wide.

The big man struggled to turn, his pants restricting his hairy legs; the brown handle was sticking from his back. Johnathan. Johnathan had stabbed him, but he was still weak and had dried blood on his head. The BreakNeck Boy took my spear and, in one motion, thrust its point into Johnathan's neck just below the chin.

"No!"

Johnathan's eyes were wide, his mouth open, and thick red blood fell onto his pale skin. My strength returned; there was no longer fear, and my legs were on fire with anger. I grabbed the brown handle and yanked it with all my strength. He shrieked and turned back, but without hesitation I skewered the blade quickly into his chest. Sadness would've been disappointed at my rage-filled stabbing—like a wild animal. My performance in a fight was typically more measured, but Johnathan meant the world to me. Screams of rage filled the air and echoed through the square from both of us. Mine were savage shouts; his were cries of pain and fear. I slashed and stabbed over and over. My aim wasn't for a specific location. No, it was wild and uncontrolled, without care where it landed, as long as it was through his body.

He didn't seem so big anymore and he did the best he could to resist me, but with every push of the long sharp metal through his flesh, strength faded, and his body became smaller. Our roles were reversed, and there was pure fear in his large brown eyes that looked at me like I was the most frightening terror his meaningless pathetic life had seen. The knife was now back as far as my shoulder would allow, and after a deep breath of the burning haze into two overworked lungs, I brought the blade down with a roaring scream, such a scream that would scare anyone.

That time the aim was careful, and his yelp of fear rang out, his hand in front of his face trying to block the final blow. The heavier blade sliced through his palm with ease, driving down towards his face, impaling his eye. I pushed down with every fiber of strength I had until the metal could go no further, and with a twist of the handle, the man's screams fell to silence, and the ground absorbed his thick body.

I was breathing so fast that I started coughing again. Sadness's voice rang in my head, and I watched my fallen enemy, ensuring he was dead. The other two weren't moving either and my focus went to Johnathan, who was still alive but struggling for air. He had a crease in his forehead from a deep frown of fear, and his light blue eyes were bloodshot.

"Johnathan, oh no, please, no."

He tried to speak as dribbles of blood fell out of the sides of his mouth.

"Kat, I'm sorry."

Tears streamed down my cheek. "I thought you liked my full name better?"

Johnathan tried to smile, but the pain was too much. "I've always loved…"

His eyes closed and his last breath released into the haze like a gentle gust pushing away a cloud. I held his hand tight as my tears fell on him like rain. The surrounding area turned dark in my grief. I hated the eastern square and that damn yellow haze. Johnathan was no more, and my eyes locked on him.

"I love you too, Johnathan."

After a gentle kiss on his forehead, I let him fall into the mud. The three BreakNeck Boys had sunk even further into the wet red earth. Gazing at them filled me with a new level of emotion I couldn't express in words. Those bastards took something from me that could never come back. I moved to the air handler, picked up the cracked bucket of cloudy water, and drank. The youngest one had a duffle bag, and the leader of that group had a backpack. Scavenging everything from the dead was a matter of survival, and it was time: ripped clothes, a dirty sheet, pouch of marbles, and pliers.

I rolled the young one over and watched his lifeless face for a moment, holding the pliers in my hand, opening and closing them. Sadness taught me to be measured and act as he would. My violent nature was a matter of circumstance from living on the surface.

They'd pay for what happened. I emptied the marbles into my bag and reached a finger into the young one's mouth, pulling the lip up so his teeth became visible. I used the pliers to grip a large tooth and pulled; blood trickled from the gaping hole in his gum. I spun my wrist, looking at the prize, the points of the roots shining in what little sunlight there was; I stuck it in the pouch. It only took a moment to do the same to the others. I wasn't entirely sure what was running through my mind at that act; were they trinkets, was I trying to fill a new void deep inside my soul, or was it something else?

Pulling teeth was thirsty work, so I took another big gulp from the cloudy polluted water, and my stomach growled again. After freeing the blade from the man's head, I spoke one last farewell to my love and departed that place for the last time. I'd never go back there again. The hunger returned with the headache. I left the ruins of a forgotten time; it was just another day living on the surface of Civil Earth.

CHAPTER 4

Schools of the Relations Station

Education on the Free Worlds' past (Henry)

"Alright, class, we have an exceptional guest with us today," Mrs. Toro said. The teacher couldn't be older than thirty. "Representative Henry McWright's the highest-ranking member for the Colonial Accord on the station. Do you remember what the highest position inside the pentagon is for each wall?"

The students all raised their voices at the same time: "Center seat."

"That's right. Of the three seats for each Free Worlds' government, the center seat's the most senior position."

Sitting center seat would be more enjoyable if I didn't have JJ sitting to my right. Maybe I should have switched seats with Christine Keng, our left seat, to get away from JJ.

A student, wearing a standard school uniform of thick uncomfortable wool with a high collar that seemed to irritate his skin—he scratched constantly—raised a hand. "Do the representatives have more authority than our station director?"

Mrs. Toro smiled. "Excellent question. It's a different kind of authority.

The three representatives from their bubbles are elected or appointed by their Free World. They help write and maintain laws that bridge the gaps between the Free Worlds and their independent regulations, customs, people, and local governance." She walked up and down each desk aisle, continuing. "Pretend I live on one of the six planets in the Colonial Accord, and I grow apples. On the Accord planets, they sell for five credits per kilogram. Now, pretend I grow such high numbers of apples, I sell them to other Free Worlds too, and this station. But on Civil Earth, a kilogram of apples sells for nine credits, on Epsilon Prime three, and on the station, twelve credits per kilo. How do we set a fair price for everyone?"

An enthusiastic young girl with rosy cheeks leaned forward, throwing her hand into the air. "The Free Worlds' Relations Policy states what's fair."

Mrs. Toro nodded, and said, "Correct. Director Rumi Houlton has a vital job. Some of your parents elected her in a vote, and in another two years, she'll have to run again. She is responsible for every portion of the station, apart from the cathedral, which the chief agents look after, and her job is to maintain our safety and make sure everything works properly. We have over seven hundred and eighty million residents in our cylinder, with different occupations, tourists, and vacationers constantly scurrying from one end to the other. The Secretary of Commerce tells us at any given time, not including the bubbles, there are up to two million visitors from across occupied space. Our station is centrally located between all five home planets for the Free Worlds, making the relations station the most popular hub for travel. Undergrads come from all the Free Worlds to attend higher education, too."

Only if they could afford it.

Another student asked, "Do they not have schools on the other Free Worlds?"

I snickered. "I sure hope so—otherwise I wasted credits sending my children to university."

They giggled innocently, and the teacher gave me a smirk while saying, "The Free Worlds have much of the same opportunities that we have. One advantage in the main cylinder is that they share their knowledge and technology, making our higher education programs desirable for certain fields of study. Some of the brightest minds in occupied space either went to secondary school or higher education here."

Mrs. Toro was smart, maybe too smart.

I couldn't help it and said, "I should pay you to come inside the forum and educate some of my fellow representatives the way you teach these children. Honestly, you might know more than they."

The students laughed. Benjamin lightly tapped my arm, reminding me of the cameras flying through the room for local news highlights later that afternoon. I regretted that choice of words, even though they were accurate— the tiniest slight created tidal waves under the dome.

"We're beginning today's lessons," Mrs. Toro said, looking at me. "Would you like to start us off?"

I cleared my throat, stood, and walked to the front of the class; the cameras followed. Benjamin was watching closely and taking notes on his PDD.

"I want you students and all residents of the station to know that we of the Capitol Forum are looking out for the best interests of all, not just our home planets. We're all the Free Worlds of Humanity, and that includes this station. At the end of class today, I'll be glad to answer any questions you have for me. Let's begin."

I paused to look around the classroom for a moment. "What are we learning about today?"

"We've been focusing on the early histories of the Free Worlds, and today's a review of our studies."

I gave a fake smile while looking at the cameras. "Ah, the end of the Years of Forgetting and the founding of the station."

Malcolm had done an outstanding job picking this class and the day's topics. It was a neutral conversation that shouldn't offend the other representatives. Especially with the invasion of Gliese that might lead to yet another war. Maybe it would be better to live on a rogue world outside that political spectrum. Rogue planets had it easy, by comparison, only needing to worry about their native population, and not every world in occupied space.

"Please, don't let me stand in your way," I said and took my seat next to Ben.

Ben whispered, "Good work on recovering, sir."

"Now class, do you remember how we started the week talking about the Great Darkness? How long did it last?"

Young hands flailed in the air. The picked student answered, "No one knows for sure, but experts believe it lasted between five and ten thousand years with all humanity falling into darkness across occupied space."

I'd seen the ruins from the Old World on different planets. Those crumbling monuments, buildings, and megastructures were all that remained from the Titans and our ancestors. People in the past had technology thousands of years more advanced than our current understanding. Then after the fall into darkness we reverted to pre-technology for a while. The Titans gave us advanced understanding, then something took it away. Leftover relics from the Years of Forgetting always displayed Titans as a separate entity to our ancestors. Maybe it was just a class difference, like Civil Earth and their tier system. For whatever reason, Titans were always depicted as two hundred and seventy-five-centimeter-tall godly giants.

Mrs. Toro continued. "Very good. Who can tell me what caused the Great Darkness?"

A different set of hands went up excitedly. "No one knows, but there are tons of theories."

"That's right. Scientists aren't certain what had the power to affect all occupied space. People lost their way, and technology reversed. Most forgot how to create electricity for a time."

Well, those children had learned absolutely nothing thus far, with our inadequate responses. Even our brightest minds couldn't answer them. Humanity had forgotten more than it could ever learn again. We knew that our ancestors, during the long period of Darkness, destroyed technology wherever they found it. Our predecessors treated advanced tech like a diseased tumor, and forcefully tried to remove it. They wanted to forget something, but why? People from the Years of Forgetting tried to erase all Old World history. Why were they so scared of our past? Some leftover depictions showed Titans as saintly angels and others as fire-breathing demons. We've reverse-engineered some Titan technology excavated in digs, but not enough.

The teacher continued. "The cause of the Great Darkness might never be known. It spread to every free, outer, and rogue world nearly at the same time, but there's great effort to find the answers."

She glanced at me, and I replied, "Yes, we spend numerous credits inside the Capitol Forum trying to answer this question. What caused the Years of Forgetting? Our smartest minds have found clues through the years, and the station sends thousands of archaeologists across the stars to dig up remains."

In truth, we representatives and the powered authorities couldn't care less; it happened, and we had to deal with the here and now. We spent too much time trying to gain an advantage over each other. I never met a representative who truly cared for the reason, it was too long ago, and we who were in power lived in the best accommodations available, eating the finest foods and spending more credits in a few weeks than working families could spend in half a lifetime.

"Humanity's extremely resilient," I said.

Mrs. Toro added, "That's right, we are. Just before the Darkness started, every planet lost large portions of their population, some as much as ninety-five percent, and a few lost all. We only know that people once lived on those planets because of the ruins. More loss followed the long period we call the Great Darkness or Years of Forgetting. But look at us now—hundreds of billions across hundreds of worlds."

A student called out without raising his hand. "My dad said a plague killed everyone."

Another raised her voice. "I heard it was a supernova."

Mrs. Toro glared at them, and it was enough to gain control. "What you all heard might very well be right, but we raise our hands in my classroom to speak. Does everyone understand?"

"Yes, Mrs. Toro."

She continued. "There are endless suggestions for what caused that terrible and dangerous time: a massive galactic electromagnetic pulse, incurable plague, total war, fanatical religious cults like the Dark Priests or Warriors of the Light on Epsilon Prime, or something else. They're all guesses. Whatever the event, some planets have unusable land, like Civil Earth, and their megacities were built in permanently damaged territories. What we know with certainty is that even after years of hardship, here, we are a united humanity."

She was doing her best to convince those young minds of our benevolence. The Free Worlds barely hung on by a shoestring, always teetering on the edge of war. Only someone born on the station or on one of the Free Worlds would be considered civilized and a part of our greater collective. There were at least forty-eight billion souls across some hundred and sixty-two planets of the rogue worlds that didn't have the rights or liberties of our Free Worlds. Most of them still lived in darkness; then there was that primitive royal family claiming the fifty outer worlds, but they could barely keep a hold over the systems closest to them.

"Which Free Worlds government has the most planets in their system?" Mrs. Toro asked, walking up and down the desk aisles. She was smart, confident, and … *Keep the box locked, Henry.*

Eager little hands flew into the air, and a student said, "The Colonial Accord."

I raised my voice. "That's right, young one. We have six habitable planets in our stellar system: Ardum, Tautrus, Lars, Pardalis, and Talbora, led by my homeworld, Uropa."

I wouldn't mind if Ardum and their ugly flower didn't exist; then I wouldn't need to deal with JJ Richmond. We'd still have five air-breathing worlds that would outnumber the rest of the Free Worlds combined.

Mrs. Toro stared at me with a half-smile. My position and personality had always attracted women and men of all ages over the years. Was that teacher falling into the same spiderweb?

A student nearby raised her hand with narrowed eyes in my direction, and Mrs. Toro called on her. "Uropa's the only natural planet in your system. The others all have seed engines on them.

"Thank you, Representative McWright, for your answer, and thank you, Brianna, for bringing up another valid point. Only four percent of the planets we reside on through occupied space formed naturally. The rest within their goldilocks zones have world seed engines—more technology from our past. Teams still work on recovering information on how they functioned, but like other innovations, that tech lays in ruins."

We Colonials were still the luckiest of all systems in occupied space. It didn't matter that five of our six planets were artificial. We'd never be able to recreate that level of advancement again, as far as I was concerned. Titans were basically walking gods with their understanding of the universe, which was why the art depictions showed them standing nearly three meters tall. Everyone knew that fairy tales of walking giants, divine beings, floating cities the size of mountains, and disappearing stars were fantasy. People entertained themselves in any way possible during the Great Darkness, and those stories were a byproduct. We were able to retrofit some technology left behind, like faster-than-light travel. It felt like a daily occurrence—archaeologists digging up old war armor space suits and FTL drives. The real breakthroughs came when we found a functioning fusion reactor.

A student near the front of the room asked, "Can we talk about the Frontiersmen?"

Mrs. Toro said, "They're an anomaly from the Old World. We don't know if those ark ships are on autopilot or controlled by our ancestors. What's known with certainty is that, based on design and Titan tech from deep space imagery, they're from our past. Frontiersmen travel on a random grid-by-grid search pattern across charted and uncharted space. It appears that they spend most of their time in FTL, which we're unable to track or predict when they'll show up, but when they do, it's usually above an air-breathing planet. Representative McWright, would you care to add anything?"

The Frontiersmen were all that remained of the superior Old World—only they found us habitable worlds. We had no reason to travel beyond occupied space.

"The Capitol Forum has tried to contact them without success," I said. "The Frontiersmen are uninterested in us and continue their random jumps through the stars. That's why our experts believe the ships have no one on board. Representatives have made attempts through the years with radio, video, light, pulse, and mathematic communications. None of those attempts had success—the ark ships do what they do and jump away. The only interaction we ever get from them is their beacon, with more power disseminating from it than we can detect from a star. When they arrive at a new planet, the beacon alerts our tracking grids, and that's it. If it were possible to get into one of their vessels, we'd gain lost knowledge of our past and enter a new golden age for all humanity, but I fear that won't ever happen."

Intelligence photos in closed session under the dome always amazed me, showing those ark ships' sheer size. They were thousands of years more advanced than us, and even our not-so-public attempts at communicating ended in disaster. The Dolrinion approach brought a smile to my face. Representative Guth of the Offensive had said, "Even if they destroy our probe, it would be a sign of interaction. Send a hundred probes to smack them in the face. Let's get something from these deaf-mutes!"

We sent it, and the probe disappeared from our sensors as it exited FTL travel, hundreds of kilometers away from their fleet, erupting into flames. The arks could track us in faster-than-light, which showed their superiority. Even if we got on one of those ships, there wasn't a guarantee we could replicate the tech, and the wars over who got those advancements first would be unending between the Free Worlds.

"Are they aliens?" asked a student.

The classroom burst out with laughter, and Mrs. Toro shushed them, saying, "No one should make fun of any question. We're all here to learn, and part of learning is to ask questions." She walked to her desk. "There's never been a discovery of advanced life other than our own. Rogue worlders might look at a Dolrinion or a Native Lowlander from Galma and think they're aliens. Educated minds know the truth. Humanity has lived in different ecosystems for thousands of years and evolved to those conditions. Kora, the homeworld of the Dolrinions, has gravity pressure three times higher than the averages of other planets. Evolution stunted their growth and gave them greater bone density. In comparison, Lowlanders of Galma live in a constant thick fog where no sunlight can penetrate. Because of that environment, their skin is gray, nearly translucent, and their pupils are huge enough to help them see in the low-lit landscape."

While speaking, Mrs. Toro brought up a hologram of a random Dolrinion, Galma Lowlander, and me, standing next to each other.

"Look at these three humans, one of them being Representative McWright. Seeing them for the first time would make you believe two are aliens, but if we tested their DNA, it would be clear that all three are human with minor changes to their genetic code. Evolution makes adjustments to adapt our bodies to certain environments."

The same student asked, "Does that mean we won't ever find intelligent alien life?"

She hesitated. "Occupied space is vast, but only a small blip compared to our galaxy. There's much we still don't know. Science tells us that going from a single-celled organism to a fully functioning spacefaring species is harder to do than we made it look. Because of our history and superior intellect, we believed that evolution was easy, something that can happen naturally on various worlds. Unfortunately, that reasoning is incorrect."

Some of the students appeared displeased with her answer, so I chimed in, "Don't feel so lonely, children. Including the Free Worlds and this station, there are at least three hundred seventy billion people throughout occupied space. With a few more evolutionary traits, there will be people with three eyes sprouting from their heads soon enough. We'll all look like aliens."

The children laughed, and Mrs. Toro went on with other classroom topics for that day, half of which were hard for me to keep my attention focused on. The lecture ended, students left, and the cameras all departed. Mrs. Toro was cleaning up her desk as I approached, and she gently pushed her thick dark hair from her eyes.

"Representative McWright, thank you for coming today. It was wonderful for the kids to spend time with such a renowned center seat of the forum."

"I would do anything for the citizens of the station, especially for someone like you. Look at what you do for these young minds. It's so important."

Her excitement was evident—she blushed—and she was having a hard time making eye contact with me. "As a teenager, I focused my studies on politics before going into teaching. I always watched you on television and even came to a few of your speeches."

I laughed. "Ah, so you were a representative groupie?"

"You could say that. Like most, I saw you like a star and inspiration—I still do."

Her face was redder, and she seemed nervous.

"I'll admit, I found it difficult not to notice your beauty and that lovely blue skirt. Our conversation will be the highlight of my week. What's your first name?"

I tried to give her my undivided attention, but in truth, the speech tonight was all I could think about. Show one face even when you feel another. Dad taught that powerful lesson and it had stuck with me over the years. Be a chameleon and appear the way you must, to blend in.

"Gabrielle. Gabrielle Toro, but most of my friends call me Gabby."

I used my PDD to send Gabby my contact information, and an alert went off on her device. She looked at it and to me with her eyes open wide.

"Gabby, if you ever need anything, I don't care what it is, call me. You can call an hour from now or next year, and I promise to do what I can to help, regardless of the need."

"Thank you, Representative McWright. I will watch your speech tonight at a local pub near my apartment. Have a wonderful day."

The exhortation to have a wonderful day was easily spoken compared to reality. The dock rally was next, followed by my minutes meeting with Mia. A checklist of events was typical for a representative on the relations station. I exhaled deeply, feeling exhausted, and it wasn't even lunchtime.

CHAPTER 5

A Programmer for the Federate Corporation

Working for the Department of Internal Security (Mace)

One minute after midnight, the start of a new day. I'd been stuck in the control room for fourteen hours with my coworkers trying our best efforts to get the new system up and running. It should have been on ten hours earlier. The entire Department of Internal Security looked terrible when we hit the activation button and it failed to boot. Everyone was so tired—rows of exhausted employees with long faces and drooping eyes at computer terminal stations. I saw at least two employees nod off at their stations a little while ago. It was easy to see because of the slight downgrade of each row and a massive screen at the bottom showing the new defense grid, which wasn't working. The stadium-style station seating reminded me of my childhood. Going to power-ball games with my dad always made me feel happy, unlike the way I felt at that moment.

Supervisor Dennis and Program Development Manager Tammy were behind Rafael and me, breathing down our necks.

Rafael leaned over from his screen and whispered, "I just finished checking all the code in the guidance system. It's all clean. The error was not there."

"Speak up so we all can hear you. You're not alone in this room, remember." Tammy's tone was crisp with authority.

Rafael stumbled on his words. "The guidance system is clean, no errors, ma'am."

She had a crooked half-smile. "Well, good. Continue your checks."

Along the opposite back wall, board of directors' member Kai Yom was still standing like a quiet cat. He was older than the others and was dressed in an expensive suit. Yom hadn't left the room when all the other high-ranking employees fled like they feared the failure would rub off on them. Board member Yom's focus was pure and unmoving, the same as it had been earlier.

Grade twenty-seven wasn't so bad, and I knew Rafael didn't mind. He'd told me numerous times over drinks after work. Better to be seven levels up than stuck in the lower levels of corporate society.

Standing next to Yom were the face cards of the playing deck, including the chief general of the Air and Space Cab, vice president of Planetary Security, and the vice president of the Department of Internal Security. So much top leadership from the Corporation in that overheated control room. Too many chefs in the kitchen. When we first tried launching the system, the number of board members, vice presidents, directors, and managers outnumbered the ordinary employees two to one. Talk about being top-heavy.

Another employee at the front of the control room raised his voice. "The main program is clean, no errors."

Dennis said, "Good to hear."

Rafael and I glanced at each other and rolled our eyes. Of course it was good to hear, you dimwit. I spent a year writing that entire program. He reviewed every line after, and if the error was in my code with neither of us aware of it, the chamber would be the last thing we saw. All the secondary systems had come from the others sitting in that poorly ventilated room. Hours had passed, and my back was stiff from going through lines of code for each programming system looking for the error. It was clearly a coding issue.

A year of preparation to initialize the new planetary defense grid, and it failed. Being the head program writer made the entire situation suck just a little bit more. I had given my word it would be faster and more advanced than any of its predecessors. Processing power when working with basic Old World technology and our Free Worlds most advanced tech took time to register when activating and firing for defensive and offensive platforms. It was the same for traveling in FTL. Defending Dol'Arem was all the brass face cards wanted. My program was more sophisticated than anything the relations station had.

The fighting on Gliese between our Corporation and the Offensive was why everyone was on edge.

Rafael leaned in again. "I knew there was nothing wrong with the main system, and the coding is perfect. You know your shit, my dude."

I smirked but that was it. Usually, I'd make a funny face or say something witty but I was so damn tired.

Dennis kicked his chair to shut him up before Tammy could say anything. "Sorry, sir."

Before observing the next line of code, I glanced at the front of the room to the right of the big screen. Standing there as always was the gigantic stone statue of the CFO who had franchised Dol'Arem and was the top employee of the Federate Corporation at that time, Allison Westbay. The statue was footed with hand-carved varnished oak, which reflected in the light of the room. A plaque at the bottom displayed her famous words that we were all instructed to live by: "If we work together, we win together." Those words were written in bold at the beginning of our four-thousand-page Federate policy and procedures handbook, which all corporate guidelines employees lived by. We were all employees from birth and had to serve the Four Sisters of the Corporation.

The next line of code was clear, and Tammy, standing behind me, whispered to Dennis. "Pont's on her way down. If we don't have it fixed in the next few minutes, we'll all get negative notations."

Great. The most dreaded words for any employee of the Corporation. I had never gotten a negative notation in my quarterly review but had seen what happened to others with poor performance evaluations. Rafael and I had positive reviews that did little in helping us advance, probably because they came from our base-level supervisor. It was better to have a negative notation from someone like Dennis than from the CFO of Genesis Foundation. Notations were equal, regardless of who gave them, they told us. Right. I'd seen employees fired from notations given by a VP level or higher. I couldn't let that happen to me. The three-month grace period to find new employment with one of the other sisters was laughable. Green Scrap Consumers would be the only place I could go if that happened, besides the chamber.

I stared at my hands. What would it be like going from typing on a computer terminal one day to working an assembly line the next? My hands weren't thick enough for manual labor, and dropping to grade-level twenty-two would crush Jamie. We'd have to sell everything and move. Such a familiar story for failed employees of the Corporation.

The next heading of code read *Radar Active Passive Omnidirectional and Directional System.* It was a waste of time to look through the RAPOD system. High-level programmers learned to write code for our space-tracking programs before learning anything else. It was the easiest system in our entire defense-grid mainframe. Wait. That was odd. The next line of code had something extra that shouldn't be there. After highlighting it and moving to the next line, I found there were mistyped subroutines too. That wasn't good.

Two rows down was the RAPOD terminal station. Dominic and Jenifer sat there reviewing someone else's program. They might have been junior-level programmers at grade twenty-five, but we all knew how to write that code in our sleep, and why didn't supervisor Henly catch it in his reviews? He stood behind Dom and Jen. His untucked shirt was smaller than his belly, and he hadn't shaved in days.

I heard Dennis breathing heavily behind me and didn't want him to see what I had highlighted yet. I nudged Rafael and sent him the page of code. He spent a few minutes scanning it and found the same errors. Perspiration dampened my forehead. When I reported that error, there was no going back. I didn't have a choice. The chamber and its small walls with large exhaust vents appeared in my mind, and I pictured Dominic and Jenifer begging for their lives.

I raised my hand slowly and the bigwigs in the back corner glared at me. My stiff bones cracked from being in the same position for so long. Dennis placed a hand on my shoulder and spent a few minutes looking over what Rafael and I had highlighted. I was uncomfortable with him so close and the stench of coffee on his breath. Things were tenser when Tammy came over, followed by her boss, a director-level employee, who then called his boss, the vice president of program development for the Department of Internal Security. It was like a small tree falling over, knocking into a larger, which in turn fell onto a bigger tree. I didn't even realize a vice president was standing behind us—another high-level employee with us peons. More chefs in the kitchen.

The vice president examined what Rafael and I showed him, and his face turned red. Writing that code from scratch was easy. He waved over to Dom and Jen's supervisor and manager and showed them the mistake. Dominic had his arms folded, eyes narrowed in my direction, and Jenifer's bottom lip trembled. Feelings of guilt overcame me, but what could I do?

The director, the vice president of my group, and the VP of planetary defense ushered all four from that computer station into a conference area. They were behind glass doors that had a clear view of the elevator bank into the underground control room we had been in all day and night. Security operators walked into the room dressed in their full battle armor with thick front covers and face shields down. They always had their shields down because of the treacherous way Dolrinions fought. Poison gas had killed countless employees since the first Franchise War. The reason the operators felt it necessary to wear them twenty sublevels underground inside the most heavily fortified building in the city of Lavlen was beyond me.

Jenifer covered her face. The way her shoulders jerked from uncontrolled crying, we all knew what was happening. The manager and supervisor turned pale, eyes opened wide. Dominic was tight-lipped and red-faced. Both supervisor and manager followed the operators to the elevator as Jenifer and Dominic opened the glass doors leading back into the control room. The upper lights flashed off the glass like the sun reflecting off a frozen lake. Both employees tried to regain their composure with little success as they walked back to their station. After watching the elevator door open and close, the vice president of planetary defense walked into the room with a stern gaze. Most bosses that senior had similar faces. I'd probably look that way too from years fighting up the chain of corporate life. He had a thick dark mustache peppered with gray.

"The error's been found and corrected." His voice carried through the room with authority.

His eyes seemed to stare right through me as he waited for a response.

I stumbled for words. "Yes, uhm, yes, sir, I'm removing it now."

As quickly as possible, I deleted the corrupted coding and hit a test run. Once the green checkbox flashed across my screen, I gave a thumbs up.

The vice president puffed his chest out and said, "This error, I'm told, was in the most basic programing system attached to the new defense grid—the last place an error should have occurred. I'm disappointed with what transpired here today. The CFO herself was witness to this failure. Manager Melesi and supervisor Henly are no longer employees of Genesis Foundation. Since the two employees over there," he pointed to Dom and Jen, "who initially made this error are still new and should have received the proper guidance from their supervisors, which they didn't get, we'll only give them one negative notation on their file."

A negative notation from the vice president of planetary defense. Dominic's and Jenifer's careers would be stagnant for years, and whoever heard of a manager and supervisor fired on the spot like that?

"Now, CFO Pont is on her way down again, and this time I expect the new system will be ready to launch."

He looked around the room at the stations where manager-level employees were nodding their heads like small wooden bobblehead dolls.

The VP of planetary defense stared at me again. He was intimidating in his formal military uniform with pins and medals that jingled as he moved.

"You four over there." The vice president pointed to our station. "You did outstanding work, and you …" He looked at me directly; I pointed to myself, unsure what to do. "Yes, you. You wrote the entire program code for this new defense system, and it's the most advanced of any Free World."

I wasn't sure if that was a question or not, but the VP of defense was gawking at me, so I said, "Uhm, yes, sir, I did. It took a year to develop the code fully, and I couldn't have done it without my coworker here, Rafael."

He glanced at Rafael, and the look itself made my friend jump in his chair.

"Outstanding work. All of you, from direct report to the manager, will receive a positive notation from me."

Rafael, Dennis, and Tammy all looked excited. I couldn't help but think that if I had messed up even one line of my main code for this design, he'd be walking me to the elevator instead of those other two, and three months after that would be a gas-filled chamber.

After a few more minutes, the back hall elevator doors opened. Security operators and the CFO Security senior operations supervisor came through the glass panels, escorting CFO Pont herself alongside a plethora of staff members. As they entered the room, all, regardless of their corporate grade-level, including the standing statue, Kai Yom, stood up straighter. CFO Pont had droopy eyes and pulled one side of her lip back, attempting to smile.

"So, are we ready this time?" Her voice was soft and hard to hear.

She was older than most in the room. The VP of planetary defense and chief general of the air and space cab both answered at the same time. "Yes, ma'am."

Rafael leaned over and whispered, "I can barely hear her when she talks."

"She doesn't have to talk any louder. She's our CFO. When she speaks, everyone stops what they're doing to listen."

CFO Pont walked over to her fellow board member alongside other high-ranking Genesis Foundation employees standing around waiting.

The VP of planetary defense stared at me again. "Program writer, what's your name?"

"Mace, sir, Mace Applegate."

His mustache rustled. "Well, Mr. Applegate, you designed it. This time you hit the launch button."

Dennis and Tammy smiled. Positive remarks for me reflected on them. He only wanted me to hit the button so he'd have someone to blame if it didn't work that time. My back cracked loudly as I stood, I had been so long in that seat, and my walk to the front terminal was accompanied by deep breaths of agony recalling what I had endured designing the system. Endless nights from home, fights with Jamie, and the stresses of following our Federate policy and procedures with the ever-looming threat of extinction from Dolrinion sentinels. I needed a vacation. It was so quiet in control, the simple click from a mouse sounded like a nuclear explosion.

Live videos on the big screen showed the satellites powering on. The large boxes stretched what looked like wings and displayed their weapons like a warrior of old pulling a sword from its scabbard. Each one of those oversized satellites had more firepower than a destroyer. Another screen showed gray boxes that turned green in succession. Thousands of those platforms circled the planet from two different sides and crossed near the equator—armed artificial rings.

A loud computerized voice spoke over the loudspeakers. "System active."

Everyone clapped and cheered except for Dominic and Jenifer. They didn't even look up from their computers as everything turned on. I didn't cheer either, but no one noticed. Were the programmers happy at the launch or happy they could go home? I felt beaten, completely drained of everything that made me happy after all that stress, just to hear a strange computer voice say that the system was active.

From a side door near the statue of CFO Westbay came lines of servers holding serving plates with glasses of wine. Were they back there that whole time waiting? Talk about wasted resources.

CFO Pont spoke. "With this success, we've entered a new age of safety for the Four Sisters to our Corporation. We've lost employees, lots of employees, on the rogue world Gliese, but with the new defense system, our safety is absolute. You've all worked hard, and for that devotion, we'd like you to toast with us with the finest vintage from the Island of New Greta on Lars."

Some of the lower-grade-level employees made sounds of surprise. At fifteen thousand credits per bottle, none of us could afford that, except the pecking roosters along the back wall.

"If we work together, we win together," CFO Pont called out with her glass up high.

The entire control room echoed her words, and after another fifteen minutes of handshaking, congratulating, and formalities, Rafael and I were dismissed by Dennis to go home.

Inside the elevator, Rafael behaved like a kid in a candy store, moving from one wall to the other, smiling.

"I can't believe it, man. We're getting a positive notation from the vice president of planetary defense! Do you realize how big a deal that is?"

The display screen showed updates from the stock market and Free Worlds markets, and that kept my attention. I was having trouble trying to snap myself out of a funk. "You'd think that designing the most advanced program in Free Worlds history would have at least earned a handshake from Pont."

Rafael crinkled his nose and shook his head. "Dude, they gave us a glass of New Greta White. We'll never have that again. That was all the thanks I needed."

"Dom and Jen are screwed. They'll never advance with Genesis Foundation, not now. Did you notice our director sent them to the elevator as the wine came out? They're going to lose a grade-level."

"They made their beds, brother. Even if they lose a grade-level, at least they still have a career here with us. Melesi and Henly aren't getting another job. The other sister companies wouldn't do it now. No way, man, no way. The freaking VP of planetary defense just fired them on the spot. Three months from now, they'll be in the chamber."

I didn't want to go to the chamber. It was my greatest fear, along with most other employees. "They're screwed if they can't get away."

Rafael frowned. "It's how we've survived since colonizing this planet. The Dolrinions want us dead. My kids are more afraid of them than Androsians."

I opened my eyes wide. "Really? I can't decide which one is worse. The widgets who want to enslave and kill us or the cybernetic psychos who want to eat us."

Rafael gave a slight laugh. "Hey, if Melesi or Henly can get the Rogue Syndicate to smuggle them off-world, they'll live in exile. If not—"

"Operators will scoop them up and toss them inside the nearest chamber to breathe in the lemon-smelling gas. It only takes two minutes—did you know that?"

Rafael lowered his head and turned away. I wasn't always this moody and felt bad for acting that way. I needed to snap out of it. The elevator door opened, and we left through the main lobby. A security officer near the entrance smiled at us. "Another long one in the vault?"

I answered, trying to act more like myself. "They couldn't keep us down there indefinitely. CFO Pont wouldn't like the way I smelled without a shower for a few days."

He laughed and we departed after scanning our employee cards.

Rafael watched me stare into the parking lot.

"Hey, man, we did a good thing tonight. You should be proud."

"Tell your wife and kids I said hello."

"I will," he said. "You and Jamie should apply for a kid now that you're over this crazy hump."

I paused. "Did you hear about Cynthia from accounting?"

Rafael nodded. "She had to terminate. I don't know what she was thinking. She needed approval from Family Management first."

"Jamie didn't want to apply before one of us got another promotion. She doesn't want to give up our lifestyle."

He smiled. "We're cool with one PDD and one car. So we can't go away every year on vacation like you two do. At least we're happy. Every day is a vacation in the Vega house."

We both laughed.

"With two kids under ten, I'd say so."

"Your wife is already a supervisor at grade-level twenty-eight. You guys should seriously apply."

"Maybe one day," I said.

A work shuttle arrived to take me a short distance to the train station.

*

The transport arrived at the train station and my train hadn't left yet. Our corporate motivational posters were displayed on the walls leading to the platform. One read: "Hard Work—there are no secrets to success; it is a result of preparation, and learning from failure," and another: "Work Together—a good team is more powerful than the sum of its parts." I never cared for that propaganda.

On the train, I sat in a window seat, closed my eyes and cringed at lower-back pain from sitting so long at my computer station. Typically, by that hour, I'd be home sleeping after a normal workday. The train carried more employees than I expected for the hour. Never let an hour go wasted. The corporate structure never slept.

It was near 2 a.m. by the time my train arrived at the station, and I yawned, feeling my eyelids get heavy. I got off the train and stepped around the corner. A MERC Guild agent with his mongrel was there inspecting people's Federate identification cards. My heart raced. Why was he there so late? I paused, feeling uncertain. It had been years since I'd seen an agent in person. The mongrel's fur was light brown, almost orange, with dark streaks. Dabs of drool hung from its large jowls, and the beast's head reminded me of a hippopotamus because of its size. The agent was near the exit platform. I couldn't avoid him.

"Good morning, sir."

He gave me a stone-cold glare, not changing his expression as he took my card. The Corin-steel armor and its glowing green lines almost put me in a trance, but the shiny pentagon-shaped badge broke my stare as he spoke.

"Applegate, is it?"

I swallowed. "It is."

The mongrel growled as it leaned closer. The sound made me anxious, or maybe it was the agent's hesitation and his unmoving stare. Two security operators came off the nearest train; they walked over and broke the agent's focus.

He gave me back my card and said, "You can leave."

I grabbed it, thanked him, and moved away quickly. The operators were conversing with him, but it had nothing to do with me. I got into my vehicle and it drove home.

On the drive home, I switched on a news channel. '… new bounty pricing for capture or death of the Black Skull Admiral, Derwin of Draco, the Dolrinion exile who is terrorizing the whole of occupied space. And now a round-up of the main news …' The newscaster went on to highlight what was happening with the fighting on Gliese. The inhabitants of that planet were unlucky because it was just outside the demilitarized zone, which meant it was only a matter of time before the fighting spilled there. All the rogue worlds inside the DMZ and Exclusion Zones were once inhabited but were now barren after our endless wars. Complete wastes of air-breathing planets, but everyone followed the laws enacted by the relations station. Gliese would be the next void world, but not because of whatever caused the Great Darkness. It would come from our own doing.

The car pulled into my driveway at nearly 3 a.m. Light reflecting through the blinds at that hour worried me. Jamie should have been fast asleep. Why was she still up?

"I was wondering if you were going to come home tonight." She sounded agitated.

"I'm sorry, babes, you know I didn't have a choice."

Jamie frowned and stared at the table. "If we work together, we win together. Do you think our corporate words apply to both working and after hours with the family? I couldn't help but think about that tonight."

Things were tense at home because of my fourteen-hour workdays and countless nights sleeping alone in our bed; she was angry with me for coming home so late. Jamie had enough of me sharing my time with Genesis Foundation and slept in our guest room more often than not.

"The new grid is active—we're all safer now. Let's go on vacation, just you and me, away from all this bullshit."

She hesitated, still watching the table as if there was something there of particular interest. "I doubt the Department of Internal Security will let you take off right after the activation. What if something goes wrong?"

I'd usually have something sarcastic to respond with, but nothing came to mind. "As long as I follow the policy book, they can't say no. I'll put the days in right away. You should do the same."

Jamie's shoulders slumped and she wrapped her arms around herself. *What did I say?* I couldn't understand why she was acting that way. She lifted her chin, and our eyes met as a single tear rolled down her face.

"The Federate policy manual is why I'm so scared. The rules are not made to be broken for employees like us. We have to do what it says." She paused and her eyes wandered. "I've got something to tell you."

I sat next to her, waiting during an uneasy pause that felt like a lifetime.

"Mace, I'm pregnant."

I stopped breathing. My exhaustion disappeared, and a pulse of rejuvenation coursed through me. I leaned in to her with arms opened wide. We embraced and kissed.

"It's ok, it's ok. I mean, with your promotion, I was going to suggest that we start discussing the possibility of having kids together now. Family Management would approve us with your grade-level increase."

Jamie cried out, "That doesn't help us right now. My next physical's in six weeks, and they'll make me terminate the pregnancy. You know the rules. We need the authorization first. They'll measure the baby's size and know that we got pregnant before getting the approval."

She was right. There wasn't any way to hide it during our employee semiannual health exam. They'd make her terminate the pregnancy. It didn't matter that I'd just created the defense grid with a positive notation. There was a good reason why our policy manual was four thousand pages. They expected us to obey, always.

"What are you trying to say?"

Jamie's voice was louder as she answered, "Mace, I'm keeping this baby!"

I thought about the year I'd given of my life to get the defense grid online, Dominic and Jenifer in the control room getting a negative notation on their files, supervisor Henly and manager Melesi who were fired on the spot and would probably be inside a chamber getting gassed in three months, and how I didn't cheer with joy when everyone else did inside the control room.

Eventually, I spoke. "Well, I told you we needed to take a vacation, didn't I? Maybe a nice long one that we don't come back from would be better. Somewhere off-world."

Jamie laughed through her tears and hugged me tight.

I kissed her forehead and said, "I love you, Jamie Applegate."

"I love you too."

Her next physical was in six weeks, and she wouldn't start to show for the next month. I had to figure out how to get us off this planet.

CHAPTER 6

Eatontown Avenue Café

You owe me or I owe you? (Henry)

After finishing my speech to the union workers, we had a small photo op with some of the dock workers who had suffered wounds in the explosion. Some had new skin with strange imprints from basic repairs to the burns. If they'd had more credits, reconstructive surgery would have already made it appear like nothing ever happened. Those workers were poor by comparison.

We were back in the transport driving through the main cylinder on our way to my favorite café inside Eatontown for the minutes meeting with Mia Stavish. I looked out the window through the main cylinder to see the artificial sky and sunlight that resonated across the station, the thick clouds moving gently in the wind and the support brace on the other side of the slow-spinning station with trees, buildings, grass, and roadways.

Ben saw me looking out the window. "What's on your mind?"

"Nothing of importance. I love the habitable zones inside the main cylinder. It's breathtaking to look up at the ground, regardless of how many times I see it."

Benjamin glanced at his PDD and opened his eyes wide. "Representative McWright, your approval rating through the localized main feed is rising after your speech in the dock."

I smirked and looked outside again. "That's from the live stream. Shipbuilders from Dol'Arem, Tier Four labor workers from Earth, Colonial Accord Labor local unions from Tautrus and Pardalis, and our colony miners in Titans' Belt—a plethora of eyes helped build the momentum for tonight."

Ben nodded, and I asked, "So, what are your plans this weekend? We had a trying week, and I think everyone deserves a good weekend."

Benjamin looked up. "Tomorrow I'm donating time at the refugee dock. I try to get there at least once per month to help give food to new arrivals, pass out clothing, and help the kids enroll in school."

I smiled. He was a good lad. The main cylinder refugee dock was busy since the rogue world Gliese invasion. The Federates and Offensive brought their fighting or occupation to rogue worlds sporadically from time to time, and a byproduct of that was new refugees and citizens for the main cylinder.

"You're a true civil servant. Look at you, working fourteen-hour days for me and then donating your free time with the less fortunate."

Ben smirked and looked back to his PDD.

After twenty minutes of driving, we arrived on Eatontown Avenue and pulled along the street, parking near the café. Mia was already there, and so were a few trucks with tinted windows and a small crowd. She had picked the outdoor seating area near the street. That was a good publicity stunt, so citizen videos and pictures would show us doing our duties as representatives to the station. Mia enjoyed the cheers from commoners due to our popularity and fame. Oliver opened the door, and I stepped out; more random people saw me and smiled. There was a cool breeze pushing softly off the flowering plants circling the seating area and tables.

I got past the bystanders and approached the table. Mia stood to greet me, wearing a traditional Civil Earth Tier One toga of silk gliding gently against her athletic shape. Tier One men and women never wore undergarments with their thin togas. They loved displaying their bodies through the fine fabric, even the overweight ones. There was no shame among Tier One. Both wrists were layered in gold, silver, and exotic rubies of different colors. Exquisite low-hanging necklaces made from the same metals lined her neck, and she wore laced sandals that went up to her calves. Mia was younger than me by nearly twenty years, and with her perfect ebony skin she was desirable.

With arms opened wide, we embraced, and she spoke in her Civil Earth accent. "Representative McWright, so good to see you."

I spoke while pecking both cheeks. "Representative Stavish, I'm glad we could get together on such a busy day."

Mia glanced at the people standing on the street to ensure they saw us greeting each other. She turned, waving her arm over the table. "I took the liberty of ordering appetizers and drinks."

Cooked finger foods of fried crackers, melted cheese, sliced cherry tomatoes, and bacon. The smell of that bacon made my mouth water. Those little bite-sized sandwiches were something I always ordered at Eatontown Café. Next to those were bowls of blueberries, olives drizzled in oil and salt, and chopped vegetables. All of it was real and not the lab-grown imitations so common across certain Free Worlds. We representatives were accustomed to eating that way for every meal, and even the Federate Corporation representatives ate real foods. For average Free Worlds citizens from Civil Earth, the Federate Corporation, and the relations station, real food was costly. Most of them ate artificial food from the dispensers. The Corporation viewed it more as a cost-effective way to save money, always looking at profits over preference.

Mia lifted a glass of dark red wine, which she knew was my favorite. "You still prefer the island of New Greta vintage from Lars, correct?"

I smirked and nodded. Mia, like all who enjoyed our level of wealth, preferred New Greta red or white. They were the most expensive, and those in the highest social order always drank one of the two from Lars, a Colonial world controlled by my Labor Party.

"You've outdone yourself as always, Mia. Have you picked our meals too? You knew what I wanted thus far with these wonderful appetizers and the wine."

She raised her chin and smiled. "Braised lamb from Epsilon Prime with fennel, garlic, onions, and all the sides you prefer."

"I'll take a shot in the dark and guess that you ordered crab-stuffed lobster claws, correct? And crème brulée for dessert?" I said through gritted teeth.

Mia's smile faded, and she raised an eyebrow. "Two for two—you know me too well, Henry."

We lifted our glasses and tapped them together. My hand vibrated slightly, and Mia added, "To the Free Worlds of Humanity—may we have long and prosperous years together."

"To the Free Worlds and its people."

That first interaction to any onlookers would appear as an innocent tease of old friends, but ordinary people wouldn't understand that it was an opening salvo to a long and bloody word game. Everything on that table and what she ordered for me was her way of showing me that she always watched and knew what happened across the station. I enjoyed coming to Eatontown Café nearly once per month and ordered the same items. I hadn't dined with her there in years, so there wasn't any reason she should know my choices by heart. Spy games were powerful tools for the fifteen of our Capitol Forum. Mia was attempting a display of dominance by ordering before I arrived. I countered by listing the exact meal she ate with Center Seat Representative Boran from the Federate Corporation when she dined there a few months prior. Mia preferred choices she was familiar with. My guess could have been wrong, but at least she knew I was watching things as closely as she.

Benjamin sat with Mia's aide Melissa, an attractive young woman. He had to be careful with his words because the game had already started.

Mia pointed to her PDD and said, "I watched your speech on the dock, very uplifting and motivating for the unions."

I needed to choose my words carefully. She might have someone listening to our conversation.

"I was transparent with my goals and policy direction for the forum next month."

She tapped her fingers on the table rhythmically. "You were, but I recall our discussion regarding the last part of your proposed changes, and you said you'd consider removing it."

Equal rights in the workplace was her issue, and allowing for the creation of a Relations Station Human Reliability Department that would govern workers' rights across the territories.

"Mia, you owe me one for the vote last month. Your bill was dead in the water and would never have come out of closed session without me. Both right and left seats for the Colonial Accord voted it down as well as all three from the Dolrinion Offensive wall."

Her bill helped reduce trading insufficiencies that had plagued Civil Earth for the better part of twenty years. I only agreed to help because it grew my wealth through Representative Laskaris of the Human Alliance. When that bill passed, it profited his family business tremendously since it was an import-export trading company on Epsilon Prime, and half its enterprise went through Civil Earth megacities. As payment, Zachery Laskaris gave me three percent ownership in the company. A win-win, which ensured Mia owed me, too.

"I owe you?" Mia sounded frustrated. "You've done for me, and I've done for you. I am not keeping score of this, are you? Who's to say we aren't already even, hmm?"

I leaned back and took another sip of wine, keeping my expression neutral.

"Henry, I can't convince my left and right seats to vote yes with those union provisions in the bill. Tier Four union workers on Civil Earth would have a field day if they believed they had equal rights to the upper tiers. There's a system on my planet that has worked for two thousand one hundred years, and the Hawks of Tier One aren't changing it tomorrow because you want to look good for some two hundred billion throughout the Free Worlds—"

I interrupted her. "Did you see the public-feed approval ratings after my speech in the dock? The general public agrees with the things I said."

Mia acted as if I hadn't spoken over her and continued. "If I helped you pass your bill, Tier Four union members would try to gain access above the ninety-fifth floor of megastructures. The families of Tier One will never accept that. Olivia's already working hard behind my back to show building administrators and other Hawk families that I'm no longer effective as center seat. If I vote yes, she'll have the evidence she needs, and you'll be sitting here next month with her. Center Seat of Civil Earth Olivia Belitz doesn't have a nice ring to it."

I inhaled deeply, trying not to let myself grow angry. "You and I both know that the caste recognition system on Civil Earth would never allow a Tier Four identification card to scan past the lower forty floors. Eighty percent of your population lives down there, and they don't call it living in the Lower Forty for no reason. That's it, forty floors and no higher. I did reword some of the writing to accommodate your world's needs."

Mia took a long sip from her wine. "The Lower Forty Tier Four refer to us as Living in the Clouds, because they believe we aren't in tune with reality, and that our heads are always off, floating around. I saw your changes, and my answer is simple: have you ever eaten deer meat?"

I hesitated, knowing there was a setup to her question, and she kept speaking. "It's popular to eat on Epsilon Prime and two of your Colonial Accord planets, I know. On Pardalis, they call it venison, and on Talbora, it's called skinny meat. There are three different names for the same food, and that's what you did with your revisions. You were on that stage during the dock rally, and I saw your crossed-out words and rewrites. You tried to find words that sound different but mean the same thing."

I felt my ears warm from the anger boiling inside and ate one of the bite-sized sandwiches, chewing long and hard. Our meals arrived emanating a light steam and a savory aroma, which saved me from saying something regrettable. We started eating, and I changed the topic. "What's on your agenda for next month in the forum?"

Mia swallowed a large chunk of crab meat dripping with butter before answering. "I'm concerned about the recent disappearances of staff who work under the dome and the main cylinder. Our bubble ambassador's aide disappeared two weeks ago, the station secretary of defense's staffer, and a Federate Corporation junior aide who worked for Representative Decelle all disappeared without a trace. I want to allocate funding for armed protection of all staff when outside the dome."

I wiped my mouth of grease slowly dripping from the moist lamb meat. "That cost will exceed our budget. You won't get those numbers in closed session without demanding more taxation."

In truth, I couldn't care less about the missing staff members; we representatives always had a plethora of staff with us like an entourage, and none of mine had disappeared. Paying for that protection would cost billions more, and Mia knew that. Her eyes wandered and she frowned. The topic troubled her.

"Our aides are essential. They know some of the most sensitive information. We can't allow whoever is taking them to find out our state secrets."

She peered over her shoulder at Melissa, who was conversing with Benjamin. Mia had been happily married for thirteen years and had two children living on the station inside the Civil Earth bubble. Her husband was from a less prominent family, which was why they kept the Stavish name. That didn't take away from the late nights working with her aide Melissa under the sheets. Mia did a terrible job of hiding her infidelities from those who watched, but it was discreet enough that the masses didn't see. Her real need for the proposed bill was her fear of someone taking Melissa and revealing secrets.

"What has the MERC Guild said regarding their investigation into the disappearances?"

Mia narrowed her eyes and tightened her lips. "The same thing they always say. They're dedicating all resources to investigating the matters. They work too slowly for my taste."

None of Tier One of Civil Earth cared for dealing with the Monitoring Enforcement Regulations Chancellery because an agent was the only person in occupied space who could walk above the ninety-fifth floor of any megastructure during Guild activities without a caste recognition card.

"I have a meeting in the cathedral after our lunch and will speak with a senior agent about your concerns."

Mia nodded. Past the flowerpots, both our security teams kept the ever-growing crowd away, who waved and called out to us.

"All the representatives make up the wealthiest among our societies. I believe we could afford the cost of personal protection for staff within our camps without dipping into the Free Worlds' budget. Tier One Hawks don't use Civil Earth Defense for protection. You pay private security."

Mia glanced at the crowds and replied, "Securitan Security Services."

"Yes. Triple S."

"In addition to my station security, I always keep five Securitan officers with me at all times. Forgive me for saying this, Henry, but I don't see how you could possibly be so worried about the Free Worlds' budget when you used a capital transport for your private political rally. That wasn't official forum business." Mia smirked.

I knew that could come back to bite me; I had to go on the defensive. "I had every intention of logging the kilometers traveled and paying for the service in full. This is tit-for-tat nonsense. I'll work with you next month on your bill if you work with me this month and tonight."

She cracked a giant lobster claw, dipped the soft meat into butter, and sucked it into her mouth. "What are your proposals for next month?"

Mia had redirected the conversation. There wasn't any reason to keep pushing.

"The fighting on Gliese between the Corporation and Offensive. Thousands died on both sides, and the native population is suffering in ways much worse. My aide sitting with Melissa has donated time on his weekends at the refugee dock for the droves coming to our station."

She waved her hand as if she was swatting my words like a pesky bug in her face. "Rogue worlds are of little concern to me. The Corporation and Offensive mean nothing. Let them kill each other by the millions. Civil Earth and the Colonial Accord have the most political influence inside the pentagon, and we're the most prosperous. The Watchful Hawks and the Mighty Hammer of Uropa, together in the forum, an unstoppable force."

Mia knew that the Federate Corporation was more financially secure than our planets, even with the war. She was just trying to win me over. The Hammer of Labor was greater than her Cloud Walkers of Tier One, but I could never say that outright.

She reached for her wine glass as I said, "So if we sit back and do nothing while the Corporation dumps much of their world finance budget into the war effort, we can push the gap even further, correct?"

Mia sipped and nodded.

"Mia, let me ask, what happens after the war? Civil Earth, the Accord, and the Human Alliance would be stuck financing the recovery efforts required by our Relations Policy. If the fighting ever made it to one of their homeworlds, it'd cost hundreds of trillions to repair that destruction. When the dust settles from war and rebuilding, we'd all be worse off under the dome, with the addition of millions more dead and emptier pockets."

She glanced at the spectators waving their hands, and said, "Of course, you're right, Henry, you are right most of the time about these things. I'll work with you on next month's agenda if you work with mine."

Our conversation at the Eatontown Café appeared like any other between two prominent officials. We were sitting there having lunch, having an apparently casual conversation, but in reality, we two representatives held the real power inside the forum for the Free Worlds of Humanity, and our words decided whether millions of people would live or die. It all came down to how we voted inside the Capitol Forum. The results for next month were being decided over lobster claws, lamb meat, and costly wine. If those waving Free Worlders knew how little control they had in their everyday lives, what would they do? Mia told me once, "Commoners don't need a brain to follow the herd, only legs."

Keep the box locked, Henry. Don't let those thoughts out. I agreed, and we talked more about gossip and whispers throughout the territories. Mia told me she was having trouble with Station Director Rumi Houlton regarding updates Civil Earth had requested for their bubble entryway into the main cylinder. I saw Rumi often at formal black-tie events and our monthly meetings with her or her staff. She was a serious individual, similar to me in age, but extremely uptight. Rumi's position came with high stresses and responsibilities that contributed to her personality flaws.

Our minutes had concluded, and I felt drained from watching my every word and timing my responses accordingly. Even when talking unofficially, a wrong sentence uttered could have lasting effects.

"Will you consider voting yay tonight?"

The wine had gotten to her head, and her pause was long.

"If you remove the provisions I originally asked, I promise to take your bill to the finish line. You've back-stepped from promises before, and we all know your abilities with words. You won't have trouble recovering when all is said and done."

I stood, called to Benjamin, and leaned over, pecking both cheeks before leaving; my ears felt warm. "Mia, you'll have my answer within a few hours."

I left Mia to her thoughts and proceeded to our vehicles. Once back inside, we went on our way to the cathedral, headquarters for the MERC Guild, at the bottom of the station. My mind wandered thinking of Senior Agent Ficco, and the next council meeting. I needed a solution to deal with Secretary Nicolas Nomikos, but I was having trouble keeping focused.

Our drive to the cathedral took roughly forty-five minutes through the main cylinder's roadways, and it gave me time to consider Mia's requests, or were they demands?

"Benjamin, how did it go with Melissa? Did you win your word game? I fear I might have lost mine."

"She didn't say much at first. After you finished your first bottle of wine, Melissa started talking. She's not as intelligent as other staff under the dome."

I smirked. Mia didn't hire Melissa for her brain, more for what she looked like with her clothes off and how she used her tongue.

"The other representatives aren't as fortunate as I to have an aide with your skills and degree."

Benjamin had studied psychology and had a doctorate in political science. He was knowledgeable and finished those studies while working for me. He was smart, but not the same quality as other staff of representatives of the five walls. Most were masters of manipulation and word games. Ben wasn't. Melissa was an outlier because she served in different ways.

"Anything useful from her?" I asked.

"Yes. We know that Mia met with two separate representatives yesterday to finish her minutes for the month. What isn't in the official log and Melissa clumsily gave up was that she also met with JJ. I looked it up on the public feed. Mia and JJ have six-minute gaps in their public records for yesterday."

An interesting development. Meeting outside of the minutes happened sporadically, but for both to go through the effort of concealing, it was something else. Why did she keep that information from me? Everyone across the Free Worlds knew how much JJ Richmond and I disliked each other. The Rose and Hammer could never agree. Mia was always secretive about her activities.

"She wants me to remove the equal rights portion of my bill."

Ben frowned and scratched at his chin. "That was a huge rallying point for the bill. Local unions are on the networks talking about it constantly. The Hammer Unions saw it as a sign of strength, showing that our Labor Party could reach out to other Free Worlds."

"I know, lad. It's a tough position. I'm between a rock and a hard place. We need the rest of my bill to pass. Without support from the Federate Corporation or Civil Earth, it's dead in the water."

No persuasion would come by way of the Corporation because of my aggressive coaxing for yay votes in Mia's bill last month. They also wouldn't want their employees to have rights superseding corporate policies. Voting yay for me would be a double slap in the face.

"Sir, I've learned an important lesson from watching you through the years." He paused as we made eye contact. "Your best weapon is a podium and microphone. It will sting to take that clause out of the bill, but you'll be able to redirect thoughts elsewhere."

That boy had no idea what my best weapon was behind the curtain. My hands were tensing up, and I felt sweat under my arms. *Easy, Henry. Keep it locked.*

"You know me well. There's still time to make a decision. Let's see what the rest of today brings."

The last stretch of roadway brought a change of scenery. The cylinder itself was shrinking. The central support beam and the other side got closer to each other, narrowing like a funnel; instead of towns, green landscape, and accommodations, the ground beneath and above changed to metal, appearing more like a standard space station or ship. Signs littered the area displaying warnings that we were drawing near to the cathedral, and then the wall enlarged ahead of our trucks, starting like a distant speck that grew rapidly the closer we went, pushing up higher until it towered over us from both sides like a mountain. The cathedral wall had an intimidating and immense persona. It was like a living structure all on its own—the illustrious grand walls known throughout occupied space. When people talked of the cathedral, it was always as a story of fable or myth. It was aged bronze with sparkling lights, making the wall appear like it was held together by magic because of its size and splendor.

At the checkpoint, Guild agents with their mongrels patrolled alongside the entrance, and they approached us. I never understood why they were so concerned. No one was foolish enough to attack. Agents were superheroes to most, and their mongrels always turned heads.

A sentry walked to the window, asking for identification. On the passenger's side, his mongrel pressed its snout against the glass, breathing deeply and fogging the clear barrier. The beast made Oliver uneasy, and he shifted in his seat and adjusted his shirt collar.

Ben's eyes opened wide, looking at the agent, and he gave a slight smile. "My uncle's an agent with the Guild. The last I heard, he was on a Civil Earth substation in one of their megacities."

"You've got good genes in your family if someone so close in blood passed the genetic screening."

"He's the first. I remember him saying there's only one agent for every one hundred and fifty-three thousand Free Worlds citizens."

"That's why the training takes so long, and lots don't pass. An agent needs to be better and smarter than everyone else."

Ben leaned to the other window to look at the mongrel.

"Ben, you're acting as if it's the first time you've seen an agent. Did you have posters, shirts, and toys of famous agents growing up?"

"All Free Worlds children did. My favorite was Senior Agent Scala because he was Dolrinion, so rare."

"Yes. Dolrinions often don't have the proper genetics for MERC Guild requirements. I've only sworn two into office through my career. Scala was the agent who went to the pirate world Martoosh and hunted the Flock family, right?"

"Yes, sir. He fought off pirate captains native to the planet and recovered all the family members' heads."

The Flock family killed two agents who attempted to bring them to justice and other law enforcement officials from the Free Worlds. Scala and his mongrel, Champ, took the family out one at a time over two weeks on that rogue world with pirate captains hunting him.

I said, "Well, you can be impressed with a senior agent from three hundred years ago. I'm more impressed with their mongrels." I turned my head to look at the closest beast standing outside our truck who was nearly eye level with me.

Our vehicles cleared the checkpoint and moved inside the colossal main sliding doors. Once through the outer doors and another three airlocks, we entered the primary staging location. The cathedral entry area was vast, like the main cylinder without the artificial aspects and vegetation. The Guild had no need for those accommodations because every square centimeter served an objective. A Guild transport cruiser drove in front of us and towered over our truck. Another came up behind and our interior speakers came alive with a voice.

"Good afternoon, Representative McWright. I'm Agent Idell. We will be your escort to Academy Hall, where your chief of staff, Malcolm Booth, is awaiting your arrival."

"Thank you, Agent Idell. We are grateful for your protection and escort."

It was all theater. There wasn't any reason for armed escort inside the cathedral. They did that as a show of respect and to justify their massive funding budget granted by the five walls. I dreaded those closed session debates when the chiefs came begging with open hands, claiming they were underfunded. Malcolm should have spoken my needs to key figures there. He'd been behind the curtain with me for many years. My presence was only a formality, and it was good for agents to see me at the bottom of our station once in a while.

Benjamin called my attention to both sides of our vehicle, where six mongrels ran with us in their full field armor of Corin steel. We were traveling at least sixty-four kilometers per hour, and the mongrels had no trouble maintaining speed. Their fur was short, different shades of brindle, brown and black; they had pointed cropped ears, cut tails, and huge jowls that reminded me of traditional mastiff breeds.

"Wouldn't it be nice to have one of those amazing animals at your side for protection?"

Oliver said, "I'm terrified of those monsters. Years ago, when I served on dome emergency response, an altercation broke out inside the dome dock. Smugglers were attempting to bring illegal weapons right through the Capitol Forum. The crew had fifty heavily armed mercenaries providing security. When the Guild unleashed their full abilities on that ship, it was something I'll never forget. Those mongrels were firing rounds from their auto guns and leaping at the fighters, tearing them to shreds. The agents had some of the most disciplined focus I have ever seen, and they had that entire ship subdued in less than a few minutes."

Agents were also armored with Corin steel, the most robust and rarest metal in existence. The auto guns were similar in power to medium-range spinners, able to lock on to targets automatically.

"You don't give yourself enough credit, Ollie," I said. "I'd put you and my security detail up against any MERC agent without a second thought. You're very capable."

I wouldn't bet five credits on my security lasting ten seconds in a straight fight with one Guild agent, but building their confidence was essential.

Benjamin added, "A mongrel's bite is stronger than an alligator. I wouldn't want those fangs anywhere near me."

"Then remind me to never find myself within biting distance of their mouth when an agent isn't around."

During the almost fifteen minutes of travel, we discussed other famous historical Guild agents and their great deeds. Past agents like Senior Agent Bishop and his mongrel, the War Horse of Duppo, the largest ever created by Kennel Hall. Agent Lockwell and her beast Goliath, the smallest mongrel in history. We also discussed a current walking legend among the Guild, Agent Dykstra, who spent most of her time tracking criminals on rogue and outer worlds. She had more successful recoveries than any other agent in history, and her neural connection worked on two mongrels, Eda and Lynx, which was considered impossible before her successful melding.

Academy Hall appeared as a massive pentagon-shaped building, big enough to house twenty years' worth of trainees. Oliver opened the door for me and six agents with their mongrels took up defensive positions, once again nothing more than show.

The mongrels panted but hadn't seemed to lose much stamina from that long run at a constant speed.

"Sir," Idell said. "It was an honor to escort you here. We appreciate all your efforts under the dome to help the Free Worlds."

He wore a tactical Corin-steel-plated vest with its glowing green lines and black flecks streaking through the war plate. I was almost in a trance, looking at the shining lines of the rare metal. His pentagon-shaped polished-bronze badge broke my focus.

I smiled and shook his hand. "It's my pleasure, Agent Idell. Without the MERC Guild, we'd have anarchy in occupied space. You honor me. Could I pet your mongrel?"

Waiting for his response wasn't necessary. I knew the answer already, but being polite while exerting my authority was prudent.

"Absolutely, sir, just give me a second, please."

He closed his eyes, which twitched slightly along with his eyebrows. The mongrel shadowing behind closed its eyes with a head tilt. It was captivating to see the wireless connection in action. That skill took agents years to master. At Kennel Hall, staff worked tirelessly, finding the proper gene splicing to upgrade the modified dogs' abilities, including mental upgrades. Agents and mongrels could communicate with each other.

They were aggressive animals, and if the agent didn't mentally subdue it before I put my hand out, I'd need a new hand. That alligator bite Benjamin referred to was genuine. Both opened their eyes simultaneously; the beast took a few steps towards me and lowered his head. I moved my hand closer. Its fur wasn't soft or rough, rather of an odd coarseness that seemed almost oily, like hair not washed in weeks. It didn't remind me of the rabbits I had as a child growing up on Uropa.

Benjamin's eyes were wide.

"What's his name?" I asked.

"Major. He was joined to me only five years ago when my last mongrel died during an operation."

Agent Idell lowered his chin, and I raised my eyebrows with interest. "That's a story I'd like to hear one day. The next time you're under the dome, stop by my office. We'll have lunch, and you can tell me the story. I know it's difficult to get over that kind of loss. The mind-meld makes you one, and a piece of you died with your mongrel."

Agent Idell looked up. "It would be a great honor, Representative McWright. Thank you."

Those types of conversations were how I developed lasting relationships on the station with those who could assist me in the future. It was how I took Senior Agent Ficco under my wing when he graduated. I molded him into the agent he was, and it had benefited me tremendously. At the top of the large stone staircase of Academy Hall, two agents stood guard, and their mongrels watched us closely.

A civilian staff member was at the top of the stairs near the doorway, waiting to kiss the rings before bringing me to Malcolm and Ficco. I was the most senior under the dome, and I had certain expectations as to how I would be treated in a place like this; while other visitors would be hesitant and fearful, I anticipated the respect of all. My dark thoughts wanted to surface, but I held them back to keep my public composure. The day was still far from over. Life was never dull on the relations station.

CHAPTER 7

A Refugee of the Free Worlds

Running away from the Alliance (Isabel)

Another dream from all those years ago. It was a common dream with subtle differences each time. A never-ending escape from a time when the twenty-one city-states were independent, following the leadership of elected prime regents. That ended with the Unification Civil War. Fourteen years ago, Athinia's Ministry of State was intact on Epsilon Prime, and the Human Alliance was the greatest power of all the Free Worlds. No more. So many people died during the war.

In the dream, Tuddy looked as he did before the war. Adam and Juliet were young children, chasing chickens in the coop and giggling. Of course, it was a dream. The children were adults of twenty-three and nineteen now, and Tuddy had been dead for nearly a year because of our resistance against New-Sparta. For years we spent endless nights moving the kids from place to place. Hiding in basements, attics, or hidden sub-wall rooms as the city-state loyalists helped us fight and stay alive while the Lyons Pride shock troops kept hunting, trying to kill my family line.

Nightmares about Isaac and Killian Lyons were common too—the Twins of New-Sparta with their city-state allies who started the war with a surprise attack to take control. The Pride came close to catching us over the years, and we spent lots of time and energy resisting them to the bitter end. That was all in the past, and the current dream was pleasant with luscious green grasslands far and wide, spanning unending miles and thick dark forests with more foliage than other Free Worlds. At least the farmland around our home was that way fourteen years ago. Each city-state only had its one major city, and the surrounding lands were villages, green lands, rolling hills, and wilderness. Such beauty, now gone.

That rural lifestyle made our people incredibly self-sufficient and strong. Cows, chickens, and huge pigs made their usual sounds as the dream continued in tranquil bliss. Tuddy rode his horse along the fence line in search of broken sections. Androids helped tend the farm, and Adam and Juliet laughed so innocently chasing more of our animals. Juliet still giggled and larked with her sneaky ways, which helped her cope with stresses, but Adam hadn't smiled or laughed in years. The smell of fresh cow pats was in a light wind. It was a typical day, and everything was peaceful—what a great dream.

On the snap of fingers, something changed and seemed wrong because the sky was changing colors like a flashing light on an intersection. It wasn't the luscious light blue of a clear day and flickered from red to blue, back and forward in a repetitive pattern. Adam and Juliet didn't notice the change. "Wake up." They were still playing with the chickens. Tuddy in the distance, "Wake up," kept riding the fence line, and the droids were collecting their daily harvest, "Wake up." What was that sound? Was someone yelling? There wasn't anyone else near, and the red flashing sky was brighter. Things in the surrounding landscape faded away in cloudy darkness. Tuddy disappeared, and past him was a looming black cloud of emptiness. My heart was pounding, and the kids slowly evaporated like hot breath in a cold chill.

"No, no, please. Come back."

There it was again, that voice and so loud. "Wake up!"

As my eyes opened, the realization of where I was hit like a ton of bricks. The refugee ship was our reality and had been for the last three weeks as we fled the Alliance. The walls were gray, as were the ceiling, floors, and everything else, gray-gray-gray, not green at all. A red alert light on the wall flashed with a buzzing alarm every few seconds. Juliet was looking down, shaking my shoulders, and Adam, with his raggedy beard from months without a shave, put what few things we had into a bag. My throat felt dry, and my eyes burned in the dreary recycled air.

"What's going on, Juliet? What happened?"

She was pulling on her hair, caressing it, and it rattled my nerves. That was something she always did when she was nervous. I needed to stay strong for them both.

"I honestly don't know. The alarms started going off for no reason, but I remember what that woman said in the dining area yesterday. We're in the Great-in-Between, remember?"

She was right—the emptiness of space stretching numerous light-years that touched on three different Free Worlds' territories. It was the most hostile region of all occupied space with regular contact from pirates, Dolrinions, Rogue Syndicate, and Androsians. We prayed to the three acolytes that it wasn't Androsians targeting us on their screens.

The ship commander chose to gamble our lives in the Great-in-Between to save on cost. Going around it to the relations station would have added weeks to the trip, and the ship didn't have enough food for such swelling numbers of refugees. The junker transport needed to drop from FTL for more cooldowns, which painted a target across the ship. The flashing lights and alarms brought my attention back to present circumstances.

"We need to go to the safe room."

"But this ship's life box isn't made from Corin steel," Adam said.

"It's still a better tactical position for us, and when have you ever heard of Corin steel being used on refugee ships?"

When the bad guys come, and there's nothing left but doom, the last place to survive is inside the safe room.

It didn't matter what the room was made from; if our distress call didn't get an answer from friendlies, enemies could get inside. I stood, slipped on boots, and tightened the laces as the lights continued flashing and the deafening sharp buzzing noise continued. We weren't strangers to that type of stress, waking in the night to flee time and time again because of the Lyons Pride and their New-Sparta Pact states.

"Let's go," I shouted and hit the release button on the door.

Gears on the door turned, making their usual clicking noise releasing air and a whoosh sound as the pressure between the hinges released. The door was almost entirely open when two passengers in the outer hallway whisked past us in a hurry, running to the left.

I squeezed Juliet's hand a little tighter and pulled her into the hallway. Adam was right behind us with our travel bag. Like our room, the hall was also gray, such a depressing sight for someone who had spent their life in the countryside of Athinia. Even the Alliance bubble on the relations station had so much green inside, with beautiful forests made to look the same way they did on Epsilon Prime. But on the ship, the landscape was pipes wrapped together at eye level running along the walls on both sides, power distribution boxes and air scrubbers scattered randomly.

We ran, trying to get to the safe room.

Adam said, "Mom, do you remember where we need to go? I think it's four levels down from here."

"Three levels down and in this direction."

A loud tapping noise came from the outer walls of the hall. I remembered that sound from the four years in mandatory military service to my state before the civil war. Uranium rounds were hitting the ship's hull.

"Someone's shooting at us. We're taking fire."

The greater question was who the unknown aggressor was in the darkness of space. Both my kids' eyes widened. Neither of them had been on a ship before, let alone one under attack.

"Let's go," I said, pulling my daughter's hand as we ran faster down the hallway.

At the center location of our vessel were ladder hatches above and below. Large screws were spaced around the metal of the domed hatch on the floor. That area was larger than the hallway of our room. The centralized common area contained an elevator bank, benches, a service screen showing information like the current temperature of the floor we were on, our ship's location, and what meals would be in the ship's dining areas. Adam ran over to the ladder hatch on the floor and cranked the lever, his veins bulging as he twisted the stiff metal.

"Why don't we take the elevator? Wouldn't it be faster?" Juliet said.

"We can't. The ship goes into pressurized lockdown when alerts are triggered. If the hull became compromised in any way on a certain level, the pressure lock ensures we don't depressurize and suffocate."

Juliet's mouth dropped. "I don't want to suffocate."

The hatch was open, and Adam raised his voice. "Down to the next level."

"Don't worry, Jules. We'll be ok once we get into the life box."

Adam held the bubble door open as Juliet climbed down, followed by me. He came after us. We were in the dead space between floors, and underneath was the next hatch to the lower level.

I opened the bubble hatch, and the small green light turned red. A ladder was built into the wall of that level, and we climbed down. A few meters to the right was another ladder hatch to the next dead space below.

A family stood there, trying to open the next hatch. The woman cried hysterically as she held an infant and her partner pulled on the lever. When Juliet climbed down to the metal floor and stepped over to the family, the woman jumped away and gasped, covering her mouth.

"Oh, goodness, I didn't see you there." She wiped away some tears from her cheek.

Her accent was from City-State Macegia. They were our allies during the civil war.

I stepped off the ladder; Adam set about closing the upper hatch to secure it and the light turned green.

The man trying to open the lever was sweating and straining. He had a stubbly unkempt face. He asked, "Do you know how many more levels down the safe room is?"

I answered quickly, "The next level."

The lower door opened, and the family climbed the ladder, followed by my family.

As Juliet moved on the ladder, I said, "We're almost there, Jules, just keep going."

Those words seemed shallow because we were in the Great-in-Between. The likelihood of someone registering our distress signal that far away from Free Worlds space was slim, and the odds of those who did receive the call answering it were even smaller.

Most heat signatures inside the in-Between would be hostile. No one had claim inside the starless void, and the Androsian Singularity was home to the cybernetic demons. It was a free-for-all here.

We would have a fighting chance inside the life box. That room wasn't a terrible position from which to mount a defense against whoever was attacking. Who was attacking us? New-Sparta wanted us dead, but Isaac Lyons would wish to make a spectacle of it. Killing us out here with no one to see wasn't his way. Military destroyers were far beyond the abilities of our junker, and in a fight we would be like a fly caught in a spider's web.

Lights nearby flickered as the power fluctuated, and the alarms stopped buzzing, but the red lights continued flashing. That meant we had switched to emergency power. The attackers would be boarding the ship soon. The Macegian man with his scruffy face was still trying to open the lower hatch. It wouldn't budge with the upper door open. His panic set in.

"It won't open until my son closes the upper door."

Adam twisted the lever bar on the hatch, but the crank appeared stiff and it creaked loudly.

The Macegian man shrieked, "Hurry up! Close it, please. Close it now."

"Calm yourself. We're almost safe. Take deep breaths."

How did he survive the war with such fear? One of the first things we all learned in military school was to remain calm. Green light: the upper hatch secured.

"Now," I said. "Open it."

Red light: the lower door opened and the family climbed down. The terminal docking doors, dining area, commander's quarters, command center were on that level, and the safe room. We were moving slower, and it took a few minutes for the strangers to get down before we started our descent. It felt like an eternity. Juliet went down one rung at a time with the flashing light reflecting off everything below. The tapping stopped. They'd be entering soon.

Jules was down, and I started my climb. I reached the grated floor and glanced down the distant hallway. The strangers from Macegia had already passed the terminal doors and turned left down the junction hallway leading to the safe room. Adam was still trying to close the hatch, but he was taking too long.

I yelled, "Leave it. We have to go."

Adam looked up at the hatch door and me, then climbed down. But his foot missed the next bar, and he fell three meters to the metal floor. My son screamed from the pain of a twisted ankle.

I leaned down and inspected his injury. "It's just a sprain, Adam. You'll be fine."

We helped him to his feet, and he leaned on us with one leg lifted.

"We have to carry him."

We held Adam's arms, supporting his weight, and I grabbed his belt to keep him steady. It was too slow, and the terminal docking door cylinder lights began spinning. Someone had docked.

"They're here. Juliet, take your brother and continue left down that hallway. You need to get to the life box."

Juliet stared at me with her eyebrows raised and said, "But, Mom, I don't—"

I grabbed my daughter's arm and talked over her. "Stop, Jules. You need to focus. Keep going, and don't look back. You're stronger than you know. It's time for you to save your brother. Now go."

Adam and Juliet gazed for a moment. There wasn't enough time to say more. On Epsilon Prime, while resisting the Lyons Twins of New-Sparta, there was rarely any time to spend with them like a typical family. For the last fourteen years since the war, life was hard for us all. We couldn't waste any more time.

I raised my voice. "Go. Both of you. I'll hold them off."

They needed time to get to the safe room. If the commander had any courage, he'd wait to seal the door. Juliet dragged Adam down the hallway, supporting her brother's weight the best she could. The terminal doors towered over me, and to the left was a breaching bar. A cranking sound came from the doors. Someone was manually overriding the locks. It wasn't Androsians. They would have used their laser cutters to slice their way in, to do the nightmarish things they did, before leaving the ship to depressurize. The enemy out in the dark coldness wanted to salvage our junker.

I grabbed the breaching bar and held on to it. It was a cumbersome metal rod with a slight curve and flat angles on both sides. That was the way to open doors after a power loss on crap ships like this one. Better equipped vessels had automatic mechanical breaching tools, but not a junker. The bar felt good and well balanced. My back was to the wall, leaning against the cold metal. Adam and Juliet were near the junction turn and would be out of sight soon. It was time to get ready for whoever was coming through the terminal.

The crank locked into place, thrashing and reverberating through the hall, and the massive doors rolled open, retreating into the wall. I squeezed my hands tightly, and my fingers interlocked around the metal. Adrenaline was pumping through my body, causing stiff fingers and clammy hands. The air from our two ships met, creating a light mist surrounding the entire entryway, and fog gently floated to the ceiling and disappeared. They were about to come inside.

*

Someone walked through the terminal door, and the sound of boots echoed on the grated metal floor. He turned to the right down the hallway, where my kids were only seconds earlier. The strange aggressor had a mask with goggles, not sealed for space—which would serve a purpose. His mask was for fear and intimidation. Someone with less experience would look at him and tremble in fear. I was not that person.

There were black straps around his head holding the mask in place. From his attire, I knew he was not a member of the Rogue Syndicate or a Dolrinion sentinel. These attackers were here to steal, loot, and pillage this transport. They were lowest of the low, criminals of all occupied space. Space Pirates of the three worlds: Leo, Martoosh, and the most famous of the three, Draco. Scavengers and deadbeats, that was all.

He wore all black, though the color had faded from years of use, and his rifle was old and beat-up. His back was to me; he was looking down the hallway leading to the safe room. As he turned, I swung the breaching bar, fast and hard, striking his trigger hand. A muffled scream emanated from behind that ugly dark mask, and his arm went down from the blow as several rounds shot into the metal grates. I spun behind him and raised the bar even higher, and with every fiber of strength, connected to the mask and the face behind it.

By that point, everything moved in slow motion. The pirate falling felt like hours, and behind him, more figures appeared, making their way in my direction. I shifted sideways and pulled the breaching bar back, arching my elbow to swing again at the next attacker. Before I could do anything, someone struck me with tremendous force. Was I run over by a truck? He was the largest man I ever saw. By all means, a giant.

I smashed against the grates, and wind cleared my lungs like a balloon losing air. Pirate guns pointed in my face, and one man stepped forward, who was better dressed than the others, which wasn't saying much. The way he stared at me was like a Tier One administrator on Civil Earth looking at someone living on the Lower Forty of Tier Four. It enraged me.

He was their captain, wearing a tactical vest with nothing beneath but myriad tattoos and an oversized pistol holstered at his side. Pirates flooded the ship, moving in different directions. I felt a sharp pain in my ribs from the giant's tackle. That bastard moved fast for his size.

The captain had a calm, balanced voice with a hint of the Colonial Accord in his accent. "Where did this ship come from?"

A subordinate standing behind gave a swift kick to my back and hollered, "Answer the captain."

I winced. "The Alliance, we came from Epsilon Prime."

His face curled into a half-smile as he looked at his underlings, who were waiting for orders. Above the captain's left eye was a hideous scar that ran past his eye and down the cheek. In place of that eye was a cybernetic implant that didn't resemble an eye at all. He lifted both arms, showing missing fingers. The pointer and middle were no longer there.

The Human Alliance had captured him before. Our militaries of the twenty-one city-states had little pity on those who fought against them. When enemy combatants became prisoners, the military would cut off their first two fingers of each hand—a sign to all that they were enemies of the Alliance states and should never take up arms again. The captain's dominant hand had replacement fingers, not professionally done but rudimentary. His metal fingers would allow him to hold a gun again, which was all a pirate needed. There was nothing in place of his missing two fingers on the left hand.

Fear crept under my skin, looking at that wicked half-smile.

He grabbed a handful of my hair and lifted me straight to my feet. He leaned in and pressed his lips to the side of my face. I attempted to pull away, but his hold was firm.

He took a deep breath and smelled my skin. "Let's go find your friends, shall we?"

"We're a refugee ship going to the relations station. There's nothing of value here."

"We shall see."

He pulled away and raised his hands from side to side, stretching them out like he was going to hug someone who wasn't there. He spun around in a circle, saying, "Let the games begin." His laugh was loud and projected through the room. "Search the entire ship, find me some credits, and take what you will. Empty their food stores and if you find someone you want, claim them. They're yours."

The pirates all shouted with glee; some moved down random hallways, and others opened computer docking stations to try and hack access to the mainframe so they could remotely open the doors. Good code crackers might unlock some living spaces, but the life box was on an isolated system and would never open from their attempts.

Someone grabbed my arm and pulled me through the hallway. Pirates were all around as we went through the junction hallway and turned where Adam and Juliet had been only moments earlier. Piping ran along both sides of the walls and openings to different common areas were spaced out sporadically. Every six meters or so was a bulkhead in case of a breach.

At the other end of that long hall, pirates were already in a shootout with someone from the junker. I hoped it wasn't Adam and Juliet. In such a confined space, the gunfire sounds were deafening. My ears rang from the loud bangs and I covered them. A few pirates were already dead, lying in their own blood, which felt sticky on my boots like sap. Another fell and rolled into me. Blood streamed from his mouth along with shallow gasps for air. I had fought in countless battles against the Lyons Pride in situations just like this, so I wasn't a stranger to the sight.

Small flashes of light sparked off the walls as bullets missing their intended targets impacted the metal. The captain took a position near me at the corner, screaming out and shooting his pistol down the corridor. The other end of that hall was the command center, and behind that was the safe room. He leaned back, holstering his gun.

"Suppression fire, keep them pinned. I'm going to toss a banger."

He pulled a proximity concussion grenade from his chest, yanked the pin while shooters across from him increased their rate of fire. The grenade left his hand and flew down the hall. The giant of a man who tackled me earlier yelled, "Take cover."

The explosion was thunderous and rumbled the entire hallway, including the metal floor grates. Even with my eyes shut, the light from the blast was so radiant I could see the back of my eyelids.

When I opened my eyes, the pirate captain waved his people forward to press the attack. The hallway was darker, nearly pitch black from the explosion, which had blown the lights out. After a few moments, the giant pirate guided us through the thick residual smoke, its smell like burned rubber. A few bodies of ship's crew members lay on the grates. None of them were real soldiers.

Some were still alive, and one was the commander—an older man with salt and pepper hair and a thick mustache; he'd been kind through the trip. Three crew, sweating in their standard light blue jumpsuits, survived the attack on the command center and were on their knees. The pirate captain walked circles around them, gawking with contempt.

"You killed two of my crew and will return that price in full. But first, what floor are your power cells located on?"

The captain stopped his pacing behind the first crew member, a young woman nearly the same age as Juliet with black marks over her face and dust on her uniform that was torn in random spots exposing her skin underneath. The arrogant ass of a pirate slowly raised his arm, pointing his pistol at the back of her head, jabbing with the barrel of the gun.

Her lips quivered as she answered, "Level J, from the main terminal docking door, go down two levels." She paused briefly to catch her breath and rub those red, irritated eyes.

The captain's half-smile returned. "Why, thank you."

Only a moment passed, and he pulled the trigger. The front of the frightened woman's head exploded out like a corkscrew shooting from a bottle of champagne. Her brain matter and thick globs of red blood littered the floor grates and dripped through to the subfloor.

Her lifeless body fell to the grates, and a second crew member, a middle-aged man, screamed with dread in his voice. He attempted to stand only to be struck with the butt of a rifle, sending him down once more.

The captain smiled again and raised his left hand with the missing fingers. His remaining fingers were clenching into a fist and he pointed one into the air.

"That's one."

He stepped over to the middle-aged man, who was now on his back with both hands raised into the air as if he was attempting to shield himself from the bullets that hadn't yet left the gun.

The frightened crewmember said, "Please, don't, please. No. I'll do whatever you want."

I pitied that crew member. He didn't realize it yet, but there was nothing he could do to prevent his fate. The captain straddled the frightened man lying on the floor.

"I'll let you live if you tell me what level the food storage is on."

"Level H, go to H, everything is there, food, repair equipment, and extra storage gear."

The captain smirked and raised an eyebrow. "Thank you kindly."

Despite those words, his gun moved slowly, pointing down at the crewman, and blasted rounds of fire and death into his chest and neck. There were no more sounds of fear from that frightened man, only ghostly silence.

The blood wasn't visible or pooling. It fell under the subfloor. Our vessel's commander had his eyes down, blank-faced, and the captain walked to him. Even an old commander who had seen much in his years couldn't pretend he didn't witness the atrocities in that room. Using his gun, the captain lifted the aging commander's chin, and they made eye contact for the first time. The commander's eyes narrowed in an attempt at defiance, but he didn't speak a word.

A gaze like that would bother most people, but the captain appeared unconcerned. He squatted down, leaning on his knees to be eye level with the commander, cocked his head to the side, and smiled. "That, commander … is two." He held out his maimed hand with two fingers pointing straight out.

Some of his crew laughed.

"Open the door to the safe room, please."

Our transport commander didn't answer, and it was impressive to see his courage. Hopefully, Adam and Juliet were in that room, but how long would the commander hold out before giving in?

The captain tilted his head to the other side, still smiling. He spoke with lingering exaggeration. "Open the door."

The captain waited a few seconds, then holstered the pistol and slapped his knees. "Ok, time for the fun stuff. Bring up the brander, heat the coils, and let's see what this old toad smells like when his skin cooks."

All the pirates cheered as the next phase of this terrible encounter began to take shape. How many inhabitants of our free, outer, or rogue worlds could be going through something similar at the same time? There were lots of human souls spread through the vastness of occupied space. How many were being tortured, killed in some horrific manner, or within centimeters of the end of their life? A depressing thought because it probably happened somewhere every minute of every day. Extreme violence was the way things were for the Free Worlds of Humanity; the strong ate the weak and the wicked preyed on the innocent. That was why we had to be strong and keep fighting because otherwise awful people would consume everything without resistance.

A huge muscular woman came into the command center. She had dark, short-cropped hair and a black tattoo covering half her face, and a crazed demeanor. Her eyes were open so wide they might have fallen out. Her outfit was different from the rest—a backpack with a cable linked to a long-handled metal rod. The rod had coils around it, and I felt the incredible heat coming from the metal, which made a buzzing sound like hornets.

The heated coils were burning red hot, and steam rose from the metal. The light was so radiant, half the room glowed orange and yellow. It was like a cattle brander but much hotter, and heavily retrofitted for a different reason, a more sinister purpose.

The captain moved his feet as if he were dancing or skipping with his arms folded behind him. He moved behind the crazed behemoth woman holding the brander, walking back and forth while the woman stared as if possessed in the commander's direction. He was trying to shield his eyes from the light and heat.

"I will kindly ask you one more time, commander." He jerked his head sharply to look at the commander again. "I would like you to open the safe room door."

Our commander gave no response. What were his thoughts at that moment? Was he putting his mind in a pleasant place, thinking of a lover, his family, or a happy time from his past, or was he bitter, cursing these invaders of his ship? Maybe he wondered how he could have made different choices to avoid this situation by traveling around the Great-in-Between instead of through it. What does one think when they're about to endure extreme physical pain and the person doing it to them was enjoying the experience like a game?

Sweat drenched the commander's body and he still tried to shield his face from the heated coils close to him. At that distance, his palms blistered like the skin was cooking in an oven. For the first time, a noise came from his mouth, but it wasn't words, only cries of pain.

The captain signaled his mad torturer to step back and halt the torment. She obeyed, using a thickly gloved hand to cover the heated coils. The cocky pirate leaped towards the bewildered victim and dropped down to his knees again, face to face with the commander.

"So, do I have to melt half your face off, or are you going to start flapping that hole right above your chin?" He pushed his mechanical finger into the broken old commander's face.

If the captain had his real fingers and jabbed me like that, I would have bitten them off without hesitation.

With a downcast expression of defeat, the commander finally broke his silence. "I-I can't open the doors even if I wanted to. Once put into lockdown, the life box door will only open from the inside. The override's in effect, and my codes are useless now."

The pirate let out a disappointed sigh and grabbed the commander's wrists, pulling them closer to inspect the newly formed blisters. After a few seconds of inspection, he sarcastically instructed the commander to have his hands looked at by a doctor at the earliest convenience. Stepping back to his torturer, the captain tapped her shoulder and spoke. "I don't like his mouth. Remove it for me, would you?"

Her face was even more grotesque with a wide grin of delight. She uncovered the coils and pointed the red-hot rod at the commander's face. He cried out in terror and kept his hands up in an attempt to block the coils.

The hot rods pushed past his hands, melting the skin off instantly, making the bones visible, and the modified brander hit its mark, driving past lips, teeth, and into the back of the commander's throat. His thick mustache disintegrated, each small hair burning back up his face like a fuse. It only took a moment for the hot buzzing coils to melt his face away entirely. It was as if his blood and bodily fluids were in a pot cooking.

I've seen some horrific things through my life, none of which compared, and that smell, what was that awful smell? Around his body was nothing but red and brown mush. The commander's head dripped with ooze from melted skin, fat, muscle, and bone.

Some of the pirate shipmates in the room were visibly disturbed, covering their mouths, squinting their eyes, or making sounds of disgust. Even the captain lost his half-smile in the end, and the only person who seemed to enjoy the experience was the crazed woman performing the deed. From the pleasure on her face, it couldn't be any clearer that she was a complete psychopath.

Some time passed as pirates made their way into the command center with things they had stolen from the living spaces, prisoners, and some came with nothing but their old beat-up rifles. One of the pirates had DDD near its end-stage. He'd be dead within the year. DNA degradation disease was a terrible way to die. The slow death. Surprisingly the captain was compassionate to that crew member.

As the spoils of their raid came in and the captain inspected what little there was, I was both afraid and comforted because he had forgotten about me standing there in the corner, but he was also frustrated with what little there was to steal. A pirate standing near me signaled to the crazed woman to turn off the coils. For the next fifteen minutes, passengers made their way into the command center as captives. The room was large enough and had no issue accommodating them. Not enough of the refugees had made it to the safe room. We outnumbered our attackers two to one, but these people wouldn't fight to save themselves. They weren't the warriors who resisted our enemy city-states.

The captain became angry, red-faced, raising his voice. He must have realized my words earlier were right because one thing refugees didn't have were valuable items or credits of any kind. There was nothing the captain could use to improve the status of his crew or ship. It was all about increased wealth and reputation for pirates who lived on the fringe of Free Worlds society— that much I knew about them. All the crew who followed that captain did so because they believed he would make them wealthy, improve their lifestyle, or bring them a grand adventure in the deep of space. If things weren't going well, the crew would take control and remove their incompetent leader or choose to leave that crew for another. Captains of lesser ships changed frequently.

The entire situation made me think of the most famous pirate known in the Free Worlds: the Black Skull Admiral—Admiral Derwin, a Dolrinion exile who commanded a fleet. He was one of the most wanted people in all occupied space.

Inside command, some of the other ship passengers couldn't take their eyes off the pile of goo that was once the commander. The refugees had sagging shoulders, folded arms, and some were sobbing. In the military, I'd boarded pirate vessels and removed fingers myself. At that moment, I was under their control, which was a new experience.

The command safe room door was secure. They had to be on the other side. More yelling came from the captain at the other end of command, but suddenly he turned, and our eyes locked. Why was he staring at me? Quickly he came, and my heart raced. He wasn't slowing down, and I closed my eyes and turned my head because he was going to barrel right through me. The captain grabbed my throat, nearly lifting me off the ground, and slammed me into the wall, my head connecting with a power box behind, pushing my neck forward. He squeezed, which made it hard to breathe. I struggled for air.

"You tried to warn me this ship was nothing more than refugees, didn't you?"

He released his grip on me so I could talk, but it took time to recover.

I answered as insolently as possible. "I did try to warn you, but you refused to listen because you're arrogant."

His half-smile returned, the same way it had before burning the ship commander's face off. "Well, we can't always have a good raid, now can we? Especially out here. The in-Between can be perilous." The captain raised his voice so all would hear. "Pirates of the Black, we have to make do with what's here. Some of you head down to H and J levels, see what's in storage. No taking passenger prizes on this raid. Have your way with them before we leave."

He turned back to me and grabbed my neck again.

"Not you. You're coming with me—a captain's prize. I like your feistiness and will have fun breaking you back in my cabin."

Crew members laughed at their leader's words.

There was no way that scum would take me in any way, shape, or form. In his cabin, alone, would be his undoing. I'd gouge that one good eye out before letting him inside of me.

The captain squeezed my throat tighter and threw me to the grates. It took all my strength to stop from smashing the metal floor. My hands were sticky from the ship commander's blood, gunk, and brain matter. Small lumpy bits stuck to my palms.

Pirates made claims, both men and women, forcing themselves onto the frightened refugees. Other crew members abused and beat passengers while some only stood around, not doing much of anything. Those pirates didn't have the stomach for violence.

For seemingly no reason at all, the invaders stopped dead in their tracks, putting hands up to earbuds and listening. Strange. I knew those wide eyes and long faces of fear, more fear than the refugees. What happened?

The captain moved fast, yelling out orders. He was mustering a defensive line, but why? Two pirates opened a sealed container and set up a tripod mini railgun. That was an effective weapon. They pointed it down the junction hallway that led to the terminal docking doors.

The pirates seemed terrified. Someone they feared was coming. We were in the Great-in-Between. There could have been anyone out there who would be just as bad if not worse than pirates. Because of the nothingness in the in-Between, any heat from engines or weapons fire would be detectable by sensors through the entire sector. Someone had heard us and was within reach, but who was it? I knew of only one thing to put such fear into seasoned scavengers, and those were the things of nightmares.

The captain was breathing heavily, screaming orders at his crew, and moving fast from one area to the next. It seemed frantic to me. All acted as if it were their first raid. Even the crazed behemoth woman who burned the commander's face off looked concerned. She reignited her modified cattle brander coils and moved herself to the command center's front, where the hallway met this room. The railgun was behind her, and with any luck, she'd step into the weapon's line of fire. The Free Worlds would get rid of a raging lunatic and be better off.

Something terrible had come, and the realization that my day was about to get a whole lot worse stirred. I looked back to the safe room, hoping that my children were inside.

When the bad guys come, and there's nothing left but doom, the last place to survive is inside the safe room. Unless the door was already locked …

CHAPTER 8

Meetings Behind Closed Doors

A vital speech with billions watching (Henry)

We continued up the stone staircase to Academy Hall inside the cathedral. Agent Idell and his escort pulled away with screeching tires as if they were going somewhere important. An older civilian staff member stood near the entrance with her head high and arms locked behind her lower back. Mia's word games clouded my thoughts, and I had a hard time understanding why she didn't tell me about her meeting with JJ and that six-minute gap on her public record. I had a slight headache and rubbed my head as I stepped on the landing. The staff member attempted a grin, but her wrinkled skin made it difficult to tell if it was a smile or frown.

"Good afternoon, Representative McWright. My name is Colleen. I will escort you to the memory room, where your staff member is waiting."

I smiled while shaking her hand. "Thank you, Colleen. Please lead the way."

Colleen led us through the doors into the lobby of Academy Hall. Statues of famous past agents littered the brightly lit area, and between each sculpture were polished pillars that held up the high ceiling. I looked up and saw my picture in a golden frame beside the other fourteen representatives. Mine was in the center, and it was from twelve years ago. I had aged a bit since then.

The back training courtyard to Academy Hall was empty. An asphalt track lined the entire perimeter, where trainees of varying ages ran with their classes. In other locations, recruits performed push-ups and other floor routines or sprinted through an obstacle course. Academy agent instructors followed close behind to ensure everything happened correctly.

We stepped near the asphalt track to watch a young class running past us singing out together. "In the academy running along, we run, run, run till the running is done."

The lead instructor singing saw us and raised his voice. "Good morning, sir."

"Good morning, sir," the young recruits echoed.

The instructor continued, "Run with us!" The recruits repeated the call, and the instructor yelled, "Just for fun. Run with us—there's more to come."

All the recruits once again repeated their instructor's words. I pushed both thumbs into the air and smiled as they passed.

Those Guild academy recruits couldn't have been older than ten if I had to guess, and one of them at the back struggled to keep up with the main group. Another instructor running with the recruit screamed at him.

"You can't keep pace with the class. You're worthless. Just drop out, and we can call it a day."

The child cried and gasped as the instructor yelled at him. That recruit would be in the memory room before year's end.

Benjamin leaned over and whispered, "Is it necessary to scream at them like that? He's a child."

Before I could reply, Colleen said defensively, "It took hundreds of years to achieve perfection in this training program. What you're witnessing is necessary to ensure the creation of an ultimate law enforcement officer who can operate in the most hostile regions of occupied space. Some portions of their training may seem harsh, but we live in a harsh reality, don't we? Terrible things happen across the Free Worlds of Humanity every day, and we need to have a force capable of meeting those challenges and overcoming them."

Ben's eyes were wide. If I didn't know any better, I'd say he thought Colleen was too old in the ears to hear his whispers.

I said, "We all trust in the Guild and how it maintains itself. Don't mind Ben—he cares greatly for people and doesn't mean any offense."

Colleen lightly nodded her head, and we walked through the grounds surrounded by recruits struggling through their physical training. With some careful maneuvering through the academy, we arrived in a poorly lit hallway where Malcolm stood. The floor was checkered tile and our shoes made clicking sounds as we walked. More pictures of agents and their famous deeds hung on display along the walls.

Malcolm said, "Good afternoon Representative McWright. Senior Agent Ficco is finishing up overseeing a memory erasure and said he would join us in a few minutes. We can wait in the next room."

Colleen bid us farewell and stayed on the closing elevator.

"It's good to see you, Malcolm." I turned to Benjamin. "You and the team wait here for me. I won't be very long."

Before we walked into the next room, Oliver conducted a security check. Inside was a two-way mirror looking into a white-walled room, so vibrantly lit that it was overwhelming; the whiteness appeared solid, with no seams to tell where the walls, floor, and ceiling met. In the center of the room a metal chair protruded from the white flooring. At the top of the chair was a head restraint, molded to cradle a person's head. Above was a cover that would descend. Wires were attached on either side of the head restraint ending in small round terminals placed conveniently where a forehead would be. Small flat glowing lights between each connected joint flashed in sequence. This was the memory room, known across all Free Worlds of Humanity.

A teenage girl sat in the chair. Her head was shaved and her forehead rested snugly in the device. She cried out and tried to free herself from the restraints.

I stepped to the window. "Another day in the memory room?"

Malcolm said, "Yes. Wiping the memories of all the recruits who failed out of the academy this week."

Her hands were clamped to the armrests and her throat was locked into place by a leather strap.

The scared teen cried out, "Give me one more chance—I only got three questions wrong on that test. I know I can bring my average back up. Please. Just give me one more chance."

Senior Agent Ficco appeared emotionless standing next to the chair, silent, his eyes narrowed and lips pulled tight. His mongrel sprawled on the floor of the white room biting at its front paws. At the other corner were two Guild civilian staff behind computer stations.

The two-way mirror rattled as the light on both sides of the chair moved up in a blinking pattern as it traveled from the floor to the head restraint and the conductors against her head. A loud humming sound came from the chair, which contributed to the vibration of the glass. There was so much force, I felt it in my legs too. The small lights between the joints against her forehead became so intense I had to cover my eyes briefly. The noise subsided, and the frightened teen frowned with confusion, unaware of her surroundings.

The room grew silent until the young recruit gasped for air like she was learning to breathe all over again. Her eyes wandered curiously as if it was the first time she had ever seen those white walls before. From her perspective, that was true. The recruit's memories had been erased from that moment back to selection day for MERC Guild training when she was five years old. She spoke, but her words and voice came out like a small child's.

"Where's this? Who are you? Momma? Where is Momma?"

"You're ok, young one. There was an accident, and we had to take care of you. Now you're going home to see your mom again. Would you like that?" Senior Agent Ficco said softly.

The teenage failed recruit, with the mentality of a five-year-old child, timidly nodded and frowned. Ficco hit a button on the chair, and all restraints released. He helped her stand and escorted her to the door on the other side.

The memory chair removed everything from a failed recruit's mind. The training knowledge was the most heavily protected secret within occupied space along with the breeding program for mongrels. When a recruit failed within the twenty-year training cycle, they were brought to the white-walled room willingly or by force to have their minds wiped.

Malcolm said, "I've seen this process several times through the years, and it still gives me chills. One minute they're recruits of the MERC Guild, and the next, they think they're five years old and have no idea what's happening."

Younger recruits had an easier time for their brains to adjust to their larger bodies. The older recruits never truly recovered, even after years of education and rehabilitation.

"A huge sum of credits goes into reeducation, physical and speech therapy, and psychological counseling. Most recruits fail, and our relations budget absorbs that cost."

Malcolm paused, watching the teen with a mentality of a five-year-old leave the room, then asked, "How many of them fail again?"

"Each class varies, but the average dropout rate is around eighty percent."

Countless recruits sat in that cold metal chair. Classes usually had two thousand recruits and graduated four hundred or less. I recalled one class only having ten graduates. New classes started and graduated every day of the year. Years ago, during one of my campaigns, Alyssa and I met with former recruits suffering from mind wipes after failing. The younger ones had recovered for the most part, but the older failed recruits were basically disabled, unable to do things that anyone would deem ordinary, like tying shoes, combing hair, or opening a bottle to drink. Their speech was slow, and they moved clumsily as if their hands were something new.

Malcolm smiled and said, "Greatness requires great sacrifice."

I corrected him. "Great things require great sacrifice." Those words came from behind a closed door in a different context. "Did you have time to speak with Ficco regarding his concerns for the next Guild council meeting?"

Malcolm answered before Ficco entered the room. "Yes. He's worried about Secretary Nomikos, since he'll be sitting in for station command's seat in the next meeting."

Nicolas Nomikos was once the vice-regent of City-State Elpis on Epsilon Prime. His state supported Athinia and my friend Liam Sideris during the civil war. Before the Allied States lost, lying nearly in ruins, Nicolas came to the station seeking support but became a refugee instead. For the last fourteen years, he'd been active in station politics and a firm supporter of Director Rumi Houlton.

Senior Agent Ficco entered with his chest pushed out, holding his hands wide as if to embrace me. Instead of a hug, he extended his hand. "Representative McWright, it's great to see you."

He was a short middle-aged man with light eyes, a shiny bald head, and a jet-black mustache goatee with gray streaks. Inside our dark room, his Corin-steel-plate vest reflected green light from the lines.

"You can call me Henry in here."

Ficco glanced at the corner where a camera was pointing in our direction. We couldn't touch on more sensitive topics. That wasn't an issue. He could always run into me somewhere on the station.

I nodded, and said, "Malcolm and I spoke regarding your concerns, and I'll assist with Secretary Nomikos."

"Great. Chief Bockrath will be pleased. Station command and that Secretary of Free Worlds Affairs is up our asses so far, we can smell their breath. Rumi's trying to change the river direction, causing anxieties for senior leadership. Human rights violations, please."

What would Nicolas have done three hundred years ago with Senior Agent Scala after his return to the station with six rotting Flock family heads?

I said, "The meeting's Monday, correct?"

Malcolm answered before Ficco could. "Yes, at zero nine hundred."

The senior agent glanced at Malcolm then turned back to me. "That guy has been nothing but a problem since he came here with his hands out like a beggar all those years ago. Station security is always swarming him because he's paranoid those Lyons Pride boys are gonna try and scoop him up and ship him back to the Alliance. The Lyons Twins still have a large bounty for the kill or capture of Nicolas Nomikos. War crimes they say, hah. War is war. His biggest crime was being on the wrong side of the field when the fighting stopped."

It was laughable that Isaac and Killian Lyons accused Nicolas of war crimes when their atrocities were countless. New-Sparta had no emotion when it came to dealing with its enemies. I couldn't speak those words out loud with cameras on us.

"War is a troublesome affair. How much is the bounty now?"

Ficco shrugged, and Malcolm said, "Twenty million credits, the last time I checked."

The senior agent's eyes widened. "I'm surprised Director Houlton doesn't ship him back herself. She's retiring after this term anyway. Hell, I'll do it for that much."

I took a step to the two-way mirror and admired the seamless white room where Ficco's mongrel was still sprawled on the floor, relaxing and licking her paws.

"I will personally request the presence of Nicolas for Monday's closed session to assist with concerns over the fighting on Gliese and human rights violations to the local population. An expert from the director's staff would work nicely. Let Bockrath know."

"We owe you one, sir."

I sighed and said, "I had lunch with Representative Stavish today. She brought some things to my attention."

Ficco laughed and raised his voice. "So, she went to you kicking and stomping her feet like a child, did she?"

Mia was Tier One from Civil Earth, one of the Watchful Hawks of the caste system, and her family was the second wealthiest on the entire planet. The woman had expectations for getting her way with things.

"Mia wants to ensure that the Guild is using all appropriate measures to come to a successful and quick resolution regarding missing aides on the station. We mustn't overlook anything."

Ficco snapped, "If she wants, I can go over to the Civil Earth bubble and round up a few Tier Four sanitation workers. We'll blame them and have a public execution. Will that make her feel better?"

Mia would like to take you back to her family residence on Civil Earth above the ninety-fifth floor and skin you alive while her staff cheer her on. I narrowed my eyes in his direction, and he stepped back. "That's not necessary at all. Mia will be satisfied with the responsible party's capture by our competent agents. Who do you think it is?"

Ficco walked to the other end of the room and hesitated. "You know I can't discuss an open investigation by the Guild. We're doing everything in our power to come to a quick, accurate conclusion. Please inform Representative Stavish that a senior agent from the investigation team will come to her next week to discuss the progress so far."

Ficco's answer was the respectful way any agent of the Guild from chief down to a recruit should speak to me. He got carried away sometimes, but Ficco knew not to bite the hand that fed him. I've guaranteed a happy retirement when the day comes.

"Thank you, Senior Agent Ficco. I wish you great success in your future endeavors and look forward to our next meeting."

Senior Agent Ficco returned to the memory room, where the next failed recruit, a child of seven or eight years, was already in the chair waiting for memory erasure.

I turned to Malcolm and said, "Mia won't help me with my bill unless I remove the provisions for the equal union rights."

Malcolm held up his PDD, hit a button, and pointed it up to the camera for a few seconds, scrambling the network so it wouldn't hear or see our conversation.

"We prepared for this possibility, sir. Let's delay the bill for next month and work on the representatives from the Federate Corporation."

I appreciated his positive thinking and said, "We can't delay—next month's center issue will be the fighting on Gliese. The Corporation will want nothing to do with my bill after that debate starts, and you know as well as I that Gliese will dominate the forum for several months."

Malcolm paused, looking up to the ceiling. "The next polling on representative approval ratings is in two weeks. If you remove the union rights portion from your bill, the rest will pass without issue, and that will make Free Worlds citizens happy, but the unions will be pissed off. The media will eat this up."

"More people will watch tonight's open convocation than vote in primary elections. I'm going to take advantage of the chaos happening on that rogue world, and after listing my bill's intentions, minus the union rights, the focus will shift to Gliese. People will forget about the unions when we show pictures of dead civilians in front of their homes cut down like animals by the Dolrinions and Corporation."

"You're right. I'll start working on next month's agenda right away."

Before leaving the room, I said, "There's one more thing bothering me. Benjamin found a six-minute gap in both Mia's and JJ's public record schedules yesterday. It appears they met in secret, and I want camera footage of this meeting if it exists."

"It concerns me that they met outside of the minutes and didn't log it. I'll find out anything there is to know about this meeting."

We walked outside to the hallway, where Benjamin and my security team were patiently waiting.

"Benjamin, remove the union provisions from my bill and send the revised bill to all representatives. After that, send a private message to Mia informing her that now we're even."

There was a bitter taste in my mouth at those words. I hated doing things against my will, and it made my ears warm as I fought to keep the box locked. My childhood rabbits flashed as vivid images in my mind, and I took a deep breath. I had no choice but to make the concessions and still needed my strength to meet with JJ Richmond later tonight.

*

I glanced outside the window of my transport to see the splendor and enchanting aura of the relations station. Below was the main cylinder and random bubble embassies bulging out and spinning in opposite directions. I couldn't see the cathedral from this far up, but the capitol dome made up for that with its blinding light that shone like a star. The station had been the pinnacle of creation for our Free Worlds of Humanity since its foundation, and seeing endless ships, freighters, and public transports traveling in different directions like a locus swarm of chaos made me proud of our higher order by comparison to rogue worlds. *This station is a beacon of light for humanity, helping guide the masses.*

Once inside the dome dock, we landed and disembarked where Stacy, my junior aide, waited with two interns. She was younger than Benjamin but heavier.

"Good afternoon, Stacy. It seems like you've had a busy day. Who are these two eager young minds?"

"Interns for your office next month, sir. They're both studying political science at the University of Talbora in our Accord. We spent all day together in the back office. Then I showed them the Capitol Forum, golden road, and the founders statue. We also visited the offices of Secretary of Defense Willock and Inspector-General Nottage."

Both young adults stared, smiling, and I asked, "Tell me, if I were having a problem with one of my Capitol Security Protection Service officers, who would I bring that news to, Secretary of Defense Willock or Inspector-General Nottage?"

They glanced at each other, and one of the energetic young students answered, "Paula Nottage, sir. She commands Capitol Security, and Secretary Willock reports to Director Houlton in the main cylinder."

"Very good. Average Free Worlds citizens have trouble understanding the detailed dynamics and toe stepping that occurs here. The secretary's office still resides under the dome from tradition, which, in my opinion, is the death of advancement."

All three faces gleamed. Stacy served well and worked numerous hours more than required during a week. At least the interns weren't from Ardum, JJ's homeworld.

"I look forward to spending time with you next month and giving you the chance to see how things work in the Capitol Forum." *Minus the backstabbing and deceiving to get things done, of course.*

Both students had twinkles in their eyes and seemed overwhelmed by all the happenings under the dome. They spoke together. "Thank you, Representative McWright."

Stacy continued, "We're looking forward to your speech tonight, sir. The students received access to sit in the amphitheater."

"Great to hear. It's a privilege and honor to be present during open session." I stepped away. "Now, please excuse my haste, but there's much to do before tonight. Good evening."

Malcolm, Benjamin, my security team, and I kept walking, and exhaustion hit me. "Ben, I would like some coffee when I get back to my office, please."

"Absolutely, sir."

"Also, call Alyssa and see where she is. I won't have time to meet her for dinner before my speech because of the revisions needed, but I would like to see her before I walk into the forum."

Ben nodded, saying he would take care of it, and moved off.

Malcolm came closer and spoke. "A conversation with our friends in the secretary of defense's office should help give us answers to what Mia and JJ were doing. They had to have met in the main cylinder of the station. After that, I'll walk out front where the media core will be to answer questions in your place."

Malcolm speaking to the media annoyed me because if not for Mia's required changes, I'd be out there talking to the press beforehand. I had to skulk in my back office doing speech rewrites on my chicken-scratch papers, then upload it for the teleprompt.

I said bitterly, "You know what should be said when standing in the grand foyer. Keep it brief. I'm disabling my PDD to think more clearly."

We entered a lift taking us to the Colonial back office behind the forum. A huge painting displaying the Accord's Golden Age by some famous artist on one of our worlds was against the wall in the hallway to my office. I smirked.

We never exhibited art showing the billions that died in our system war during the integration. That was how things worked in the Free Worlds—

accomplishment through torment and death, then forgetting the terrible things that happened to get there. We loved showing off successes, regardless of how small.

Benjamin was inside my office, standing near the Hammer of Labor on display near the sideboard. Oliver took his usual location near the window and my chessboard.

"See something you like, lad?"

Ben smiled. "I always feel a sense of excitement when I see the Labor Union Hammer. It's a relic of our past and commands such power."

I went to the handle and grasped it. "It is inspiring. There's great power in Labor."

Engraved into the mallet was the emblem of each union that made up our Labor Party. The symbol for the Entente was in one corner with the number twenty-three carved deep.

Ben replied, "It's funny how even when they etched the union emblems into it, the Twenty-Third is opposite Sadie Enama's union."

"Yes. We're in a constant struggle with FIW in our shadow war."

Ben laughed. "That's all conspiracy theories from crackpots."

I raised an eyebrow, "Oh? AMT, FOOE, CSA, and FAA, alongside the others, are always doing battle behind the curtain for control. To the public, we appear unified. The truth is something different. After election season things get … interesting. Years of experience showed us how to keep ourselves civil even when they aren't."

Ben maintained a focused stare as I continued. "Two drunks left a bar and were found the following day in an alleyway with defensive wounds and their PDDs and valuables gone. Well, that was a robbery gone bad. Someone driving home on a rainy night after working a double shift slipped off a bridge and drowned. An accident in bad weather. Another fell down a flight of stairs and snapped their neck, suicides, or workplace deaths. The common denominator is that all those examples are delegates, shop stewards, or leaders for their respective unions. Any smart person adding the numbers would see those seemingly unfortunate deaths occurred at rates three hundred times greater than any other Free World. The unions are constantly working against each other vying for control."

All of that as we fought off the greater threat, the Rose Party of Ardum.

Ben lowered his head. "I got you some food too, figuring it would be late before you could eat again."

He really was a loyal lad and would do so well with our Hammer of Labor on Uropa.

"Thank you, Benjamin. I'll see you after open session. There's one more thing I need from you. Go to Civil Earth's back office and speak with Mia's chief of staff. See if everything went as planned with my revisions. I haven't heard from her."

"Yes, sir. I'll take care of it. Alyssa said she would be sitting in her usual seat in the theater."

I nodded, and Ben left. She knew that her dress needed to be something on the conservative side. All too often, she wore tops that exposed more of her breasts than necessary. That, with her constant flirtatious personality ... *keep the box locked, Henry.*

I was angry, but sat and worked on my revisions with a shaking hand. Thanks to politics, I had a lesser speech that would have to do.

Oliver spoke. "Sir, the time."

Damn it. I was running late for the minutes meeting with JJ. We left my office and stepped into the lift down a level to JJ's office. As the lift doors closed, I saw someone running towards us from the other end of the hall but couldn't see who it was. Was that Malcolm? Couldn't be. He was out front speaking with the media. Lots of staffers worked in the building. It could have been anyone.

I stood outside JJ's office, observing the dark oak door of hand-carved roundels—a typical Ardum design, their rose appearing in multiple locations. A deep gouge below my eye level damaged the door, which made me happy. My disgust and anger boiled over every time I saw that Ardum door. Memories of my mother leaving us for Ardum were trying to surface, but I held them back.

I cleared my throat. "I'm here to see Representative Richmond."

A security officer said, "He's expecting you, sir. Please go in."

The door creaked open, my heart raced, and I felt more saliva in my mouth as the adrenaline pumped through my veins. JJ stood near the window overlooking the well-maintained flower gardens of our back offices' main entrance from the outer yard. His bright strawberry blond hair was long in a top knot, which made him look like a woman from behind.

He turned, and I saw his freckled face.

"Good evening, Representative McWright. It's a pleasure to see you on such a wonderful day." His tone was welcoming, which was odd.

My mental stamina lacked the ability to handle another word game after this long day. JJ had a sideboard in the same location as mine, and in place of the Hammer of Labor was a glass canister with a single Ardum rose, the symbol of his Rose Party, the Rose of Enduring. It was thriving in the sand, a display of its resilience.

I glanced back at JJ. "Representative Richmond, I'm glad this day finds you well."

We embraced, and he waved his hand, pointing to a chair near his desk. We sat at the same time. His chair was higher so he could look down at all sitting across from him. We were still eye level though because of my height—JJ was shorter and heavier than me.

"I saw your public log today. You met with Mia to conclude your minutes."

My pause of suspicion made him smirk.

"Yes. We discussed next month's agenda and where things might stand with our fellow representatives."

His expression was hard to determine. Was that a smile or something else?

"I assume that my name came up in your discussion with Mia."

I gave no response, and after a moment of silence, he said. "I think next month we should focus on the Colonial Trade Company transport attacks. No one boards the ships, nor are the contents taken, besides a few random incidents from the data logs recovered. After attacking and destroying the company transports, the aggressors move on without explanation. These attacks are problematic and should be the Accord's primary focus. I believe the Black Skull Admiral is responsible. All efforts should focus on his capture."

JJ wanted us to concentrate on the Colonial Trade Company because the Richmond family had deep connections with its headquarters on Ardum.

I stared at him without speaking, and he said, "Oh bloody hell, Henry. You still treat me as if we were fighting the war before our Golden Age. Ardum and the Rose of Enduring aren't trying to kill anyone from the Hammer of Labor anymore. It was nearly two thousand years ago."

He knew my mistrust for Ardum, Pardalis, and Talbora festered in my youth due to a deeper loathing of his planet and party.

"Uropa won the war."

Lars and Tautrus were still behind Uropa since the war.

JJ scratched at his beard. "You hate the Rose Party because of what happened with your mother, right? She's still on Ardum in an assisted living home."

It wasn't time to fall into one of his traps. I redirected the conversation. "I don't understand your blaming Admiral Derwin from Draco without proof. It seems absurd, even though such a renowned outlaw figure would, of course, garner attention. Bounties for the Black Skull Admiral have increased each month for the last two years. The MERC Guild, local hunters, private bounty specialists, and Free Worlds' law enforcement have tried hundreds of times to capture or kill Derwin without success. Do you believe anything will change now? Besides, he's a smart Dolrinion and does things for profit and fame. What's happening to the Colonial Trade Company has nothing to do with either. No, the issues for next month's agenda will be different."

"And what will the headline issue be for next month?"

"The fighting on Gliese, of course."

JJ sat back in his chair. "Well, you're the center seat from our Accord, and I lean on your judgment in this regard."

As JJ spoke, his eyes widened, and a mischievous smile appeared. Why was he so happy? The sound of muffled arguing came from outside his thick oak door. Irrelevant at that point. I was bothered by that damn smile. Most of our meetings ended with red faces and shouting. Why was JJ so happy?

"I watched your comments from yesterday as you walked down the golden road with the news reporters. It was interesting that you decided to walk the road when you left the forum instead of taking the back office's normal means. What you said … was concerning."

JJ slowly stood and dusted off a bookshelf behind his desk. If he wanted to become a janitor, I'd readily accommodate him with a job. After a moment, he said, "Word games."

"Come again?"

"You told me once, long ago, that we representatives always played word games with each other under the dome."

"You're only half right. What I told you was that we played word games and should watch what we say in public. I gave that advice freely when you came to this station, sitting there so innocently and confused in the left seat."

JJ was unmoved and said, "You know, before I came to this station, in my early political career with the Roses of Ardum, I heard such amazing stories about your abilities as a politician. People said that you were the puppet master pulling all the strings up here and that almost all Free Worlds' laws and decisions on this relations station had some level of involvement from you. People from all six worlds of the Accord spoke of you as some mythological figure who could shoot bolts of lightning at will."

If he only knew the things I'd done for all of humanity, not only here under the dome, but throughout all occupied space, he'd remove that obnoxious smirk and apologize. It was wishful thinking on my part. The slithery Rose and Mighty Hammer would never agree.

"Even though you were from a rival world and party, I tried to take you under my wing. However, you bit the hand that offered to guide you and did whatever you pleased regardless."

JJ's grin was even more full, and it made him look like a damn clown with his red hair. All he needed was a red nose and big feet. Maybe he could juggle for me while I waited for him to speak.

After a lengthy delay, he said, "I haven't changed much at all since that time, Henry, but you have. You're no longer the strong influential leader of the past. What I see before me now is an aging man who has lost his way, circling the drain, trying his very best to swim away from falling down the pipes into oblivion."

I gazed at him scornfully.

"Speaking of always watching what you say, I saw your visit to the classroom this morning. The news highlighted specific words you said about reeducating fellow representatives. Do you recall saying that?"

I snapped back defensively, "Yes, I recall saying that, and moments later praising my fellow representatives and the work we do in the forum."

JJ stopped cleaning and sat back down. "My mother once told me, always tell someone good news first. If you start with the bad news, they'll not hear one bit of the positive words and sulk on the negative comments. That's precisely what happened with your statements, and you helped me hammer the final nail into the coffin, which would not have been possible without those remarks."

I was confused. What was he referring to, a nail in a coffin? Usually, I wouldn't give anything away to JJ, especially without proof, but I was tired of these games and antsy to get to the center platform for my speech. "Your public record from yesterday is missing six minutes. Interestingly, Mia is also missing six minutes at the same time. Why did the two of you meet with each other?"

JJ leaned in and looked at me as if he'd just had a sexual experience. "I'm so glad you brought that up. This moment is truly great, and I had numerous thoughts in my head today about how our conversation would play out. You have not disappointed, Henry, not in the slightest. Today will be one of the greatest moments of my career with the Rose of Ardum."

I rolled my eyes. "Why will this be one of the greatest moments in your career?"

That red-haired clown answered, "Henry, your bill is dead. I spent days working on ways to dismantle what you worked so hard on. Up until today, it seemed hopeless until favor fell to me with Mia's help. The Dolrinions are stubborn people, and without them, I couldn't hope to get the votes."

I was angry. "There's no reason for the Dolrinions to back out—they don't have unions on Kora, only slaves, and I made the revisions required by the Federate Corporation and Civil Earth. All other listed bill items will benefit all Free Worlds."

"The Dolrinions were deeply offended by your comments in the school. In fact, after local news highlights aired, Center Seat Representative Sharrar from the Offensive burst through my door looking for blood. The Dolrinions call him the Iron Fist of Kora, and from the way he punched his way into my office, the name makes complete sense. It took all six Capitol Security officers to hold him back, and he swore to speak with you himself on Monday."

I looked down, running those words through my mind, and JJ kept talking. "I believe when Sharrar says speak, what he really means is beat you to within a centimeter of your life, but what do I know of Dolrinion sentinels?"

My ears were warmer, making me uncomfortable, and the pressure in my body was elevating like a teapot with its nozzle covered.

"This is a first. I've made the great and powerful Representative Henry McWright speechless. Well, while you sit there contemplating, let me fill you in on more of my accomplishments today. You sent your revisions thanks to me having Mia push you into doing so at the last minute, do you recall?"

Of course I recalled, it only happened a few hours prior, you redheaded clown bastard. How could he have pushed Mia like that? He's not powerful enough to sway her. What does he have on Mia, or what did he offer for her obedience?

"After you sent your revisions, if circumstances were normal, we would have all voted yes, but, you see, with Mia's help, the Federates and both right and left seats of Civil Earth voted no. Getting Right Seat Olivia Belitz to side with Mia is an accomplishment in itself. Of course, the Dolrinions were all too eager to vote no right away after your offensive remarks, though they did have to side with the Federate Corporation. Dolrinions siding with

Federates while they kill each other in droves on the rogue world Gliese—oh well, we both know this is politics under the dome."

I hated him. "How did the vote go?"

JJ laughed loudly. "Ten to five. You got all three representatives from the Human Alliance due to your new relationship with Left Seat Representative Laskaris and, of course, our very own Left Seat Representative Christine Keng, the loyal scratching Tigress from Lars."

I stood, my ears flaming, and said, "It's no matter. I have a speech to give and will deal with this in my opening comments."

It wouldn't be the first time I had given a speech making it up as I went along. I planned to speak from the heart and explain what happened. I walked to the door of JJ's office.

JJ raised his voice. "Have you not checked your PDD at all in the last forty-five minutes?"

He was right. My PDD was silent while I wrote my revisions.

"No, I have not."

JJ laughed again even louder and said, "This is perfect. I couldn't have planned it any better if I tried. Henry, we voted your bill down forty-three minutes ago exactly with an emergency declaration. We didn't need you, since this bill is yours. Then fourteen minutes ago, we voted again. Mia Stavish announced to the entire Free Worlds' news core out front that your speech is withdrawn due to your last-minute changes."

"How did that vote go?"

JJ chuckled some more, answering, "You're always interested in the finer details, aren't you? That vote was more on your side, eight to seven. Mia, left seat of Civil Earth, the Dolrinions, center, and left seat for the Federates, and I voted against letting you speak. You got all your previous yay votes, including the right seat of Civil Earth and the left seat of the Corporation. Those who voted against your bill but voted to allow you to speak only did so trying to play both sides of the coin. It appears some still want to remain in your favor to a degree, or maybe they believe you really can shoot lightning bolts from your ass." JJ bellowed with laughter. "It's no matter though, the vote was still eight to seven against you, and even though Mia backstabbed you today, she'll probably be asking for a favor tomorrow because that's her way. One day the sky is red, then green, red, and green, back and forth with her."

Was JJ playing another trick on me besides what he said? White specks appeared and floated in the air. No, it was not a trick; those were stars buzzing around my head because my heart was pounding out of my chest. It was hard to breathe, and my tongue felt like thousands of pins and needles poked inside my mouth. Dark thoughts were trying to push through to the surface of my mind, and I held them back.

I grabbed my PDD and saw three missed calls from Malcolm, two missed calls from Benjamin, one missed call from Representative Keng, and one missed call from Representative Laskaris. My wife hadn't called at all. Alyssa probably had no idea what was going on. I turned the silencer off and looked up at JJ, seeing a big red blob outlining his body because of my raging anger. Around the perimeter of the office, Capitol Security officers looked at us. I wanted to go over that desk but couldn't with witnesses.

My PDD rang. It was Malcolm again, and I sent it to voicemail.

JJ spoke. "I know your power behind a microphone with cameras on you. There is no greater weapon inside the five walls. From the beginning, I have tried to minimize your strengths wherever possible. That's why the Rose Party sent me here."

"You and your withering flowers will feel my full strength one day. It will not be today or even tomorrow, but one day when you think you're ahead and everything is going precisely the way you planned, I'll be there to put your face down into the mud. Lightning bolts are nothing compared to what I can do."

JJ smiled again as I turned away and walked to the door. He shouted out one last time, "Representative McWright, where are you going? We haven't finished our required minutes for the month!"

My ears were so hot I could have roasted a marshmallow with them; evil thoughts competed for space in my head, and I didn't shut them out this time. My PDD rang again; I looked and was surprised at the person calling. I thought of hitting the voicemail button, but I answered it at the last second while the thick oak doors with a fist imprinted into the wood closed with JJ still inside.

CHAPTER 9

Civil Earth
Living in Tier Four

Working for Air Restoration Services
in building thirty-three (Daniel)

The alarm clock was going off. It was morning. Work started in an hour for another double shift. I exhaled a deep sigh thinking of my three double shifts per week so we could live in our small two-bedroom apartment in building thirty-three. The Lower Forty—armpit of Civil Earth.

It still felt strange waking up in that room. Amber and I moved in a few months ago after Dad passed from the Galmaree flu. Kofi said that virus came from the rogue world Galma, but who in the Lower Forty knew about things like that? Most of us never left our building, let alone the city line before. Kofi was a talker. Maybe he didn't know either. Dad worked hard for thirty-five years, and that cramped apartment was all he had to show for it.

Amber was still asleep, her back leaning against the wall because the bed was so small. *She's so beautiful.* I didn't mind squeezing into a single cot together. I loved taking deep breaths and smelling her next to me. She stirred, pushing her long black hair away from perfect golden skin, and mumbled, "Good morning."

After giving her a gentle kiss, I said, "Go back to sleep, my love. It's early, and you worked late last night."

Amber snuggled into her pillow. Late nights working at Smitty's Bar on the second floor exhausted her.

I took a few short steps to the other side of the room and looked at myself in the small mirror. I flinched and covered my nose from the smell of my tattered work clothes hanging on a hook. When was the last time I cleaned them? At least a month, maybe more. What could we do? It cost too much to clean them more often.

The toga-wearing Cloud Walkers didn't have smelly clothes. I glanced at my caste card hanging on a lanyard near the dresser. It had a large bold number four with a picture of my face. I looked at my work bag with the Air Restoration Services logo on the side. The only way out of this depressing scenery was through an airlock to the surface or joining up with Civil Earth Defense.

I took a few short steps across the hall to the bathroom, gazing longingly at the shower, wishing it was Thursday. The faucets wouldn't work until Thursday. It was only Tuesday, and I felt so dirty. The air vent above rattled away, and it was rank with a smell of eggs. That was more pleasant than last week.

Inside the living room, I glanced at the crossbar latch as a memory of my childhood came back to me.

"Don't! D-d-don't anybody move!"

The robber's hand shook as he pointed the gun at Mom, and sweat dripped off his face. Uncle Terrance took a step towards the nervous thief and he turned, firing his weapon several times.

I was a young kid and remembered wiping the blood from my face as Mom screamed. Uncle Terrance's mouth was open wide and his eyes rolled back. That lowlife killed him to steal our food rations from the dispenser. He killed my uncle over food.

Lilly rustled on the pull-out mattress near the television, and I quietly moved into the kitchen. I was swiping through the food choices on the dispenser screen, what few there were, and Lilly woke from the noise.

"Good morning, Oppa."

I smirked and replied, "Good morning, Lil."

She rubbed her eyes as I placed a tin bowl under the spout and pushed the button for breakfast whites.

"Breakfast whites. The food of champions."

Lilly giggled with a yawn. "The chunky bits aren't oats. I don't care what the administrative authority tells us."

"Who knows what this junk is? It tastes so bland." I turned to her and hesitated. "I spoke with Tobias. You're all set for the Fleet Branch test."

Lilly narrowed her eyes and leaned back. "I didn't ask you to do that. I only graduated from school a week ago. Give me some time to figure out what I want to do."

I watched the white semi-thick substance slowly pour into the bowl as my stomach growled. "If you join up, they'll give you two hot meals per day and double rationing. Tobias has lived in Tier Three as a captain for eight years now. He's getting promoted to major soon and going up to Tier Two. I want that for you, Lil."

My sister bit her lip, and her face was flush. I put my tin on the hot plate Dad built for us before he died, and turned it on.

Lilly said, "You fixed it?"

"I did, last night. It needed a new copper tube. I snagged one from one of the broken air handlers at work."

I looked in the corner of the kitchen where Dad had stacked old machine parts. Dad got most of those items from the machines he fixed inside Defender Corps barracks across the city line. He taught me how to make machines to heat our food. So few of us in Tier Four had such trade skills.

"Don't forget," Lilly said.

I turned back and disconnected the hot plate. The administrative authority would come to investigate our power consumption if I left it on too long.

After sitting down and mixing some salt into the breakfast whites, I took another deep breath.

Lilly giggled. "Preparing yourself to eat that crap?"

I smiled. "Come on now. Commercials say everything we need like vitamins and nutritional requirements are in these meals from the dispenser."

That didn't excuse the terrible taste or hunger that remained after eating. Our attention went to the back wall near the apartment door. The television turned on automatically, displaying the Civil Earth flag, and music began to play.

Lilly sighed. "An official broadcast from Tier One."

The volume increased and echoed outside our apartment from the public speakers. Building thirty-three's administrator Iris Unon appeared. He had perfectly trimmed facial hair that shone, as if globs of wax were molded into the hair, in the spotlight beating off his face. Unon's toga was bright violet and green. Gold and silver chains covered his neck so tightly it seemed like they were choking him. The administrator had a smug grin, which irritated me. A typical Tier One Cloud Walker look for anyone living above the ninety-fifth floor and higher.

Lilly said, "That man is so disconnected from the world, he wouldn't know what a foot was if it kicked him square in his ass."

We both laughed as Unon spoke. "Good morning, fine citizens of building BZ thirty-three. We of the Three-Three need to keep our spirits high. I'm proud to say that workflow production is up by five percent from last quarter. All tiers will be glad to know that our esteemed leaders fight for us each day inside the Capitol Forum on the relations station. Center Seat Stavish, Right Seat Belitz, and Left Seat Nasby brokered a bill last month that reduced our planet's trade deficit with the other Free Worlds. This ensures better pricing for all floors."

Administrator Unon's smile widened. "Crime in our building is down thanks to the efforts of our glorious defenders. Civil Earth Defense offers better food, education, and living for all. The Lower Forty are encouraged to join. It nearly makes me want to join myself."

Lilly laughed. *Not sure why anything on the relations station affects someone like my family and me in the Lower Forty floors.*

"They only do what's in their best interest, not ours," Lilly said.

Iris Unon's voice carried through the room. "With CE Day approaching, I want to remind everyone that checkpoints through our building are operating at one hundred percent. Everyone should give extra time when leaving their dwellings due to increased traffic. Remember, we are the birthplace of humanity, and every Free World looks to us for guidance. Let's be good role models and show all how to be productive and efficient."

Administrator Unon gave one last smile displaying his fat rosy cheeks, and the screen cut to black. I had forgotten that Civil Earth Day was approaching. There were always problems with that holiday. Floors above forty celebrated with music, food, drink, and fireworks, while the Lower Forty went to bed hungry and wondered what the holiday's point was in the first place. Tier Four had no desire to celebrate the rebirth of civilization that had brought our caste system to life during the Age of Innovation. People in the Lower Forty would prefer the Years of Darkness any day.

"Oh joy, another year where they give us a child's-portion-sized muffin from the dispenser with a cream filling and tell us it's a celebration." Lilly sounded like a typical teenager with an attitude.

"Lilly, you shouldn't talk like that. If the wrong people heard you, we'd be in trouble. Mom and Dad saved extra credits every year to give gifts and cook real eggs on Dad's hot plate. You remember. They loved hosting every year with friends."

For one day each year, the troubles and heavy burdens of Tier Four wouldn't be in our minds. A small break from the dreads of our lives, and it was nice.

Lilly spoke defiantly. "Dad's dead, and Mom hasn't said anything about doing a get-together this year. When I brought it up, she cried."

"This will be the first year without Dad. She's grieving. We need to keep her distracted. Maybe a party isn't the best way to do that."

Honestly, Mom's DNA degradation disease was getting worse with each passing day. She wouldn't be able to do anything anyway.

Lilly shook her head. "It doesn't matter. The Caste Freedom Fighters said they would disrupt every public event this year. I wouldn't be surprised if the administrator cancels the holiday."

Lilly was young and didn't understand that Tier One would never cancel a world holiday, especially one celebrating our caste system's founding. I nodded and continued to eat my puddle of white gunk. After finishing, I walked to the door, touched the crossbar—still secure—and looked at Lilly. "Don't forget your Civil Earth Defense officer's test today."

She tightened her lips and adjusted herself on the couch, ignoring my words and watching the television.

I raised my voice. "Lil, please answer me."

She turned with a frown. "I won't forget."

"Remember, if you take this test and score well, Mom will have better care through government insurance. DDD requires advanced help, especially in her stage."

She lowered her brow and stared at the floor, her eyes wandering. Lilly knew how bad the disease was, and Mom was already blind in one eye, had lost her left leg from the knee down, and her jaw was starting to lock into place. It was the uncurable bane of our genetics; I remembered what the doctor said when she received her diagnosis.

"Individual strands of DNA that make her who she is can no longer hold themselves together, and pieces will erode at random, causing strange side effects. It will eventually kill her. There is no cure."

Some medications helped treat it by alleviating the symptoms or slowing down the degradation, but that was all. All tiers suffered from the disease, which gave people in the Lower Forty some satisfaction. They thought DDD was karma to punish the Cloud Walkers, but it affected everyone the same way.

Before leaving, I said, "Remember, don't answer the door to anyone you don't know and check the locks."

Lilly rolled her eyes. "I know, big brother, you tell me every day." Her tone became softer. "Have a good day at work. Mom and I are happy you and Amber moved in to help with everything."

I smiled. "I know, sis. I'm not going anywhere. When Mom wakes up, tell her I said to have a good day."

I had twenty-six minutes to get to work, so I gripped my work bag a little tighter. People sometimes gave me a hard time moving through the building, but when they saw Air Restoration Service emblems and heard my words, "Let me do my job so you can breathe," most would leave me alone.

The ceilings in the transit hub were high, and thick metal pillars were scattered throughout the area. Benches and display screens littered the surroundings plus vending machines with artificial food and drink choices. The hub was busy that morning with travelers going to and from work. At the far wall were large clear tubes big enough to fit fifty people on small trains that went through the city line to other megastructures. I never needed to go on one of those because my job kept me here in building thirty-three.

Elevator banks of thirty or forty doors lined the walls. We always had to wait for an elevator. The long faces and worn clothes of tired working-class Tier Fours around the hub gave them away without sight of their caste cards. Upper tiers didn't have the problem of worn out, musty work outfits from years of hard use. Most of us worked ten to fourteen hours a day, seven days per week.

Civil Earth defenders stood guard in full battle armor near each elevator and train tube scanning station. Their sleek and well-fitted armor shone in the light. The metal reminded me of aluminum foil, polished, and I could see my reflection in it if I got close enough.

I was never much for violence, but their main weapon always fascinated me because of its mechanics. The pistol rested easy on their hip and could turn into a fully functioning battle rifle with one button push. The noise of grinding gears as it changed impressed me because each part needed to work perfectly as it locked into place.

I could take that weapon apart and figure it out in a day. Dad helped teach me that talent, and Mom got angry when I took apart things in our apartment when I was young.

Fourteen minutes to get to work. Crap. I was distracted.

After scanning my card and passing the defenders I waited for an elevator.

The elevator was full of people going to work like me. As the elevator descended, a display screen at the top of the car showed Free Worlds news.

The newsperson spoke. "Upset on Friday last week when Representative Stavish from Civil Earth announced the sudden cancellation of Representative Henry McWright's speech—the most senior member in the forum. A fellow Colonial Accord Representative JJ Richmond had this to say ..."

The camera view changed to an expansive area with two of the biggest staircases I had ever seen. Giant white stone pillars and pretty flags and banners were in the background.

A short well-dressed red-haired man said, "There was no choice but to cancel his speech. Representative McWright sent his revisions to the bill at the eleventh hour, just before beginning open session. His speech was to air live across every network. Everyone in the Free Worlds of Humanity would be watching—and it would have had lasting effects. McWright is my fellow representative from the Colonial Accord. I pleaded with him not to commit to these changes so late in the game. He disregarded my counsel."

The news anchor continued. "Confusion is running amuck under the dome regarding the sudden changes. McWright himself was at a union rally on the station earlier in the day, making his bill's points clear. We tried reaching out to Representative McWright, but his chief of staff, Malcolm Booth, wouldn't allow any contact with the center seat representative."

Another man was on the screen, older, with a balding head. "Much more is happening here than the five walls are letting on. Revisions will occur, and Representative McWright will bring his original bill to a vote next month. That much, I'll promise. Representative McWright will press on, but right now, he's unavailable for comment. Thank you."

The news anchor spoke. "Political pundits are skeptical about next month's agenda because of the invasion of the rogue world Gliese by the Dolrinion

Offensive and Federate Corporation, missing staffers under the dome, and the attacks on the Colonial Trade Company transports by the Black Skull Admiral Derwin."

I'd never met anyone from another world before and wouldn't know the difference between a Colonial or Human Alliance citizen. Everyone could spot a Dolrinion because of their peculiar appearance and height. I only knew Tier Four people and Tobias, who visited from Tier Three when he could. None of that news benefited my family and it was irrelevant here. I had to make sure my family could eat and didn't care about attacks on another planet. It was so far away from Earth.

The elevator stopped on random floors; people got on and off, and when we stopped on the sixth floor, which was the lowest apartment level, a sensation of grief overtook me. I always felt bad stopping on that floor. It wasn't fair to those living on government assistance and unemployed. A horrendous smell engulfed the entire elevator car. Everyone covered their faces and made sounds of disgust. The rotten-egg smell in our apartment vent was better than that stench.

A mother and daughter stepped onto the elevator. The little girl couldn't be older than five, and she was coughing. Not a surface cough, which everyone recognized.

Her young mom spoke. "Cover your mouth, darling."

The mom attempted a smile, not making eye contact, and looked down at the floor. I got the impression she was embarrassed by her own and the young girl's appearance. I would be in their situation. It wasn't their fault they were born and raised in the lowest levels. Their clothing was old and didn't fit properly, and was ripped and torn. It was filthy, and I felt so bad for them. Unfortunately for Tier Four, the sight was typical. Some from the sixth floor wound up on the surface, a death sentence.

The elevator stopped on the second floor. Half the people, including the mother and daughter, got off. The second floor always had most of our megastructure's pedestrian traffic.

That transit hub was significantly larger, with more bustling activity than the hub I came from on the upper level. The elevator doors remained open for a few brief seconds. People moved in different directions and stores, street vendors, entertainers, and local community organizers conducted their daily routines. Defenders stood everywhere in groups of three.

Two others remained in the elevator, custodial employees by the look of them. We traveled to the first floor; the doors opened again and they got off. It was tough working on the surface in the yellow haze. Everyone working outside needed to keep their caste card because defenders wouldn't allow anyone back in without one.

Kofi had told me about a construction manager who worked on the surface for thirty years. She went through the same airlock door every day, speaking to the same defender guards, and was well-liked by all. One day on a job site, she fell from a scaffolding, receiving only minor injuries. Once the workday concluded, they all went back to the airlock to return inside. The manager's caste card was gone, displaced in the fall. All the workers entered the airlock one at a time, scanning their cards, waiting for the green light, and proceeded inside.

The manager went to the defender and explained the day's incident, but the defender sergeant wouldn't allow her to enter. She and several employees spent hours looking for her card without success. She had no choice but to remain outside.

Her company applied for a new card, but without priority clearance, it took months to obtain a new caste recognition card. Company employees would go out daily to supply her with food, new respirator filters, and water.

Weeks passed, and the trauma of being out on the surface took hold. She looked worse with each passing day, like she'd only slept for a few hours, and the haze was making her weaker. She had interactions with surface dwellers, and bruises on her body made it clear that bad things happened.

Six weeks later, her company received a new caste recognition card, and the owner, a Tier Two elite living in the Upper Twenty-Three, and other supervisors, came out to present the card to her. What they found was a nightmare.

The manager's body was naked. Someone had tied her arms and legs, and her skull was caved in from beatings. Terrible things took place at that location, and everything that her company brought outside daily was missing. In her right hand, she was clutching a bloodstained white long-cut sock. I couldn't bear to visualize it. Who would do such a terrible thing to someone?

Civil Earth Defense determined a surface gang killed her. What irony—the day she received a new caste card was the day she died. They were ruthless animals out there, all of them. Wait, that wasn't true. I let my emotions get the best of me. Tobias lived on the surface for two years after his dad disappeared. His family saved his life and got him back inside. Tobias was a good person. He suffered from a terrible surface cough that reminded me of someone with bronchitis or pneumonia, but much worse. T said his lungs looked like someone rubbed a cheese grater along the inner lining.

Life was hard, living in the Lower Forty, but I'd take living inside any day over the surface. I wouldn't survive long out there, that much I knew.

*

The elevator doors opened on lower level five, and I hurried to punch in. The lighting was dim, not nearly as bright as the upper floors. Some corners were pitch black. Six minutes before my shift started.

I put my belongings away in the locker where a few coworkers talked shop. Like normal, Kofi was there blabbering away about a mainline air system he had trouble with yesterday. He was seasoned and knew how to fix most issues, so if the mainline was giving him trouble, something was seriously wrong with it.

"Daniel, this handler isn't functioning correctly, and I already checked the gearbox and loops from the inside. They're all fine. I went outside and looked down, and everything seemed ok. What do you think?"

My coworkers asked my opinion on tough projects. They all believed I could fix anything attached to our building. Maybe they were right, or perhaps not, I didn't know. It could be annoying at times.

I answered the same way I always did. "You need to go through the checklist. Easiest to hardest and clear each item one at a time. It's patience that fixes problems, not band-aids or haste."

They all grinned and repeated my words as I spoke.

Kofi laughed. "If we had a credit for each time you said that, we'd be living in the Middle Thirty."

Everyone echoed his laugher. Dad had taught me the phrase and how to live this lifestyle. His work ethic was outstanding, and I learned everything from him. We left the locker room, and I cleared the attendance area door as morning muster started. Our supervisor Chrissy was already taking attendance. She called my name as I entered the doorway.

"Here," I said.

Chrissy glared at me from her tablet, peering into my eyes like she was burning a hole in my soul. "Yes, you're here and lucky to have stepped into the room when you did."

She looked above me at the wall clock and pointed to Kofi with the others behind him. "The workday already started. You all are late."

Kofi replied defensively, "We're here and ready to work."

Chrissy hardened her face and pulled her lips in so far, they disappeared. "Not today, you aren't. Punch out and go home. Maybe tomorrow you'll be here on time."

Kofi and the others opened their eyes wide; they seemed lost for words. Chrissy was always harsh with air restoration workers. They didn't argue and left. Chrissy would've fired them if they tried to fight with her, especially with everyone else sitting in the room. They wouldn't receive credits for that day since we didn't get paid time off.

Why did Chrissy always have to be so mean? Missing a day of work would cost them food from the dispenser. Their children would go to bed hungry one day the following week, and that was sad. That kind of incident was what made people join up with the Caste Freedom Fighters.

Chrissy almost smiled after her worthless victory. She lifted her head high, apparently pleased with herself for a moment, then started the day's rundown, talking about work reports from the previous shift. "The night shift left us with a leaky bag as usual. Kofi was working on the mainline in section 7544 off our main building. He was unable to fix the issue, and the night shift sent two technicians outside too. It's still broken."

Chrissy looked like she needed to either pass gas or was confused by a crossword puzzle she was attempting to solve. Finally, she said, "Daniel, clear your schedule today. You're going out there to see what's wrong. You have better luck than the rest of these techs."

Luck had nothing to do with it, but I'd never tell her that.

"That's all, everyone. Get to work, and Daniel, try to fix the system before the end of your shift today. You take forever to fix things at times."

Chrissy didn't understand. I had to take my time going through the checklist one at a time to solve the issues.

Everyone left; my coworkers quietly muttered about what happened to Kofi and the others. They needed to talk lower, or Chrissy would send them home too. There was no time to waste, so I moved fast through the lower level to a maintenance elevator that led to one of the smaller adjacent support buildings.

My cracked work tablet showed everything attempted on the broken handler. Those tablets were the closest things we had in the Lower Forty to a PDD. There wasn't a choice. I had to go outside and check the main box on the side of our air purification building. The technicians had done everything they could inside. All the air restoration techs hated going out there. At the outer door to the support building roof, I fastened my respirator and checked the filters before swiping my card to go outside.

The haze was thick, moving gently away from my body as I walked through it. Sanitation and engineering workers on the surface had to schedule escorts to go outside. Sometimes surface dwellers attacked the trucks. But I didn't need Defender Corps protection up there. No one could reach me on that roof.

Down the building ledge was the mainline intake box. It was off. That wasn't good. I hooked into a winch near the edge of the building to hoist myself down the side. First, the checklist: hook in, winch secured, helmet strapped on, and the pulley was tight. *Easiest to hardest, Daniel.*

It didn't take long to jump into the work. I took off the mainline cover and oversized filter. The inside components reminded me of all the appliances I disassembled and rebuilt as a child.

Hours went by with me hanging over the side of that building. During first break, there was no choice for me but to remove the respirator and breathe in the yellow haze. The smell reminded me of something sour, like spoiled milk, but not as bad. Our Tier One benefactors told us that short durations of exposure wouldn't harm us, and I had to hope that was true. I ate two dry tacks that tasted like chalk, and they dried my mouth, but the coffee helped.

The city line was quiet, and my sight was limited. It was still a marvel, the sheer size of each building—rows of megastructures with their support buildings and the reddish-brown mud lining the streets. My break ended, and I continued working for another few hours. I heard a sound in the distance. Was it screaming? When I stopped to listen, only the wind resonated in the landscape. My nerves were getting the better of me.

For lunch, I ate more tacks, and that time there was some butter paste to spread over the top. To relieve myself, I peed on the side of the building. I was sure Cloud Walkers wouldn't mind.

The project was extremely time-consuming, and the workday had nearly ended. I finally reached the inner gearbox and found some broken reels inside. The replacement pieces were in my belt pouch, and it didn't take long to rebuild the box.

Once it was reassembled, I flipped the switch, and a roaring engine noise blasted out, reverberating through the surrounding buildings.

"That's it!" I screamed, wiping sweat from my forehead. I took a deep breath and hit the pulley button. "Time to go back inside."

The crank was pulling me up the side of the building when, without warning, the rope line holding me jerked up and down. The winch above made a grinding noise, and I fell two meters at first and sprang back up another three. There was nothing else I could do but grab the harness rope and squeeze.

A much louder sound came from the roof. Black smoke was gushing through the yellow haze. The rope line dropped me again another three meters and came to a grinding halt. My shoulder and body smashed against the side of the building. Again, another three meters dropping until the line stopped; it swung me back and forth like a pendulum. It happened again, and again it swayed me like a rag doll. After seconds of sheer terror, the rope gave out entirely, and I fell to the wet, muddy ground.

It took me some time to recover and gather my composure. I was angry. When was the last maintenance checkup on that stupid broken machine? Fear took me instantly because of what happened to the construction manager. After another frantic moment of checking, I took a deep breath of relief—the card was still secure on my neck. At least I could get back inside.

An airlock should be two hundred and seventy-five meters or so to the north. I walked in that direction with my heart racing. I'd heard frightening stories of what happened to people on the surface. I wondered if the old sheds leaning against my megastructure could tell any tales; they were in ruins and must have been hundreds of years old.

I was halfway to the airlock when something became visible in the distance. Outlines of people were moving in my direction. There was nothing to my left or right, only two enormous megastructures and the red wet mud beneath my feet—nowhere to hide.

They were clearer through the haze, two adults and two older teens with rugged appearances and tattered clothes; they needed a bath. All were malnourished worse than Tier Four. The surface dwellers scowled at me in confusion; they must have been able to tell from my outfit that I didn't belong. My dirty Tier Four clothing was nicer than theirs. All four had cut long socks on their right arms, which reminded me of the construction manager's story.

"Who is he?" the teen girl asked.

The older man answered, "Not sure."

"Is he the one who's been killing us?" The teen boy had an angry frown.

The older woman said, "Nah, he ain't doing any killing to our members. Look at him—he's from the inside for sure."

They inspected my gear and took special notice of the belt pouch and backpack. I also had a tool bag clipped to my belt behind me.

With an evil-sounding giggle, the teen girl said, "Maybe he comes out to clip us off. Gets his rocks off or sumthin'. A little sport before going back inside." Her speech was slurred through the gaps in her teeth.

"Nope, can't be, because he's Tier Four. Those airlock defenders won't let him out and back in every day without questioning what he's up to out here." The older man looked thoughtful.

The giggling teen girl was getting angry. "All alone, are you, insider? No shiny armor suits keeping you safe. They did this to my teeth, and other things too." She touched herself between her legs.

All four pulled makeshift weapons of some kind from their waists. The man had a pipe; the woman pulled a small pocketknife; the boy wielded a long, broken piece of wood with nails sticking from the end, and missing-teeth had nothing but her fists. She continued to giggle at me.

I was never a fighter. Growing up, Tobias would defend me in school when others gave me trouble. He was the warrior, not me. If he'd been here, I wouldn't have to worry. My lack of experience made me scared.

I took a few steps back. "Listen, I have food and tools you can have if you let me pass."

The older man smiled, his yellow teeth resembling the haze. "After we kill you, your stuff is ours anyway."

My heart dropped, and I moved further away. "I have family that depend on me inside. Please, let me pass."

The woman smirked, her evil intent clear. "And if they were here, we'd kill them too. It's the way, you fool."

Sinister giggles from the toothless girl persisted. I was scared and angry. My family needed me, and if I died, they'd lose the apartment and go down to the lower levels. I wouldn't allow that to happen. I took a few more steps back and pulled a metal hammer and a large heavy wrench from the tool bag. There were four of them, but only three had weapons.

The older man seemed pleased, observing the tools in my hands as if it were sport. "Good, now it will be fun to kill you, insider."

He leaped at me, swinging down the skinny broken pipe. I used the wrench to block his blow, and the shock wave of metal on metal rattled my hand and arm, echoing loudly across the landscape. In one motion, I raised the hammer with my other hand and swung it down, striking his head just above the left eye. Blood spewed from the gaping hole. The man's eyes rolled back and closed as he fell with my hammer embedded in his skull.

From my blindside, the older woman came at me too quickly for a response. There was a sharp pain under my right arm that streaked through my body like lightning. I tried to step away from the agony, but the teen boy was waiting with his wooden nail weapon. The nails struck my left arm, embedding into the skin. As quick as the nails went in, the boy pulled them out.

I screamed so loud that it boomed through the muddy streets. I tried to run away and tripped over my own feet, falling to the red mud. The wrench was gone too; I must have dropped it. I rolled over to face the attackers. It was evident that I was a terrible fighter. The three surface dwellers stared down, grasping their blood-soaked weapons. Realization of my outcome hit like a ton of bricks. This was it. I was going to die on the surface of Civil Earth surrounded by strangers and yellow haze.

The teen boy spoke to the giggling girl. "Your turn to do something. Have a swing at him."

She picked up my wrench from the muddy ground and moved closer. She only took two or three steps before stopping to look back at the teen boy who was gasping for air, a gurgling noise coming from his mouth. A sizeable knife protruded from his throat just beneath the chin. It gleamed then disappeared as he fell to the mud.

Someone new had come; an older teen girl became visible through the haze and shadows. Her deadly knife was tied to a long utility pole. She was taller than average and had a more confident demeanor. Her head and shoulders were held high. Tears slowly dripped down her cheeks, and she looked sad and angry at the same time. Her skin was dark, and she had thick wavy hair that curled down to her shoulders.

The woman lunged at the newcomer with her pocketknife, but she swatted the older woman away like a fly. The confident teen was faster and moved with grace, calculated grace. The small knife dropped to the mud as the end of her pole smashed the woman's hand. She swung her blade end around and drove it into the older woman's upper chest. Within seconds the woman was down, holding a gaping laceration.

The first teen girl was already moving to attack the newcomer. The oversized wrench landed a powerful blow, and she shouted, but within one blink of my eyes, spun around and pushed her long pole into the giggling teen's face, and the girl dropped to the mud with blood coming from her mouth. She wasn't giggling anymore, and if she'd had any teeth left in her mouth, they'd be in the mud beside her. As the girl fell, the new dominating, prideful teen pushed her spear into the final attacker's chest.

All four aggressors were down, and the teen newcomer glanced quickly at them. She moved with such perfection. I stood slowly, making a grunting noise from the pain. My uniform had blood all over it. Once on my feet, I turned to find the newcomer's long shiny blade pointing at my throat. I raised my hands nervously to show that I wasn't aggressive.

"I'm not with them—please don't hurt me."

She looked at me with narrowed eyes and lowered her blade. She glanced back at all her defeated enemies once more. "I know you're not one of them, or you'd be dead already."

The older woman was still breathing shallow puffs of air. The newcomer walked over to her and thrust the long blade into her throat without hesitation.

"You were amazing to watch. Much better than me."

She looked at me. "You did a good job. I was watching and waited for the right moment to help."

"I've never done anything like that in my life—I was scared."

"Being scared is good—it keeps your senses strong. If you froze, that would be bad. Freezing is weak. You tumbled like a clumsy dummy and dropped your tools, but you didn't freeze."

She might have been young but she commanded knowledge of someone much older. *Living on the surface must age people considerably.* The newcomer rummaged through all of the fallen foes' belongings, scavenging whatever she could find.

"I was trying to get inside building thirty-three's airlock, but they were on me halfway to the other side—"

She cut me off. "You were out in the open. You can't get yourself caught in the open on the surface. That's how you die out here."

I was unsure how to respond to that and felt faint from blood loss. The newcomer did something peculiar next. She had small pliers in her hand and bent down slowly to each body, reached into their mouths and pulled a tooth the same way a dentist would. She dropped each tooth into a small pouch that was nearly full of teeth and looked like a bag of popcorn. As she performed those barbaric deeds, tears streamed from her eyes. Was she feeling pain or anger? I couldn't tell. Her confident demeanor, although gone, reminded me of Lilly.

I asked, "Why are you doing that to them?"

She wiped tears away and moved to the next body. The dead giggling girl had no teeth, and after inspecting the mouth, she forcefully pulled a fingernail from a hand.

"These people that attacked you are BreakNeck Boys, one of the surface gangs. Three weeks ago, they killed someone important to me."

"You feel a great sense of loss."

"Yes, these teeth are my compensation. Maybe trophies, I don't know."

I stood next to the man with my hammer still embedded into his skull. The teen came over and dropped down to remove a tooth from his mouth. I carefully placed my hand on her shoulder.

"You don't have to do this anymore. I can help you."

The newcomer pressed her lips together and frowned before pulling away.

"You're an insider and wouldn't know what I need or don't need to do."

I reached into my workbag and pulled out two tacks for her to eat. When she saw the tacks, her eyes opened wide; she grabbed them like a wild animal and devoured them quickly, as if she was afraid I might try to take them back.

I spoke again. "I can help you if you let me. You saved my life. Let me return that kindness."

She didn't say anything because her mouth was full of the hard, dry crackers.

"What's your name?"

The girl hesitated and swallowed while wiping another tear from her eye.

"My name's Kathryn, but I prefer people call me Kat."

CHAPTER 10

Surviving in the Great-in-Between

The strong-willed refugee (Isabel)

We were still in the command center of the refugee ship with the pirates and their arrogant, cocky captain. Someone else had come, and I wasn't sure who it was, but everyone was scared. They had long faces of dread. I prayed that Adam and Juliet were inside the safe room.

The captain's yelled instructions to his crew made it clear why the pirates were on edge. On his wrist, he had a command bracelet; it was an older model but still functional, which gave him control over ship systems. He lifted his wrist and used his other hand with its metal fingers to flick the display up as a hologram.

The image was what I feared. Another ship had come next to the pirate vessel and docked with it. Our three vessels were side by side. It was a harvesting monstrosity, twice the size of both our ships combined.

Androsians. Horrors of the Free Worlds that made children hide under their blankets when they heard a clatter at night. The oversized ship was the greatest fear for any commander or captain observing an uplink screen. Androsians were part of humanity—a twisted, dreadful and corrupted form of us. They were still human and made the pirates look like religious choir singers by comparison. Androsians committed unspeakable atrocities to people.

The Androsian Singularity inside the Great-in-Between caused their madness. The first of them were brilliant scientists and engineers from Civil Earth and the Colonial Accord who were studying the singularity. Prolonged exposure degraded their mental capacity to reason. A normal human brain understood that shooting a stranger in the face for no reason isn't normal behavior. For an Androsian, skinning someone alive was as ordinary as sneezing.

Those grotesque monsters suffered from the Androsian Effect—a new form of insanity. All their pain receptors and nerves were gone so they felt nothing. Androsians performed body modifications to each other regularly without sterilization or anesthesia.

Reports from survivors of attacks contained references to experimentation on victims, torturing for fun, and women often became prisoners for breeding since Androsians couldn't procreate independently. The nightmarish monsters were also omnivores, consuming anything they came across, including people.

I couldn't imagine the pure hell it must be for people taken to breed. Those poor women would spend each day near the singularity, slowly losing their humanity while forced to make babies for those monsters, and the children would grow to become deformed predators.

I regained my focus and looked back at the life box door. Adam and Juliet must be inside unless they were hiding somewhere else.

"Shipmates of the Black, be ready. Our craft has gone dark, and the terrors have come," the captain yelled.

His exaggerated mannerisms and dramatic facial gestures were gone because it was no longer a game. We'd all die on that ship. I had seen firsthand what vessels looked like after Androsian stalkers went aboard.

Our ship's power turned off, and the emergency lights were no longer spinning. It was pitch black. The pirate crew set up battery-powered lamps shining directional beams down the hallway that led to the terminal doors where the pirates entered earlier. The rest of the command center had no light except faint glimmers from the spotlights.

Small arms weapons fire rumbled from the junction hallway. Flashes of light bounced off the distant walls, combined with screams of terror. The gunfire grew louder, and there was another noise, a strange screeching like a wild animal, followed by something sounding like a chainsaw. It sent shivers down my spine as more screams filled the room. Those shrieks wailed like death. I searched the back of command for anything I could use as a weapon, but nothing useful was there. All noisy commotion ceased at the same time. It was eerily silent, so quiet I could hear people nearby breathing.

The captain called out again, "Be ready. Be ready."

From the far junction hallway, someone turned the corner, running in our direction with the spotlights reflecting off him. It was a pirate and he screamed in pain, his entire upper body covered in blood, like paint. He had a missing arm, torn from the shoulder joint, and clenched in his other hand was the missing body part, flailing up and down as he ran straight at the lights.

All that blood couldn't be his. The scared defensive line tensed up, and everyone raised their rifles a little higher into the air. The missing-limbed pirate had only come halfway down the long hallway when something silver and bright emerged from the center of his chest, jerking him forward violently. The shiny pointed object sparkled in the spotlight, and long metal tangles burst from the point of it and wrapped around his body. The long tangles were flexible like rope but metal, and they engulfed his entire chest. It reminded me of squid tentacles. In one motion, his body was pulled back to the junction hallway and around the corner leading to the terminal docking doors. His screams fell to silence once more as he vanished into the black.

A pirate crewmember squealed, "That was Fe-Fe-Felix!"

The captain said, "Good, we needed a new navigator anyway. Be easy, my shipmates. We can beat them back. Remember who you are. Draco is with us. The Pirate Black runs through our blood the same as in our Black Skull Admiral. We'll do him proud this day."

So they were from Draco, one of the three pirate rogue worlds where the Black Skull Admiral Derwin resided, past Titans' Belt. Pirates loved harassing miners and using that gargantuan barrier that spanned hundreds of light-years across as a buffer between the Free Worlds. I didn't notice any black running through Felix's blood and guts.

There was another animal-like noise that screeched through the command center, but that time it came from behind. Pirates turned and looked through command, squinting their eyes in the darkness to see better. Nothing dangerous was in sight.

Someone turned one of the spotlights to inspect the back wall of command. Another pirate moved through the rows of computer stations, trying to find the source of the scream. Again, another cry, and it was closer to me. I jumped back against a side wall as the hair on my arms raised. There wasn't a way in or out of that room, other than the junction hallway, and the safe room blast door was secure. Where was it coming from? Nothing was back there.

A few pirates cautiously walked to the back of the command center looking for a source. Lights beamed from their rifles as they inspected under and over every object. One of the pirates near the back wall stopped in his tracks at the sound of scratching from above. Nearby were computer systems, life support scrubbers, and ventilation. *Oh no, the ventilation.* It was recessed high into the ceiling and wasn't wide enough to fit a grown person, but maybe something smaller.

The pirate raised his rifle and the light shone up into the recessed ceiling; his eyes opened wide, and he appeared to become sick from whatever was up there. There was a shout of fear as he fired a steady stream of bullets from his weapon into the vent. More pirates took his side to assist, but what the captain and I both noticed was that everyone's focus wasn't on the right spot. No one else was observing the junction hallway.

The captain yelled, "Hold your positions. Stand fast."

It was too late; something dreadful was moving down the hallway.

Patches of skin were randomly placed on its upper body and it had no hair of any kind. Right above its eyes was metal, nothing but metal, forming a helmet across the creature's head. Spikes pushed out from both sides of the jawline, extending out like elephant tusks. Its eyes were hideous with evil poise and bloodshot focus. I thought of that monster as an *it*, but no, that wasn't true. It was a part of humanity, only our most dreadful form. The creature was an Androsian stalker, apex alpha predators of all occupied space.

From the stalker's shoulders down to the elbow were what looked like typical human arms with gashes in areas of the skin, revealing sophisticated mechanical systems beneath. At the elbow, substantial modifications made both forearms thicker than the biceps. On the stalker's right hand was a saw wheel spinning with the chainsaw sound I heard earlier. Abruptly the wheel turned, folding one hundred eighty degrees into the metal forearm, and disappeared. In place of the spinning saw wheel were fine-pointed fingers with surgical equipment like drills, scissors, laser cutters, and staplers.

After another moment, these tools retreated another one hundred eighty degrees, and the cutting wheel returned. The stalker's left hand consisted of a sharp harpoon with long wriggling tentacles dragging on the floor. That was what yanked the one-armed navigator back through the junction hallway.

From the stalker's waistline down all was metal, which flexed and moved from side to side. Its lower body resembled a serpent as it slid fluidly from one side of the hallway to the other. The flexible metal body extended back nearly five meters in length. Each metal link of the snake-like body was silent while in motion, but a strange soft moaning came from behind the stalker's main body.

As the creature got closer to command, the moaning grew louder, and what was making those sounds sent another chill down my spine. Spaced out along the serpentine body were mounted poles extending upward, reaching higher the further away from the main body they went. The nearest mount was flush with the metal body, and each after that increased in height by twenty centimeters. At the top of each pole was a head, and, sickeningly, their eyes and facial muscles moved. The moaning came from those heads because they were somehow alive.

At least seven heads lined the serpent body, all diverse through the spectrum of humanity. A Dolrinion sentinel with his smushed face and oversized nose like all the people of the Offensive was at the back on the longest pole. The middle was a small child's head, and she was crying as any child would under those circumstances, while the very first head was unbelievable to comprehend. It was the navigator Felix, and his eyes were frantically moving from side to side in confusion and panic.

He screamed, "Help me, please."

None of the other heads talked in comprehensible words. Maybe it took those heads so long ago that their brains were only shadows of their former selves. That Androsian stalker was the most horrifying and fearsome thing I had witnessed in my entire life. But the captain and his crew weren't looking down the hallway. Their gaze remained at the back of the command center. I looked up at the recessed ceiling vent where the pirate had fired his rifle—and tensed up. The pirate and other crew who had been shooting into the vent were down, and the surrounding area was freshly painted with blood.

Something scurried rapidly across the ground at waist level. It was so fast that I couldn't see what it was in the darkness. There was a strange clatter of clicking as it went past me. Other pirates were still searching the dark back wall of command.

The snake-like stalker was at the entrance, and the crazed woman with her heated coils turned her head to see the huge metal monster next to her. She shouted with fright, roaring so loud the sound drowned out all other turmoil in the vicinity. Refugees observed the stalker for the first time and screamed the same cries of fear. The heads lining the metallic body turned with anger and shouted back at the frightened refugees. The crazed pirate pushed her hot coils into the stalker's chest. There wasn't an immediate response from the creature. It looked down at the brander, which steamed red hot, disintegrating what little flesh remained, then the coils touched the metal underneath.

Small flakes chipped away from the stalker's chest plate, changing to burned black ash. The stalker frowned in a fury, observing the flaking metal, and it yelled with the same animal shriek as earlier. Its jaw unlocked, opening more extensively than any regular mouth should. A watermelon would have fitted inside with ease, and what made it worse were the teeth—metal with sharp points extending out like shark teeth.

She quivered with fright, which seemed ironic because only a few minutes earlier, she was the one filling everyone with fear. At that moment, she was nothing more than prey. The stalker lunged forward, taking her head entirely into its massive mouth, and with one chomp, her lifeless body fell to the grated floor. There was a crunching sound as her head was crushed into small bits by those unforgiving sharp teeth, and the crackling crunch was dreadful. Within seconds, the captain was screaming orders to the railgun crew who opened fire on the stalker. Bright streaks of light from the railgun littered the air like glowsticks. Rounds penetrated the surrounding walls and opened large holes in the metal chest of the snake stalker. It retreated down the junction hallway, slithering left and right before turning out of sight.

Behind me, more refugees and pirate crew were dead. What was it that brushed past my leg? The chaos in that room would get us all killed. People ran in seemingly random directions, screaming, crying, shooting weapons at invisible enemies without concern for those near them, and dead bodies were everywhere. Things had fallen apart so quickly. My attention drifted to the raised ceiling area where the ventilation system was. Long dark hair hung down from above the raised ceiling and two small watery and bloodshot eyes, filled with hate, gazed at me from above.

The head was attached to a small body with eight metal legs. It fell and landed upright as a cat would. That Androsian was a child, no older than nine, and she was another thing from someone's nightmares. Her hands and upper body were the same as any nine-year-old girl, but her lower body had modifications that made her look like a spider. Wait, no, there was a tail too. Not a spider but a scorpion, reminiscent of the black-tailed scorpion on Kora. More small Androsians moved at the back of command, ripping at both refugees and pirates without prejudice. They maneuvered unnaturally fast and had more strength than any child should.

143

The Androsian girl let out a terrible scream of rage and charged in my direction with more agility than I ever saw before. Her tail curled up and pointed over her head into my path, and she had similar metal teeth to the snake stalker from the hallway. She was almost on me. I grabbed the conference table to my left and pushed it down to create a barrier between us, then moved back against the sidewall, but it trapped me. She pulled herself over the top of the conference table slowly and came straight for me, shrieking.

My heart dropped into the pit of my stomach, but before she cleared the table, her head exploded into a thousand little pieces. Small bits of flesh showered over me as her body slung over the thick table. I used the back of my arm to clean the pieces of blood and meat off my face.

The captain was standing above me, holding his maimed hand out; the other was holding his oversized pistol, smoke gently floating above the barrel. I hesitated—this didn't fit with what he'd done before.

"We need to get out of this room before we all die." The captain pulled me to my feet. "Forget what happened five minutes ago, the here and now is all that matters."

He grabbed a rifle from one of his dead pirates and handed it to me. "Don't shoot my crew. Follow me, and we might yet survive."

Regardless of my distaste for him, I knew from experience that he was right. I nodded, and we moved to the main hallway that led to the junction.

"What's the plan?" I asked as other pirate crew and two refugees came to join us.

"The junction hallway common rooms—I saw ladder stairs leading up to dead space. We'll go up another level or two and work our way to the opposite end of the ship where the life pods are."

"The Androsians would shoot us if we launched."

He smiled and raised his chin. "We'll secure ourselves inside and stay quiet. Once they finish up here, they'll leave. It would take them great effort to get to us if we secured ourselves inside the pods. People always run to the life box when evil comes for them."

"When the bad guys come, and there's nothing left but doom—"

The captain interrupted. "Ah, yes, what a splendid rhyme. But I bet you didn't know there's a second verse to that poem, did you?" I shook my head. "When the safe room's closed, and all must hide, the life pods are where we survive."

"Never heard that one before, but I wish I thought of it earlier." The life pods were much closer to our quarters than the damn safe room.

We went into the junction; people were still fighting inside command, and others had gone into survival mode, fleeing or hiding. The pirate who tackled me earlier was with us. He gave me a contemptuous stare when he saw the rifle in my hands.

The captain noticed. "Easy, Jack, we'll settle up later. I'm sure she'll want that too. Right now, we need all the help we can get. Besides, she can handle herself. I'd even bet she was in the military."

If he only knew the things I had done in my life. "Jack, is your name?" He nodded, and I said, "Big Jack would sound more accurate."

The captain laughed again. "He's Jack the Giant. A famous Pirate of the Black."

Jack the Giant. That man was well over two meters tall. He was the biggest person I had ever seen—another first on a day of firsts. At the junction hallway, the captain looked past the corner to see what lay beyond the hall. Our group consisted of three additional pirate crew not counting Jack and the captain, and two refugee passengers with makeshift weapons.

At the hatch inside the gym, the captain climbed the ladder stairs built into the wall and opened the top hatch. It only took him a moment to crawl inside, and then he poked his head down with a thumb extended.

I grabbed the ladder stair, but Jack pushed me aside and said, "I'll go first. You won't be up there alone with the captain."

He was a big dumb brute, but loyal to his commander. After Jack got up the ladder, I followed and the others after me. The last pirate crew member who was guarding our flank had a foot on the bottom rung when something pulled his attention away from the ladder. He turned and fired his rifle, screaming with fear. After a few short bursts, a new Androsian was on him, maiming his body as it slashed with sharp blades.

Jack and I looked down as a big female stalker with pointed arms jabbed and sliced the pirate as if she were filleting a fish. There wasn't anything we could do to help. I grabbed the heavy hatch door and pulled it down as Jack lobbed a grenade into the room below. The metal grated plank flooring under our feet rumbled in the explosion.

Jack said, "The grenade was mercy. No one should die like that."

I couldn't agree more. I'd take a grenade over being mauled to death like an animal any day. Only seven of us remained, and we kept climbing to the next level. That floor was strange because of its quietness. The lighting was all out, but some sidewall display screens were still operating and giving us our only illumination besides our rifle lights. Right under our feet, people were dying by nightmarish butchers, but on that level, all seemed tranquil.

We carefully followed the inner ship to the other side. At the other end of the vessel, we reached another elevator landing area with benches against some walls and larger display screens flickering from the power disruption. Blood covered the metal floor, and syrupy gore slowly rolled down the screen of one of the displays. Something had happened there already, and the sight made everyone uneasy. We had three different directions to choose from. All three means of egress were gloomy and quiet, and everyone raised their weapons higher.

"The secondary terminal docking doors are two levels up at the end of this middle hallway."

"The pods are past those doors. We'll move that way," the captain said.

He waved his hands, and everyone slowly pushed down the hall, trying to cover all access points. The only sound was our boots on the grated floor. We moved up through two levels unmolested. I was surprised we had that much success. The secondary terminal doors were before us. One at a time, we climbed up the open hatch from the dead space below. There were three egress directions, and they were pitch black with no light source. The captain, Jack, a refugee, and the female pirate crew member were out of the hatch alongside me. Behind us was an elevator on the other side of that landing across from the secondary terminal doors.

We heard a noise from behind; everyone turned and pointed whatever weapon they had in that direction. The female pirate ran over to the elevator control panel and hooked up a screen from her bag. She was trying to override the pressure lock. Another odd noise from the opposite direction. Jack turned to face the sound, and another pirate crew member popped his head out from the ladder hatch with a rifle pointing in the same direction.

"We won't make it to the pods on this level. Time to go higher up in the ship," the captain yelled.

The code-cracking pirate said, "I've almost got it."

From the third hallway between Jack and me, a scrambling noise drew close, and something became visible in the beam of my rifle light as I turned to face it. I took a knee and opened fire with the old beat-up rifle. Steady, accurate rounds ripped through the stalker as it clawed its way towards us. Each shot that penetrated did little to slow it. Small bursts of blood spat out from each round that pushed through flesh. But still, it came.

In the hallway Big Jack covered another Androsian stalker that was coming through the darkness on four legs like a dog. Jack's rifle sang with fire, but the stalker ignored him and lunged to the pirate standing on the ladder hatch with most of his body still inside the dead space below. The stalker grabbed hold of the pirate and they both fell down the ladder. Jack closed the hatch leaving one of our refugees and a pirate still inside. I brought my aim higher, firing at the head of the stalker attacking in my hallway. The captain shot at it too, and after multiple headshots, the stalker slumped to one knee, screaming out in rage as foam and blood leaked from the sides of its metal mouth. I stood taking two steps forward, pulling the trigger one last time, and killed the monster.

The captain came over, observing our fresh kill. "That right there is a conversation starter if I ever saw one." He turned back to Jack. "How many people from occupied space can say they killed an Androsian stalker?"

Jack shrugged, unsure, and I said, "It will only be a conversation starter if I survive to tell the story."

Another animal-like screech came from Jack's hallway.

The code-cracking pirate spoke. "That's it, the elevator's working again."

She went inside, followed by Jack and the teenage male refugee. The captain and I were moving to the elevator door when I felt something wrap tight around my leg. He grabbed my hand to keep me from being pulled back, but he wasn't strong enough. There was a brief tug of war that ended with me falling to the metal floor further away from the elevator door. Three stalkers emerged out of the shadows and glowered at me. The elevator doors closed with everyone inside. I was alone with three demons and my rifle was across the landing almost out of reach.

Two of the stalkers climbed up opposite ends of the wall as if they were insects, scaling up with ease. One opened the upper hatch, and both went inside the dead space, presumably to chase the elevator. I was alone with an Androsian, who still had my ankle wrapped like a lasso. It was now staring at me without expression, and that scared me. It had two different color eyes that didn't match in size. It was obvious they came from two different victims. Metal skull sockets were visible, outlining the eyes with no skin covering. Sharp metal teeth chattered together while it watched me without moving.

It lifted its arms from the darkness, and fear took me. All the fingers on each hand had long sharp-bladed nails reflecting what little light was present. The expression on the stalker's face turned to malice as it stepped forward, eyeing me like I was food. It scowled as driblets of spit fell from its mouth. A new sound came from behind—a grinding of electronics and gears. Two heads attached to angled poles peeked over the shoulders of the mismatch-eyed Androsian. It had three heads in total. Jointed poles pushed the new heads higher and must have been connected to the stalker's shoulder blades behind it. Both the extra heads snapped their jaws repeatedly. The additional heads were similar to those attached to the snake stalker, including Felix's, back in command. The three heads eyed me balefully.

The heads were complicit and acted with the stalker in unity, unlike the heads we'd seen in the command center. My breathing became uncontrolled as fear filled my body. The mismatched eyes of the stalker moved right over me, and its two biting heads arched down and got closer, inspecting my face. The Androsian and its two extra heads made a gurgling noise. Then the creature dug its sharp-bladed nails into my upper thigh, pushing through pants and skin with ease, like a knife in butter. I screamed. Blood streamed down my leg while the three-headed monster made another sound that might have been laughter. The two heads arched closer and began biting my arms. It hurt; they weren't causing serious damage though, only gnawing on my flesh with normal teeth, barely breaking the skin, but using enough force to leave marks on my arms.

I couldn't understand what was happening. The mismatch-eyed Androsian was next to me, and I could feel its breath on my face as it swayed from side to side, peering into my eyes. I saw the faint reflection of my glowing green eyes in his pupils, and the stalker raised his hand. The nails grew, doubling in size instantly. With one hand, he grabbed my shoulder, and the extended nails dug through soft tissue and scratched the bone. I felt the vibration in other parts of my body. I screamed louder, and the two complicit heads mocked my shouts. I closed my eyes, wishing it were a nightmare.

When I opened them, the stalker was using his other hand to rip out the larger brown eye from the metal socket. The sound of ripping as the nerves tore made my stomach upset. It fell into my lap with the pupil pointing up. The stalker appeared unfazed by the violent act. Extreme anxiety took hold; I had green eyes, bright green eyes, like my father and children. We were the only family that had the genetic glow, an anomaly. This thing was going to take my eyes. I attempted to pull away, but the intense pain in my shoulder was too much.

The stalker's blood-covered hand with those long sharp points moved slowly to my face. As its bladed fingers got closer, the biting heads followed the blades carefully as if they were helping to guide the nails. My heart raced. I was terrified and tried to think myself out of the moment. Adam and Juliet, my father and my husband, before the civil war; thoughts streamed like a river, but it didn't help. The thin metal nails were like surgical instruments pushing into the skin. My eyelid was no match for those blades. I'd never screamed so loud in my life. Again, the two biting heads on their angled mounts copied my cries. The pressure in my eye was unbearable, and an instant later there was a pulling sensation. I blinked rapidly, but something was wrong. Everything on the right was black as if someone pulled a veil over that side. When the realization of what had happened sank in, I looked up with my remaining eye to see the stalker carefully dropping my green eye with its slight shimmering glow into his empty eye socket.

The stalker grinned a terrible sneer. It was wicked and frightening. What made it worse was my long optic nerve hanging from its eyelid. The entire experience was insane, and there wasn't any way to stop the torment. *Wait, a noise. What was that sound?* A tumultuous thud rattled against the opposite side of the landing area, and the red cylinder lights of the secondary terminal docking doors spun and an alarm blared. Someone had come. That thud was a ship docking. On the other side of our refugee ship was a pirate ship and an Androsian ship; now someone else was on this side. The huge doors swung open, and the Androsian snapped his head in that direction. My eye fell to the floor and rolled to the entrance.

A beam of light brightened the landing area and steam engulfed that side of the room upon the meeting of two air types. The Androsian forgot about me and moved closer to the docking doors. It took a position on the ground like an animal, reminding me of a tiger right before leaping to attack. The creature grabbed the grated metal floor, and the two biting heads pushed forward past the main head, now missing an eye, and gazed into the mist.

There was a silence that seemed to last a lifetime. All three heads growled. Something pushed through the steam with lightning speed and slammed into the stalker. The smaller bulky figure drove the cybernetic monster into the elevator wall near me.

It was hard to see the commotion with one eye soaked in blood and sweat. The short, fast figure threw the Androsian across the entire length of the landing area where it smashed into the opposite wall near the terminal doors, crushing all the piping.

I cleaned my eye out enough to see who had come—a Dolrinion sentinel, covered in thick battle armor from head to toe wearing a heavy face shield and helmet. His shoulders were protected by massive pauldrons that overlapped the chest armor. No one else in the Free Worlds would fit into that armor because of its shape.

Above one pauldron was a light beaming in the direction of the stalker. Behind that light was a Dolrinion battle rifle, a superb weapon for any soldier. On the other side was a mounted auto gun with ports for rockets and solid rounds. The sentinel's chest was so broad it could have acted as a table fitting several people comfortably to feast. More cumbersome armor covered his legs, with sizeable circular knee guards overlapping shin armor.

The sentinel's legs were as thick as a silverback gorilla's but shorter than an average human's. Dolrinions were small but incredibly powerful. When he moved, mechanical components displaced throughout his armor, making sounds as the metal undulated. The symbol on his chest showed that he was a gunnery sergeant and, judging by the dents and damage to his yellow and brown armor, he must have been a veteran of hundreds of battles. His chest plate displayed several rows of small emblems shaped like thick handcuffs pressed to a star design. The shapes indicated his confirmed kills. On his hip, resting easy, was a scabbard housing the famous Dolrinion tip knife—a ceremonial blade essential to the Offensive's way of life.

That battle-hardened sentinel was shorter than me by several centimeters. My father always said, "You'd have a better chance of winning an argument with a rock than a Dolrinion. Don't waste your time debating with them."

The Androsian stalker and sentinel observed each other for tense seconds, like two killers deciding the best way to exterminate their enemy before attacking. The sentinel pulled his battle rifle; the stalker's nails grew even longer and the sharp points sparkled in the glow of the sentinel's shoulder light. Once again, all three stalker heads hissed with disapproval.

Dolrinion sentinels had appeared through the mist and stood along the open terminal docking doors, close to where my eyeball lay. Sentinels had a strong prideful sense of duty and honor. None would interfere with them in single combat.

Both combatants screamed and charged fearlessly at each other.

"For the Offensive," the sentinel shouted, driving for the creature.

The stalker's cry was a bone-chilling shriek of terror—rounds from the auto gun on the sentinel's shoulder fired, penetrating flesh and metal. Large holes opened on the stalker caused by the armor-piercing bullets that didn't dissuade its advance. The demon continued rushing forward. They connected in a single violent crash. The stalker swiped its sharp nails, breaking the battle rifle in two, but, undeterred, the sentinel landed a powerful punch knocking the stalker off balance—an opening for the veteran sentinel. He capitalized on the advantage, grabbing one of the biting heads still connected to the angled pole and snapped his arm back, removing the long rod with the head chomping in his direction. All the spectating sentinels screamed in deep, bellowing approval.

The stalker jumped into the air and kicked both legs, smashing against the considerable chest-plate armor of the sentinel, which launched him against the back wall close to me. In a fluid motion, the missing-eyed stalker reached back and pulled the remaining angled mount rod, removing it from a connector on its back. It straightened the angled pole, locking the joint in place, and then tossed the rod with accuracy like a spear, with the biting head at the end. It landed in the stomach of the sentinel pinning him into the wall.

A grunt came from the sentinel, and his shoulder auto gun opened fire on the stalker, pushing it to the opposite wall near the terminal doors. He pulled the spear from his body and it screeched as the armor rubbed against the metal pole. A waterfall of blood fell over the sentinel's battle armor, falling through the grated floor. Our ship's floor had drunk more blood that day than any other since its creation.

The gunnery sergeant broke off the biting head from the end of the Androsian lance and threw the spear back at the stalker, who was fending off armor-piercing bullets from the auto gun. The spear had the same effect and drove the stalker into the wall, pinning it there as the grievously wounded sentinel limped through the terminal landing area. Halfway to the stalker, he stumbled to one knee, clutching his wound.

The line of silent sentinels stomped their feet in unison, a show of encouragement—something Dolrinions did instead of clapping their hands. The injured gunnery sergeant seemed rejuvenated. He recovered and stepped to his pinned enemy. A sigh of frustration came from the stalker as it gazed at the sentinel with hate. The gunnery sergeant lifted his face shield, which made a whooshing sound as it moved. The wrinkles on his face overlapped each other—not wrinkles of age, rather drooping skin from the high gravity of Kora—and he had a massive nose. Blood leaked from both sides of his mouth, thickening over a cropped goatee.

"Impure abomination, your end comes at the hands of Force Command Burning Star. You may have killed me, but I'll live long enough to watch you die. Duty, valor and glory to the Offensive." His voice was deep and rasping.

"Duty, valor, and glory!" the line of sentinels called out.

He removed his tip knife from its sheath, still holding the open wound with his other hand. The knife blade had serrated edges from the handle to the midpoint, and at the point on its reverse was a significant barbed edge that extended beyond the normal curvature of the blade. I could only imagine the pain of that weapon driving into flesh, and the removal would cause more damage from the barbed point.

The gunnery sergeant forcefully plunged his serrated knife into the stalker's head, pushing through the metal and bone. The creature closed its one remaining eye and died against the wall. The wounded sentinel took two steps towards his comrades but fell to the grates, more blood spewing from the open hole in his body. Groups of sentinels charged out in all directions—up, down, and across our vessel. A colonel came through the little mist that remained and went to his fallen soldier. His face cover was up, and he had long gray hair overshadowing his facial features.

"You won your individual combat with witnesses, my brother of war. You served me loyally—you have an exemplary duty record, proving your valor beyond count in the field. Today's glory is yours."

For the last time, the wounded gunnery sergeant spoke. "I go to the memory stone, to rest with my Force Command brothers and sisters."

He had one last breath of air, and then closed his eyes forever.

"You earned it, sentinel. I will ensure your name finds its place on the stone."

The colonel stood and took notice of me against the wall, covered in blood. Behind the officer, dozens of sentinels spread out into teams moving through the hallways. One group opened the lower bubble hatch and opened fire on something below.

My head felt heavy and the room started to spin, then everything turned dark and I closed my eye.

*

I opened my eye and breathed in a long solid breath of air. At least I wasn't dead. There was a throbbing pain in my right eye, and I winced. I was still in the terminal docking area with the elevator behind me. Things had changed; refugees and pirate crew sat nearby with their hands bound to thick metal bracelets connected on a chain.

Sentinels were all over, standing motionless like stone. Force Command Burning Star. All Dolrinion Force Commands had a battle standard and specific color for their armor. I knew who we were dealing with when I saw the colors and cuffs pressed to a burning star.

Someone had taken care of my missing eye; there was a patch covering the hole where my eye had once been, and a familiar voice was speaking to me.

"The widget medic took care of your wounds. They were pretty rough with you, but you didn't even flinch. She cauterized and bandaged your shoulder and leg too."

The pirate captain was next to me with Jack the Giant, the young refugee man, and the female code-cracking pirate. They survived both attacks.

"Be careful how loud you say that word. Dolrinions get angry when people call them widgets."

The captain's sarcastic half-smile returned. "They get angry about everything."

"How long was I out?"

"At least an hour. They fought hard through each level, and it took some time. The stalkers retreated to their ship and left with several passengers and some of my crew. What you see here is all that remains."

I shook my head. "No, the Androsians would never retreat unless severely outnumbered, and even then, it's not a guarantee."

Big Jack said, "The Dolrinions have a hunter group out there collecting new slaves."

Armadas, fleets, battle groups, quick ready cluster, and hunter groups— all the fancy names for our Free Worlds militaries. My missing eye was sticky goo resembling chewed gum on the floor. Someone stepped on it, and that made me angry. A surgeon could have put it back with some plastic surgery and healed the tissue damage as if nothing happened. That option was no more. Wishful thinking regardless, because we were all at the mercy of Burning Star.

Another high-ranking officer waddled into the landing area without a helmet; she had a commanding appearance but was irritated by our presence. Her voice was deeper and scratchier than the dead gunnery sergeant.

"I'm Major Rancour. Behind me is Colonel Bowick. We're the ranking officers from this hunter group detachment of Force Command Burning Star."

Many of the refugees gasped or cried out at that name. All educated Free Worlds citizens knew what Burning Star represented. Each of the ten Force Commands served a purpose to the Offensive as a whole. First Ones specialized in industry and education, Tacoma focused on diplomacy and governance, and BlackRock were experts in the occupation of foreign territory. We were unlucky. Burning Star were masters of collecting people.

The slave trade was barbaric, and no one else did it in occupied space but the Dolrinions.

"You're all slaves of the Offensive. You can take comfort in knowing that if we hadn't come, you would all be dead after the Androsian assault. We'll bring you onto our destroyer, provide medical assistance, and give you sustenance."

A refugee said in a hoarse voice, "But, ma'am, we're Free Worlds citizens and slavery's illegal against us."

The major's face turned bright red. She walked over to the refugee, and Dad's words were loud as if he was standing next to me. "You would have better luck winning an argument with a rock than a Dolrinion."

The major stood above the chained refugee, and without hesitation, she punched him in the face. Her superior power, both naturally and from the battle armor, was behind the blow. His cheekbone shattered, and the eye instantly swelled.

Major Rancour turned and yelled, "Medic."

She walked away from the broken-faced refugee, inspecting everyone else sitting nearby. "This ship's registration is that of a refugee transport heading to the relations station. Your logs were easy to read. We have access to refugee port applications from the station. Every one of you has revoked your citizenship of the Human Alliance. Per the law established by the Capitol Forum under the dome, and under the Free Worlds' Relations Policy guidelines, every single one of you is no longer a protected class. The same as these pirates."

No one spoke a word. Everyone looked both scared and confused—another sentinel standing across the landing area ordered us to rise and fall into line. My mind raced.

I asked the captain, "Did they open the life box door?"

He shook his head. "No, they left it alone. The people inside the safe room will be ship crew anyway and citizens of the Free Worlds."

I remembered the terrible things the pirate captain did to me and the people of the ship. I leaned in to him as if I wanted to whisper into his ear. He moved closer, and I pulled my head back as far as it would go then smashed it forward, striking his nose. A loud crack emanated from his face, and he shouted. Jack tried to move in my direction, but a sentinel was on us in seconds.

"Knock it off, or you'll find yourselves tossed out of an airlock."

The captain laughed as blood dripped to the floor. "Don't worry, Jack. Remember, I said we'd settle up after the Androsian attack, didn't I? It looks like she got a head start on that."

We walked single file through the terminal docking doors into the airlock. The only windows on that ship were in the airlock, and when I looked out, Dolrinion warships littered the surrounding blackness of the Great-in-Between.

Major Rancour spoke to the old graybeard commander. "We lost eighteen sentinels and killed five stalkers before they fled. Our gunships engaged, but the Androsian harvester jumped into FTL."

We were too far away, moving into the Dolrinion destroyer for me to hear anything more. As we walked into the hangar bay, my life and especially my kids flashed through my mind—such transition through the years and so much hardship.

First, I was the daughter of a regent for years in the powerful city-state of Athinia before the Unification Civil War and our state's demise. As a young teen, I was an aide to the center seat representative of the Human Alliance during secondary school studies at the relations station. Next, I served, rising to captain in my city-state military while my dad became the prime regent of our world, on and off several times through the years. I was a wife, mother, resistance fighter, city-state loyalist leader, widow, refugee, pirate captain's prize, survivor of Androsian mutilation, and now a Dolrinion slave.

I laughed out loud because the last four of that list had all happened in one day, and it wasn't even lunchtime yet. I wondered what the afternoon would bring? The captain and Jack narrowed their eyes strangely at me.

"What's your name?" the captain asked.

It took me a moment to stop laughing, and I answered, "Isabel. My name is Isabel Sideris."

He peered into the blackness of space from the airlock windows then looked down. "I'm Captain Gideon," he said after a moment of silence.

I turned back, observing the Dolrinion slave ship, and sobbed. This might be the last day I ever saw Adam and Juliet. Tears streamed from my left eye. What a day, living in the Free Worlds of Humanity.

CHAPTER 11

Closed Session Under the Dome

A day in the Capitol Forum (Henry)

Loud banging rang out across the chamber from the Dolrinion Offensive podium stand. Center Seat Representative Sharrar, or as sentinels of the Offensive called him, the Iron Fist of Kora, slammed his massive, mighty hand onto the podium. Echoes blasted through the pentagon's five walls in the lower amphitheater. The acoustics in the enormous open forum dramatically enhanced that sound, as they would a concert.

Representative Sharrar yelled, "I'll not stand here and let the Federate Corporation representatives accuse our Offensive of war crimes. They're the reason for this fighting on Gliese in the first place!"

More screams from both sides blasted along the five walls. Left and right seats of the Offensive stood and yelled like drunks at a bar. The Federate wall was more of the same, with cries of insult. Anyone looking into that room would fear for our future because the fifteen representatives in the theater controlled the Free Worlds' fate. Not counting laws passed inside the forum, the homeworlds took our counsel, and given the current situation, things were bleak.

The domed ceiling inside the forum was sparkling white, with gold crown molding around the circle between the dome and sidewalls. Stylized designs ran along the Capitol Forum amphitheater walls—it was a marvelous sight. I glanced to the round marble stage, the center of the five walls, which had five steps leading out from the circle on all sides. I would have given my speech from there if not for JJ and Mia. My hand squeezed into a fist.

The weekend after my canceled speech involved nothing but planning how to deal with the betrayal of those sitting inside the pentagon, until a ship carrying refugees from the rogue world Gliese landed inside the refugee dock that Sunday. Countless vessels had come with people from the rogue world, making them citizens of the Free Worlds, and there was no reason to suspect anything else when the ferry arrived.

The transport doors opened, and soldiers from Gliese poured out, shooting everyone inside the dock, including people from their own planet. The soldiers' armor, weapons, and equipment were rudimentary compared to the Free Worlds', but pure panic engulfed the station. Security officers and citizens of the main cylinder working in the dock died. For the first time in recent memory, the entire station went into lockdown with a total travel ban, while the MERC Guild investigated the cause of this unprovoked attack. Surveillance footage showed how effective station security was in stopping the aggressors. Our MERC Guild quick-reaction force was in the dock within minutes and engaged the rogue world soldiers.

MERC mongrels leaped from one soldier to the next, firing their auto guns. Those huge beasts were such an advantage to agents, but even with that benefit, two mongrels, one agent, thirty-two station security officers, and one hundred nineteen civilians and refugees died.

We suspended all actions under the dome for three weeks of mourning for those lost in the attack. The incident helped drown out the political turmoil that would have had the media eating me alive. Now their focus shifted to the rogue world Gliese.

The sergeant at arms to the Capitol Forum called the chamber to order. Once the voices reduced to a murmur, Mia Stavish rose from her center seat, perched higher than the left and right on an elevated platform, to speak.

"Representative Sharrar, you're speaking out of turn. The floor is still open to the Federate Corporation. Now please, return to your seat."

The Iron Fist of Kora gave Mia a hard look and ground his teeth. He turned and waddled back to his center seat. The Dolrinion representatives all wore full battle armor without their helmets inside the forum. They already walked strangely because of their shape and size, but that armor made their movements seem clumsier. The three Dolrinion representatives' armor were each different colors and designs according to their Force Commands.

I said, "Representative Orwick, please continue."

Cassandra Orwick from the Corporation glanced at me and then looked back to her teleprompter, and continued to ramble on. While she talked, I lost my focus, looking at the only straight wall where Civil Earth's representatives sat, and staring at Mia. She played me for a fool and I hadn't forgotten what she did.

Cassandra Orwick was still talking at the Federate podium.

"You will see in our Corporation's after-action report, which we shared with all here under the dome, the situation is dire. Our sister companies have brought food, medical aid, and temporary housing for this rogue-world population in all areas under our control."

She flicked her wrist and a holographic image displayed above center stage showing Gliese. Half of the world was blue and the other half was red. A substantial area between both colors was gray—not under either side's control. The marshlands of Gliese were where all the resistance on the planet operated under local control. The Frogmen of Gliese, special operations soldiers, conducted daily hit and run raids and set up traps for both Federate and Dolrinion forces.

Before the invasion, this marshland area was not inhabited by natives of the planet. During Gliese's buildup to defending against the Free Worlds, the military constructed small infrastructure inside the marshes where high numbers fled during the initial landings.

Attacks were so frequent that flight above the marshlands and the upper atmosphere became restricted. The native military did the best they could with the technology available. No rogue world could stand against one Free World invasion army, and that planet received two. The initial resistance lasted thirty-six hours in total, but their changed tactics produced better results. Occupation was always harder than invasion.

Representative Orwick concluded by saying, "And with that, I yield the remainder of my time."

She walked back up to her right chair of the Federate wall.

I cleared my throat and said, "We thank you for your time. Closed session of the forum now calls for opening statements from the Human Alliance of Epsilon Prime."

Left Seat Representative Zachery Laskaris stood and walked down the steps to his podium surrounded by polished white terrazzo tile. He and I had been in each other's good graces for a few months. We worked closely to pass a bill that profited us both tremendously. Even though I hated that world's current situation and would always loathe Isaac and Killian Lyons for murdering Liam, politics were politics.

Representative Laskaris spoke. "Good day to you all here under the dome. Because of the recent terrorist acts by the rogue world population of Gliese, we of the Human Alliance would like to take the rest of this month to mourn those that were lost. We relinquish our time today and give it to the center seat representative of the Colonial Accord."

Whispers broke out from the other walls, and Mia Stavish narrowed her eyes at me. I glanced at her and looked above, past the pentagon-shaped walls to the amphitheater with its stadium seating where onlookers observed open session. It was empty and the whispers resonated through the seats.

She stood and said, "We of the forum thank you for your time. Closed session now calls for statements from the Colonial Accord of Uropa, Ardum, Tautrus, Lars, Pardalis, and Talbora."

Mia sat, expressionless, and kept staring at me.

I stood and said, "I would like to thank my esteemed colleagues from the Alliance for giving me their time today. In turn, I'll give this time to my friend, Left Seat Representative Christine Keng."

JJ Richmond, sitting to my right in the lower seat, chuckled under his breath.

Today's closed session belonged to JJ, our right seat of the Accord, and since he and I disagreed on pretty much everything, the clown would go in his own direction with policy. That was one of the great foresights of our station founders. They ensured that each representative would have a voice in governance. We took our turns each month, and as luck would have it, JJ was to give opening remarks to steer policy under the dome for this month. Since Zachery relinquished his time to me, and I, in turn, gave it to Christine, JJ would now need to wait another three months before spewing his Rose Party bile into the forum. It was a small victory for me, but I'd take what I could at that point.

Nicolas Nomikos, being a career politician, grinned as he glanced up at JJ, knowing full well what was playing out. The secretary of Free Worlds Affairs sat in our guest seat near the Colonial podium. I had kept my promise to Senior Agent Ficco and brought Nicolas to closed session. Even with the warning I gave to the Alliance representatives beforehand, they still gawked at Nicolas. The Alliance would need to bite their tongues because the MERC Guild's concerns had to take priority at this moment.

Christine Keng slowly walked down each step, keeping her unforgiving gaze stern. The Free Worlds knew the Angry Tigress of Lars for her aggressive demeanor, governance style, and general personality. The woman's passion and short temper, added to her constant yelling when she spoke, made rivals show fear and colleagues admire her. She never surrendered or admitted defeat inside the Capitol Forum. I always respected Christine's strength.

When she reached the podium and spoke, her voice carried her hostility across the five walls. "This month has been very troublesome with the issues in the port and the continued fighting between two of the Free Worlds' governments here in the forum. There's also shame along these five walls as a result of the actions of a few, and it was disgraceful." She looked back at

JJ and continued. "Center Seat Representative Henry McWright has been a shining light of hope here on this station for twenty-two years. He created the food equality bill, ensuring that not one Free Worlds citizen ever goes to bed hungry. He helped co-author a bill sixteen years ago before any of us were here that adjusted currency spending more efficiently within the MERC Guild."

Christine pointed to Jaxson Boran at the Federate wall, speaking louder. "Even you, the center seat representative of the Federate Corporation, complimented his way of re-managing spending at the Guild. For the genius accounting mind of Tri-Co to say this publicly means a great deal. After the Unification War, Henry McWright also helped the Human Alliance by allocating vast sums of Free Worlds credits to rebuild the city-states. He looks out for us all and puts his priorities behind the needs of the many. It's our responsibility and duty to do the same for him. I call for a revised version of Henry McWright's bill to be brought for a vote in open session."

Christine turned and walked back to her left seat without speaking another word, and she gave JJ a stare that would scare a grown man out of his shoes. JJ was looking at his nails and pretending to clean them, seeming uninterested in his surroundings.

Zachery Laskaris at the Alliance wall said, "I second the motion."

Michael Decelle from the Federate Corporation added, "I third the motion."

The rule of three stated that a bill couldn't go to open session without three representatives from three walls voting it through, not counting the bill's author. There were subsections to the rule of three regarding other actions here under the dome. Christine and Zachery's votes were a given, but Michael was a surprise. He voted both ways the night of my speech, saying nay to my bill and yay to allow me to speak. It appeared the left seat representative from the Corporation might want a favor down the line that didn't line up with his other seats.

Closed session opening statements were always short and to the point. There was no need for dramatics or theater when cameras were off, the amphitheater was empty, and special guests were not in attendance. Even the balcony for the outer worlds was empty during closed session.

I stood and said, "We thank you for your time. Closed session of the forum now calls for opening statements from the Dolrinion Offensive of Kora."

I took my seat, and both the center and left seats of the Offensive stomped their feet. Right Seat Representative Guth waddled to the podium with his chin and shoulders high. As Guth moved, sounds of gears rolling came from his battle armor.

Guth spoke in his deep voice. "Force Command Tacoma, along with our fellow Force Command Representatives Sharrar of First Ones, and Halku of Command Overwatch, demand action by all in this forum. The Offensive didn't instigate this war on Gliese. We've abided by the restriction laws enacted right here under the dome and never crossed the DMZ without being provoked by the Federate Air and Space Cab. Our intelligence from Force Command Overwatch clearly showed that the Corporation began their invasion massing forces in Gliese's system long before we arrived."

The Corporation representatives jumped from their seats, roaring once again, and so did the Offensive.

Dolrinions were incredibly stubborn, proud, and quick to anger. I remembered Liam Sideris saying something about winning an argument with a rock before winning one with a Dolrinion. Guth was from Command Tacoma, and of the ten Force Commands, they were the easiest to deal with when negotiating. Still, that wasn't saying much when talking about Dolrinions. Their usual form of bargaining was with a battle rifle.

Representative Guth continued after the Federate representatives calmed down. "We currently occupy forty-two percent of this rogue world. The Federates are in control of forty-four percent. The remaining fourteen percent are those marshlands that the primitive locals use to stage their attacks. Even after an orbital bombardment, they still resist us. The natives are even firing on our ships with ground-based defenses, so we have halted all activities around that zone. The Offensive wants this area currently under the control of the Corporation."

He used his hands to highlight the hologram in an area of mountains on the rogue world next to the marshlands. "That area accounts for one percent of the total planet size. Once our Force Commands have this mountain, we'll begin a crushing campaign against the Frogmen in the marshes."

Representative Sharrar ground his teeth, and Halku looked down and mumbled to himself. The Offensive was precisely that, always on the offensive, and hardly ever attempted to negotiate a resolution. War was a way of life for Dolrinions, and their society depended on it to survive.

Offensive battle groups weren't advanced enough to take on the Corporation Air and Space Cab without committing every Force Command to arms. The Federates had the most advanced ships of all the Free Worlds. As far as a strategy was concerned, the only way for the Dolrinions to assault that mountain would be drop capsules, and the Offensive wasn't able to get their ships close enough to drop them because of the Federate fleets and ground defenses of the Frogmen.

Somehow, the Frogmen had acquired Free Worlds' weapon technology when getting ready for the invasion, either from the Rogue Syndicate or pirates from Draco, Martoosh or Leo. If the Dolrinions could obtain control of that mountain, they would stage a constant barrage of mortar fire on the marshlands.

Representative Guth looked at the Federate wall. "If the Corporation gives us this mountain willingly, we will stop all hostile actions against them on the planet and focus on occupation of the territory we currently hold."

Our guest, the Secretary of Free Worlds Affairs, Nicolas Nomikos, sitting in the seat near our podium, spoke. "Might I ask you, Representative Guth, the current status of the rogue world Gliese population in your occupied territories? How many of them are on slave worlds for the Offensive?"

All at the Human Alliance wall scowled at Nicolas. Secretary Nomikos was once vice-regent of the city-state Elpis before the civil war. When defeat was imminent, the regent of Elpis sent Nicolas to the relations station seeking aid.

Representative Guth's face turned so red I thought his head might explode. He raised his voice. "A rogue world doesn't fall under the Free Worlds' Relations Policy. The only harvesting on Gliese was for labor in the war effort. Might I remind you, Secretary Nomikos, if the Federates hadn't initiated their invasion in the first place, we wouldn't be anywhere near that planet or its primitive population."

Left Seat Representative Michael Decelle of the Corporation jumped from his seat, yelling, "I'll not sit by and let you lie in this sacred forum amphitheater. Our intelligence services received accurate information that your Offensive were the ones who invaded that planet first."

Once again, both sides jumped from their seats, howling at each other. It took several minutes for the sergeant at arms to silence the shouting.

Nicolas said, "Gliese might be a rogue world, but our relations station is feeling the pressure from your war. I need not remind you of the attacks in the refugee dock only three weeks ago. It was our station's blood that spilled, not yours. There's also severe strain with the mass numbers of refugees flooding here from that planet. The main cylinder doesn't have the housing or resources for all of them. To date, two hundred and fifty thousand have ventured through the refugee dock. Given the low technology level of Gliese, finding these people productive jobs to contribute won't be easy."

Representative Guth smiled. "If you are so troubled by these primitives, I will notify a supreme general from Force Command Burning Star to come to the station immediately. They would be more than happy to take them all for you."

All on the Dolrinion wall erupted into laughter. Dolrinions were the only Free Worlds civilization with slavery. Tier Four on Civil Earth were nearly the same thing, but officially only the Offensive collected people. There was a time that the Dolrinions kept their reaping to the United Union and its fifty hellish wasteland worlds. The forum's representatives banned harvesting from their planets a generation ago, and the union had tried to gain recognition as a Free World ever since. As long as Mia Stavish and I were representatives, it would never happen. I glanced up at their empty balcony again.

Nicolas narrowed his eyes. "That's very inappropriate indeed, sir. This station is the pillar of the Free Worlds, holding us up strong and always looking out for the best interests of all." He pointed to each of the five walls, one at a time. "All of you represent the five fingers of humanity. Fingers can't function without a palm, and this relations station is the palm of our species. We need each other and will only function properly if all five fingers close to the palm at the same time."

Random representatives around the pentagon cheered and clapped, including our Angry Tigress of Lars.

Guth laughed again. "Hey, Nicolas, I got a finger for you right here."

The Tacoma supreme general pointed his middle finger at Nicolas, and once again, all on the Dolrinion wall burst out with laughter. The Alliance representatives joined in too.

The Silent Lion said sarcastically, "Now, Representative Guth, that was highly inappropriate." Christopher Floros, the right seat representative for the Alliance, was known as the Silent Lion because he rarely spoke. Even when it was his month at the podium, he usually yielded the time to one of the others from the Alliance wall. When he decided to speak, it was advisable to listen.

Representative Floros retired from the Lyons Pride Intelligence Services of New-Sparta and then was appointed to this station by Isaac Lyons. Of all in the Capitol Forum, his words were the fewest, and more often, he gave responses by merely motioning with his hands. Christopher was a dangerous man and always appeared to be in deep thought. He dressed formally with his gold lion's head lapel pin shining bright.

"We will make no concessions at all until the Corporation gives up that large mountain range. There's nothing else to say." Representative Guth sounded defiant.

The Offensive wall stomped their feet as Guth marched back to his seat.

I stood and said, "We thank you for your time. Closed session of the forum now calls for opening statements from Civil Earth of the planet Earth."

I took my seat. Mia's betrayal was like a skin burn that wouldn't heal. As dark thoughts surfaced, I pushed them away. *Keep the box locked, Henry.*

Right Seat Representative Olivia Belitz walked to the podium. She was wearing a colorful yellow and orange toga with a beautiful bohemian headpiece of white pearls over her intricate hairstyle. Olivia was young with bright blue eyes and light hair. Her family was the wealthiest of all Tier One on Civil Earth and had an exciting rivalry with the Stavish family. The Belitz family commanded a massive personal fleet of ships and private security. They could invade a rogue world and conquer it without Civil Earth Defense if they wanted.

The Civil Earth representatives all wore colorful togas with beautiful jewelry each day. Just like their eccentric forum seats, they dressed the same way as a show of superiority.

Olivia spoke. "Good morning to all representatives here in the pentagon. Civil Earth will relinquish our policy direction this month because of what transpired in the dock. Instead, per our center seat's request, I yield my time to Right Seat Representative JJ Richmond's concerns for this month. We demand that the MERC Guild investigate the attacks on the Colonial Trade Company transport vessels. We believe the Black Skull Admiral Derwin is responsible. After the destruction of these ships, everyday goods' costs are on the rise, and vital food shipments do not reach their final destination. Our Free Worlds markets are in complete disarray due to the numerous vessels that are lost."

That bastard JJ; I wouldn't have thought he had such a snare over Mia to push his issue through Civil Earth. He threw his head back with a smile. Mia, on the other hand, looked like a defeated dog glaring at the ground. Something was happening, and I needed to find out what. JJ had once again outmaneuvered me.

He stood and spoke for all to hear. "Representative Belitz, you're a true professional of the five walls here under the dome. I look forward to the MERC Guild findings on their investigation, and I know that the Colonial Trade Company of Ardum will be pleased."

He glanced at me before sitting down, and I felt my ears burning. Olivia gave JJ and Mia a dirty look. If I had to guess, she wasn't pleased to have given up her time. How much did Mia sacrifice for that request, I wondered? Something interesting must have transpired for Olivia to concede her time.

We concluded the session after another ten minutes of formality. Then all representatives left through rear doors along each pentagon wall that led directly into the back offices behind the Capitol Forum.

"So, I outsmarted you again, did I?" JJ was clearly trying to taunt me.

He wore his formal Ardum attire of a bright red frock coat with intricate lacing and buttons throughout. His clown hair was up in its usual bun. I wanted nothing more than to take him behind the curtain.

"Have you ever seen the Uropa flower before?" JJ frowned without speaking. "It's the most beautiful flower in occupied space, making your Ardum Rose pale by comparison with colors of red, blue, green, and purple. It takes three years for the flower to mature and come into bloom. If the flower isn't cared for properly, it'll wither and die. Even a drop of water more than recommended can kill the plant before it flourishes."

"Are you going to take up a new profession as a florist when you retire? I promise to be your first customer."

I chuckled. "No, that's not my plan. I'm just educating you to know that all good things come in time. With the right nourishment and care, the best outcomes will happen precisely when they're supposed to."

Before he could respond, I turned and went down the hall to my office building. The Angry Tigress of Lars went to JJ, coming within a centimeter of his face, wide-eyed and angry. She turned and walked away as he stood there, still trying to make sense of my comments.

CHAPTER 12

From the Surface to Tier Four

Learning to adjust to the Tier system (Kathryn)

There was so much stuff inside that room—more things than I ever saw outside. Plastic cups, tissues, towels, gowns for changing, pillows, doctors' instruments scattered through the room, and Daniel's hospital bed right in the middle. How could someone need so much stuff?

Daniel looked different than he had outside; he was clean, not wearing tattered clothes. He had short dark-colored hair and golden skin. He was a good-looking man and seemed humble so far. Without him and his childhood defender friend Tobias Norcross standing on the other side of the room, I wouldn't have gotten back inside. Tobias came to the surface and gave me a Tier Four caste card.

The new card hung around my neck on a lanyard, with a picture of my face visible, and in large lettering the number four, for my caste.

Daniel said, "Kathryn, did you hear me?"

"No, my mind was wandering."

Daniel had been in that bed for five days due to the infection suffered from his wounds. He told me his job supervisor, some witch of a woman, surprisingly came and said to him that they would pay him temporary disability until he could return. She was happy with something he did on the building before he fell.

"I said you couldn't stay here in the hospital with me anymore. The staff is giving me grief over you living in this room with me." Daniel's speech was labored and he held the side of his stomach.

I was defensive. "It wasn't my fault—that nurse snuck up on me, so I reacted. Hesitation is death on the surface."

Daniel took a deep breath. "That nurse was only coming into my room to give me medication. You had your back to the doorway, and that doesn't count as sneaking."

Tobias added, "Kathryn, you're not on the surface any longer. I rushed the reinstatement for your caste recognition card and gave assurances that you would behave. If you start breaking people's noses every time they walk up behind you, Civil Earth Defense will march you back outside."

I gave Daniel and Tobias a look of irritation and folded my arms in defiance. They both started laughing at the same time.

Tobias said, "Danny boy, you told me, and now I believe you. She's just like Lilly. Even her mannerisms are the same."

Daniel winced and grabbed his arm as he laughed. "I told you, T, she's a fighter, and her defensiveness reminds me of Lilly."

Tobias coughed. That was a surface cough, he spent time outside.

He spoke after recovering. "Kathryn, I know exactly what you're going through right now—believe me, I do. Living inside will be an adjustment for you but only for a short time. Things will fall into place quickly, I promise."

After dropping my arms, I asked, "How long did you live on the surface for?"

Tobias sighed. "Did my cough give me away? I was out there for two years hunting city line moles, collecting water from air handlers, and hiding from the surface gangs. My aunt and uncle applied for a new caste card, and it took two years for me to get back inside. You're fortunate, Kathryn."

"You can call me Kat. I've always preferred that name." I paused for a moment. "You both should know I appreciate everything you did. It's not something taken for granted. I'm a survivor, though, and even if you hadn't brought me inside, I would have lived out there another fifty years, at least."

That was my stubbornness talking; the truth had been something different, but that was for me and me alone.

Daniel smiled and said, "Based on how you moved out there, defending me and taking out those gang members, there's no doubt of that. You saved me, Kat, and I'll forever be indebted to you. My family would have stood no chance in the Lower Forty without me coming home that day."

Tobias said, "Speaking of your family, your sister took the Fleet Branch officer's test and scored off the charts. She's still resisting, but maybe you can speak to her. Whenever she says yes, I can get her into the academy quickly. Based on her score and personality, within five years, she'd be Tier Three commanding a destroyer."

"That's terrific. I had my doubts that she would take the test. It'll help Mom when Lilly graduates the academy."

I spoke bluntly. "You told me your mother has DDD near its end-stage. She won't be alive to move up in the caste."

Daniel and Tobias looked at me oddly. They didn't say anything, but kept their eyes fixed on me. Beating around the bush wasn't something done outside.

"Sorry," I said, "for the last seven years there hasn't been much time to talk softly or watch what I say to people. There's no time for things like that on the surface. I was only speaking from my own experience out there. People with DDD die fast. Maybe in here, things are different."

"I know you didn't mean anything by that comment, and in truth, you're probably correct." Daniel paused. "She's my mother, and hope is all we have in the Lower Forty."

Tobias put his hand on Daniel's shoulder and said, "Rest easy, Danny. It's time for me to head out and walk these lower floors. It's been a while since I've been down here."

"It hasn't changed much, T. New faces, but the walls still look the same as they did when we were kids."

Tobias laughed and walked to the hospital room door before turning to me. "Kat, let him sleep. You've hardly left his side. Come with me and let's stretch our legs a bit."

I stood cautiously and looked at Daniel.

He nodded. "Go with Tobias. He's a good man and wouldn't try to harm you. I'm not going anywhere."

I narrowed my eyes, grabbing the pouch of teeth on my belt. "If he did try to harm me, I would make quick work of him. Besides, I'm not worried about T. Anyone willing to come out on the surface alone to get me is good in my book."

Tobias smirked and continued out of the doorway. We left the hospital and walked into the general common area on the second floor. Tall pillars stretched from the floor to the ceiling. We moved through the crowds of people; their clothing was much nicer than anyone's on the surface. Life on the inside seemed easy by comparison.

Insiders had more meat to their bones, too. They must eat every day to look like that. Tobias wore a long solid dark-colored shirt with jeans. His clothes were better than the other people around us, and it made me wonder.

"What tier are you?"

Tobias hesitated, looking at the common area and its people. The way he observed everyone reminded me of myself. He watched their hands and body language for possible aggression. It was something Sadness taught me.

"I'm currently Tier Three because of my Defender Corps service with Civil Earth Defense."

I took a step back and said, "Wait, Daniel told me about you and your promotion—soon you'll be Tier Two."

A few people near us gave Tobias suspicious looks. T grabbed my arm and walked away from the common area to a side bench away from people.

"Please be careful what you say here. We're in the Lower Forty right now. Some down here don't understand and wouldn't care to understand. If the wrong person heard you …" He paused again, looking around. "I lived on the surface for two years, Tier Four for eighteen years, and spent the last seven years in Tier Three. Yes, a promotion's coming, but the things I had to do for it …" He shook his head. "Orders from command in the past … I still get nightmares. The caste system's horrible, and I wish it didn't exist, but it does. There's nothing I can do. I'm a sheepdog in a world of hungry wolves."

He also had nightmares about his past. Mine were from the things I'd done outside to survive. I was deliberately vague. "I have nightmares every day. I also dream of Johnathan."

Tobias leaned back and raised his eyebrows. "Who's Johnathan?"

I wiped a tear from my eye as it spilled and started to answer. "He was my—" But before I could say anything more, my cough returned and overwhelmed me. Phlegm and blood were in my mouth. I used the back of my hand to wipe away the thick globs.

Tobias said, "Your cough's worse than mine. I have a friend on this floor back at the hospital who you should see. She might be able to help with the symptoms."

After recovering, I said, "That cough wasn't too bad, don't worry. We aren't outside where it would betray us through the yellow haze for all to hear."

Tobias's face contorted. "Lots die when a surface cough gives away their location. I've seen it myself." He paused again before saying, "Many times."

He was out there years ago. The great flood was something everyone who lived on the surface knew about from traveling stories.

"Were you out there before or after the flood?"

T narrowed his eyes and hesitated. I could tell he didn't want to answer me, but he spoke at last. "During the flood. The year before the dam broke, and a year after. I remember hearing the water before it rushed through each block of our city line. The power of that water is the only thing I have ever seen that could move the yellow haze."

My eyes and facial expression must have given me away. The year after the flood was the hardest year in the history of surface life since Civil Earth came out of the Great Darkness. He was out there during that awful year. Tobias

Norcross was much stronger than I thought, and he didn't brag about these accomplishments. It seemed that these things made him sad.

I said, "My last three weeks on the surface, I did things." I stalled, thinking of the teeth. "Terrible things that felt right. But now, now after thinking about it, I'm not sure. Revenge became my primary motivation after Johnathan died."

Tobias noticed me clutching the tooth-filled pouch at my waist. "Daniel told me about what you were doing to the BreakNeck Boys out there. Everyone on the surface did awful things the year after the dam collapsed, and I can tell you for a certainty that nothing you did while out there is a testament to who you are as a person. We do what we must to survive, that isn't the real us. I've committed terrible sins for the Defender Corps and wish I could take them back, but this is the way things are in the Free Worlds of Humanity."

"You're a glass-is-half-full kind of guy, Tobias. I believe the people we are in those desperate survival situations is our true inner nature that's forced out. When things are going well, people show a false face."

Tobias smirked. "We can agree to disagree. Come on, let's get your lungs checked out."

We walked back through the common area of that floor. People were going about their business. A mother near me was yelling at her young kids who were fighting with each other, those tin-suit defenders walked in groups of three observing everything going on, and someone stood on a ledge speaking out to everyone passing by.

We got closer to listen to the woman speaking with passion.

"And that's why I tell you all the caste system is our undoing. The Caste Freedom Fighters are not terrorists like these defenders here, and their Tier One puppet masters above like to tell us that they are." The woman pointed to the three tin suits standing nearby. "The Cloud Walkers use the defenders, water rationing, and food from the dispenser as a measure of control—eat when we tell you to eat, shower when we tell you to shower, and breathe when we tell you it's ok. Civil Earth Day is approaching, and it's time for us to stand up and say no. No, we will not eat breakfast whites anymore while our bellies growl from hunger every day. No, we will not let you tell us which floor we can walk on and live on without any say."

I looked at Tobias and asked, "What's she talking about?"

"People in the Lower Forty aren't happy with the caste system. We'll talk more about it with fewer ears around us."

The woman kept talking as tin-suit defenders moved in and pushed people out of the way, yelling orders at everyone to move along. Two defenders grabbed the angry woman and restrained her. The crowd shouted at the tin suits, which made all the defenders draw their sidearms, which extended into long rifles. The guns made a noise as they grew in size. Those weapons made everyone stop and step away cautiously.

Tobias yanked my arm. "Let's keep moving before there's more trouble."

I said, "Trouble doesn't bother me. I still don't understand why those people were all mad. Stick them on the surface for a week. These Tier Four people will realize just how good life on the inside is."

Tobias puffed his nostrils. "People are creatures of habit. They've all lived here for so long that it's easy to find things wrong with life. Even some in Tier Three and Tier Two might feel the same way. It's human nature to want more. Things in the Lower Forty aren't great compared to the Middle Thirty and Upper Twenty-Three."

The hospital entrance was in front of us, and we walked inside.

*

I sat on a small bed in the emergency room with curtains around us for privacy. I heard people on all sides, but I couldn't see them through the hanging sheets. The sounds reminded me of sickness and pain. Tobias was in the chair next to my comfortable small cot. I never had something like that outside.

A beautiful woman in a long white coat walked in. She had something on her neck that didn't look familiar. Her skin was smooth, brown, and clean and she had beautiful long dark hair. Tobias was paler with light brown hair and hazel eyes. Since I didn't have to look over my shoulder for the next bad

177

thing to come out of the yellow haze, I took notice of the way people looked. Before I went outside, I remembered my mom telling me that our Free World was the most diverse of all the others. I was darker than both of them.

She spoke. "Tobias Norcross, as I live and breathe. What are you doing here?"

Tobias turned red and glanced at the floor, apparently looking for an answer to her question. His commanding, confident demeanor was gone, his shoulders drooped lower and he seemed to shrink.

He said, "Courtney, hi, hello there. It's good to see you again after so long."

Courtney smiled. He was clumsy with his words. I looked at them staring at each other and cleared my throat, so they'd notice me.

Tobias stumbled on his words. "Yes, yes, we're here … I mean, I'm here to bring Kathryn to see you. Daniel was able to get her back into the building after she'd lived out on the surface for seven years."

It didn't take a genius to see he had feelings for Courtney, and her body language seemed to me like she felt the same way for him.

"You got me back inside, not Daniel. He asked you to do it for him after I saved his life."

From what I'd seen so far, Tobias didn't like taking credit for anything. Even something positive.

Tobias rubbed the back of his neck. "Well, yes, I got the card, but it was Daniel who, well, that doesn't matter now." He looked at Courtney. "She has the cough. It's much worse than mine. Can you please check her out for me?"

"For you, Tobias, I would be glad to help." She walked over to me. "My name is Doctor Lameira, but feel free to call me Courtney."

Courtney pulled the strange-looking thing from her neck and placed the ends in her ears. She started to reach over to my chest, and I instantly reacted, striking her hand away, but before anything else could happen, Tobias had my wrists locked in his large, powerful hands. He was faster than me, and that was a surprise.

"So sorry. I wasn't thinking. It was a reaction. I'm so sorry."

Tobias said, "It was your instinct from past experiences living outside. I know this, and so does Courtney. She specializes in helping people recover from living on the surface. Be calm and know that she won't hurt you, we promise."

There was something about Tobias that I trusted, especially after learning more about him. I turned to the doctor. "Please accept my apology for hitting you like that. That won't happen again."

Courtney was discomfited after my slap, pushing hair away from her face with a shaking hand. After a moment, she said, "It's ok, it's ok, I should have warned you before walking up to you that way. My mind was on … something else. That was my fault."

She was thinking about something else; I peered at Tobias; *she was thinking about you, dummy.*

Courtney stepped forward again and started to examine me. She asked me to cough, to breathe deeply, and she also placed her hands against parts of my body. She brought over a device on wheels. "Breathe normally, and don't move. This machine is going to scan you from head to toe so we can see a picture of what you look like inside."

I had seen what people look like on the inside countless times before but never myself, which would be interesting. The machine had a large paddle-like device with lights, and it made a strange noise. It moved quickly from my head to my feet several times and then stopped. Courtney and Tobias both looked at a screen together, and from the expressions on their faces, something was wrong.

Doctor Lameira whispered to Tobias.

I said, "If you're talking about me, speak up so I can hear. There's no point in sugar-coating things. Surviving alone the last seven years outside wasn't done lightly. Just tell me what's going on."

If they only knew the number of people I'd killed to survive out there. Only part of my statement was a lie. Five years were by myself, but the first two years on the surface were with Sadness, and he trained and protected me during that time.

The doctor walked over to me, placed her hand on my shoulder and said,

"Your body's healthy for the most part. You're malnourished, but in general, not in bad shape. But there's a lot of mucus sticking to the walls of your lungs. You also have some serious scar tissue, and your breathing capacity's barely fifty percent. Lung damage like this is common for people who have lived on the surface. Your case is more advanced because you were out there for a long time."

I thought of Sadness. "I met an older person years ago before he died. He told me he lived on the surface for eighteen years. Two years later, his lungs finally had enough. It took two days for him to die with me beside him. His cough was much worse than mine, and there was so much blood in his mouth. It looked like someone was choking him to death as he slowly turned blue and finally died. I held his hand for two days, and he told me to take his things when he was gone. It took twenty years for the yellow haze to kill him, and my time was shorter than that."

What I didn't tell Tobias or Courtney was that his name was Sadness, that he was like a father, and that he taught me everything I knew.

Tobias said, "Most people who come back inside have only spent one to three years out there. It's rare for someone to come in after surviving five years, let alone seven. You're a survivor, Kat, and this won't kill you, but will make things harder. You'll have to use twice as much energy and feel twice as much strain when doing physical tasks."

Courtney stepped closer. "There are medications I can give you that will help heal some of the less damaged tissue, and a device called an inhaler that you can take whenever it's hard to breathe. I will also give you something to help reduce the mucus levels in your lungs—"

"Do you use these medications, T?"

"The pills, yes, not the inhaler."

I looked back at Doctor Courtney, folded my arms, and said, "Just the pills for me. No inhaler."

The doctor smiled. "As you wish, little fighter. Let me scan your caste recognition card first to see what you're eligible for."

She scanned my caste card on a small machine then gazed at T strangely.

Tobias asked, "What can she get with her current status?"

"A three-day supply. There's no listed recent family history, so she isn't eligible for government assistance."

Tobias walked over to me, stared for a moment, then glanced around the room. If he was thinking, I hoped he'd tell me what was going on because I couldn't read minds.

"How much is a month's worth of the medicine out of pocket?"

Courtney answered, "Three thousand five hundred credits."

T's eyes opened wide and he rubbed his neck again. "Can you increase my dosage so I can give her what she needs?"

"No, my attending physician signs off on medications prescribed to Tier Three and Four. He would never let me increase your dosage like that."

"I don't need those medications. I was doing just fine on the surface without any of that stuff." I was annoyed.

T and Courtney stared at each other. He asked, "Does she need to have the meds?"

"Kathryn has significantly more damage than you. If we do nothing, she won't survive another ten years.

"There's a charity program here at the hospital. I'll get you two weeks of the medication, but after that, I won't be able to get more." She turned to T. "You need to come up with a way to get her these meds."

Tobias stuck his head out of an opening in the curtain, observing people moving through the emergency room. "I'll speak with Daniel and see what our options are."

I was seventeen years old, and another ten years would make me twenty-seven when I died, based on Doctor Courtney's opinion. That was a long life, and probably longer than I would have survived on the surface. Sadness was much stronger than me, and things might have been different if I could have come in sooner. The words that came out of my mouth were that everything was fine, but the truth ... the truth was that it was tough to breathe.

CHAPTER 13

Trying to Flee the Corporation

The Applegates learn the hard way (Mace)

One week had passed since Jamie told me she was pregnant. That weekend we made our plans to leave Dol'Arem and the Federate Corporation forever. Jamie said she didn't want to stay in our home any longer because of our plan. She didn't feel safe, and honestly, we were both paranoid. After the weekend, I felt like people at work were watching me and knew what we were plotting to do.

Thinking about my paranoia after the fact, though, all my coworkers were looking at me with admiration because of our success with the defense grid launch, nothing more. News spread like wildfire regarding our positive notation from the vice president of planetary defense.

Before work ended, I asked Rafael to meet with me for lunch at Tiff's, a local bar near work. Coworkers always went there once a month for happy hour after work. Meeting Rafael would look like a normal gathering, only a day off from the usual time.

Micromanaging our work activities was life in the Corporation; we were always watched and scrutinized. Our sister companies and the posters in public spaces said that Human Resources was always watching.

I submitted twenty vacation days and surprisingly, Denis and Tammy approved it for me. They were still in good moods from the positive notation.

Jamie walked into our hotel room where I was changing out of my work clothes into something more comfortable. "Did you talk to Rafael about meeting him this weekend?"

"Well, good to see you too, babes. How was your day?"

Jamie was twisting the ring on her finger. She gave me a half-smile. "Sorry, I'm very focused right now."

She walked to me, and I held her lower back as we kissed.

"How was your day, Mace?"

"I thought it would bother me more when I walked out of the lobby to my car for the last time, but I honestly felt nothing."

"I was afraid all day today. Every time my manager came into my office, I jumped, thinking security operators would arrest me at any moment. They drill it into our heads that our sister companies are always watching."

"Maybe they are, and maybe they're not. Who knows what the truth is? The only thing your manager knows for sure is that he will need to stop being lazy for the next twenty days while you're away."

Jamie's manager was lazy and always pushed everything onto my wife. She was extremely effective as a supervisor, which meant she did his job as well as her own.

She said, "You're right. He'll have to work now instead of sitting doing nothing all day." She held her belly and looked down.

"Go take a hot shower and relax, babes. I'm meeting with Rafael tomorrow for lunch, and there's nothing we can do until then. The night is ours, so let's make the best of it."

"That's a good idea. Let's order room service and unwind."

Jamie went into the bathroom and I brought up the service menu on our entertainment screen. I heard the shower turn on while scrolling through the food options.

I raised my voice. "They have bacon cheeseburgers and fries." That was one of her favorite meals. I mumbled to myself, "Even though it's all artificial, the taste is better than other Free Worlds artificial burgers. That's what I've heard, at least."

The drinks menu had tons of options. Jamie wouldn't partake, but that wouldn't stop me from having a few. That would be the best stress relief at that moment.

The shower door opened, and Jamie peeked her head out, saying, "Mace…"

I turned. She was completely naked, the light blonde hair on her head matching that between her legs. She glowed in her perfection. No one could compare to Jamie in my eyes.

"Want to join me?"

My heart skipped a beat, and I had to admit she found a better way to relieve the weekly stresses than drinking.

"Absolutely, I do!"

I ran to the bathroom, ripping off what clothing I had on. Jamie giggled as I fell before reaching the door, trying to pull my pants off. When I cleared the shower door, we kissed—long, wet, open-mouthed kisses. Her tongue felt fantastic against mine and it excited me.

After we finished, Jamie's face was glowing. "That was exactly what I needed."

I was still holding her. "I can't believe I lasted that long. We haven't done it in a while, and I was sure that I'd finish in seconds."

Jamie laughed, and I said, "Seriously, I had to go over program code in my head to keep me distracted so that I wouldn't go too soon."

Jamie smacked my chest and smiled. "You stop it, Mace Applegate. Get out of this shower so I can wash my hair."

I grinned. "Yes, ma'am."

Back in our room, I felt sorry for us. We only had a few belongings with us—three travel bags with our clothes, and our most prized personal possessions, which could fit into one of the bags. What we had was all we would need to start a new life somewhere in occupied space. I'd prefer the relations station or one of the Colonial worlds. My programming skills and

Jamie's work ethic and abilities would secure us a good life.

The idea of leaving Dol'Arem was easy to think about, but making it happen was a whole different monster. Employees who'd tried to flee found themselves inside a chamber. First, operators would parade them around a courtroom live on the main feed. After proceedings they were marched to a chamber where gas filled their lungs. I wouldn't allow that to be our end. No, Jamie and I would raise our baby together.

After some time, Jamie came out of the bathroom, and we spent hours relaxing, watching our entertainment screen, and ordering room service. Jamie got the bacon cheeseburger, and I ordered the lemon chicken with rice and peas.

Spending quality time together in that hotel within our hometown felt like a real vacation, regardless of the constant stress lingering over our heads. Chewing on that artificial chicken in its thick lemon sauce had my mind wandering and I laughed.

"What's so funny?" Jamie raised an eyebrow.

"Remember that abandoned home on Clark Street when we were kids?"

"Yes, yes, I do. Matt, Erin, Mehul, and Jasper all brought food and drinks but no sleeping bags. I stole some alcohol from my parents' bar, and we had some green leaf too."

Green leaf had different names on different worlds, but the effect was always the same. It made people hungry, relaxed, and everything seemed funny, even when things weren't.

I said, "Yup, that house was empty for five years and had roots growing up the walls. I was scared to stay there because of all the horror stories we heard from friends. You had more courage than everyone, and even stayed in the basement that night after Erin's dare."

Jamie's laugh was mischievous. "Wait, I didn't stay down there."

I looked at her, confused. "You didn't?"

"No, silly, there was a window and I climbed out."

"Where did you go?"

"I went home and slept there that night while you all stayed inside that humid creepy house. I set my alarm clock and came back the next day before any of you got up."

We both laughed. I couldn't believe that for all these years I thought she stayed in that damp basement all night long.

"You are a sneak."

Jamie playfully slapped my arm and we continued eating. We grew up together, and it wasn't until our senior year of secondary school that we started dating. She was always more daring than any of our close group of friends, willing to take risks and try something new. I remember her going skydiving on her eighteenth birthday as an act of defiance because her parents always said no.

I said, "You've always been smarter than me, babes."

Jamie smiled. "I wouldn't say smarter. You're the program-writing genius of Genesis Foundation, not me. I'd say I was always more willing to try things other people wouldn't. Remember that old train bridge over the Amway river? Everyone was too afraid to jump, thinking the water was shallow."

It took me a moment to remember. "I forgot all about the Amway death bridge."

"Oh, please, no one ever died jumping into that river. I leaped off and never came close to the bottom."

Jamie's personality was what made me fall so hard for her in those years. That Amway train bridge was a part of the first rail system on Dol'Arem, and it ran through each of our major cities on the largest continent.

After talking more and enjoying each other's company, Jamie kissed me again, and it led to the second round. We hadn't spent that much quality time together since before the defense-grid project almost a year earlier. She jumped on top of me, taking control of the entire experience. If it were possible to get pregnant twice in a row, she would've had twins in her belly by the morning. I lasted longer the second time around, and after we finished, we lay naked in our comfortable hotel room bed and fell fast asleep.

Through the night, I rolled around restlessly; my thoughts woke me several times. Did she have twins in there? Was it a boy or a girl? Would the baby look like her or me? We needed to get off Dol'Arem. I woke up several times on and off as the sun rose. I would have to function on only a few hours' sleep that day.

Before long, it was time to shower, but Jamie didn't join. I suggested that she go to the hotel spa and pamper herself. My gut instinct told me it might be the last time she could do such a thing for a long time. We'd have it hard enough rediscovering ourselves without being employees of the Corporation. That day was for her, and she deserved it.

We ordered room service again and enjoyed some blended eggs and toast.

Jamie spoke abruptly. "We should go to Galma."

"Why Galma? It's a rogue world controlled by the Syndicate, and the technology level is low by contrast."

"We can't go to one of the Free Worlds or the relations station. Genesis Foundation and the MERC Guild have the authority to take us there. On Galma, no one would bother us."

The thought of Galma made me nervous. "But on the relations station, I could utilize my programming abilities to find work."

Jamie shook her head. "Oh yeah, and with that job, we can afford twenty-four-hour protection from station security? Remember the Federate bubble up there has almost a million employees living in it. I'm sure Representative Boran—and especially Representative Decelle—would love the opportunity to have us arrested. They have a chamber ready to go in that bubble just waiting for us."

She was right. It was foolish to think we would cruise up to the relations station or the Accord worlds and live happily ever after with no recourse for our actions. Even if we applied for sanctuary, the process would take time, and we'd be defenseless.

"You're right. I didn't even think about that. Last week when you told me you were pregnant, there was a MERC Guild agent and some operators in our local train station checking people's identifications."

Jamie's eyes opened wide, and her voice became higher pitched. "Agents and their mongrels are dangerous. We must do everything we can to stay away from them."

"Galma it is, then. It should be cheaper because that planet is closer than the relations station." I chuckled. "Do you think they have beaches in the highland mountains of Galma? I don't think we'll be getting much sun in the lowland fog with those albino-looking natives."

"Don't joke about them. Native Lowlanders are cannibals."

I smirked and shook my head. "No, only the Androsians eat other humans, and the odds of a ship running into them are slim."

Before Jamie left, she turned to me. "Mace, please be careful today." She cradled her belly. "We must protect our child."

I placed my hands on her stomach and kissed her gently. "I don't know anyone who ever got hurt going to Tiff's for lunch and a beer. I'll see you this afternoon and hopefully have some answers on getting off this planet."

We embraced once more, and she left. Before long, it was nearly time to go. I decided to leave early and wait for Rafael at our corner table inside the bar. I wanted to drive the full distance into the city this time to avoid the train station and unwanted eyes. The MERC Guild agent was still fresh in my mind. We had to do everything we could to avoid any authority, which was the reason I disabled the GPS tracker in my vehicle.

*

Driving in, I once again passed the ruins of our world seed engine. Images of the millions of bones in those mass graves uncovered within the last few hundred years stirred in my mind. What were the people like before the Years of Forgetting? What changed everything, and how did they die? How many employees had the Federate Corporation walked into the chambers through the last seven hundred and forty-five years? Were there newer mass graves somewhere else on the planet for ex-employees? The manager and supervisor from the control room the night we launched the new defense grid would find themselves in the ground soon enough with gas from a chamber filling their lungs.

Out of all the creative ways to kill an employee, why did the Corporation choose gas? The Dolrinions made gas their primary method of exterminating us on battlefields of the distant past, so why did our brain-dead leaders believe it was the best way to kill their own? Honestly, I couldn't answer these questions, and they were frustrating to think about, so I stopped.

I arrived at Tiff's bar and parked my vehicle on the automatic belt loop that would store it. I stepped out to the walkway that was busy with pedestrian traffic, which was typical for a block inside the city of Lavlen. Corporate-grade-level twenty employees performed their jobs polishing shoes, collecting garbage, cleaning streets, or painting buildings.

I walked into Tiff's, looking at the surroundings. The main bar was located centrally with stools for tired employees after the workday. Music with a fast-beating bass played loudly. I couldn't even hear that sound from outside, but when I entered, it was so loud I couldn't hear myself think.

Above the bar were several entertainment screens; when I looked at each screen, the music level decreased, allowing me to hear precisely what was showing. Tiff's bar had noise-canceling technology, which allowed employees to talk to each other in peace.

I went to our usual corner booth and took a seat. A holographic display with the food and drink choices appeared as I sat. I ordered my favorite Federate pale ale and waited for Rafael.

When he arrived, we greeted each other in our usual embrace.

"What's up, dude?" Rafael sounded excited.

I held a napkin up that read, "Do you have your PDD?"

He shook his head, saying, "No, Ness has it. She always hangs on to the PDD when the kids are with her."

They only had the one PDD like most with kids in the Federate Corporation at grade-level twenty-seven. The Corporation could track them, so Jamie and I had left ours at home.

"Why are you acting weird?" Rafael furrowed his brow.

I said, "Let's get a beer and a shot for old times' sake."

Of course, he agreed, because we had some good times together over a shot of bourbon and beer.

After the shot came and we ordered an appetizer of artificial fried wings glazed in honey sauce, I spoke. "I don't have time for small talk, so I'm just going to come out with it. You and I have been best friends for sixteen years."

Rafael held up his beer and tapped it to mine. "Yes, brother, you were the best man at my wedding."

He was loose after the bourbon, which was good.

What came from my mouth next would scare any employee. "I need your help now more than ever."

He smiled and said, "Anything I can do for you. All you need to do is ask."

I took a deep breath, delaying for a moment. Once those words left my mouth, they could never be unsaid, and I would have no choice but to live with the consequences, whatever they might be. We were backed into a corner with no other options. I was putting all the weight of Dol'Arem on his shoulders, and I knew that wasn't fair. We were so desperate.

"Jamie is pregnant."

Rafael's eyes opened wide, and he frantically looked around the bar as if he was expecting Federate operators to jump out of closets to arrest us both.

"And she's going to notify her doctor to have it taken care of, right?" he said quickly.

Rafael already knew the answer to his question. I wouldn't have told him otherwise. Maybe we should have ordered another shot before having this conversation.

"No, she's keeping our baby."

Rafael again looked around the bar quickly, and I hissed, "Will you relax? No one is coming to arrest us for having this discussion."

"How do you know that? Are you an expert on this kind of thing all of a sudden? I mean c'mon, man, you have it made here. Your wife is a twenty-eight supervisor, you just designed the system that will protect our planet for another one hundred and fifty years, at least, and you got three positive notations from your supervisor, manager, and the vice president of freaking planetary defense. How can you be talking like this now?"

I took a sip of beer and measured my response before speaking. "When you look at your children's eyes every night before they go to bed, do you think to yourself that you would give them up for the things you just listed?"

Rafael lowered his eyes to the table, and murmured, "No. I wouldn't give them up for anything."

I put my hand on top of his. "Then you know exactly why I am doing and saying this."

He tapped the menu screen and ordered two more shots, finished off his first beer and ordered another. "So why are you telling me this? What do you want me to do?"

"I need to see your cousin."

Rafael leaned back in the bench and stared at the table. There was a sheen of perspiration on his head. Neco was a low-level member of the Rogue Syndicate here on Dol'Arem and Rafael was close to him.

"Right when you told me Jamie was pregnant ... I knew why you asked me to come here today."

"The only thing I'm asking you to do is walk me into the door and introduce me to him. Then you can walk away, and I'll do the rest."

Rafael wavered, shaking his head. "I don't know, man, I don't know. If I bring you to him, I'll become an accessory after the fact."

"Rafael." His eyes met mine. "Jamie and I have already decided to try and do this. The only thing standing between us both being walked to the chamber or getting off this planet is you."

It wasn't fair of me to say that to him. Rafael wasn't being given a choice and now had to suffer my burden. I just threw him into the water with circling sharks.

Our shots and new beers arrived with the appetizer. We took the shots right away and began eating. Rafael sucked down some honey-glazed meat and wiped his face before speaking.

"Fine, I'll bring you to meet Neco, but I gotta warn you. He is a little off in the head."

We drove together through the city of Lavlen, Genesis Foundation's capital on Dol'Arem named after the founding CFO during the franchising of this world. At the lower end of the city was the Hollow Ward, an area of low-income corporate employees and small businesses.

It was incredible seeing the difference between two streets as we crossed. Everything changed, from the cleanliness of the sidewalks to the design of the buildings. Rafael's cousin worked in a laundromat that serviced big business corporate employees who worked a few streets over in the high-rise buildings.

I parked my car on the street. Employees nearby gave us suspicious stares; they looked mean, steadfast, and unhappy to see us, with folded arms and frowns. They were grade-levels twenty through twenty-three, which were the lowest paying in all of Dol'Arem. The laundromat was right in front of us, and there was graffiti all over the brick walls of the building. Rafael walked inside first, and I followed behind. The humidity and heat overwhelmed me instantly, and there was a smell of mildew.

Neco was behind the register sweating horribly and looked like he hadn't showered in a month. He had a PDD that he was playing with on the countertop, and that surprised me. His grade-level was twenty-one or lower, and he shouldn't be able to afford the monthly payments for a PDD.

Neco glanced up as we entered and smiled. "Ra-Ra-Raffy, what's up, baby? It's so good to see you, cuz." He had a gap where teeth should have been and one black tooth near the middle of his mouth. His hair was thick and puffed out numerous centimeters, and he had tattoos on his face and neck. Both pinky nails were black too.

Rafael smiled and hugged his cousin. "NeNe, what the hell are you up to, cuz? It's good to see you. How's Auntie Iris?"

Neco shrugged his shoulders. "I dunno, I haven't seen her in a few months. She isn't happy with me, you know."

Rafael said, "Aah, moms are never happy when it comes to their kids. They always think we're going to be the next sister company CFO."

Neco giggled and twitched. "Dat's true, dat's true."

Every ten seconds or so, Neco twitched his face to the side, lifting his lip slightly, and shook for a few seconds. The convulsions were bizarre, and I understood what Rafael meant when he said his cousin was off.

Two corporate employees from big business walked into the store. One handed a ticket to Neco and the other dropped off two expensive suits. Even though this was two blocks into the Hollow Ward, it was still close enough to the corporate buildings that high-grade employees would come to have their things cleaned because of the price. Neco serviced the employees, who then left. He looked at me with a skeptical grin on his face.

He twitched and asked, "What's he want?"

Rafael looked back at me and then to his cousin. "He's here with me, cuz. I need some help, and I can't do it without you."

Rafael glanced at the PDD on the counter.

Shaking his head, Neco said, "Don't bother with that. It's an off-network PDD. The Corporation can't listen in or track me. My boys gave it to me, you know."

Rafael tapped his shoulder. "That's what we're here for, Neco, your boys."

Neco pulled his lip in, and it twitched. "What you want with d-d-dem?"

Rafael closed the laundromat door and turned on the neon *closed* sign. Neco yelled and twitched. "Cuz, don't d-d-do that. My boss sees dat, I'm-ma getting fired again."

Rafael stared at his cousin seriously and spoke in a firm voice. "Cuz, I've always looked out for you, you know that. I helped you get two jobs over the last five years, and you know if you got fired from this job, I would get you another one if your Syndicate boys didn't help."

Neco looked down, and said, "I know, I know, you a good man, cuz."

"Well then, I need your help. My brother here." Rafael pointed to me. "He needs to get off-world right away, and he isn't coming back."

Neco said, "What makes you think I can do that?"

Rafael spoke louder. "Because you work for the Rogue Syndicate on this planet—and don't lie to me and say you don't."

Neco, twitching uncontrollably, said, "I'm just their go-go-gopher. I got no authority to do nuttin' for them."

I spoke. "We aren't asking you to put us on a ship to get off-world. We're asking for you to put me in front of someone who I can pay to get my wife and me out of here."

Neco stopped twitching and stared at me long and hard.

"You do this for me, cuz, and I will buy you some new clothes, make sure you got a new job when this one goes tits up, and always have your back like I have since we were kids. You see this man here. He's my best friend, like a brother to me. If you help him, you're helping me, cuz."

Rafael picked up the off-network PDD and handed it to his cousin. "Use this and call whoever you need to, set up something and help my brother here leave."

Neco, still looking down and banging his hand on the clothing order machine, waited for a few moments and then said, "I don't need to call nobody. I can get your brother a meeting with the Bum Bum."

I frowned and asked, "What is a Bum Bum?"

Neco stared at me with his eyes wider; was it fear or something else? I couldn't be sure.

"He's da Butcher of Lavlen. Big one for the Syndicate here, and if you can't convince him you deserve to leave, he gunna make you gone for good."

Well, what would one more body be in the mass graves of Dol'Arem?

CHAPTER 14

A Slave of the Offensive

Two eyes are better than one (Isabel)

"Izzy bear …" I heard in my dream, "Isabel, what are you doing here?" My father's voice was as clear as the last time we spoke fourteen years ago.

"Dad, what's happened? My PDD was going off with an alert message saying 'Please stand by for official information from the Ministry of State.' Nothing else came after that."

My father had a long face with heavy eyes. Anxiety and despair had taken him. Standing in that room, the great and powerful Liam Sideris had an appearance that matched his age.

He spoke. "You shouldn't be here in the city. The capital isn't safe."

"Who attacked us? You were just elected as prime regent again. No one would be foolish enough to attack Athinia now. We are the acting City-State-Prime."

My father had been regent of our city-state for thirty years. He ruled as the planet's prime regent two separate times, and that would have been the third. The regent vote for the next prime regent position took place two weeks prior. The majority of Epsilon Prime's regents representing their own city-states cast their votes. They voted eleven to nine, with one state not voting. His win was legitimate.

After a brief pause, Dad said, "Isaac and Killian Lyons weren't happy with the results. Our states have been at each other's throats for months now, and since I made Isaac look bad at the last regent assembly meeting, the vote became the tipping point. They mounted a surprise attack three hours ago on nine city-states."

"Which states aren't fighting?"

My father sighed. "Both Aetós and Rhódmore declared neutrality. Their militaries are idle while we burn. Lémas betrayed us, siding with New-Sparta, which allowed our enemies to invade three Allied States taking us completely by surprise. While Delfa, who didn't vote at all and thought they were allies to the Lyons Twins, is begging for our help. We're outnumbered ten to nine, and four of the states on our side are under heavy bombardment. They can hardly defend themselves. Both in space and here on the ground, the invasion's underway."

My heart raced. "I could hear explosions in the distance from the farm. Tuddy's there with the kids right now. He already started calling local village militias to rally at our home and was taking calls from defense post commanders."

Dad nodded and said, "They started by attacking our land border defense systems. That's probably what you were hearing. So many have died already, so much death. We were complacent, so complacent." He was sobbing by the last sentence.

I put my hand on his shoulder and tried to comfort him the best way possible. He was taller than me and because his skin was darker than mine, the green in his eyes was even brighter, with a slight shimmering glow.

"Our military is strong, we can hold them back. I know it. If we can establish a defensive line and turn the area between our enemy states' advance into a killing field, we might be able to hold out until cooler heads prevail."

My military training and service came out into words like flowing water. Dad shook his head as two state military generals walked through the door.

He regained his composure enough to speak. "Gentlemen, status report?"

Both generals looked like they had just found out someone important to them had died. More importantly, a strange aura of defeat surrounded them. A blind man could see it on their faces.

The higher ranking of the two said, "Prime Regent Elect Sideris, sir, the information coming in is still not totally accurate, there's a lot of jamming going on by the aggressing states. But what we have learned with certainty is that ..." He paused and glared at me then back to Dad.

"You can speak in front of my daughter, General."

"Yes, sir, sorry. We've lost at least half of our forces in the opening attacks. We were caught completely off-guard, and our defenses were overwhelmed. But our conscripts are holding the newly established front on the northern end of the state ten miles inside our borders."

He stood straight and waited for Dad to speak. Dad stared down at a table map showing all the city-states around the planet. Athinia was lucky because only Iskhoros shared a border with us, the others were our allies.

He finally said, "Iskhoros has a powerful ground military. Can we hold them back with our low numbers?"

I was woken from my dream abruptly by someone next to me inside our cell. After being captured, the Dolrinion destroyer transferred us to a slave cruiser, and all the refugees and pirates from the refugee vessel had been shoved into a small room together. There were slim roll-up cots for us to sleep on, one toilet with no doors or walls for privacy, and a sink. The pirate captain Gideon showed some of the refugees that holding the cots up could be used to block the view of people using the bathroom. Of course, because of his personality and nature, Gideon loved to use the toilet with no one blocking the sight of his naked body while sitting on the bowl, smiling and pushing out whatever meal he ate a day or two before.

We were in that room for two weeks, and the sentinels who guarded us didn't engage in any way except to bring us food. Interestingly enough, Captain Gideon had kept his pirate crew in line. Some of them tried to steal food from a few of the refugees in our cell. Gideon beat one of the crew members who led the theft, and that stopped any further attempts. The big one, Jack, was always at his right side, keeping an eye on everything.

The older refugee woman that woke me said, "So sorry to wake you, dearie. But this fell out of your pocket, and I didn't want anyone to steal it from you."

She handed over the picture that I had kept close to me since we left Epsilon Prime. It was Tuddy, my kids, and me, all on the farm, and we were smiling. The kids were younger in that picture, but it was such a happy moment that brought me joy.

"Thank you so much. This picture means the world to me, and I would have been devastated if I lost it."

The older woman smiled. "The best things in life are the family you love, the things you do, and the memories you make."

I smiled back as she stood and walked to the other corner of the cell and sat down.

The captain had kept his distance from me since I broke his nose. The pirate who was able to hack the pressure lock of the elevator on the ship when the Androsians attacked us had spent some time talking with me. Her name was Nina, and she grew up on the relations station's main cylinder. She told me she had joined with Captain Gideon eight years ago when rival pirates attacked her ship, and the captain saved her.

Nina had short-cropped hair that was buzzed on the sides, with two long braids near the front. She had tribal tattoos on both sides of her head, and a nose piercing. She was paler than me with light brown hair and brown eyes.

She saw me awake and came over. "How did you sleep?"

She had been overly kind to me these past two weeks. Before that, she was attacking the refugee ship and caused the separation anxiety I was going through over my kids. But I knew that surviving alone would be impossible. Regardless of how I felt, from my experience, real strength was in numbers, not attitude alone. All the refugees on that slave ship weren't dependable.

"The sleep was ok, the dreams were not," I said.

"Epsilon Prime again?" I nodded. "You've been dreaming about that almost every night."

On the other side of the cell was the glass blocking us from the rest of the ship. After observing it, I said, "The civil war is always in my dreams … and the way things were before."

Nina looked at the barrier glass too and pointed to the sidewall near the metal door connected to the glass. "Do you see that panel near the door? Behind that is the motherboard interface for the door. If I had my tablet still, it would take less than a minute to get it open."

I frowned. "That would only solve one problem. We're on a Dolrinion cruiser with hundreds of battle-hardened sentinels. The command staff from that destroyer came onto this ship with us to see our transfer to the planet. I doubt our ragtag group of bewildered refugees and malnourished pirates stand a chance versus all of them."

Nina grinned. "You don't know how capable the captain is. If he wants to do something, he always finds a way to make it happen."

Thoughts of what happened on the refugee ship with the Androsians stirred into my mind, and it brought up a memory of something Gideon said.

"Nina, what did he mean during the Androsian attack when he said, 'The same black runs through our blood as the Black Skull Admiral.'? I've noticed the pirate crew have those black-colored tribal tattoos. When I was in the Alliance military of my city-state, we had fights with pirate ships, but I always assumed there was no real organization or sense that pirates work together."

Nina raised an eyebrow and answered, "Draco, Martoosh, and Leo, are the worlds with organized pirates. We here are all from Draco, and that world flag color is solid black. You may notice we have no official uniform, but all our clothing and tattoos represent this color."

"It's your battle standard and how you display the planet you represent. The three pirate worlds are known to all in the Free Worlds, and the only reason they've never organized an attack was because of their paranoia with each other. The Free Worlds are too busy trying to kill each other to worry about Draco, Martoosh, or Leo. Besides, Titans' Belt acts as an effective barrier, and as long as the pirate worlds don't disturb trade from the belt, the Capitol Forum couldn't care less."

She nodded, and said, "Yes. The three pirate worlds have a structure with rules and laws. We don't get along with each other and fly different flag colors. Martoosh are Pirates of the Brown, and Leo are Pirates of the Burgundy. We never work together, and besides attacking ships like yours, we fight each other constantly."

Listening to her about this topic was interesting. No Free Worlds student ever learned anything about that, especially not me in the military academy, secondary school on the relations station, or primary school on Epsilon Prime. Things that happened on rogue worlds rarely made it to the ears of Free Worlds citizens. What happened across all occupied space, I wondered? Almost all planets with humanity were technologically inferior to the Free Worlds, but people were still people. How many of those worlds were harvested by Force Command Burning Star to become slaves of the Offensive?

The metal door of our cell slid into the ceiling and a pressure-release hiss echoed through the room. Three sentinels in battle armor waddled inside. The one in the middle had a lieutenant bar at the center of his chest.

He spoke in a rasping gruff voice. "Slaves of the Offensive, hear me. We will be exiting faster-than-light travel within the hour and landing on your new home. I'm here to give you a quick rundown of expectations when we are planetside."

The lieutenant walked through the cell from one wall to the other and turned away, holding his nose. We did smell awful.

"We'll select a few of you to work directly for commanding officers. You will maintain their barracks rooms, preparing food, cleaning latrines, and removing the trash. The rest of you are going to a work camp to join slaves already there. They'll show you how we mine our raw materials and ensure you follow the proper protocols in place."

An older refugee raised a shaking hand but didn't speak. The lieutenant looked down with a hard face and walked to him. The man cowered into a ball. He had cause for concern.

The officer sentinel stared at him for a moment and said, "Speak."

The man lifted his head, shaking, and replied, "Are we working in the mines subject to your planet's gravity pressure, sir?"

Most of us understood his fear. The refugee looked like he hardly had the strength to lift a mining pick, let alone swing it in Kora, the homeworld of the Offensive's gravity.

The lieutenant and the other two sentinels laughed mockingly, and said, "No, weakling. You wouldn't survive twenty minutes on Kora. Only generational slaves live and work on our homeworld, those who have the strength to survive with our gravity pressure and who give humanity the name it deserves. You're the bottom of the barrel when it comes to people. It would be dishonorable to allow you anywhere near the memory stone."

He backhand slapped the refugee who asked the question and spoke louder. "That's your first real lesson as a slave of the Offensive. You do not ask questions—you perform, work, and obey. If you do your job, we will ensure you are fed well, have warm clothes, and a comfortable bed to sleep on at night. We give you this promise. Provide for the Offensive, and we will provide for you."

The lieutenant waddled over to the old woman who gave me back my picture and glared at her. She must have been ten years older than the man he just struck over the face, who was bleeding from his nose, and he had to be in his late sixties.

"We are going to the rogue world Pomona, and everyone will do well to remember that name because you will all die there." The Dolrinion officer looked back at the woman. "Some will be too old when we get there. That is a shame for you."

He waddled out of our room into a common area and other cells across the hall. The other two sentinel soldiers followed him out.

One turned to us and said, "When this door opens, you're all to line up and file out one at a time. When you clear this doorway, you will feel the gravity of Kora inside our ship. That will subside once on Pomona. We'll direct you where to go from there."

The sentinel left and the cell door closed behind him. Conversations erupted in our cell.

Nina looked at me and said, "You should come over with me and speak to the captain. I'm not asking you to like the man, but you have something the rest of these people don't."

She stood and took a step towards the other side of the cell where Gideon and Jack were. Nina turned back to me. "Besides, two eyes are better than one. He's missing the left and you the right. Together you have a pair." She smiled and continued on her way.

I looked at Gideon and thought about some of the things he did to me on that ship—and that my kids might be dead because of these pirates. *No, they're not dead.* I refused to believe that. I had to deal with the current situation. If we were placed into a camp with other slaves, surviving by myself with one eye would be impossible. I stood and slowly walked over to Nina, who was now leaning against the wall next to Gideon and Jack.

Gideon was talking with his small group. "I know this world they're bringing us to—it's a dual sun system near the exclusion zone several light-years away from the DMZ."

The young male refugee who was with this group during the Androsian attack asked, "What's an exclusion zone?"

Gideon smiled and spoke sarcastically. "History lesson time for little Ethan here. The exclusion—"

I talked over him. "The exclusion zone spreads out fifty light-years across and connects to Dolrinion space. There's a similar-sized exclusion zone on the Federate side of the demilitarized zone as well, and per article three of the Free Worlds' Relations Policy, neither side can establish any foothold in that area. All the rogue worlds there were abandoned or killed off by both sides."

Everyone stared at me with wide eyes. That was the first time I'd expressed myself with more than an angry look since we got here. I probably knew more about the Free Worlds than any of them.

Gideon wore an incredulous arrogant grin, and said, "Aren't you just a bundle of knowledge?"

I tapped my nose and glared at him.

My words seemed to amuse him. Gideon smiled broadly. "Yes, my broken nose is healing nicely from your hard head. Remind me to never get that close to you again."

Under both his eyelids, even the mechanical eye, there were dark black bruises that had only just started to heal. His swelling had gone down much since the first few days here, and it hadn't stopped him from being … well, being him.

Nina asked, "What's our plan on Pomona?"

Gideon glanced around the cell and answered, "We're going to be good little slaves to start and do what they tell us while we pay attention to everything around the camp. Jack and I have spent some time in Free World and rogue world prisons. We will do what we must to blend in, and, more importantly, find more Pirates of the Black."

Jack, in his slow speech, said, "A good number of our shipmates won't stick by us once we get planetside. A few loyal ones will, but some of them are already drifting away."

Captain Gideon waved his hand. "As long as they still have those tattoos of the black, they aren't going to drift anywhere but where I tell them. They know the price for the marks, and if they want out, I'll take what's mine by right. Draco has rules, and all from our ship are bound to them."

Ethan spoke excitedly. "I want a place on your crew. On Epsilon Prime, I was alone. I knew what awaited me on the relations station—nothing but a life of poverty with no family. What you see is all I have. My hands are yours, Captain."

Gideon smirked at him and patted his back. "You'll have to prove yourself in time, but for now, you can stay with us. Besides, Jack's taking a liking to you."

Youthful eager ignorance. My excitement and motivation when I first joined the Athinia Guard at seventeen years old was the same. Ethan couldn't be older than nineteen from his look, and he had the same level of obliviousness as I once did.

Gideon turned to me and asked, "And what is your plan, Isabel Sideris? You still blame me for everything that happened. Will you keep holding on to that anger or work past it to achieve a similar goal?"

What I would've liked to do was beat him over the head with the metal prybar from the refugee ship. What happened to that pirate when the terminal docking doors opened? I never saw his face. *Did the Androsians take him?* More unproductive questions.

I said, "There's no plan yet, and when I decide, I'll make sure you're not the first person told."

I walked away, remembering Gideon smelling my face, choking me, and treating me like property. He also saved my life from the stalker girl with the scorpion body. I turned back at the captain's frustrating grin. He annoyed me.

I sat back down on my sleeping cot and turned so my missing eye faced Gideon. My blindside covered half of the cell, and it made me feel better to keep his bothersome face out of my vision for a while.

The refugees and pirates around me looked scared. The most capable people in that cell were Gideon, Jack, Nina, and me. That wasn't a good sign because bringing myself to work with Gideon was beyond my abilities at that point. Nina had been enjoyable company for the past two weeks, and some kind of human interaction was necessary to survive. Maybe staying close to his group but not joining up with them would be a better alternative.

*

An alarm was going off, and the ship shook violently. We were entering the atmosphere of a planet. I moved quickly, placing my back against the wall and straightening my legs on the ground. Gideon and his group had done the same. They knew what was about to happen too. Others didn't. A few even stood, including one of the pirate crew. Dolrinions never entered a planet's atmosphere casually. Combat hard drops were ferocious and unsafe, but it was the quickest way to land, especially if a ship was under attack.

It was hard to hear my voice over the alarm, but I screamed, "Sit down, fools, this is a hard drop through the upper atmosphere—sit before we cross the threshold."

Only the people closest to me could hear what I said, and they all copied what they saw me doing with my body and breathing. The ship jerked forcefully up and down, and the two standing fell to the floor, crying in pain. They had each broken both their legs—bone was pushing through their pants. I could see them screaming, but the alarm was louder.

My body was being subjected to tremendous pressure, and the only thing helping me was my previous training—breathing in and out to the best of my ability and tightening every muscle in my body. *The hard drop should only last a minute or two.*

The alarms stopped and the shaking slowed; we were in the rogue world's atmosphere. I've never been anywhere near this planet before. The damage caused in that drop was clear to see even with one eye. Besides the two who broke their legs, everyone else seemed ok, but I wasn't sure. Their shouts made it hard to concentrate.

Several more minutes passed, and finally, the cell door opened. At first, no one moved, but Captain Gideon yelled, "You heard those widgets before— stand and line up before they come in here and start cracking our skulls."

Everyone stood up together, cautiously. People got in line near the entrance, but on the ground, the older woman who gave me back my picture lay there lifeless. I walked over to her and checked her pulse. She was dead. A combat hard drop wasn't for the weak of body. Her death made me sad because she was a good person who didn't deserve that fate.

I stood and got into the line, gazing at the two screaming on the floor with their broken bones. Gideon took a position behind me.

He said, "Say goodbye to these two. They're dead for sure."

I was annoyed. "No sympathy? One of them is yours, I believe."

Gideon brought on that same damn smile as always and said, "Sympathy does them no good. Their life is still over because of their stupidity."

"Will the sentinels just come in here and shoot them?"

He laughed to himself and pointed. "No, do you see that circular outline on the back wall over there? That's an airlock. The Dolrinions will leave whoever is here alone. When they go back out into space, the airlock door will open." He made a whistling noise, wiggling his fingers like they were flying away. "They'll drift into the great black of space."

I narrowed my eyes and said, "At some point on this planet, I'm going to take one of those mechanical fingers and shove it up your ass."

"Promises, promises."

We all marched out in single file into the larger common area. It had the typical bleak appearance of a military combat vessel with metal walls, metal floors, and dim lighting. People from all walks of life came out of the other cells. Many of them were rogue-world natives. Some might be Federate Corporation employees, which would be illegal because they were Free Worlds citizens. Who was going to argue that point here? The three-times-pressure gravity of Kora weighed down on us all. Some of the weaker prisoners were having trouble walking, hunching their backs as if they were carrying a heavy bag.

Groups of sentinels stood in the area with their helmet covers down and battle rifles in hand. All the people coming out of the cells were much taller than the sentinels—except for the children; it disgusted me to see the children.

Loud screams emitted from inside most of the open cell doors. As the marching line passed by more cells, we saw other severely injured people inside. They were too ignorant to have known what to do during a hard drop. On the back wall of all those cells was the circular outline of the airlock opening. All injured captives would be ejected into space when the cruiser left.

Behind me in order were Gideon, Nina, Ethan, and Big Jack. Before long, we arrived in the dock of the ship, and behind an elevated platform, Major Rancour and Colonel Bowick pridefully looked down from the balcony as they observed their newest slave harvest.

Gideon spoke quickly. "Listen to me carefully, Isabel. When we get outside down the ramp, they're going to start yelling at us and make everyone run—to try and cause panic. The sentinels want to weed out the people with poor health and those who can't hack it. It will be chaos, people running in different directions. You'll see several chain-linked fences that push us all into a funnel. Near the end of the funnel are openings that lead into separate paths divided by fences. Stay with us when we get to that point. Slaves are divided randomly by the opening in the fence. Each opening is a different work camp. I told all of my crew to go to the opening at the far right."

Somehow Captain Gideon was knowledgeable about the inner workings of Dolrinion slave worlds. We cleared the airlock opening and moved down the ramp; the gravity pressure subsided. I hadn't responded to Gideon yet.

The captain shouted at me, "Damn it, Isabel, don't be so stubborn and answer me!"

It sounded just like how Tuddy, my father, mother, and commanding officers in the guard used to speak to me when I was angry or ignoring them. I had the same strong-willed personality as Mom.

The sentinels shouted and our speed increased. They fired their rifles into the air and threw nonlethal riot control spark grenades.

I answered rapidly, "I hear you, Gideon."

People trampled each other in confusion. Some cried, screamed, pushed, and lost their minds. Panic had set in. The ground was sandy, and people's faces got pushed beneath it.

I lost the captain and his small group. Someone pushed me to the ground as they ran past and feet stepped on me as I attempted to stand. It was difficult to breathe, and I had sand in my face.

My heart was racing as someone abruptly pulled me to my feet. It was Big Jack. His strength was unmatched by anyone there since he stood over two meters high. People bumped into Jack and stopped dead in their tracks because running into him was the same as smashing into a concrete wall.

"Thank you."

He casually nodded as if he was somewhere else and not involved in any of this anarchy.

The fence openings were in front of us, and slaves had been smashing into the sizeable thick metal posts while trying to go through one of the entrances. My body slammed hard into a group of people at the far-right opening. There was a significant buildup there of people trying to go one way or the other.

Everyone stuck in that pileup was screaming, scratching, swinging hands, or biting at random others. Jack barreled through them all into the opening. I was unable to move until Big Jack made a gap through the people. I used all my strength to push past two people stuck near the post while trying to squeeze into the clearing, but it wasn't working. Someone pulled on me from behind.

A large, panicked man, trying to pull himself into one of the open fence clearings, was holding on to me.

I yelled, "Let go."

He couldn't hear me through his uncontrolled screams. I kneed him between his legs, and when he bent forward, I punched my palm into his nose at an upward angle.

Blood seeped from his mouth and nose, and his eyes rolled back into his head as he fell to the sand. Gideon was in the entrance to the far-right fence holding on and he reached out to me.

"Isabel, grab my hand."

I lunged forward with all my strength and grabbed him. Captain Gideon pulled me into the entrance with him, Jack, Ethan, and Nina.

We were ushered through the fence and made it out to a clearing; everyone who came through our opening stood there breathing heavily. Sentinels lined the perimeter and watched us. We all tried to catch our breath after the ordeal, and behind us we could still hear the chaos, screams, gunfire, explosions, and deaths of those who hadn't made it through a fence opening yet. Those poor children from the ship were enduring that torment too.

It was clear that Gideon's message had been well received. There were at least twenty from our cell on the Dolrinion cruiser standing there. Strength in numbers.

A sentinel captain walked over to inspect us. He seemed agitated by our presence judging by his grunts and frown. "There's too many in this group. I count fifty-four. Camp Folth wanted less than fifty to fill their losses."

The captain took a few more steps left and right and then came to Gideon and me.

He looked up at us and said, "These five here, send them to Camp Uolmar. They can always use a few more over there."

Several sentinels grabbed us: Gideon, Jack, Ethan, Nina, and me. They took us through a gate and made us get into the back of a truck. Ethan tried to resist only to receive a well-placed rifle butt in his face.

All that effort to stick together with the larger group was for nothing. That large man I hit with my palm near the gate entrance might be dead for all I knew, and it didn't even matter.

Ethan gazed with wide wandering eyes and said, "What do we do now, Captain?"

Gideon appeared frustrated. He spat then wiped his mouth with the back of his hand. "What do we do now? Now we survive ..."

CHAPTER 15

A Dolrinion Sentinel of the Offensive

The Hero of Gliese (Askar)

Another proximity alarm went off in no-man's-land. It wasn't the inferior natives of Gliese this time. They continued to resist us and deserved credit for that feat, although maybe their energy was in the wrong place. They couldn't hope to win now. Red Legion's initial invasion was only two months ago, and it was horrific. They killed countless natives, and even now, locals died at a rate of five to one.

Native special service soldiers, known as the Frogmen of Gliese, have changed their tactics. They rig explosive devices in random locations within our control and have killed sentinels each day. We've occupied and conquered various rogue worlds over the last eighteen hundred years, but Gliese was the first to utilize such duplicitous tactics.

Brothers of war told us that one of the locals working for Brim Fire committed suicide in the same manner that sentinels from Force Command War Dogs did when defeat was inevitable—by detonating a charge on his body. The native stood before a table of officers, stared at them with pride, and said, "For the people of Gliese, this is our revenge."

Dishonorable treachery, but we Dolrinions should also be ashamed of some of our actions on this world. Force Command Red Legion took the new style of resisting our Offensive's occupation personally. The Legion decimated entire neighborhoods and towns for no reason. Innocent civilian populations across our occupied zones were tortured and killed for sentinel deaths hundreds of miles away. The Legion was earning its nickname of Red Death—for every one sentinel killed they slaughtered men, women, and children from Gliese without pause.

The proximity alarm came from no-man's-land, so it wasn't the Frogmen attacking again. Small skirmishes with the Corporation across the front had tested our defenses over the last few weeks. The Frogmen attacked from the marshes and the Federates from the battlefront. It made sentinels wonder if they were working together.

Another proximity alarm activated further down our wall, facing out to no-man's-land. Trouble was on its way; I needed to get into position and send an alert through the LENS to my squad cluster of little pebbles.

I ran to the front line where Force Command First Ones had built a three-foot concrete and steel pillared wall that spanned the entire planet. My pebble squad called it the victory wall, stating our eventual triumph was on the other side into enemy territory. Our automated defense turrets—bumbles—were spaced every forty-five meters or so.

The bumbles' motion-sensitive trackers fired medium-range explosive rounds now from two different locations. The turrets shook awkwardly, like stumbling drunks swaying from side to side. My LENS wasn't alerting me to any incoming fire or movement tracking, which was strange. More alarms went off, and my Force Command BlackRock brothers and sisters came out of entrenchments, barracks, and command buildings. They were just as confused as me.

I looked over the victory wall and saw explosions from our bumbles. My chest rumbled in the immense pressure and percussion even through my battle armor. There was a heavy smell of gunpowder and metal in the air, but no enemy in the scorched lands. My pebble squad joined me, and Corporal Soli spoke.

"Master Gunnery Sergeant Askar, my LENS isn't tracking any movement. What's going on, sir?"

The corporal was younger than me by forty years, at least.

We watched the explosive round detonations getting nearer, and the turrets kept firing, turning closer to each other. I'd been a sentinel of Force Command BlackRock for forty-six years and never seen deception like that. I glanced at the young warrior faces around me. *I'm nearly triple their age. Why am I still here?*

"The rounds are striking the ground and moving closer to the wall, but nothing is visible at that location. Be ready for anything. The Corporation has no honor."

Hundreds of sentinels came up from the rear, including our camp commander Colonel Zilath, running for the wall. The colonel was a legendary warrior who had seen more years and battles than most. They called him the Gray Boulder for his age and steadfast determination. He was older than me by fifteen years. The colonel's confirmed kill count was so high that both sides of his chest plate were full to the maximum capacity with etched emblems.

Our bumbles kept firing at the ground, striking several rounds per second with dirt and ash scattering all over no-man's-land. The area between both front lines was nothing but mud and death. Everything was scorched, the trees, structures, and grass all gone, soot and ash replacing what once was. It was like there was an invisible target there moving closer to us.

The bumble weapons fire hit the victory wall; steel pillars and concrete dispersed like dead leaves in the wind. Both turrets continued to fire, and I realized what was happening.

I said, "Rock sentinels, hard armor at that location under the ground. Move to the trenches now."

The pebble sentinels all stared at me in confusion but followed my order and moved to the nearest trench. None of these pebbles would question a master gunnery sergeant.

What I thought went through my LENS to our control building and then to the other sentinels in the camp, including our Gray Boulder commander.

Hundreds of rock sentinels moved to defensive positions, but it was too late.

Dirt and stone erupted through the ground where our bumble turret rounds still fell with little success. The long mechanical arm extended out nearly four and a half meters. The end of the metal arm had three high-caliber uranium spinners, and they opened up a few seconds apart, firing hundreds of rounds in short bursts. Both bumbles burst into flames, and secondary detonations went off caused by the explosive rounds inside our defensive weapons. What was this new terror attached to below the dirt?

The spinners turned and shot bursts at our camp buildings, killing sentinels inside and in the immediate area. Caretakers of the memory stone would be busy after this battle, etching new names of our fallen.

I shouted, "Bring down that death arm, give it everything you have, sentinels."

The young warriors yelled with approval and engaged. Sentinels around camp did the same with zero results.

"Sentinel Soli, Corporal."

He couldn't hear me over the loud noise of battle, even though I spoke through the LENS. I banged on his helmet cover, and he turned back to me.

"Use your rail tube. We'll cover you."

Corporal Soli nodded and left the trench to take a position behind some metal transport boxes to our right. That wasn't a good position to fight from but would serve for him to fire his tube.

I looked over our hardpoint position. The spinners were turned to another trench position.

"Now, sentinel, shoot now!"

The corporal came out from behind the metal boxes, took a knee, and fired. The round struck perfectly, hitting the three uranium spinners, but instantly, the spinners turned to the corporal and fired their uranium rounds. Soli's armor was no match. His body blew apart into shards as if he were a log of wood going through a woodchipper. In one continuous motion, the spinners turned in our direction and fired.

"Cover."

My pebbles ducked low in our trench as heavy penetrator rounds ripped through the ground. The zipping sounds of weapons fire were loud, and I could feel the warmth of heated uranium streaking overhead. The eyes of all my squad were wide, and they were scared, not a good look for BlackRock sentinels.

"Sentinels, that was a good death for the corporal. He has earned a place on the memory stone, as will you all. Show the Corporation no fear. We're rock strong and will win this day."

Another rail round hit the three spinners. One of the platforms slowed and stopped firing. Sparks and smoke radiated from the weapon. There were only two spinners left engaging other squads. It was time to make a move.

"Sentinels, when I give the order, all of you engage that arm, suppression fire with your rifles, grenade launchers, and shoulder rockets—empty everything you have at that monstrosity." There was authority in my tone as I raised my head high.

They spoke at the same time, "Yes, sir."

I turned to the pebbles. "Duty, valor and glory to the Offensive!"

All called out, "Duty, valor and glory." That was how a squad should sound during combat, and I was proud of them.

The smoke was thicker on the spinners, and flames waved from the top of the weapon. Through camp, sentinel bodies lay in the mud, their black armor matching the dirt. It was time to move. I jumped from the trench and ran as fast as my old legs would take me to the destroyed metal boxes. What remained of Corporal Soli squished beneath my feet. I picked up his rail tube and aimed at the devil arm.

"Rock Sentinels, give it hell!"

It was a marvelous sight—dozens of rockets, grenades, and bullets streaking through the air to the death arm. My sentinels looked like veterans with their performance. I aimed and fired the rail tube. The bright streak of light hit the dead center of the spinners. Only one of the weapons still fired— the other two had stopped spinning—and it was still engaging my squad. Another sentinel was down. I fired again, and this time a massive explosion overwhelmed the uranium spinners attached to the long metal arm.

Cheering broke out across camp and sentinels threw their arms into the air. I lifted my face cover and took a deep breath of the combat air. Sulfur, gunpowder, and rotten eggs were the aromas that filled my nostrils. Including Soli, we lost three sentinels from my squad. Only six remained in my rock cluster. I walked to the pebbles and observed them for a moment. They had post-battle long faces, but they held their heads up high.

"Report," I said.

A sentinel stepped forward. "Bruises and scratches, nothing more. We're in working order and ready to fight, sir."

Her name was Uva, and she didn't realize it yet, but her stepping up to answer me got her promoted.

"Sentinel Uva, battlefield promotion. You're now Corporal Uva and our cluster's second in command. I'll notify my superior at the earliest convenience."

She lifted her helmet cover and her eyes opened wide in a hard, strong face. Corporal Uva would make an excellent officer one day.

She said, "I'll not let you or the Offensive down, sir."

"There's no doubt of that, sentinel."

The ground beneath our feet shook like an earthquake accompanied by a strange sound of grinding. I nearly lost my balance. Dirt pushed up from the earth into the air where the death arm had collapsed. A huge metal body appeared through the soil and rock. It was massive. That's what the spinners were connected to.

I had never seen a weapons platform like that before—a humongous cylinder machine with track wheels on both sides, and at the front was a powerful laser drill. Additional death arms with more uranium spinners at each end sprang up from the round body. We'd had trouble with one arm and couldn't take that machine alone.

Both sides of the main body displayed the Federate Corporation's emblem reflecting off the myriad fires through camp. I hated the shapes and designs of that flag.

"Take cover," I said.

We had no choice but to hide under our trench as thousands of rounds poured out from the multiple death arms in all directions and bullets nearly struck us before we could duck down.

The streams of hot lead subsided and I lifted my head above the trench; the strange-looking machine rolled through camp in the direction of our command building. Perfect timing—an alert blasted through my LENS, and the Corporation emblem reflecting off the metal armor exploded. Its thick metal peeled back in shredded layers. Multiple armor penetrators blasted into that machine of death.

Behind us, rumble tanks steamed forward. They were thick battle tanks with a low profile and five massive tank barrels on both sides stretching out meters. It fired in succession from ten barrels.

Four tanks rumbled to the Federate target, decimating the machine. The tanks roared as they passed our position and the ground shook, and they left deep imprints in the mud under their massive weight.

Sentinels cheered and threw their hands into the air, but it was short-lived. Behind us at the victory wall, numerous towering Federate battle bots climbed over and opened fire. Our bumbles would have held these bots back if not for the death arms removing our defenses.

Two of the six bots had substantial damage from crossing no-man's-land. Our minefield covered every square centimeter on our side of the crossing. Bot carcasses that had encountered our defenses littered the field across the entire planet.

Colonel Zilath showed his valor and the reason he was our commander. He ripped off his helmet and threw the heavy metal down before screaming with such ferocity that hundreds of sentinels could hear his cries of war.

"Rock Sentinels, this will be our finest day since coming to occupy this world. Duty, valor, and glory to the Offensive. Fight with me!"

Hundreds of sentinels screamed, "Duty, valor and glory!"

The colonel pulled his renowned Corin-steel short axe, responsible for at least half his confirmed kills, and held it high in the air as he charged headlong at the battle bots.

Every sentinel through camp had regained their strength through his bravery and their cries of battle echoed in the landscape. We followed our commander storming towards the towering bots, to victory or death, it made no difference. The rumblers engaged too, firing round after round. This was the greatest combat I had seen in ten years—our Force Command wasn't on Gliese during the initial invasion.

"Earn your place on the memory stone, sentinels. Victory for the Offensive."

My pebbles charged with me and shouted once again, "Duty, valor and glory!"

I grabbed a sack of explosive charges from the trench and the rail tube before moving on with my squad. Streams of smoke from thousands of shoulder rockets blanketed the sky as they moved like a flock of birds straight for the bots. Bright beams of rail tubes fired from other positions in camp, and the giant bots attacked with the variety of weapons platforms scattered on their upper bodies.

Two rumble tanks were already in flames with black smoke rolling and tumbling into the sky, but they took down three battle bots before meeting their end. Another heavily damaged bot stomped down, squashing sentinels as it moved quickly through camp, and it was running right for Colonel Zilath. I closed in on the colonel to assist him as he threw his Corin-steel axe at the bot. It embedded itself several centimeters into the armor cover plating, but the bot continued straight for us.

Colonel Zilath's shoulder rocket fired, and he shot his battle rifle. The bot would step on the colonel, and I couldn't allow that to happen. A steel pillar that had been part of the victory wall before its destruction was on the ground.

I picked up the steel beam, my battle armor grinding from the tremendous weight, and ran next to the colonel, who was still screaming, staring his enemy down without fear. The bot's size blocked the sun as we stood in its shadow; the machine lifted its leg and stepped down to us. The commander helped me put the pillar into place and the heavy leg crashed down onto the steel. The whine of mechanical components not getting their way reverberated from the joints of the bot. The victory wall steel was too durable to overcome.

I pulled the rail tube and said, "Clear from behind."

The colonel looked back and tapped my helmet. "Clear."

The last rail round ripped through the straight leg, removing it from the battle bot's body, and it lost its balance and fell straight back to the mudded dirt like a tree falling. I ran up the chest plate, holding an explosive charge in my hand.

Colonel Zilath's Corin-steel axe was in front of me, buried deep. With a swift tug of the handle, a large gaping laceration became visible. Glittering lights and wires pulsed from inside. I pushed an explosive charge into the gap and pressed the timer button.

I leaped from the bot. "Take cover."

A massive detonation with fire and ash scattering in all directions destroyed the battle bot. Sharp shards of metal pierced my back, and one large piece penetrated my armor, pushing out of the left pauldron shoulder guard. My pebble squad engaged the other heavily damaged bot. It was missing one of its connector arms and dark plumes of smoke glided upward from the machine.

The newly promoted Corporal Uva was in command of my squad cluster engaging the bot; it took notice of them and shot medium-range automatic rounds at them. Three more pebbles died, and Corporal Uva became its next target. The bot fired a rocket round directly at her, and a smoke trail followed behind as the rocket whistled. Her battle armor showed lacerations from the explosion, peeling the armor back, exposing the wires and techno gear beneath.

I ran to my cluster as Corporal Uva stood, ripping her damaged helmet off. Blood leaked from her mouth, and areas of her armor appeared to have been fused to her body by the heated blast. I called her name and tossed one of the explosive charges from the sack. She caught it and gave me a stone-hard glare.

Corporal Uva closed her eyes and took a breath of the battle-scented air before turning with a frown to the bot closing in. She screamed, "I go to the memory stone with pride!"

Uva leaped into the air right at the bot as she hit the detonator on the explosive charge.

A fire burst detonated and massive secondary explosions pushed me off my feet. It took a few moments to recover, and Colonel Zilith helped me stand. The battle was over. We were victorious.

The colonel said, "A glorious death. She earned her place and will live forever on the memory stone."

I agreed with the Gray Boulder, though thoughts of these young pebble deaths under my command over the years burned in my head. So many young faces all perished in service of the Offensive to live forever in the stone halls of eternity.

Sentinels in camp started the post-battle recovery process. I looked for my squad cluster and realized that they all died. I was alone again, and emotion hit me like a ton of bricks. For the second time since arriving on Gliese after the invasion, my cluster squad all perished in defense of the victory wall. I felt cursed.

Colonel Zilath pointed to my shoulder and said, "You should have the medics look at that, sentinel."

A sharp piece of metal wet with blood stuck out several centimeters from my left shoulder, the liquid seeping down my armor.

"Only a flesh wound, sir."

The colonel smiled and laughed. "You're rock hard, sentinel, a true warrior who gives our Force Command pride."

He saw that I was holding his Corin-steel axe.

I handed it over and said, "This belongs to you, sir."

The Gray Boulder glanced at the axe and then to me. "Thank you, sentinel." He turned to face the rows of sentinels standing nearby and yelled, "Force Command BlackRock, fall in and listen to your commander."

When more sentinels had crowded around us, the colonel continued. "This master gunnery sergeant earned his elevated promotion because of his many years of tremendous service. He's shown us what it means to be solid as a rock. From this day forward, Askar will be known as the Hero of Gliese for his actions since arriving on this world."

The sentinels all cheered, and Colonel Zilath leaned in, his voice a whisper. "I've watched you closely, sentinel, and I know you lost your last cluster too. Keep your focus. I have plans for you in the coming weeks. The Offensive needs hardened veteran sentinels who know their place and how to perform."

I closed my visor to hide the water swelling in my eyes at the cheering and the colonel's words. I didn't deserve any of that; those young pebbles should still be here, and an old sentinel like myself should be long dead and gone. Why was the memory stone still denying me after all these faithful years of service? Every sentinel who completed the Rite of Passage with me forty-six years ago was long dead. My end should've come one hundred times over, and it saddened me to think about the longing I had to go to my resting place in the stone halls.

I took a deep breath and said to the colonel, "I am yours to command, sir."

CHAPTER 16

Civil Earth Day

This year was very different (Daniel)

The workday was over, and my body felt like it ran a marathon. Next week my stitches would come out, but there was still tenderness when I moved in certain ways. Chrissy was back to her usual self, giving me a hard time at work again. She was meaner than expected, and I wondered if it was because she had been nice to me in the hospital. When I opened my eyes in that room and saw her sitting next to me, it was a shock. My face must have given that away. She told me that she put in the disability paperwork for my injury, which wasn't guaranteed to be approved, but her Tier Three boss somehow agreed to allow me to take time off. We were lucky that the boss accepted the request because Lilly, Amber, Kathryn, and my mom would have been affected if I didn't get paid for last week.

Tomorrow was Civil Earth Day, and this year, we decided not to host a party because of Dad's passing. Lilly and Amber agreed that it would be better if we skipped the holiday. Amber and I still saved our money throughout the year, and because of my cautious nature, we would be celebrating tonight instead of the real holiday tomorrow.

Who knew if those Caste Freedom Fighters would try to do something in our building during the events? I'd rather us play it safe and hunker down in the apartment with our steel crossbar secured on the front door.

Since we decided to use the credits saved this past year, Amber and I would go to dinner at a third-floor restaurant. We hadn't eaten real food in so long it'd be great to taste something fresh. Even after paying for our expensive dinner, there would be some extra credits left over, so we planned to surprise Lilly and Kathryn so they could go out and have fun too. They were kids and should get out and enjoy the night, especially Kathryn. That teenager was the most capable person I knew, but she had also been through so much hardship already in the short years of her life. Maybe even more than Tobias.

I made it back home and inserted the key into our apartment door. Lilly hadn't locked the crossbar, and that annoyed me. Opening the door and walking inside, I saw Lilly sitting on the couch with a smile on her face.

"What are you so happy about?"

There wasn't a reason to get into an argument over the door. Tonight should be memorable for the girls.

Lilly said, "Kathryn and I went to the donation center today and spent most of the day there waiting to get her some new clothes. We found a few things, and I sewed the holes in a nice dress that she's trying on now. I think you'll be surprised."

The donation center clothes were much better than what she was wearing outside on the surface. Tobias said he would try and buy her some new things when he got a chance, but it'd be good for her to dress up when she went out with Lilly.

"That's great news. How's Mom today?"

Lilly turned away from me. "Mom's been sleeping all day. She's getting worse. She can't eat solid food anymore and only drinks smoothies from the dispenser."

"Mom's lived with this disease for five years. The progression is different for everyone, and she might be entering the next stage," I said. "I'll check on her and see if she needs anything."

The bathroom door opened, and Kathryn came into the room wearing a sundress with straps exposing her shoulders. The dress had flowers on it in patterns, and she wore defender military jump boots. Kathryn's face was made up, Lilly's work without a doubt, along with straightening her hair. She looked beautiful; it shocked me because outside, she was a completely different person.

"Kathryn, you look wonderful. I almost didn't recognize you."

Kathryn frowned and glanced down at the dress. "Stop looking at me, dummy."

Lilly laughed. "Kathryn refused to take off those boots. She said she wants to be ready for a fight, and she can't do that wearing flip flops or heels."

Kathryn played with the dress and pulled faces that indicated she was uncertain about how she felt, almost uncomfortable in her own skin.

I said, "Being ready for anything is good. The Lower Forty might not be as bad as the surface, but people," I paused, "people are still people."

Kathryn grinned. "That's why I keep my knife tucked into these boots. It hides well."

She pulled a small handle out from her sock and pushed a button, whereupon a sharp spring-loaded blade extended out of the handle, clicking as it locked into place.

Lilly laughed. "Kathryn's my bodyguard from the college boys on the second floor."

Lilly and Kathryn got along well with each other. Their personalities drew them together quickly as if they'd been friends for years. It was a good thing. Amber came out of our bedroom wearing a dress, and she glowed in her beauty like she always did.

"How was your workday, love?"

"Coming home was the best part."

I hugged and kissed her gently on the lips. She wrapped her arms around me, and both Kathryn and Lilly made joking sounds like they were grossed out by our affection.

"So should we tell them?"

Lilly asked, "Tell us what?"

Amber said, "You might as well. Our reservation is in an hour, so we'll need to leave soon."

Lilly and Kathryn came closer to us. "You know that this year's different than last year. Amber and I have been saving our credits like we do every year for the CE Day party. We decided that you girls should have a good night tonight. We're giving you one hundred credits to go out and have some fun."

"Obsessions. Some of my friends planned on going there tonight and I told them we couldn't go because of the cost. Kathryn, we're going to dance and have some fun tonight. I'll make some calls—two of them are leaving next week to start their academy training with Civil Earth Defense." Lilly sounded excited. She grabbed the wall phone and ran into the bathroom to make her calls.

Kathryn shrugged. "What is an Obsessions?"

Amber said, "It's a club for teens and young adults down on level two. They have food, music, and dancing. You're still seventeen, so the bar won't serve you."

Feeling uneasy, I said, "Lilly's eighteen and can order drinks."

"Daniel, trust your sister. She's not going to do anything bad."

I nodded. "I'll go get changed, and we can leave in a few minutes." Turning to Kathryn, I asked, "Are you good?"

Kathryn narrowed her eyes. "Why wouldn't I be good?"

I chuckled. "Never mind."

In the bedroom, I changed into something more appropriate for a third-floor restaurant. I looked in the small mirror at my stitches, and a memory of something Tobias said in the hospital room came back.

"Daniel, her lungs are in bad shape, and without the medication, she'll be dead in the next ten years. There's something about her that seems familiar to me. Maybe it's just because we both lived on the surface, but I don't know. I feel a sense of responsibility for her now."

I said, "What can we do? I'll let her stay with us for a few weeks, but she can't live with me permanently. If the Civil Earth Administrative Authority catches her in our place without registration, we'll be in trouble. I can't afford to keep her in the apartment."

"One thing at a time, Danny boy. Give this to her. It's two weeks of medication."

Tobias handed me a bottle half full, his name written on the side.

"It's yours? What are you going to do without it?"

"Don't worry about me. Just try and keep Kathryn under control while you have her. I fear coming back down here to find out she killed people trying to talk to her. Also, scratch my name off the bottle label, so she doesn't know."

I simply said, "Me, control her? I'd have an easier time telling a Cloud Walker what to do."

The memory faded, and I got dressed.

The girls were in our living space, talking to each other on the couch.

I said, "Lilly, make sure you two eat before going out tonight. The food at that club is expensive compared to the dispenser."

"We'll eat before we go. Besides, Kathryn's a cheap date. All she wants to eat is breakfast whites."

Kathryn widened her eyes and grinned. "That food is delicious."

We were all surprised at that.

Amber said, "I've never met someone who likes breakfast whites before. That's a first."

"She likes when I heat the food for her," Lilly said.

Kathryn's grin widened. "That food tastes much better than eating sewer moles."

Amber and Lilly both made sounds of disgust.

Kathryn raised her chin; to me, she was acting as a seventeen-year-old girl should—showing off a little and bragging about her surface accomplishments. Typical for someone of her years, and it was good.

Looking in the kitchen, I said, "Lilly, please remember to turn off Dad's hot plate before you leave. We have to be careful, especially since Kathryn is staying with us."

Lilly rolled her eyes and folded her arms the same way as Kathryn. "I know, Oppa. Don't worry so much—go out and have fun with Amber tonight. You should get drunk and enjoy the night."

Amber raised an eyebrow. "A drink or two does sound nice. It would be great for someone to serve me and not be the one catering to everyone else."

Before leaving, I went into Mom's room to check on her. She was in bed under the blankets. She rolled over and looked at me.

"How are you feeling? Are the stitches still bothering you?"

That was Mom, dying of a horrible disease, and only wanted to know how I felt.

"There's still some tenderness, but everything's good, Mom. How are you?"

She winced in pain and opened her eyes. One was blinded, cloudy, and didn't move to focus the way her other eye did. She had lost so much weight the first year after her diagnosis, and now, in the next stage of that terrible disease, a strange sour odor excreted from her regularly.

"Everything's fine, my son. Don't trouble yourself with thoughts of me. Life's a full circle, and mine's almost complete." Mom had certainty in her voice.

I grabbed her hand and held it with care. She did her best living in the Lower Forty to take care of my sister and me. It was so emotionally painful to see her like this.

"Don't speak like that, Mom, you've got good years left. Dad would have wanted you to live on and be happy."

She started crying. "I want to be with your father. This world's too much for me now."

I wiped some of the tears from her face, and said, "We still need you, Mom, especially Lilly. Dad would want you to fight on and stay with us."

"Lilly doesn't need anyone. You know that. She's smarter than both of us, and you, you are just like your father. I have no worries about you after I'm gone. When Lilly leaves, you and Amber should have a child. Grow the Lu family name and live a long, happy life. You deserve it, my son ..." Her voice trailed off.

A child? Mom wanted us to replace her with a new life. She wouldn't survive long enough to see a grandchild, and that made me sad. I was unsure how to respond to her, so I said the only thing that came to mind.

"Can I get you anything before we leave?"

After a moment of pain, Mom said, "Just some tea, please."

I kissed her forehead. "I love you, Mom."

She smiled. "I love you too."

It only took me a few minutes to make the tea and bring it to her. After that, I went back into the living room where the ladies were still talking.

"Alright, girls, have a good night, and please don't get into trouble."

Lilly stood and said, "Wait, before you go. Let's take a picture."

She grabbed her camera and placed it on the table. Lilly took charge, telling us where to stand near the side of our couch in the living room. The order was Amber, me, Kathryn, and Lilly. The camera flashed.

"Ok, time to go. Have a good night out, girls. We'll see you later," Amber said.

Amber and I walked out of the apartment, and secured the door lock. Once inside an elevator from our transit hub, we were alone and went down to the third floor.

"What did your sister say about going to the Fleet Branch Academy?"

"She told me she would think about it and give me an answer after CE Day. Tobias already set everything up for her. All she has to do is walk into a recruiting station and say her name."

Amber seemed uneasy and gave a blank stare. "The thought of her in Civil Earth Defense scares me. It's a dangerous life. I hear the stories all the time from drunk defenders in the bar."

"Fleet Branch is much safer than the Defender Corps, and besides, there hasn't been a real war between Civil Earth and the other Free Worlds since before we were born. Things are peaceful right now aside from the fighting on that rogue world."

Amber pursed her lips. "Things are peaceful until they aren't."

We arrived at the third-floor transit hub, which was not half as congested as the second floor. The people were more professional and put together than the crowds of unemployed wandering on the second floor. The restaurants and other areas were visited by the higher class of Tier Four on the third floor. Even though we were in the lowest tier, some were more well off than others, as if there was a secondary caste system within the Lower Forty. Regardless, our floors didn't compare to the Middle Thirty, Upper Twenty-Three, or Living in the Clouds.

We made it to our restaurant, and the host greeted us at the door.

"Good evening. Did you make a reservation with us tonight?"

Amber said, "Reservations under the name Lu."

The host scrolled through her tablet. "Ah, yes, will you dine with our artificial or fresh menu tonight?"

"Fresh menu, please."

The host smiled and walked us to our table, where she handed over a tablet showing the menu and drink options. Most of the customers in the dining area were business professionals eating, socializing, and drinking. It was rare for me to be near people of that standing, given my profession.

Amber saw my uneasiness. "Are you ok?"

"Absolutely. People gazing, that's all."

A server came to the table and asked if we were ready to order. Amber was excited; she ordered a fresh salad with blue cheese and bacon bits. I ordered a grilled chicken sandwich with cheese and tomatoes. The server asked if we wanted an appetizer, but we turned that down because there were only enough credits left for dessert.

Amber also added two vodka and club soda drinks, and while enjoying our beverages, she spoke. "What's the plan for Kathryn? She can't stay with us much longer."

That question had bothered me for weeks. It was hard providing for Kathryn in our apartment. We barely had the finances to sustain four people, and now with her, the stress level was through the roof.

"Tobias and I are trying to figure out a plan. She'll only be with us for another week or so."

Amber stirred her drink. "It's hurting our pockets to have her in the apartment. Another week should be fine, but we can't afford to have her with us any longer after that."

"I know, but remember that I'd be dead right now if not for her. She saved my life, and we owe her." I was defensive.

"Unquestionably, we owe her. But at what cost? Our family can't suffer paying back that price. We don't make enough credits to support Kathryn."

I nodded, agreeing, but dropped the subject. We ordered another round of drinks, and after another few minutes, our meals arrived with a fantastic aroma. Real food always smelled amazing. We savored every moment, eating slowly. It would be at least a year before we ate something real again.

Civil Earth grew real food in the fertile regions unaffected by the yellow haze. Only the Cloud Walkers and the Upper Twenty-Three had access to local fresh foods. We finished our meals and another three drinks.

"I'm drunk," Amber slurred.

We laughed, and I said, "Me too."

Amber's eyes opened wide. "After dinner, let's go down to the second floor and walk the market. We don't get to enjoy a night out often, and I want to make the best of it."

The shopping market was full of street vendors and kiosks, with performers singing or doing some sideshow acts attempting to earn credits from spectators. Some were subpar, but others amazing to watch.

I smirked and said, "Sounds good, my love."

The waiter came back, and we ordered one slice of cheesecake. As the server was halfway back to the kitchen, Amber raised her voice. "Two shots of Red Mud whiskey, as well."

He gave us an odd look, probably because of our excitable behavior, but we couldn't care less. By the time we ate in that place again, he wouldn't be working there. Before long, our shots arrived with the cake.

Amber lifted her glass. "Here's to family. Happy years with happy tears."

I raised my glass, and because the drinks had made my head fuzzy, I said quickly, "My mom wants us to have a baby."

Amber leaned back, looking slightly shocked, and quickly tapped her glass to mine, taking the drink down in one big gulp. She said, "Maybe we should have a baby. After Kathryn leaves and Lilly is off to the academy. It's not a bad idea."

Her initial expression had made me think she didn't want a child. "Your look had me thinking differently."

She smiled and said, "It was just the blunt way you put it. That's not usually your way."

I agreed. "The alcohol's made me bold. Let's eat and go down to the second level."

We finished and paid two hundred and fifty credits for the meals, which made me gulp. That was a lot of credits. We left and headed down to the public market. In the elevator, we laughed and held each other close, kissing deeply. It felt so good. Before the elevator doors opened, I hit the emergency stop button, and the car shook from side to side as sounds of brake pads screeching against the metal echoed through the car.

Amber said, "Why did you do that?"

I looked down at my pants, which pushed several centimeters out. When Amber saw, she broke out into laughter. It took a few moments for the swelling to subside, and I hit the release button.

The second-floor hub was alive, with people moving one way or the other, dozens of conversations taking place, and random display screens showing Free Worlds news feeds overshadowing everything. We held hands and pushed past the heavy congestion. I noticed more defenders than usual in groups of five.

It took us almost fifteen minutes to get from the elevator to the market, where we spent two hours shopping. Amber bought a new shirt, and we purchased another drink from one of the bars in the area.

As the night wound down, our legs grew tired, and we moved back into the direction of the transit hub. We stopped for some time to watch an entertainer playing a guitar and singing. She was terrific, and her joyful voice carried across the open fountains and seating areas.

There was a commotion behind us of people shouting in unison. We turned to loud chanting and people holding their fists in the air. They had signs that read "Tier One" with the words crossed out.

Some screamed, "No more caste, it won't last."

Others yelled, "Tier Four, we deserve more."

The protesters weren't violent but were incredibly disruptive, which forced the performer to stop playing. At the other end of the open area, a large group of Civil Earth defenders pushed aggressively through the shopping crowds, not caring who they cleared from their path. The defenders had big sticks, half as long as arms.

I grabbed Amber's hand and guided her away from the rising panic.

"We need to get out of here."

We shoved past people and got to the sidewall away from the protesters and defenders who were on opposite sides of the fountain. Others who happened to be in the wrong place at the wrong time were also trying to push their way free of the area.

A defender spoke into a megaphone. "Disperse immediately."

There was a brief break in the tension, but the defenders smashed their bats against the skulls of protesters and pedestrians alike without waiting for any response. Blood sprayed from savage blows as bats cracked on heads. Two defenders with blue-barreled rifles jumped onto the stone wall of the fountain. They took their time aiming at protesters and shot. The guns made sounds similar to regular rifles, but they fired blue paintballs. People struck with the markers instantly had patches of skin and clothing change to blue. That paint would dye their skin, and they'd be unable to remove it for months. Defenders used those types of weapons to identify disruptive individuals that could later be placed under arrest when spotted with blue paint on their skin. It didn't matter who got away. Eventually, all would go to a holding cell. Innocent bystanders not involved got hit with the paintballs. We hugged the wall and crept around the protesters away from the chaos. Splat sounds hit the wall right above my head and trailed behind me. The protesters were no match for fully armored defenders. Defenders beat back a few of the activists and sprayed anyone nearby with crowd-control liquid. People screamed, and the strong odor made it hard to breathe.

Amber and I managed to escape from the market, pushing past others who froze or went in their own directions. We made it back to the transit hub.

"What were those people thinking to come into the market square like that?" Amber was struggling to talk and breathe at the same time.

I said, "It was foolish. People won't change anything causing disruptions like that. The upper floors don't care about protests down here. All that happens after these disturbances is that the Defender Corps tightens their grip."

Amber frowned. "Were they Caste Freedom Fighters?"

"No, the CFF is more calculating in their actions. They wouldn't cause a spectacle protesting in public, but rather antagonize others to do so. The freedom fighters act quietly without anyone noticing them, and they wouldn't think twice about setting off an explosion to kill the defenders with civilians nearby. If those activists had been acting under the influence of the freedom fighters, lots of people would be dead right now."

Amber rubbed at her lip with the back of her finger. "Things are getting crazy in this megacity."

Life in the Lower Forty of any megacity line was crazy. Usually, Amber had a more positive outlook on things. My cautious nature didn't allow me to think the way she did. If we kept to ourselves with our heads down, the world would hopefully leave us alone.

Because of the commotion, we decided to take a different way back to the transit hub, down a hallway leading around the other side of the hub that also passed Obsessions. Maybe we would spot Lilly and Kathryn to make sure they were ok.

It was too hard to see inside as we walked past the club. Big men with barrel chests stood guard while drunk teens stumbled near the entrance. None were Lilly or Kathryn. Amber and I moved on through the public hallway. At the next corner, defenders blocked off a dead-end portion of the hall that led to a garbage disposal unit. Caution tape was up, driving people away from the separated space.

Amber pointed past the garbage container where a young man was lying, apparently dead. "What's going on in this building tonight?"

"The actual holiday is tomorrow, and things will be worse. We need to get home."

We got back to the apartment. I turned the key and opened the latch lock and we both went inside like bulls in an antique store.

Amber laughed as she stumbled into our living room, kicking our side table.

She looked back at me and slurred. "Shush, be quiet!"

We both laughed again and I said, "You're the one making all the noise. Besides, the girls aren't here, remember?"

"Oh yeah, that's right." She stared at me through her lashes.

We got closer and kissed. I held Amber's lower back and carefully guided her into our bedroom. Inside our room, we undressed slowly. Amber pulled off my pants, and I removed her shirt. Our kisses were deep and zealous. I caressed her arms and lightly touched her body. I climbed into our tiny bed and put my back against the wall, leaning on my right side. Amber got in, still kissing me.

The walls were thin, and sound trekked with ease. We needed to keep our voices down. My stitches were painful, but the alcohol and the brain between my legs didn't care about the soreness.

After, Amber smiled and closed her eyes. We lay there for a few minutes recovering our breath, and finally, she rolled over.

"I'm going to set up an appointment to have my birth control removed because there was only one thought running through my head as you finished."

"What thought is that?"

She hesitated for a moment and her smile widened. "I want your baby inside of me …"

CHAPTER 17

The Meetings That Change Worlds

Behind closed doors (Henry)

Malcolm said, "I had the attorneys do what you asked, and it's all here, just requiring a signature."

I nodded, flipping through some of the pages with highlighted tabs that needed to be signed. Per Free Worlds' Relations Policy, any agreement ratified under the dome must be in written correspondence. Digital copies were kept on backup and not acceptable for official seal.

"Are you sure this is the best idea, sir?"

His concerns were understandable. This decision didn't come lightly. What choice did I have? *Sometimes, to get the results needed, unpleasant concessions must occur.*

I said, "I did want to keep this a little while longer but don't forget, I paid nothing for it and made millions of credits in profit for merely casting a yay vote. No, it's time. I must gain an advantage over JJ before things get worse."

Malcolm looked up at the ceiling and tapped his fingers on the armrest of the chair. "I hoped we would save this for something further down the line when you're up for reelection again."

Benjamin raised his voice. "Now's the right time with elections only a year out—there's no point in waiting. If we can't get Representative McWright's popularity up with the middle class and unions on Uropa, he could lose his seat."

Malcolm gave Ben a cold look, the same glance someone would give gnats continually buzzing around their head. He said, "His numbers weren't as low as we anticipated in the approval polling. Expectations were worse because of his bill and speech cancellation. While on the subject, where were you during that fiasco?"

Benjamin's face turned bright red. "I was doing exactly what Representative McWright wanted. We've already been over this. How many more times do you want me to repeat myself?"

"Your story remains the same, yet, when I look back at the cameras from that night, you went to the Civil Earth back offices to speak with Mia's chief almost thirty minutes late. Video evidence doesn't lie, boy."

Ben jumped from his chair with his fists clenched as if he was getting ready to fight. Malcolm did the same, although he had to look up at Ben.

"I hadn't eaten or used the bathroom in several hours—I spent my entire day working for our center seat. Sorry that I needed to do something normal people do. After going to the Civil Earth offices, they detained me," Benjamin insisted.

Malcolm stepped closer to Ben's face, having to raise his head even higher to look into his eyes. "If we find out otherwise, I promise you I will—"

My fist slammed into the desk with a noise like heavy pallets falling on concrete. It was excessive, but I needed to end this charade. Everyone in the room jumped.

I was furious. "Will you two stop! You're arguing like children competing for my favor. I'm not a parent picking between which child I like better. Both of you have skills I need equally. Now, this nonsense will stop immediately, or I'll take both of you to the nearest airlock and throw you out into space myself."

Malcolm and Benjamin seemed to shrink several centimeters, and my ears burned. Both men meekly sat back in their chairs.

After regaining control of myself, I realized that Stacy, plus another junior staff member, was in the office. They looked frightened. Malcolm had seen real rage behind the curtain, and this paled by comparison.

Benjamin said, "Sorry, Representative McWright. I shouldn't have spoken out of turn."

Malcolm added, "Sorry, sir. The stress of events lately has gotten to everyone. It won't happen again."

I sat back in my chair and ran my fingers through my hair before speaking. "I understand your feelings, gentlemen. This past month has been interesting, if not unprecedented. We've been through a multitude of hardships before, and this will not be our end. It is only the beginning."

Both men turned their heads, saying nothing but glaring in different directions. Malcolm and Ben hated each other so much, and it would need to be dealt with before long because it was hindering their productivity.

Benjamin got an alert on his PDD. "Sir, Representative Boran is ready for the minutes meeting."

I stood, clearing my throat as I picked up the prepared paperwork, and said, "Gentlemen. The wheels are already in motion. We either jump on the train or die as it rolls over us. Benjamin." He jumped from his chair. "You'll accompany me to both meetings today, and after, I want you to take my PDD and continue going about my public schedule. Go to each location listed and stay for the preset time."

"I won't let you down."

I smiled, placing one hand on his shoulder, and said, "I know you won't, lad." I turned to Malcolm. "You will pursue your investigation into what our right seat of the Accord has on Mia. There's a leash around her neck that's being held by JJ. In twelve years here under the dome, I've never seen Mia Stavish so weak."

Malcolm stood. "There's progress, and I will have answers soon."

"You have been with me for many years, Malcolm, and have yet to let me down."

We all walked to the door. Before stepping out, I turned to Stacy and the junior aide whose name I had all but forgotten, and said, "Please forgive us for our unprofessional conduct, Stacy. We shouldn't have acted that way."

Stacy smiled. "We're all here to serve you, Representative McWright. Whatever happens here, happens for a reason, and it doesn't matter as long as we meet your goals each month."

That was the exact answer expected from a junior aide. Stacy would have a place here for years to come. Benjamin was behind me with Oliver and my security team in tow as we walked through the door.

*

The Federate Corporation's back office was very different from the Colonial Accord's. Tasteless and dull, in my opinion. I walked to the giant statue carved from marble and polished to pristine brightness. The figure was Allison Westbay, the CFO of Tri-Co, who took Dol'Arem in the first Franchise War. She appeared to be an attractive woman, and I wondered how much the statue exaggerated her features. Was she truly that beautiful? Did the sculptors use their skills to make her appear more striking than she really was?

An employee of the Corporation came over. Her face was bland and emotionless.

"Good morning, Representative McWright. It's a pleasure to host you in the Corporation back office. I will escort you to Representative Boran's office."

With a smile, I said, "You lead, and I will follow, my lady."

Finally, a slight smirk came from one side of her face. Federate employees acted like robots with dull, uninteresting personalities in my experience. The same was true under the sheets. Alyssa's nature spoiled me.

The Federate Corporation had incredibly advanced technology and utilized androids and robots with artificial intelligence for lots of aspects of their daily life. Employees probably used machines to satisfy urges of a more carnal nature too.

We reached the fourth-floor hallway, and although the same shape and size as our Colonial building, it had a different look with white-painted cinder block lining the walls. The flooring was a faded carpet that had to be older than my deceased grandparents. Spaced out along the wall were motivational posters.

One of the hanging reproductions had writing in bold letters: "Respect your fellow employees, work together and achieve a common goal."

Another read: "If we work together, we win together."

Oliver and Benjamin trailed behind as I opened the ordinary-looking wooden door into Representative Boran's office. The carpet here was even older than the one out in the hall, and his office was boring and gloomy. The man sitting behind the representative desk was anything but plain, dull or ordinary.

Wearing a costly suit with a rare model wristwatch that was just shy of a million credits in worth, Representative Boran had an air of confidence. He was unusually tall and disproportionately lengthy. His arms and legs seemed like they were entirely too long for his body. While utterly bald on the top of his head, two small metal boxes above his ears protruded from short-cropped gray hair only visible around the ears and the back of his head.

The metal boxes were uplink implants that wealthy people had surgically connected to their brains so their minds functioned as a PDD; they had no need to carry a device. The implant could link to a starship, control satellites, and use thoughts to search any database within the Free Worlds, among other things. It was expensive and rare to see, and similar to the implants used by MERC Guild agents to speak with their mongrels.

The center seat representative was listening to one of his aides speaking, with his elbows on the armrest. His large hands were steepled together. His fingers were so long, more than double the length of mine, and the way he held them reminded me of a spider web. Boran, without a doubt, was the spider.

It was never comfortable to look at his odd shape, especially when standing so close, but his form was not the reason most in the Free Worlds feared him. The powerful brain of Jaxson Boran was more dangerous than a nuclear missile.

Under the dome, he was known as the Man of Many Numbers because of his accounting and financial abilities. Representative Boran had two doctorates in the study of accounting and mathematics. He had been a board member for the Corporation and the vice president of accounting and spending management for Tri-Co before becoming a representative on this station.

Jaxson finally stopped talking to his aide and took notice of me with a light smile, as if he didn't know I was standing here waiting for him. "Good day to you, Representative McWright."

He waved his long inhuman-looking fingers over his desk, inviting me to take a seat.

I moved to the chair. "Representative Boran, it's always a pleasure to meet with a fellow center seat."

I sat, and we patiently waited for all staff members to leave besides the chosen few, including his chief of staff and Benjamin, who was seated at the rear of the office.

The center seat stared through me with a smirk on his face. Anyone else sitting across from this man might cower in fear. I was an entirely different entity altogether, and he knew this, but we played our little games regardless.

Jaxson finally spoke. "I found Representative Laskaris's actions predictable during our closed session. You've been on each other's sides for some time now."

"Evidently, everyone was able to predict my intentions. JJ saw it coming from across the station and countered with Civil Earth doing his work for him."

Jaxson chuckled awkwardly and said, "Yes, yes. I was aware that Civil Earth had decided to push forward Representative Richmond's agenda. Though I was surprised that it was Olivia Belitz who swooped down with her talons," he continued sarcastically. "The Stavish and Belitz families working together. Math couldn't account for how much those two hate each other."

"It was also a shock that your left seat voted yay for me to reintroduce my bill for open session. He went against your wishes, it would seem," I said defiantly.

Jaxson smiled, his eyebrows low, ignoring my comments, and said, "There's no equation for what happened in closed session when you played your games and JJ played his, but if there were and it was a test, you would have failed horribly, the same way as when you didn't anticipate JJ working against you the night of your speech."

The Man of Many Numbers indeed.

I had to change the topic. "How's the war on Gliese going?"

"You told me this once before my election to this station that war is a troublesome affair but sometimes necessary."

"I remember that conversation—when you were still a vice president with Tri-Co, speaking of your former title—the most recent replacement hasn't worked with me the way you once did."

Representative Boran waved his fingers in the air and said, "She's a cautious employee and wasn't promoted to do the things that I achieved."

"Different times require different tactics."

Jaxson raised his eyebrows and drawled, "*Yes.*"

"And how is your sister company these days?"

He looked pleased with that question. "Did you know that Tri-Co is the oldest of the four sisters that makes up the Corporation? Our flag has four pillars, and the largest pillar at the top is for my sister company."

Of course, everyone knew that Tri-Co was the largest of the companies and commanded the most seats on the Corporation board of directors. Genesis Foundation was the next biggest, followed by Excalibur Industries and Green Scrap Consumers. The four sister companies and their small businesses under the umbrella encompassed the entire Federate Corporation as a whole, with everyone an employee from birth.

I decided to play along for the time being. I would play ignorant.

"I may have heard that at one time or another. Now I understand better why you and I get along so well. Uropa is the oldest, the financial and political power of all six Colonial worlds. Our flag is the same, with Uropa's circle being the largest around our Hammer of Labor."

Jaxson smiled again and said, "*Yes, yes,* we tower over the rest and know that it's the older sibling's job to lead the way for the younger ones. Only we know what is best for the Free Worlds of Humanity."

If his head were any bigger, he wouldn't be able to leave the office without getting stuck in the doorway.

"Is that why you led your younger sisters into the war on Gliese?"

The representative narrowed his eyes while leaning his face on his overly long fingers as he considered his response.

"We went to war because of the intelligence received from a confident source."

I already knew how that intelligence came to Jaxson Boran's uplink implants on his head. "And it's small wonder why the Silent Lion thought it would be beneficial to give both you and Center Seat Representative Sharrar counterintelligence stating that both sides were invading Gliese. The fourteen others who sit in the pentagon, including those of the Human Alliance wall, know Representative Floros's words to be few. When he does speak, it's usually to cause chaos and does nothing but benefit himself and New-Sparta. Isaac and Killian Lyons have their reasons for the things they do, I guess."

The real face and colors of Center Seat Representative Jaxson Boran became visible. He had an evil expression on his face like a wild animal about to eat its prey without a second thought.

Jaxson said, "Have you ever seen the Federate battle bots we use in combat?" I nodded, and he continued. "My sister company designed and manufactured those fearsome machines of war. If you were to go to Gliese today and travel the planet in areas under Federate control, you'd see that all operators from Tri-Co, Genesis Foundation, and Excalibur Industries utilize our bots. The latter two sister companies have purchased over one hundred and eighty thousand bots since the fighting started."

I said, "Lots have taken notice of Tri-Co stocks on the Free Worlds and Federate markets increasing dramatically of late."

Jaxson's smile returned. "*Yes*, the numbers never lie, Henry. Our three younger sisters have invested heavily in the war effort, as have an array of wealthy private investors from all the other Free Worlds, not including Kora, of course. The armor worn by operators is manufactured by Tri-Co as well. So, you can see that although this war has taken hold of the station and unintended events have occurred, the money is flowing faster than ever."

I grinned and asked, "What's the mathematical calculation regarding the countless deaths since the fighting started?"

"Numbers, numbers, and more numbers. Add a few and subtract some more. We've lost one hundred and twenty-six thousand Federate operators to date. Do you know how many Dolrinion sentinels we estimate dead?" I shook my head. "Over six hundred ninety-eight thousand on the wrong side of the sod—that's a ratio of five and a half to one. Have you seen any sentinels lately with missing legs, I wonder?"

He laughed to himself as if that was the greatest joke ever spoken and then continued. "You see, our battle bots are the first in during the fighting, killing several sentinels, at which those ignorant jarheads smile and charge the bots thinking they're hurting the Corporation with every bot they destroy. That's ridiculous, obviously. All they're doing is making Tri-Co more profits since we manufacture and sell these weapons back to our sister companies who beg us to make more. My fellow Tri-Co board members haven't been this pleased since we invaded Dol'Arem seven hundred and forty-five years ago."

This was precisely why he was a board member and the center seat representative for the Corporation. Boran could squeeze credits out of anything and make the Federates money. All the dead bodies were nothing more than numbers to him, equations that needed to be solved by any means necessary to turn a profit. For someone like Jaxson, the outcome of these events was irrelevant because they wouldn't directly affect him in any meaningful way.

I said, "Your yearly profit margin will far exceed this year's expectations, which will mean a nice bonus for you."

Someone like me understood death very well, and when death was unavoidable, I agreed. But regarding a decision without regret that has killed high numbers of rogue world natives and Free Worlds soldiers for no reason other than finances, I was undecided, and would require more reflection. I couldn't help myself and said, "What do your numbers say about the two hundred million dead natives of Gliese?"

Jaxson leaned in, pressing his fingers against his lips for a moment. "The bodies are what always change opinion on war, especially when they're innocent people and children. Have you noticed that the Corporation has spent large amounts of credits on humanitarian aid? We're going out of our way to ensure that no one on our side of the planet dies unjustly. Can the Dolrinions say the same for their side? I think not. Besides, the Free Worlds' governments should be happy because there's another way to look at our fighting: we feel like we're doing the Dolrinions a service. They're so fixated on those religious beliefs of immortality of the soul with their silly memory stone. With our battle bots, we're simply providing them with the means to go to that wretched rock. Dying in glorious combat or something like that, I believe, is what they say."

Dangerous didn't begin to describe Representative Boran. One military-grade fusion warhead didn't have the power to kill two hundred million eight hundred twenty-four thousand people with one blast. All Jaxson had to do was use his uplink connection to speak with the board of directors, and poof, so much destruction. They followed his lead, and regarding the invasion on Gliese, the Free Worlds would never know the truth. My deeds had been terrible behind the curtain, but I had never killed an entire planet for profit.

The Federate Corporation as a whole wasn't evil, no, only the man sitting before me, and sadly for employees on Dol'Arem, Jaxson Boran was in complete control.

I said, "Can I ask what your numbers say regarding the vote on my bill during open session?"

Representative Boran looked at me seriously. "That math is simple, and it doesn't favor you with both your right seat and Mia plotting against the bill. Henry, I'm a realist, not a theorist. There is no way your bill will pass a second vote when the last vote was ten to five."

I kept myself calm. "The past is the past. I know that you're worried about voting yay during open session because then you'll have JJ and Mia against you."

He added, "And the Dolrinions. To have two walls as guaranteed nay votes for any bill that I put forward doesn't leave much room for error. I wonder what it is that Representative Richmond has on Mia. He's wrapped his little rose vine around her neck and she has submitted to his will. Even the Silent Lion, our pentagon Master of Spies, doesn't know the answer to that intriguing question."

"We will have the answers shortly. Balance inside the five walls will return, I promise."

Boran nodded. "Stability is necessary for us to function properly inside the forum."

Jaxson didn't like that JJ was getting his way, and his opinion helped me. Everything I had prepared for was ready, and the time to make my move had come.

I was confident. "I have a proposition for you—it will help bring harmony back by uniting two walls, which everyone would believe to be impossible."

The Corporation center seat's eyebrows lifted high, and he touched his long fingers together once again. In a drawn-out tone, he said, "*Proceed.*"

"Have the Corporation relinquish that one percent of landmass, give it in good faith to the Dolrinion Offensive so they can start shelling the marshes on Gliese. What do you care about the natives and Frogmen? Nothing, of course. In return, I'll give you three percent ownership of Metak Agathon, the import-export company belonging to the Human Alliance. My charge will be half the current value of that percentage."

Representative Jaxson Boran seemed to grow in his chair. He closed his eyes, and his chief of staff started feverishly typing away on his PDD.

The chief spoke. "Fourteen million credits, sir."

Jaxson said, "So fourteen million credits for something valued at twenty-eight million. You're ok with that?"

"Absolutely."

Jaxson closed his eyes again. After a few more moments on his PDD, the chief answered, "Around nine hundred million credits, sir, and is projected to grow fifteen percent over the next five years due to the new trade bill passed two months ago."

Boran smiled and said, "Ah, now I see. Zachery Laskaris's family owns Metak Agathon. He gave you that three percent ownership as payment for voting yay. If I recall, you did much of the legwork convincing others to vote in favor, including me. This can't be all that you want. "

My confidence was higher. Jaxson was an innocent bug flying into my spiderweb.

"You are correct. I also want a yay vote from your entire wall on my bill during open session."

"*Aaah*, the true meaning of your offer."

I said, "As you say, the numbers never lie. My next minutes meeting is with the Iron Fist of Kora. I'll inform him of our negotiation to surrender the mountains if he agrees to have the Dolrinion wall vote yay on my bill. With the Federate Corporation, Dolrinion Offensive, Human Alliance, the Angry Tigress of Lars, and my vote, the numbers are simple. Eleven to four if my math is correct, but you should check to be sure."

Jaxson leaned back, and I waved Benjamin forward. He brought the legal document surrendering my Metak Agathon ownership, placing it in front of the center seat.

Boran looked as if he'd just had a satisfying sexual encounter.

"I don't think the Federate Corporation needs to hold this mountain range any further, and it's time for us to restructure our battle lines across Gliese."

Using his uplink implant, the representative scanned each page of the document. A flashing light beamed from the side boxes to his desk. The wording was straightforward; I had my team write it in three languages: Uropa, Dol'Arem, and Civil Earth's Language of Humanity. Jaxson grabbed a pen from his desk and signed the document.

Our meeting drew to its conclusion. It was time to meet with the center seat of the Dolrinion Offensive. Sharrar was still angry with me over my comments in the classroom with the schoolteacher Gabby. He had nearly broken JJ's office door with one solid punch. Was my meeting with Jaxson going to be the easiest or hardest of the day? I couldn't help but wonder.

*

We walked outside the Corporation back office and strolled the path leading away through the flower gardens that flourished between each office walkway. Numerous tourists came to observe the stunning exotic flowers from across occupied space. Capitol Security kept onlookers away from entering our offices, but most only came to see the flower beds and arrangements.

The gardens bloomed with all colors of the spectrum that quickly overwhelmed the senses and would make any rainbow appear insipid by comparison. Some of those flowers seemed so alien that I found myself uncomfortable near them. Capitol Security officers stood strategically throughout the area.

We had to pass our Colonial office first, Civil Earth, and the Alliance offices before getting to the Dolrinions. It meant my legs would get some exercise that day. When the capitol dome construction was nearing completion, the builders thought it wise to keep the Corporation and Offensive access limited from each other in every way possible. The first Franchise War concluded, and their hate for each other raged on.

Benjamin said, "Representative McWright, are you worried about seeing Sharrar after he punched his way into JJ's office because of your comments at the school?"

"No, Sharrar's a proud, stubborn old sentinel who did that to save face and appear as a typical supreme general of the Offensive."

The real reason Sharrar wouldn't do anything was that he knew if he laid a hand on the center seat representative of the Colonial Accord, three hundred million Colonial Marines would answer his aggression by eliminating his entire command. A Colonial Marine Hellfire was enough to make anyone second guess fighting our Accord.

Benjamin looked away, stewing on my words for a moment. "Dolrinions frighten me, sir. They're easily angered, and I have seen a fight break out on this station before with a sentinel in battle armor. The sentinel threw the local like a paperweight and broke his back. Even the famous unbeaten Black Skull Admiral is a Dolrinion."

I said, "Dolrinion physical strength is superior to the rest of humanity, generally speaking, but it's their battle armor that gives them such an overwhelming advantage. Have you ever seen sporting events of professional fighters? Dolrinions without their armor can lose the same as anyone else. A real fight between two aggressors can go either way. In my opinion, the fighter who takes the lead early on and capitalizes on any weakness will always win. If it comes down to it, take off your shoe and use it as a weapon to beat someone to death. Always throw the first punch and try to overwhelm your opponent. The overall outcome of a fight is easy to see in the first minute. What makes the Black Skull Admiral so fearsome isn't his abilities as a Dolrinion, but rather people's fabled impression of him. Everyone hears stories of the famous Admiral Derwin, and without ever witnessing his real skills, they fear him from the start. For the Free Worlds of Humanity, perception is reality."

Father taught me lots of the things I told Benjamin. More memories of Dad came to mind, but I pushed them away. Benjamin nodded, and we continued to walk, passing our Colonial office and then Civil Earth's.

Ben seemed lost in thought for a time. "Sir, why did Representative Floros give false information to the Federates and Dolrinions causing the invasion?"

"Why do representatives of the forum do anything at all? Everyone has a rationale that makes sense to one person or another. The Silent Lion has his reasons, and I would surmise that those motives align perfectly with Isaac and Killian Lyon's plans for the Free Worlds."

Benjamin's face grew long. "The Human Alliance always seems so passive in the forum. They rarely become confrontational with any of the other walls."

Liam Sideris came to mind. He was such a force on Epsilon Prime and had strong leadership ties on every other Free World. He was a good man, something that was in short supply these days.

I said, "Before the civil war, Epsilon Prime had one of the most active standing military forces of any Free World because of their independent city-states. Twenty-one states in total and five of them thought some of the others would attack for one reason or another at any given time. Military service is and was mandatory upon graduation from secondary school for everyone. Now, in the aftermath of the Unification Civil War, only the states that sided with New-Sparta can keep a standing army. Nearly all city-states who supported Athinia live in poverty, worse than outer or rogue worlds. The radical Lyons Pride treats those states like animals. Its citizens are beaten, detained, raped, killed, or any other manner of perversion that comes to your mind. Since Epsilon Prime's military conscript force is half the size it once was, Isaac and Killian Lyons depend on espionage and misdirection to accomplish their goals."

Ben asked, "What are their goals now, sir?"

I smirked. "Destabilization of every other Free World inside the pentagon."

Now my aide looked even more confused. If I didn't know any better, I would say smoke rose from his head from all that thinking.

He turned to me and said, "I don't understand, sir. You're friends with Representative Laskaris. The two of you have worked closely with each other, but you know what's going on behind closed doors."

Ben would have to stay with me another ten years before he was ready to follow a political career with questions like those. He wouldn't last one term in the battleground politics of Uropa. He had much to learn about the inner workings under the dome.

"Friendship, enemy, lover, acquaintance: nothing but words. The mutual benefit we provided each other recently helped us both increase wealth and influence, which is the overall goal inside the five walls."

We arrived in the lobby of the Dolrinion back office and felt the gravity pressure of Kora. Their dismal display was by far the worst of any under the dome. The flooring was a dark color of poured concrete, and the walls were of the same material. Common chattels were missing from the lobby, such as statues, pictures, furniture, intricate designs of local art, or staff to greet us.

War was the only type of art known to Dolrinions. Standing strategically around their lobby were sentinels on guard against the walls. Near the center of the lobby was a recognizable item known to all within the Free Worlds. Ben and I went over to observe that small marvel.

"Is that the memory stone?" Benjamin said, sounding awed.

A large chunk of rock, dark purple with green sparkles, was before us, and a faint humming sound emitted from the stone. I could see my reflection in the smooth surface, and the floor beneath glowed bright yellow, reminding me of the faint glow on a horizon as the sun set behind a mountainside. Ben had never set foot in the Dolrinion back office before today.

I laughed. "This piece broke off from erosion. Look under, do you see the yellow glow?" Ben nodded. "That glowing area was once attached to the main stone on Kora. I saw it in person. Regardless of my opinions on their religious beliefs, the stone mountain is huge and a magnificent sight. It's just shy of a kilometer high and spans almost twenty-nine kilometers in length. When a sentinel earns a place upon death, caretakers etch their name. The yellow glow is emitted from the carving for all time. Here, touch it and feel the vibrations."

We each touched the warm, smooth surface. I could just feel the stone vibrating, and the noise reminded me of an electric razor, only quieter.

Benjamin looked back at the sentinels, who stared us down with hatred.

I said, "Easy, lad. They won't do anything because you're with me."

Dolrinions were exceptionally protective of that rock. We made our way to the fourth floor; the hallway was the same colors and material as the lobby, with bulkhead doors every twenty meters as would be expected on a ship. Maybe sentinels worried about a dome breach.

Three Capitol Security officers were outside Representative Sharrar's office. He never allowed them in, and if he had his way, he would've removed them from his service. The general didn't permit them inside the Dolrinion bubble either.

"Good afternoon, gentlemen."

The lead officer respectfully said, "Representative McWright, it's a pleasure, sir. Representative Sharrar is waiting for you inside."

I raised my finger to give instruction. "Listen carefully. No matter what you hear inside this office, you will all remain outside. Do I make myself clear?"

Benjamin, Oliver, Josue, and the lead security officer for Sharrar were wide-eyed.

I reemphasized. "Gentlemen, do I make myself clear?"

They still wouldn't answer, so I raised my voice. "You must listen to me—don't interfere. I need to deal with Representative Sharrar in my way. If you come in, it will appear dishonorable to the general. Dolrinions aren't like us."

Oliver tried to speak, but I talked over him. "Ollie, don't come in."

All agreed uneasily. They nodded, looked down, or moved away from the door.

"Good. Now open the door and close it behind me."

Representative Sharrar's office door was a thick metal bulkhead with huge screw heads outlining the frame. When it opened, a loud creaking echoed through the hall. I stepped inside, and the security officers complied with my orders, securing the door behind.

Sharrar, the Iron Fist of Kora, one of five supreme generals to Force Command First Ones, the largest and first command of the Dolrinion Offensive, stood behind his desk, looking at a holographic display of the rogue world Gliese.

When Sharrar saw me, he waved the hologram away and ground his teeth. The sound was like scraping a rock against concrete. He screamed, and I took a step forward, glaring at him. The Iron Fist threw his massive desk upside down several meters away, and he charged straight for me, still shouting with fury, spit flying from his mouth.

Again, I stepped forward, keeping my expression the same. Sharrar stopped a centimeter from pushing through me and stared up into my eyes. His teeth still scratched together and thick veins bulged from his short wide neck. Sharrar was making sounds like a wild animal growling. Still, I didn't move or change my focus. Undeterred, I waited for him to speak.

After another moment, he lowered his shoulders and said, "Sit down, Representative McWright."

"Thank you, Representative Sharrar."

The Iron Fist turned and waddled back to his seat. The walk was short since his desk was on the other side of the room. JJ had made a crucial mistake when Sharrar burst through his door. Representative Richmond more than likely turned white as a ghost with pure fear in his eyes. Sharrar was a shark. When blood was in the water, he attacked to devour the weaker target.

I was not prey and came here from a position of power with personal pride and confidence. Dolrinions respected strength and scorned weakness. We both sat, and Sharrar took some time to calm himself while still breathing heavily.

He said, "You smell of Federate filth. Did you enjoy your meeting with the Corporation scum?"

"They're weak of body but strong of mind, and that is the only reason they succeed. The Federates do not have your honor."

The general nodded his head with a grunt.

I said, "My comments in the classroom before the scheduled speech in open session were displayed improperly on the news. I would never intentionally insult any of our fifteen from the pentagon. You know my respect for the five walls is firm."

Sharrar snapped his teeth again and raged. "You always find fancy ways to say things, Henry. Half of the time, when you speak, it comes across as an insult." He raised his voice louder. "Don't trifle with me."

"No games or tricks, Supreme General. I'm here to make amends with you and I've already started by working out a deal that will benefit the Offensive considerably."

Representative Sharrar folded his arms and narrowed his eyes. Dolrinions had such trust issues with everyone; even their Force Commands viewed each other warily and there were often fights between generals and their armies.

He asked, "What did you do?"

I answered steadily, "I negotiated the surrender of the mountain range on Gliese. The Corporation is preparing to retreat from that area and turn it over to Red Legion."

Sharrar's eyes opened wide. His face betrayed his feelings. "How?"

"How isn't important," I said. "What's important is now you can begin your campaign against the marshes and those Frogmen."

The general's face grew flush. "We can take those marshes without that mountain if we want!"

I stood from the chair, stepped towards the door. "Fine. I'll go back to Boran and revoke the deal. There's nothing you need to give to the Corporation in return. But, since you don't want it, I bid you a good day."

Sharrar hastily replied, "Wait, don't go." He sighed. "Tell me what you want in return."

I turned and smirked at the general. The wheels of change continued to spin here under the dome. Open convocation would be quite different that month indeed.

CHAPTER 18

Obsessions

Old habits are hard to break (Kathryn)

Daniel left with Amber for their date. Daniel, Amber, and Lilly were great people, but they didn't understand me. How could they? Tobias understood. He lived outside before and knew real pain. I was forever indebted to Daniel, but continuing to live there was hard for me.

Lilly said, "Kathryn. Are you ready? Tonight will be so much fun."

She put music on the display screen and danced through the room. She looked silly, and it made me smile. She ran over to me and grabbed my hands, but my body didn't move to music like hers. I felt awkward.

"I don't know this song."

Lilly shouted over the music, "Don't worry, just dance, dance like no one's watching."

She was undressing right in front of me, nearly naked in a bra and underwear, still spinning around and singing. Her skin was visible where the underwear should cover it. That was odd.

"Something's wrong with your underwear."

Lilly laughed. "You have so much to learn. Let's start with something simple."

She ran into the bathroom and returned with a small box. We sat on the couch, and I was uncomfortable with all her exposed skin so close to me. Lilly opened the box, which contained a small vial.

"We call this *funny herb* on Civil Earth, the liquid form of it, at least."

I asked, "What's so funny about it?"

Lilly giggled. "You're hilarious. It's only a name. The Corporation calls it green leaf, Alliance calls it marifeer, and I have no idea what the Colonial or Dolrinion name is."

"What does it do?"

Lilly raised her chin with a half-smile. "It makes you feel amazing inside, dulling your senses and perception. You'll feel nothing but happiness and complete relaxation."

A memory of Sadness during my training on the surface stirred.

Sadness had said, "Remember, you must always keep your senses strong, be ready for anything at all times. Right now, five Rockland gang members could come around the corner of that building, and we would need to be at our best to survive. You must be able to see a situation and know every possible outcome based on your surroundings. Think of what your enemy might do before they even know themselves."

I remembered responding to him, "I don't understand."

He rarely smiled and would only curl his face up on one side from time to time, amused by me. I was younger when he taught me most of these lessons.

"You will in time, child."

Lilly brought me back to the here and now with a slap to my arm. "Hey, Fleet Branch cadet. You're off in the clouds flying around or something."

I punched her hard in the arm, and she winced.

"Damn it, Kathryn, that hurt." She lifted a small metal pipe. "Ok, do you want to try this or not?"

I pulled my lip in and folded my arms. "No, I don't want anything that won't keep me sharp. Sorry for punching you."

She smoked her pipe and got up, still dancing. After a few minutes, Lilly put some clothes on. Her body was remarkably skinny, her ribs visible, and it reminded me of people from the surface.

Lilly went to the dispenser and swiped her finger across the display screen. "Breakfast whites for you again?"

"Yes."

That food was excellent, and after eating it, my belly didn't growl the way it always did outside. Lilly heated the food on that plate thing near the dispenser, and we sat down together to eat. For herself, she made something called alternative meat, which was a dark brown color with small chunks.

Lilly said, "One of the guys coming tonight is joining the Defender Corps."

"He wants to be a tin suit? Why?"

Lilly narrowed her eyes. "We all hate the defenders, but families in the Lower Forty can't afford for their children to hang around after secondary school. Delano's decision is twofold—he wants to help his family, but also his father is forcing him to leave. If the family made more credits, maybe he wouldn't need to join, but we live in reality, not in a world where everything works out like a fairy tale. Daniel and Amber want me to join Fleet Branch for the same reason. I think he wants to get rid of me."

"That's not true at all," I said defensively. "In the hospital, when Daniel and Tobias talked about you and the academy, they said joining up would get you into Tier Three. Your life would be better in the Middle Thirty. They said something about your mom going with you."

"Who are they to decide what's best for me? I can make those decisions myself. Besides, Mom won't live another five years. Any idiot can see that she's nearing the end."

I looked down and said, "I told Daniel the same thing about your mom."

Her eyes turned red and filled with tears. At least she knew her mom. I couldn't remember much about mine. Lilly saw that I was glaring at her with pity. She looked irritated and punched my arm. The hit was weak, but she could have it for free.

She said, "Enough buzzkill talk, we're going out to party like rock stars tonight. Finish up, and let's go."

Some of the things she said were hard for me to understand. We finished eating, and my surface cough started again. Daniel had given me half a bottle of pills that came from Tobias. I wondered where T got them since the cost was so high. Maybe Doctor Courtney and T found a way, but I knew they couldn't afford the meds.

"What's the guy's name we will see tonight? You like him, I think."

Lilly smiled. "Delano, we went to school together."

Her glow reminded me of my feelings for Johnathan. I reached down into my boot to ensure the pouch of teeth was still there—that dress didn't have anywhere to store them. Lilly saw me grabbing the small sack and looked curiously.

"What's in that little bag?"

Unsure of how to answer, I quickly snapped, "Just a reminder that I am not ready to forget yet."

"It's time to leave. Everyone should be there already. Don't worry. I'll introduce you to the group—they're great."

We left the apartment, and for some reason, I felt like we had forgotten something, but nothing immediately came to my mind. The thought vanished as we moved quickly through the hallway to the transit hub.

On the second floor, we pushed through the crowds of people. I watched everyone carefully, but Lilly seemed uninterested. Around the next corner, loud music overtook all other sounds. We were at the entrance where two big guys checked caste cards. Their muscles made them easy targets for someone like me. I'd run circles around those slow giants.

Inside, the club was filled with commotion. People stumbled around, dancing, drinking, eating, and talking. The music was so loud I could hardly hear myself think. Strobe lights in beams of green, yellow, red, and blue shone down from the ceiling. The flickering lights turned on, off, and changed color with the music. Large windows were on the opposite wall, and past the glass was our city line.

I had tunnel vision with everything around me and walked over to the windows. Another memory stirred of the strobe lights bouncing off these windows. Seven years ago, these strobes were clear to see from the red mud surface.

Sadness had said, "Those lights up there are your reminder that they don't care about us. The people inside are soft. They eat, drink, and enjoy life while we starve out here and kill each other for scraps. Only you can protect yourself and do what's necessary to survive. Many will try to take advantage. You must always be ready."

As Sadness spoke, my young mind absorbed everything like a sponge. He also trained me to use bladed weapons among countless other things.

Lilly ran to me, pushing on my arm to get my attention. "Hey, are you ok?"

I leaned in to speak in her ear over the loud music. "These strobes were always clear to see from the surface at night. The yellow haze blocked the stars, but these lights shone through the sky, and those on the outside watched them."

Lilly said, "You'll never go back out there again. Tobias and my brother wouldn't let that happen. Come on—I want to introduce you to my friends."

We went to a table where her friends were socializing with each other. They all appeared so innocent and naïve. From their smiles, I could tell none of them had ever experienced real pain. Lilly named them one at a time, but I wasn't paying attention because I didn't want to be there.

We took a seat in the booth, and I watched Lilly make a fool of herself, flirting with Delano, and acting silly with her friends. That Delano guy obviously liked her. He carefully caressed her arm as they talked, and she touched his leg.

A few minutes of boredom passed, and all at once my heart raced, and I couldn't breathe. I ran to the bathroom and hid in a stall, trying to calm my nerves. Sweat dripped from my face, and my hands were clammy. What was happening? I was so nervous, and it felt like the walls were closing in.

I sat in that bathroom stall for what felt like hours, but things returned to normal after some time. It took me a few minutes to clean my face in the sink and regain myself. When I left the bathroom, I noticed that Delano was no longer sitting next to Lilly. He was at the bar ordering drinks, and three older guys hovered near Lilly. She attempted to push the largest of the three away. It was clear that she didn't want those guys near her. They wouldn't leave and even grabbed at her hips and touched her without permission.

I moved closer, carefully watching the jackasses. One of Lilly's friends tried to intervene without success. The other two guys pushed her friend away with ease. Lilly stood and attempted to walk away, but the large man pulled her close and tried to kiss her lips.

His dumb friends weren't paying attention to their rear, which left me an opening. I moved fast and kicked the large man in his knee. He screamed and stumbled to the ground. Again, I kick him, this time on his upper back, and he rolled across the floor. The two dumb friends realized what was happening too late and moved in my direction. Before they did anything, the huge security guys around the club grabbed all three jerks and removed them. The men gave me dirty looks but offered no challenge to security.

Lilly jumped up and hugged me. "Thank you, Kathryn, I was so scared."

Oblivious, Delano returned with drinks in hand, asking what happened. He wouldn't make a good tin suit, not paying attention to his surroundings. He was weak, and Lilly shouldn't be with him. All of them were weak.

"Maybe we should leave," I said.

Lilly rapidly said, "No, not yet. Don't worry. Those idiots are gone now."

I remembered what we forgot when we left the apartment. I yelled at Lilly, punching her arm. "We left the hot plate on in the apartment."

Lilly cringed and shouted back, "Ouch, damn it, Kathryn. We're already here. It's been on for hours. Forget about it. Daniel and Amber will turn it off when they get home."

Daniel had warned us how important it was to turn it off. I was annoyed and wanted to leave, but Lilly was ignoring me. It took almost thirty minutes to convince her to go. She was annoyed by my constant bothering. She leaned in and kissed Delano goodbye. I'd never seen people kiss like that before. I only nodded to Delano to say goodbye. We finally left, and my ears rang from the music. Lilly looked angry and wouldn't speak to me.

"What's wrong with you?"

Lilly cried, "You wouldn't stop bugging me. I had plans tonight, you know. Delano's family is away on business somewhere in the city line. We were going to stay at his apartment tonight. I wanted to sleep with him. It might be the last time we ever see each other. He could die serving Civil Earth Defense."

His chances of dying were slim, considering most of these tin suits stood in the transit hubs doing nothing all day. There was no point in arguing with her.

"I didn't mean to interfere with your plans. I wish you understood how hard it is for me here. I'm so uncomfortable."

She didn't say anything, but her eyes showed me she was thinking. We continued through the hallway, turning down another junction. That hall was empty and quiet, which reminded me of being caught in the open on the surface. As we approached the other end, two men stood to the right, blocking our path. My senses heightened. The men were the two friends of the larger guy from the night club.

I turned to see that he was behind us with a satisfied grin on his face. Damn, how did I not notice? His expression reminded me of the BreakNeck Boy who attempted to rape me. They backed us into a dead-end near a garbage disposal unit and dumpsters lining the wall.

Lilly had a look of dread as she whispered, "What do we do?"

The larger man called out, "Well, if it isn't the two tease bitches from the club."

He was confident because of his size and strength. Another memory of Sadness's words came to me. "People will always underestimate your abilities because of your size. I will teach you to use that as an advantage—to move faster than everyone. When your enemies are overconfident in victory, you can calculate how to capitalize on their mistakes. Do something unexpected to throw them off. Confusion is a powerful weapon—change the direction of events to control the situation."

I said softly to Lilly, "Don't worry, I will handle this." I turned to the larger man and raised my voice. "I'm glad you caught up with us."

He had a dumb puzzled stare. "You are, why?"

With a teasing smile, I unbuttoned the top lace of my sundress, exposing more of my skin. The man was staring with a terrible smile. He was drunk and dumb.

"Because I was jealous. I wanted your attention. What makes her better than me? That's why I kicked you."

All three men laughed, and the larger one said, "Don't you worry, doll. There's plenty of me for the both of you."

We approached each other, and the stench of liquor on his breath was overwhelming. The man kissed my neck. I could feel his penis push against my body through our clothes. What he didn't realize was that I had the knife from my boot in hand, and with a button push and a snap of the blade locking into place, the moment was mine.

My knee went into his groin, and he shrieked like a child before falling to the floor. One of his idiot friends moved to grab me, but I was too fast. A quick slice of the blade across his forearms made him scream. These insiders were weak. The third man did nothing and ran away in fear.

I turned, but my face took a tremendous blow from a savage punch. I fell, but before the larger man did anything further, Lilly jumped on his back. It didn't take more than a moment to recover as Lilly lost her grip and fell and he faced her.

Before he could react, my knife landed in his neck, cutting through skin and meat. The slice was perfect, contacting with his jugular vein and external carotid artery. Blood pulsated from the open gash, and death would be quick. Pure terror overwhelmed his face as he fell to the cold metal floor with blood spraying everywhere.

I grabbed Lilly's hand, and we ran down the previously blocked hallway leading to the transit hub.

Lilly said, "We can't go home after this. We should head to Delano's apartment and wait for him."

When we made it to the apartment, neither of us had any way of sending him a message. Lilly and I waited for an hour until Delano came home. We explained everything, and his fear on hearing the story convinced me that he didn't stand a chance of surviving in the military. We settled down for the night. I slept on the couch in the living room while Lilly went into Delano's room.

I could hear Lilly through the walls yelling out strangely. They had sex more than once through the night. Good for her; he was weak, but if he made her happy, I guess it was ok. We woke the next morning and left.

Once inside the elevator, Lilly spoke. "After what happened last night, I've made a decision … I can't defend myself the way you can. It's pathetic. I'm going to join Fleet Branch. I'll tell Daniel today."

"That's the smartest thing you've said since we met."

The elevator doors opened, and we walked down the hall to the apartment. Something was wrong; Daniel and Amber were standing in the hallway arguing with tin suits.

Lilly said, "The defenders must be here because of last night. They'll send us up to the prison mines on Lunar One."

"Stay quiet and let Daniel talk for now."

Daniel saw us as we walked up and gave Lilly and me a look of disappointed frustration.

Lilly said, "What's going on?"

A tin suit answered, "Your apartment violated numerous building codes under the administrative authority of our megacity. There was a huge power usage increase from this apartment all of last night. Every sensor in this building alerted us."

Lilly and I looked at each other, realizing what happened. The damn hot plate. I narrowed my eyes at Lilly and punched her arm.

She cried, "Damn it, Kathryn," and punched me back, harder than last time.

Daniel yelled at us both, and the tin suit asked, "Do both of these girls live in this apartment? Only four people are registered here."

Daniel stumbled on his words, "Uhm, no, sir. No, Lilly lives here. Kathryn's only visiting."

I couldn't see the tin suit's face with the cover down, but he would have looked mistrustful if I could. Daniel wasn't a good liar. Tobias was down the hall headed in our direction. He wore a formal military uniform of light gray and blue. The fabric was stiff and appeared uncomfortable to wear. His last name, Norcross, was in large lettering across the jacket.

I smiled, but it faded quickly in the face of T's firm, angry gaze. The tin suit stood at attention when he saw Tobias, and the soldiers walked away to speak. Then T went down the hallway with Daniel and Amber. I grew frustrated, wondering why they wouldn't talk to us. They kept looking back while chatting, and it made me feel uneasy.

All three came back, and Lilly said, "Why are you acting so weird?"

Tobias retorted, "You know precisely why, Lilly. You have two problems—the first is the hot plate, which was an immature mistake. The second is what happened in that hallway near the garbage disposal."

I was shocked, and Lilly looked the same. T continued, "Girls, you realize that nearly every square centimeter of this building has cameras, right? The only reason a team isn't here to collect you both is because of the video evidence. Those three boys planned to ambush you in that hallway. It's clear what their intentions were."

Daniel said, "Wait—we saw the scene of a murder last night." His expression changed to horror. "Was that you?"

Lilly raised her voice defensively. "They tried to attack us."

Daniel turned to me and said, "Kathryn, you need to go with T. You can't stay in our apartment any longer."

I squeezed my fists—I was angry. "You're kicking me out because I stopped those guys from having their way with us?"

Lilly added, "Oppa, she saved me."

Tobias said, "Kathryn has no choice but to leave because of the hot plate. Our building authority will check this apartment weekly now, and if they catch Kathryn here, well, everyone will have problems."

Daniel, with tears in his eyes, said, "If I could do anything else, you know I would. You're one of us, family. We're only looking out for your best interest."

Uncontrollable tears fell from my eyes, and it made me mad. I felt betrayed by those I trusted and I didn't like showing my emotions.

"Where am I supposed to go?"

Tobias said, "With me. We need to talk. Go inside and grab your things."

I snapped back, "What things? I own nothing."

Lilly said, "That's not true. We bought you new clothes, remember?" She ran inside the apartment—the tin suits were still inside—and returned with a bag nearly full. Through her tears, she said, "Take the bag too. It's yours."

We hugged each other as if we had been friends for years.

I whispered, "Don't forget to talk to your brother about Fleet Branch."

Lilly wiped a tear away. "I'll talk to him."

I punched Lilly's arm. "Stop crying. Don't be a buzzkill."

She laughed and punched me back. "Now you're starting to catch on."

Daniel hugged me and said, "I wouldn't be alive without you."

I said farewell to Amber, and then Tobias led me down the hall to the transit hub. He didn't speak or acknowledge me as we walked. Once in the hub, we got into a private elevator off to the side that the tin suits used.

T hadn't looked at me yet. I wanted to speak to him but I was scared. He coughed, worse than last time I saw him. If he was on his meds, the cough shouldn't sound like that. The elevator traveled down, all the way down to the surface floor.

The doors opened to the airlock hallway I came through when I entered this building. I was nervous, and the hair on my arms straightened with goosebumps. I felt like I was going to be sick. "Why are we down here?"

Tobias didn't answer. We were in a tunnel where tin suits stood guard. When they saw T, they all jumped to attention.

One asked, "What can we do for you, sir?"

In a commanding tone, he said, "Open the airlock. I'll only be outside for a few minutes."

The tin suit lifted her face cover and gawked at me with a grin. "First one of the day."

The airlock opened to the yellow haze and red mud. We walked outside with the haze gently pushing past us, and the damp mud squished on our feet. The door closed as fear and anger took hold of me. T glanced left and right, still ignoring the fact that I was there.

I cried out, "So that's it? Tossing me out like yesterday's trash?" Tears streamed from my face. "I don't want to be alone again!"

T took a long breath of the haze and said, "When you came back inside, you didn't leave the surface where it belonged." He pointed out in the open. "Out here."

He coughed more, and I asked, "The meds you gave Daniel for me, it was your prescription, wasn't it? Why? Why did you do that for me?"

Tobias recovered. "Because I care about you. Years ago, I was you. The only difference is that when I came back in, I left all the shit that happens on the red mud where it belonged. You can't hold on to the past with hate."

I regained my composure. "I'm afraid to forget Johnathan. I've forgotten so much. I don't even remember what my parents looked like."

T smiled sadly. "I can't remember what my parents looked like either. We tend to forget the most important things. You may not remember your parents, but you did love them and Johnathan. Keep those feelings alive, forever, right here." He pointed to my heart. "We're more alike than you know, Kathryn."

I grabbed my pouch of teeth and looked at it for a moment. Tobias put his hand on my shoulder. "If you come back inside with me, these must stay here because it's the past, and we are only concerned about your future."

My mind whirled with thoughts of pulling teeth, Jonathan, and the older boy I killed last night. I blurted out, "I'm fucked in the head."

Tobias laughed ruefully. "We live in the Free Worlds of Humanity. We're all fucked in the head."

I smirked, but changed it to a frown. "Johnathan. I don't want to forget him."

T hugged me and said, "You won't. Honor his memory by being a better person inside with me."

I stared at him, confused. "With you?"

Tobias raised his chin. "That's right. You and I are going to stick together. I'll look out for you, and you do the same for me."

Wiping some of the tears away, I said, "Do you promise?"

He pointed to my pouch. "Yes, Kat, I promise. Now leave those where they belong. We have a busy day ahead of us. I can't adopt you without filling out mountains of paperwork on the fourth floor."

I was utterly surprised. "Adopt me?"

Tobias swiped his caste card to open the airlock door. "That's right. I'll be your big brother like Daniel is to Lilly. You'll move in with me in the Middle Thirty and become Tier Three."

The airlock opened, and I gazed at Tobias with happiness and disbelief. We walked back inside, and the tin suit with the grin looked at us in confusion. As we passed her, I tossed the pouch of teeth.

"Here," I said, "you can keep these. I don't need 'em anymore."

She opened the sack and screamed in disgust while Tobias and I laughed our way back to the elevator.

CHAPTER 19

The Hollow

Two worlds meet as one (Mace)

Three days had passed since meeting with Rafael and his crazy cousin Neco. Jamie had grown restless from all the waiting. When Rafael received word, he'd come to the hotel and tell me so I could meet this Bum Bum person. We knew we could find out at a moment's notice and have to move quickly. It felt like waiting for operators to escort me to a chamber. It was horrible. Jamie had not turned the entertainment screen off for days. She watched the news with constant anxiety.

"Babes, our faces won't pop up on the news, believe me. We haven't committed a crime yet. Until the meeting, this entire thing is only an idea."

"Operators take employees for the wrong ideas. You know this. I don't understand what's taking so long. Three whole days? Nothing takes three days." Jamie sounded frustrated.

"It's not even dinner time yet. Rafael's still at work. He might come today."

Jamie shook her head and said, "We need to get off this planet."

We hugged, and I guided her to a chair, rubbing her back to soothe her. "There will be a ship for us. Order some dinner and rent a movie, pick something funny for us to watch. I'm going downstairs to stretch my legs and check our vehicle."

My wife's nervousness came as a surprise because she had always been the more unshakeable of us. The pregnancy had changed things. Jamie pulled away from my hug and said, "Please, be careful. Keep your eyes open for anything that looks off."

I smiled. "Don't you worry, Mrs. Applegate. I don't know anyone who ever got hurt going down to the lobby of this hotel. Order us some dinner and unwind. I'll be back in a little bit."

I kissed Jamie, stepped out into the hallway, and looked both ways. Her paranoia was rubbing off on me. My eyes wandered, looking for operators the same way Rafael peered around at Tiff's. *Relax, Mace, everything's fine.* Down in the lobby it felt good to stretch my legs. The truth was that I came down to drink at the bar because alcohol calmed my nerves.

Two beers and a shot later, after paying my tab, I went outside for some fresh air. The sun was setting over the horizon in colors of red, yellow, and orange. It was clear that day with a light breeze and perfect weather for our climate. The rogue world Galma probably didn't have sunsets as lovely as Dol'Arem. Most hated the Corporation, including me, and I was committed to leaving, but there was a sense of loss about departing our planet forever. It was my home.

Time to go back upstairs; Jamie would start to worry. I turned to walk back inside, and my heart dropped into my stomach.

"Jeez, Rafael. You scared the crap out of me, dude."

Rafael seemed bewildered and his forehead beaded with perspiration. "Sorry, brother. Didn't mean to startle you, but we have to go right now. Neco called me at work before I left and told me to get you to a bus stop on the corner of the cleaners where he works. You have to be there thirty-five minutes from now."

"It takes forty-five minutes to get into the city from here."

Rafael said, "Yes. So we need to go right now. Hurry."

"But Jamie, I need—"

"You can't," Rafael said louder, "there's no time. She'll understand."

We sprinted to his vehicle and got inside without a second thought. Rafael took manual control of the steering wheel and peeled out of the parking lot. I never saw him drive in manual before or so aggressive. His focus was precise as he gripped the steering wheel. He was committing lots of corporate moving violations speeding through the streets.

"Do you have your PDD on you? I should call Jamie and let her know what's going on. She'll think something happened to me."

Rafael didn't respond right away because he was paying attention to the road, weaving in and out of lanes.

He said, "No, sorry. Ness has it. Don't worry, when you come back with a way off-world, she'll understand. Once we get to the bus stop, you need to take the 292 Lower Hollow and get off at the corner of R Street and S Avenue."

"What do I do after getting off the bus?"

Rafael shook his head. "No idea, Neco didn't tell me anything else."

Rafael pulled his arm down and jerked the vehicle wheel hard to the right. I slammed into the glass and he almost hit a slower vehicle.

"Careful. It's ok. The buses have display screens on them. I can call Jamie there."

Rafael said, "No, don't do that. Neco said no PDDs or communication of any kind during this process. He said someone from the Corporation is always watching and we can't risk getting caught."

We drove on, my white-knuckled hands gripping the dashboard in fear like I was on a roller-coaster. We entered the outskirts of Lavlen, our sister company's prize. Employees throughout Dol'Arem referred to Lavlen as the crown jewel of Genesis Foundation and the city of dreams. Even though we were only the second largest of the sister companies, our capital city was envied by all.

Our progress slowed because no one else was driving with manual control. There were only five minutes left before the bus arrived. Thankfully Rafael's aggressive driving got us there in time. The bus was at the stop and I wasted no time jumping out of the vehicle before it came to a halt.

I shouted back to Rafael, "Thank you for everything. I'm forever in your debt."

"Don't thank me yet. Good luck in the Hollow."

On the bus, bottom-grade-level employees gave me angry glares. My clothes gave away what grade-level I was. If there had been more time, I would have worn something less conspicuous.

In the bus seat, my nerves overwhelmed me. Even a crown jewel had sharp edges and impurities. No jewels were flawless, and the Hollow was that flaw. There wasn't an issue with low-income employees for me. I wasn't stuck up. My concern was that the highest crime rates on all Dol'Arem came from the Hollow. Employee gangs and the Rogue Syndicate had total control.

Years ago, operators attempted to change things. They were unsuccessful with budget spending tripling the initial estimates and losses of life heavy on both sides; Genesis Foundation gave up on this area. Employees still followed the Federate policy and procedures handbook at face value because all were all bound to the rules regardless of where we lived, but other regulatory policies that would be common in the suburbs where my home was were ignored in the Hollow. Public works barely went into the district.

Fifteen minutes passed, and we arrived at the corner of R Street and S Avenue. I got off the bus and stared up at the street sign. It took me a moment to realize, but when I did, I laughed. Employees on the street side-eyed me.

"R Street and S Avenue," I said to no one in particular.

What a clever idea. R and S for Rogue Syndicate. What irony; if the MERC Guild or operators ever came, they might laugh too. I sat near the street sign and waited for several minutes. Scary-looking employees watched me from across the street. Did they think I was an operator? I ignored them and looked elsewhere, and before long, someone tapped on my shoulder, which frightened me.

Neco said, "You re-re-ready." His face twitched.

I stood and adjusted my shirt. "Absolutely."

He waved his hand, and we walked to a building on the corner with that funny street sign. The rundown, dilapidated construction appeared abandoned. One hundred years ago, it might have been a warehouse storage facility. We stopped at a solid metal door with exterior opening hinges and a broken light above.

Neco pounded on the door. When it opened outward, I moved to avoid impact. The design of this door was similar to an airlock on a ship. Extremely hardy-looking employees greeted us inside; they looked like any common criminal would with scars, angry faces, tattoos, and unkempt hair. I wanted to laugh with nervousness, but I resisted it.

As we moved further into the building, the appearances of the Syndicate employees became more intimidating. They all had guns in their hands, which increased my fear. Neco noticed my uneasiness.

He said, "Relax, my man. Da Bum Bum gave you safe passage here tonight. Nobody gunna touch you un-un-less he says so."

At the center of the building, a large storage area was full of huge boxes, crane lifts, and catwalks above. There were outlines of people up there looking down. The lighting was sparse, with three hanging lamps below the catwalks spaced out across the entire room.

At the other end of the room was a single oak office desk with a huge man sitting behind. He stood to greet us, wearing a formal suit of blue pinstripes and an elegant tie. He was a giant, standing more than thirty centimeters taller than me.

He had a dark complexion with no hair on his head or face. When he grinned, it filled me with fear. There were gold implant outlines around each tooth and drilled into the center of each were diamonds, one per tooth. His shoulders were so broad he'd need to turn sideways to enter my home.

He extended his oversized hand to greet me, his face still curled into that dreadful smile. I couldn't take my eyes off those diamonds. After a moment of reluctance, I reached out and shook his hand. Neco stood next to the desk, looking down at the floor.

I cleared my throat to speak. "So, you must be, well, the one they call Bum Bum?"

The fancy-suited man narrowed his eyes at me and his smile faded. The hair on my neck stood straight up.

After a brief pause, he smiled again. "Mace Applegate, it's a pleasure to meet you."

He called me by my name as if he had known me for years. Bum Bum's accent was Colonial, but not of any particular world.

"Some call me Bum Bum, you may call me by my real name, Silas."

We took our seats, and I blurted, "Bum Bum and Silas sound nothing alike."

Silas laughed and said, "Before joining my current employer, I spent some years in the amateur fighting circuit traveling throughout occupied space going by the name Bum Bum. My adventures brought me to all the Free Worlds, including Kora. I have contacts and friends from all walks of life throughout dozens of systems."

His massive shape made sense if he was a professional fighter who traveled the stars. The Syndicate must have loved people like him. The street signs outside were still in my mind, so I said, "R Street and S Avenue? You might as well put a sign out front that says 'We are here.'"

Silas bellowed with laughter, his enormous chest rising and falling. "Employees come seeking favor with me. You're the first to notice my joke. That street sign is exactly the reason for purchasing this property." He stopped laughing. "Neco here tells me you want transport off-world for you and your wife. Is this correct? Where do you want to go?"

"Yes, my wife is pregnant, and we're keeping the baby. We need to get out of here before the end of this month. Her physical is soon, and if they see the baby, you know what happens. We want to go to Galma."

Silas sat back in his chair and glared at me. "Twenty thousand credits for you and thirty thousand for your wife."

"Why so much more for Jamie?" I said in disbelief.

Silas gave me a sharp, piercing—and frightening stare. "Don't forget who you're speaking with, Mr. Applegate. An attitude like that in the Hollow can get you killed." He lowered his shoulders and continued in a more mellow tone. "The difference is quite simple. Your wife's traveling with two, not one. With all the recent attacks across the emptiness of space of late, those risks cost more. Black Skull Admiral Derwin himself could be lurking about when the transport exits FTL for cooldown, or worse, Androsians. You're paying for protection as well as travel."

I uttered without thought, "We only have twenty thousand, though."

Silas smiled. "Well then, you can leave—she must stay. Or you both stay. It makes no difference to me."

I leaned back in my chair and looked down at the desk. How could that be it? Why did I say how many credits we had? It took us years to save that money, and we thought it would be enough. No one could loan us thirty thousand credits, and even if someone would, we'd never be able to pay them back.

"Can my wife go for twenty thousand credits? I'll stay here. She and the baby are all that matters."

I heard the desperation in my own voice, and Silas must have been able to see it in my face, but his smile persisted. "We're not negotiating. Your wife's thirty thousand credits."

I had no idea what to do. Our only options were to go into hiding or terminate the pregnancy. No, I wouldn't give up that easy. We would hide until they caught us. When they did, the operators would walk us to the chamber with our baby in hand. My mind raced in different directions.

Silas said, "Perhaps I can rectify your current predicament—that is if you are willing."

"Yes, please, anything!"

Bum Bum's gold outlines and sparkling diamonds shone in the dim lighting.

"You work for the Department of Internal Security for Genesis Foundation." He paused and I didn't speak. My shoulders tensed up. "That wasn't a question, rather a veracity. The Syndicate knows everything about you, Mace. The genius mind of Mace Applegate, creator of the new defense grid across Dol'Arem. I would appreciate some assistance with a program-writing issue."

Silas snapped his fingers and a young woman with oval eyes and short red-streaked dark hair walked from a corner of the room. She placed a laptop on the desk before me. It displayed program code, some kind of data collection code. This type of writing wasn't something I knew.

"What do you want me to do with this?"

Silas said, "Arkie here developed the code. When it's active inside our off-network PDDs, the program can steal information from Federate-issued devices, like names, addresses, bank account codes, and other personal information."

"I wouldn't know the first thing about this type of programming," I said. "It has variables that I've never learned. My specialization is different."

Arkie snickered. "I already programmed the main code. We don't need you for that."

Silas said, "We need you to go to your job and copy the firewall program used by Internal Security. Put it on a drive and return it to us."

My heart raced … the firewall program. Was he crazy? Words were easier than actions. Our systems at Internal Security had safeguards to block access to applications, especially that one.

Silas saw my reaction and spoke. "Don't waste your time telling me the reasons you can't do this. I don't care, really. Do you want off-world? I'll grant your wife, unborn child, and you passage if you copy the firewall program and pay twenty thousand credits. A transport is ready to go as soon as you are."

While I sat there pondering all the reasons why it was a horrible idea, and knowing that my options were severely limited, Neco stepped forward.

As he twitched uncontrollably, he said, "Ma-Ma-Mace, this be da way to go. My cousin Rafael would tell you the same. The chamber smells like l-l-lemons, and you will be there if you don't do dis."

Silas glanced with a smirk at Neco. The Syndicate master knew he had me dangling over a fire, and there was nothing I could do but beg him to take me off before I burned up into ashes.

"What choice do I have?"

Silas insisted. "None."

"Well then, it looks like I'll be going back to work tomorrow."

Silas looked at me with satisfaction and said, "Good. Since we agree, Syndicate blood is how we seal a contract."

He pulled a small knife from his desk drawer. It had a serpent head of gold near the butt, and the snake body coiled around the handle up to the cross guard. The blade was beautiful and something I had not seen before. What blood did he mean? Silas saw my nervousness and waved his hand at me.

"Relax, all things within the Rogue Syndicate require blood. You'll understand in a moment."

He cut a small notch into his palm, only enough to draw drops of blood, then turned the handle to me and said, "You do the same, but hear me well, Mace Applegate. Once we shake hands and our blood meets, you're bound to this deal until its failure or completion."

My hand extended slowly. The blade was heavy.

"And what happens if I should fail?"

He studied me for a moment before answering, "The Rogue Syndicate seals these contracts in blood. Only blood can pay for their failure, whether it be yours or someone you love. We always get what's owed to us one way or another."

I pulled my hand back in fear as if a biting dog had snapped its fangs at me. He really was the Butcher of Lavlen. This situation was the most dangerous I had encountered in my life. How did it come to this? The mass graves of Dol'Arem from the Years of Forgetting stirred in my mind again. So much death before and now.

Arkie said, "If you want to leave the planet, you must seal the contract. It's our way. Shake his hand."

I slowly brought the knife to my hand and pressed the cold blade into my palm. Silas and his gold-outlined diamond teeth reflected off the steel. There wasn't a choice. As easy as breathing, the blade sliced my palm and my shoulders flinched from the cut. Silas hardly moved for his slice. How many contracts did he seal in blood?

We extended our hands slowly and shook. It felt strange with the warm thick liquid squishing against our palms. The deal was complete, signed in blood. Neco handed us a towel to clean ourselves. Silas said things that alarmed me, and something didn't seem right.

"The deal is official and complete, correct?"

Silas said, "Yes, our blood is a perpetual agreement now."

"So can I ask you a question without any consequence? Our deal's final, and I am bound to its arrangement."

Silas cocked his head curiously, and said, "You may ask your question, though the answer might be something you regret."

Part of me didn't want to ask. If what I believed was true, it would only anger me. I needed to know the answer.

"If I wasn't Mace Applegate and came into this room to meet with you. What would the price for my pregnant wife and me have been?"

His evil smirk returned once more and his eyes narrowed. With sureness in his voice, he said, "The cost? In that situation, it would be the standard rate I charge people trying to flee."

I pressed my question. "What's the standard rate to leave Dol'Arem?"

Silas laughed and answered in a deep, dreadful voice, "Ten thousand credits per person, of course …"

CHAPTER 20

Camp Uolmar

What color do you represent? (Isabel)

Processing through the camp's intake was nearly complete. Dolrinion doctors looked us over, made us shower, and gave us vaccinations to protect from illnesses common on this rogue world of Pomona. Going through that process, receiving the booster shots, reminded me of the Unification Civil War on Epsilon Prime.

Days after I visited my father at the state building in Athinia, just after the surprise attack, he made a decision. Dad asked me to travel with him to the relations station to visit an old friend there who was, at that time, the left seat representative for the Colonial Accord. Henry McWright tried to help us without doing so publicly, but there was always something about him that didn't sit well with me. Dad and I had vaccination boosters before going to the station. Once we arrived in the Colonial bubble in secret, Henry greeted us in the dock.

Henry said, "Liam Sideris, my good friend, it's a pleasure to see you but a sadness under these circumstances."

Dad wasn't himself. At that time, his eyes were heavy with dark lines, and he seemed frail. He said, "Henry, these are hard times for us indeed. We must be quick and get back as soon as possible."

Henry brought us to his residence in the Colonial bubble, where we spent the night. I was surprised to see a left seat representative living in the ambassador apartment, but that was irrelevant to the issues at the time. Over dinner, we talked about the war.

Dad said, "Henry, we're desperate at this point. Of the nine city-states on our side, Gelarhcret has already surrendered, and Elpis will fall soon enough. City-State Iskhoros currently occupies thirty percent of our northern border. We've established a battle line, but reinforcements from New-Sparta will arrive in weeks to drive us back further. We need troops and supplies."

Henry shook his head. "Liam, you know I would do anything to assist you. I owe you so much already, but the Colonial Accord and other Free Worlds inside the forum have declared non-intervention. This war is a Human Alliance issue—a resolution must come from the city-states. None of the Free Worlds wants to be involved in another war right now. The Lyons Pride has already rounded up two of the three dome representatives. Anyone inside the Alliance bubble against New-Sparta is missing. It's madness on this station."

My father twirled his food with a fork as a child would for several minutes as if he wasn't paying attention. "I'm desperate, Henry. We've already lost this war. The outcome is as clear to see as the food on your plate. All I want to do is buy time for my people, and those of our ally states. The volunteer groups from this station have already been to Epsilon Prime with refugee ships a few times. Any other resolution will take weeks to come to fruition. Millions more will die before then."

Henry sat thinking for some time. "There may be something I can do to help you. It will be highly illegal, and if discovered, I must deny any involvement."

"Anything, Henry," Dad cried out, sitting up high in his chair. "To save my people, I'll do anything."

Henry called to his head security officer. "Oliver, be a good lad and have the others wait in the den for me, would you?"

The security officers all left the room, and Henry studied me for a few moments, which made me uncomfortable. He had lust in his eyes, in my opinion, but later, when I mentioned this to Dad, he said it was ridiculous and that Henry was a man of honor.

Henry spoke. "From behind the curtain of Colonial politics, I've had various dealings with the Rogue Syndicate. An underboss of the Syndicate is here on the station. I can arrange a meeting for you."

My father looked confused, and said, "I don't understand. What can the Syndicate do for me? They're petty criminals. We have them on Epsilon Prime."

Henry laughed. "You have planet cells of the main organization on your world, not the leadership from Galma. The organization of the Syndicate on every Free, outer, and rogue world combined has a more robust economy than your entire city-state."

I remember saying, "Contracting the Rogue Syndicate to fight our war would be dishonorable to all our ally city-states. We would look like rogue-world overlords or worse, pirates."

Dad gazed at his plate once again, debating a response, and Henry cleared his throat. "War is a troublesome affair, and sometimes terrible things must happen to ensure there is a positive future."

Dad said, "We have no choice, Isabel. How it looks doesn't matter. All that matters is that we buy enough time for people to flee."

My memory faded away as a Dolrinion sentinel grumbled at me to move along. They let us retain our clothing, and that surprised me. The sentinels checking our belongings hardly did anything but lightly tap the clothes after we stripped down to shower. Smuggling something into this camp would be easy, based on what I saw.

Gideon, Jack, Ethan, Nina, and I all stood there naked, waiting to get our clothes back. Because of his size, Big Jack's tattoos made him look menacing. Those arms were massive, and his tattoos were solid black covering both biceps. Gideon had a tribal sun tattoo on his left arm with a beautifully designed star map around the sun. On each side of his chest was a tribal skull tattoo. One of the skulls had a bright colored red eye. That was the only different coloring of any tattoo on his body, so it seemed like that skull signified something important. More elaborate tattoo shapes had been created down his ribs, all the tattoo coloring in black. When I looked up, Gideon was watching me with his obnoxious smile.

"See something you like there, Izzy?"

I rolled my eye and turned away so my empty eye socket faced him. Sentinels gave us our clothes back. I felt uneasy hearing Gideon call me Izzy. We got dressed and walked out of the building down a narrow path to the camp entrance.

A sentinel escorting us spoke in a thick voice. "Slaves of the Offensive, welcome to your new home, Camp Uolmar."

We moved closer to the camp entrance; a sizeable fenced wall surrounded the entire camp. The fence was at least six meters tall with barbed wire at the top. Spaced out evenly across the fencing were guard towers with huge spotlights at the top.

Next to the entrance, six dead bodies with flies buzzing on their rotting flesh were nailed spread-eagled to the wood. Some looked fresh, and others looked like they had been there rotting for weeks, the skin near their lips stripped back to the nose and chin. The sentinel stopped us at the entrance and pointed to the bodies.

"Look here at these slaves. There are only two things that will put you on this wall next to them. If you try to escape or cause any harm to sentinels, this wall will be your final resting place. Provide for the Offensive and the Offensive will provide for you. Work in the mines by day, relax, eat well, and sleep in comfort by night. Do you all understand?"

No one answered right away, and the sentinel raised his voice. "I said, do you understand?"

Gideon smiled and saluted the sentinel. "We understand you, commander, slave master, sir. We'll provide all that you need and not challenge your authority, sir."

The sentinel waddled over to Gideon, looking up at him with scorn. He said with zero emotion, "I am not a commander."

He turned back onto the path accompanied by the mechanical noises of his body armor, driving us forward.

Sand covered the ground and cactuses and random patches of palm trees were scattered in the distance. Though the appearance was that of a desert, the temperature was moderate.

We walked into camp through multiple levels of fencing. To our left was a medical building constructed from popup materials common among Free Worlds' military services. Several slaves stood outside the building. Some looked injured, and others appeared as though their injury might be inside their head and not a physical one.

A man with a long beard was against the fence near the medical building peering through the fencing. He had massive broad shoulders and thick braided long hair. The bearded man was tall but not as tall as Jack. I doubted anyone else was that tall. The man's expression reminded me of the crazed pirate woman on the refugee ship with the hot coiled brander. His eyes were wide open and he stared wildly at us.

He shouted in our direction, "Fresh meat for the grinder! Fresh meat for the grinder! Fresh meat for the grinder!"

That man had brown tattoos on his entire upper chest and different shapes and designs across his chest and arms. We ignored him, continuing forward, and Gideon looked over, smirking at the man.

As we passed, the man grew angry and asked, "What color do you represent? Which of the three Bs do you fight for? What's your color? Answer me."

I got closer to Nina and said, "He's a pirate like you."

Nina shook her head. "Not like us. Did you see his tattoos? He's of the Brown from Martoosh."

She had already explained the three pirate worlds to me and their colors, black, brown and burgundy.

"Your rival, your enemy."

"Yes."

Once we were inside the main camp area with its rows of portable popup bunk buildings, the escorting sentinel spoke.

"Find a bunk with open beds. The work crews are already out for the day and will return in an hour or two. Once they get back, you can learn your responsibilities. All of you will be on the picking line tomorrow."

Gideon smiled and waved at the sentinel. "We are here to obey."

He bowed his head, keeping his eyes on the sentinel. He was clearly cynical with his exaggeration. The sentinel stared at Gideon with narrowed eyes, looking unsure if he was being mocked or praised. After a few moments, he muttered to himself and waddled away.

Ethan asked, "What's the plan, Captain?"

Gideon snapped his head at Ethan, holding his smile, and answered, "We find a bunk, of course."

Big Jack put his arm around Ethan and added, "We look for someone with tattoos from Draco. That will be a good start."

Jack talked to Ethan like he was his younger brother. We moved through the rows of bunk buildings observing our surroundings. Slaves were maintaining the bunks, and after some time, Gideon spotted someone with black tribal tattoos like his.

"Ah, there we go. Some Draco blood."

He approached the older man who seemed frightened to see us. Gideon said, "Shipmate of the Black, Draco is with you."

The feeble man tried to run away but fell over some buckets. Jack picked him up with ease and spoke, raising his voice. "What are you doing, pirate?"

The man shook as he replied, "We aren't allowed to say those words anymore. Not here. Not anymore. Ezra will kill you if he hears you speak the words of Draco."

Gideon turned red and narrowed his eyes as he stepped to the shaking man and slapped him across the face.

Nina said, "Pirate, you're speaking to a captain of Draco. Stand up and show some respect."

The man took a few moments to stand and calm his nerves.

He wiped the blood from his lip. "I'm sorry, sir. Things have been different around here for the last few months. My name is Matthew. I was a shipmate of the *Midhalla* before Force Command Burning Star took us."

Gideon asked, "Where's your captain?"

Matthew shook his head. "No captain, not anymore. Ezra killed him."

Big Jack asked, "What about your first mate?"

"No first mate, not anymore."

Nina added, "Ezra killed him?"

Matthew nodded.

Gideon appeared unconcerned. He rolled his eye and sighed. "Ok, Matty, who's running your crew now?"

"Geoff, our ship quartermaster, but ..."

Gideon stepped closer, bending his neck to gaze into Matthew's eyes. He took his hand with the mechanical fingers and moved Matthew's lips as if Matt was talking, but Gideon spoke.

"This is where you finish your sentence and leave nothing out, pirate."

Matthew said, "Geoff's running things with us now, but he listens to Ezra and does whatever the Pirates of the Brown tell him to do."

Gideon stepped away from our group for a moment and paced back and forth in thought. "Would Ezra happen to be tall, thick of build, braided hair with a long beard? Seems to be a bit touched in the head?"

Matthew frantically nodded so fast I could hear his neck cracking. "Yes. That's him. He spends most days in the medical building when everyone else is working. The only time he goes to the mines is when he wants to do something bad. His Brown Pirates fill his daily quota, so the sentinels don't care."

I spoke. "You said Ezra has been killing your fellow pirates since he got here. Why don't the Dolrinion guards intervene?"

Matthew frowned at me after looking at my arms. "You aren't of Draco."

Gideon said, "She's under my protection—answer her."

Matthew obeyed. "No, the sentinels don't care what happens between slaves in camp. People die every day, and new slaves come to fill the losses. The Dolrinions keep to themselves as long as we don't mess with them or the quotas."

Gideon looked at his subordinates and then back to Matthew. It was as if his eyes spoke to Nina and Jack, and they understood their captain.

"Shipmate Matthew. You now report to me. I'm the highest-ranking Draco pirate here. You'll do nothing that Geoff tells you without clearing it with me first. Is that understood?"

Matthew nodded again.

Gideon said, "Good. Bring us to your bunk then, and we'll wait for everyone to return. It's long past time that some things change around here."

We made our way to the bunk, following Matthew, and I asked Nina, "What did he mean when he said a shipmate of the *Midhalla*? It seemed like that point had great significance."

"Ships and captains are well known to all from pirate worlds. The name of a vessel is important. Draco is large, with settlements and population centers everywhere. The best way of knowing a pirate is by the fame of the captain and ship they follow."

Matthew pointed to a popup bunk building and said, "Here, Captain. Our bunk with all that remains of the Draco Pirates." We walked inside, and Matthew continued. "Captain, might I ask your name and ship?"

Gideon smiled and said, "Everyone in this bunk will hear the name at the same time. No ruining the surprise, Matty."

The bunk beds were arranged in rows and the space was cooled by ceiling fans. They had a small pantry area, showers, secluded bathrooms, and four walls with a roof. That made me happy to see—some privacy at last.

I asked Nina, "How do your tattoos work? I noticed Gideon has many. You have a few, and Matthew only seems to have one or two. The crazed Ezra's entire upper body is tattooed."

"We earn them. Pirates from the three worlds only get new ink for an accomplishment, like raiding a ship, killing an enemy, finding great wealth, or any task that benefits the crew and ship. Once an objective is achieved and witnessed by shipmates, the pirate earns colors. The more tattoos you have, the greater your renown. Those black-covered arms you saw on Jack took him twenty years to accomplish. They are our badges."

"So that Pirate of the Brown Ezra is a formidable enemy if he has such numbers of tattoos covering his body."

Nina said, "Yes, we've never heard of him before, but those tattoos say everything we need to know about his abilities."

More time passed, and we heard a commotion from outside. The work crews were returning from the mines. The bunk doors opened, and tired and dirty slaves came inside. They were diverse in age, sex, and race. All were covered in black soot, and they were in desperate need of a shower. They stared at the six of us oddly, the whites in their eyes standing out in their sooty faces.

A man stepped forward. "Who are you, and why are you in our bunk?"

Gideon smirked and replied with irony, "Before me stand the true colors of Draco. Look at the black covering their bodies, my shipmates. A sight to behold and something the Black Skull Admiral himself would be proud to see."

The question-asking man said, "I am—"

Before he could continue, Gideon talked over him. "I know very well who you are, Geoffrey, quartermaster of the *Midhalla*."

"And who might you be?"

Gideon strolled from one side of the bunk room to the other, observing the pirate slaves before him, and then answered with confident poise.

"Captain Gideon, at your service."

Some mumbled to each other, and others' eyes opened wide. After some commotion, Geoff said, "Gideon of the *Viathon*?"

"Not anymore."

The low talking continued between the slaves. Gideon and Jack removed their shirts, revealing huge numbers of tattoos. The bunk slaves appeared impressed by the overwhelming number of marks on both Gideon's and Jack's bodies.

"I am now Captain Gideon of the *Abernath*."

Geoff paused. "If you are Gideon, then he must be Jack, the Giant."

Jack's head went high into the air, and he bellowed, "I am he, first mate of the *Abernath* to Captain Gideon."

"The deeds of both of you are legendary, but I don't understand, why leave your father's ship?"

Gideon answered, "It was time to seek out riches and earn colors without my father's shadow behind me."

His comments reminded me of my experience on Epsilon Prime living in my father's shadow for my entire life. The Daughter of Athinia is never spoken of without Liam Sideris coming to the speaker's mind.

Geoff giggled to himself and said, "Much good that did. You're here with us as a slave now."

Some of the other pirates laughed too. Gideon's expression turned to malice, and he walked towards Geoff the same way he did to me on the refugee ship when I thought he would walk right through me. Geoff raised his hands, but Gideon stopped before walking into him.

"Take your shirt off, Geoffrey." Geoff tried to object, but Gideon covered his mouth and yelled, "I said, take off your shirt now!"

Geoff complied; only three tattoos were visible. They were small in comparison to those of Gideon and his crew.

Gideon looked Geoff over and said, "Now I see you have a right to mock me because of your accomplishments." Looking down at his own body covered with tattoos, he continued. "You are now all under my command since your captain and first mate are dead. Jack and I will be running things, and things are going to change. Is that understood?"

Only half the pirates replied with faint unconvincing answers.

Jack raised his voice. "The captain has given you an order. Speak up like the Black Blood of Draco or by the eternal flame I'll be cutting tongues out tonight."

All shouted, "Understood."

Gideon called out, "Shipmates of the Black, Draco is with you."

The pirates all returned his call, including Nina and Jack. "Draco is with us all."

Geoff did nothing, and Gideon noticed.

"What about them two?" Geoff pointed to Ethan and me, looking resentful.

Gideon said, "Ethan here wants to join us and will earn his ink shortly. Isabel," he turned to me, "she's under my protection and will be left alone."

Some time passed, and after other conversations, people started to lie down in their beds. I took a bottom bunk with Nina taking the top above me. Gideon and Jack were next to us, Gideon on the top. Before I closed my eyes, Gideon made an obnoxious noise to get my attention.

I snapped, "What do you want?"

He chuckled with a smile. "I just wanted to tell you to sleep tight and don't let the Pomona bugs bite."

My eyes narrowed at him. "I really do hate you."

Gideon laughed louder and rolled over. An hour later, I woke to Nina sneaking out of her bed. She was focused towards the other end of the bunk room, where Geoff was sneaking out of the main entrance. I got out of bed and followed her to the door.

She stole a look outside. After a few moments, we both went out and followed Geoff, who carefully snuck halfway to the other side of camp, moving through the shadows. Ezra stood near a bunk waiting for him, and the two spoke for several minutes. Ezra appeared annoyed by whatever Geoff was telling him, and I realized Matthew was correct when he said their quartermaster had betrayed them.

Nina whispered, "We have the proof we need. Let's get back to the others."

We carefully crept back to our bunk and went inside. To my surprise, everyone was up and waiting. It was startling to see all eyes looking at me when we opened the door.

Nina spoke to Gideon. "He was with Ezra telling him everything that's happened, no doubt."

Gideon raised his chin, grinning. "Pirates of Draco, Quartermaster

Geoffrey has betrayed the Black and will be dealt with swiftly. Everyone be ready."

Sometime later, the door to the bunk creaked open. Geoff stepped inside, and the lights came on. A pirate closed the door so that Geoff couldn't escape, and some others restrained him. After a brief struggle, he stopped fighting, breathing heavily like a panting dog. That was fear on his face.

Gideon stepped between two pirates and said, "You've betrayed the sacred code of Draco. By my authority as a Captain of the Black, you've lost your right to wear our colors."

The pirates restraining Geoff ripped off his clothes, leaving him naked. They pushed him to the floor, his chest facing up, and held his arms out wide. He cried in terror.

"Please, no. Don't do this. I had no choice—Ezra would have killed us all."

Big Jack pulled a large knife from one of the trunks next to the bunk beds and Geoff screamed louder, flailing uncontrollably. Gideon took the knife and slowly approached the frightened man.

The captain of Draco spoke with confidence for all to hear, "Geoff of the *Midhalla*. The Black of Draco is too good for you now. You're banished from our service and must give back what doesn't belong to you any longer. Our color is sacred, and you do not deserve it anymore."

Gideon carefully sliced at Geoff's flesh, stripping away the skin from the biggest tattoo on his body. Small flaps of skin loosened with each cut. Blood soaked the floor and squirted everywhere. The first tattoo was no more. In its place was exposed muscle tissue and red gore.

The captain handed the knife to Jack, who cut away the second black tattoo of Draco. Halfway through the slow slicing, Geoff passed out from shock or blood loss. Jack finished fast and handed the blood-soaked knife back to Gideon, holding the sliced skin in his hand.

Captain Gideon walked to Ethan, handing him the blade. The boy looked down at the knife and over to Jack with a frown.

Gideon said, "Ethan, if you wanted to join my crew, this is how you prove yourself to me. Complete this task, and tomorrow the first ink of black will be yours."

Ethan slowly took the knife and gazed at Geoff's body. His breath was heavy and sweat seemed to appear out of thin air. Everyone watched his hesitation. Big Jack walked over to the boy and whispered in his ear. After Jack's words of encouragement, Ethan bent down, pushing the sharp edges of the knife into Geoff's skin. All the pirate spectators, including Gideon, Jack, and Nina, pounded their chests in unison while watching Ethan's work.

Strips of flesh peeled back as the boy held the flap of skin with one hand and the blade in the other. Each piece he stripped away was tossed to the floor. All I could think, watching that horrific display, was what the hell was wrong with us? Even in a place like this, people couldn't help themselves from acts of extreme viciousness. Humanity was barbaric, and we were nothing but savages.

CHAPTER 21

Copying the Firewall

Subroutines and ulterior motives (Mace)

After leaving the building with Silas and getting on a bus to return to my hotel, I logged on to the display screen and pulled my vacation day for the coming week. When I arrived back at the hotel room, Jamie slapped my face, crying hysterically.

"Mace, what happened to you? When you didn't come back, I thought someone had killed you."

Jamie's words confused me. Why would the operators kill me when placing me under arrest? She was flooded with emotion, and her hysteria affected her rationality. I explained everything that had happened and especially what Silas said and did to me. Jamie was agitated by his games. It didn't matter, because we had dipped into our savings in the hotel. We were down to sixteen thousand credits; even if we were regular employees trying to get off-world, we wouldn't have the twenty thousand. If I could get the firewall program from Internal Security and return it to Silas, he should let us leave. Hopefully, it would be enough with our diminished funds to buy us two tickets off the planet. I was taking a chance, but what choice was there?

I went back to work. When I arrived, some of my fellow employees stared at me. Most knew about my vacation time. *They're all nosy and should mind their own business.* Outside the Department of Internal Security was a giant statue of Genesis Foundation's CFO Victor Lavlen, standing to one side and grasping both lapels. He gazed up at the sky. Our current CFO, Pont, would get a statue when she died too. Critical Employees of our Corporation got recognition like a statue or a building named after them. The only thing I'd receive if things didn't work out was a lemon-scented chamber.

Once on my floor, I went to my desk. Rafael saw me and came over with a perplexed look on his face. We hadn't seen each other since he dropped me off. It was too risky to speak on the phone.

"What are you doing here?"

"Had to come in. There was no choice. We don't have enough credits to leave."

"Dude, Ness and I can loan you the credits. How much do you need?"

I looked down with a resigned smile. "Thirty thousand credits."

He gave me a blank look, and that was all the answer I needed. Who had that many extra credits lying around?

I pushed an external drive from my pocket into the computer at my desk. "The only way we're getting away is if I do something for them."

"This is really dangerous. The Corporation's going to catch you. They oversee these systems carefully." Rafael's gaze wandered around the office.

I looked up at him and said, "What choice is there?"

He shook his head and left. Based on how worried he has been from the start, it was probably the last time we would ever talk. Coming back to work to access this program was pushing the boundaries of our arrangement. These actions were treason on a spectacular level. He had a family to worry about, and they couldn't suffer for his mistakes in helping me.

Once logged on to our Federate computer terminal, I brought up the defense-grid program that took one year of my life to design and almost ruined my marriage.

I used to upload the defense program into a simulation system for testing.

In another cloud folder was the firewall program used for cybersecurity here on Dol'Arem. There was an entire employee floor dedicated to the firewall program in our building; they maintained it daily. I couldn't just copy the program from the cloud and drag it over to my external drive. That would immediately alert my computer to the system core, and security employees would be at my desk within minutes. No, for me to do this, I needed to drag the program into the simulation system and act as if I was trying to run tests on both programs working with each other. We had completed these simulation tests over the past year, so I had an idea of how to justify my actions if questioned.

With my hand on the computer mouse, looking at the screen, I realized that if it didn't work, the chamber would be the last thing I ever saw. My nerves came back, creeping up my spine like a rising tide, and my right hand shook. I clicked on the firewall program and dragged it over to the simulator. Once I let go, there was no turning back. Releasing the mouse made a sound like a nuclear explosion in my head. But something was wrong. A red box popped up stating that a supervisor level of grade twenty-eight or higher must authorize that program's use in the simulator. An alert went to Dennis.

Butterflies filled my stomach, and my hands became clammy. Sweat seeped out of nowhere all over me, and I was breathing heavily. I needed to calm myself before he got here. *Relax, Mace.*

Dennis turned the corner to my cubicle and said, "Mace, I was surprised that you took back a vacation day today. Now my PDD's gone off, saying you were trying to run a simulation with the firewall program. What's going on?"

I swallowed deeply. "Good morning, Dennis, great to see you. Yes, I took back a vacation day because I couldn't sleep thinking about the monthly system update my grid program will perform for updates. There are areas of code that will conflict with the internal securities firewall."

Dennis looked at me like I was speaking a language he didn't understand. "We ran firewall simulations already, didn't we?"

"We did, but the update log portion was the last part I wrote after everything else was already working properly. We never looked to see if the firewall would conflict with the defense-grid updates. You can check with Rafael if you want, but this is the only reason I needed to come in. One year of my blood, sweat, and tears went into designing this. If it failed after the first month because of the firewall, well, we would all look bad. That wouldn't be good, especially after all of us receiving that positive notation from the vice president of planetary defense."

Dennis's frown and hesitation showed that he was confused. "Mace, you're the best employee that has ever worked under me. Look at your dedication to the Corporation. You can have access to the firewall program. I'll send a report to Internal Security."

Dennis swiped his badge and pressed his thumb to the fingerprint detector. The red screen on my computer changed to green and displayed "Access Granted." Dennis patted my back and walked away with a smile from ear to ear.

The hard part was over. If Dennis were smarter and less lazy, he would have reviewed my grid program himself and seen that what I stated wasn't true. The monthly system updates wouldn't interfere with the firewall at all. There was a subprogram I put into the main defense program used by Rafael and me to add notes that we could refer to from time to time. A hidden program inside the main program. Once I dragged the firewall program into the simulation system, the entire code was visible.

With a few clicks, the firewall copied into the sub-note program, so it would not be detected at all. Another click for the simulator and it came back clear. Anyone looking shouldn't know what I did. A copy of the defense-grid program was now on my external drive. Copying that program wasn't an issue since I had all of that information on my secure home system anyway.

Accomplishing that task brought a great wave of relief over me even though my nerves were going crazy. There was no point in arousing any suspicion. I acted as if it was a regular workday for the rest of that morning.

It was lunch and time to go. My coworkers knew I went out for lunch once a week. That was my intention today. No one needed to know I wouldn't be returning ever again. Before I cleared the doorway, someone spoke to get my attention, and it frightened me.

Dennis approached me. "Mace, I need you to come with me for a moment."

The clamminess in my fingers was back, and my heart was pounding out of my chest. There was no way around whatever Dennis wanted. Running away wasn't an option because operators were throughout the building.

"Is everything ok?"

Dennis raised his head. "Come with me, and you'll see."

We went down the hall, and Rafael peered up from his cubicle wall, looking worried. We stepped into a conference room where Tammy, our manager, sat at the head of the table. *They've caught me!* I frantically looked left and right to see if there were operators in the room.

Tammy glanced up from her PDD and waved her hand over the table. "Mace, please have a seat."

I hesitated for a moment but complied, and Dennis sat across from me at the other end of the table.

"Dennis has informed me of what you did today."

My chest pounded so hard it sounded like musical drums. My breath was heavier, but I did my best to calm myself.

She continued. "Anyone from Genesis Foundation who's that worried about their work to leave vacation just to check the program is a model employee."

Dennis said, "That's right, Mace. I told her that you came in today to run some simulations regarding your monthly update program. Tammy was very impressed with your dedication."

If my idiot supervisor had only added a few extra sentences to what he said to Tammy, there wouldn't be praise coming from her mouth. He left out the bit about me checking the firewall program with my program's monthly updates. Tammy was smarter than Dennis, and she would've known something was off with my reasoning.

Tammy said, "We're recommending you to our director for grade-level promotion."

"Promotion?" My mouth opened wide.

"Yes. You have proved yourself in our division, and now the time has come for you to take the next step in our sister company."

If only things were different. Jamie was grade twenty-eight, and for me to have the same grade-level would be such a big deal if we stayed here. If this promotion had come months ago and we applied for a birth permit, our baby would be born here on Dol'Arem in a stable environment as well as love and a good family. It didn't matter. Those were dreams because the current situation wasn't changing, and even with the promotion, without the permit, Jamie would have no choice but to give up the baby. *We must leave and never look back.*

I gave a fake smile and said, "Thank you both. This means the world to me. My wife Jamie will be thrilled to hear this."

Dennis grinned. "It's a big deal for you both. Maybe now the time's come for children. Family Management would quickly approve you with two twenty-eight-grade-level employees in the same household."

I nodded but wanted to cry at his words. "You're right. That's a discussion I shall be having with Jamie immediately."

Part of me wished we could pawn off her pregnancy with the doctors and just stay on Dol'Arem, but that would never work. With one hundred percent accuracy, the Corporation doctors would be able to determine the date of conception. We would have still broken the Corporate Policy.

Tammy stood, followed by Dennis and me. We all shook hands and left the conference room together. Rafael was looking over his cubicle in our direction. My thumb went into the air to try and calm his anxiety. He disappeared behind the cubicle wall.

The stairwell was the best option to leave, and maybe it would help my anxiety to walk. The stairwell door was closing behind me, but before securing all the way, it swung open and slammed against the wall. The sound startled me. To my surprise, Dominic came barreling through the door. His face was red, and he had watery, narrowed eyes. Dom grabbed my shirt and pushed me into the opposite wall.

Spit flew from his mouth as he spoke. "I got demoted a grade-level because of you."

"Dom, I had no choice. If I hadn't raised my hand in that control room, my job would have been in jeopardy. I have been at my grade-level for years. They wouldn't demote me for missing the error. They would terminate me."

Dominic punched me in the stomach and yelled, "You could've deleted it without saying anything. My wife wants to leave me now because we'll have to wait at least five years to have kids."

The punch was painful; the shock traveled up my chest and I gasped for air. After recovering, I said, "You know as well as I do that someone's always watching what we do. I had Dennis and Tammy behind me that night breathing down my neck."

Dominic studied me for a second but changed course and punched me again, this time in the face.

I cried, "The people you should really be mad at are your supervisor and manager, not me. They reviewed your code and found nothing wrong. It's their fault, not mine. But what does it matter? They'll both be in the chamber three months from now, and you know that."

He let go of me and leaned against the wall gazing over at the other side of the stairwell landing. Another employee opened the door.

I waved my hand and said, "Everything's ok here. We're friends just messing around. Have a great day."

The employee left, and Dominic walked to the door. Before opening it and walking out, he turned to me with sad eyes. "I hate this Corporation so much and wish I could leave. Look at what they do to us. We're just as bad as a rogue world."

He left me to my pain, and after a few deep breaths, it was time to continue down the stairwell. With a fresh cut on my head and pain in my stomach, the main entrance was a bad idea. The operators would notice the wounds on my face and question me.

There was a fire exit at the bottom of this stairwell. At the bottom, I swiped my badge to open the door. Genesis Foundation would reprimand me for using this door on my next scheduled workday, but it didn't matter. I'd never return.

Auto-drive, in a case like this, was a blessing. As the vehicle pulled away, in the rear-view mirror I saw a MERC Guild transport truck parked outside the building. That was odd; the Guild hardly ever came to the Department of Internal Security. Especially this building because it was so secure. Guild trucks were easy to spot because of the large opening in the back for transporting their mongrels. There was a sizeable mounted weapon on the top of the truck and flashing lights. The coloring matched their Corin-steel chest plates with glowing green lines and black flecks. They didn't make the trucks with real Corin steel because there wasn't enough metal in existence.

Once back at the hotel and in our room, Jamie asked, "Did you get it?"

I smiled, pulled the external drive from a pocket, and said, "Yes, I did. It was a piece of cake."

Jamie stared at my head. "Except for the marks on your face. What happened? Did someone hit you?"

The fresh wounds were tender to the touch. "It was unrelated. Dominic confronted me in the hall. He was angry because of what I told you about."

"That's ridiculous. It was his error, not yours. If I were a supervisor in your division, he would lose his job immediately," Jamie snapped, looking irritated.

I couldn't help but smirk. "That's the grade-level twenty-eight Jamie I love. You sound like yourself again."

Jamie smiled at me while inspecting the cuts on my face. She kissed my cheek and held me. It felt good to be close to her. It would be great to stay longer and spend time with my wife, but there wasn't any. The quicker this firewall was turned over to Silas, the faster we could leave Dol'Arem and get away from the Corporation. I wasted no time and left the hotel, driving to the laundromat where Neco worked.

Neco was inside and saw me in my vehicle. He closed the store and came over, saying, "Y-y-you got it?" As usual, he twitched while he talked.

"Yes. Do you want me to park my car for the bus?"

Neco shook his head and said, "Nah, man. We drive through the Hollow today. N-n-no problem."

He got inside my vehicle, and we drove to the building on R Street and S Avenue. Once we arrived, Neco directed me to park in the back near the loading dock. There was a large rolling door there where trucks could pull in. Neco pounded on the door, and it raised. Several employees with intense-looking faces were there, holding rifles, like last time. We walked through a hallway that led back into the storage area. Again, I saw shadows on the upper catwalk, standing guard in the dark. I sat at the desk and waited for Silas.

A strange noise came from a different back room. The sound reminded me of someone cleaning a rug by smacking it with a paddle. Every time the noise echoed, a grunting sound followed. It was a person making that noise. Was he working out punching a heavy bag? The echo continued for another five minutes until eventually the back door opened.

Silas walked through the door, followed by Syndicate members. The Bum Bum wore a purple suit with pinstripes and a black button-down dress shirt. Blood covered his hands and forearms, soaking through the blended fabric.

He'd need to get rid of that expensive outfit, but I didn't think he cared based on his expression. It was a look I'd never seen before in a person. He seemed almost possessed with focus and hate. It was terrifying. *The Butcher of Lavlen indeed.*

When Silas saw me, he smiled, his diamond-studded teeth sparkling in the light. He extended his hand to shake mine but pulled it back when he saw the blood drenching his hands.

"Mace Applegate, back so soon? Hopefully, for your sake, you come bearing gifts." Silas turned to one of his Syndicate lackeys. "Go find Arkie. Tell her to bring her computer at once."

My mouth got me into trouble. "Is everything ok?"

Silas let out an odd sound, halfway between a laugh and grunt. "Oh, this? It's nothing for you to worry about. From time to time, Syndicate cells on the Free Worlds go through changes the same way they do on Galma.

297

Sometimes others in our establishment don't accept those changes. The Syndicate rewards those who take what they want by force. It shows a drive and desire that the bosses on Galma appreciate. Someone here who works for me was feeling ambitious, hoping to change leadership in our cell. Obviously that didn't happen. As I told you before, Syndicate blood is how we seal our contracts. Leadership positions come to those who take it with blood too. What I did to him ..." Silas paused, looking at the dried blood on his fists for a moment. "Is for all to see."

"For all to see what?"

Silas raised his chin and smirked. "Who's in charge here."

Arkie came into the room, walking past Neco to the desk. She placed the computer on the table and turned it to me.

"Add the firewall program to my script."

"It will take me a few minutes. I'll need to write some subroutine code."

Arkie rolled her eyes and said, "Duh. Do what you need to do."

I inserted my external drive to the laptop and started the code-writing process. Arkie hovered behind me, watching everything I was doing. With the drive in place, all I needed to do was hold Control and push S. I'd finish this task but had every intention of anonymously sending a copy of the entire skimming program to friends at Internal Security. Employees in my building could fix the firewall to block this program once Jamie and I were safely on Galma.

Silas leaned closer. "Arkie, is he doing everything correctly?"

"As far as I can tell, yes. He types extremely fast and writes code better than anyone I have ever seen before."

Arkie's attention went to Silas as she spoke, and it gave me the time I needed to save the file to my external drive.

Silas's glittering diamond teeth seemed to brighten. "Our intelligence on him was correct. You see, Mace, this is why I couldn't charge you and your wife twenty thousand credits to leave the planet. I knew your skills would work better for the Syndicate in this way."

I gave him a fake gesture of acceptance. If he knew that this program would stop working in a month or two when I sent the code and this building location to my sister company, he'd probably kill me right now. After completion, Arkie simulated a successful test run. The excitement was plain to see on her face.

Silas laughed and said, "Mace, you've done it. Now, after your credit transfer, the deal is done."

I stared at him cautiously. "I only have sixteen thousand credits. We were unable to secure the additional four thousand you needed."

His smile faded quickly, and he looked at me like I was an animal that just urinated on his kitchen floor.

Arkie said, "He did more for us than four thousand credits' worth, sir. By tomorrow afternoon, we'll have millions in our off-world accounts. Galma is going to honor us for these deeds."

Silas lightly banged his fist against his desk like he was debating whether to break my neck or let me leave. Another moment or two went by, and he smiled again. "Ok, I'll let it slide because of your accomplishment." He glanced at the blood on his arms again. "And frankly, my hands are tired of beating people to death for one day. Neco, bring it over."

Neco came with a PDD in his hand and gave it to Silas, who continued. "This is an off-network PDD. Tomorrow it will ring. The voice on the other end will tell you where to go and when to be there. By this time tomorrow night, you'll be on a ship traveling to the rogue world, Galma. When you're there, make sure you visit the Stumble Inn. It's the best social club in all occupied space. The prostitutes are superb, and the gambling tables with live music will make time pass by like you're in a dream. The owner and I are close friends."

I grabbed the external drive and placed it in my pocket along with the off-network PDD. I pulled my lips in at this butcher of a boss. "Our deal is done?"

Silas kept scratching dry blood from his knuckles and lifted his head. "It is, once you place your thumb on Arkie's PDD for the credit transfer. Now we're friends, Mace Applegate. You've done the Rogue Syndicate an excellent service. Shake my hand and be on your way."

We extended our hands to shake, but a loud explosion rocked the front of the building before they met. It felt like an earthquake. I instinctively took cover on the side of his desk. Gunshots rang out near the outer front door with the broken lamp and external hinges. Syndicate members were screaming and scrambling all over through the chaos.

Silas yelled to his members, "Everyone to the front, now!"

Another Syndicate employee came from the front, running to the back room with the shipping containers and overhead catwalks. He was yelling out with fear.

"It's a MERC Guild ..."

He couldn't finish his sentence because a mongrel had caught him and bit down on his head. Blasts of gunfire in the background rang through the open room. The humongous beast shook the Syndicate member's body from side to side until his neck snapped. With one more violent shake, the mongrel tossed the employee to the ground like yesterday's trash.

The mongrel lifted its head high and stood proud on all four legs in an undaunted posture as Syndicate employees closed in. It looked in our direction with a growl. Foam and blood dripped from its jowls. Even with the dangers around, the beast was unconcerned. Why should that monstrous animal care? He was the pufferfish in that room, and all of us were small guppies.

The mongrel had thick chest armor of Corin steel, and an auto gun with high-caliber rounds was clear to see as sparks jetted off the metal armor from bullets impacting the surface. Big slabs of the steel lined the animal's back for additional protection. After a few more rounds hit the armor, the beast dashed away like a grasshopper jumping through high weeds. The mongrel was so fast the shooters couldn't keep up with it, hitting the concrete floor instead.

Silas got my attention. "Mace, leave now. Go out of the back door. The Guild's here for me."

I heeded his warning and ran to the back wall. Before walking through the doorway, I turned. Up on the catwalk was a MERC agent engaging the shadow lookouts up there. He fired his rifle and Syndicate weapons shot back. Flashes lit up the area, making everything visible for brief seconds between the shots.

The agent's skills in battle far exceeded those of the Syndicate members. He engaged one target at a time, snapping his rifle to the next as if he had done this a thousand times before. He moved methodically, firing and moving from one to the next, and appeared never to miss. The mongrel below the catwalk leaped from one dark corner to another, biting chunks of flesh from employees while its auto guns shot at others.

Arkie grabbed her laptop and ran past me, screaming, "You better get out of here."

Neco followed her, running by, and he took my hand to lead me away.

"M-M-Mace, follow me."

He pulled my arm, leading into the back hallway, but before clearing the doorway, he fell forward. Bullets had struck his back and passed through his chest. He hit the ground, blood covering his body.

Without twitching, Neco said, "Leave this place. Go now."

I looked into the warehouse one last time and saw Silas jump onto the mongrel's back. He ripped at the auto guns, removing them with enormous force. The former amateur fighter showed his previous skillset, locking the mongrel into a headlock with his powerful arms.

The beast fell to the ground, trying to shake its head to free itself without success. As powerful as the mongrel was, it couldn't shake free of the Bum Bum. For a moment, it appeared that Silas would subdue the animal, but his assured expression changed to shock when a long blade pushed through the gold-plated diamond teeth.

The agent was behind Silas driving his knife through the back of Silas's head and out of his mouth at the other end. His diamond teeth glittered like snowflakes as they gracefully fell to the cold concrete floor covered in blood. There were still Syndicate members everywhere, and more gunshots buzzed out through the room. Both agent and mongrel took cover behind shipping containers.

That violence was more than enough for one lifetime. I ran through the hallway where Arkie had fled moments earlier, and got into my vehicle outside, taking manual control as I peeled out of the parking lot. When I got to the front where the broken lamp post and the thick metal door once were, I saw a MERC transport on the curb near the entrance. A considerable hole replaced the metal front door where the agent gained entry. Local low-grade-level employees crowded nearby, keeping their distance and observing the bodies and smoke, the sound of gunfire ringing through the streets from the battle still raging inside.

The drive home felt like a lifetime. All I could do was run the events through my mind. Silas had said the Guild was there for him. In the hotel room, Jamie listened to everything that happened. We checked out with our untraceable cash card. By the next day, we'd be on our way to Galma. After what we'd been through, we deserved a reprieve. With any luck, nothing else should go wrong. I knew for sure that I hoped never to return to the Hollow again in my life.

CHAPTER 22

Open Session in the Forum

A night for all to see (Henry)

"There's no reason to worry now, girls. Henry and the other representatives have corrected the processing methods of those refugees down in the dock." Alyssa wore a self-assured smile.

Beth, the mildly attractive wife of our ambassador to this bubble, said, "Well, still, it's a dreadful affair. Those primitive rogue-world barbarians coming up here the way they did to kill such high numbers was terrible. Molly and Paavo have done so much through their organization to help the people on Gliese."

Molly grinned. "To date, our transport ships have brought ten thousand refugees. We've also donated enough food for two hundred and fifty thousand people living on the Federate side of the planet."

Molly and Paavo were the owners of a nonprofit organization that helped sustain rogue and outer-world populations who were less fortunate and unable to provide essential services for their people. The reason Molly was smiling was that for every ten credits received in donations, they only used half for these services. The rest went into her and her husband's pockets.

Hadlee raised an eyebrow and pulled her thin lips in. "Why bring those primitive rogue-world people here to the station? Don't we have enough issues with the minor citizens of the main cylinder?"

Hadlee was a three-times-divorced and once-widowed billionaire who collected most of that fortune from her past husbands. She was now an entrepreneur and private investor for the main cylinder. Though Hadlee was in her late sixties, she always surrounded herself with younger, more attractive men.

Paavo said, "One thing we do differently than the other volunteer groups is to prescreen the refugees we have brought here. If the refugees don't possess trade skills of some kind or desired training that would be useful here or on one of the six Colonial worlds, we won't remove them from the planet. Operating in this manner is how we assure refugees aren't becoming reliant on government aid."

Alyssa, Beth, her husband Warrin, and Hadlee all praised what Paavo said. I smiled but couldn't care less. These issues paled in comparison to what I did daily under the dome. That evening's public forum session was all that mattered.

Warrin, our half-witted bubble ambassador, said, "Henry, is all in good order for tonight's open convocation? We in the embassy were deeply troubled by what has been occurring between you and Representative Richmond. The Hammer and Rose parties oppose each other, but the actions between you two appear personal."

His comments irritated me, and my ears warmed. Warrin was a finger puppet to Sadie Enama, Chair of Uropa. He was there to spy on us representatives, especially other union members. That woman had always feared my influence with the other unions. She wanted control of the Hammer. As long as I was still alive, it would never happen. Warrin, with his fat face and rosy cheeks, was a buffoon in our political arena.

I replied with a question. "Will you be attending tonight's open session?"

Warrin jiggled his face up and down and smirked. "Absolutely. Nothing's more important in all occupied space."

Alyssa put her hand on my leg, knowing that my anger was flaring. "Henry's more than ready for tonight. He has been quietly preparing for some time now."

I smirked at my wife. She wore a low-cut black dress. Her smile was bliss to look at as I played the grand game with other prominent figures of our Accord bubble.

"Many issues that have reached boiling point will be rectified tonight in the pentagon thanks to heavy negotiations conducted by me," I said with a meaningful gaze at all.

Our gathering was a monthly socialization with the women my wife called "the Girls" and their husbands. Alyssa spent time with these women weekly, and they all thought in their infinite wisdom that dragging their husbands along once every month would develop a friendship between us. An idea that couldn't be further from the truth. If I had my way, I'd put these men into an airlock and open the outer door without a second thought.

Hadlee said, "So sorry to say this, but I won't make it tonight. I have already scheduled a social gathering at my home with some lovely young couples that I've become fast friends with."

Hadlee was once striking in her youth, which was what attracted her rich husbands. Now she had grown old and let herself go. Alyssa had told me in detail that the gathering she was referring to was a meeting of young couples in their twenties and thirties who enjoyed switching partners. They spent hours in the same room having sex with each other. Hadlee enjoyed her events so much because she got to sleep with all the men. She usually brought along a random partner that she had been spending time with to join in with the wives. She loved more youthful men and only hosted events to make herself feel better about what age and time had done to her body.

Alyssa licked her lips. "That sounds like fun. Maybe Henry and I should join you the next time you host." She winked at me, and reached under the table to rub her hand on my inner thigh. She had made comments to me in private about the gatherings. As usual, my wife was playing her little games with me.

Hadlee smiled. "You two are always welcome. In fact, Molly and Paavo came to my party last month and had a grand time."

Molly and Paavo became visibly uncomfortable, and Molly stumbled her words. "W-we only stopped by briefly, yes, briefly."

Alyssa laughed and retorted, "Please, Molly. There's nothing wrong with expressing yourself erotically with others. Experimentation's a delightful experience, and something more people should be open about. Everyone in this bubble is always so uptight and reserved."

Beth said, "Here on this station, we're the leaders of our Colonial society. What we consider to be normal is normal regardless of what anyone else thinks."

Warrin slapped the table. "Well said, darling. I'll toast to that."

He lifted his glass of New Greta red and held it high in the air. Everyone followed suit.

Alyssa said, "To the leaders of the Colonial Accord here on the relations station. May we continue to lead the way for the rest of our people."

Paavo and Warrin echoed together, "Hear, hear," and took a sip of their wine.

I lifted my glass and finished its contents. Hadlee's small yelping dog barked. It was a tiny animal that reminded me of the rabbits I had as a child on Uropa. Father bought them to help me with my anger. She hushed the dog by slapping its snout.

Warrin said, "Henry, what are your plans for dealing with Representative Richmond? It seems to me he's been upsetting the balance of things lately. The Roses are a dreadful party. They always seem to act without reason."

I narrowed my eyes, staring at Warrin, whose expression became uneasy.

"I think you've asked me enough questions for one month, Mr. Ambassador. The five walls are always going back and forth with each other. It's like a game of table tennis—the ball gets hit to one side and then the other."

"Yes, but unfortunately for you, your teammate's attempting to spike the ball down on your side." Warrin snickered.

That pompous ass at the other side of the table challenged me with his words. Not only were my ears feeling hot, but my face became flush. Ambassador Warrin Neises was now a target for my list. I'd deal with all of them in time.

Alyssa said, "Now, boys, enough of that boring political talk. There are more interesting things occurring, believe it or not."

Beth leaned closer to the table. "Oh yes, I almost forgot, next week's your birthday, isn't it?"

"Splendid. Alyssa, will you be hosting a gathering like the last few years?" Molly asked with excitement.

"Sorry, girls, not this year. Henry and I have decided to spend time quietly—he has a surprise and won't give away any hints. The day before, we ladies can do something together."

Hadlee said, "Isn't that fabulous? A romantic night for just the two of you. Henry, what's your surprise? What do you have in store for our lovely leading lady?"

"Trade secrets, ladies. I'm sure you'll hear all about it the day after."

The waiter came over to hand us our bill for the day's meal. We were in one of the best restaurants inside our Colonial bubble, and had consumed six bottles of New Greta red and eaten elegant exotic dishes from across the Accord. There was smoked pork jowl with honey sauce, scallops with Meyer lemon confit, lamb salad with couscous along with other dishes. Everything served was real, as to be expected for people of our social standing.

Each month, when we got together, we took turns paying for the meal. This month was our turn. However, Warrin had angered me with his comments. I glanced at the receipt for a moment, then smiled and handed it to him. He had a perplexed look on his face and his eyes opened wide.

"Warrin, would you be a good lad and take care of the bill this month for me? I'll take your turn next time."

Warrin turned to his wife and the others at the table, clearly unsure how to respond. Of everyone there, he was the least wealthy. Sure, he could afford it, but the cost would affect him more than the others. The wine itself was ninety thousand credits. Small victories can lead to positive results.

Warrin meekly said, "I could never say no to the center seat representative and Labor Party leader."

He took the bill as drops of perspiration appeared on his forehead. I'd make sure to cancel this monthly chore when it was his turn to pay again.

We all said our goodbyes and left. Alyssa grabbed my hand and upper arm as we walked out of the restaurant with my security team, Oliver, Josue, and new security officer. We'd had a hard time finding a third officer who understood my needs. It took a few years to find Josue. Alyssa's security officer Zoey was also with us. She had that same somber look as always.

Alyssa leaned in, whispering to me, "What you did to Warrin was perfect, darling." She kissed me gently on the cheek.

"Oh? I wasn't sure how you would feel since you're so close to Beth."

Alyssa rolled her eyes and said, "Please, she's dull and always acts like an outer-world prince's concubine. Beth would lick the scraps from our table if I asked her to."

I smiled at my wife and kissed her. Alyssa's personality matched mine perfectly. She looked at all people like they were beneath her, and that confidence was what made her so successful.

Alyssa continued, "What are you doing for the rest of the afternoon before open convocation?"

"Benjamin's waiting for me at my office. Malcolm will join us, and then we have a meeting at station command with Director Houlton. We need to wrap up some issues before tonight."

Alyssa said, "Do you have any preferences on what I wear for open convocation?"

"The long blue dress with those silver sparkle designs. It's my favorite. That one is the proper length. It covers your breasts better than the dress you're wearing now."

Alyssa smirked and looked down at her cleavage. "You know I wore this for you. I love catching you staring at them."

"I'd like a much closer look when we get home tonight."

"Don't you worry, Henry." She leaned in and continued quietly, "Tonight I'm going to take you like it's our last night alive."

*

Benjamin was in the transport with me outside of the station, traveling to station command. Control for all government, security operations, station quality management, and our Free Worlds communications central grid came from command. Our ship traveled to the center of the main cylinder. Once inside that dock, a tube elevator would transport us to the center of the cylinder. This was where the artificial light was generated from—and the fake sky visible throughout the cylinder. Visiting station command was always hard on my stomach because of its location. The artificial gravity for the main cylinder came from the rotation brace near station command. Since the central brace rotation was right above command, people who worked there constantly experienced vertigo. The gravity at command was off because of the proximity to the brace. People working there were used to it, but I only visited a few times a year. The visit was crucial for that night's actions.

Benjamin said, "Is everything ok, sir? You seem lost in thought."

I turned to Ben and tapped his shoulder. "All is well. I was thinking about the endless things that must happen before tonight."

Ben had a blind date a few weeks ago he told me about at the time and I had forgotten.

"How was that date you had? It was something set up by one of your friends if I remember correctly."

Ben looked down. "Actually, it didn't work out. She wasn't my type."

"That's unfortunate. What was wrong with her?"

"I like women who are more, well, more outgoing. She seemed too timid for my taste. But I paid for the meal and even walked her home."

Maybe he got lucky after all. "Did you take your date inside?"

Ben blushed. "She invited me in and kissed me, but no, I didn't. I turned her down and went home. That isn't the kind of person I am, sir. I wouldn't have felt right taking advantage of her like that."

"You're a better man than me, Benjamin. I wouldn't have been able to stop myself from having a go at her." I sighed. "You're a good lad and will make a woman happy one day."

"Thank you, sir. I know the right lady is out there for me. I'm just biding my time for the right moment."

Ben and I sat in silence for the rest of the trip. When we arrived, our ship had priority clearance to enter through the dock. Rows of space vessels waited outside for authorization to enter. Our ship passed them all. The dock had significant traffic because it was a commercial port and busy compared to our dome dock of the Capitol Forum. Seeing the industry ships flying in all directions made me proud of our Free Worlds of Humanity.

Malcolm waited inside the dock for us. He was clearly focused, preparing for our meeting, which I liked.

"Good afternoon, Malcolm. Is everything ready?"

Malcolm said, "It is, sir. I have everything we need."

"Good. When we get up there, I'll initiate with Director Houlton. After the formalities finish, you take over the conversation. You know my troubles near the rotating brace. It'll take all of my energy not to get sick."

Malcolm nodded. "No problem, sir. Everything will go according to plan."

Malcolm taking point would be a good reminder for Benjamin as to why Malcolm was my chief of staff and not Ben. Malcolm handed me a pill to help with my vertigo. The last thing Director Houlton needed was me getting sick on her desk when I shook her hand.

We went through two doors that looked like an airlock to the elevator tube. There were station security personnel near the entrance, and these trained security officers were under the control of Director Houlton. Security services of the main cylinder were nearly four million strong. Even though the security of the main cylinder dramatically outnumbered our Capitol Security under the dome, they paled in comparison.

The tube lift jolted up towards station command, and the views from inside as we elevated were incredible—rolling lawns as far as the eye could see, and busy residents moving about like ants. On one side of the station were streets with businesses and bigger apartment buildings. On the other were residential homes, parks, and sporting fields. We were too far away from the higher area of the main cylinder to see the industrial business park of Maintown and its myriad skyscrapers.

Malcolm asked, "Isn't next week Alyssa's birthday?"

"Yes, it is. I bought tickets to the Colonial Phantom Performers."

Malcolm puffed his nostrils. "That's a treat. I knew the group had come up to the station from Pardalis, but I thought they left already."

"Their final performance was last weekend. I spoke with the group's owners, and they agreed to extend their stay for another week at my request. Alyssa has no idea that they're still here. She will be pleasantly surprised when I tell her."

Malcolm seemed pleased, but Benjamin appeared distressed.

"Ben, are you ok?"

He swallowed. "Yes, sir. I can feel the gravity changing as we get closer, and it's making my stomach upset."

"Malcolm, do you have any more of those vertigo pills? It looks like he might be suffering from the same issue I have when coming up here."

Malcolm looked at Ben with little concern for his well-being and said, "No, sorry. I only had the one."

The elevator doors opened to station command where employees moved purposefully about in the lobby area. Security personnel in full combat gear were placed strategically.

A receptionist greeted us. "Good afternoon, gentlemen, Director Houlton's expecting you. Please follow me."

The director's office doors opened. At the opposite end a solid piece of plexiglass overlooked the entire main cylinder. Rumi could amplify the vision on the glass to zoom in and see either end of the cylinder. Rumors claimed that she sat up here most days, spying on people.

It was a marvelous view, and I would enjoy spending time looking at the station if it didn't make me sick. Rumi stood near the glass with her hands clasped behind her. She was motionless, staring out, and I wondered who she had her eyes on. The director turned with a self-assured smile.

"Representative McWright. It's a pleasure to host you here at station command."

The room spun around me. I closed my eyes and took a breath, trying not to fall over.

"Director Houlton, I hope this day finds you well."

Rumi said, "Your appearance would indicate the day isn't finding you very well at all. Or is it our gravity field here at the core that's making you uneasy?"

She was toying with me. I had to keep my composure and play along for the time being.

"You know me too well, Rumi. I feel like I'm fishing in the great green ocean of Uropa with six-meter swells right now."

Rumi laughed and waved her hand to seats near her desk. "Well then, sit down and try to relax."

I took a seat with Malcolm next to me. Benjamin sat in a chair along the back wall keeping his PDD in hand. When I gave him the signal, he was to send a message for me.

Rumi continued. "To what do I owe the pleasure of this last-minute get-together today? Don't you have a busy night? Open convocation will command large viewing figures tonight because of the refugee dock attack."

"Yes, tonight's crucial, but I'm here for something even more important. The topic is sensitive to station security, and it simply couldn't wait."

Rumi's confident smile changed to apprehension. "Station security? Is there an issue I need to be made aware of?"

"My chief of staff, Malcolm Booth, will take over this conversation and advise you of the issues at hand."

I waved my hand to Malcolm, who sat up in his chair and got himself ready.

"Director Houlton, something occurred under the dome that has never happened in the seven hundred and forty years since this station's creation. It's a gross violation of core security and a top official from one of your subordinate offices is involved."

Truthfully, neither of us was sure that what happened had never occurred before. But the dramatics were necessary.

Rumi looked at me blankly then back at Malcolm and spoke sharply. "You had better explain yourself and leave nothing out."

Malcolm stood and placed his PDD on the table. He hit a button that displayed a hologram from security camera footage in the Civil Earth back-office hallway of the fourth floor. Visible in the camera screen was the door entrance to Center Seat Mia Stavish's office.

"This was obtained by the MERC Guild as part of an ongoing investigation into some nefarious activities happening under the dome. We originally thought it might be the Rogue Syndicate conducting illegal operations meant to undermine the legitimacy of the Capitol Forum. However, after further research, the truth was discovered."

Malcolm hit play on the PDD, showing a standard day in the back office. Mia entered her office twice during the day. The video was in high-speed mode, so everything happened rapidly. The end of the day showed cleaners vacuuming and dusting, painters doing touch-up work on the walls, and late staffers leaving.

Rumi said, "Am I supposed to be impressed with this? It looks like a normal day in the back office. Additionally, I would love to know how you acquired internal footage from Civil Earth's office. The MERC Guild should never have given you this—it violates the Free Worlds' Relations Policy."

I waved to Ben to send the message.

Malcolm leaned closer, pointing his finger at the hologram. "The more interesting issue, which is why we're here, you can see ... right ... now."

The timestamp on the hologram was 03:45. Three individuals entered Mia's office with ladders, drills, and other surveillance equipment.

Malcolm said, "What you're looking at, Director Houlton, are three special service officers who work under your secretary of defense, Aldemar Willock. We've already verified using facial recognition who these men are."

Rumi sat higher in her chair as if it was the most uncomfortable thing she'd ever sat in and cleared her throat. "Aldemar wouldn't have had anything to do with this. It looks like these three have gone rogue and did this without Aldemar's knowledge."

Malcolm said, "Before standing to your statement, I would ask that you continue to observe this video."

Another thirty sped-up minutes went by, and then someone stepped into the video frame. Malcolm paused the footage where a clear image of Secretary Willock was visible, receiving a device from one of the men walking out of Mia Stavish's office.

I leaned on the armrest and glanced at the video. "If I'm not mistaken, that appears to be Secretary of Defense Aldemar Willock."

Malcolm chimed in. "You're not mistaken, sir. The MERC Guild's confirmed that this video is legitimate with no alterations."

Rumi looked like someone had just kicked her between the legs. She stared at Malcolm, the video, and then me, unsure how to respond.

"Speaking of the MERC Guild," I added.

We sat for another minute of uncomfortable silence. The intercom on Director Houlton's desk warbled. "Director Houlton."

Rumi was annoyed. "I'm in a meeting and should not be disturbed right now."

The voice said, "Yes, ma'am. Sorry, but there's a Senior Agent Ficco from the MERC Guild here to see you. He's already walking in. I was unable to stop him."

I smiled at Rumi. "Right on time."

The doors to Rumi's office opened and Senior Agent Ficco, with his monstrous mongrel, walked inside. The mongrel's snout was low, sniffing around the room, then it found a corner and lay down. Ficco smiled at us and grabbed a chair from the other side of the office. He dragged it across the floor and placed it at the corner of Rumi's desk where he sat down, lifted his feet, and put them on her desk.

"Howdy all. Did I miss anything important?"

Malcolm said, "We just finished up at the part where you should take over."

"Good." Ficco stood and walked behind Rumi's chair. "After seeing this evidence, the Guild conducted a cyber investigation and found numerous violations on Capitol Forum networks. It appears Secretary of Defense Willock had his security officers hack the storage for the dome camera systems and delete this video that Malcolm showed you. I'm guessing that's why he was willing to expose himself on video entering the Civil Earth back office. What Secretary Willock didn't know was that all recordings have a secondary backup in the Citadel."

Rumi shuffled around in her seat listening to Ficco. "We found video evidence of a less professional nature on the off-network spy cameras inside Representative Stavish's office."

The senior agent hit a button on his wrist and a hologram image of Mia, naked, in her office with her head between the legs of the young aide Melissa was displayed. Melissa was also naked, sitting on Mia's desk with her legs spread and arching her head back, yelling out in pleasure. Melissa grabbed Mia's head forcefully while Mia licked her and jabbed at her with her fingers. It was a delightful video that would get anyone with a sexual appetite in the mood.

"I wonder how that tastes?" Ficco's voice was thick with sarcasm. "This video then found its way onto a secure-link private server inside Secretary of Defense Aldemar Willock's office. The link was accessed three separate times, according to the Guild cyber division. Once in Asbury Park inside the main cylinder near the entrance to the Civil Earth bubble."

The camera changed to a location in Asbury Park, the hologram displaying JJ Richmond sitting on a bench next to Mia, showing her the video on his PDD. Mia looked extremely disturbed, which made it clear that JJ was blackmailing her. She was happily married with two young children. If that video ever got out, she would lose her position as center seat, and her family name on Civil Earth in Tier One would lose clout.

Ficco stepped back towards his seat still talking. "It was reviewed by Representative Richmond when he was alone sitting in the pentagon waiting for a closed session to start. The representative must be a lonely fellow based on the next video."

The hologram display changed again, this time to JJ sitting in his left seat, watching the footage and rubbing himself between his legs.

"And a third time by ... oh, wait, that was me," Ficco said. "Let's just say it was a lonely night and an excellent video."

Rumi raised her voice. "Representative McWright. This senior agent has gone too far, and I—"

Before she could say another word, I slammed my fist down on the table in the same fashion as when Malcolm and Benjamin were arguing in my office. Rumi yelped.

"You will sit here and listen to everything the senior agent has to say or so help me this will be your last day on this station as a director. Aldemar works for you, and by extension, his actions are yours," I said sharply.

Rumi stumbled on her words. "I-I-I ..."

But before she could say anything else, Ficco spoke over her. "This evidence, as Center Seat Representative McWright has pointed out, is conclusive enough to show that votes inside the five walls of the forum have been swayed through a conspiracy that started right here in station command."

"I had nothing to do with this."

I smiled and said, "No, you didn't, but perception is a reality here on this station. We can make this go away quietly for you. However, first, you'll terminate Aldemar immediately, and tonight when everyone is sleeping, your staff will remove those cameras."

Agent Ficco added, "We have also seized the private server, but we won't take it offline until after open convocation tonight."

Rumi frowned at me. "And what of Representative Richmond? This evidence is enough to remove him from office."

Removing JJ had been my dream for a long time. I promised myself I would destroy his career. In truth, if this came out, he would lose his right seat position only to return to Ardum and take up the mantle there as an inspiration to his Rose Party. No, when he fell, it would be in such a way that his life would be over.

"That is for me to worry about, and you will forget this conversation ever happened after we leave your office."

The intercom system crackled again. "Director Houlton, ma'am."

Rumi sighed. "What is it now?"

"Secretary of Defense Willock is here for you."

Rumi gazed at all of us sitting in the room, then said, "Well, send him in."

*

"Hear ye, hear ye. All rise for the honorable representatives of all the Free Worlds of Humanity," said the sergeant at arms wearing his formal evening cape and jerkin studded with the most beautiful rubies and jewels found across occupied space. The pentagon shape of our five walls inside the forum was appliqued to the back of his cape. He also wore a ceremonial sword, a part of his dress attire, for special events. The blade was more for show than anything else.

The sergeant was in his mid-sixties and had been a commanding officer with station security a lifetime ago. He earned many honors and badges for heroic deeds throughout his career. When he became sergeant at arms, an honorary position awarded to those with standing such as his, the representatives of the forum had a Corin-steel sword made for his belt— replacing the old blade of standard high-grade metal. He helped keep the animals in line during session.

Music played as all the representatives entered by seniority from their wall's rear door. Center seat first, right seat second, and left seat third. People up high in the theater looking down clapped and cheered, and the echoes blared across the inner dome with deafening percussion.

Open convocation had always been my favorite part of being a representative. I loved the roars and applause from the thousands in the seating above. Camera drones hovered nearby recording and streaming the event live on Free Worlds network feeds. Unfortunately, these events didn't air in prime time. Only special occasions like the speech I was supposed to give before its cancellation would have that honor. Still, billions would watch, and all news agencies across all Free Worlds would show highlights in their rundowns.

After everyone had entered and was standing behind their respective seats, I spoke. "All inside the Capitol Forum and the various citizens of all Free Worlds, we begin tonight's open session with a moment of silence for the souls lost in the attacks on the refugee dock. We honor those lost and those who fought hard to ensure our safety."

Everyone in the forum lowered their heads. It was so quiet inside the amphitheater the slightest sound echoed throughout the chamber. When the moment ended, I continued. "Esteemed colleagues of the five walls, our honored guests from the outer worlds and all citizens of the Free Worlds, I declare the commencement of open convocation for the Civil Earth month of September. Let our issues resolve in agreement and elegance under the Free Worlds' Relations Policies."

Cheering once again broke out across the forum, and certain representatives also clapped. Once the commotion calmed, I said, "The forum calls on Civil Earth to begin tonight's convocation."

All sat, except for Representative Olivia Belitz, who would discuss the same issue she brought to our attention in closed session. During open convocation, the only walls that could speak were those who brought up issues during closed session. The Free Worlds that passed on time could still speak but only to give their time away. Olivia adjusted her toga and jewels as she walked down to her podium.

Her voice carried with brightness and a bold undertone. "Good evening to all of the Free Worlds and our honored guests from the outer worlds." She waved her hand in the direction of the seating area to the three sitting on the balcony representing the Nejem Royal Family, who controlled the outer worlds.

"This month, Civil Earth has decided to dedicate our time to an issue that was brought to our attention by Right Seat Representative Richmond of the Colonial Accord. The Colonial Trade Company is the largest transportation public corporation supplying multitudes of goods you fine Free Worlds citizens purchase daily. Recently there've been attacks on ships traveling through occupied space attempting to deliver important commodities to our territories. Without provocation, vessels disappear from RAPOD tracking. We agreed in closed session to dispatch a special unit from the MERC Guild to immediately investigate the cause of these strikes. The Guild will bring the attackers to a swift end so that the costs of daily products won't impact anyone on a Free World. We of Civil Earth make this promise to all."

The forum burst out with roaring applause, cheering uncontrollably. JJ smiled and glanced up at the cheering masses, and then he looked at me. I turned my head away from him, expressionless. *I don't want to give away the game just yet.*

Olivia concluded. "I yield the remainder of my time, but before concluding, the Civil Earth wall wants the Free Worlds to know something important. We are all mourning the losses in the refugee dock caused by the terrorists of the rogue world Gliese. Tier One of Civil Earth has donated survivor benefits to the families of those security service officers from the main cylinder to ensure that their bills are taken care of for life. The children and significant others of all who died will have their homes and future education paid for in full."

The entire forum erupted in applause again. That was a genius idea that I was sure Mia orchestrated. I was jealous that I didn't think of it before her. Olivia returned to her seat.

"Thank you, Representative Belitz. The pentagon now calls on the Federate Corporation." My voice was even toned and clear.

I sat and covered my mouth to hide the smile behind my hand, so Mia and JJ didn't see.

Right Seat Representative Cassandra Orwick from the Federate wall stood and walked down to the podium. She said, "Good evening to all on the relations station and the many living on the Free Worlds across occupied space. I wish good fortune to our honored guests from the outer worlds as well." She paused for a moment, looking at the audience above the five walls. "Gliese, the name of that rogue world, has been in conversations everywhere.

At work, at home, and in social gatherings. This planet's name pops up in discussions more frequently than the scores from the latest professional power-ball games. After much debate with my fellow representatives and the board of directors from Dol'Arem, we've decided you deserve the truth." She pointed to the spectators in the upper seating area. "The truth is that before yesterday we representatives were failing you."

Commotion and muttering overshadowed us from up in the amphitheater.

"Both the Federate Corporation and Dolrinion Offensive couldn't agree on concessions that would help ease tensions on Gliese. In closed session, our conflict with each other matched that of the fighting on Gliese. Our forum battling made it difficult to come to a compromise agreement. If six representatives couldn't agree with each other in private under the dome, how could millions stop fighting on Gliese to start the healing process? There was no end in sight to our hostilities until someone stepped up to help. Someone in this pentagon spent countless hours behind the scenes trying to resolve our differences. His concern was for the safety of all Free Worlds and showed care for the civilian population of Gliese. By helping both Free Worlds governments, the representative I speak of gained nothing. No influence, fame, or reward came from his help. He did all of this for the greater good, and after much debate, our Center Seat Representative Boran made the decision that we should recognize his efforts in helping us come to an accord."

When Representative Orwick said the word *accord*, Mia and JJ turned toward me. My smile must have been evident through my hand now. Mia was smart enough and saw what was going on, but JJ wasn't.

"Before recognizing this representative, I'd like to call on Representative Guth from the Dolrinion Offensive to come to the podium."

The onlookers above had trouble remaining quiet while watching history in the making. Representative Guth waddled to his wall's podium, his battle armor making cranking noises with each step he took.

Once he reached the podium, Cassandra said, "Representative Guth. We will be turning over one percent of the landmass mountain range on the outskirts of the marshes to the Offensive. As I speak, our forces are already withdrawing from the mountains, which we have renamed the Mountains of Hope. Hope seemed like a fitting name because we hope that this exchange will help bring lasting peace to our two Free Worlds societies."

Guth gave Cassandra a sharp glare and said nothing for a few moments. The amphitheater was silent once again, awaiting the supreme general's response.

Representative Guth raised his eyebrows and smirked. "With these concessions, we of the Offensive Force Commands have agreed to a two-month ceasefire to open further negotiations with the Corporation. All of this wouldn't be possible if not for the efforts of the representative you speak of."

Representatives Guth and Orwick looked in my direction at the same time.

Cassandra said, "Center Seat Representative Henry McWright of the Colonial Accord. We of the Federate Corporation thank you."

Guth added, "And we of the Dolrinion Offensive salute you for your efforts."

My heart racing with excitement, I got up from my center seat and took a few steps forward, holding my head high.

"Your kind words are appreciated, my fellow representatives. I was merely doing my duty as an elected official here under the dome. My efforts would've been in vain if not for both center seats of your walls. Representatives Sharrar and Boran, I thank you for all you did to make this effort possible."

Both center seat representatives stood and bowed their heads. The loudest cheering of the night blasted through the entire forum with thunderous radiance, more intense than for any professional sporting event.

I turned to walk back to my seat and stared at JJ with a grin. His face was extremely red, more so than his hair, and he appeared confused, trying to figure out what was happening. I looked up at my beautiful wife in her lovely dress. Alyssa blew me a kiss and half-smiled, watching me work the room.

Guth returned to his seat, and Representative Orwick spoke again.

"Nothing further needs to be said this month. The Corporation yields the remainder of our time." She returned to her seat.

I announced, "The Capitol Forum now calls on the Human Alliance for opening statements."

Representative Laskaris walked to the podium, his shoulders raised, with an inviting smile at all in the amphitheater.

Zachery said, "In light of the attacks committed by the terrorists from Gliese, the Alliance has agreed not to address our concerns this month. We representatives of Epsilon Prime willingly give our time to Center Seat Representative Henry McWright of the Colonial Accord."

More chatter from above as the civilian population and honored guests tried to make sense of his statements. Mia, who observed me carefully, stood to turn the Alliance time over.

Before she spoke, Representative Laskaris said, "One moment, Representative Stavish, if you will. The Alliance does have one important announcement to make. Since the start of the fighting on Gliese, this station has been weighed down by refugees flooding the main cylinder. We've been made aware that the number has now reached nearly one hundred and fifty thousand frightened human souls. After various conversations between the representatives of our wall and the Lyons Twins of New-Sparta, the Alliance has decided to take one-third of all Gliese refugees off this station and give them citizenship on Epsilon Prime."

The amphitheater cheered and applauded. That was genius political flair from the Alliance. Well played indeed, but as I'd said earlier to Rumi, perception was a reality here. Little did these cheering commoners know that the refugees brought to Epsilon Prime would be forced into city-states who supported my very dear friend Liam Sideris during the war. Some of those states were so poverty-stricken and filled with death that the refugees would have been better off staying on Gliese. They might have even fared better on the Dolrinion side of that rogue planet.

Zachery took his seat and Mia spoke out. "The forum now calls on Center Seat Representative Henry McWright of the Colonial Accord."

I went to the Colonial podium fingering my Hammer of Labor charm. Our Left Seat Representative Keng spoke for me during closed session, but I would never avoid a chance in the spotlight; my position was too important. I smiled, looking at all up in the amphitheater.

"Good evening to all Free Worlds of Humanity. Last month, I attempted to help all union-working Free Worlds citizens with a bill that would benefit everyone. Through deception and lies, my bill and my speech became prime-time news because of a last-minute cancellation by an emergency vote right here in the forum. Conniving treachery, perpetrated in secret behind my back by a small minority within the five walls of this sacred forum, was to blame." I glanced at Mia and JJ. "However, positive changes and goodness always find a way to overcome evil intent. When strong people refuse to stand down in the gathering darkness, our light will always find a way to succeed. We are the Free Worlds of Humanity, and humanity is resilient, thriving, and advancing through all perils. I once again present my Union Labor Rights Bill to the forum for a public vote. My bill gives all union workers a five percent increase in pension funding, guaranteed medical for retirement, and the ability for collective bargaining during contract negotiations. Each Free Worlds' government would be bound to this law under our Free Worlds' Relations Policy."

What I didn't say was that I had removed the higher pay and the equal rights portions of the law that Civil Earth and the Federates didn't want in there. I had to do this for the Man of Many Numbers, Jaxson Boran. What I was giving the unions was trivial because collective bargaining was still managed by Tiers One and Two on Civil Earth, and the Federates had their way of dealing with it. Dolrinions would ignore this Free Worlds Policy like they did others. Policy inspectors from the Capitol Forum never returned from Kora, so there wouldn't be an issue at that end.

"Before I call a vote to the floor, there's one additional topic to present. Our Civil Earth and Human Alliance friends did well to honor with generosity the families of fallen security officers as well as innocent civilian natives from the rogue world Gliese after careful consideration with leadership of

323

the Labor Party on Uropa. Under my guidance, they agreed to live up to our Colonial Accord name. We're the breadbasket of Humanity, and our fields are bountiful. We of the Labor Party will donate one hundred million tons of real food to the rogue world Gliese to help feed the starving populations there, the cost of this challenging task paid for in full by the six worlds with additional donations from the Labor Party."

The entire forum emitted screams of joy. Everyone clapped and yelled with pride. I never spoke to anyone from Uropa or the Labor Party for permission for that monumental action. They'd have no choice now. I couldn't let Civil Earth and the Alliance get all the credit for charity. Besides, Jaxson Boran and Sharrar had added that last-minute concession to the agreement. Fifty million tons would land on the Dolrinion side of Gliese then find its way to Kora. The other fifty million tons would fall on the Federate side, then find its way to Dol'Arem. The natives of Gliese would never see one crumb of that food.

"I now call for a vote in the forum for my bill."

The sergeant at arms walked to the middle stage of the pentagon, his shoes clicking on the tile. "Under chapter one of the Free Worlds' Relations Policy to the Capitol Forum of the relations station, I call to order for a vote. The pentagon will hear the nays first."

JJ jumped from his seat like a bottle rocket and yelled out loud for all to hear, "Nay, I call nay to this bill."

Many audience members above made sounds of disapproval.

Mia rose from her seat, apparently reluctant, slower than a flower coming into bloom. "I also call nay," she said softly.

Left Seat Representative Xander Nasby of Civil Earth stood, but when he realized that no one else was standing, he quickly sat back down. JJ peered from one end to the other anxiously. Olivia Belitz smiled while staring at Mia. She appreciated the game. Mia glared down at the ground, clearly knowing she was powerless to act.

The sergeant at arms said, "The nay count is two. The forum will now hear the ayes."

My vote was automatic, so there was no need for me to do anything. I turned around and looked at JJ with a smile on my face. One by one, everyone else in the forum stood and said, "Aye," for all to hear.

After the final call, the sergeant continued, "The votes are all tallied. Thirteen ayes and two nays. Representative McWright's bill passes open convocation."

Cheering exploded across the entire forum, and the sounds resonated so loud, the walls shook as if an earthquake took hold of the amphitheater. I looked at the crowd with a feeling of accomplishment. There was even a slight breeze on my face from the overwhelming shouting and clapping. JJ was sitting low in his chair.

I walked to him, leaned down to his ear, and whispered, "It looks like I can still shoot lightning bolts from my ass."

JJ glared at me, squinting his eyes, and said, "You told me in my office that when I think I'm ahead and everything is going precisely the way I planned, you'd be here to put my face down into the mud."

I smiled at him and said, "Do you see mud under your feet? No, what I told you would happen has yet to manifest itself. Tonight was only a small appetizer of the meal I intend serving you one day."

I turned and glanced over at Mia, who looked foreign compared to her typical aplomb. It was rare to see her in this form, given her abilities inside the forum. When our eyes met, she regained her composure enough to nod her head in my direction.

The Dolrinions took their podium time and kept it brief like always. The sergeant at arms called an end to open convocation after additional formalities. All representatives left the pentagon and the spectators above did the same. Mia came to the center stage and waited for me. I took my time to approach her, smirking.

"You play the game well, Henry."

"It took some effort, and I had to make some sacrifices, but all worked out in the end."

"Regrettably, I'm still in a bad place with JJ. I'll remain under his snare for some time. There's no choice, especially with Olivia working her claws into my back."

I gently lifted her chin, and our eyes met. She appeared like a beaten animal that was once wild, a queen of the plains, now nothing more than a zoo creature crushed and broken into submission.

"No, you won't." I pulled an external drive from my pocket and handed it to her. She stared at it in confusion. "This is the video that JJ was using to blackmail you. The Guild seized the server holding the video. There's no longer any evidence of the contents. What you have in your hand is the only copy left. I met with Rumi this afternoon, and she terminated Secretary of Defense Aldemar Willock. He was the cause of the misfortune that befell you. Tonight, the cameras in your office will be removed at my direction."

Mia didn't respond right away; it took her a moment to process everything. She gave me a heavy stare of concern. "Wait. You had everything resolved this afternoon? Why did you not tell me sooner? I could have voted with you and not alienated myself."

I smiled at her and said, "You played me for a fool the day of my speech and bill. I sat through lunch with you at the café while you knew exactly what was going to happen to me that night and did nothing. I watched you speak to the press out front with a smile. No, I wanted tonight to happen exactly the way it did. Maybe next time something like this occurs, you'll come to me first before making bad choices that lead you into a corner."

We had another moment of pause as Mia thought to herself. Before leaving, she asked one last question. "Now what?"

I laughed and answered, "Now? Now, I'm going home to have sex with my beautiful young wife …"

CHAPTER 23

Arriving on the Relations Station

There's a first time for everything (Adam)

The new ship's commander, who was the chief engineer before the pirates, Androsians, and Dolrinions boarded the ship, had announced that we had finally arrived at the relations station. Mom, the honorable Isabel Sideris, Daughter of Athinia, always talked about this place like it was something from a fairy tale. She would tell Juliet and me how all the Sideris children for ten generations went to secondary school here at the station. She said that the smartest minds across all the Free Worlds either went to secondary or higher education in the main cylinder. I guess that made my sister and me fools since our education was cut short because of the civil war. Most of my childhood memories were of living in fear as the Lyons Pride hunted us from one village to the next. The Pride killed Dad; that was something I constantly visualized, watching him fall to the ground and close his eyes for the last time even though I wasn't there when he died. I fantasize that his death was heroic.

Dad's death broke Mom. She never recovered, and resistance leaders believed she lost her way. After she renounced her leadership of the city-state loyalists, the movement had trouble continuing. People lost hope without a

Sideris leading the rebellion. I would never forgive her for giving up the way she did. Mom would still be here right now if it weren't for her poor decision-making. Now I had to take care of Juliet and figure out our next step.

"Adam, after we check in through the refugee center, we should reach out to Henry McWright. Mom said—"

"I know what Mom said, but Mom isn't here. I have to keep us safe now. It's my job, and you should remember that."

She stared blankly at the wall as if she saw something there. I shouldn't have talked to her like that. My emotions were all over the place. There had been screens in the safe room showing the rest of the ship. I watched the Androsian butcher Mom like it was a game. Then the Dolrinion slavers took her. There was nothing we could do. I had tried to open the safe room door, but someone inside the room held me down. We resumed our trip to the station with no other interference, but it took an extra week for the engineers to get the engines working again.

"Jules, we'll be ok. After we register, we'll request an audience with Representative McWright. I remember what Mom told us."

Mom said that the Lyons Pride spies were all over the station. We had to be careful about what we said and who we talked to; there were only two people we could trust, and that was each other. Mom also told us that Henry McWright and someone named Nicolas Nomikos might be able to help, but we should be cautious even with them. Nicolas was from City-State Elpis, and that state was our staunch ally during the civil war.

The commander's voice came across the intercom. "All refugees, the station cleared us to enter the dock. Please gather all of your belongings and meet at the secondary terminal doors."

Juliet seemed excited. "We're finally here." She ran around our room, packing what little we had into our bag.

"Remember, we can't tell anyone our last names here. The station's a dangerous place that we know nothing about."

Juliet gave me a funny look. "Come on, Adam, lighten up a bit. Mom taught us everything ..." Jules paused and looked down, then lowered her voice. "Everything we need to know about this place. I miss her."

"She's still alive," I said. "We saw the Dolrinions cuff her and take her onto their ship. If anyone can help us get her back, it will be Representative McWright."

We arrived at the secondary terminal door; what was left of the passengers of the transport were there. Honestly, we all looked terrible. The ship's cameras had captured it all, and images of Mom displayed on the screen inside the safe room flashed through my mind. Mom shooting Androsians, being attacked, losing her eye, and the fight between that sentinel and the Androsian who attacked Mom. The great Isabel Sideris of Athinia, warrior daughter of the honorable Prime Regent Liam Sideris, had become a Dolrinion slave. Some of the refugees on our ship who knew us but remained quiet seemed sad to see Mom dragged away.

The terminal door opened, and a light mist formed where the air from the station met the atmosphere of our ship.

The new commander called out, "Alright, this miserable trip is over. Now get the hell off my ship."

Everyone filed into the brightly lit docking area. There was so much happening—people entering and exiting different vessels. I hadn't seen such an assortment of people in one place since visiting Athinia's state capital before the Unification War. Juliet was young when we visited together, and she wouldn't have remembered. Her eyes wide open, Juliet looked like a child. Soldiers in combat gear holding rifles stood ready throughout the area. They reminded me of Lyons Pride. Hundreds of transport ships were clamped down with humongous metal bolts as more passengers disembarked, and the ceiling was so high, many vessels could move around with ease.

"What do we do, Adam?"

"Keep walking. Someone will direct us."

Another refugee from the ship, dark circles around his eyes and a bandage on his nose, stood next to us. It was the young man that gave me an attitude the day after the attack. He said he thought my mother was foolish for trying to fight the pirates. Mom and Dad taught Juliet and me how to fight and defend ourselves. They told us it was the responsibility of every city-state citizen to know how to protect themselves—especially those who lived in Athinia.

Most people remembered their first fight. Mine was in primary school with a teasing boy. The second was with someone living in the home of those hiding us. It made me angry to think about my childhood.

There was an unpleasant smell in the dock, and from the look of everyone, including us, lack of hygiene was to blame.

A soldier standing on a platform was yelling orders. "If you're from the rogue world Gliese, follow the yellow line on the ground. It will direct you to processing."

A person standing next to the soldier was speaking another language. *That must be a translator.* We learned the Language of Humanity before the civil war started. That was the language the soldier spoke. The other language must have been from that rogue world.

The soldier continued. "If you're from the outer worlds, follow the green line on the ground. It will lead you to processing."

Someone standing on the other side of the soldier spoke in yet another language.

"If you're from one of the Free Worlds, please follow the red line on the ground."

Juliet pointed to a thick red line with arrows leading away from us and got excited. "The red line's here. We should follow it."

People dispersed in one direction or another. Juliet and I, along with others from our ship, stepped onto the red path. An older teenager who slept with Juliet during our trip walked over to us. He wasn't that attractive, but served his purpose, keeping Jules busy during the dreary days in FTL. I caught them two different times in our quarters.

My sister was extremely attractive, even more beautiful than Mom was at her age. I told Jules he was beneath her, but things worked out the way they did. The older boy should consider himself exceptionally lucky. He'd never have someone as attractive again in this life.

He spoke to Juliet. "My parents are making us go claim refugee status with the outer worlds. But there's another line that the security officers don't say anything about for whatever reason. The gray line leads away from the other colors. If you follow that line, you can try to claim refugee status at another location in occupied space like another Free World, Titans' Belt, or a rogue world away from all the fighting. For whatever reason, my parents want to go to the outer worlds. I wanted you to know before I left that I'll miss you."

Juliet said, "I'll miss you too. Maybe one day we'll meet again."

He looked at me and I rolled my eyes at him. "She was way out of your league, and you know it. You better count your blessings because you'll never have someone like her again."

He gave me an angry grunt and walked away without saying anything. That boy never appreciated my blunt speech.

Juliet glared sourly at me. "Why'd you say that to him? He was nice to me, and I enjoyed his company."

"After the attack on the ship, your choices were slim. You had him or that overweight refugee with the missing leg. There wasn't anyone else to spend time with besides me."

Juliet was defensive. "That's not true. One of the ship crew was interested in me until the new commander put an end to it. I've always preferred men older than me, anyway."

The ship crew member she spent time with had to be nearly forty-five. My sister had always been like that with relationships. She lost her virginity to a man who owned the house we were hiding in. Mom and Dad at that time were busy leading attacks on New-Sparta with the loyalists. They didn't pay attention to what was happening with their kids.

The man who owned the house was so old compared to Jules. He had his way with her a few times before I hit him over the head with a pipe. When Mom and Dad came home, I lied and told them that Lyons Pride soldiers had come into the house and did that to him. We packed up and left before he woke up.

I had endless memories of trying to defend Juliet after the fact when things that shouldn't happen to her did. Maybe that contributed to my anger and hate. Everything seemed so dull all the time. Mom thought of me as a little boy who couldn't defend himself; that couldn't be further from the truth. Mom would probably be dead soon anyway.

We got into line. Ahead was a high portable fence with pillars; soldiers on this side of the fence surrounded a desk where people used fingerprint systems to check identities. People behind the fence held posters and chanted loudly.

"Peace on Gliese. Peace on Gliese."

"Millions dead, it will spread. Millions dead, it will spread."

Juliet asked, "What are they talking about, millions dead? Peace on Gliese? I don't understand what's going on here."

I put my arm around Jules and led her forward. "It doesn't concern us. We need to find someone who can get us to Henry McWright."

The soldiers and workers at the table concerned me. Once we placed our finger on the detector, it would show our real names. Other people nearby in the dock away from the desks, wearing regular clothing with military boots. They weren't getting into line, only standing around viewing everyone. Something about them looked wrong. Could they be Lyons Pride?

Juliet said, "Adam, look over there." She pointed seven meters away from the table. "MERC Guild agents and their mongrels."

She was right. There were three MERC Guild agents in full combat gear with three mongrels patrolling the lines, watching everything that was going on. I'd never seen real Corin steel before. Those glowing green lines with black flecks across the chest plate were recognizable anywhere. There was so much firepower in that dock. It was as if the station were going to war.

Juliet said, "Remember what Mom told us? The agents work for the representatives of the Capitol Forum. If anyone in this dock can help us get to Henry, they can."

She might be right. "Let's see if we can get into the station on our own first. If it doesn't work, we will go see them."

Our turn was next; one of the women in civilian clothing but wearing military boots stared at my sister and me. Our eyes gave us away. We had the bright green eyes of the Sideris family. The same eyes my mom, grandfather, and several generations of our family had. After the war, the Lyons Pride killed anyone they found in Athinia with green eyes to ensure that no one was left who could have shared our ancestry. Our eyes were more brilliant green than past family members because Dad also had green eyes but without the glow.

The woman waved to another wearing the same clothing and boots. I stepped up to the screen and placed my thumb on the detector. The civilian staff member behind the table called for the attention of the lead soldier. Now the woman watching who reminded me of the Pride stepped over to see the computer screen. Everyone's eyebrows went high in apparent disbelief.

I asked those behind the table, "Is everything ok?"

The civilian staff member mumbled, "Uhm. Y-yes, give me a moment, please. I'm waiting for a commanding officer to come over."

A few more security officers moved closer, and four shady civilians with military boots who must be from the Lyons Pride closed in on our location. Our situation turned bad quickly.

I yelled to Juliet and grabbed her hand, "Run to the MERC agents, now!"

We sprinted away from all the watching eyes. Jules and I were good at this. We'd run from the Lyons Pride hundreds of times on Epsilon Prime. Most of the time, we were woken from sleep to flee. Both security officers and civilian-looking soldiers closed in behind us, and one nearly grabbed Juliet's arm before we made it to the Guild agents. Their mongrels leaped in our direction, snarling as their auto guns aimed. Juliet and I raised our hands.

I shouted, "We're not a threat."

The lead agent said, "Identify yourself. Why did you run to us?"

"My name is Adam Sideris. This is my sister Juliet. We're the son and daughter of Tuddy and Isabel Sideris and the grandchildren of the former Prime Regent Liam Sideris of City-State Athinia on Epsilon Prime. Representative Henry McWright is expecting us."

He wasn't expecting us, but at that point, it didn't matter.

People around us opened their eyes wide like deer looking into headlights. The MERC agents wore full facemask covers, and the lead agent took her mask off. She carefully observed the security officers and Lyons Pride sneaks dressed as civilians pointing their weapons in our direction. Her pause felt like hours, but then she tapped a device attached to the side of her head and called out loudly.

"Senior Agent Korson, ID number 674-132-11M. I need an extraction team in the refugee dock. All call, I repeat, all call to every available agent. I have high priority VIPs in the dock for an immediate extraction."

The three mongrels moved quickly behind Juliet and me. They faced the security officers and Lyons Pride sneaks, growling at them all with their auto guns pointing at both groups. The other two agents stepped next to Juliet and me, aiming their weapons at everyone behind us.

The security officer in charge said, "They need to come with us per Secretary of Free Worlds Affairs Nicolas Nomikos. We have orders to take them to station command here in the main cylinder."

More security officers in the same armor pushed through the spectating refugees and ship transport haulers. The officers looked confused but took up positions with the other station security officers, pointing their weapons at the Pride and agents alike. I could identify three groups here—station command, the Lyons Pride, and MERC Guild, all viewing each other like enemies during the civil war.

The woman in civilian clothing with her military boots pulled a badge from her waist in the shape of a lion's head of gold, the symbol of the Pride.

She spoke forcefully. "By order of the Lyons Pride of the Alliance bubble and the Lyons Twins of New-Sparta on Epsilon Prime, the Sideris siblings are coming with us."

More civilians with combat boots pushed past the groups that formed, and some of the people in the crowd shouted slurs at the Lyons Pride. Those onlookers must have been from the Allied States before the civil war. Lyons Pride sneaks stood behind the senior agent who called for help. Even with these odds, the agents looked unfazed by the various threats around them.

The senior agent stared at the ranks over her shoulder and in front of us at the pointed guns. She was exceptionally focused, appearing to calculate who she would shoot at first. The other two agents did the same. Things grew quiet, and time seemed to stop.

A hovercraft that reminded me of a small helicopter with dual blades on both sides glided above the stalemate. MERC Guild agents descended on ropes with their feet locked into place. Mongrels leaped from the craft, taking positions to form a perimeter.

The odds were better with six additional agents and their mongrels ready to fight. These agents had more substantial armor plating, much thicker and more intimidating.

Within seconds, more agents pushed through the angry crowds of spectators, still shouting, and some even pushed a few Lyons Pride sneaks. The main cylinder security officers and the Lyons Pride were surrounded by the power of the MERC Guild.

The hovercraft above had two bubble pods with massive weapons that reminded me of cannon barrels. Inside, agents aimed huge turrets at both Pride and security officers. My sister's hair blew in the wind formed by the engine blades of the craft.

The Lyons Pride sneak leader had despair on her face. She looked at Senior Agent Korson. "You have no right to take them—this is an internal city-state matter of Epsilon Prime. The Relations Policy gives us precedence."

Senior Agent Korson narrowed her eyes at the Pride commander and walked to her quickly, her mongrel beside her. Some of the security officers and Lyons Pride aimed their weapons at the senior agent as she approached, unfazed by their weapons.

"As far as I'm concerned, the only higher authority on this station than the Guild are the fifteen representatives of the Capitol Forum. If you disagree with my assessment, or you," she pointed to the security officer in charge, "we can shoot it out right here and let those left standing, claim justification."

Her mongrel growled; the sound reminded me of a tiger but more dreadful. Within seconds, two more hovercraft flew above with weapons pointing at the scene, and another smaller transport ship appeared directly above Juliet and me. Everyone froze, and all three groups stared at each other.

Juliet grabbed my hand in fear, and I pulled her close to me. The Lyons Pride commander took two steps back and looked down in submission. The other civilian Pride sneaks lowered their weapons too.

The security officer in charge shook his head and raised his voice over the engine sounds and wind. "No, the highest authority in the main cylinder, which is where we currently are, is Director Rumi Houlton, not the representatives of the Free Worlds. The Sideris siblings are coming with us to station command."

Senior Agent Korson chest-bumped the security officer, pushing him back several centimeters. She retorted, "Oh, yeah? You say one thing, I say another. We can fight it out and see who's right. Do you really think Rumi's in charge of this station? The cathedral and capitol dome squeezing the main cylinder would be interesting to see. You're not ready for that, nor do you want to be the cause of it."

Mom had told us that the main cylinder was initially built to support the capitol dome and that hardline politicians and social leaders from both sides crossed paths often on who had the authority to do what there. That didn't take into account the embassy bubbles, which were separate structures attached to the main cylinder.

A few tense seconds passed, but the security officer lowered his head and weapon. Another MERC Guild agent pulled Juliet and me back so the small transport could land. The agents nearby directed us into the craft. Once inside and strapped into our seats, I looked over at Senior Agent Korson, who helped us. Her face was stern with a hardness I'd never forget, but she nodded as if to say farewell and you're welcome before turning and walking away. Our transport shot into the air with immense force, lifting at least seventy meters; it had plenty of room to maneuver since full-size ships could fit into the dock. The Guild agents operating our transport flew us away from that mess of a scene.

Juliet shrieked when she turned her head in the direction the craft was flying. My eyes were wide for a moment, seeing the metal wall of the dock. We were traveling too fast and would surely strike, but before impact, two sliding doors retracted into the wall, large enough to allow all three MERC ships to pass through.

The tunnel was long and, based on the symmetrical lights we passed in patterns every few seconds, our speed was high. Outer doors opened, and we cleared them quickly to something we'd never seen before. It appeared as if we were on a planet, with sunlight and puffy clouds. But when looking up past the clouds, I saw green grass on the ground. The same was true when looking down. How was that possible?

I followed the ground from one side to the other; it made a complete circle, reconnecting to the point I originally looked at. There were buildings, trees, and roadways. Every part of the cylinder was alive with activity and aircraft. Juliet's look reflected my surprise, observing that fantastic sight. It seemed like magic.

"Maybe Mom was right—this place is like a fairy tale."

Juliet smiled. "It's amazing here. Look at this place."

"Agent, can I ask where you're taking us?"

"The cathedral. Center Seat Representative McWright's on his way down."

We flew for another hour, passing wonders of construction—parks, forests, villages, towns, small cities, lakes, rivers, and mountains. In the distance, something grew higher and higher as we got closer. A massive wall was clear to our front, more significant than the dock wall from before. Weapon pods on the wall moved in different directions. Below, agents with their mongrels patrolled the main entrance.

Juliet said, "It's the cathedral. We grew up hearing stories of agents and this place, and it's here, we're here."

She was right. As children, we had toys of famous agents in history. I was always fond of Senior Agent Scala. The way he decapitated members of the Flock family and brought the heads back here to the station fascinated me. Juliet liked Chief Ashton and her mongrel Tinnius, one of the most mammoth beasts ever produced by Kennel Hall.

The hovercraft flew into an airlock opening along the wall. The interior of the cathedral looked alien compared to the main cylinder, reminding me of a regular space station because of the metal walls, floors, and chunkiness. Agent transports lined one wall near a staging area of a hangar.

When we landed, the agents brought us to a building; they treated us well, offering food, water, and clothes. We sat for two hours before the doors finally opened. A tall man walked in, well dressed, with pale skin, light brown hair, and blue eyes. He had a commanding, confident presence and held his head high. He was handsome for an older man, having an inviting, sweet smile. It had to be Henry McWright. His suit was well fitted, including a vest, and a golden chain with a gold ornament of a hammer or mallet.

Juliet's puppy-dog eyes looked up through her lashes in a submissive, coquettish way. It was clear she found him attractive too, which irritated me. She always had men groveling at her feet because of her beauty. I was also desirable, in my opinion, and women had come at me countless times, but my interest wasn't in them. Juliet turned twenty a few weeks ago. On her birthday, the older teen she was sleeping with gave her a night to remember. I spent the evening in our refugee ship's common area. A night like that at some point this year would be great, maybe even with Henry.

Henry spoke. "Adam and Juliet Sideris, you have no idea what a pleasure it is to meet you both. I'm Representative Henry McWright of the Colonial Accord. Your mother and grandfather were—"

I cut him off and said, "We know all about you, sir. Mom told us to seek you out when we got here. The Pride is still hunting us though, even this far away from Epsilon Prime."

Henry nodded and studied me for a moment. "Yes, the last time your mother came here was after the war had already started. They stayed with me for a brief time, and I quietly helped your grandfather, but it was all in vain. Athinia still lost the war, and now the Lyons Twins control the planet. The Pride will always try to capture you because of who you are. The Green Eyes of Athinia, in the flesh, standing here in this room."

Juliet said, "We've heard so much about you through the years. It's great to meet you finally. I've imagined what you looked like from all the stories our mother told us."

Henry gazed at Jules, and from the way he was staring, he found her desirable. Once again, it was happening. I spoke up to break his focus.

"The MERC agents saved us in the refugee dock. If not for them, we would be in the hands of either the Pride or those security officers in the battle armor."

Henry said, "Yes, Nicolas Nomikos is the Secretary of Human Affairs here on the station, and he was once a vice-regent of Elpis. I had no idea he was seeking you out. More than likely, he wanted to use you as a tool to anger the Alliance representatives and their bubble. I'll not let him use you for politics. I owe much to Liam and will do everything in my power to help."

He and Grandpa were close, but how close? I was young when he died and had no memory of my grandmother because she passed before I was born.

"The security officers said the agents had no authority to take us. Is that true?"

Henry smiled. "Technically, it is. In the main cylinder, those security officers and all who work for station command are the highest authority there. But I'm the real power of this station, and the Guild is one of our main tools throughout all occupied space. What happened in the refugee dock was a big deal and will bring some headaches for me soon. Nothing like this has ever happened before, but I guess there's a first time for everything."

CHAPTER 24

Two Steps Forward
One Step Back

Something unexpected (Henry)

It was Alyssa's birthday, and she couldn't have been more excited. Her surprise was a marvel to see when the celebrity chef had food cooking as she woke up. The aroma was her alarm clock that morning. We were on the back terrace, enjoying mimosas with our delightful food. The chef made crepes Suzette with a side dish of tornado hash browns and eggs benedict. There were different berry sides, including one of her favorites, cape gooseberries.

Alyssa said, "Breakfast is wonderful, Henry. What a delightful surprise, waking up to a wonderful smell that brought a smile to my face."

"Glad to hear it, my love. The day is yours. My PDD is on call forwarding to Benjamin for the entire day. Only my immediate staff will be able to reach out to me if needed."

Alyssa smiled and took a sip of her mimosa. "And do you have a gift for the most beautiful woman on this entire station? The leading lady of the highest-ranking member under the dome should have something as elegant as her, something to show off, perhaps."

My wife enjoyed expensive and rare gifts. Each year, expectations increased for me to outdo the last. It grew ever harder to find something more extravagant. But this year, I'd found something incredibly unique that would be awe-inspiring, and that feat was hard enough. I paused for a moment while she stared in anticipation.

"Come on, Henry, you know I hate to wait for anything."

I pulled her gift from under the table and placed it in front of her. There was a sparkle in her eyes as she looked at the professionally wrapped rectangular box. Alyssa grabbed the gift hastily and tore the wrapping off. Having it gift-wrapped was two hundred and fifty credits, but that paled compared to the item inside. Alyssa hesitated with a smile on her face. She glanced at me and then down at the box again. She opened her gift, and an even brighter sparkle gleamed in her eyes, reflected from the item.

"Oh my, Henry," she said with exhilaration, "I have never seen anything so beautiful before. What is it?"

Alyssa delicately lifted the jewel, observing the marvel of the gems, a faint glow emitting from each. A small silver Corin-steel clasp held the gemstones in place around a thin necklace made of the rare steel. Each jewel's color was clear as a diamond, but each stone had a brilliant blue hint of light.

Alyssa held it up to her neck and asked, "Would you?"

"Of course, my darling."

The necklace clipped on with ease. It fit perfectly and rode high enough so any outfit she wore wouldn't block the view. The jewelry was light because of the glowing green and black-flecked steel.

"Ollie," I said, "please go grab a mirror from the bathroom downstairs so Alyssa can see how stupendous she looks wearing her necklace."

Oliver complied and hurried back with a small handheld mirror. Alyssa observed her reflection, and I continued, "The jewels have no name. They're one of the rarest items in existence."

"What are they?"

"Colonial miners found them in Titans' Belt. Belt scientists analyzed the gemstones to discover they're all that remains of a planet from millions of years ago. The asteroid the miners excavated was the last known piece of the world. These jewels were buried deep in the core. The belt scientists wanted to send these to the Uropa Free Worlds Museum, and the miners tried to keep them for their odd religion. Thankfully, with the help of Macaroy Garner, our Labor Party union leader in the belt, and some large sums of credits, the mining director helped these gems fall off the back of a shipping hauler and find their way here. They're utterly priceless. Do you see the blue glow in each stone?"

She nodded.

"Those were rare gases from the planet when it was still a solid body. It's a chemical reaction that will take millions of years to dissipate. The clasp at the back and holding clips for each stone are Corin steel, the strongest, rarest metal known. What you're now wearing is the last item in existence of a planet that could have once had life on it, long before humanity reached out to the stars and before the Titans of the Old World."

Alyssa turned and kissed me. "Oh, Henry, it's the best gift you've ever given me. I love it and you."

Not only was it the best gift I ever gave her, but also the most expensive. That small item cost more than the entirety of the three percent of Metak Agathon I sold to Representative Boran. Her happiness was all that mattered.

Alyssa said, "I'll wear it today and won't take it off until bed tonight."

"I'm glad to hear that. Now finish up breakfast, and we will start your day."

"What are we doing next?" Alyssa was excited.

"Next, we're going for a couple's massage at your favorite resort and spa. After lunch there, I have something for later tonight." I waited so her anticipation could build. "We're seeing the Colonial Phantom Performers at the Performing Arts Center here in New Wick."

The smile on Alyssa's face was wider than the one she displayed when opening her gift.

She was quite joyful. "The Phantom Performers? I thought they returned to Pardalis already? Their last show was this past weekend."

"The owners of the group's company and I had a conversation. At my request, the performers are here for an extra week."

Alyssa jumped from her chair and kissed me, stroking her tongue against mine. She pulled back and purred with delight. "You're the greatest husband in all of humanity."

After breakfast, we got dressed and left for the resort and spa. It was strange not receiving any notifications on my PDD at all. There'd be at least five calls, twenty messages, and another fifty or one hundred bulletins on a typical day. To be honest, I enjoyed the thrill of those calls and messages. I could give up one day for my wife.

After lunch, we traveled back home to spend the afternoon together. I anticipated some intimate time and tried to initiate with Alyssa as she undressed from her spa clothes, but she shook her finger, saying in her usual teasing tone, "No, no, that's the grand finale tonight after the show."

Another one of her little jokes that I found exhilarating; it made me want her even more. I went back out onto the terrace to observe the overlook of New Wick, our bubble city named and fashioned after the capital city of Warwick on Uropa. I loved it here and enjoyed spending time on the terrace.

Alyssa joined me after some time and said, "Where are your thoughts, love?"

"Nowhere, in particular, just taking it all in. Our lives here on the station always move at a thousand kilometers per hour with little time to see what it's all for. Sitting down and relaxing is nice."

Alyssa curled up next to me and put her head on my chest, looking out at the view. "It's wonderful here. I hope we never leave."

A few more minutes of sitting in peace went by until my PDD rang boisterously. It shouldn't have happened since call forwarding was active.

Alyssa looked enraged and glared at my PDD. "I thought you had that off today?"

"I did. It shouldn't be ringing." Something must have happened that couldn't wait. "I have to answer this, love. Malcolm wouldn't bother me unless it was important."

Malcolm started talking before I even said *hello*. That was strange behavior for him.

"Sir, I'm sorry to bother you, but you need to be made aware of a situation down in the refugee dock."

I was irritated. "What could be so important in the refugee dock that you would bother me on my wife's birthday?"

"Sir, Adam and Juliet Sideris, the children of Isabel and grandchildren of Liam are in the custody of the Guild. Station security officers inside the dock tried to detain them under the orders of Nicolas Nomikos, and the Lyons Pride also attempted to seize them. A three-way shootout nearly happened, but the agents were able to deescalate the situation. The kids are being flown down to the cathedral as we speak. They specifically asked for you, saying their mother told them to seek you out."

Malcolm kept referring to them as kids; however, if my memory was correct, they should be in their twenties. I jumped from my chair, pushing Alyssa's head away, my heart beating uncontrollably. Liam's grandchildren were here at the station? How did they get off Epsilon Prime without Isaac and Killian Lyons stopping them? Lots of questions needed answering.

"Have my ship prepared. Contact the chief agents and advise them I'm coming down right now. There's no time to waste. Tell the Guild to put extra agents on the siblings for protection. No harm can fall on them—they're critical to the future of Epsilon Prime."

Malcolm said, "Chief Agent Ashton's already giving me grief about violations to the Free Worlds' Relations Policy with the Guild taking Adam and Juliet."

"Don't worry about Ashton. I'll deal with her. The other chief agents want more control anyway and wouldn't care. Ashton's stricter with Guild mandate policies and probably angrier that Ficco relayed my order to the dock agents without her knowledge, more than likely," I said hastily.

After I hung up, Alyssa glared and her face was flush with fury. She shouted, "What are you doing? Today's my birthday!"

"Love, I'm sorry, but you have no idea how important Adam and Juliet Sideris are. Not only do I owe it to their grandfather, but the future of the Human Alliance depends on their well-being."

It concerned me that Isabel wasn't with them. Colonel Tuddy Sideris died, but Isabel should still be alive. Where was she?

I turned to Alyssa. "This situation is much bigger than you or—"

Alyssa slapped my face before I could finish. "I've already stopped listening to you. Now go, go do what you always do, be the center seat representative you are, and leave once again on urgent business."

I took her hands softly. "Alyssa, please. You have the tickets for tonight's performance. Go, take one of your girls and enjoy the rest of the night. I must go down to the cathedral and won't return until tomorrow. I promise to make this up to you."

Alyssa sat back in her chair, staring out over the terrace. She waited for a moment and said, "Just go."

I gathered my things and ran upstairs. Zoey, Alyssa's security officer, remained. Oliver and Josue rushed out with me, and another new security officer met us in the lobby. The trip was two and a half hours traveling outside of the station. That time helped me prepare for how to interact with the grandkids of the man who taught me much in my early political career. Liam, the Unifier, greatest man I ever knew.

*

We arrived at the cathedral dock and were given priority clearance to enter. After leaving the transport, Senior Agent Korson joined us on the walk to meet Adam and Juliet.

She said, "Representative McWright, sir. I have concerns about what transpired on the dock."

"I watched the video of what happened on my flight over here. Your Guild training is flawless, and the actions of the agents at your command were perfect. You held your ground against a much superior force. I'll be putting you in for commendations for these brave actions."

She appeared uneasy. "Yes, sir, but there was a lot of treading on feet going on up there. The Lyons Pride and station command officers both wanted them. I'm afraid of the repercussions when all is said and done."

Senior Agent Korson's reference was to what happened when agents' actions were ruled unjustified by cathedral magistrates. Korson, who helped shield Adam and Juliet in the dock from station security and Lyons Pride, would lose her titles, get branded as a rogue agent, and brought to the memory room for excommunication if the cathedral magistrates found her actions in the refugee dock unjustified.

I smiled at her and said, "Don't trouble yourself with the finer points of politics. I'll take care of those issues. Director Houlton will do what I tell her, and I'll speak to your superiors and go to the Hall of Justice myself to deal with the magistrates."

"What about the Alliance?"

I replied without answering. "You can return to your post now, senior agent. Once again, you did wonderful work."

We went into the building where Liam's grandchildren were. Guild agents and mongrels patrolled the area in high numbers. Maybe I was crazy to worry and request additional security for the Green Eyes. This was the heavily fortified cathedral. No one could get in here without clearance.

Before walking into their room, I took a breath to prepare myself. I felt nervous, which wasn't a common emotion for me. The door creaked open to the unnaturally bright green eyes of the Sideris family. Genetically it should have been difficult for all direct blood of a family to have the same color eyes, but this trait had followed the Sideris family for countless generations. Liam's wife had blue eyes, but his daughter and her kids all had the green glow. Two influential young adults stood before me, but there was no way they knew just how important they were to the Free Worlds.

I smiled and said, "Adam and Juliet Sideris, you have no idea what a pleasure it is to meet you both. I'm Representative Henry McWright of the Colonial Accord. Your mother and grandfather were—"

Adam talked over me. He had a strong-willed personality like his mother and spoke with attitude.

We talked for a moment and it reminded me of the last time I saw Isabel fourteen years ago when the civil war started when I allowed her and Liam to stay in my residence. If Liam hadn't been there, I would have tried to take her under the sheets. She was gorgeous, and I was a single man at the time. Her daughter was even more stunning, or maybe it was only her young age.

For the last fourteen years, I'd quietly tried to undermine the Lyons Twins of New-Sparta. Not actively; instead with passive subversion. The working relationship with Left Seat Representative Zachery Laskaris had benefited us both for a time, but my true loyalty had always been with Liam and Athinia. Zachery and his father Donovan of City-State Aetós were still treated as second-class citizens on Epsilon Prime. The Chrysós Aetós waited until the very end of the war to choose a side in the fight. That was why Zachery and I got along so well. Things would change because of my open defiance, declaring myself for the Green Eyes of Athinia.

Adam asked, "The security officers said the agents had no authority to take us. Is that true?"

He was pestering me about that, too.

I smiled. "Technically, that is true. In the main cylinder, those security officers and all who work for station command are the highest authority. But I am the real power of this station, and the Guild is one of our main tools throughout all occupied space. What happened in the refugee dock was a big deal and will bring some headaches for me soon. Nothing like this has ever happened before, but I guess there's a first time for everything."

JJ Richmond and his Rose Party of Ardum would try to use the incident against me. My own Labor Party might give me trouble because of this unheard-of action. The more I thought, the more I questioned myself.

"I must ask, where is Isabel?"

Juliet said, "The Dolrinions took her."

Adam added, "Pirates attacked our ship. We hid in the safe room, and my mother stayed back to buy us time. She fought them and was taken captive."

"I thought you said Dolrinions took her?"

"They did, but other things happened first." Juliet's eyes went to the floor.

Adam said, "After the pirates were on the ship for some time looting and ransacking everything, we were boarded again by Androsians—"

"You saw Androsians on your ship?"

"Yes, they came on the ship and started doing terrible things. Never seen anything like it before. It was something out of a horror movie. Even behind the safe room doors, everyone was terrified. With the help of Mom, the pirates fought the stalkers with little success, but she killed one."

I snickered. "A true Sideris to the bone. Isabel's a warrior, and I know she ran the resistance for years with the loyalists on Epsilon Prime."

Adam narrowed his eyes; he looked troubled and even annoyed. He was fascinating, and I looked forward to learning more about him. He continued, "One of the Androsians got Mom near the secondary terminal docking door and mutilated her. It removed an eye and almost killed her. But then the secondary doors opened, and the Dolrinions came onto the ship."

"I've never heard of a single vessel being boarded by all three groups at the same time. You hit an unfortunate trifecta."

Juliet said, "Mom survived. The Dolrinion medics patched her up and took her with the pirates off the ship in slave cuffs."

That gave me hope. "Isabel's a slave to Force Command Burning Star. That's good news."

Adam, looking confused, asked, "How is this good news?"

"Because I know where she is now. There are three supreme generals of the Offensive under the dome that I have a good working relationship with at the moment. I can trade them for her release. If the pirates took Isabel, we'd never see her again."

Adam's and Juliet's eyes opened wide, and they looked hopeful. *My actions are for you, Liam. I'm going to save your family.*

"Ok, listen to me now, tonight you'll stay here. I need to arrange some things for you both, and it will take me a day to get the wheels moving. Tomorrow night you will become guests inside the Colonial bubble. We must keep you safe. You're under my protection, so rest easy because nothing is happening to you here."

Both thanked me, and I left in a hurry. Alyssa was angry and did not expect to see me tonight. I felt guilty and wanted to return to her since it was her birthday. A surprise might smooth things over to a small degree. Maybe there was a chance of amends for leaving the way I did.

We got into my transport, and I spoke to Oliver. "Get me home as fast as possible. I've got an angry wife to get to."

It took two hours, and we finally arrived back in my apartment lobby. I wished the doorman a good evening and got into my private elevator to go up to the penthouse. All three security officers were with me. Whenever we entered my apartment after being away, they cleared the house before the new officer went back down.

Alyssa should still be at the performance; maybe I could set up some candles to surprise her when she got home. The elevator doors opened and we walked inside. Strangely enough, the lights were on. We walked into the kitchen area where Zoey, my wife's security officer, stood guard near the spiral staircase up to my bedroom. Her eyes were open wide as if she saw a ghost. Something unexpected was happening, and it made the hair on my neck stand straight up.

In a stern voice, Oliver asked, "Security officer, what are you doing here?"

"I'm here with Alyssa, sir."

"Where's my wife?" I snapped, jumpy with anger.

For the first time, Zoey didn't look somber. She seemed insecure, like a child, looking down at the ground, her shoulders drooping.

"She's ... she's upstairs, sir."

The tickets to the Phantom Performers were on the granite countertop in the kitchen. She never went to the show, and something wasn't right. I felt it in my bones.

"Oliver, don't let anyone move. I'll be right back."

I used the other staircase in the living room to go upstairs. My office was above our bedroom, overlooking it perfectly. The lights were off in the office; no one would see me. Each step through the dark room came with an echo, like a slapping and moaning, and it grew louder the closer I got to the catwalk. That sound was familiar to me.

Once next to the railing, I peered down to see Alyssa on the bed, bent over on all fours like a dog with her face down into the pillow, squeezing it with all her might. She yelled loudly into the cushion as a young man took her from behind. He clutched her hips and backside and her skin pushed up through his fingertips. Every time he moved into her, she shouted louder. He was doing it faster and harder than I ever could, the young bastard. I could hear their skin slapping together, and the noise infuriated me.

Alyssa was utterly naked, but she was wearing the necklace I gifted her. He grabbed the costly jewelry, pulling on it as Alyssa arched her head back and moaned, looking up at the ceiling. His movements were even faster as he pulled harder on the necklace. The Corin steel and gemstones disappeared into her neck, choking her, and based on her expression, she enjoyed the sensation.

Part of me wanted to go down there and kill them both, but I hesitated. Who was that younger man? Only the back of his head was visible, and nothing came to mind looking at his bare ass. Alyssa turned her body and kissed him passionately. She pushed him down on the bed, and his face finally became visible. My heart skipped a beat. No, how was that possible? It couldn't be. I had to rub my eyes to be sure.

That bastard, who did he think he was, fucking my wife? So many things ran through my head. Alyssa got on top of him in a position I'd never seen before. She had never done it to me like that. He squeezed her breasts so tight. Those were mine; he shouldn't be touching them.

Memories scrambled through my head like eggs in a bowl. When that young bastard was looking at her butt, when he said he wanted to remain here and not return to Uropa, when he told me last week how he liked more outgoing women … there was no one on this station more outgoing than Alyssa. I never made that connection when he said the words. He told me he was biding his time waiting for the right moment. *Benjamin, you scum, I'll make you pay for betraying me.*

I turned and walked away, still listening to the slapping of their skin connecting. Alyssa cried out loud with delight. Back downstairs, Oliver, Josue, and the new security officer were standing next to Zoey, who looked terrified when she caught my eye.

Zoey was much shorter than me, and seemed to shrink as I stared down at her. That complicit bitch never told Oliver or me what was going on. I grabbed her by the throat, squeezing, and she ground her teeth, struggling to breathe. Oliver restrained her arms, and Josue removed her sidearm. We could still hear Alyssa moaning upstairs.

"How long has this been happening? Answer me quickly and truthfully."

I released my grip on her neck so she could speak.

"They've been sleeping together for over a year."

One year? All of this with my lead aide for a year. Malcolm was right when he said something else must have been going on the night Ben went missing for thirty minutes before my speech. Benjamin probably had Alyssa in the forum's back stairwell, fucking her against a wall behind the amphitheater.

I snapped back, "Have there been others besides Benjamin?"

Zoey didn't answer, her eyes going to Oliver. Ollie punched her in the stomach and said forcefully, "Answer the representative now."

She exhaled dramatically and gasped, "Yes, there's been others. But not for the last year. The others were before Benjamin. She hasn't been with anyone else since Benjamin."

My eyes circled the room, looking at each member of my security team. It was hard to think while my wife's moans of pleasure were still audible from upstairs.

The new security officer was to my right.

"What's your name?"

"Pietro, sir."

I glanced at Oliver and said, "Take her. We're bringing her behind the curtain."

Oliver and Josue dragged Zoey to the elevator in the foyer. She attempted to resist, but my two officers were stronger than her.

I turned to Pietro. "I want you to remain here. Alyssa hasn't seen you yet. You were down in the lobby this morning before I left. When she asks you where Zoey went—"

He interrupted. "When Mrs. McWright asks me where Zoey went, I'll tell her that Zoey had a family emergency and had to leave. Dome headquarters sent me to replace her."

I wanted to smile at him but didn't. That damn moaning sound still resonated down the stairs. Based on what I'd seen so far, Pietro would work out quite nicely.

"You're her new protection officer. Zoey won't be returning."

"Yes, sir. I won't let you down and will keep you informed on all her actions."

After everything that had taken place recently—fighting from beneath my fellow representatives, clawing my way back to the top of the forum—this, of all things, this? In my own house, Alyssa, you vile woman. *No one does this to Henry McWright.* I walked out of my home with the darkest thoughts from the recesses of my mind flowing freely. This time I let them flood my imagination without pushing them away, like a bathtub of water overflowing without end.

CHAPTER 25

Black, Brown & Burgundy

The Free Worlds of Humanity are not free (Isabel)

We had nearly finished another workday in the mines. Four days had gone by since Gideon, Jack, and Ethan cut the tattoos off Geoff in our bunkhouse. After slicing away Geoff's flesh, they dropped him at Ezra's bunk door. He was now with the Brown Pirates. To me, it seemed like an unnecessary provocation. If the Brown Pirates had much larger numbers, why egg them on to a fight? Nina told me it had to do with their code of honor as pirates, which made me laugh to myself. I've learned my entire life that all pirates were nothing more than brigands who would sell their mothers for wealth. However, some recent events countered that view. I still saw them as brutes who did terrible deeds, but they had another side too. In some ways, the strongest of them compared well to conscripts in the Athinia State Guard.

I spent the last few days observing everything happening in camp. Our workday started at sunrise. All slaves had to be outside for inspection at the same time every morning. If someone was late into line, the sentinels put them in the oven for that day. Several small wooden boxes lined the command staff building nearby. Built with old wood and splintering, they could barely fit a person inside. The boxes had narrow slits so the occupant could get fresh air, but after hours inside, the planet's heat could kill. Most died, and those who did survive spent the next few days inside the medical building. The oven was the primary form of punishment besides getting nailed to the wood along the fencing out front.

After inspection, we marched in single file through the front gate where the sentinels made sure to show us slaves nailed to the wood and any new additions that day. The march to the mines took forty-five minutes; from the number of steps it took to get there, I knew that the distance was slightly over three kilometers.

There weren't any roads, but the sand path was packed down from millions of feet walking it for countless years. The views were decent enough with rolling hills, sand as far as the eye could see and palm trees. On the downslope of our hike, thousands of slaves became visible in the distance ahead. The scene reminded me once again of the civil war.

After Dad met with the Rogue Syndicate and made his deal, we returned to Epsilon Prime from the relations station. When we got home, we learned that the battle line previously established had collapsed, and a new line formed twenty-four kilometers from the state capital city. Tuddy had taken command of the main battle line and saw to the defenses there. During his masterful strategy at that time, he earned the nickname Stonewall of the Allied States, a name the Twins despised. Our neighbors watched the children near our farm in the south after a failed attempt to steal them by Lyons Pride sneaks.

It took an additional week for the mercenaries hired to come to Epsilon Prime. I remember standing in the streets of our city and watching the soldiers marching out to join the main battle line. Music filled the air and streamers drifted in the wind, falling over everyone like early snows before winter. People danced in the streets with smiles. It was a celebration, and citizens cheered loudly as the mercenaries moved out of the city.

Those mercenaries were poor excuses for soldiers compared to our Athinia Guard. Dad had to empty our state coffers to pay the Syndicate for these troops. There was no more money left, but Dad said it didn't matter.

There wouldn't be an Athinia as we knew it for much longer. Refugee ships still landed almost daily, removing citizens from our city-state, and people needed time to flee. By that point, I had reenlisted as a major in our city-state military with strategic command. I helped organize our strategy along with other capable military minds—those that were still alive after the initial attack. My grandfather was in my thoughts often during those days.

Keon Sideris was considered one of the greatest military minds in Athinia's history. Historians referred to him as the Fighting Sideris for his abilities in battle. Grandpa fought the War of Oppression against New-Sparta.

That war was five city-states against five city-states with Athinia on one side and New-Sparta on the other. Athinia won, and Epsilon Prime lived in relative peace until the Unification Civil War. Everyone from the older Alliance generations knew the name Keon Sideris. He coined the famous battle cry of Athinia. In combat, he would scream "Banue Na'yah," meaning freedom from tyranny.

Three months after the mercenaries had left the city, the Lyons Twins marched in their Parade of Victory down the same street where we celebrated months earlier. The Lyons Pride wore their extravagant shiny dress battle armor and marched in lockstep with each other to our State Capitol. The Pride had fancy pauldrons shaped like lions' heads that glistened in the sunlight. The arrogant Twins had smirks on their faces that made Athinians angry, but we could do nothing. All held New-Sparta state flags and clapped as the soldiers went by. Those who didn't participate or made insolent comments were scooped up immediately and never seen again.

When I regained my focus, I started coughing from all the soot and ash in the dark and gloomy cave. There was a level of moisture in the air that never faded, and it made the heat sometimes unbearable. The sharp dark-colored rock always felt wet and constant drips fell from it. The workday was nearly over, and my shoulders and arms were fatigued. I swung my pickaxe a few more times, breaking off pieces of the wet ore we harvested in the mine.

I paused for a moment to wipe the sweat from my forehead as Gideon turned a corner and startled me, speaking sarcastically.

"Well, aren't you the good little miner? I'm surprised you haven't filled your quota already for today."

I was breathing heavily. "I filled my quota three hours ago. This pile's for tomorrow's quota."

Gideon laughed in his usual obnoxious manner. "That's a good thought, but it won't work. After the slaves leave the mine for the day, sentinels clear every corridor and passage to make sure no one tries to stay behind. Any additional ore on the ground won't be here tomorrow."

I narrowed my eye as my stubbornness got the better of me and countered, "We'll just see what happens tomorrow, won't we?"

Gideon sighed. "I don't know how your husband put up with that very thick head of yours." He emphasized his next words. "Ok, let me help you give more ore to the sentinels for free."

We hammered into the thick sharp rock for some time until I stopped for a few seconds to catch my breath again.

"I've never understood why we call it the Free Worlds of Humanity. There's nothing free here—it's all an illusion. Even if we weren't picking away in this mine, we'd still be slaves to the worlds we call home. Free, outer, and rogue planets combined, nothing more than slaves, all of us."

Gideon studied me for a time. "That's not true at all, Isabel—the Free Worlds are precisely what you say. But the rogue worlds are the freest places in occupied space. You look at me and our world Draco thinking that we are nothing but animals. You believe that on our rogue world, we roam around terrorizing each other daily. If you were to go to Draco today, you'd see villages, people living in peace, children going to school and playing games. Yes, the living conditions are harder, especially on a world like Draco, but life there is good. Rogue planets have much that you would see on a Free World without all the arbitrary rules and regulations. Sure, the technology level on Draco is nothing by comparison, but what does that matter? We have running water and basic needs. There are exceptions to this, of course, but the well-known rogue worlds are exactly how I explained. We're the real free worlds, and we didn't need to create a space station to justify that freedom."

I shook my head. "That can't be true—you're always fighting with each other, one captain trying to overcome the other and outdo each other for fame and glory. Other rogue worlds have barbaric overlords, and war spreads like a sickness without vaccines."

Gideon laughed. "That's what you see in the deep black of space. We don't fight each other on our homeworld. It's against our law for any pirate to fight another while on Draco. If there is a disagreement, they must leave the planet and settle it on our moon or in deep space. The other major rogue worlds are the same. Have you ever been to Galma?"

I shook my head again, and he continued, "People live well there even with the Syndicate running the Highlands. The Lowlands aren't what the stories claim. Albino Lowlanders don't eat people like Androsians. The Free Worlds of Humanity are the real prison, Isabel."

I snapped back in defiance, "Well, we're slaves on a rogue world right now."

Gideon smirked. "A rogue world controlled by a Free World, isn't that irony?"

I resented him now. "I don't want to speak with you anymore today."

"No problem, let's get out of here. The workday's over, and we need to get back with our group."

Gideon walked away back into the mine. I waited a few minutes, then followed. Our march back to camp was the same as when we came, only this time we were all covered in black soot. At camp, all slaves went to their bunks for a shower. Showering was my favorite part of the day.

All bunks reported to the mess hall for meals. It was a large popup building that had round tables with stools for up to ten people each. There were hundreds of tables and long lines to get food. Surprisingly, we ate real food with high calories to sustain us—cooked chicken, pork, rice, different kinds of pasta, bread, and vegetables. The mess hall didn't have restrictions on consumption. Excess food was wasted on Pomona. Nine Allied States, including Athinia, starved to death daily, and this food could have saved thousands of lives.

There wasn't any alcohol in camp, but it didn't stop some from trying to ferment their own with fruits and yeast from bread inside bunkhouses.

Since the incident with Geoff, there hadn't been any reprisals. Ezra and the Brown Pirates had been keeping to themselves, but Gideon believed they were waiting for the right moment to strike. One Pirate of the Black died in the mines when a rock wall collapsed. Strangely enough, the next day, the same thing happened to a Pirate of the Brown. Aside from those two incidents, nothing else happened.

Even after a long day's work, people enjoyed leisure time after eating in the mess hall. Every night slaves formed teams and played power-ball. The champions of the yard were Ezra's Brown Pirates, and they enjoyed enforcing made-up rules for what could and couldn't happen in the yard. Sentinels placed bets on which groups would win each game. I met other slaves from Epsilon Prime out there. To my surprise, I saw two slaves who were once professional power-ball players from City-State Macegia. That state allied with Athinia during the war. They were a small state but strong and produced some of the best athletes in all of the Alliance. The two former professional players I spoke with said they were on a ship traveling to Uropa in the Colonial Accord for vacation. Force Command Burning Star attacked their vessel and enslaved the survivors. I kept hearing stories of Free Worlds citizens being taken and forced into slavery even though it was illegal. I figured Burning Star battle group commanders had quotas to fill, and if harvests were unsuccessful outside Free Worlds' territories, they attacked anyone within range.

I spent a great deal of time in the yard befriending the former power-ball players. They introduced me to other slaves that were once from the Alliance. Most of them were from the Allied States siding with Athinia during the Unification War. Some came from Elpis, Macegia, Gelarhcret, Corinetus, and Syrac. None of them said outright that they knew who I was, but some made faces of disbelief, giving away their thoughts. My eye gave me away. One slave in particular, named Bacon (or so dubbed by his fellow bunkmates), had leathery skin and always smiled when he saw me. He never spoke any words, but would look into my green eye and smile wide. He earned his name because the Dolrinion guards put him in the oven nine different times for his actions, though honestly, it seemed to me that those actions were because of his simple nature. Gideon joked and said that the reason Bacon acted that way was that his brains cooked in the oven like a nice crispy piece of bacon.

Syrac was always Athinia's closest ally throughout history. Our two city-states were known as the sibling states, and both had representation in each other's Ministry Offices. City-State Syrac had a strong ground conscript force and put up the most significant resistance to New-Sparta during the war. Even after Athinia surrendered, Syrac continued to fight for another month. They'd paid for their defiance to the Lyons Twins with years of torment. Of all the former allies of Athinia, Syrac suffered the worst. They claimed that the air always smelled of death inside their state. It might have been true. The death toll on Syrac was higher than any other Allied State because of their work camps, execution centers, and treatment by the Lyons Pride.

The sun had gone down, and the spotlights from the tower guards shone through camp. A bunkhouse near us made a pit fire like they did most nights. They enjoyed the cool air surrounding the fire and talked. Gideon, Jack, Nina, Ethan, and I joined in to socialize and enjoy the breeze under the stars. Wood crackled through the flames and embers glided into the air like starship engines in the black of space. The sound calmed me, and I loved the smell of burning wood. It reminded me of home.

Ethan scratched at his new forearm tattoo, which looked like a wave with intricate designs and patterns. It was small, no bigger than five or six centimeters, but detailed. The skin around the tattoo was red, and the black scabs were peeling. Pirates in our bunk tattooed him by hand with a small wooden rod for tapping, and a needle on another rod. Nina told me all tattoos they earned came by the needle tap.

It was easy to fade away into thought gazing into the flickering fires. A beautiful young woman sat with the group and she began to sing. Her voice was magical, and everyone nearby stopped what they were doing to listen.

"We hammer away until the end of each day, always working with our bones hurting. But we keep our hope, hope, hope, that these things will change. When morning comes, and the three suns rise, we hammer away, each and every day. Away, away, I wish I could fly, away, away, please take me away."

This young woman with her amazing voice continued to sing, and some of the slaves listening, cried. They were tears of joy at her perfect heavenly voice; even Big Jack had a single tear rolling down his face. He wiped it away and continued to listen with a smile.

I whispered to Nina, "Her voice is great. Where are the people in this bunkhouse from?"

Nina leaned closer, still listening. "They're all generational slaves. Every one of them was born here."

I was surprised; that young woman would be a superstar on one of the Free Worlds of Humanity with a voice like that. Because of circumstance, she was nothing more than a slave spending her nights by this fire.

Later on, we returned to our bunkhouse for the night. It was time to sleep, and I drifted off, but woke and turned to see Ethan in his bottom bunk with Nina under his blanket. She was on top of him, rocking her hips as they kissed. Good for Nina, even though Ethan made more noise than her. Others in the bunk might be awake, but none cared enough to pay attention. There wasn't privacy in the bunk racks, and I would have bet this was a common occurrence. Nina gazed at me while I watched her. She smiled, moving her hips faster. I rolled over and closed my eye.

The next morning, we all lined up for inspection again, thousands standing there as the sentinels walked the lines counting. Once complete, we set off on our march to the mines. Nina was next to me, and I couldn't stop thinking about what she did last night.

"So, Ethan, really?"

Nina raised her chin and grinned. "It was a reward for earning his first tattoo and joining the captain's crew. Besides, a woman still has needs, even in a place like this. For me, that's all it was. I got off, and I feel better for it. Poor little Ethan, though. I think he's in love with me now. During processing in the intake area, I saw his manhood. It's disproportionately enormous."

Nina laughed before continuing. "I was so impressed and couldn't get the size of that thing out of my mind, so I decided to take it for a test drive."

We giggled together, and for one reason or another, Gideon's naked body was in my mind.

"Gideon's pretty large himself."

Nina raised an eyebrow. "He is."

"Have you been with him?"

"Never," she answered, "he doesn't take women the way other captains do."

Her statement made me curious and my narrowed eye must have shown it. "He tried to take me on the refugee ship. He said he would have fun breaking me in his cabin."

Nina shook her head. "No, that was a gimmick. Captains must act a certain way, and if they don't, their crew won't respect them. Gideon said the same thing to me when he took me onto his father's ship as first mate. Once inside his cabin, he gave me a separate bed and didn't touch me. After a few weeks, Gideon integrated me into his crew, where I have been ever since. He would have done the same thing for you. Especially after watching you defend yourself against us."

An image of the first pirate who came onto the refugee ship when I knocked him out with the metal prybar came to mind. There was more to the captain than I initially believed, but it was hard to see past his obnoxious, arrogant attitude.

"That's interesting."

Nina said, "Truth be told, Gideon has only been with one woman, but it was before I joined his crew. I heard the stories ... she's a captain now of her own ship. They had a falling out when she challenged him to be first mate of his father's ship."

"Who's his father? Others keep talking about him too, yet no one's said his name."

Nina grew uncomfortable. "You'll have to ask Gideon. It's not my place to say anything further."

Before we talked anymore, the sound of someone yelling blasted through the air. I turned to the side and saw Ezra marching faster than everyone else with Geoff and all the Brown Pirates following. He hooted, "Move out of the way, you weaklings! Us Martoosh will show you how to do some real mining today. As captains of the Brown always say, Us Martoosh will lead the way!"

All the pirates behind him called out in approval and marched faster, walking past us to the front of the line.

Nina looked concerned.

I said, "Remember Matthew's words? Ezra only comes to the mines when he wants to do something bad."

Nina waited for the last Brown Pirate to pass. "We need to speak with Gideon."

We arrived at the mine entrance where the sentinels handed us our pickaxes and mining helmets with headlamps. Gideon and Jack were near the cave entrance with other pirates of Draco. Nina and I went to the group.

Gideon said, "We all know what's going on here. Jack and I have a plan. We'll split into three groups and go deep into the mines. Jack and his shadow Ethan will lead one, Nina'll lead another, and I'll take the third. After those brown shits spend time trying to find us, they'll grow impatient and split off to cover more ground, that's when we'll strike, picking them off little by little."

I spoke bluntly. "What about me?"

Gideon snorted. "Now you want to be one of us?"

I narrowed my eye. "No. I don't."

"Exactly. You do whatever it is you do. You aren't a Pirate of the Black, so there's no reason for the browns to bother with you. Go find your pile of ore if it's still there and continue with your workday. You'll know our outcome on the walk back to camp."

They left me to my anger. It was strange for me, not being a part of the action, when I had led countless assaults against the Lyons Twins on Epsilon Prime. Was I angry not being included because of my past, or did I feel that way because of an attachment growing inside of me for the people of our bunkhouse? My initial intention was only to stay near them for protection, but Gideon, for all his loathsome ways, had a way of bringing people together.

I walked inside the mine where I'd left my pile of ore from the previous day, but it was gone. Gideon was right. The sentinels took it. All that extra work for nothing. There was a dense dust cloud in the mine that day. I decided to move up the shaft to an outer rim to get some fresh air. My lungs could use the break with today's work. Tunnels pushed out to the side of the mountain. Sentinels built the outer shafts for airflow to the inner primary mining area.

A few hours passed, and I took a break, stretching my stiff arms and legs. Near the edge of the tunnel, overlooking mountains and sand, I sat. Those three suns hurt my eyes, the brightness reflecting off the coarse surface, and there were no visible clouds. A sound from behind broke my focus.

"Isn't this a surprise, what do we have here?"

I turned, but the dark tunnel made my unfocused eyes blurry. When the voice stepped into the light, my heart dropped with a similar feeling I had when the Androsian ripped me from the elevator before I lost my eye. Ezra, Geoff, and two Brown Pirates were behind me. I stood and took a few steps forward, away from the mountainside ledge. I had the pickaxe gripped firmly in my hands. They outnumbered me, and Ezra counted as two by himself.

Geoff said, "That's her right there—Captain Gideon said she was under his protection. I think she's his prize."

Ezra smiled. "If she's good enough for the famous Captain Gideon, she's good enough for all four of us to take a turn. No sloppy seconds. I go first, you three watch."

I screamed with fury, "I'm nobody's prize, and the first one of you to try and touch me will lose their prick!"

All four bellowed in laughter, and Ezra said, "Even with a missing eye, she's a bottle rocket. Geoff, do me a favor and go fetch her."

Geoff grinned and ran straight for me. I held the pickaxe level with both hands. He grabbed the axe and pushed, but I rolled backward and kicked my feet up, pushing his body over the ledge and down the side of the mountain. We could all hear Geoff's cries and grunts as his body slammed from one sharp edge to the next, falling several hundred meters to his death. I regained my footing and smiled with delight as the three stared at me with wide-open eyes of astonishment.

Ezra appeared bewildered. "Well now, isn't that interesting?"

He and his pirates roared again, laughing together as if the sound of Geoff's death was the greatest joke ever told.

Ezra's expression changed to a deep frown, and all three men came towards me fast. I tried to swing the pickaxe, but Ezra caught my blow like a toy.

He punched my stomach, and I fell to the ground. The other two picked me up, holding my arms, and bent me over a large boulder in the tunnel. Ezra grabbed my belt, pulling on it to remove my pants, but stopped when another loud voice resonated through the tunnel.

"What do we have going on here, I wonder? There appears to be a role reversal happening before my eyes. Pirates of the Brown usually take it in the brown. You should be lying on that boulder, and she should be standing behind, having a go at your backside. Not the other way around."

The pirates holding me down let go to glare into the dark. I didn't hesitate and ran away from them in the direction of the voice. Someone walked out of the shadows. It was Gideon, but he was alone.

"Where's your group?"

"Taking care of something else at the moment. I wanted to check on you." He looked over at Ezra. "It appears I came at the right time."

Ezra slammed his chest with a clenched fist. "You come here alone and talk this way? I'm going to show you how it feels to take it in the brown, Gideon of the *Viathon*."

Gideon said, "You know who I am, but I don't know you."

Ezra pounded his chest again even harder. "I'm Captain Ezra of the *Moonsea*."

Gideon tilted his head, lifting one eyebrow. "Never heard of you."

Ezra's face turned flush with rage and he squinted, shouting, "Not yet you haven't. But after I kill the famous Captain Gideon and Jack the Giant, my name will be legendary on Martoosh."

Gideon looked unmoved and pointed to the tattoos on both his arms.

"Many before have claimed they'd kill me. Their failures are now ink on my body."

Ezra grumbled, "Aah, you have never faced a more capable captain than me."

Gideon smiled obnoxiously. "You know, I never understood why you Brown and Burgundy pirates always acted so tough when facing us Pirates of the Black. Of the three Bs, black's the strongest. Have you seen what black does when it's mixed with other colors? It always consumes, rarely giving way to anything else. Black's also the last thing people see when they close their eyes upon death, fading into nothingness. We always win in the end."

Gideon glanced at me and wiggled his fingers. "Now, run along, you. I've got lessons to teach to these simpletons."

I hesitated, then said, "There's three of them. I can help you."

He gave me a cold look and screamed, "Run, now!"

Without pause or fear, Captain Gideon turned back to Ezra and walked with purpose at all three Pirates of Martoosh. I did what he told me and left, but it felt wrong. As I ran down the tunnel, the sound of a scuffle breaking out was behind me.

I cleared the mine and saw other Pirates of the Black huddled together. Jack came over and said, "Where's the captain?"

I looked down, ashamed, and answered, "He made me leave."

Jack grabbed my arms, lifting me off my feet like I was a stuffed toy and spoke louder, "Where is he?"

"Still in the mine with Ezra," I yelled.

Jack and other pirates tried to run inside the mine, but sentinels stopped them. A few minutes passed, and Ezra cleared the tunnel opening with a smile on his face. Only one other Pirate of the Brown was with him. Gideon must have killed the other. Ezra rubbed himself between his legs as he walked. Jack screamed with belligerent wrath, trying to go after Ezra, but the group held him back. It took eight to restrain our giant.

Tense moments passed, and two Dolrinion medics came from the cave with a gurney. Gideon was face down on the stretcher with a sheet over his body. He was alive, but there was blood dripping from the sheet. His face was swollen with thick globs of blood where they beat him.

A sentinel said, "Is this one with you?"

Jack answered, "Yes."

"Take him. He'll need to spend a few days in the medical building and get stitches for the tearing in his ass."

Dolrinions weren't sensitive with their words. Gideon's eyes were open, but his gaze seemed to come from a mind that wasn't there. No smile, sarcasm or joking demeanor, just a blank stare of emptiness. Why did he sacrifice himself for me?

I made a fist and tapped it against my hip. "Damn you, Gideon. I told you to let me stay and help. It was three against one. You didn't stand a chance without me."

Nina ran over and grabbed my arm to pull me away. "Now's not the time. We can talk to him later."

The walk back to camp felt like an eternity. I ran everything through my head, second-guessing all my decisions that day. What if I did this or what if I did that. None of it mattered. What was done was done. We arrived back at camp, and Jack took Gideon into the medical building.

I asked Nina, "What were the groups doing in the cave? Why did Gideon come to me alone?"

"We ambushed different groups of the Brown Pirates who were trying to find us. Jack killed Ezra's first mate and two others. My group killed four, and Gideon was going to take Ezra, but he wasn't with his flock. Gideon left right away because he had a feeling they were going for you since Geoff wasn't with any of the Brown Pirates. Gideon's group killed two before Gideon ran to find you. In total, we killed nine and lost four, but the shame to Gideon is worse than all their losses. It makes him look weak."

"I killed Geoff, sent him flying over the side of the ledge in the air tunnel. There were two other Brown Pirates with Ezra, and only one came back, so the count's eleven, not nine."

Nina exhaled a sound of approval. "That's good news we need to spread in our bunk. Jack should hear it too. He might be sour with you for not staying with Gideon, even though he told you to leave. Jack's so loyal to the captain. He loves him like family."

Jack and Ethan finally came from the medical building. Jack gave Nina and me an unpleasant gaze before speaking. "The captain wants to be left alone for the night."

My stubbornness and agitation flared. I ignored Jack, walking past him into the medical building. The giant yelled at me to stop. Once inside, I went to Gideon, waiting for the medic to stitch his wounds, and sat next to him. I slowly brought my hand to his and held him without speaking. Gideon looked past me at the wall, unwilling to acknowledge my presence.

I couldn't contain myself any longer and said, "Why did you give yourself up to Ezra? You did that to protect me, but I don't understand."

Gideon was motionless for some time, still glaring past me. Finally, he turned his head, staring into my eye, and spoke two words softly that pierced through my body like I was standing in water as lightning struck.

"Izzy bear."

I pulled my hand away as goosebumps covered my arms. "How do you know that name?"

Gideon took a deep breath. "Your father referred to you by that name a few times on my visits to the Athinia Capitol building during the war."

With disbelief, I asked, "How's that possible? When? What were you doing in Athinia?"

He'd known who I was the entire time. When I told him my full name as we walked onto the Dolrinion slave ship, I didn't think a random pirate captain would have any idea who a Sideris of Epsilon Prime was. Now I remembered him gazing out the airlock window after I said my name while we walked into the slaver's ship. He realized who I was at that moment.

Gideon said, "Your father contracted the Rogue Syndicate during the civil war with mercenaries."

"I know. I was in the room when he decided to use the Syndicate."

"Yes, you were," Gideon allowed, "but what you didn't see were the drops of millions of tons of supplies, food, munitions, and equipment for the soldiers. Each week, supply ships arrived for the nine Allied States fighting the Twins of New-Sparta. I flew dozens of missions into Athinia delivering goods. My father was contracted through the Rogue Syndicate to use our Draco ships to bring in the essential supplies your people needed. The Syndicate doesn't care who they take money from, and it was cheaper for them to use us instead of their own ships. By that point, the entire northern border of your state, with its production factories, had already fallen into enemy hands. Your father and I worked closely with each other for three months before Isaac and Killian Lyons publicly executed him on the State Capitol building steps. When Aetós declared for New-Sparta, and their fleets blockaded the atmospheres of all nine Allied City-States, those bastards captured me and killed most of my fellow Draco Pirates. I watched the live execution of Liam the Unifier from a prison cell with fresh wounds on my hands from where those Golden Eagle assholes removed my fingers."

Gideon lifted his maimed hands to look at the missing fingers. "Your father was a humble, caring person who didn't lie or cheat to get ahead. That's something quite rare in the Free Worlds of Humanity."

His speaking of fathers made me wonder, so I asked, "Who's your father? Everyone talks about him around here like he's some fabled figure. You said you live in your dad's shadow. Well, you know my dad, I've lived behind him my entire life." The captain gave me an uncomfortable look, and I pressed my question. "Tell me."

Gideon closed his eye, taking another deep breath of air. "I'm the son of the genuine black-blooded leader of Draco, the one who puts fear into people's hearts when his name is spoken out loud. He renounced his Force Command and forsook the memory stone in disgrace only to rise as the greatest ever seen in the three pirate worlds. My last name is Derwin. I'm Captain Gideon Derwin, son to the legend himself, Admiral Derwin, the Black Skull Admiral ..."

CHAPTER 26

Off to the Academy

We have much in common (Kathryn)

It had been two weeks since Tobias adopted me, and the time had gone by in a flash. T's place had two bedrooms like Daniel's down in the Lower Forty, but with much larger rooms. There were two dressers and a closet in the bedroom. Lilly needed to hang her clothes on strings against the living room wall near their TV in Daniel's apartment. I had so much room to store things but didn't own enough stuff.

The air smelled cleaner without the rotten-egg aroma from the vents. When we first walked the hallway of our floor's apartment, I pointed out the spacing between each door. Middle Thirty floors had only a quarter of the door entries for each apartment. Tobias said that was because only twelve percent of Civil Earth lived in Tier Three. So many more people squeezed into the Lower Forty.

T wouldn't let me go out on my own. He wanted me to wait and learn how to behave correctly first. Speaking of learning, he was making me see a tutor every day. She was an old woman who gave me an attitude when I answered her questions incorrectly. Her name was Renee, which seemed like an old person's name. Tobias laughed when I told him.

Renee was teaching me things that I didn't fully understand. Why did I need to know that there were six planets in the Colonial Accord, and their population in total was over one hundred and forty-three billion? Why did I need to know that the Human Alliance had twenty-one city-states and that the current ruling state, New-Sparta, went to war to take control? The memory stone on Kora, the Androsians who killed and ate people they caught, four sister companies of the Federate Corporation and the mining colonies in Titans' Belt. So much information about useless things. The places Renee made me learn about were so far away from me.

Tobias said I should consider myself lucky that I didn't need to learn a new language. He told me the Language of Humanity was what we spoke here on Civil Earth and that every other Free World learned our speech as a second language. It was also spoken at the relations station. Renee and Tobias kept bringing up the relations station. I couldn't understand why it mattered to learn about that place either. One thing Renee did teach me about that interested me was when Civil Earth left the Great Darkness. The Years of Forgetting had always fascinated me when I was outside visiting the square, and its ruins from the Old World.

Renee couldn't tell me much about the Old World because no one knew, but she did tell me about the time just before we came out of the Great Darkness. She said, "For one hundred years before entering our Age of Innovation, Civil Earth had powerful rulers spread out across the entire planet—warlords, wealthy families, criminal organizations, and smaller groups run by elected leaders. During that time, the ruling body of each group started forming coalitions with each other. As the coalition grew and the number of people under the main body increased, those who would become Tier One came up with a new way of managing the masses. The caste system was born from that time in our history."

I hated the caste system, and when discussing it with T, he made a face like he was uncomfortable with my history lessons too. But the legends of walking giants, floating cities, and disappearing stars excited me. I'd heard the stories of giants from the Old World before, but never anything about the other two.

During one of my study sessions, I had another feeling like I'd had the night in the club Obsessions with Lilly. My chest became tight, and I couldn't breathe. Renee saw me sweating and struggling. She got me a glass of water and asked me to explain my feelings. She wanted to know what I was thinking about just before the sensation. My thoughts were about Johnathan's death and living on the surface. After talking some more, she said she thought I had a panic attack. I didn't understand how panic could attack someone and wondered if that was the name of a person. Renee said she would talk to Tobias, but he hadn't said anything to me yet.

Over dinner last night, T told me we would be leaving after his promotion to the rank of major. He said, "Next week, I'll be getting my bronze leaf. After that, we're leaving for the rogue world Nim."

Renee had told me about rogue and outer worlds. There were one hundred and sixty-two rogue worlds in occupied space that we knew of and fifty outer worlds controlled by King Sallu Nejem and the royal family. The outer worlds had over one thousand princes and princesses across fifty planets near the edge of occupied space, who all claimed to have ancient royal blood from the first Exalted Ruler of the Union.

I asked him, "What's a bronze leaf, and what will we be doing on Nim?"

Tobias told me, "Do you see the captain's bars I have on my uniform? It's how defenders identify my rank. The bronze leaf is the symbol used for major. This promotion comes with new responsibilities that will require us to go to one of the Civil Earth colonies on the planet Nim. I'll be second in command of a garrison that protects our outpost there."

I'd never gone far from building thirty-three in my entire life, and now T was taking me to another planet. I was excited to think of traveling on a spaceship to another world.

"After that promotion, you're going to Tier Two."

Tobias grinned and took another bite of his food before saying, "We. We will be going to Tier Two together. You're my only family now, so I'd like you to pin the rank on my uniform during the ceremony. It's a great honor and it would mean a lot to me if you did it."

It felt good being needed and having someone who looked on me as family. I told T, "I have one condition. You need to invite Doctor Courtney to the ceremony and then take her out to dinner to celebrate."

Tobias coughed his water back into a cup before conceding, "Ok, I'll invite Court, and you're pinning my rank. We have a deal."

I regained my focus. Tobias was next to me on a train; it was the first time I'd been on a train inside the clear transfer tubes that linked one location to another inside the city line. From my window, I could see the yellow haze, thick, leaving no area untouched, and the moist surface. We were on our way to meet Daniel and Amber to say goodbye to Lilly. She was starting her academy training.

Viewing the surface and seeing some people walking out in the open brought another memory of Sadness. I was very young, looking up at a passing train, and was hit on the head by a rock.

Sadness said, "Stop drifting off. The here and now is what matters, not what's happening up there."

We were in the open, passing from one building to the next, when Sadness snapped sharply around at a noise. Five outlines appeared through the haze. There was nowhere to go because we were already halfway between buildings. When the five became visible, we could see their headbands. They were Rockland gang members.

One crowed, "Look what we have here. An old man with his … something."

Another one said, "She ain't his daughter, they don't look anything alike."

Sadness carefully observed each one. "Move along, and you'll live to see tomorrow. Attack us, and everyone will die."

The leader of the group laughed and said, "You're old and blind. There's five of us and two of you."

"No, only one, she doesn't count. It's five versus one."

Sadness let his lip curl up into an attempted smile, and said, "It's four versus two."

The gang members looked at each other, confused, as Sadness glanced back at me and said, "Stay back, child, and watch everything that happens."

He turned fast, pulling a knife from a hiding place on his body and threw it at the leader of the Rockland group. The blade struck him in the eye, and he fell back to his death. Two of the other gang members looked like dummies, unsure what to do. The other two pulled weapons and moved to attack Sadness. He made quick work of them both, moving more gracefully than I ever could, even now. The first gang member lost his footing on a rock. Sadness pulled the headband down over the Rockland guy's eyes and pushed him back where he fell into the mud. The second came in fast, but Sadness punched him in his throat and drove the knife under the man's chin. The gang member with his eyes covered was dead before he could remove the headband.

The two frozen dummies finally moved and got on opposite sides of Sadness. With extreme focus, he watched them pace in circles. But my protector started to cough and fell to one knee. The gang members advanced and beat him with their legs and fists. One of the dead gang members had a sharpened stick lying in the wet mud. I picked it up and wasted no time, the way Sadness taught me, *don't hesitate and thrust with accuracy.* The spear pierced the back of one man's neck, and he fell to his death. I watched the dead gang member for a few moments to make sure he wasn't moving, as my years of lessons taught me. That was my first kill while living on the surface, and I felt no remorse. The last gang member kicking Sadness came after me. I was inexperienced at the time, and he overcame me quickly. But before long, Sadness got behind and put him into a chokehold. I watched Sadness strangle the life from the last of our five aggressors as he battled his surface cough.

After that incident, it became clear that my protector's time was almost over. He was spitting up blood and wheezing as he breathed.

Sadness said, "My time's nearly over in this life. We'll need to speed up your training so that when I close my eyes for the last time, I can leave this world knowing you'll survive with everything I taught you."

He always treated me like a daughter, and I wondered about his past.

I asked Sadness, "Did you have any kids on the inside?"

He told me he had a son still alive, and that it was just the two of them.

The memory faded when Tobias hit my arm and said, "We're almost at the city port."

"How long will Lilly be gone for?"

"The Academy training facilities are on the other side of the planet. Anyone who joins Civil Earth Defense, whether Fleet Branch or the Defender Corps, goes to the same location for training. Basic training is five months, then Lilly will spend another five months off-world in her special skills instruction."

"Special skills?"

"Yes, basic training's where she learns everything to become a part of Civil Earth Defense. Basic teaches recruits teamwork, self-control, defensive tactics in hand-to-hand combat, rifle training, physical fitness, officer classroom instruction, military tactics, and command discipline. After Lilly finishes that training, she'll move on to Fleet Branch instruction out in space. Lilly's test score pegged her for command staff training."

Tobias told me that the academy would change Lilly. I had grown close to her and hoped she didn't change too much. Lilly gave me the picture of Daniel, Amber, her, and me that we took inside Daniel's apartment.

We arrived at the city port; there were large planes and ships everywhere. Tobias said visitors from off-world came through the port too. People scurried about one way or another, and some dressed in ways that didn't match the caste system. They were from other worlds, and we would soon be on another as well, which was exciting.

Lilly came over and punched my arm. I saw her coming but let her have that hit for free.

I smiled at her. "Are you all ready to go save us as one of those tin suits?"

Lilly smirked. "I'm not joining the Defender Corps. Fleet Branch doesn't wear battle armor. Next time you see me, I'll be all dressed in uniform."

"Be careful out there. You won't have me to save you when things go wrong." I winked.

Lilly hugged me and said, "Maybe the next time you see me, I'll be the one protecting you."

Daniel and Amber came with a smile. Amber leaned in and kissed my cheek. I wasn't used to affection, but it felt nice.

"You look good, Kathryn," Daniel said. "How are you?"

"Still trying to figure things out, but good. I've got a full month's supply of the medication for my lungs and bought some new clothes."

Daniel said, "Once T adopted you, his military benefits kicked in right away. You'll never have an issue going to see a doctor again."

I glared at T and back to Daniel. "He's making me see a tutor every day."

Daniel and Tobias laughed, and Tobias said, "She's getting a crash course in international relations and Free Worlds social studies."

Lilly snorted. "When we meet again, you'll be a scholar of the Free Worlds on the relations station."

I folded my arms in defiance, then pointed my finger at the sky. "I couldn't care less about what's happening up there."

Daniel placed his arm on my shoulder. "It's important to know these things, especially after you get into Tier Two with Tobias. The people in the Upper Twenty-Three are book smart. They won't be kind, especially if you don't have a basic understanding of society within the Free Worlds of Humanity. Stay sharp with those airheads up there."

Young recruits were walking onto the plane. They all had large duffle bags for their academy training, the same as Lilly's hanging on her shoulder.

Lilly said, "I think I'm ready to go."

Tobias said, "Don't think you're ready. Know you're ready. You've always been a confident young lady. Keep that confidence, and be sure of your decisions and actions. Trust in yourself—it will help you go far in the academy."

Lilly took a deep breath with confident poise and said again, "Ok, I know I'm ready." She turned to hug Daniel. "Love you, Oppa. Take care of Mom, and I'll see you after graduation."

Daniel gave a half-sad smile. "Love you too. Everyone will be fine while you're gone. Don't worry."

Lilly hugged Amber and said, "Watch out for my brother. He needs you more than he knows himself."

Tears rolled down Amber's cheeks. "We'll miss you. Please be careful."

Lilly looked at Tobias. "Thank you for the extra push when we talked after what happened at the club. It helped me to make my decision."

Tobias only nodded.

Lilly came to me. "Try not to kill too many people while I'm gone and don't be a buzzkill."

I smiled and gave a playful sound. "T made me promise to try my best. I haven't been out of his apartment too much lately, so it shouldn't be hard."

Before Lilly got onto the plane, Daniel gave her a wristwatch like the one I had when I first went outside.

She stared at it and smiled. "Thanks for fixing this. After training, I'll always wear it to remind me of my family."

Lilly turned, went up the ramp and onto the plane spinning her head back several times to make sure we were still there. The door closed and the aircraft moved down the enclosed runway before leaving through a hangar into the yellow haze.

For no apparent reason, Tobias laughed. The three of us looked at him in confusion.

"What's so funny?"

T recovered. "I remember when I first went onto that ship. Lilly walked in there with a smile. What she didn't realize was the academy instructors were already waiting for her on the plane, screaming in her face and dumping her bag the minute that hatch closed. They do it to all the recruits at the same time—they make them get down and do push-ups for each item missing. It's a trick, of course. Almost every recruit probably had their bags filled the proper way. The instructors have a list that includes at least six or seven items that weren't on their original list. They have to do twenty push-ups for each missing item while the plane is taking off."

Daniel laughed but I was concerned.

Amber said, "What's so funny about that? They're setting them up for failure right away."

Tobias shook his head. "No, what they're doing has a purpose. The first six weeks in the academy is nothing but breaking the recruit down and making them feel like they do everything wrong. That's why I told Lilly to keep her confidence, no matter what happens. After the breakdown and those who can't hack it washout, the instructors build them back up again with confidence using teamwork and unity. Her first week there will not be easy. It's called hell week for a good reason."

My hell week on the surface lasted seven years. If I could survive that long outside, I was sure Lilly could handle a few rough months of training.

Amber still looked uneasy, and Tobias continued, "Don't worry, she'll do just fine. What they do to the recruits is all simulated stress. None of it's real. Because of her test score, Lilly's in the officers' program. That portion of the academy isn't as physically hard as Defender Corps training. When Lilly graduates, she'll be a second lieutenant and already have rank over most of her defense peers."

I asked T, "Do all tiers go to the academy together?"

"Tiers Three and Four go to the same training location. However, if the Tier Three recruit is in the officers' program like Lilly, they graduate as a first lieutenant. All Tier Four officers graduate as second lieutenants, and most of them spend their entire career at that rank or one grade higher. Only luck or circumstance gets a Tier Four officer to captain."

Daniel said, "You don't give yourself enough credit. It was your skills as an officer and your heroism that got you to captain, not luck."

T glanced down uneasily, rubbing the back of his neck. "Most Tier Three officers make it to captain eventually, but then stay stagnant for their careers too. That stagnation's also the reason Tier Four officers stay at their grade-level so long. Tiers One and Two always get promotions first, and they go to a separate training academy, graduating as captains. By the time a Tier One officer is in their third year of service, they're usually a major or lieutenant colonel."

"Isn't that annoying? Because Tiers One and Two are born into their caste, they get to outrank people with experience?" I was irritated.

Daniel added, "She's right—you've been a defender for how many years now, fifteen?"

"Sixteen years and five months."

"Exactly my point. Sixteen years, so with all your experience in the field and your numerous promotions, you have to listen to some silver-spoon Cloud Walker who has no idea what they're doing and only outranks you because of their Tier One caste."

Tobias smiled uneasily. "Being a defender does have its drawbacks, but those officers you refer to depend on the seasoned lower ranks to run field operations. After my next promotion, Kathryn and I are leaving for the rogue world Nim, to defend our colony there. The colony commander's a twenty-five-year-old Tier One full-bird colonel. If I'm lucky, she'll depend on my experience when making command decisions."

I asked, "What if you're not lucky?"

"My orders would stand, and I'd follow her commands."

Daniel said, "Her orders could get you killed."

"That's how it's been my entire career. I do the best I can with what they give me."

The city port had tons of restaurants, and Tobias suggested we grab a bite to eat.

Daniel and Amber seemed uneasy, and Daniel said, "We don't have the credits to eat out."

Tobias waved his hand. "I got you, Danny boy. We're eating real food for lunch today. It's my treat."

I remembered what Daniel said when I was living with him. They saved their money for an entire year to eat real food at a restaurant on CE Day.

The ground-level shops and stores were in the common area of the port, which had an open floor plan and was more extensive than the second floor of building thirty-three. Above were additional levels overlooking the main floor, and to the sides were elevators guarded by defenders. Since that area was shared space, the tiers briefly mixed together. Tiers One and Two scampered quickly with their well-dressed security escorts following close behind. People from the inside were strange to me.

We picked one of the restaurants, and the attendant gave T and me a hard time when we scanned our caste cards.

She said, "Sir, ma'am, you should go to the second floor for a meal. This area's for Tier Four dining."

"We're fine at this establishment, thank you." Tobias gave her an annoyed look.

We sat together in a booth. Tobias, Daniel, and Amber ordered a beer. I was happy with clear water; the water outside from the air handlers always had a strange taste and bits floating around.

A waiter came to our table and asked what kind of menu we wanted. The question was confusing.

"A menu that has food on it would be a good start, you dummy."

Tobias slapped the back of my head. "That isn't what he meant. Real food menus, please."

The waiter scanned T's caste card again before bringing the menus over. The people were uptight in the city port. We ordered our food and talked about random things. Tobias and Daniel talked mostly about their childhood.

I asked Tobias, "How old were you when your father died?"

Daniel and Amber opened their eyes wide with awkward expressions, looking at me then at T.

Tobias took a moment of thought. "My father didn't die, he left."

"What does that mean, and what about your mom?"

Daniel cut in. "Maybe we're not in the best place for this conversation. T doesn't want to talk about that in front of Amber and me."

Tobias shook his head and said, "No, it's fine, there's nothing to hide, and you already know my story." He turned back to me. "My mom died giving birth to me and Dad raised me by himself. When I was younger and knew Daniel, my dad was a first lieutenant in the Defender Corps. When he was promoted to captain, the same rank I am now, we moved up to Tier Three.

One day shortly after, he didn't come home. I was only eight years old at the time. Within a few days, the defenders came to my apartment and kicked me out. I wandered through the lower public floors for a while until they sent me out to the surface. You know most of the other parts of that story. When my aunt and uncle got me back inside, we inquired about what happened to Dad. Civil Earth's Administrative Authority had no record. He was here one day and gone the next."

That was similar to my story. "My parents died when I was ten, and the tin suits forced me out of my family's apartment into the Lower Forty to wander, just like you."

Tobias's and my story were similar, though he didn't have a Sadness to protect him like I did when he was out in the yellow haze. That was twenty-five years ago, the same time Sadness was out there. I wonder how things would have fared for T outside if he'd met my fierce protector.

CHAPTER 27

Galma

A visit to the Stumble Inn (Mace)

We were finally near Galma. The ship's captain told us we'd be exiting faster-than-light travel within a few minutes, ready to land. Jamie was excited to get off that junker, although the last few weeks had been relaxing in spite of the conditions. There was only one functioning shower on the entire vessel that all ex-employees shared. Jamie had taken one shower since leaving Dol'Arem, and I hadn't had the opportunity yet.

After the incident in the Hollow with the agent, I went home and told Jamie what happened. We packed our belongings and checked out of the hotel. One good thing that happened as a result of the attack was that I was able to retain our sixteen thousand credits. We transferred them to a new cash card, ensuring no one could trace us. Jamie said the Guild could track us through the bank, and we knew that once our sister company discovered that we had left, our accounts would be frozen. Cash cards were how we'd spent credits since leaving our home.

The night of the attack, we went to a rundown motel near the city spaceport. I figured it would be better to be closer when the phone call came.

However, I got the location wrong. When the PDD rang, the voice on the other end told us to head to the consumable docks at the other end of the city. Green Scrap Consumers, a sister company to the Corporation, owned that dock. All imports and exports for Lavlen came through the consumable docks.

The captain waited for us near a shipping container where suspicious characters stood guard with firearms. We gave the captain the Syndicate PDD and he smiled. We had to go inside the container where other employees of the Federate Corporation anxiously waited. All inside were frightened, and I realized what we had been going through was also happening to various other employees. Lavlen was only one city. I wondered how many different locations on Dol'Arem had something similar happening.

Employees were fleeing from all four sister companies. Some were as high as grade-levels thirty-one and thirty-two. Even the rich and those with the highest prestige of our mighty Federate Corporation tried to escape. Once on the transport, the captain made everyone go through a UV light to remove any unwanted pathogens from our bodies. Then he gave us booster shots so we wouldn't contract any of the known diseases on Galma.

Over the last two weeks, Jamie and I had spent time speaking with other ex-employees going to Galma. Some of them intended to stop off there before continuing somewhere else. One of the grade-level thirty-two ex-employees said he'd purchased a ship for his family and intended fleeing to uncharted space to find another world to call home. I thought that was a death sentence since there would be no way for him to find an air-breathing world by randomly jumping across space. He'd have better odds returning to Dol'Arem and living out his life unseen. How could anyone think that strategy was safe? Only the Frontiersmen could find new worlds, and no one had seen them in years. Jamie believed that pirates would attack that employee before he made it past occupied space.

There were two other couples in the same situation as us. One of them already had two children, and the other was a young couple pregnant with their first. We spent more time with them than any of the other ex-employees.

The first family were employees of Tri-Co; the husband was Jerry, and his wife, Allison. Lots of women from Tri-Co took the name after Allison Westbay, first Tri-Co CFO on Dol'Arem. Their parents probably thought it would show favor with their sister company. Their kids' names were James and Trever, who spent most days running throughout the ship with energy and smiles I hadn't seen in years. Jerry and Allison were unable to get the approvals from Family Management before getting pregnant.

Brent and Danielle, former employees of Excalibur Industries, were the other couple. They already had names picked out for their baby. If a boy, Malcolm, if a girl, Jenifer. Both names were nice. I decided to speak with Jamie about our baby.

Jamie said, "I think we should wait until the baby is born. We'll look at his or her face and decide a name."

Not a terrible idea. We hadn't had any scans yet to make sure everything was ok with her pregnancy. For all we knew, there could be something wrong with the fetus. That would be irony if we spent all that effort fleeing the Corporation only for Jamie to lose the baby once we got to Galma. I shouldn't think of such negative things.

I regained myself as the captain called out over the loudspeaker. "All former employees of the Corporation. Grab your personal belongings and meet at the airlock door on level thirty-two. We need to go over some things before we let you disembark."

"What do we need to talk about now? He's already spent days lecturing us about how things work on Galma. If I have to hear him say one more time how amazing the Stumble Inn is, I might punch him." Jamie was annoyed, rolling her eyes while listening to the loudspeaker.

I said, "He did tell us one useful thing. Remember what he said about the Lowlands? If someone wants to disappear forever, the Lowlands of Galma is where to go."

"It would be so depressing down there in the fog. The sun never shines, and I think those Lowlanders would freak me out. They look like aliens."

I said, "There are no aliens, babes. You know that."

We walked to the airlock door staging area. There were large windows on both sides of the airlock looking out, the only windows on the entire transport. The ship was still in faster-than-light travel. Other passengers came into the staging room. Brent and Danielle walked up to Jamie. Allison and Jerry came shortly after with their boys, who ran everywhere like madmen again.

Brent said, "We're almost here. I can't wait to get off this damn ship and breathe some fresh air."

Jerry asked, "Why does the captain want to speak to us again? The guy never shuts up."

"Jamie was wondering the same thing. I'm sure he wants to go into another detailed story about the do's and don'ts of Galma."

The ship exited FTL, and my attention focused outside the window where Galma was visible. Rings of orange encompassed the world, which otherwise looked similar to most air-breathing planets except for the thick dark gray patches. At first, I thought those were clouds, but after looking closer, I believed that was the fog from the Lowlands. All the green we saw was the mountain Highlands. The main Galma port was in the Highlands, and from what the captain had already told us, the Stumble Inn wasn't far from there.

The inn had its own private port, but we didn't have the stature to enter that way. We passed the rings, and small cruisers appeared instantly like a magic trick pushing up through the rings. They took positions around our transport. One of the other ex-employees standing nearby became nervous, rubbing her neck vigorously as she looked out of the windows.

She shrieked, "Those ships are taking up an attack position. Are they going to shoot us before we make it to the planet?"

The captain came out from a hallway and said, "Relax, woman. Galma always escorts ships into its main port. If they wanted to kill us, their defense grid would have already shot us."

The defense grid was visible outside only after the captain spoke. Galma didn't have huge numbers of satellites. The Corporation grid was like two artificial rings circling Dol'Arem, but Galma's satellites were spaced out far apart and looked old. That was probably why they kept cruisers inside the planet's orange rings—for additional protection.

More of the captain's crew came into the staging room and stood near their leader, who was at the airlock door. Something seemed wrong because they had rifles and dreadful expressions. The other passengers became agitated and nervous. Jamie squeezed my hand.

The captain spoke in a commanding voice. "Listen up, all of you. I want one single line here." He pointed to the floor. "You will come up to me one group at a time and deposit one thousand credits onto my PDD. If you don't, your group won't be able to leave."

Others standing in the room became angry and called out, "We already paid for this trip." Others shouted, "We don't have a thousand credits."

The captain pulled his sidearm and pointed it at everyone offering resistance. The noise level reduced immediately.

"If you don't have the credits to pay, you'll be required to stay on my ship to work off your cost. Consider it a form of indentured servitude. Don't worry. A thousand credits will take five to six weeks of labor, and then I'll drop you off on another rogue world."

Some ex-employees seemed to be ok with that explanation. I could hear Brent talking to his wife. "We can stay here for a little longer. I'll work for both of us and explain that you're pregnant. Then whatever world they go to can be our new home."

The captain asserted, "If you try to resist us, my crew will shoot you and leave your dead body in the spaceport. Don't test us. We've done it hundreds of times before."

Our ship was entering the atmosphere of Galma. The captain looked over his shoulder, where flames licked at the windows. The nervous ex-employee who thought the cruisers would shoot us sat on the floor and put her back against the wall.

The captain gave her an odd look with his lips pressed together and said, "Woman, you're crazy. We aren't doing a hard drop into Galma. If you haven't noticed, this isn't a combat vessel. Our approach is a soft entry and it will take several minutes before we get to the port. Get the hell off my floor."

She stood, breathing heavily, and walked back to her husband, who didn't say a word. The captain shook his head and pointed to the woman's husband.

"Take her to see a doctor when you get off my ship. Something isn't right in her head."

His crew laughed as we passed the clouds, and the flames dissipated. Jamie and I were at the end of the line. We weren't paying attention when everyone lined up. We had the credits, thankfully, on the cash card.

We landed, and the captain smiled. "Welcome to Galma, the most visited rogue world in occupied space."

The airlock door opened, and people moved one group at a time to pay the new fee. Some could pay and left. Others couldn't afford the cost and went to a side room where crew members stood with their weapons.

Allison and Jerry walked forward with their kids and said, "We only have seven hundred and fifty to give."

The captain bit his lip in agitation. From what I'd seen so far, only half of the ex-employees could afford the cost.

The captain said, "Ok, since I'm in a generous mood, I'll divide the amount between the four of you. One must stay behind. The others can get off."

He didn't realize Allison was pregnant, which was good. He would count her unborn child as another person.

Jerry looked at the captain and said, "My family will leave. I'll stay and work off the cost. When I pay back the fee, you can have more free time out of me until your ship returns to Galma."

The captain nodded. "A fair deal, indeed."

Jerry transferred the credits, and the captain waved his arm to the airlock door. Allison shook her head frantically and sobbed, tears streaming down her cheeks. The boys were crying too.

Allison cried, "I won't know what to do without you. What am I supposed to do?"

Jerry embraced her. "You take care of our boys anyway you can. I'll be back, I promise."

James's and Trever's little faces were wet with tears as Jerry hugged them both.

"You boys be strong. You must keep your mom safe. Do whatever she tells you, and don't wander off. I'll see you soon."

Allison and her boys, still overwhelmed with tears, left the ship. Jerry wiped the liquid from his eyes and moved into the room where the other bewildered ex-employees waited.

Other groups had their turns. Some were able to pay and leave, and others weren't. Danielle and Brent's turn came and the captain grinned.

Brent said, "We don't have the credits to leave. My wife's pregnant. With your permission, I would like to work for us both. I'll do double shifts if I must."

"That's not an issue. Please." The captain pointed to the room where Jerry and the others were.

Danielle looked back at Jamie and sighed. "Good luck to you two. Maybe in a few months, we can meet again."

Jamie smiled at Danielle. "We'll be here when you get back."

There were a few more groups ahead of us before it was our turn.

I whispered to Jamie, "We have the extra credits. We could pay the two fifty for Jerry and a thousand for Danielle and Brent."

Jamie shushed me. "That money's all we have, Mace. We need to look out for our family, not other employees."

We went to the captain, and he gave Jamie and me the same unwarranted smile as the others. "You're the last group. I have a rule for those that are last. You must pay fifteen hundred to leave, not one thousand."

Jamie snapped back, "You crook. Does the Syndicate know what you're doing here? We already paid so much money to guarantee our transport to this planet."

The captain pressed his lips together, looking at us with scorn, and said, "This is my ship, woman. You don't tell me what I can and can't do on my ship. You paid the Syndicate for transport to the planet. If you look behind me, you'll see that we have fulfilled that arrangement." He glared at me. "She has a mouth. That will cost you another five hundred."

Crew members laughed, and I could see Jerry, Brent, and Danielle watching our predicament.

"I'll pay, sir. Please excuse us, and we thank you for the safe trip to Galma."

The captain showed me his PDD with the number two thousand in bold lettering. I scanned my cash card, and the screen turned green.

"Now get off my ship, both of you."

Jamie and I were cautiously moving to the airlock opening when Brent spoke up. "Captain, where are you taking us next?"

The captain licked his lips and strolled to the room containing all the ex-employees who couldn't pay. "Next, you ask? Next, we're going to rendezvous with the hunter crew waiting for us outside this system so you can become slaves of the Offensive."

The captain hit a button on the door, and it closed faster than anyone could get to it. Their screaming voices faded as the door closed. The crew members laughed with the captain. Another crew member with his rifle stopped Jamie and me from walking down the ramp.

The captain turned to us. "Let those two go. They paid the fee. We've got at least three thousand per head on the cattle inside this room." He tapped his hand against the sealed airlock door. "Let's go. We're out of here."

*

Jamie and I rushed down the ramp. I could feel my heartbeat in my throat. Once we got to the bottom, Jamie shouted with anger. "That son of a bitch. He took the Syndicate money for sending us here, made us all pay an extra thousand, and will take those who couldn't pay to Force Command Burning Star for another three thousand per person. He's a greedy devil."

I was still in shock. "That captain's probably been doing it for years. How would anyone know? As far as the families are concerned, the significant others who don't come back must have died or whatever. The Syndicate doesn't care either. Half of us were still able to get off the ship. Silas told me he normally charges ten thousand credits per person to leave Dol'Arem.

I'll bet only two or three thousand of that goes to the transport vessel. That ship captain would do well working in one of the sister companies of the Corporation."

Jamie narrowed her eyes., "That's not funny, Mace."

What I said wasn't meant to be funny. My mind was becoming numb to the twisted games that we of humanity played on each other. Allison and her boys waited near the exit door, looking in our direction.

Jamie saw her and turned to me, "Don't tell her what happened. She's already terrified of being here alone and will want to stay with us."

"How can we not tell her? She'll be hanging here for the next year or two, waiting for her husband to come back, and he never will."

"If you tell her, she'll break down. Allison needs to be strong for her young kids. Hope's a powerful emotion. Let her hold on to it and believe that her husband's coming back."

She was right and I nodded. "I won't say anything, but how do we get her away from us? She doesn't have credits or a clue what to do next."

Jamie turned her head, looking around, and said, "The Stumble Inn. Tell her we're going to the inn for a meeting. Her kids won't be allowed inside, so she has to wait here for us."

I didn't want to argue with my wife anymore, but the whole thing was terrible. We were going to leave Allison here helpless and alone with two young kids. We might have been just as bad as the captain.

Allison's eyebrows drooped as she gripped her boys' hands tightly. "Was everything ok? I saw you two running down the ramp fast, like something was wrong."

Jamie said, "Everything's fine. We couldn't wait to get off that ship. The captain said they would be back sometime before the end of the year."

Allison smiled, pushing hair from her face and I narrowed my eyes at Jamie. She was good at playing off the moment.

"That's good news," Allison said. "Can I ask, would you mind if we tagged along with you for a while? Jerry was the planner, not me. I don't know what to do now, and we have no credits."

I opened my mouth to speak, but Jamie blurted, "Sorry, we have a meeting up at the Stumble Inn with some associates. Your kids won't be allowed in. Wait down here for us. We'll come back later and find somewhere to stay."

Allison seemed to shrink. "Ok, that sounds good. The boys can sit here with me and count ships as they come into the port, won't we boys?"

Her children had tears and their eyes and answered timidly, "Yes, Mom."

Jamie and I said our farewells and moved away quickly. I felt so guilty, leaving them alone with nothing.

"Jamie, this is wrong."

She grabbed my hand, tugging me along. "Our family's all that matters, Mace. We need to protect our child."

The Galma port had sizeable upper-story walkways above us going in different directions, held up by massive concrete pillars. Vendors stood nearby, trying to sell goods. The sky was visible because there was a transparent dome above us. Ships came and left sporadically. All around us were people from different worlds, some with the famous togas of Civil Earth's Tier One with armed security, and others had the olive and brown skin of the Human Alliance. Various groups were there from the outer worlds, based on their long braided beards and head covers, and the women had hijabs. Outer worlds in the inner system of planets had hot climates with constant red sandblasts. The bulwark worlds surrounded Helana, the home planet of the Nejem royal family.

Jamie pulled on my arm to get my attention. I turned to what she was looking at, and my heart dropped. Five Dolrinions in battle armor moved through the sea of people parting down the middle as if they were an unstoppable force everyone was trying to get away from. The suits made sounds of gears rolling as the soldiers waddled through the crowds. The sentinels were shorter than any adults in the port. One of them glanced at me with a cold glare as he passed. It felt like he knew I was from the Corporation just by looking at me.

"Their armor's black with the spiral circle emblems. They're sentinels from Force Command BlackRock," I said.

I wondered how many of those emblem deaths represented Corporation employees. We pressed on and asked a stranger where the Stumble Inn was; she pointed up a giant mountain and told us that we could take the sky lift if we didn't want to hike.

Looking past the sky lift in all directions, I could see nothing but huge mountains, some high and others no more than hills. It seemed like there wasn't any flat land on the entire planet. Grass and trees were numerous wherever jagged stone edges and boulders weren't pushing out of the ground.

On reaching the sky lift, we purchased tickets. Large T-shaped steel beams protruded from the ground connected by a pulley system. On the pulley-wire, spaced out every six meters or so, were pairs of wooden seats with a safety bar across at chest level. People waited for the chairs to pass under them, then they sat and brought the bar down.

Jamie and I handed the tickets to a gray-haired man with loose skin and missing teeth working the lift. He attempted a crooked smile, saying, "Enjoy the ride. Next stop, the Stumble Inn."

The lift swooped in behind us without warning and startled Jamie as the seat hit our backsides, pulling us up the hill fast. It reminded me of an entertainment ride. I pulled the bar down so we wouldn't fall out. We peered at the landscape, which was spectacular and beautiful. Countless mountains without end marched in every direction. We saw structures built right into the mountainside of the closer formations that would fall into the black fog of the Lowlands if not secured into the bedrock. Towns, small developments, businesses, and larger structures were all built intricately through the sharp edges and stone. The architecture was impressive, appearing to work through the stone rather than clearing it for the foundations. It looked so foreign.

I said, "I don't understand. We've always learned that rogue worlds were barren wastelands. The technology here is inferior to the Corporation, but this place is great."

Jamie nodded, still amazed by the sights. People hiked up and down the mountain. Some seemed to be relaxing in the grass, eating and enjoying the scenery, and others looked as though they were fishing in ponds.

Jamie squeezed her eyes shut. "Oh, no."

I turned my head, and my initial reaction was to hold my hands up in front of my face to block the rock wall we were cruising towards, but before striking the sharp jagged side, the sky lift pulled up with extreme force. We cleared the wall with a meter to spare.

Jamie and I both laughed. "Maybe not as beautiful as I initially thought."

We reached the top of the hill and got off the sky lift, running away before the next seating basket behind us came through. A walkway for travelers went further up a hill, and we followed it until we reached a massive cobblestone structure. It was a castle with wide cylindrical towers that spanned at least fifty meters spaced out along the top of the vast structure. Each tower had a pointed round roof that was brightly lit up by spotlights moving to the rhythm of music. The colors were beautiful, changing endlessly. The walkway went directly to the castle wall midpoint, where an arched entryway cut perfectly into the thick cobblestone.

Above the massive opening was a holographic sign spinning in circles that read "Stumble Inn." People of all ages from dozens of worlds followed the walkway to the entrance. At the door, intimidating men stood close by watching everyone. Their size reminded me of Silas. The Syndicate owned the establishment and ran everything in the Highlands of Galma. I wondered if Silas started as one of these bouncers before he worked his way up in the organization.

A short, skinny, balding man with a peculiar-looking mustache that curled out past his face and arched inward stood near the opening. He wore a patterned maroon silk vest and an oversized bow tie with dress pants. He was slapping his thighs and shouted with excitement at everyone entering the inn.

"Welcome, welcome, welcome. Free, outer, and rogue worlds combined. One and all are always welcome."

He jumped onto a small, elevated stage, and bent down, holding his arms out to the sides. "Whatever world you travel to throughout all occupied space, people know of the Stumble Inn. All your heart's desires and deepest fantasies are inside, and best of all, our doors are always open. You might not stumble in, but we guarantee you will stumble out. Come inside and see the marvels of humanity. Gamble, drink, and party until your hearts are content."

His words stimulated the crowds who paid the doorman and rushed inside. Some young, excited partygoers were near us.

I asked one of them, "How much does it cost?"

He was an eager young man. "Fifty credits per person."

Jamie said, "They charged us fifty per person to get up that lift. We have to pay two hundred just to walk inside."

"Our remaining credits won't last long at this rate."

The yelling man with the strange-looking mustache raised his voice. "Our first floor has the main entertainment and the biggest bars you've ever seen. The second level has the casino, live betting, and VIP suites. The third level houses our gentlemen's and ladies' clubs as well as the private showrooms. The fourth level is for guests looking to spend the night. Visit our basement level for the nightclub Cell Block. Be careful down there—some go in and never come out, ha ha. Access to the upper floor is for our lovely Syndicate benefactors only. Now go on in, enjoy the entertainment, drink libations, and try to pace yourselves."

We paid the doorman; he stamped our hands and waved us inside. There were fantastic displays of lighting, artificial fog, laser lights, and holograms everywhere. Customers drank, danced, and some in less populated areas appeared to be having sex.

Jamie leaned in to me and said, "Prostitutes earn their incomes everywhere."

"You'd think that they might find a private place for it, not out in the open. It's like no one cares."

Behind each bar, up high on platforms with long poles, men and women danced in provocative clothes. One of the women hung from the side of the pole, holding on with her legs. I'd never seen anything like that before. Jamie saw me staring at the woman and slapped my arm as the dancer giggled and waved at me.

We followed the walkway because we weren't even inside the inn yet; that was only an outer courtyard with nothing but the night sky above. Another set of doors led into the castle.

Every thirty seconds, a single large mushroom firework went off in different colors shimmering above the courtyard. People looked up at the pretty display with happiness—those that weren't doing the deed with a naked body under or above them.

"This place is wild."

Jamie said, "We're not even inside yet."

At the main doors, still outside, two young adults, one male, and one female, no older than eighteen, came to us with inviting smiles. The man grabbed Jamie's hand, and the woman took mine. Each kissed us gently on the lips and said, "Looking for some company tonight? We'd love to join you in a private room."

Like the name of the inn, I stumbled on my words, trying to reply, but Jamie had less reservation. "We're fine. Thank you for offering. Maybe another time."

They curtsied or bowed, then walked up to two more people and played the same routine. We went through the castle's main entrance into an open hall party room. In the middle was a slow-spinning stage with a band playing music. Patrons danced near the stage, drank at bars, and ate rich food that looked real. The patterns and shapes in the fabric of the carpeted floor moved to the music—spinning flowers and designs changing form as they drifted through the carpets. We were near one of the walls and I noticed that the entire party room perimeter had steps leading into tiny individual spaces with narrow beds, pillows, erotic sheets, and sex toys. A thin red curtain provided a barrier between the small room and the main public area. Some curtains were closed and others open. Within the open ones, extremely attractive men and women wearing next to nothing tried to entice patrons inside.

"There's even more sex workers in here than outside."

Jamie said, "At least in here, they have privacy."

Halfway through this room, a strange noise that reminded me of wild animals came from behind us. We turned our heads to see an oversized cage moving automatically on the floor. Inside were chimpanzees swinging on tree limbs. The enclosure carefully traveled by guests without bothering them. Other pens came too, throughout the party room, containing exotic-looking animals. We saw sixty-meter constricting snakes, white tigers, hippopotamuses, and one enclosure had a scorpion the size of a horse.

It was the black tail scorpion from Kora. The creature's tail was featured on the Dolrinion flag because of its power and aggressiveness. They lived in the southern waste of Kora and were incredibly hard to kill. The scorpion's tail struck the cage every few seconds, scaring some guests but making others laugh and drink more.

In the next room was another stage with a band playing a completely different type of music. This room looked nothing like the first. Spaced out along the ceiling hung swings with erotically dressed young men and women. They moved from side to side, laughing and waving at guests underneath. Every few seconds, water spurted out from the ground in a stream arching across the room past some of the swings. The streaming water fell into different holes a few meters away. There was a lazy river traveling through the room with guests and staff inside tubes swimming along as they drank, smoked, and smiled. Acrobatic dancers, jugglers, and hoop jumpers moved gracefully around the room, reminding me of a circus.

An attractive young lady with sparkling silver across her skin, lying on a surfboard, was floating in the air. On her back was a device holding long cylindrical shot glasses. She smiled while offering customers shots as she floated from corner to corner. Her legs hung off both sides of the surfboard and she acted like she was swimming in the air.

"I need a drink, babes."

Jamie palmed the side of her head and said, "I'd like a glass of wine to be honest with you. One small glass won't hurt the baby. The stress of this past month has gotten to me."

I looked through the room and said, "Let's grab a drink then go up to the next level. We can check this place out and get a room on the fourth floor."

A crowded bar nearby drew our attention. We found an opening near the end where the stairs and curtained prostitutes were. Jamie stood behind me as I stepped up on the first stair and leaned over the bar to order a drink. The red curtain to my left was open. A woman with slumped shoulders leaned against the wall looking down. She was pretty but appeared sad, and ashamed of the outfit, which barely covered her nearly naked body. She tried to use her arms to conceal herself.

After ordering our drinks, I got a closer look at the prostitute's face and realized she had bruises and cuts that were only starting to heal. She lifted her eyes and saw me looking at her.

"Do the people who pay you to go in that room do this to you?"

She shook her head, answering, "No. The Syndicate made some of the fresh marks on my face. The older marks were gifts from the people who sent me here from the relations station."

I opened my eyes wide in disbelief, and took a step back. "The relations station? Why are you here? You're a Free Worlds citizen."

"My former employer didn't like that I was hiding information from him. My loyalty was to his wife, not him. It seems like you were not a fan of your former employer, either. Why did you leave Dol'Arem?" I must have looked curious, because she said, "Your accent's from the Federate Corporation. That's how I knew."

"What was your former profession?"

She turned away and hesitated. "Security officer in the Capitol Forum. I was a protector for the representatives."

"What's your name?"

She hesitated again. "Zoey."

Before I could say another word, someone put their hand on my shoulder. I turned, and my heart dropped into my shoes. Arkie was there next to Jamie with a proud smile, her chin held high. She didn't die during the MERC Guild agent attack in the Hollow Ward.

"Hello, Mace. I'm glad to see you made it. Your presence is needed upstairs."

I stared at Jamie and then back to Arkie, who continued, "Would you kindly follow me please."

The lie we told Allison before coming up to the inn wasn't a lie, after all. We had a meeting, but who with was another question altogether.

CHAPTER 28

Terrible Deeds

A special mission of the utmost secrecy (Askar)

They gave me another cluster squad that was younger than my last. The new sentinels were nothing but small pebbles fresh from the Rite of Passage, and I felt terrible looking at their novice-young faces. We were huffing it through local towns to another camp, and every morning our LENS gave us reports regarding conditions across the front lines and other news from the Offensive. The updates ran for two minutes and were filled with positive stories to help encourage our young warriors. Gray Boulder told us the truth that many camps across the entire front line suffered attacks like ours. Sentinels died in high numbers, victims of the death arm machines, and some camps were overrun.

We were redeploying forces by taking advantage of the temporary ceasefire enacted on the relations station. Our camp's success was minor compared to others across the planet. The further from the last base we marched, the clearer the differences between how BlackRock and the Legion handled the occupation became. Red Legion controlled the area we were huffing through. The Red Death had groups of Gliese natives on their knees near the area we were moving past.

A lieutenant gawked at the locals, "It's a simple question you should be able to answer. Where are the Frogmen hiding?"

Another sentinel from Force Command First Ones next to the lieutenant, repeated her officer's words in the native tongue. The First Ones sentinel's armor was different, with turquoise and white outlines, not as thick as the Legion armor. He also had more technology on his war plate. In place of our shoulder rockets, he had a satellite with small drones lining the hardware down his back and a sizeable robust pack for equipment.

Force Command First Ones focused more on classroom studies, education, engineering, and building. Combat was secondary for the first command founded.

The Red Legion lieutenant paced from one local to the next then stopped in front of one. "Answer me, primitive weakling. Where are they hiding?"

The bewildered native wrinkled his nose and narrowed his eyes, shaking his head. The lieutenant glanced at a sentinel standing behind, pointing a rifle at the local's head. The look from a commanding officer was all that was needed, and the sentinel pulled the trigger. Blood and brain matter littered the ground like grass seed thrown before a summer's rain.

The lieutenant continued to the next native, also on his knees. That one was a teenager, and the First Ones sentinel translated the question again.

The teen shouted in his tongue, "The Frogmen will avenge us!"

A different sentinel standing behind pulled her tip knife and cut the teen's throat. Locals standing nearby cried and some covered their eyes. My squad of pebbles dragged their feet, witnessing those horrors.

"Eyes forward, cluster squad. Don't concern yourself with Red Death's actions."

The squad all swung their heads to the sentinel at their front and kept marching.

I despised the Legion's actions, but what could I do? Deeper into town, homes were in ashes, and some areas reminded me of how no-man's-land appeared. The surroundings looked that way as punishment by the Reds for

Frogmen attacks. All that remained of the scattered homes were concrete foundations. It was the same every time.

Two locals ahead of us were on their knees, completely naked, with visible ribs and drooping skin from malnourishment. The man was filthy with long hair and an unkempt beard. He made hand gestures, asking for food. Sentinels ahead pushed him away, huffing past, and a gunnery sergeant hit him in his chest with a battle rifle. The second naked native, a woman, bent down to console her partner as they both shook uncontrollably. They cried and motioned with their hands, begging for food. Another huffing sentinel kicked the woman in her face. They lay in the mud holding each other in fetal positions.

I moved ahead of my cluster squad and took a knee next to the befuddled locals. Then I pulled a small ration container from my side and gave it to them along with portable emergency water pouches. The natives opened their eyes wide in what appeared to be a desperate smile. I could only guess that it was appreciation in those watery eyes.

I lifted my hands, motioning, and spoke. "Eat slow. If you eat this too fast, it could kill you."

They didn't understand me. I shouted to the First Ones sentinel standing off to the side with a squad of Red Death. Both turquoise and deep red battle armor approached.

The Legion sentinel was the interrogating lieutenant, and she gave me a hard look and narrowed her eyes. "What are you doing, master gunny?"

Based on her armor design, I knew she was a husk commander. Her right arm pauldron extended from her shoulder across her chest and down her arm to the elbow. Husk commanders controlled drop capsules and had a short life expectancy because their primary role in the Offensive was to drop into heavy combat and hold a battle line to establish a front. Commanders of husks had the shortest fuses of all sentinels. There was no time for patience when every second meant life or death for hundreds.

I answered, "Giving them some of my rations, ma'am. I wanted the First Ones sentinel to translate."

She screamed at me with fire in her eyes. "Who do you think you are, feeding primitives under Legion control?"

It took me time to think of an adequate answer, but before I could do anything, the Legion lieutenant pulled her tip knife and stabbed the naked man behind his head, killing him instantly. The husk commander, hissing like an animal, stepped on the female local, who was still holding the rations I gave her, and drove her blade through the side of her head; her arms fell motionless as she died. The Legionnaire spat into the mud and walked away.

Before the First Ones sentinel left, he turned and said, "The Red Legion suffered great loss during the invasion. Her name's Lieutenant Ballo. She was in the first wave of drop capsules here. Some of her best sentinels died from local defenses. She hates these natives with a passion now."

He left, and I fell back in with my squad, still thinking of how helpless those natives were before Ballo killed them. There was no honor in those deaths. The further we huffed, the more First Ones we saw driving dozers and digging holes in the dirt. The fresh-dug holes down the road had hundreds of bodies inside of dead natives, a byproduct of Frogmen attacks against us.

Their ages ranged from incredibly old to toddlers, and none were soldiers. These holes and bodies were a disgrace to the Offensive, and it angered me immensely. Sentinels should act with a warrior's honor. The deaths of innocent natives were a massacre and something the Legion had become known for throughout all occupied space.

I'd heard of past Red commanders like Colonel Deveraux, who committed the genocide of Caladorn on the rogue world Enzah some four hundred years ago, and other famous leaders from that command who spent years conducting liquidation missions on multiple planets within the exclusion zones on both sides of the DMZ.

Our relations station representatives negotiated the surrender of the mountains above the marshes. The Federates called them the Mountains of Hope. Leadership changed the name to the Red Mountains for the blood that would spill from occupying them. The Legion had spent day and night shelling the marshes with massive artillery strikes. The Frogmen continued to elude our firebomb explosions. It wouldn't take much effort to turn those artillery cannons to face the Corporation's front line and wreak havoc.

My pebbles stared into the holes at the hundreds of dead. That sight wasn't the best way to break in a new squad. I lifted my faceplate, covered my nose and flinched. The smell of bloated dead bodies was something no one could get used to.

"Rock sentinels, don't lose heart. You won't treat natives like that. Our command has spent hundreds of years perfecting the art of occupation. If natives obey our rule, we occupy with reason over force. BlackRock doesn't have mass graves in territories held by our boulder commanders. My squad, especially, will take care of how we treat Gliese natives. We fight against warriors, not children."

A rock captain walked past us and tapped my pauldron, saying, "Good lesson, master gunnery sergeant." He looked at my face, and his eyes opened wide. "You're the Hero of Gliese. I didn't recognize you at first." The captain focused his eyes on my squad. "Sentinels, a walking legend among our Force Command is teaching you, so listen to everything he says. Follow his lead, and your name will find its way onto the memory stone when you die."

He moved away from us, conducting line inspections. The day after our camp's attack, my face was across every Dolrinion LENS in the Offensive in their nightly report. My actions and LENS recording appeared like a movie for every sentinel's helmet in occupied space, even Colonel Zilith's speech. Sentinels began calling me the Hero of Gliese. That name felt like a thousand stones on my shoulders, and the thought made my eyes water as I huffed.

I closed my shield faceplate so no one could see the tears. I was not a hero. The fact that I was still alive was nothing more than a curse on my soul. *Take me, memory stone, take me home to be with those who fell before me. Take me to rest with my Force Command in the stone halls of eternity, please.*

It was some time before I recovered, and one of my pebbles spoke. "Master gunnery sergeant, we only arrived planetside last week. On our transport, we saw videos and heard about the new Federate weapon."

I lifted my faceplate and said softly, "Death arms."

The private nodded. "Yes. I wanted to ask, sir." He turned away for a moment looking at our surroundings. "Do you … do you know what our strategy is against those monstrosities?"

I took a deep breath. "Relax, Private. You won't fight one alone. No-man's-land now has mighty seismic charges in addition to the minefields. Those underground diggers won't get through again."

Both the Federates and our Offensive had taken advantage of the ceasefire. Added defenses went up daily on both sides. Force Command Overwatch advised us that the Federates had built a six-meter steel wall across their entire front line. Their wall was more substantial than our victory wall, and we wondered if they did that to mock us, since all knew the Federates were better builders than Dolrinions.

Our formation huffed through two more towns occupied by the Legion. Much of what we saw in the first town had also happened here. Every other home or business scorched to the ground in ashes. Destroyed primitive tanks and jets littered the surrounding landscape. Every so often, we passed skeletons from the invasion never cleared away by the dozers. Outside each town, Force Command First Ones buried natives in the ground. If the planet were alive, it wouldn't need to eat for another thousand years.

It took all afternoon of marching to reach our new camp. I was glad we made it because my armor was almost depleted and in need of a recharge. If combat were to break out, we didn't have enough emergency recharge boosters for the entire platoon.

Our new camp looked the same as the old one with the victory wall where no-man's-land started. The barrier wall had more bumbles than our last camp, and near the bumbles, spaced out across the front, were rumble tanks holding the line. The rest of the camp consisted of the same portable popup buildings, sleeping bunks, mess halls, latrines, supply buildings, ammo dumps, repair depots, and one large brick building that might once have been a school or administrative structure of the rogue world. Our command staff occupied the building.

My squad and I brought our gear into a bunk for unloading. Inside, along the wall, were recharge stations for battle armor, single cots with supply chests stood in rows in the middle, and the heads and showers were in the back. Some of these pebbles had long faces and let out loud grunts as they dropped their bags.

"Unload your gear and hit the racks. Our shift's in five hours, so sleep off the march."

Before I removed my battle armor to inspect for repairs, my LENS alerted me to report immediately to our command building. That was strange. I stepped into the charging station and hit the emergency recharge button. My squad gave me puzzled stares.

"Continue what you're doing, sentinels. I'm needed at command. Here's a good lesson for everyone—make sure your armor's always charged. You could walk out that door nearly depleted when battle breaks out. Without power, you'll die fast."

The pebbles echoed together, "Yes, sir," as my armor completed a power boost, giving me a ten percent reserve.

I left the bunk and moved to the command building. The ground at our last camp was mud and dirt. Since the death arm attacks, all camps had thick concrete poured throughout to help deter diggers. Walking on the solid surface felt better on my knees. Through the past year, my age was overwhelming the burdens of a sentinel's life.

A commanding officer nearby raised his voice at other new pebbles outside a bunkhouse. It reminded me of my two previous squads. Thinking of those excellent sentinels made my eyes water again. I closed my faceplate once more to hide the emotions. Watching the newly promoted Corporal Uva sacrifice herself to earn a place on the memory stone had hit me the hardest of all that died. She was an excellent warrior and should still be alive. Maybe if I'd acted faster during that assault, I might have been able to get to my squad more quickly. *Damn these old knees.*

Two sentries stood at the entrance to the brick command building. They ordered me to halt before entering.

I lifted my faceplate. "My LENS alerted me to report to Colonel Zilath."

One of the guards said, "It's you." He turned to the other guard. "It's him, the Hero of Gliese. A pleasure, sir. Colonel's waiting on the second floor."

Before entering the building, I removed my thick, cumbersome war helm, relieving the heavy strain from my back. Even with powered armor, that helmet was heavy. My eyes were wet again as I took each step up the stairs, but I had to choke back the tears. I couldn't dishonor my command by looking weak to the Gray Boulder. On the second floor, two more guards snapped to attention when they saw me. The new title brought new respect from my fellow sentinels, and it made me uncomfortable.

A sentinel said, "The colonel's waiting inside, sir." As I walked inside, he carried on, "We're proud to be in your brigade, master gunny."

Inside the colonel's office were holographic display screens showing the front line's current status across the entire planet. When he saw me, the colonel waved the display away and stood.

I straightened my back to attention, hearing my old bones crack. "Colonel Zilath. Reporting as ordered, sir."

The Gray Boulder grinned. "Relax, master gunny, take a seat."

I hesitated, looking around the room. That treatment was uncommon for me in my years of experience. Two sentinels stood near the colonel's desk, and from their light battle armor and color, I knew they were from Force Command Overwatch. Their armor was thin compared to that of the other commands, with light gray coloring and gunmetal outlines. It wasn't true battle armor because most from that command rarely set foot near a front line.

Force Command sentinels viewed Overwatch as untrustworthy spies. They deployed elements with the other nine commands all the time. A barracks or mess hall always grew quiet when Overwatch sentinels walked inside.

The Gray Boulder saw my hesitation.

"You've done nothing wrong, sentinel. They aren't going to detain you. It's quite the opposite. They're here to recruit you, so take a seat."

My commander's statements confused me; I sat. "Recruit me, sir?"

Colonel Zilath stood and turned, looking from a window over camp with his arms clasped behind him. He said, "Our deadlock with the Corporation for control isn't changing for the time being. The truth is … we're losing. The ground war's all but frozen. The Frogmen have crippled us. We can't operate properly, and the Federates keep coming up with creative ways to kill sentinels."

One of the Overwatch sentinels added, "Overwatch isn't blind. The Corporation's killing us quicker than we can kill them. All commands here are holding on for now, but the Offensive can't hope to maintain forever with these losses."

I looked around, still uncertain of why he told me these things. "Why are you telling me all this? I'm nothing more than a master gunnery sergeant who follows orders. Our discussion seems like something that should be occurring between supreme generals, not me, sir."

The Gray Boulder grunted. "Master Gunnery Sergeant Askar, you're the Hero of Gliese. That's exactly why you're sitting in this room." The colonel waved his hand, and a display hologram showed a man and woman walking through a spaceport.

The other Overwatch sentinel said, "These two Federate Corporation former employees fled to the rogue world Galma. He's Mace Applegate and was previously a gifted program writer for Genesis Foundation. The woman's his wife and of little concern."

Another video displayed Dol'Arem, the Corporation homeworld.

"Those two artificial rings in the video are the Federate's new defense grid," said the first Overwatch sentinel. "Mr. Applegate wrote the entire code. Even better for us, he's fled the Corporation with his wife. Mace-plus-one are on Galma, for what purpose we aren't sure. The Corporation's scrambling all resources to recover him, and Representative Michael Decelle, the Huntsman of the Corporation, is itching for the opportunity to track them down himself. We need to capture Mace first."

Gray Boulder said, "If we could disable that grid, Dol'Arem would fall in days. This rogue-world war would be nothing by comparison. An opportunity of such magnitude might never present itself again."

"But why me? There's plenty of Red Legion war heroes who could handle the task more efficiently than I could. Younger ones too."

The colonel gave a loud sigh. "Did you know that over half of our Force Command has never set foot on Kora? We've always specialized in occupation after a war's end. Many of our sentinels are born, complete the Rite, and die, never feeling Kora's true gravity. Gliese is a special situation, and we've had to assist with the war efforts. Your own words are why Overwatch believes you're the best choice for the mission. Youthfulness isn't always the better choice over experience."

"Have you seen what Red Legion's doing to the locals?" the lead Overwatch sentinel asked but kept talking without waiting for an answer. "If we had a champion of the Legion go to Galma with us, that sentinel would kill half the planet before recovering Mace Applegate. We need someone who understands how to operate on a rogue world with a native population. Maneuvering in secrecy is crucial for the success of this mission. As your colonel stated, Force Command BlackRock specializes in occupation. Your command's scattered across half of all occupied space. It's common for the black armor plate of BlackRock to visit Galma."

"You said, 'go to Galma with us.'"

Colonel Zilath said, "Yes, Askar, you'll assist in recovering Mace Applegate. Overwatch Sentinel Negal will be in command with you as his second. Sentinel Mith here will be in support. She's an expert on the Rogue Syndicate and has studied Galma extensively."

I lifted my chin and asked, "Negal, what rank are you? Overwatch never displays rank or kills on armor. I'd like to know who's leading me."

He raised an eyebrow with a strange grin. "I'm a major. Do you know the reason we don't display our rank? Overwatch is the absolute authority within the Offensive. We're always watching everyone and everything. During an investigation, every sentinel within the Offensive from general down to private is subject to our efforts. Not displaying our rank ensures every sentinel respects our authority."

I turned to Colonel Zilath and said, "I'm yours to command, sir. You want me to go and capture a Federate employee? I'll bring honor to my Force Command."

"I knew you would, master gunny." He gripped his belt. "There's one more thing. You saved my life in our last camp and deserve recognition."

I interrupted. "Sir, I need nothing. I was doing my duty to our command and the Offensive."

Colonel Zilath lifted his hand to silence me. "I'm your commander, and this decision is final."

The colonel pulled his Corin-steel axe from his belt with its glowing green lines and black flecks and placed it on the table in front of me. "They call me the Gray Boulder. You're old for a sentinel, and I've got you beat in years by at least fifteen. My wife died long ago, and both children. The youngest passed two years ago fighting Androsians in the Great-in-Between. The eldest, lost here on this world a day after our command arrived. Once I die, my family name will die for all time. I want you to take my axe and use it to avenge our losses here. Capture Mace Applegate and add more spirals to your chest plate using my axe in glorious combat."

All could see my hesitation. "From time to time I'm called old for a sentinel. My response is always the same. I may be old, but I've got one good fight left in me. The same's true for you, sir. I'll do my best to honor you."

Colonel Zilath smiled. "Glad to hear that, gunny. We're giving our Overwatch friends BlackRock armor to blend in. Armor in the air in one hour. Gather your things, and prepare yourself."

With any luck, I would complete my mission and bring pride to our Force Command and the Offensive. Then hopefully, my life would end so that my soul could finally rest in the memory stone for eternity with a successful completion and my death. Was I asking too much for both?

CHAPTER 29

The Red Circle

Another Perpetual Agreement (Mace)

Arkie led Jamie and me from the bar where she had confronted us. Jamie frowned, no doubt wondering who Arkie was.

I leaned in to whisper, but before I could say anything, Arkie spoke up. "Mrs. Applegate, I'm one of the Syndicate members who assisted in getting you off Dol'Arem. My former employer in the Hollow Ward set up your departure."

Jamie raised her shoulders as if ready to engage in a debate. "You didn't do a good job. The ship captain demanded another thousand credits from each of the groups trying to leave. Those who couldn't pay were put into a holding room. The captain told us they'd meet up with the Dolrinions to transfer custody."

Jamie sounded like a supervisor of the Corporation. She needed to remember that Galma was hostile for people like us, and we had no protection.

I tried to emphasize Jamie's point in a friendlier tone. "The captain's selling them as slaves. It doesn't look good for the Syndicate. Those people paid for safe passage, and he denied them the right to get off his transport. Dolrinions aren't kind to employees of the Corporation. Being slaves is the best outcome for them if they're lucky."

Arkie didn't say anything and led us to the opposite side of the room to an elevator where enforcers wearing long black coats waited. One of them pushed the elevator button, and a small machine gun hanging from a shoulder strap under his arm swung out from his jacket. Inside the elevator was another enforcer who pushed the penthouse button.

Arkie said, "Every so often, captains do what it was you told me. I know that captain and will speak to my sister about punishing him for his actions."

"Who's your sister?"

She grinned. "The Rogue Ronin, second in command here at the Stumble Inn. She has powerful sway on Galma. We're going to see her and her boss."

The elevator opened to a long hallway. The ceilings were tremendously high with crown molding and detailed emblems along the entire length. On one side of the hall were windows spaced out along the thick cobblestone. The other side had wallpaper with designs that moved the same way those on the floor did inside the bar downstairs. The floor was a polished tile of different colors. Between each window were more enforcers dressed the same way as those who were by the elevator.

At the other end of the hallway were two huge gloss cedar doors which squeaked as they opened. Inside, enforcers stood guard along the perimeter. A circle of red carpeting surrounded by gold rails with one opening was in the room's center. At the center, inside the railed circle, several steps led down to seating. It was like a mini-amphitheater for small gatherings. A short man leaned against the rails at the opposite end with an unnecessary smile and hands in his pockets.

He was nearly as short as a Dolrinion with salt and pepper hair and a goatee that angled down to a point. Diamonds like the ones in Silas's teeth lined his hairline, jutting out of his skin. Both his ears had large diamond studs too. His attire was formal, but the colors were bright orange, yellow, lime, and lavender.

Behind him was a tall, athletic woman who resembled Arkie, with the same golden skin and long thick jet-black hair with dark red highlights. Under her eyes were identical diamonds that followed a pattern to the sides of her head. She looked serious and emotionless with tight lips and a frown; she glared at Jamie and me. The Rogue Ronin wore a leather trench coat with tail flaps extending down to her ankles, tactical pants with pockets on the sides, and a leather belt with pointed spikes. A long sword on her left hip inside a leather sheath extended past her jacket. Her shirt had laced beads tied around buttons.

Behind both diamond faces, golden frames lined the wall in several rows. The frames were all standard in size, but there weren't pictures inside. White fabric lined every frame and most of the higher-level pictures above had red handprints of all different shapes and sizes inside. The lowest row of frames only had two red handprints at one end. The rest were all white. Some of the prints at the top were faded.

"Mace Applegate, what a pleasure to meet you. Arkie's filled us in with everything you did for the Syndicate on Dol'Arem." The pointed-goatee man spoke with overwhelming confidence.

I cautiously said, "Glad to make your acquaintance Mr …?"

"Mr. Jaboo. True Syndicate bred and born here on Galma. Our organization's grown so large, most members never get a chance to visit the homeworld. That doesn't matter. When we send out orders to cells on any planet, all obey."

My wife said sharply, "We thank you for the Syndicate history lesson, but fail to see the reason for forcing us here."

Jamie still didn't understand. He was a Syndicate boss, and if he was anything like Silas, that monster was capable of inflicting pain and torment my wife couldn't imagine.

Jaboo narrowed his eyes, taking his hands from his pockets, and stared at Jamie for a moment. He turned to me and smiled again. "An issue arose when the MERC Guild agent attacked the warehouse."

"Silas fought bravely. He took on the mongrel with his bare hands but died."

Jaboo laughed to himself while shaking his head. "Silas and I worked closely with each other for a long time. If he'd been born on Galma, he would've been part of top leadership. I warned him about purchasing that location in the Hollow. Always too ambitious." Jaboo paused in thought. "He fought a mongrel with his hands, you said? Doesn't surprise me. I watched Silas break a man's back just by twisting him. The Bum Bum was freakishly strong."

The thought of Silas doing that troubled me. However, the street name in the Hollow made me smirk, and I said, "R Street and S Avenue. When I first got there, I had the same thought."

Jaboo nodded. "Yes, that was Silas's way. He was cocky and always thought of himself as untouchable."

"The MERC Guild are formidable adversaries. There's a reason they're so popular in movies, and there are college courses dedicated to their deeds and history. People across the Free Worlds see agents as celebrities."

Jaboo said, "On the Free Worlds, the Guild can be our biggest problem. But here, little concern. We allow them on Galma when they pay tribute. Agents must clear their actions with us, of course, but we let them meddle about as long as they don't interfere with us. In fact, hunter agents recently left our world having collected a wanted felon in the Lowlands. From the latest communication across my feed, another agent will be arriving shortly. This has nothing to do with why we asked you here. Arkie will explain the details."

Arkie walked to the rounded gold rails and waved her hands down to the seats. We stepped into the circle and sat. Jaboo and the Rogue Ronin did the same. The red carpet reminded me of blood; the way Silas spoke in the Hollow, everything in the Syndicate required blood.

Arkie said, "This is my sister." She pointed to the Ronin.

Jaboo chimed in, "My second in command and chief enforcer."

Arkie continued. "Mace. My laptop's gone. Destroyed during the MERC attack."

With wide eyes, I shook my head. "No, I saw you run past me during the shootout. You had the laptop in your hand as you were leaving."

"I did, but the agent shot me through the wall as I fled." She pulled down her shirt to show me two fresh gunshot wounds on her arm and shoulder. "I barely got out of there alive. That laptop's in hundreds of pieces on the warehouse floor. Because of Corporation tracking, we didn't link it to a network. I lost everything."

"Even your original program code?"

Arkie looked down at the red carpet, nodding. "Yes."

Jaboo said, "Arkie told us she could rewrite the entire code, but she'll require the firewall program again. That's where you come in."

"What do we get in return for this deal?"

Jaboo laughed maliciously, and he narrowed his eyes so tightly they nearly closed. "What do you get? You get nothing. Well, you get to keep your miserable life. Fulfill your contract, Mr. Applegate."

There was no fear in me at all. Images flashed through my mind of the last few months—Jamie telling me she was pregnant, the meeting with Neco, meeting Silas in the Hollow, him swindling me to get his way, the assault by the MERC agent, our travel to the planet and what the captain did to all the passengers. I was done and didn't care anymore.

I leaned forward in the chair, lifting my head high, and said, "No. When I first met Silas and agreed terms with him, we drew a blood contract." I raised my hand to show the scar from slicing my palm. "Then Silas told me the truth—that he'd lied. He charged me fifty thousand credits to leave when everyone else who flees only pays ten thousand each. I was bound to that contract so I couldn't protest. I handed Arkie the firewall, and Silas told me the contract was complete. We got on a ship and came here with hope. When the transport landed, the captain demanded another two thousand credits. Anyone who couldn't pay is currently en route to a hunter fleet. Those passengers are still Federate employees as far as the Dolrinions are concerned and will become terrible prizes or toys. Those two Free Worlds are at war if you didn't already know. Sentinels hate employees on a level never experienced by anyone across occupied space. It's embedded in their DNA.

Jamie and I would be on our way to that fate if things had gone differently."

Jaboo's face was flat. He didn't appear to be breathing as he listened to me ramble on.

But I continued anyway. "So no, Mr. Jaboo. My contract completed the minute I handed Arkie the original code. Under Syndicate law, I fulfilled my obligation, and honestly, I'm tired of these twisted games."

My heart now raced with fear, and the goosebumps on my arm gave that fear away, but I kept my shoulders high, looking at Jaboo with unwavering eyes. His look was cold as he scratched at the diamonds on his head.

"How about this—you give us the code, or I'll shoot your wife in the head."

One of the enforcers leaned over the railing and pointed the barrel of his gun into Jamie's head. She closed her eyes tight and bit her lip but didn't move or make a sound. I kept my eyes on Jaboo without blinking or giving any expression to my anxiety.

"If you shoot my wife, you'll need to kill me too. Then the firewall's lost forever, and nobody wins." He didn't need to know that I had the external drive in my pocket.

Another minute of complete quietness passed, and by that point, the hair on my arms stood straight in the air. Adrenaline coursed through my veins and my mouth was dry. With one word, Jaboo could kill us both. The effort would have been easier than breathing. But he didn't; instead, the Syndicate boss smiled and laughed loudly. He waved away the enforcer behind us.

"Ok, ok. It was worth a shot. I misjudged you, Mace." He glanced at Jamie. "You should be careful, darling. He didn't even flinch when I told him I'd kill you." Jaboo turned back to me. "What do you want for the code?"

"Silas charged me fifty thousand credits. I learn from hard lessons, and ask for the same."

Jaboo tapped his fingers on his knee, reflecting on my words. "But you didn't pay fifty thousand. You still owe twenty. So, I counter with thirty."

Thirty thousand credits with our current amount would be more than enough to keep us alive here. We could even leave for another planet. He would give us one more thing as well.

"Thirty thousand and Zoey's freedom."

The eyes of everyone sitting in the circle opened wide in confusion; even the Rogue Ronin, who had yet to move her face, did the same.

"Who's Zoey?"

"The curtain prostitute closest to the bar where Arkie found us. She has fresh marks on her face and said you gave them to her."

Jaboo laughed. "What's wrong, Mace? Your wife not giving enough action?"

I shook my head. "No, nothing to do with that at all."

Jaboo stopped laughing. "Fine, twenty thousand credits then, and you get her freedom. She's been nothing but trouble. We beat her almost every night so she'll do her job and sleep with patrons. You'll have no luck with that one, I promise."

"It's a deal," I said. "Please put the credits on our cash card and allow Jamie to go downstairs and free Zoey. The firewall is yours, a perpetual agreement, as Silas put it."

Jaboo pulled a knife from behind him that was more elegant than the one Silas had. The butt was set with a large diamond, and the handle was solid gold in patterns of vines moving down the grip. Along the vines were more diamonds styled like berries growing on the golden brush. Jaboo cut a small notch into his palm and handed me the blade. I did the same, and that time didn't wince from the cut. We shook to seal the deal with our blood as we sat in the Red Circle. The droplets that fell onto the carpet didn't stain.

Arkie waved a PDD over my cash card. I kissed Jamie, who looked at me in disbelief, and whispered, "I promise to explain everything downstairs. Go and wait for me with Zoey."

Jamie tightened her lips and hesitated but left the room with two enforcers at her side. Arkie placed her laptop in front of me. I inserted the external drive, at which Jaboo looked at me askance; he must have realized he could have killed me and taken it for free. I had the entire code for Arkie's program on my drive, but no one needed to know that. Any delay in the Syndicate's ability to steal money from innocent people was good in my book.

"How long will it take you to rewrite your code?"

"Four or five months. It took me several years to write it the first time, but I know much of the code by heart now."

I copied the firewall program onto her laptop and removed the drive, placing it into my pocket. "It's done."

Jaboo turned to Arkie. "Are we good?"

Arkie reviewed the code quickly. "Yes. He did it. We're good."

Jaboo's face turned flush. He stood and took a few steps towards me with hate in his eyes. "Good. Now, radio the enforcers to shoot his wife in the head." He turned behind. "Ronin, you kill him for me, please. Take his head so I can stick it at the top of the castle for a few days."

My heart dropped in shock, and fear crept down my spine, the same way it did when I first met Silas. I peered around the room. Should I run? What could I do?

Arkie shouted, "You can't kill him. The blood contract—it's our most sacred law, especially inside the circle."

Jaboo snapped, "Don't try and lecture me on what I can and can't do. I was born here, a Syndicate pure blood, and will do as I please. Ronin, kill him now!"

The Rogue Ronin stood and drew her sword in a single motion. The blade glistened with perfection and the sharp edge sparkled in the light. Her eyes were locked on me with the same unwavering cold stare. She glanced at her sister and Jaboo. I blinked rapidly and almost missed her sword as it sliced across the gold railing behind me, the blade screeching as it dragged across the metal. Jaboo's evil expression changed to surprise and then fear before his head fell to the red-carpeted circle at my feet. His body collapsed as if his bones disappeared and all that remained was skin. Blood streamed from his open neck like a glass of wine turned on its side, the thick red liquid soaking into the carpet. None of the trench coats moved or did anything. They held their positions like statues. The Ronin sheathed her sword and stared at me then placed her right hand into a puddle of Jaboo's blood, allowing her hand to become completely saturated. She left the circle and went to the next empty picture frame and carefully placed her hand on the open canvas.

I remembered Silas with his bloody hands coming back to me when he said leadership was taken with blood by those having high aspirations. The bosses on Galma desired those traits.

I looked at Arkie and said, "Your sister's the new boss now?"

"Yes. Leadership this high can only be taken, not given. That's what all those handprints on the wall are, sealed in blood, the same way as contracts."

The Rogue Ronin came back to me and, for the first time, opened her mouth. "We apologize for his actions. Blood contracts are unbreakable. The Red Circle is sacred, and we owe you for these mistakes."

I was sure of myself now. "Another ten thousand credits, a firearm with ammo for Zoey, anything else a bodyguard should have, and some new clothes for her should settle things."

The Ronin gave a crooked half-smirk. "Consider it done, Mr. Applegate."

Arkie escorted me from that dreadful room, but before I left, the Ronin said, "You'd do well in the Syndicate, judging by the way you displayed yourself here. There's a hidden strength inside you."

Strength? I nearly shit myself, but she didn't need to know.

I cleared my throat. "Recent events have changed me. I've seen enough death for one lifetime."

The Ronin pushed her lips together and tilted her head. "It's called experience. The more experience you have, the better off you'll be in this cruel existence."

Arkie led me out, but all I could think was that regardless of where we went in occupied space, free, outer, or rogue world, people were the same, twisted and uncaring.

At the elevator, I asked, "Why do they call your sister the Rogue Ronin?"

Arkie peered over her shoulder. "She was born here. I wasn't. Our mom left Dad while she was pregnant with me and claimed refugee status on the relations station. I was born a Free Worlds citizen. Dad was a medium-level Syndicate enforcer like all the enforcers you've seen. He taught her everything she knows about fighting. Our father was a great warrior, and that sword belonged to him. As she grew older, my sister became well known as a hunter for the Syndicate. Whenever the bosses put out a contract, she would travel occupied space and bring back heads. Before long, she became one of the best. I didn't meet her until I was seventeen years old. She was already twenty-five and had collected over two hundred contracts. That's when I joined, and she took me under her wing. Every advancement within the Syndicate that she's received was through blood."

The more I learned of the Rogue Syndicate, the more I feared their organization. Two hundred heads? They were ruthless, and the Ronin had seen more death than I ever would.

Back at the bar where we previously ordered drinks, the enforcers were still next to Jamie and Zoey, watching them closely. Jamie wasn't happy. Her arms were folded as she leaned against the bar.

Jamie slapped my cheek when I got close enough. "You were going to let them shoot me?"

My face stung and I rubbed it.

Arkie said, "Your husband learned from his meeting with one of the most ruthless underbosses of the Syndicate. What he did saved your life. Jaboo was going to kill both of you, and my sister prevented it."

Another trench coat appeared with a bag he handed to Zoey, whose perplexed stare couldn't have been any more obvious.

"What's going on?"

"Mace purchased your freedom. Consider yourself lucky. Jaboo was growing tired of the nightly beatings. You made a terrible curtain worker. Maybe you'll do better at something else," Arkie said concisely.

Jamie lowered her eyebrows and lightly shook her head. "Why did you want her freed?"

"Zoey was a dome security officer for the Capitol Forum. She protected representatives, and I was hoping that by getting her out, she'd agree to stay on with us and keep you safe until the baby is born."

Zoey glanced sternly at Jamie and her stomach, and without saying anything, she took the bag and walked behind the curtain. When she came out, Zoey's appearance was intimidating; she wore tactical gear that would be usual for any soldier without battle armor including a vest similar to those worn by law enforcement to store equipment and a pistol at her waistline. The items on her body seemed to make that short woman grow several centimeters instantly. Zoey put on a dark brown zip-up leather jacket and stepped between Jamie and me.

"I'll keep all three of you safe."

Jamie's eyebrows were high and her mouth opened wide. "Mace, this was all to protect me?"

"Yes. Capitol Security is trusted to keep representatives safe. I think Zoey can manage a few stragglers like you and me."

Arkie escorted us out the same way we came in through dancing, drinking, and sex. As we cleared the courtyard, she said, "We won't see each other again, Mace. Take care of yourself. I wish you and your family the best of luck."

We made our way to the sky lift and explained everything that had happened in our lives for the last few months to Zoey, who sat quietly listening.

*

At the bottom of the sky lift, Jamie took a deep breath and looked around. "What's the plan now?"

"Some food and a place to sleep." I turned to Zoey, who was watching everyone passing us. "Do you know anything about this area? Is there a hotel we can stay at?"

Zoey hesitated as her hyper-focus moved from person to person. "Galma's not like the Free Worlds. You won't find hotels. They mostly have small inns and taverns with accommodations above the bars. The Lamp District might be the best place to start to the south of the spaceport."

Jamie seemed distracted by passers-by who were laughing and talking loudly. "Lamp District?"

Zoey didn't say anything and took two steps behind Jamie as two locals wearing thick jackets like it was winter stepped back and moved around us. Zoey's grudging gaze was worth more than theirs. "Those two were going to try and pickpocket you. I watched them do it to a few others before they walked this way. What sister company did you work for, and what was the closest city?"

"Genesis Foundation and we lived outside of Lavlen." I turned to Jamie. "Did you see how fast Zoey moved? She saw what we couldn't."

Jamie smirked. "I understand now."

Zoey brought her attention back to us. "The Lamp District's similar to Lavlen's Downtown, just not as big. It has small shops, taverns and inns, brothels, and apartments. It's cheaper than the Stumble Inn. Do you have credits?"

We had forty-four thousand credits on the cash card after the day's events.

"Yes. We have enough for everything, including your pay."

Zoey narrowed her eyes. "You paid me more than enough already. Food and a bed at night are all I need."

Jamie smiled. "Mace, I've never been more impressed with you. I was mad at first and thought you'd lost your mind. Now it all makes sense." She lightly caressed my cheek. "Sorry for slapping you."

Even though things were looking up and Jamie was leaning in to kiss me, I wondered where Allison and her boys went off to. We passed the railing where she said they'd wait for us counting ships. Did the boys run off again as they had at times on our way to Galma?

It took nearly twenty minutes to get to the cobblestone streets of the Lamp District. Great metal posts spaced out along the sidewalks supported oversized hanging lamps with flames giving off light. Bugs swarmed the lights in the night sky. Most building roofs were pitched steep forming points at the top, and the slatted wood planks overlapped one another angling down the frame. It was darker than Lavlen at night, but the atmosphere was nearly the same with people moving this way and that. Vendors lined the streets, patrons ate in outdoor dining areas, and teens caused mischief.

We had only been on the street for a short time when Zoey noticed a commotion at the next street intersection. She put her arm up to stop us from continuing, watching the situation carefully. As quickly as we saw the gathering, it split down the center and people moved away from the street in different directions. A MERC mongrel slowly pawed its way between the onlookers.

The mongrel lowered its head, sniffing, then raised its snout high, its moist black nostrils opened wide into the air. Zoey slowly lowered herself to the hard stone where she watched the beast and carefully pulled her sidearm from its holster. Zoey seemed to know the animal's intentions already. The mongrel closed its eyes, twitching to the side, and opened them in our direction.

Jamie squeezed my hand, and she was trembling. "We need to leave."

Zoey said, "It's here for you two. Did you tell me everything?"

"Absolutely."

The mongrel growled, and I realized. "That's the same mongrel that attacked the Syndicate in the Hollow."

Its auto guns moved from side to side as if it were clearing the tracks so it could shoot us more easily.

Zoey shouted, "We need to move now."

She led us down an alleyway with endless doors on both sides. There was a vendor cart nearby, and Zoey pulled it sideways on the street and apples and trinkets rolled away.

"Go to the end and turn right. If the door's locked, kick it in."

I grabbed Jamie's hand and we ran down the hard cobblestone. The door was locked, so I started kicking, but it was secure. Again and again, I kicked. The mongrel peeked its head over the turned cart; Zoey took aim and shot several rounds, forcing the beast to retreat from the incoming fire.

I kicked again, repeatedly, praying for the door to give way, and finally it flew open scattering splintering pieces across the stone. We fled into the doorway, and Zoey followed shortly behind, just in time, as several loud crackles went off with zipping sounds from bullets aimed at her. At the top of the stairs, Zoey pulled on a dresser and shouted for my help. It was burdensome and heavy but it eventually fell sideways like a falling tree, tumbling down the staircase with drawers and the items inside falling out. The mongrel came to the doorway and stopped. The oversized dresser reached the bottom stair and stood straight up acting as a temporary deterrent. Huge, powerful paws pushed over the top.

"Move—keep going."

We went through several rooms, then pushed open two swinging doors to a balcony. The distance across wasn't far to where another balcony stood, but underneath was a two- to three-story drop to that damn cobblestone.

"Jump to the other balcony," Zoey called out.

Jamie didn't falter. She got a running start and leaped across as she had years earlier off the Amway death bridge in her skydiving adventures as a young teen. I swallowed deep, imagining the fall if I didn't make the jump. Jamie had more guts than me.

Jamie raised her voice. "Come on, Mace, you can do it."

Well, I don't know anyone who's died from leaping across a balcony on Galma while being chased by a MERC mongrel, so why not? I jumped, and Jamie caught my hand. Behind, Zoey pulled a small tank from the kitchen stove and waited patiently near the balcony. The mongrel sprang to the top of the staircase, and while it was still in midflight, Zoey tossed the tank at it and fired one bullet from her gun. A powerful explosion erupted in the apartment as Zoey leaped away from the flames to our balcony.

We went out to the cobblestone streets where the entire incident started. Many people were on the roads looking in our direction. We quickly moved away but stopped again when Zoey lifted her arm. Someone was pushing through the same crowd as before. A MERC Guild agent took two steps out, his eyes narrowed and his lips pressed together; he seemed agitated by our presence. He was focused as if he'd done this hundreds of times before.

Behind us, the mongrel came from an alley, growling, singed fur on one side of its body exposing skin that was already blistering. The auto gun was in pieces and no longer functioning. Saliva dripped from both sides of its jowls.

The agent still wasn't moving, just standing and staring at us; Zoey did the same. Jamie's hands shook uncontrollably, and I grabbed one to try and calm her even though I was afraid too.

Zoey whispered, "When I start shooting, go to the street to our left. Keep running, and don't look back."

Without waiting for a response, she lifted her weapon. The agent did the same, and they fired their guns in unison. Jamie and I ran the way Zoey had told us to. Small plumes of smoke rose from both weapons at each discharge. Clinking sounds of empty round casings echoed between the gunshots. Sparks illuminated the agent's Corin-steel armor, and Zoey's body jerked as bullets impacted her tactical vest. She followed us, moving sideways, still firing her weapon. Neither the agent nor Zoey showed any restraint and were methodical in their movements.

From the opposite street, a black truck screeched across the cobblestones to a halt. Syndicate enforcers with rifles and black trench coats jumped onto the road and engaged the agent, the mongrel, and Zoey. Our protector shot two rounds and dropped one enforcer with ease. Automatic fire overshadowed the agent's and Zoey's guns. The enforcers turned their focus on the agent and his mongrel as we ran.

A fat man with a thick brown beard drove by in a taxi. He spoke with a heavy gruff accent. "Some wildness going on in the Lamp District tonight, let me tell you. Where it be you looking to go?"

We got into the vehicle. Zoey looked out the back window and said, "Take us to the mid-crossing."

She pulled a few flattened bullets from her vest and dropped them on the floormat.

Our driver opened his eyes wide. "You goin' down below?"

Jamie protested. "The Lowlands? No, not down there."

Zoey said, "He's tracking you two and his mongrel has your scent. It can sniff you out for sixteen kilometers. The fog in the Lowlands has a powerful odor. The mongrel's senses won't work well. Agents die as often as they don't down in the Lowlands of Galma."

"Jamie, remember what the captain told us? If someone wants to disappear, the Lowlands are the best place to go."

The taxi driver interrupted. "It's true. People go down low and don't come back. Things different down there, but you hide with no problem. You need to be careful. People be disappearing down there for some time. Nobody knows why. They here one, gone the next, poof. Why you got a Guild agent following you anyways?"

Jamie said, "It must be for you, Mace. You were in that warehouse with Silas when the agent attacked. He tracked us here."

"It could be that, or maybe the Corporation asked the Guild to recover me. I'm a threat to them because of the defense-grid program."

Zoey didn't say a word. She only watched and listened, keeping her thoughts to herself.

"I'd bet you lived and worked around agents on the station your entire life, Zoey." She nodded. "Do we stand a chance hiding from him and his beast?"

Zoey turned back to the window behind and said, "He appears to be here alone, which isn't typical this far away from the station. One on one, I don't stand a chance against him. Not while he has the mongrel. I've trained inside the cathedral with agents and know their ways. I'll do everything in my power to keep you safe. I made a promise. One thing's certain—my job just became a whole lot more interesting."

CHAPTER 30

Pushback

Rabbits can help with anger (Henry)

I had three visits in my back office already, and it was not even ten o'clock in the morning yet. First, all three Dolrinion representatives came praising me for what happened in the refugee dock with Adam and Juliet Sideris. The supreme generals wanted to use the Guild to attack station command and take control. Typical Dolrinion mentality—the Offensive always wanted to attack everything. I'd never seen the Iron Fist of Kora, Guth, and Halku smile so much before. Guth had drawn up battle plans and stated he'd lead the assault. It took great effort to calm them down and convince the generals that one war on Gliese was more than enough for now.

Mia arrived shortly after telling me how much of an uproar I'd caused on Civil Earth. Tier One had started kicking out MERC agents from substations across Earth. Tier One leadership, including Olivia Belitz's father, Jaden Belitz, said, "What's to stop these agents from grabbing me for no other reason than one of the representatives on that station saying so?" *He exaggerates.* Taking Adam and Juliet in the dock wasn't the same as going above the ninety-fifth floor on Civil Earth and detaining someone from Tier One without cause.

There was more pushback than I had anticipated from what happened. My second round of scolding had commenced with Civil Earth Representative Belitz, Alliance Representative Laskaris, and my very own Accord slithery rose JJ lecturing me. As they raised their voices, my attention was elsewhere, looking at Benjamin sitting against the back wall of my office, typing away on his PDD. Was he messaging Alyssa?

Zoey was dealt with and should be having sex twenty times a night in the Stumble Inn. She'd be dead within a month because, with her level of training and personality, she wouldn't be able to sit there and take it night after night. My rage flared when I caught Allyssa. Who did Zoey think she was? What right did she have to hide what was happening? I was the most senior member under the dome and wielder of the Union Hammer of Labor. Oliver, Josue, and I beat her repeatedly before turning her over to the Syndicate. Each punch against her body brought joy to me; it was like punching a heavy bag, listening to the connecting sound and hearing her grunts and screeches of pain, blow after blow. The Syndicate captain that took her said he'd break her into the new job on the long trip to Galma. It gave me even more pleasure to watch them drag her tiny bruised and bloodied body away. She could barely lift her head after the thrashing we gave her.

Alyssa hadn't gotten over me leaving on her birthday, which only made my ears boil more, knowing what she did in my bed with that bloody minge bag over there, typing away. That was nearly two weeks ago, and I was doing everything in my power to keep clear of the bedroom. It was easier with Adam and Juliet staying in the apartment as a suitable buffer, so I didn't strangle Alyssa in her sleep.

The Green Eyes of Athinia were interesting characters. I'd spent some time getting to know their personalities, along with their strengths and weaknesses. Juliet seemed to have a naïve simplicity with a carefree attitude. Adam was more complicated, with a fierceness that reminded me of myself. He grew annoyed easily during simple discussions. A memory of my dad teaching me how to deal with my anger came to mind, and I knew of ways to help him deal with his issues. But first, I needed to get through this ridiculous meeting.

Olivia said, "Henry, you need to give them back. Either to station leadership or Representative Laskaris. You can't keep them. Secretary Nomikos is drafting up an order, and with Rumi's signature, we'll have no choice."

Olivia was unlikely to get Rumi to sign that waste of paper while she was under my control.

Zachery Laskaris, sitting at the other end of my office, spoke over Olivia. "Henry, you've got no idea how much pressure the Alliance embassy bubble's under from the Twins. The Green Eyes must go to New-Sparta."

"You want me to hand them over to Isaac and Killian, who will behead them on the steps of Athinia's State Capitol building and place their heads on the point of the central dome as the Twins did to their grandfather? Don't act like you and I hadn't talked before about Liam the Unifier and the way things were before the war." Zachery looked down, almost ashamed, as I continued. "Adam's twenty-three, and Juliet's twenty years old. They're more than capable of deciding for themselves where to go. Don't tell me what I must or mustn't do. Everyone in this room has committed one unfavorable action or another in their time under the dome."

My eyes narrowed in Benjamin's direction as I finished the sentence and heard that slapping sound of his skin connecting to Alyssa as she cried out in pleasure.

JJ said, "Henry, your Chair of Uropa spoke to Representative Keng and me. She wants you to return to Uropa immediately. Labor Party and Red Rose leadership agree with each other for once."

JJ had something to do with that, I'm sure. Who did Sadie Enama think she was, ordering me back to Warwick? I was the center seat representative, elected not appointed, and keeper of the Hammer for our Labor Party. Union leaders from the Labor Party were pissed off with the hundred million tons of food sent to Gliese. Because of my decree during open convocation, our party had no choice but to supply the food begrudgingly.

"Chairperson Enama needs to wait, I'm afraid. Things require my attention here. Uropa can see me by year's end."

JJ knew well that the chairs of the Colonial Accord worlds could request our presence but had no authority to demand anything. The elected leadership of the six worlds were responsible for the individual planets of their election. Decisions that affected the entire Accord came to votes by the chairs and had to have representative approval, which was why all six worlds voted together for representative elections. If there was a stalemate between chair votes, the representatives cast votes to break the tie. Our decisions on the relations station affected all the Accord worlds together, plus all the other Free Worlds. We representatives had no authority to declare war; that power remained exclusively with the chairs of our Accord.

Representative Belitz said, "Henry, we really don't need to argue the finer points. Regardless of Rumi's intent, her deputy director and other secretaries are of a different mind from her. They want to restrict all fifteen representatives' access to the main cylinder. The Guild's never undermined station authority before in such an obvious way." She glanced at JJ and Zachery. "The rule of three applies."

Of course, Olivia would bring the rule of three into that conversation. Getting two other wall representatives to agree with my taking Adam and Juliet would have been impossible after all the favors and maneuvering for my union bill. Any direct action that was deemed immediate or time-sensitive required that three representatives from three walls sign off in approval.

"Rumi will have the final say in any decisions, and I believe we can discourage her from any harsh actions." I frowned. "I'm well aware of the rule, Olivia. Twenty-two years on this station, I've forgotten more than you know about things here."

Olivia folded her arms and clenched her jaw while JJ lifted a curious eyebrow. He was probably trying to figure out what I had on Director Houlton. My bothersome red-haired clown stepped forward before speaking.

"There will be an inquiry into the actions taken by the Guild. You're going to be the center of attention for violating the Free Worlds' Policy."

I had told Ficco to keep an eye out for any Sideris family members after hearing unconfirmed reports that they left Epsilon Prime. Honestly, I never thought they'd come here since lots of survivors from the war fled to rogue worlds. Ficco took things too far at times, as in this case; keeping an eye out for them didn't mean grabbing them. Regardless, I wasn't disappointed with the results.

"When will this inquiry take place?"

"Next week in closed session with a legal team, witnesses, and Senior Agent Ficco," Olivia said with her chin high.

I stood from behind my desk and leaned forward. "I haven't admitted to taking any action through the Guild regardless of your accusations. Adam Sideris claimed I was expecting him, yet I had no idea he was coming, or I would've greeted him myself at the dock. Your inquiry's a waste of resources and time, but I look forward to it." I turned to Ben. "Benjamin, see our guests out please."

Everyone in that room could let the door hit them in the ass for all I cared. Olivia tapped her finger against her lips, glaring at me, and left, followed closely on her heels by JJ.

Zachery remained behind. "Would you do me a kindness and talk alone for a moment?"

I agreed while the other representatives and my backstabbing aide departed.

"Henry, my father told me in confidence that the prime regent cabinet meetings aren't going well on Epsilon Prime. Don't underestimate Isaac, his devotion to the Acolyte of Darkness makes him …" Zachery paused, seeming fearful of saying the words as if his religious idols would strike him down for speaking. "Unpredictable. Killian always disliked your power within the Free Worlds and wouldn't hesitate to see you die of some random accident, apparently bad luck. I know your capabilities too—all under the dome know what Henry McWright is capable of, but don't believe for an instant that you're the only one in occupied space who can do such things. A reckoning is coming, and I won't be able to help. The Lyons' rage has no rival."

Lyons' rage, please. Even when they wrote those words, everyone knew the truth. Isaac and Killian grew up on the streets, poor, with nothing. Now they had the masses believing that a lion raised them. My ears were hot to the touch. Lyons' rage, huh. Henry's fury would cover the Lyons Twins like hot lava from an active volcano devouring everything it touched.

"Henry, your ears are red."

I ignored that statement and said, "Is Aetós still viewed as second class on Epsilon Prime? Before the war, your regent voted for Liam the Unifier as prime regent. Your state even assisted Keon Sideris before our time during the War of Oppression. Why didn't Aetós declare for the Allied States right away? The Chrysós Aetós, with mercenaries hired by Liam, might have turned the tide. Isaac will never let your city-state live down its hesitation to fight for the pride."

Zachery looked swiftly from one end of the room to the other as my words saturated him like a showerhead on full blast.

"It's too late for pondering the past now. Could have, would have, or should have doesn't matter. The here and now means everything. Nine city-states are in ruins while the others continue. Aetós alone can't change anything now."

He was right; his state was stuck, Rhódmore paid life debts with hostages to keep their compliance with the Twins, Bokós and Thebos fought with each other constantly. Zacynth, an Allied State, had an entire civilization hiding deep under the bedrock of the Stairway Mountains waiting for their chance to strike, and billions had fled during the civil war and wanted revenge. Isaac and Killian Lyons' power hold wasn't that secure. Zachery didn't see it based on his look, but when the time came, he might see the other side of things.

I extended my hand. "Thank you for the warning, Representative Laskaris. Please tell your father I said hello. Have a wonderful rest of your day."

Zachery frowned and didn't move, but reluctantly left my office after another moment. Benjamin returned and Oliver and Josue glanced at him before turning away.

"What's our plan to deal with the inquiry, sir?"

My ears were so hot I could boil water. I saw images in my head of me wrapping my hands around his throat and squeezing. The sounds of him gurgling as he attempted to inhale while my hands tightened were as real to me as him standing there. The room became blurry, and I saw the same floating specks in the air as I had in JJ's office when he canceled my speech.

"Sir? Are you ok?"

"Yes, fine, thinking of things to take care of soon. Don't trouble yourself with the inquiry. It won't be my first or last—Ficco's good under pressure. I want you to take my PDD and spend the rest of the day going about my public schedule. I've got things to do and don't want eyes watching."

"No problem, sir. I'll go right away." He took my PDD and left.

I turned to Oliver and took a deep breath. "It's taking every bit of energy I've got not to grab that boy when he speaks."

Oliver waited, looking back at the door, then said, "I saw your hand shaking while you were talking to him. Keep your focus, sir. With the inquiry, more eyes will be watching things throughout the station. Josue and I already spotted new bodies the last few days."

Spies who worked for the Free Worlds' governments and station director's office. They were always watching. I changed into disguise before leaving the office, and our new security officer put on my suit and sat by the desk looking out of the window every few minutes. People in the gardens would think I was in my office or out with that sleazebag aide. We used the back hall into the amphitheater of the forum and crossed past the Dolrinion seats, stepping through their door. Rifles greeted our entry into the Dolrinion back office, dark holes of gun barrels like black pupils staring us down. All it would take was one trigger-happy shooter, and that would be the end of Henry McWright wearing a hooded sweatshirt and sneaking into a back office. *Oh, that'd be a fitting end.*

Oliver stepped in front of me and shouted, "Center Seat Representative Henry McWright of the Colonial Accord is here to meet with Right Seat Representative Guth!"

We cleared the doorway, and I removed my hood.

"Why did you come through the back?" a sentinel captain asked resentfully.

"Too many eyes under the dome today. You know the Federates are always watching."

The captain grunted with a head nod and stepped back.

A Capitol Security officer said, "Representative Guth's not expecting you today, sir."

"He'll want to speak with me, I promise."

I paced around the chunk of memory stone in their lobby as the sentinel heads followed me for some time, but one of Guth's security officers finally came to the lobby and escorted us to the third floor.

Guth was wearing his Tacoma blue and orange armor and had an inviting smile as he waved his hand over his desk to display a hologram of the station with blue outlines marking the interior and red dots for strategic locations.

"Changed your mind, have you? Here's our action plan. Your Colonial Marines will attack here." He pointed to one of the red dots. "I'll send my Tacoma forces here." He pointed again. "The Guild will pour out from the cathedral and overrun their battle-line defense holding our two armies back."

I shook my head. "You misunderstand my intentions. I didn't come to discuss attacking the station. Besides, Force Command Tacoma concentrates its efforts on politics, diplomacy, and maintaining the memory stone, don't they?"

Of all the Force Commands, Tacoma and First Ones were viewed by the other commands as weaker for their fields of focus. I shouldn't have challenged Guth that way, but my mind was busy picturing Benjamin's naked arse, and that damn slapping sound was like an earworm.

Guth narrowed his eyes in defiance and said, "All Force Command sentinels can fight a ground war. Shooting a battle rifle and killing with a knife's the first thing Dolrinions learn to do after walking. I would march into battle proudly with any Tacoma sentinel at my side. Tacoma's strongest diplomatic negotiations are through the barrel of a rifle."

My father always told me the same of Tacoma, and his other teachings were more impactful all those years ago. It was strange that I was thinking of him more since spending time with Adam Sideris.

"The Red Legion and War Dogs specialize in ground wars, but all Dolrinions are more than capable. The same way Force Command Steel

Talon focuses its efforts on battle groups and space warfare. A destroyer from Force Command Brim Fire, JackHammer, or Steel Talon will inflict the same level of damage as a destroyer from Red Legion, Burning Star, or BlackRock."

I said, "Force Command Burning Star's why I'm here."

He smirked. "Interesting. Christopher Floros ran into me in the main cylinder yesterday, asking about Burning Star. He said it was just happenstance that we ran into each other. Obviously, he planned it. What makes you both think I can help with another command?"

"Because your brother-in-law's one of the five supreme generals of that command. You're a supreme general of Tacoma and have tremendous respect in the Offensive. He's a leading supreme general of Burning Star. The conversation shouldn't be difficult. Will you tell me what the Silent Lion wanted?"

Guth scratched his evenly cropped mustache goatee and grumbled. "The same thing you're here for—Isabel Sideris. She's on Pomona in a slave camp laboring for our war efforts."

"I'm surprised you're keeping her there. She would be considered a VIP hostage on any of the other Free Worlds." He must have been able to read my anxiety.

The representative shook his head and waved his hand. "Aah, she's nothing to us. We couldn't care less about those city-states. Half of their world is in ashes and all they care about is a family with green eyes that look like they spent too much time next to a fusion reactor."

I smiled. "They are unnatural looking, aren't they? Those green eyes are a symbol of hope to the Allied States and loyalist fighters. Billions who fled the Alliance during the war need those fusion eyes for leadership."

Guth didn't reply, only shuffled through paperwork on his desk as if he didn't hear me.

"What did the Silent Lion offer you for her release? I'm willing to make a better deal."

"Floros offered me credits. Millions of them, but what need do I have for that? Becoming a supreme general's extremely difficult but lucrative. I've got fifty lifetimes of financial goods. He'd need to do better."

Credits would never suffice with Guth. His home on Kora was a functioning military base with two thousand slaves working the grounds for his family—a wife, and five warrior children; it was extremely uncommon for Dolrinions to have so many offspring. Guth was one of the wealthiest of any supreme general.

"I've got something else you want—an even trade, one life for another. The intelligence you could extract would impress all the commands, and when you finish, send him to fill the lost shoes on Pomona. If you'd like, I'll also send you locator beacons of a few refugee ships leaving from Galma. You give me one, and I'll give you thousands, including the first offer."

Molly and Paavo could afford to lose a few of their refugee ships on the way back from Galma. It would bring joy to me to hurt some of Alyssa's friends.

The representative sat back in his chair, scratching his facial hair again. "Keep talking."

*

When I entered my apartment building, there was a ruckus in the lobby. Adam was against the wall with two Colonial police speaking to him. Another young man was on a stretcher with medics tending to massive wounds. I knew who he was, based on his shoes, even though they had blood painted across them. He was the son of a high-level businessman here in New Wick. His face was a pile of mush, with broken bones pushing his skin out, deep gashes, swelling, and thick globs of blood staining his skin. Adam's shirt looked like he used red spray paint to change the color. Everyone looked at me.

"What's going on here?"

An officer stepped closer. "They fought. The bloody mess in that stretcher made an advance on Adam's sister that led to a physical confrontation."

Oliver said, "A physical conflict between two adults under Colonial Law shouldn't draw charges. As long as the fight was consensual."

"That would be true if both parties were citizens of the Colonial Accord.

He isn't."

I stepped between Oliver and the officer. "There's no issue. Take Steven to the hospital. I'll speak to his father and pay for plastic surgery. He'll look like himself again by next week."

The senior officer didn't accept my offer. "Representative McWright, I know who you are. Colonial Charter Law's clear. I must take him into custody."

Everyone in the lobby, including that bloody mess on the stretcher, watched our predicament. I was over that nonsense for one day and sighed, looking at the wall clock because I was tired of wasting time. The senior officer had a wedding ring. I'd bet he had children.

"Oliver, give me your PDD, please."

Ollie handed it over. I logged into the embassy bubble's secure network and took a picture of the officer's face. I was surprised he had even passed the entrance test for his position, judging by his dumbfounded glare.

"What are you doing?" the officer asked with concern.

"I'm locating your home address and sending the Guild to arrest your wife and children. They'll be brought to the cathedral for interrogation until Adam's release," I said irritably.

Both officers froze in place, and the senior stumbled on his words. "Re-Re-Representative McWright, there's no need, sir. We're leaving."

"Take Steven to the hospital for his treatment."

"Yeah, I mean, yes, sir."

I can't trust anyone in this bubble. For all I knew, Nicolas Nomikos or the Twins had paid these two tin shields to whisk Adam away once he was out of my grasp. Once everyone left, Adam laughed to himself.

"Could you really order the Guild to do that?"

I grabbed his shirt and dragged him to the penthouse elevator doors with Oliver and Josue following. Some of the blood from his shirt stained my sleeve and jacket.

"The Guild wouldn't detain people just because I told them to. That's not how they operate."

Adam said, "But that's what the Guild did in the refugee dock."

I sighed. "Technically, I didn't give that order. A high-ranking senior agent did." I changed the topic. "Why did you beat him up so badly? From the way he looked, you gained the advantage quickly. After he was down, you continued to beat him. Why?"

Adam turned away and looked at the elevator buttons as if they would give him the answer to my question.

"I wanted to punish him for what he said. It felt good to keep hitting him. The more my fist connected to his flesh, the more power I felt inside. If the lobby worker hadn't pulled me off, you would've returned to me still pummeling him."

The way Adam talked reminded me so much of myself when I was his age. Memories of my dad's lessons ran through my head of him showing me how to deal with my anger; it worked most of the time. Maybe my experiences could help Adam.

"When we get upstairs, go change your clothes and take a shower. After, meet me on the terrace."

Adam agreed while playing with the dried blood on his knuckles. Flakes of it gracefully fell to the floor. Inside my apartment, we went in different directions. I stepped into the kitchen, where Pietro stood guard near the staircase to my bedroom.

"Anything to report?"

"No, she went to the gym this morning, then came home and has been upstairs all afternoon."

Juliet came into the family room wearing a colorful T-shirt and tiny tight teal shorts. Her beautiful young dark olive-colored legs accentuated that smooth and stunning youthful skin against her shorts. My heart sped up with tension, blood rushing between my legs.

Juliet seemed excited as she smiled. "Hello, Henry."

"Good afternoon, Juliet. I heard you had some trouble with Steven in the lobby."

She lifted her head with a slight half-smile and said, "I didn't know that was his name. The boys always make comments to me. When Adam started punching him, I left and came upstairs." She looked over at the television. "There are interesting channels on the display screen."

"We call them televisions here."

Her smile widened. "Yes, one channel's all about the station. It talks about everything. Question—the station security officers, they're different than Capitol Security Protection Services, right?"

"They are. Station security officers are the law enforcement and military of the main cylinder. They report directly to station command, controlled by the secretary of defense and director's office."

"But then why's the secretary of defense's main office under the dome? Shouldn't he be in station command? Also, Capitol Security officers that protect the representatives report to dome headquarters and don't follow the orders of the secretary of defense, correct?"

She was eager to learn, and I admired that. The way she smiled reminded me of my first wife when we started dating in our youth.

"The first hundred years on the station were very different. The founders and working authority had to go through countless trials and experiences to figure out what worked and what didn't. Originally the secretary of defense was responsible for the representative's security. As time went on the relations station became more robust. Did you know the first citizens of the station were all refugees from rogue worlds? That was the main purpose of the cylinder, and to an extent, it still is, which is why the refugee dock's always bustling with activity. Changes came when it was realized that all station command offices and jobs of the main cylinder shouldn't be involved with activities under the dome since they're independent entities with two completely different tasks. Capitol Security has policies and functions differently from station security. Most of our capitol officers protect everything under the dome, including the Capitol Forum, and golden road. The best among Capitol Security work with direct protection for the representatives and their families. There are other divisions too, but Capitol Security is a fraction of the size of station security. Everything has a beginning."

Juliet raised an eyebrow. "You have children on Uropa, don't you? Do they have protection?"

"Yes, they do, because even on Uropa, threats can lurk around any corner. Dodgy types look for ways to hurt people like me any way they can."

Juliet grabbed my hand, guiding me to the couch near the TV. We sat together, and she faced me with her legs crossed on the sofa and a broad smile. Her eyes were so bright, that close they almost seemed to glow turquoise, and she smelled fantastic.

"What else can you tell me about this place?"

My gaze wandered down her legs, which didn't have any imperfections, not a crease or dimple in sight. The shorts rode up her thighs because of the way she was sitting, and the thin material arched up high. There was an outline between her legs, bulging out at both sides to perfection. She smiled playfully under my long gaze.

I turned away quickly and said, "There's lots of interesting things to do. For the time being, you must remain in the Colonial bubble for your protection. When the time's right, you and your brother can explore the station freely."

"There must be somewhere in the Colonial bubble we can go for fun. I want to dance, drink, and do the things that normal people enjoy. Adam and I have spent years hiding. We would sit quietly in hidden rooms behind a wall for days doing nothing. Mom and Dad were always gone, trying to undermine New-Sparta in any way they could. Life was boring for years. Mom tried to hide us in our room on the refugee ship too. She said our green eyes made us stand out. We even wore colored contacts constantly."

"Your mother was only trying to protect you and Adam. So many people want to hurt you, use you, or put you on a trophy wall to show off. The Green Eyes of Athinia have so much power within the Free Worlds."

Juliet looked curious. "What do *you* want from us, Henry?"

Before I could answer, Alyssa walked down the spiral staircase, her voice thick with attitude. "Thanks for saying hello to your wife when you got home, Henry."

Alyssa gave Juliet a sharp look, her lips pressed tightly together, and Juliet let go of my hands and moved back on the couch away from me. My cheating wife was jealous of Juliet because of her beauty and age.

I stood and cleared my throat. "I just got home and haven't made it upstairs yet. How was your day?"

Alyssa rolled her eyes and said, "My day was fine." She looked at Pietro. "My new security officer ..." She stopped before finishing the sentence. "When's Zoey returning?"

Of course she wanted Zoey back. She'd followed Alyssa like a shadow and kept her mouth shut at what my bitch of a wife was doing, who she was doing. Alyssa's issue now was that she couldn't spread her legs without me knowing.

I glanced at Pietro then back at Alyssa. "There's some restructuring happening at Capitol Security headquarters. Zoey's being promoted. I have reached out to her on your behalf, but she's so busy no reply has come yet."

Alyssa appeared unconvinced. "What about her family emergency? Did you ever find out what happened?"

"Yes, her mother passed away from illness. I sent flowers on your behalf for the services held this past weekend."

Alyssa narrowed her eyes and glared at Juliet before walking into the kitchen, grabbing a snack, and slamming cabinets to show her frustration. She walked back up the stairs and stopped halfway, staring at me. "Maybe tonight, you'll sleep in our bed rather than staying up entertaining house guests all night."

She gave Juliet another look and left towards the bedroom. My ears burned hot with rage. It took every bit of effort I had not to do or say anything. *Keep the box locked, Henry.*

Juliet's voice eased my anger. "She doesn't like me much, does she?"

"Alyssa hasn't been herself for the last few days. Don't worry about her."

Juliet stood, came to me and pecked my cheek. "I'm going to take a shower. Please consider what I said about taking us out."

She turned and left, heading to the guest rooms off the back hallway. I watched her walk away, observing that impeccably shaped body. I stepped out to the terrace with two glasses and a bottle of high-end bourbon. There was a slight breeze blowing through my hair and the smell of a city alive with activity; I truly loved the sounds of New Wick—vehicles, and people on the streets and birds in the air. After I poured the drinks and relaxed, Adam came out and joined me. I handed him a glass of bourbon, and we tapped glasses. He sat and took a sip.

"How long have you had these anger issues?"

He said defensively, "My anger's a strength, not an issue."

I smirked. "You might not realize it, Adam, but my entire life is anger. An unadulterated rage that boils deep inside of me and wants to burst out constantly. It takes every bit of energy to keep it inside. My father taught me when I was young to channel my anger in other ways. You must always have two faces. The face you want everyone around you to see and the face you keep in private that only comes out when others aren't watching."

Adam's frown relaxed and he swirled the ice inside its glass.

"What did he teach you?"

After a brief pause with memories of my past spinning through my head, I answered, "Have you ever had pet rabbits?"

CHAPTER 31

Game Time

A challenge that I couldn't deny (Isabel)

Another dream from years ago. No, not a dream, a terrible nightmare, and there wasn't anything I could do to stop it. Picking the saddest recounts of my life was hard, but of every memory from before and after the civil war, that night's dream was one of the worst. The good thoughts were so few and far between the dreadful ones.

I was yelling, pushing my way through crowds of people who stood there and watched helplessly. My eyes burned with the brown contacts because of uncontrolled tears flowing from both eyes. I saw the naginata blade raised high above the executioner's shoulders, the handguard designed like a lion head biting down onto the cold steel. Even though the sun was behind thick clouds that day, and everything appeared gray in the distant landscape, those ruby-red bulging lion's eyes glistened so bright. The red shining with a backdrop of white stone on the staircase to our State Capitol building was what I remembered most from that nightmare. All those years later, the onlookers were nothing more than faceless shadows, but their outlines made it clear what they were.

The blade came down in one swift motion past Dad's neck, clinking against the hard surface, as Tuddy grabbed at my arm, pulling me back. Those bastard Lyons Twins stood there proudly smiling with their heads and shoulders high. Dark thick red blood flowed from his open neck, slowly turning the white stone red, dripping down each stair of the building Dad spent a generation working from to keep Athinians safe. His head landed upright, and I spotted our Sideris family bright green eyes wandering. I couldn't see Dad's face before the blade's slice, but I noticed after. First, he looked angry, narrowing his eyes, then shocked with a strange frown, and finally, fear as his eyes opened wide before rolling behind. That was it; Liam the Unifier died with the people he spent a lifetime protecting watching helplessly.

I clawed towards Dad's body, but still so far away, and Tuddy wouldn't let go, holding me back. I felt blood dripping down my hands as open wounds stung where I clenched my fist so hard. I screamed out the words cried loudly by my father and grandfather for years to rally our people and Allied City-States. "Banue Na'yah, Banue Na'yah!"

It was no use; the greatest reformer in the history of Epsilon Prime, who brought peace and stability across all twenty-one states like never seen before. The man that performed an impossible feat by getting Warriors of the Light and Dark Priest radicals to negotiating tables, something never accomplished by anyone in Alliance history. All these things were for nothing in the end. I'd never forgotten the fear on his face before closing his eyes.

The Pride were in the crowd, and some of them saw my distress. As they closed in, pushing through people like thick hedges, Tuddy drew his weapon and fired at them. Panic and chaos erupted, ruining the Twins of New-Sparta's ceremony. Year after year, they celebrated that day as a world holiday.

Rebels who would later become the city-state loyalists assisted us in escaping the chaos of the Twins' grand event. Most of them fell, including innocent bystanders. Our Capitol building had a sharp point at the top from which our flag once flew, and that was his final resting place. For the first few weeks, it decayed and birds pecked away, then mold grew until nothing remained but his skull. Tuddy told me to stop going, that I was punishing myself, but I couldn't stop.

I was awakened by Nina, trying to console me. The thumping of my racing heart was so intense. There was a vibration in the back of my throat.

"You were screaming something I didn't understand and shaking in your sleep."

Nina used a sheet to pat my head.

"You're sweating profusely, Isabel. What was your dream about this time?"

It took a moment to regain myself and answer, "The execution. I was there, only meters away when it happened. I see it in my dreams often." I looked down and choked back my emotions. "Banue Na'yah, it's the language of Athinia, a famous saying that means freedom from tyranny. The Fighting Sideris, my grandfather, started it during the War of Oppression."

Gideon watched me from his bunk. When my eye met his, he rolled, pulling a sheet over his shoulders. Since the incident in the mines, he hadn't been the same. Who could blame him? I couldn't imagine feeling that helpless, and I went through Androsian mutilation. Gideon's demons overshadowed any positive thoughts, the same way they did for me.

His words in the medical building ran through my head. How was Gideon son of the Black Skull Admiral? Did he really work with Dad during the civil war? None of what he said made any sense. Before the war, I'd used Admiral Derwin as a way to scare my children when they misbehaved.

"You better go to sleep, or the Black Skull Admiral will fly down and take you. He likes taking children who misbehave."

Terrible, I know. But numerous parents of the Free Worlds did the same. Hunters and law enforcement agencies had tried for years to track Admiral Derwin. All failed.

Since that horrific day in the mine, four more pirates from our bunk had died. Big Jack killed three Brown Pirates during fits of rage inside the mine; funny how Ezra ignored those deaths and kept his distance. He feared our giant, I believe. Jack would make quick work of that crazed lunatic. I'd spent so much time with these pirates, and it angered me to think of the senseless deaths.

Gideon protected me from Ezra. Captain of Draco, the same man that treated me like a piece of meat on the refugee ship, that man sacrificed his body to keep me safe. Gideon, Jack, Nina, and Ethan have grown on me, the same way conscripts in a battle trench would after spending months fighting together.

Nina told me that everything Gideon did was theater to keep his pirates in line. I couldn't believe that at first, but now … now other emotions stirred, and I almost felt ashamed of them, like I was betraying myself. If Dad trusted Gideon, maybe I could.

Ezra ruled camp in ways that reminded me of the Lyons Twins of New-Sparta. Intimidation, fear, and death always keep people in line. Even though the slaves in camp outnumbered the Pirates of the Brown massively, they wouldn't stand up and fight back. Not yet, at least.

Ezra banned us from the yard after working hours. We didn't have the numbers to challenge them outright, so Jack had us honoring that proclamation. Things in camp were already depressing enough, and now without a way to socialize with others during group time or playing games, the Draco Pirates lost heart. Power-ball, socializing, and sex were the only ways to relieve tension in camp.

Besides Nina and Ethan, others snuck in each other's beds at night, and sounds of squeaking bunks were common. I was surprised there weren't more pregnancies in camp; stress had much to do with that. Sentinels weren't concerned when a woman was with child. They worked the mines the same as everyone else. Others helped swollen bellies by filling quotas, but that walk to and from the mines was taxing on our bodies. Those marches weren't for sore backs and swollen feet.

A new day had begun with our walk to the mines, and Gideon joined us for the first time in two weeks since the attack. I went to him and he turned away, looking into the distance and taking a deep breath of the desert air.

"How are you?"

He gave me a side-eye and frowned. He said sharply, "Nothing for your concern, Isabel. I'm fine."

"Why did you …?" I paused. "Why did you sacrifice yourself for me? Knowing Liam Sideris wasn't reason alone."

"It was my captain's word. I told all on day one that you were under my protection. The word of a captain means everything to pirates. Anything that happens to you reflects on me. Especially with those in our bunk."

Could those be the only reasons? He was acting more stubborn than me.

"Is that it?"

Gideon turned his head, staring at my eye. We looked at each other for a long while, and time seemed to stop before he spoke.

"The only reason you'd care about."

I squeezed my lips together tightly. There was so much I wanted to tell him but couldn't bring the words from my mouth. *It's been so long.* What could I say?

"You're a loaf of stale bread, Gideon. But when someone's starving, even stale bread can taste good. We aren't done yet. After we get out of here …"

That was all I could say without giving away more.

Gideon raised an eyebrow. "After?"

"Yes, there's always an after. I've survived too much hardship on Epsilon Prime to die here. This place will not be my end."

He smirked. "That's the first thing you've said in some time that I agree with. You've earned a new name." Gideon emphasized his words while pulling something from his pocket. "You've got a heart of fire, Isabel Sideris. We should call you Fireheart of the Alliance. That sounds much better than that daughter name the city-states gave you. I've also got a gift."

The Draco captain opened his hand to reveal a black cloth patch. I slowly took it, stretching the expanding strap. Since we arrived here, I'd only had medical gauze covering the hole in my head. Now I would look like a pirate. I smirked.

"A real pirate patch."

Gideon said, "Aye, you can look like a real shipmate of Draco now."

He sounded more like himself, confident and commanding. It was good. The crew needed him to be more like himself.

"I have an idea about fixing our issue with Ezra in the yard. It'll take some effort today in the mines—a few people need convincing to work with us. I'll need some pirates from our bunk too. The most athletic and capable."

"You'll have 'em."

Once at the mine, we grabbed our hard hats, picks, and walked inside. I moved deep into an underground tunnel to find Finlay Petrid and Sven Vlahoses, the two professional power-ball players from Macegia. Without them, the plan wouldn't work. It took some time, but I found Finlay at last, deep inside the mountain where the only light came from our headlamps.

He swung away and grunted as sparks jolted from his pick striking rock. Even after all these years, he still had the body of a professional player, and he used that strength to help other slaves who couldn't make their quotas daily. It was honorable.

Finlay raised his headlamp in my direction. "You never come this deep in."

I didn't say anything and stepped next to him, chipping away at the rough, jagged edges of sharp rock. Small particles of stripped stone jetted into my face with every slap of iron against its surface. I gave it a few moments before responding.

"I wanted to speak with you and help fill everyone else's quotas."

He smiled and swung his pickax into the wall. I didn't want to jump right into a conversation. Instead, I helped him with that sizeable boulder for some time. There was a heavy cloud of thick black haze in the tunnel, and I periodically coughed and gasped for air. How the hell did he work down here every day?

Finlay halted and watched me struggling for breath. "So, what's the real reason you came this far down?"

"Did you know that I played power-ball at Bordertown secondary school on the relations station near Maintown district? Received a partial scholarship because of my abilities."

Finlay lowered his brow. "Are we comparing sizes? I received a full scholarship to Macegia state college. You know the rest of that story."

"I'm not comparing sizes, yours is obviously bigger, but can you still use it? That's the greater question. I need you and Sven, two others, if you've got them."

He turned and swung his axe again showing little interest. "Ezra banned you and the pirates of Draco from playing the game."

"He did, but I want to challenge him for control in a power-ball game. Most of our team would be pirates from my bunk. With you, Sven and two more. I've seen Bacon play, he's a bit of a brute, but good enough. He'll join with another if I ask."

Finlay stopped swinging and said, "What makes you think they'll play for you? Because of who you are?"

I narrowed my eye at Finlay and stepped away.

"Come on, Isabel. Every slave from Epsilon Prime in camp knew who you were the minute you came into line on the first day. You may only have one eye, but we all knew—the other one didn't lose its color. Right here in the mine, it glows faintly like a small flashlight or lighter: Liam's daughter, the Daughter of Athinia. Your name alone won't earn their allegiances, well maybe Bacon, but he doesn't know any better. Besides, why would I want to risk my life to play Ezra? He leaves Sven and me alone as long as we keep our heads down."

I folded my arms. "Unless he wants a woman from your bunk for the night. You know, I remember watching you years ago before the war during the Olympic Series on Civil Earth. Jarred Edgely from the Accord was your biggest rival, and he'd always challenge you on camera, during weigh-ins, and I remember the fistfights. Your competitiveness was inspiring. So many looked up to you. In your entire career, you never let a challenge go unanswered. Now the Martoosh Pirates have taken your manhood, and you cower in defeat."

He turned, breaking eye contact with me, and I pressed him further.

"Even now, after everything, I fight on. I was captured as a slave, mutilated by Androsians, taken as a pirate captain's prize, fought the Twins of New-Sparta as the city-state loyalist leader, held my husband Colonel Tuddy

447

Sideris, Stonewall for the Allied States, as he died because of Killian Lyons, dragged my children from one hidden room to the next, night after night, fleeing from the Lyons Pride, and I watched as the executioner decapitated my father." Finlay had shame on his face and looked down. I raised my voice. "I screamed with rage the words cried by millions, including Macegia, through the years—Banue Na'yah! Banue Na'yah! Freedom from tyranny. I screamed those words with fists clenched so tight, pushing through the crowd to try and save Liam the Unifier. I still have the scars to prove it. Tyranny's what your life is while Ezra has control."

In my outburst of passion, I pushed my palms into Finlay's face so he could see the lumpy marks across my skin. He gazed at me, unsure how to respond, but then his eyes opened wide as he lifted his chin and spoke with pride. "Banue Na'yah."

I put my hand on his shoulder, thanked him, and moved away. My lungs craved some fresh air after all that dust. Travel took time because of sharp rock, pitfalls, and no real walkways. Finally, a faint light pushed through the dust cloud. I turned off my headlamp and moved through the thick particles floating through the air. Around the next turn was sky, but something was happening at the opening.

Gideon, Big Jack, Ethan, and Nina were standing at the ledge of the mountainside. Ethan was closer to me inside the tunnel keeping guard, doing a terrible job, and looking in the wrong direction.

The Draco captain carefully put his fingers around the cylindrical portion of his mechanical eye and turned until it fell out of its housing. A cybernetic implant canister no longer than a thumb stood in Gideon's hand. Small flaps like wings kept it upright. He pushed a few small buttons and the device that would normally act as his eye started spinning, slowly at first, but the speed increased rapidly, like a tornado. A screeching sound so shrill I had to cover my ears echoed through the tunnel, the noise amplifying off the stone walls. It pierced through my entire body.

A flash of beaming yellow light, brighter than a sun blast into the air, pushed up and past the clouds. The spinning cylinder was moving even faster when a ball of light followed up the beam and disappeared.

I went back down the tunnel, so they didn't see me. That was a high-powered signal amplifier. Gideon had sent out a distress call. If he had that damn thing the entire time, why did he wait until now to send it?

The workday was complete, and I barely finished my quota before its end. We were on the march, and Gideon caught up to me.

"How did your little mission go? Accomplish your plan?"

I stared at his mechanical eye, flicked the implant with my finger, and said, "I had as much success as you. When were you going to tell me you had that in your head?"

Gideon pressed his lips together and sighed. "Ethan does a lousy job at watching out for unwanted snoops, it seems. What you saw has happened every day since we started working the mines. Minus the day we attacked Ezra and when I was laid up. There's no way for me to know if my signal was received until someone comes into the system and sends a reply." He spoke more precisely. "What's the matter there, Izzy? Afraid we'd leave and not invite you along?"

With certitude, I said, "You won't leave me."

He tilted his head. "I won't?"

"Nope, not after everything we've been through together. Besides, I owe you for saving me from Ezra. It's the way of Athinia. Call it a life debt." He grinned as I said, "I've grown on you."

Gideon chuckled as a light breeze blew through our hair. "Something's bothering me. You're a Sideris of Athinia, daughter of Liam, and both your kids are the same."

"Well, I'm glad you've figured that out after all this time."

He shook his head. "Now you sound like me. No, my question is, your husband Tuddy, why did he have your last name too?"

Hearing Tuddy's name gave me pause. I missed my husband and felt guilty. Was I flirting with Captain Gideon? What had happened to me?

"Tuddy was a farmhand and lived with my family since he was ten. I was only eight. We grew up together. Dad unofficially adopted him when his parents died. By my sixteenth birthday, teenage hormones had taken over, and we ran off to the barns as often as we could. When I turned eighteen, Tuddy asked Dad for my hand. He took the Sideris name at my father's request. Dad always said Tuddy was one of us anyway, and it would bring honor to the family. If I'd taken Tuddy's name, that would've been it for the Siderises of Athinia. Now, I have a question for you, Captain Gideon Derwin. How's the Black Skull Admiral your father? You don't look Dolrinion, and why is he the only admiral pirate? Everyone hears horror stories of him, and children always believe he's lurking in every dark corner."

Gideon raised his chin. "I asked you something personal, so now you ask me in return? Well, it's only fair. I was born in the Colonial Accord on Talbora. After my communal integration ended, they accepted me into one of the main cylinder's universities on the relations station for higher education. In school, I had a gift for mechanical engineering. You saw what my eye could do. I made this nifty device myself. My transport to the station was a junker. We stopped dozens of times for FTL cooling. It only took one stop before Draco Pirates led by Captain Derwin attacked."

My eyes opened wide, and he kept speaking. "That's right. He wasn't always an admiral. We'll get to that. I fought them, the same way you did when we came onto the refugee ship. They nearly killed me, and he took me under his protection, teaching me the ways of Draco. I instantly fell in love with the lifestyle and looked at Derwin as a father. I never knew my father, so even with Derwin being as dangerous as he was, it was more than I ever had. Years of earning tattoos, and my renown, he officially declared me his son within minutes of the Battle of the Bs conclusion. I became first mate of the *Viathon* a year after that."

"Battle of the Bs?"

"Yes, that's where my stepdad took the title of admiral and solidified his position as the greatest pirate leader of the three worlds. It's also where I got this," he tapped the metal cover holding his implant. "Nearly twenty years ago, the most renowned captains from Draco, Martoosh, and Leo came together for peace talks. Black, Brown, and Burgundy were going to try and create a lasting truce. If successful, we'd have had a navy large enough to challenge a society like the United Union."

I interrupted. "None of the pirate worlds had destroyers, carriers or battleships, though."

He nodded. "True, but at that time, the three worlds could've mustered thousands of cruisers, frigates, and light gunships. I may not be a military expert, like you, but I've seen a shield of flames from destroyer flak fail with enough missile fire."

He used that term the same as Dolrinions—a shield of flames. Suppression flak cannons were for stopping incoming rounds during battle and how everyone from junkers to Chrysós Aetós heavy carriers prevented attacks. Defensive flak wall, firewall, or shield of flames, any way you named it, the outcome was the same—massive exploding cartridges attempting to disperse incoming rounds. Based on the weapons of our Free Worlds, flak suppression was the best way to overcome attack or jumping into FTL.

Gideon continued. "There was a hope that we could set ourselves up as an independent empire. Much like the founders of the relations station did for the Free Worlds of Humanity." He puffed his nostrils. "Fate had other plans for the three Bs. You see, we met in a secluded area inside Titans' Belt with the mightiest ships from all pirate worlds. I was there, and the sight was marvelous. Endless rows of ships in any direction like schools of fish. Random miners from the belt happened upon our gathering and called in all Free Worlds mining colonies for aid. Military barges can't operate inside the belt—they'd be torn to pieces in minutes by endless rocks. Miners are hardy people, fighting their own battles. They used their powerful rounded scout ships to launch a surprise attack. Because of our untrusting nature, Black, Brown, and Burgundy thought each one was responsible, and all retaliated. The fighting lasted for twenty hours straight with so much flak, missile, cannon, and uranium rounds streaking across space. Even friendly ships destroyed each other, unintentionally. The three Bs and the Belt, that fight was a massacre with legendary captains from all three worlds dying—a dreadful day. When the flashes of light dimmed, and the last cannon barrel melted, Captain Derwin was one of the last commanders standing. He took control of the remaining Draco vessels and declared himself the Black Skull Admiral. I lost friends."

"I've never heard of this before," I said in disbelief.

"I doubt any from the Free Worlds know the tale—why would they? We're only rogue worlds and insignificant to the relations station and its followers."

"Maybe that will change one day."

Gideon slapped my arm and smiled, speaking with enthusiasm. "Enough of that. So, tell me, what's this grand plan?"

I brought my finger up, shaking it from side to side. "No ruining the surprise. You need to wait until we get back to the bunk like everyone else."

Gideon shook his head. "Isabel Sideris, making jokes? Hell must be freezing over."

*

In our bunks, all showered like any other day, and once everyone was near, I spoke up. "Those of you who play power-ball need to follow me into the yard, now."

They glared at me in confusion and frowned. One asked, "Why?"

"We're going to challenge Ezra for control of the yard." My voice was loud and confident.

They laughed, and another said, "We don't have enough players to challenge 'em."

Another added, "Aye, we're missing four, and why would Ezra accept anyway?"

I jumped on one of the trunks, looking down at them, except for Jack, who was still taller than me, and I yelled, "I've got our players, and Ezra will accept because of his pride. We'll challenge him in front of each slave. I'll stare through him like he's nothing."

Mathew, our bunk porter, said, "What does it matter? The Martoosh Pirates are better than us at the game anyway."

"Not with Finlay Petrid and Sven Vlahoses on our team."

Their eyes opened wide. Even these rogue worlders knew Finlay and Sven.

Gideon smirked and jumped onto the trunk. "With them boys playing with us, we can beat Ezra and his shit-stain pirates."

All in the bunk called out with approval as Gideon cried, "Shipmates of the Black, Draco is with you!"

Everyone answered, including me, "Draco is with us all!"

Gideon and Nina smiled when I uttered the words of Draco with them.

An uneasy pirate still asked, "Are you sure you can convince Ezra to play us?"

I lifted my chin high and stared at him. "Ezra wouldn't dare deny us. Follow me, stand by my side, and show unity. Let's go."

We poured out in the direction of the yard, moving fast, with focus, and it felt like storming enemy forces with a battle line. Slaves from camp gathered before mealtime. Ezra saw us approaching and frowned as he, with his Brown Pirates, met us. The Martoosh captain saw hundreds gathering around to watch.

He hollered, "I already warned you, the yard's off-limits."

I shouted back so all could hear, "We've come to challenge you."

Ezra appeared intrigued by my statement with a half-smile and eyebrow raised. "Challenge us to what? How many pirates from both sides can die faster, is it?"

His pirates standing behind laughed, no doubt believing those comments were clever.

Gideon stepped closer. "If that were the competition, we Pirates of the Black would be winning. Nina, how many brown stains have we killed so far?"

"Fourteen, rotting in the ground."

Gideon gave his usual smile and the Brown pirates seemed angered by it. "And how many have we lost?"

"Only eight."

Gideon raised his voice, emphasizing his words, "Only eight? It appears we're winning."

Before Ezra could respond, I yelled, "Killing each other's not my challenge to you, Captain Ezra." I picked up a power-ball and threw it at his chest. "This is."

He caught it, and I kept talking. "A game of power-ball here in the yard for all to see. If we win, control of the yard goes to us."

Ezra shrugged. "What do I get if we win? You're already banned. What's in it for me?"

He threw the ball back, and I caught it. Looking at the gathering crowds, I already knew he wouldn't say no; he couldn't afford to look weak.

"If you're too frightened to face us in a simple game, turn and go to chow. Everyone would know the truth." Slaves were muttering to each other, and Ezra noticed. "You tell me, Captain Ezra, what do you want if you win?"

Ezra's nose crinkled as he looked at the spectators, then his eyes opened wide with a lustful smile and desire. He peered at me before speaking. "You. If we win, I get to finish what was started in the mine before Gideon interrupted us. You become my permanent captain's prize."

The Martoosh shipmates snickered at their captain's words. If they won, Ezra would take me night after night in his bunk and probably allow his pirates to have their way with me too. I would become a working slave by day and a sex slave by night.

Gideon protested right away. "No deal, Isabel, don't agree. If he wins—"

"If, Gideon. If he wins."

I turned back to Ezra and said, "You have a deal. If we win, the yard's ours. If you win, I'm yours."

Ezra giggled and screamed, "You don't have a full team—good luck playing us while you're missing a few defenders, guards, or runners. Who'll play for you? None of these slaves dare to challenge us. They know better."

Finlay and Sven stepped forward in our direction along with Bacon and another player from Syrac, one of the Allied States. Bacon smiled and glared with narrowed eyes at Ezra, who seemed taken back by Bacon's crazed appearance.

"We'll play with the Daughter of Athinia and her team," said Finlay.

Ezra grew angry. "Fine. You've got a team. Doesn't matter. Tomorrow after dinner we'll play, and after I win, you'll sleep in my bunk permanently, on the floor, like the dog that you are, except for when I want to take you."

The Brown Pirates turned and went into the mess hall. Finlay and Sven nodded their heads at me and left. Bacon smiled and stared at me before the Syrac player pulled him away. Big Jack, Nina, Ethan, and Gideon gathered, and Gideon was worried.

Nina said, "Well, that's one way to stir the hornets' nest."

"You should use Jack on the guard line. He's never played the game before, but he could stick his arms out and bearhug three of them at the same time." Gideon sounded nervous.

Jack added, "If you need me, I'll play this silly game. I don't know the rules though—I've never played before."

After dinner, our team met near the bunks to discuss our strategy and who would play what position. Finlay and Sven came to help since they were the two professional players and had more experience than the rest of us combined. Ethan got excited and said, "It's a great game and pretty simple. It has four fifteen-minute quarters."

Jack frowned. "What are the rings for?"

"The three circular rings at each end of the field are stacked on top of each other. The bottom ring at waist level is the largest and easiest to throw or kick the ball inside."

Ethan said, "That gives you one point."

"The middle ring is half the size of the one underneath at chest level."

Ethan added, "Worth three points."

"The hardest ring to score on is at the top of the stack—at eye level—and it's only a few centimeters larger than the ball itself."

"Worth fifteen points. Lots of pro games end without anyone throwing for the top circle. It's really hard to get points on that one." Ethan was becoming even more excited.

"Players can kick, throw or headbutt the ball into any ring. The only time the clock stops is when the ball goes out of play, the player running with the ball in hand is tackled, or a team scores. Games are fast paced with no timeouts."

Jack made a grumbling sound. "Where do the players stand on the field?"

Ethan said, "Teams have two defenders near the three rings, four runners split evenly on each side of the field near the midpoint, and four central players on the guard line. Guards are the biggest players on the field and do most of the tackling and fighting. That's where you should be, Jack."

Ethan was right; a guard position was probably the best place for the famous Jack the Giant. We'd have four Pirates of the Black from our bunk including Jack. Ethan, me, Finlay, and Sven's group would be a good team. Ethan had played the game for fun his entire life.

Jack seemed uneasy. "Why can't I just kill their players when we start? Wouldn't that be easier? This silly game confuses me."

Finlay said, "Jack can't play. He'd be a burden for us because he doesn't understand the rules and has never played before. Players on the guard line do more than just hit the ball when it drops off at the start of the game and tackle each other. Guards need to know when to push with runners or fall back with defenders to help."

Finlay was probably right. When games started, the ball dropped from above between both guard lines. The lines would fight it out for possession while trying to pass the ball to a runner or defender. Finlay was a runner, and Sven was a defender.

Jack looked confused and tilted his head. "I've changed my mind. I don't think I should play."

Another Draco pirate stepped in for Jack and Finlay nodded. "Ignore the top ring. Don't even bother throwing for it. You can watch one hundred professional games and only see one successful toss into the top ring. For the first two quarters, throw and kick for nothing but the bottom circle. Trust me. Sven will hold most of their points back on defense. We want to go slow and steady."

Most players, when throwing for the bottom circle, tossed it underhand or kicked. Scoring on the middle ring usually consisted of throwing overhand

and good players could kick the ball into the center with ease.

I said to Finlay, "I remember you winning the Epsilon Prime Olympic series scoring on the top ring."

He sighed. "That toss was complete luck. I was aiming for the middle ring when I threw the ball. My adrenaline was too high, and I overextended my arm. That toss put the game into overtime, and we won. We won't be doing that tomorrow."

After practice and calling it a night, we returned to our bunks. We'd all work the mines in the morning, and the spotlights from the Dolrinion guard towers shining across camp told us how late the hour was. Gideon, Jack, and Nina had watched us practice the entire time.

On the walk back, Gideon came to me and said, "Do you believe you can win against Ezra's team?"

"I watched the Brown Pirates several times. They're good, but not that good. Most of them run up and down the field tackling, punching, and kicking aimlessly without real strategy. Ezra's terrible. All he does is pound everyone into the ground."

Gideon lowered his head and spoke with concern. "Ezra will be pounding you every single day if you fail. I already told Jack, if our team loses, that night we're going to storm Ezra's bunk and fight them all to the death. It'll be a suicide run, but I won't stand by and let him take you like that. Not after everything."

There was more to Gideon's feelings than he was letting on. He appeared more troubled than ever before. I wasn't used to that kind of treatment, not since Tuddy died.

I said, "You're still injured. Only you, Jack and Nina, have a fighting chance. Others from the rest in our bunk, well, they aren't you."

"It doesn't matter. I'll kill every one of those brown shits myself before Ezra sticks his prick anywhere near you."

I tried to respond, but Gideon moved ahead with Jack to the bunk. Nina came to me with a smile. "You know, I've noticed the way you look at the captain now. It's different than before."

I blushed and looked away, almost ashamed. "Things changed in a short time. I'm still not positive exactly what I feel because I tend to keep things bottled up, even from myself."

I wouldn't tell Nina the truth. I was feeling more than I should, and it made me uncomfortable.

Lying in bed that night, I found myself restless and unable to sleep. Anxiety about the game crept through my skin. Nina got out of bed and went into Ethan's bunk again. I looked over at her hips moving up and down under the sheets as they kissed passionately. Nina was the one making noises this time. I watched longer than necessary. It would be nice to feel a man's body against mine again. It'd been so long. I turned away to see Gideon staring at me from his bunk bed. He glanced over at Nina with Ethan then back at me. We locked our eyes, and I felt warmth between my legs with a pulse that made my heart race with excitement and fear. Quickly I turned my head and pulled the sheet over to hide from the world.

*

Work in the mine was slow that next day. Gideon made sure that our entire team stayed close together in case Ezra tried anything. Jack thought they might try to kill one or two of us before the game. We finished our work and went back to camp, passing new bodies nailed to the wood, and as usual, the sentinels made us stop and look. One was still alive, begging for water and pulling at the rods that tore his skin.

We showered, ate a light dinner, and went out for our game. Word had spread across camp, and sentinels were placing bets on the outcome. One way or another, things were going to change that night.

The time had come; both teams were on the field at their respective ends. Normal power-ball grounds had dark green artificial turf to help absorb tackles and falls. This field was packed sand, like everything else on Pomona, and felt hard like concrete when I grabbed some sand and rubbed it through my fingers. Before taking the field, Gideon came to our huddle with Jack and spoke as thousands of slaves cheered in the background.

He spoke with confidence. "You're not just representing Draco Pirates, or Allied States of the Alliance tonight. You're representing them." He pointed to the cheering crowds. "Look at their faces—that's hope in their eyes. They need you to win so things can change. Don't just play for yourself—play for them. Be their voice." Our team yelled with encouragement. "Besides, brown's a shit color anyway!"

All laughed, and Finlay brought us together for the huddle. His voice was thick with passion. "You heard Gideon, they're shit, and we're strong. Do it for everyone. It's our night."

He shouted the well-known slogan of his former team, the Macegia Raptors, "What time is it?"

Sven and the rest called back, "Game time."

We ran out to our positions with Ethan and one of our bunkmates on the left side and Finlay and me on the right as runners. Sven and another bunkmate were playing as defenders, and Bacon with the rest took our middle guard line. Bacon had a menacing smile that put fear into the players facing him. Ezra's pirates fanned into their positions, Ezra taking the middle away from Bacon.

A few tense moments passed in complete quietness. Then the whistle blew, and the ball dropped off. Ezra pushed one of our guards down and took possession. He passed to a Brown guard who moved in Ethan's direction.

Finlay and I went to the middle of the field while two of our guards pushed to chase the ball. The Brown Pirates ran the ball downfield quickly. A Brown runner threw aiming for the middle ring, but Sven blocked it immediately, recovering the ball midair as he rolled and threw back to our side.

Like the professional player he was, that entire block, recovery, and return were over in one continuous motion. The ball came to me. I caught it and moved to the right field edge. Finlay was so fast, running to the Brown rings, none of the defenders could keep up with him. I kicked the ball over the defender's heads; Finlay recovered and quickly tossed it into the middle ring, a Brown Pirate defender only arriving after he scored.

Ezra screamed, "No. Cover him, you fools."

The game went back and forth in our favor for the entire first quarter, and by the end, the score was Black ten, Brown four. Finlay scored most of our points. He dominated the game.

The second quarter went much like the first. Ezra kept hitting our guard line and even knocked Ethan with a hard tackle causing blood to stream from his mouth, but those hits couldn't stop Finlay. When the Brown Pirates did get the ball, Sven and Bacon were able to stop them most of the time before reaching our rings. By the end of the second quarter, the score was twenty for Black and twelve for Brown.

During halftime, Finlay was tired and had a long face. He said breathlessly, "We're performing perfectly. Keep going the way you are, and the game will be ours."

"Can you keep up? You're playing three runner positions out there by yourself."

Finlay smiled, shaking his thumb and pinky. "Don't worry. I can hang."

The third quarter drop-off was imminent and the Brown Pirates were angry and frustrated. A whistle blew, and the ball fell. Bacon recovered the ball, shouting with rage and shaking opposing guards off him. He threw it to Finlay, who went to the central running position and crossed to the right side. A Brown guard came in fast, but Ezra tackled Finlay from the side, landing on top of our pro-player. The takedown turned into a pileup, which was common in the game. Everyone fought for possession as the whistle blew. Referees removed bodies one at a time.

Finally, Ezra, but something was wrong; he had blood all over his chest and an enigmatic smile. Finlay was on the sand, blood gushing from a massive slice on his neck. It was a gaping wound, and Finlay gurgled as he struggled to breathe.

I ran to him and yelled, "Someone, give me something. We need to put pressure on the wound."

Bacon pulled his shirt off and handed it to me. I wrapped it on Finlay's neck and stared into his terrified eyes as tears streamed down his face. Blood trickled from his mouth and his arms and legs shook furiously in what appeared to be a seizure. A few more moments passed, and his eyes closed. Finlay was dead.

I pointed a blood-soaked finger at Ezra and screamed, "You did this, bastard."

Ezra laughed. "I did no such thing. Search me if you'd like. I've got no blade. There must've been a piece of glass in the sand that he slipped on during the stack."

Gideon was defensive. "You know that's bullshit, Ezra."

There was nothing we could do. Finlay was gone, and the game had to go on. We brought in a backup player to take Finlay's spot. Sven had tears streaming down his face. Once the body was cleared, the referees called for a center drop-off as if the game was starting a quarter.

Our team was demoralized. Even with Sven on defense, the Brown Pirates gained an advantage. By the end of the third quarter, the score had changed in favor of Ezra—twenty-two for Brown, nineteen for Black.

We were about to start the final quarter, and I needed to encourage our team.

"Listen to me. We can still win for Finlay. Bring up your spirits, and don't give in to Ezra and those brown bootlickers. The crowd are still cheering for us, hoping for a win. I've spent time with each of you for the last month or so, you're all my battle brothers and sisters. Everyone here is a Sideris of Athinia, my family. I'd fight and die for each of you. I ask that you do the same for me. Don't let Ezra walk off this field with me as his prize. Fight him here on the field with your sweat, blood, and tears. For Finlay."

Sven's face was set with anger as he puffed his chest out, shouting, "What time is it?"

"Game time."

The fourth quarter started. We gained ball possession in the first drop-off. With a few passes, we scored. Twenty-two Brown, twenty Black. Ezra's team became overly aggressive, striking our players with immense force, even when they didn't have the ball. Bacon was giving better than getting and never seemed to care when he got hit, as if he didn't feel it.

Halfway through that quarter, the scoreboard read twenty-eight Brown to twenty-four Black. Sweat and heavy breathing from exhaustion was a normal look for each of us now. Gideon wore a disturbing glare, pacing from side to side at the field edge.

Ethan gained possession on the next drop-off and scored with only two minutes left and the scoreboard reading thirty-two Brown to twenty-eight Black.

Sven said we needed to play more defensively. He wanted two of our guards to fall back and play with the defenders near the rings. The runners would have a harder time scoring, but it would ensure Brown didn't extend their lead any further.

Before the next drop-off, Sven yelled to us runners, "You need to push yourselves, more than you have the whole game. If you can get close enough, go for the middle ring. If you can't get close enough, kick for the lower circle."

The whistle blew, and another minute went by with our defensive strategy working. Brown couldn't score again, but we were also having trouble scoring. We kicked the ball several times without success. Ethan tried to rerun the ball but got tackled. Sven blocked another attempt at our rings. He saw me midfield and kicked the ball so hard I had to run to catch up to it. I took control and ran faster than all game—twenty seconds on the clock. Downfield, I passed to Ethan. A guard from the centerline ran to tackle him. Ethan threw to me, and I kept running. Ezra came right for me like a heat-seeking missile.

I screamed with rage and ran straight for the long-bearded captain. He yelled back with spit shooting from his mouth and crazed angry eyes as he charged. But those eyes opened wide when Bacon, with more ferocity than anyone else on the field, barreled through Ezra like he was a piece of paper blowing in the wind. That hit was the most intense all game, and Ezra's feet were high in the air. I jumped over both and threw the ball for the middle circle before the guards could take me. I was much further away then I should've been. If Finlay were there, he'd be yelling at me because I overextended my throw with too much force.

The clock had three seconds left when the ball passed through the top ring perfectly—fifteen points for Black. Everyone standing near the field edge shouted with joy. Final score, forty-three Black to thirty-two Brown.

Gideon, Jack, Nina, and our entire bunk ran in to celebrate. The crowd's cheers were explosive and almost deafening. Gideon lifted me up and spun me in the air, cheering out for all to hear. Sven walked off the field to where Finlay's body was covered by a sheet, and sat next to him. He sobbed and kissed Finlay's lips while caressing his face. I had no idea and felt terrible that Sven had lost his partner because of one of my ideas. Finlay was a great man and deserved a better end to his story.

Ezra screamed at his shipmates and slapped a few of them. It took some time for the commotion to settle, and Gideon to put me down. Ezra wasted no time and charged through our group, coming straight for me. Jack and Gideon stepped in front as a barrier to his charge.

Ezra bellowed, "Challenge. Captain's challenge!"

Jack roared back, "I thought you'd never ask."

Ezra shook his head and pointed at me. "No. I challenge Isabel."

"She's not a Pirate of the Black. You can't challenge her." Gideon's voice was thick with wrath.

Ezra squinted and said, "Don't play dumb with me, Gideon. Your honor's at stake. You declared the first day in your bunk for all to witness that Isabel was under your protection. Under the Pirate Code, you can't refuse me. I'm a captain and have that right."

Jack pounded his massive chest. "Don't show fear of challenging me, Captain Ezra."

"I have no fear of you, Jack the Giant. I saved a special spot on my back for your death. Isabel has shamed me, and I challenge her first. Tomorrow after dinner. She'll meet me under our sacred law."

The crazed Brown captain stormed away with his mates following. Everyone was looking at me with worry in their eyes.

I asked cautiously, "So what happens now?"

Gideon sighed and said, "Tomorrow, you face Ezra in single combat."

CHAPTER 32

A Trip to Nim

Learning is fun (Kathryn)

Another lesson with Renee, like the others we had already each day. Tobias was working at the Fleet Branch space dock, getting ready for our departure in a few days. My astute instructor was teaching me more specifics about populations of the Free Worlds. Astute: that was a word she taught me, which meant smart or perceptive. Her lessons bored me so much, and sometimes I became frustrated when something she showed me didn't make sense.

"Civil Earth?" she asked, tapping her finger on the table.

"Thirty-nine billion. Before the Federate Corporation founded Dol'Arem seven hundred and forty-five years ago, the number was much higher. The Free Worlds lost billions of their populations when the Corporation called its employees and people with skills to come find a home and new start after the Frontiersmen discovered the planet and CFO Westbay was able to hold back the Dolrinion Offensive. Before that time, there had been only four official Free Worlds governments, and the Federate Corporation was nothing more than a multinational conglomerate."

"Good work," Renee said. "What about the Federate Corporation?"

"Fifty billion."

"Human Alliance?"

They had that terrible civil war that nearly destroyed half of the planet.

"Before or after the Unification Civil War?"

Renee's lips pressed together before she answered, "Both."

"Current population, twenty-six billion. The civil war only lasted seven months, and at the time, the Secretary of Free Worlds' Affairs from the relations station estimated that sixteen billion died from both sides. At least four billion more fled and went into exile on different worlds. So, forty-six billion before that happened."

"Good. Now the Dolrinion Offensive."

"The Dolrinions don't release birthing statistics. No official number exists, but estimates range from forty-five to fifty-five billion." I paused. "Are all Dolrinions warriors? From what you've taught me so far, it seems like they can only earn a place on the memory stone by fighting in wars."

Renee raised an eyebrow and maintained her stern expression. She usually became angry with me when I spoke out of turn during a lesson. But surprisingly, she answered. "No, that's not how it works. Sentinels earn a place on the memory stone by serving their Force Command and the Offensive as a whole. There are different ways to serve, not just war. Slaves do manual labor, most factory work, farming, and other jobs of that nature. Sentinels perform administrative, management, development, sciences, and teaching just as I provide for you, besides being soldiers. They're all warriors regardless of careers."

Renee pulled her PDD and started typing. She was probably giving me a lousy grade again. At the end of each week, she provided a full report to Tobias on my classes and performance. Usually, they were bad. I didn't trust her.

"Here, watch this video. It's from a documentary film on a famous sentinel named Lieutenant Colonel Willington."

"Why do they only have one name? None of the Dolrinions you've told me about so far have a first name, just their rank and last name."

Renee said sharply, "Dolrinions have no use for a first name. The family name's all that matters. Some earn more famous titles like those I taught you about already, General Sharrar, the Iron Fist of Kora, or Colonel Limeth, the Chain Maker from Burning Star. There's also a new name circulating within the Dolrinion bubble about a sentinel named Master Gunnery Sergeant Askar from BlackRock. They're calling him the Hero of Gliese."

I frowned; Renee had taught me about that war … I mean that genocide.

"He must be a terrible person to earn a name like that. The pictures you've shown me have so much death and destruction. How could anyone be called a hero for what's happening?"

"Enough questions for now." Renee was annoyed with me. "Watch the video. You'll need to know some of this information for your last test before leaving Earth, so pay attention."

My excitement had been palpable for the last few days. I couldn't believe we were leaving Civil Earth and going on a ship to another world. From the surface to Nim—that might make an interesting story one day. Doctor Courtney gave me some shots she said would boost my immune system from viruses common there. I didn't care for the shots but I was happy that Tobias asked her to come to his promotion ceremony and dinner after. He didn't chicken out. T always got nervous around Courtney.

The video began with someone speaking while a picture of Kora, the homeworld of the Offensive, zoomed in. Bright red, yellow, and orange colors streaked across the planet and a large purple blotch stood out. That purple color was the memory stone.

The lower portion of the planet was sandy with little green. The middle had mountains that were different from the purple of the memory stone; all the clouds were yellow, and snow covered the top.

"Each citizen of the Dolrinion Offensive, from the time they can walk, learn that duty, valor, and glory for the Offensive is all that matters in life. The Dolrinions believe in an afterlife but only for those who have earned the right to have their name carved onto the memory stone. They trust that the memory stone's eternal, and it can preserve their souls indefinitely. Dolrinion sentinels have their deeds evaluated when their life ends. Senior sentinels from the sentinel's command perform that assessment, and Tacoma caretakers, who maintain the stone, carve all names upon its surface. Specific work tasks have the same influence on decision-making for name engraving. You could be a frontline battle sentinel or a galley cook, and both still earn the right to have their name engraved on the memory stone. If both provided for the Offensive while sticking to the principal belief in duty, valor, and glory for the Offensive, then their names would be etched."

The video cut to a stage where a sentinel with a microphone was standing, speaking out to a large crowd of Dolrinions. The red and yellow of the sky indicated to me that they were on Kora.

"The famous Force Command First Ones sentinel Lieutenant Colonel Willington, who has special recognition on the memory stone for his service and deeds and never saw one day of combat during his entire career, was an example of a place earned by providing for the Offensive. Willington oversaw warehouse supply for every Force Command during times of conflict. In the second Franchise War with the Federate Corporation, Willington's supply chain never broke. The siege of Arbur, on the rogue world Pilic, lasted eight months. Force Command BlackRock was completely cut off from supply for endless weeks. Food had all but run out, and weapons supply was running low. The lieutenant colonel took command of the supply transport personally to smuggle relief provisions to BlackRock three separate times during the siege. Willington rewrote all guidelines for proper supply storage and delivery. Even the relations station uses his written works. Sentinel Willington's final public speaking event before his death was an inspiration that all Dolrinions live by."

The audio of Lieutenant Colonel Willington speaking increased so I could hear his rasping voice. He wasn't wearing a helmet, and had short-cropped gray hair and a thick gray mustache.

Willington said, "Duty, valor, and glory to the Offensive. You may look at my job title of warehouse supply commander and think to yourself, where's the sense of duty sitting behind a desk all day? Where's the valor in delivering supplies? Where's the glory in that job? My response is simple: the memory stone doesn't care about your job title. The stone cares for only one phrase, duty, valor, and glory. Duty: I showed up for work every day for fifty-seven years and was always present for my day-to-day tasks. Valor: during the siege of Arbur, all Force Command supreme generals advised me to give up on the surrounded BlackRock contingent. Offensive Command was ready to write them off as a loss. I refused and made three supply deliveries through heavily entrenched enemy blockades for our brother and sister sentinels. All said it was impossible, and I made it happen. Glory: having been the commander of warehouse supply for years and serving my Force Command for more time than most live, I've never failed to deliver supplies and food to anyone of the Dolrinion Offensive. There's great glory in keeping your people fed and well-armed. So, I tell you all this—it does not matter what you do for the Offensive. Make it yours, and follow the founding principles, duty, valor, and glory. Do that, and you will find your place within the memory stone to live forever."

That video cut away and the first voice continued. "Lieutenant Colonel Willington died two months after his final speech, and got special recognition on the memory stone for his long years of service and outstanding performance record."

Renee took her PDD back and asked, "Any questions?"

"No, I'm good."

She cleared her paperwork and stood. Renee never told me when our lessons ended for the day; she just got up and walked out of the door without saying anything. But this time, she turned and said, "Have you had any more panic attacks?"

I peered at the table and lied. "No, everything's been much better up here in the Middle Thirty, thank you."

Renee flared her nostrils. "If Mr. Norcross gets promoted a few more times, you'll need to find a new tutor. They'll never allow me above the ninety-fifth floor to be sure."

"That would be terrible," I said sarcastically. "Whatever would I do without you?"

My old-in-years teacher opened the door to leave and turned back to me. "You'd walk around with nothing but the air in your head. That's what you'd do. See you tomorrow, Kathryn."

She left, and my heart started to beat quickly again. I needed to breathe in and out slowly, so I didn't have another attack. I'd had three since Renee helped me with the first one.

The PDD in my pocket rang. T gave me that thing two weeks ago, and I didn't understand how to use it fully, only to call him or pick up when he called.

I answered, and Tobias said, "Are you busy?"

I replied jokingly, "Oh, yes. I've been counting the spots on your lovely wall for the last hour and got to three hundred so far. Loads of fun, you dummy."

Tobias laughed. "Ok, ok, enough of that. Listen, I want you to come down to the barracks. I'm sending the location now. The PDD will give directions. You've been cooped up there for long enough, and Renee told me your lessons are going well."

Renee said what now? That was a shock. She'd always snapped that my answers were wrong.

I said, "It says I'll be there in fifteen minutes."

"You better hurry up then. Before it's too late."

We hung up, and I put my boots on. I liked the tactical pants defenders wore when not in their armor. I hitched my pants up and slipped into a long-sleeved fitted shirt.

When I got to the barracks entrance, four tin suits were there with rifles in hand. One of them turned his head to me, but I couldn't see his face through the shield cover.

"T told me to come down here."

They looked at each other but didn't speak as the airlock door opened. Tobias stepped through, and everyone jumped to attention.

"It's ok, defenders. She's my kid sister. Kat, scan your card and follow me."

I scanned; the red light turned green, and we went into the barracks. The halls were vast, and tin suits stood guard along the walls. Other defenders not in armor were running all over the place carrying boxes, pushing carts and other things.

"How was your lesson with Renee?"

"That woman has it in for me. She's always yelling and saying I have nothing but air in my head."

T laughed. "She used to say the same thing to me during my lessons."

I was shocked. "She taught you?"

"You bet," he said. "When I first came back inside from the surface, Renee was the tutor who got me up to the level of all the other kids my age. She specializes in helping people who lived in the yellow haze."

I looked ahead and sneered. "I'll be glad when we go to Nim and leave her here."

T smiled and looked ahead as well. We arrived at the dock, which was massive. The ceiling was so high big ships could fly here with ease. Giant military spaceships with their ramp doors open were clamped down to the dock, and there was something else I'd never seen before. Robots with defenders inside stepped through the dock, loud mechanical sounds following each step forward. They had short arms without elbows, cannon holes, and oversized gun barrels attached. Those machines weren't towering, huge things; they were much taller than people and I had to strain my neck to look up at them. I only knew that the Corporation bots were automated because T had told me, and these had defenders powering them. One of the robots steamed toward us with upper vats pushing vapor as it moved quickly in our direction. The front was solid metal with a narrow slit of transparent material so the person inside could see out. I stepped to the side behind Tobias, away from the machine that stopped centimeters away. The top hatch opened, and a man popped his head out.

"Captain Norcross, is that the little rascal you've been telling me about?"

"It is, Captain Benzo." T turned to me. "Kathryn, this is our armor officer from the fourteenth Armor Division and my friend, Captain Rehan Benzo. He's a warthog pilot."

Rehan jumped down, put his arms high on his hips, and gave me a long confident smile.

I said, "Tobias has friends?"

They both laughed, and Rehan shrugged his shoulders. "Yes, even the infamous Captain Norcross, soon to be a Tier Two major, has friends. He's a nice guy, sometimes."

Rehan had brown skin and dark hair with long sideburns. He was attractive, but that nose was huge. How could he fit that thing inside the warthog?

Tobias said, "Rehan's coming with us to Nim."

I glanced at one of the spaceships nearby. "It seems small to fly to another world in that."

Rehan looked behind. "That's only a hopper. We use it to bring our supplies and troops up to the fleet ships in orbit."

"Larger vessels that you're learning about with Renee are different," T said. "Destroyers, battleships, capital ships, and such can't enter a planet's atmosphere. Only cruisers, hoppers, and other small vessels can. These hoppers will bring us up to a detachment fleet."

"Did you take her to the simulation room yet?"

Tobias shook his head. "Not yet, was going to bring her now. You wanna join us?"

Rehan smiled. "Hell yeah. You bragged so much about how tough this little rascal is. I want to see her in action."

I narrowed my eyes and folded my arms. I didn't like that name.

"At least I don't have a big nose like you, dummy."

Tobias slapped the back of my head as Rehan laughed, outlining his nose with a finger. "I'll have you know, little lady, that this nose gets me laid more times than I can count. The women in this city love it."

We traveled through the busy dock and went to another level to a massive training room with padded floors and defenders working out and performing drills. Some ran on a track, others lifted weights, and two were inside a ring wearing protective gear and punching each other, which confused me.

"How are they supposed to win with all that padding? It'll take forever to knock someone out like that."

Rehan laughed again, and Tobias answered. "They're not trying to hurt each other, only train for a real fight."

I frowned. "Real fights are how you train for real fights."

I pictured Sadness with one of his lessons, but the memory faded when we entered the next room. Weapons lined one wall, and behind plexiglass that divided two rooms from each other was a massive area resembling the surface but without the haze and broken-down multistoried buildings that reminded me of ruins from the Old World. Debris littered the floor as if many battles took place there.

"What's that?"

Tobias said, "A simulation room. Every barracks and most destroyers or higher ships have them. You can train in real time to fight fake enemies."

"Fake enemies?"

T hit a button on his PDD, and I jumped back when a holographic person with a knife appeared a meter in front of me. I knew he was fake because of a red outline around his entire body. I circled him, and the eyes followed me. He appeared angry like I wronged him in some way.

Rehan said, "He can't hurt you. Do you see the scoreboard back there?"

He pointed to the wall where a counter showing kills, deaths, number of enemies, weapons, and points lit up.

"That keeps score of how you're doing. Every enemy killed or maimed will earn points. The simulation's extremely lifelike, so if they're only hit with a nonlife-threatening injury, they won't die and keep fighting. The minute one of the holograms gets you with something that would kill in real life, game over."

"It's not a game." Tobias narrowed his eyes. "I'll show you how it works, Kat."

T grabbed a blue training pistol from the wall of weapons. He pushed a button, and the small pistol turned into a rifle, making strange grinding sounds as it changed shape. Tobias pointed the gun at the floor, getting it balanced in his hands, then returned it to the original size and removed his real weapon, handing it to Rehan before holstering the training one.

My new brother went into the room, past the plexiglass, and the scoreboard behind us lit up, making a buzzing noise. A voice said, "Norcross simulation commencing."

I looked back into the room to abrupt sounds and saw numerous enemies appear in the distance. They were all charging towards T.

Rehan said, "You're going to love this." He rubbed his hands together.

Two new holograms appeared less than a meter away from Tobias; he had to act quickly and pulled his pistol, firing from his hip to take them out. Then T changed the gun into a rifle and ran right at the targets while keeping his body low. They were already shooting at him, and Tobias took cover but returned fire. The scoreboard made a noise every time he killed a hologram. They came at him from all directions, above in the decaying buildings and on the ground from behind boxes and wreckage. T never stayed in one place for too long. He was constantly moving and shooting. Even though the bullets were fake, sparks streaked off multiple hard surfaces.

Two more holograms came from behind debris, and Tobias fought them with his hands. He pulled a knife and moved with grace. It reminded me of Sadness but it wasn't the same kind of fighting. One of the holograms landed a punch, and T stumbled.

"Wait, the hologram hit him? How?"

"Wireless nerve stimulation. The holograms can't do real harm, but punches, kicks, pushing, or hitting with an object will stimulate a response."

T ended that enemy quickly, but before he could move any further, a simulated grenade explosion engulfed him.

The scoreboard buzzed loudly and said, "Simulation terminated."

He took a moment to recover and came back to us, breathing heavily.

Rehan raised his voice. "Damn, Tobias, that was one hell of a show."

T's eyes were heavy and sad. He didn't like doing these things but had little choice, being a defender. I could see it in his eyes. I wasn't there for *him*. He brought me to the simulation room for *me*.

Tobias said, "You want to give it a try? You haven't killed anyone in a month or so, and I don't want you to have any sudden urges with the Upper Twenty-Three on Nim."

I looked at the wall of weapons that was mostly firearms. "Never shot a gun before. No guns on the surface. My weapon of choice outside was always a spear with my knife fastened to the end."

Rehan chuckled and went to the wall where he pulled a long rod hanging on hooks. Before handing it over, he pushed a button and a blade extended. Big nose handed me the spear.

"This good enough for you, little rascal?"

I looked at him, irritated, narrowed my eyes, and said, "It should do."

Before he could react, I grabbed the spear and spun away from them, twisting the rod in my hands to get a feel for the weight, moving the way Sadness taught me, turning my body and the spear as one. I lunged forcefully forward, striking in the direction of the simulation room with a roaring scream.

Both T and Rehan had their eyes open wide.

"I guess she's ready to give it a try then." Rehan snorted.

I stepped through a sliding door into the simulation room and found a good spot near the middle away from debris that would impede my movements. Broken objects and piles of junk not far away would end me if I tripped while fighting. I was confident and in a good location.

Tobias asked, "You ready?"

With my chin high, I answered, "I'm always ready."

A loud noise buzzed, and a voice yelled out, "Simulation commencing."

Hologram figures appeared everywhere, holding edged weapons. I took a long easy breath, minding my foot placement. Sadness schooled me in everything he knew, and I wouldn't fail. My skin was sensitive as a light breeze blew against my arms, giving me goosebumps, and I had heightened hearing. Someone was coming at me from behind. I lowered myself and spun, letting the hologram run into the blade. Another came, and another. A blunt end of someone's weapon hit me. I felt resistance as my spear connected with his face. They kept coming wildly at me with bladed weapons, clubs, and knives. I had to utilize my full training to work through their advances. Blocking, striking and blocking some more, using the surroundings and even performing some of the flips and spins Sadness showed me near the end of my training. I didn't have to use those abilities often on the surface. No one was good enough to warrant such force.

They surrounded me. Time to move. I ran up the debris pile and threw my spear at a hologram coming for me. Center mass, a perfect throw. Another target nearby swung a blade at my waist, but I leaped over and grabbed the spear as I rolled. With a quick jab, he died. The execution of my attacks was textbook. Sadness would be proud. More holograms appeared, and the world around me slowed. I could see the strikes coming at me as if they were crawling. Incoming aggression went down with perfect defense, and I countered every hit with a death blow of precision. These holograms moved like savages, hacking drunks, flailing their arms, but not me. They couldn't counter my foot placement.

A hard blow took my face and stunned me for only a moment. I rolled away from the hologram and used a countering move to hit that aggressor just under his ribs near the heart.

Another twenty seconds passed and I removed lots of holograms trying to attack. Then the simulation stopped with a buzzing sound and voice speaking. "New record, new record."

It felt good to move that way again, but my breathing was intense, and my chest felt tight. I left the simulation room; Tobias and Rehan stared at me strangely. Rehan's mouth was open wide. T glanced at him and closed his mouth by pushing on his chin. He took the spear from my hands.

Tobias asked, "Where did you learn to fight like that?"

It took me a moment. I was breathing heavily. "Someone on the surface taught me how to fight."

"Sadness?"

I nodded, and Rehan shouted, "Dude, she was using Agamo Verk!"

Confused, I asked, "What's an Agamo Verk?"

T gave a crooked half-smile and said, "It's from the Old World. When Civil Earth came out of the Great Darkness, during the Age of Innovation, a so-called prophet named Agamo Verk, who had knowledge from the time of the Titans, taught his followers. The caste system was still young, and the Hawks didn't have a solid hold on everything during those years. Agamo taught two hundred followers how to fight, using what he called 'Purest Defense.' Of those who learned from him, thirteen became masters."

Rehan added, "Purest Defense seems a bit cocky until you see for yourself. But some believe it means something else. Agamo's library burned down when the Cloud Walkers came for him."

T agreed. "Agamo Verk had texts and written documents from before the Darkness. He claimed to know the truth of the Old World and showed his followers items inside the vaults. Once Tier One found out, they came for him. By then, six of his trained masters had already left Civil Earth—in those days, even Tier Four could travel to other worlds. We have records of where three went. The others—it's unknown."

"Where did they go?"

Rehan said, "One went to Epsilon Prime, another to Uropa, and the third went to Galma."

"The other seven were hunted down by Tier One and killed along with their trainer Agamo," Tobias said. "The Hawks banned that fighting style because it was so advanced and powerful. All his supporters and the vault library went up in a blaze."

Rehan countered, "Not his daughter, though. Agamo had a few children with women that weren't his wife, if you get my meaning, and his oldest child from a side girlfriend was twenty-five and a master herself. The Hawks weren't able to find her, and she taught her children, who continued teaching others."

Tobias looked down. "We aren't sure how many people know the ways of Agamo Verk here on Civil Earth. Some claim there's only a handful, but really, it's less than that. Even the master who fled to Uropa died after trying to open a studio. Epsilon Prime had more success, that master became obsessively dedicated to their faith of the acolytes and the door of life. He joined with the Warriors of the Light and taught them to master the fighting form. Years later, one of their own betrayed the Axiom and brought his mastery to the Dark Priests, which is why to this day, only those two groups truly grasp it." T frowned, glaring into the simulation room for a moment. "There're so few left. We'll talk more about Sadness, but for now, don't use that here. They'll take you right away."

Rehan laughed. "Tobias, man, I think she could kick your ass in a fight."

Tobias looked worried, and peered at me in deep thought.

*

I was taking a shower because T told me to clean up before the ceremony. When I went back into my room, there was a dress waiting for me on the bed. I peeked my head into the hallway and shouted, "T, where did this dress come from?"

"Courtney picked it out for you to wear tonight. There will be a few people there. You need to look the part."

I was frustrated. I slammed my door and paced near the bed feeling hot. I'd never worn a dress before. It sparkled with strapped lacing and small bows of light blue. It took me some time to put it on, and I gazed into the mirror, confused.

"My boots look strange with this dress."

Tobias knocked on the door and came in. "Kat, you can't wear the boots tonight. I promise no one will try anything. You don't have to wear heels. Courtney bought flats that match the dress."

T looked handsome in his formal defense uniform of light blue like the sky past our yellow haze. The jacket was thick, and his shoulders had padding. Tonight would be his chance to get with Doctor Courtney.

Tobias sighed. "Ok, it's time to go. You ready?"

"Are you ready? This whole thing tonight is for you, not me."

He bent his head and looked away as we left the apartment together.

We were in the head row with a humongous stage ahead of us. Steps led up on both sides and Building Administrator Iris Unon was at the podium speaking. He was a fat, strange-looking man. Near the rear of the stage were special guests. The two most important on the left side, the Stavish family, wore togas with gold jewelry from head to toe. Their daughter was Center Seat Representative Mia Stavish on the relations station. Next to them were two generals, from Fleet Branch and the Defender Corps. Others were there too, but I lost interest after watching the first few. All of them lived above the ninety-fifth floor.

The Cloud Walker spoke into the microphone. "Tobias Norcross has proven his worth to the caste system time and time again. He put down the riots in city one twenty-eight earlier this year that could have destabilized the entire planet, since that city, as all know, is our transfer hub for all real food on Civil Earth. He fought in two campaigns against rogue worlds that threatened our off-world colonies and has taken on pirates that raid shipping lanes in deep space. This man has never refused an order given to him by his superiors and always finds a way to succeed."

What a joke. Only the Cloud Walkers and Tier Two get real food daily. They'd be the ones destabilized from not getting their precious meats.

The Defender Corps general said, "Don't forget about his success against the mining revolts in Titans' Belt. He was a lieutenant, and four different commanders failed to gain a foothold on those rocks. Norcross did it with half a company after their captain died in the landing."

Administrator Unon smiled and replied, "Ah, yes, the Titans' Belt revolts. Clearly, every defender present tonight can see that with the right attitude and performance record, anyone can move up in the caste. As your administrator of building thirty-three and with great pleasure, I call to the stage Captain Tobias Norcross."

The auditorium erupted into cheers and clapping. Behind were thousands. I'd never seen such numbers of people before. Tobias made it sound like there would be a few spectators and nothing more. Typical T, always making things seem smaller and brushing it off like nothing. I didn't like how uncomfortable he was when Unon bragged about his accomplishments. T squirmed in his chair and rubbed his neck.

Doctor Courtney nudged my arm as she clapped. I started clapping too, and we watched Tobias walk to the stage, saluting the generals before moving to Administrator Unon to shake his hand.

"This man standing next to me has lived on the surface, Tier Four in the lowest levels, then worked his way through the Defender Corps to Tier Three, and now after years of dedicated service, with approval from above, moves to Tier Two, a promotion not seen in centuries." Unon turned to T. "You should be proud of yourself, Tobias Norcross. Please say a few words."

T slowly grabbed both sides of the lectern and leaned forward, glancing from side to side and down at me, letting out a slight smile.

"Everything I do is for the Defender Corps and Civil Earth."

The rows of defenders behind jumped from their seats, cheering loudly. Courtney stood and pulled me to my feet. We clapped again, and she leaned in, "That wasn't Tobias talking—they told him what to say before he went up there."

"It didn't sound like him at all."

Administrator Unon went to the microphone again and waved his hands, signaling to the auditorium to quieten.

"Now for the promotion. Who will be holding the tier codebook for you?"

Tobias answered while side-eying me, "My sister. Kathryn Norcross."

I took his last name after the adoption. It didn't matter. I never cared for my last name, anyway. T was my family, and that was all that mattered. Unon directed me to the stage. Reluctantly I did it and stood next to my brother. The crowd was much bigger from up there, and drone cameras flew above shining lights at us. Too bad Daniel and Amber couldn't come; the Cloud Walkers wouldn't allow any civilian Tier Four into the chamber. That annoyed me because only a few months ago, I wasn't even Tier Four, and in mere moments, I'd be Tier Two.

Unon handed me a book, and T put his hand on it and held up the other. A general came holding the bronze oak leaf pins, and an older woman removed Tobias's captain's bars while speaking.

"Captain Tobias Norcross, do you solemnly swear to uphold the tier codebook laws of Civil Earth while fighting to keep all in the caste system safe?"

"I do."

"And do you swear always to follow the orders of Tier One and those of Civil Earth Defense?"

Tobias answered like a robot, "I do."

"Then, by the power invested in me under the authority of Civil Earth Defense, I proclaim your promotion to major official."

Administrator Unon said, "Additionally, I authorize your Tier Two elevation under the laws of our tier code as laid down by the Watchful Hawks of our founding twenty-one hundred years ago. Tier One peered from above with clear sight to show us the way. Everyone, please join me in celebrating his promotion."

Everyone in the auditorium, including those on this stage, clapped and cheered vociferously. Tobias smiled with reluctance. I knew T. He was uncomfortable. The administrator handed Tobias a new caste recognition card and took his old one away. The new card had a different appearance from his old Tier Three card with a silver frame, more intricate patterns, and bolder lettering. Even the cards got nicer, the higher up the caste system someone goes.

Unon went back to the podium and raised his voice. "I present to you Major Tobias Norcross, the newest member of Tier Two!"

More cheering vibrated the stage. Tobias slowly lifted his hand into the air and leaned over to Administrator Unon, whispering something. The fat man narrowed his eyes, looking at me, and spoke away from the microphone.

"Oh yes, here, take it, for you, young one."

He handed me a new caste card and snapped his fingers in my face sharply. "Don't make me wait all day. Give me your old card quickly."

I didn't like that toga-wearing buffoon, and I knew my expression gave me away. I handed him the lanyard. He snatched it away and threw it on the podium before turning to face the spectators with a fake smile.

"Those invited, please join us for refreshments in the back assembly room. The rest of you, we bid farewell, and keep fighting the good fight for Civil Earth."

Everyone in the back area was Tiers One and Two. Doctor Courtney was the only Tier Three person apart from those working the event. It was all a charade and fake. Some congratulated Tobias, but others were doing something else or bragging about their self-worth and accomplishments.

Courtney said, "How are you holding up?"

"Still here, thanks to you."

"The medication has been helping you," she said with a smile. "Your cough's less frequent than before."

T started coughing as Courtney finished speaking, and he stepped away from a conversation with ones and twos. Some of the Cloud Walkers crinkled their noses, giving him a distasteful glare. I wanted to punch them in the face, but I'd promised him I wouldn't. Tobias told me most of the upper tiers would never accept us after his promotion. We'd always be seen as less because we were born down below.

Doctor Courtney had an inhaler, and he took it reluctantly. Tobias never used the inhaler, but that night was different. Surface coughs make people that high uncomfortable. Administrator Unon, with two Tier Ones, approached us.

"Major Norcross, I'd like to introduce you to Carmine Stavish and his wife, Sariah."

Tobias opened his eyes wide. "Sir, it's, um, a pleasure, yes, a pleasure to meet you and your wonderful wife."

I remembered Renee hounding me about our representatives under the dome.

"Mr. and Mrs. Stavish, we're honored by your presence at my brother's ceremony, and we're both extremely grateful for the hard work Center Seat Representative Stavish is doing for our Free World inside the Capitol Forum."

Damn it, Renee! She'd been working on my speech, so I would stop talking like a kid and sound more educated, but where the heck did that come from? Courtney had a wide smile, and Tobias looked like someone kicked him between his legs. Carmine was watching me with a stern face and narrow eyes as if I was a bug that he wanted to squash with his fingers.

"You two are related? You look nothing alike."

He spoke down to us like we were his servants. I had my pliers in a small pocket near my hip and thought of using them. Carmine wouldn't last fifteen minutes outside.

"I adopted Kathryn, sir." Tobias was cautious with his words.

Sariah Stavish, wearing a purple toga and big golden beams in her ears that were stretching the earring holes to an unnatural size, said, "Isn't that wonderful."

Besides the beams in her ears, she had golden chokers around her neck that made it longer than normal. It was unnatural, and I wondered if her neck would bend in half without those gold rings.

Carmine responded to his wife, sounding utterly uninterested in the conversation. "Yes, wonderful, indeed."

I blurted, "Do those rings hurt?"

Both Tobias and Courtney tried to interject, but Sariah smirked, laughed, and raised her hands to silence T and Court.

"No trouble at all for her to ask a question. She's still young and new to Tier Two. Give her time to learn our ways." Sariah lowered her head to me, saying, "No, darling, it doesn't hurt at all."

Both Cloud Walkers left, and Administrator Unon glared at me like he wanted to wrap his hands around my neck and squeeze.

After a moment, he turned to Tobias. "I'd also like to introduce you to the most prominent member of Tier Two in our city, and most of Civil Earth, Orson Outler."

Orson was dressed in a business suit. He had curly hair, dark eyes, and a short thick beard. Others were near him, catering to his needs. The way he carried himself would make someone think he was Tier One without a toga.

Orson shook T's hand. "Welcome to the Upper Twenty-Three, Major Norcross. I'll be hosting an appropriate party for the upper tiers in my apartment tonight. Much more entertaining than this mediocre display. I invite you, and your ..." He paused and gave me a cold look. "Your sister to come to enjoy the festivities. Tier One will be attending, including our administrator and the Stavish family."

Tobias's eyes flashed at Doctor Courtney. "Thank you, Mr. Outler, but we promised Doctor Lameira dinner tonight."

Courtney smiled and said, "That's alright. You can't refuse such an esteemed Tier Two businessman who offers you food."

Orson threw his head back with satisfaction at Courtney's answer. "What tier are you, Doctor?"

She answered, looking down, "Tier Three, sir."

Orson clapped his hands with excitement. "It's no bother. Tonight, you'll join us on the Upper Twenty-Three. Attend my party, and then Securitan can escort you back to the Middle Thirty. Mike," a man with strange light flickering boxes on the sides of his head stepped next to T, "give her caste card access for my apartment tonight, please."

Mike closed his eyes for a few moments, then opened them. "Done, sir."

Orson's voice showered over us. "Good, it's decided then. Everyone's coming."

*

The elevator door opened, and all of us looked around in awe. Neither T, Doctor Courtney nor I had ever been above the seventy-sixth floor before. Beautiful tiles lined the floor, the walls were white, and chandeliers hung from the ceiling. Waterfalls spaced out evenly along the sidewalls fell into small openings that led under the tile. There were detailed designs along the corners of the ceiling that Courtney said was something called crown molding. Soft music played that would put me to sleep if I were sitting. The air had a funny smell that Tobias said reminded him of lavender. Two well-dressed guards stood by the elevator.

"T, are those guards in the suits defenders?"

He shook his head. "No, a private security company. Securitan Security Services."

Courtney added, "Triple S."

"Yes, they protect high-level Tier Two and all of Tier One. Orson's part-owner of the company. Jaden Belitz, head of the most powerful Tier One family, is said to have ten thousand guards in his service. They could invade a lesser rogue world with numbers like that."

"Why do they need protection? Civil Earth Defense ensures no one gets above a floor beyond their caste card. It doesn't make sense."

Tobias hesitated, watching one of the waterfalls. "People like to feel safe. For Tiers One and Two, it's a display of power showing what their wealth can afford. Taxes pay for the Defender Corps, but it wouldn't look right if the upper floors used defenders for personal protection."

"What floor are we on now?"

"Ninety-five. Last floor before Tier One."

"Wait, that doesn't make sense. Tier One floors start on ninety-seven. What's on ninety-six?"

T hesitated again, this time looking up at the detailed chandelier above our head as we walked past. "Civil Earth Defense and Triple S use that floor as a security buffer for Tier One. It's essentially a barracks level for both."

Apartment doors were spaced out by at least sixty meters. Living spaces up there had to be huge. At the end of that hallway were two solid white doors with golden handles hanging from the center. More fancy suits stood on both sides, and one asked to scan our caste cards.

Inside, I instantly got annoyed. The entryway was larger than Daniel's entire apartment, with ceilings several stories high and walkways overlooking. How could people live so well up here? People on the surface killed each other for mole meat, and these entitled quacks were eating real hot food from servers walking by holding shiny metal plates. A server stopped, offering something I couldn't pronounce if my life depended on it. T and Court shook their heads, but I pulled the tray and removed several of the decorative morsels, shoving them into my mouth.

T slapped the back of my head, and I punched his arm.

Courtney's eyes wandered and she blushed. "Will the two of you stop? You're fighting like children."

Musicians playing piano and violin were performing in the massive living room. It sounded lovely. Orson stepped in our direction with his entourage in tow.

"So wonderful that you came. Please enjoy the food and festivities. Doctor Lameira, would you be able to entertain yourself for a few moments? I want Tobias and Kathryn to join me in the study."

Courtney smiled and said, "I think I can manage. Thank you."

Orson led us into a smaller room with large bookshelves and a massive television screen. Several Togas and others were there lounging. The screen was divided into smaller sections with different camera views looking at the surface. I knew that yellow haze and red mud right away. Everyone in the study was excited, yelling, clapping, or laughing while they watched. T froze with a strange stare. He turned to me with his shoulders low. What was going on?

It took a moment, but then I realized, the television showed Rockland gang members fighting with a group of surface dwellers. They were killing each other, fighting over food.

Orson had a closed-mouth smile with one side curling up and watched our reaction. In a mocking tone of voice, he spoke. "I know the two of you lived on the surface for some time. Would you tell me who the likely winner will be?"

Tobias looked at the television, Orson, and then me without speaking.

I blurted, "Rockland gang's going to win. The other group isn't a gang, just randoms sticking together trying to survive."

Another well-dressed Tier Two man retorted, "Damn it, girl, I bet a million credits on those random people to win."

Orson walked to the television screen while speaking. "Yes, we do this at least once a month, dropping food supplies in by parachute near a location where surface rats gather. When they go for the food, we bet on who will get it as they kill each other. It's wonderful sport."

Tobias saw my anger raging; my hand was shaking. Johnathan's dying face in the eastern square was all I could see.

A Tier One woman gave a slow laugh. "You two lived out there. Maybe sometime in the distant past we placed bets on you two fighting."

The room turned red in my anger and my heart raced. The BreakNeck punk that tried to force himself on me and countless others I killed to survive out there were plastered across my thoughts. I pulled the pliers from my pocket, opening and closing them with my fingers, and took a few steps towards Orson, but Tobias stopped me and took the pliers from my hand.

Triple S guards standing nearby moved in my direction but stopped when T grabbed me. The Cloud Walkers and Tier Two didn't realize what I wanted to do; only the trained eyes knew.

Tobias thanked Orson for inviting us and we left, T squeezing my hand. We found Courtney standing out on a terrace overlooking the city line. T pushed me into a chair. It was dark outside. The air was fresh and the stars sparkled like some of the Tier One jewelry the Togas wore. I'd never seen stars without the haze overcast before.

Courtney said, "What happened?"

"My lovely sister here was about to do a root canal on Orson Outler."

He handed the doctor my pliers, and she opened her eyes wide.

"What? She didn't touch him, did she?"

"No, I stopped her before she got anywhere near him. Thank the Titans. Securitan would have thrown us over the terrace if she touched him." T glared at me and pointed to the pliers. "Why do you still have these?"

My voice was thick with anger. "You told me to throw away the teeth. You never said I had to get rid of the tool I used to pull them."

Doctor Courtney crinkled her nose, curled her lip, and dropped them. She wiped her palms on her dress as if her hands were dirty.

I cried, "Doctor Courtney, they're sitting back there, placing bets on surface dwellers. Right now, people are killing each other in the wet red mud. They starve and die while these assholes sit here eating wonderfully decorated food, drink, and watch us kill each other for fun."

Tobias kneeled by my side and said, "Not us. You're not out there anymore. We live here, Tier Two, now. Don't forget that."

Tears filled my eyes and streamed down my face as I struggled to speak. "All I could think about was Johnathan while they were placing their bets. He died in my arms, and I killed three trying to prevent it."

T glanced behind to make sure no one was near and hugged me. "I know, Kathryn, believe me, I know. They're scum. All of them up here, we aren't like them. We're better. You and I can't change the system by pulling teeth. We need to be smart and do it the right way."

I felt desperate as another panic attack threatened. "I want to go home, please. Let's just go home."

T nodded, and we left the party together. Back at the apartment, I went into my room. Courtney and Tobias hung out together for most of the night. At one point, I woke and thought I heard the same noise as when Lilly was having sex with Delano in his parents' apartment, but maybe it was a dream.

The morning came before long, and I dragged myself out of bed, feeling extremely tired. I sat in the kitchen to eat breakfast from the dispenser while drinking coffee. Before long, Tobias's bedroom door opened.

I smiled. "Good morning, Doctor Courtney, want some coffee?"

She blushed and raised an eyebrow. Courtney was trying to leave before I woke up. She pushed the hair from her face. "No, I must be going." She went to the door, but before stepping out, said, "Kathryn, take care of yourself on Nim. Be careful, please. It's not a Free World, and things will be different."

I lifted my glass of coffee. "Thank you. I survived for seven years on the surface. I promise Nim won't be the end of me."

She smirked. "Take care of Tobias, would you?"

"He's my big brother now, and I won't let anyone hurt him."

Courtney left, and T came out a few minutes later with his packed bag. He glared at me and narrowed his eyes. I did the same and folded my arms.

"Are you ready to go? We need to be downstairs in twenty minutes."

"Let me get dressed. My bag's in my room."

We left our Tier Three apartment for the last time and went to the barrack's space dock from the day before. Soldiers were lined up, and others running around like crazy. There was so much commotion it was overwhelming. Rehan saw us, and he gave a wide smile, his shoulders high.

He tossed me a bottle of water and said, "Drink up, little rascal. The flight up to the ship's going to dehydrate you."

Tobias was yelling orders at other defenders in the dock. When he came over to Rehan and me, the big-nosed captain saluted and spoke sternly. "Major Norcross, my armored column's loaded and ready to go, sir."

T smirked at Rehan and yelled out in a commanding voice, "Alright, defenders. Load 'em up and move out. Armor in the air in fifteen minutes."

Everyone else lined up then moved to different hoppers. T grabbed my arm and guided me to a line of civilians boarding several other transports.

"You'll take this ship up with other officer family members. We won't see each other until we get onto the destroyer that's taking us to Nim."

I stared with disapproval, and he laughed. "Don't worry, Kat. You won't be alone."

Tobias turned his head and looked behind me. When I turned, I opened my mouth wide in disbelief. Renee was there, smirking, with a packed bag over her shoulder.

When she saw my face, she frowned and said, "What? Did you think I'd let you go to Nim without me? Don't look so shocked, Kathryn. You have much to learn still before our studies conclude. Don't be so upset—learning is fun."

CHAPTER 33

A Night Out
in the Colonial Bubble

People never understand (Adam)

"The whereabouts of Isabel Sideris, daughter of former Regent Liam Sideris from City-State Athinia, are currently unknown. Some sources claim she's still hiding on Epsilon Prime. Others think she's on the rogue world Galma, and one source inside New-Sparta advised she's dead."

A picture of Juliet and me in the refugee dock appeared on the television screen while the news voice continued to speak.

"The whereabouts of both Adam and Juliet Sideris, son and daughter to Isabel, are officially unknown at this moment, but the report obtained by this news station places them inside the cathedral, which the Guild has denied. Witnesses to the incident inside the refugee dock say that Guild agents took Adam and Juliet on the orders of Center Seat Representative Henry McWright of the Colonial Accord. If true, this would be highly illegal under the Free Worlds' Relations Policy. No official statement has come from the Capitol Forum yet."

Juliet said, "All of these people need to mind their own business and not be worried about what you and I are having for breakfast each day. It's ridiculous."

My sister was only half correct. People should mind their business, but our family name came with a long history within the Free Worlds. Eighteen different Siderises of the past had been representatives on the station, and eight of those served long enough to be center seat for the Alliance. From what Mom told me, the better part of four billion people who fled the Alliance during the war would rally behind us and fight. That was why Henry wanted us, and that was why I hated my name. Mom also told us that those from the Allied City-States who fled would try to seek us out if they knew we were alive. News spread like wildfire that we were on the station.

I said, "Our name comes with a level of responsibility, Juliet. Try not to forget that."

Juliet stood and stretched her body after sitting on the couch for hours with me. "We need to get out and do something tonight. Let's talk to Henry when he gets home."

She spoke his name like they'd known each other for years. It annoyed me to hear her talk like that. She was right—we had sat around doing nothing, and it felt eerily similar to the way we hid from the Pride on Epsilon Prime. The past was always in my thoughts.

"I agree. We need to get out and do something. When Representative McWright comes home, we can speak with him."

There was a noise from the foyer. Alyssa walked down the hall and gave Juliet and me an agitated stare. She wore a dress that exposed her legs and breasts more than necessary, in my opinion. The representative's wife carried bags from a long day of shopping. She placed them on the kitchen counter and walked over.

"Oh, you two are still here. Henry hasn't found more suitable accommodations yet, I see."

She narrowed her eyes at Juliet. Alyssa saw the way her husband looked at my sister. It must have been such a foreign situation for the wife of a center seat. Alyssa had gone on for years, always being the center of attention around Henry and media reports surrounding him. She was an attractive woman, but her overconfidence was less appealing to me. She didn't match up to Juliet in the slightest. Age was the biggest divider between the two, and unfortunately for Alyssa, there was nothing one could do about the erosion of time.

I said as kindly as I could, "Juliet and I appreciate your hospitality. We will do our best to stay out of your way until Representative McWright can find us more appropriate housing."

Alyssa rolled her eyes and went up the spiral staircase to her room.

The security officer that followed her daily stood at the bottom of the stairs. He waited for a moment and spoke. "You two should be less confrontational with the representative's wife."

"If you didn't just hear, my brother was very polite to her. That woman hates us," Juliet said.

The security officer nodded. "You aren't quarrelsome with your words. It's your eyes. You look at her in a way she isn't used to."

"How is that exactly?"

He hesitated, peering up the stairs before answering. "Like she's beneath you."

Juliet sat on the couch and giggled to herself, then said in a soft voice, "Because she is."

Henry returned before long, and he appeared tired.

Juliet ran to him with a smile. "Good afternoon, Henry. How was your day?"

He seemed pleased. "Much better now, thank you."

Even in his current state, he had such a confident and desirable persona. Henry turned to me and asked, "How's everything here?"

"Good. Besides Alyssa, no one came up or went down. A few birds flew into the large windows near the terrace—fascinating day to be sure."

Henry didn't say anything and just watched me as if he wanted to tell me something but had reservations.

I said, "Can we do something tonight, please? We've been stuck here for some time now, not able to leave your apartment, and it's driving Juliet and me crazy."

Juliet added, "Yes, take us out dancing tonight, Henry. We need to have some fun. It feels like we're hiding in people's homes on Epsilon Prime again, so boring."

Juliet and I knew the dangers that lurked around every corner for us, but we had grown up running from those dangers nearly every day. Even though there was a chance that something could happen to us, we didn't care because that had been a fact of life for the last fourteen years.

"I'm sorry for the last few days. Tensions are high under the dome and in the main cylinder. My fellow representatives are causing more trouble than I anticipated. That's why I had to recall the Capitol Security officers who were protecting the two of you. I don't want you wandering around the bubble without protection. Even though you're here, hardliners would try and harm you if given a chance. You can't trust anyone, unfortunately."

"Not trusting people was the first thing our parents taught us during the war." Henry made a sound of approval as I talked. "Juliet's twenty years old, and I'm twenty-three, nearly twenty-four. We've never been to a bar in our lives."

He scratched at his chin. "Think on this subject no more. I already planned on taking you both out tonight to celebrate."

Juliet was excited. "A celebration? What are we celebrating?"

"I've secretly negotiated the release of your mother." Juliet yelled with joy, and Henry smiled. "Some of the finer points are taking shape as we speak. In a few weeks, your mother will be sitting here speaking with us."

I wondered if it was weird that I felt no emotion at that news. Did I not care? Why was I so numb to normal positive emotions? The only feelings that drove me were hate and anger.

I gave a generic response. "Thank you, Henry, we appreciate everything you're doing for us."

Henry's smile came my way, and it made my heart flutter. There was something about the way he carried himself that made him incredibly attractive. My sister gave him the same puppy-dog eyes.

Alyssa walked into the room wearing a different outfit than before and glared at us coldly. "And what are we so happy about?"

"Alyssa, my love, we're going out tonight to have some fun."

Alyssa frowned at Henry. "Aren't there more important things you should be doing than going out tonight? Your aide Benjamin's been missing for two days."

Henry put his hand into the air and said, "Don't trouble your thoughts on Benjamin. The MERC Guild's doing everything they can to locate him. Six different aides are missing in total. The Guild's already fully committed to solving this crime. Malcolm's working hard to help find him. The two of them were close friends. There's nothing more we can do tonight. Why don't you join us?"

Alyssa grabbed a bottle of wine from the refrigerator, and snapped, "I think I'll stay in and party alone tonight, thank you."

Henry's strange wife left back up the spiral staircase. I might have overthought his reaction to Alyssa walking away, but I swore Henry almost seemed happy watching his wife go upstairs in anger.

With his chin high, Henry said, "Adam and Juliet Sideris, tonight will be a night for you to remember. Go shower and put on something nice, because after dinner you're going out with me."

Henry went upstairs, taking the other staircase near the front of the apartment. Juliet danced in excitement. "Adam, we've never been to a bar before. It'll be so much fun."

She ran off to her bedroom down the long back hallway to get herself ready. There were a few rooms down that hall, including mine. At the end of the hall was a long mirror with a statue of some famous Labor Party union leader from the past, holding the Hammer of Labor. It was strange to me that an entire civilization was run by unions, but people probably thought that our city-states were weird too.

We ate food from the artificial dispenser that was common on Civil Earth.

It was odd. Before the war, living on the farm, we only ate real food. Juliet didn't remember that time, but I did.

Henry was upstairs for quite a while, and at one point, we heard faint yelling. A short time later, he came downstairs with bright red ears as if the sun had been beating on his head all day. He said, "Are you ready to leave?"

Juliet raised her voice joyfully, "We've been ready since we arrived in the Colonial bubble."

Henry chuckled. "Good, let's go."

*

The music was loud and the lighting low, with beams of colors streaking across the dance floor to the beat. Partygoers of all ages, dressed to the nines, danced and enjoyed the festivities. The drinking age for the Accord was only eighteen compared to twenty-one in the Alliance, and the clientele ranged from young to older than Henry. He paid for a private booth, and attendants came multiple times, providing food and drinks. The three security officers formed a perimeter nearby.

Juliet yelled over the music while dancing in her seat, "Another."

Henry waved to a waiter. "Another round for us."

Booths lined the walls of the club, and high-top tables were scattered randomly. Some of the dancers were grinding against each other provocatively. I'd never seen anyone move like that to music before.

The attendant brought over three shot glasses to go with the beverages we were already sipping. Henry passed them out.

"You both know how important your family is. Not only to your city-state but the planet as a whole." Henry's words were less guarded, and judging by his speech, I believed he was drunk. "There's billions who hate the Lyons Twins and will fight for you. Word's spreading that you're both here with me. Loyalists will come. That's the long-term plan for us."

Juliet raised an eyebrow. "For us?"

"Yes, Juliet." Henry placed his hand on hers. "My commitment to this cause started long before watching the executioner take Liam's head on the steps of the Capitol building fourteen years ago. Behind the curtain, I've done much to try and help your family by undermining New-Sparta as often as I could. Because of what happened in the refugee dock, I've declared openly for Athinia's previous ruling political family. There's no going back now. I'm committed to seeing your mother and the two of you return to Athinia as its ruling authority. The Sideris family has a rich history of prime regents, regents, vice-regents, prime generals, representatives to this station, and city-state advocates. The Green Eyes that glow with hope have existed since the Years of Forgetting. Many respect, hate, and fear the name *Green Eyes of Athinia*."

"When you say it like that, there's a lot of pressure for Juliet and me to step into the Sideris family shoes. It leaves much to live up to," I said, concerned.

Henry gently placed his hand on top of mine, holding it, and grinned. "You'll not step into another's shoes and walk, lad. You'll make your own shoes and run miles in them. Both of you will decide how your family will be remembered one thousand years from now. Your actions together will determine the future, not the Sideris family members who lived before."

Henry holding my hand made me swallow deep. He was an inspirational speaker, and what he said motivated me to be a better person. He raised his shot glass.

"Adam and Juliet Sideris, lift your glasses and toast with me to the future."

We tapped our glasses together, calling out at the same time, "To the future."

Juliet made a funny face. "I'm drunk." She laughed.

Henry said, "Good. There're two perfectly acceptable reasons to be intoxicated. The first is to celebrate something positive—an accomplishment or overcoming an immovable object."

"What's the second reason?"

Henry's happy expression changed to serious as he answered, "To mourn a great loss. Something I've not done since Liam died."

A moment went by, and then Juliet slapped the table, grabbing Henry's arm. "Dance with me, Henry. The music's great, and I feel amazing. Dance with me."

Henry stood and looked in my direction. "Will you be joining us?"

I shook my head. "No, I don't dance. The drinks will serve for now."

Juliet and Henry were enjoying the music as they danced together. Others did the same. Thankfully, they weren't moving sensually like some of the others. It was more friendly and innocent, but I knew my sister. She wanted to sleep with him. From what I had seen of Henry so far and the way he was helping me manage my pain, I didn't think he was interested in her. No, he wouldn't want Juliet.

After a few more drinks with some food, we left the club. The artificial night sky was bright with stars and constellations—not real stars from outside the station, rather the way it would look from Uropa. The city streets were busy with traffic and pedestrians moving from one place or another. Juliet stumbled along, drunk as a skunk. I had to support her weight, typical. I always held her up when she made terrible decisions.

Once back at Henry's apartment, I helped Juliet into her room and threw her on the bed. She was all I had, and I knew I cared for her in the best way I was capable, but she irritated me at times. I closed her door and went to the living room and the television. My head was fuzzy from the drinks, and based on the way the room moved around me, I was probably drunk. Henry came in after a short time and sat next to me.

"Your sister drank more than she could handle," he said. "Did you place her on her stomach in case she gets sick?"

There was little thought in my head when I threw her onto her bed.

I lied. "Of course I did."

Henry looked at the screen showing media footage of the fighting on Gliese. Some clips had Dolrinion sentinels in red armor firing massive artillery cannons from a mountainside. Other images showed Corporation operators standing next to a machine with a drill and arms that had uranium spinners on the ends.

"Is it always like this?"

Henry opened his eyes wider looking at me curiously. "Is what always like this?"

I turned to the screen. "The Free Worlds trying to kill each other and doing everything possible to gain an advantage over one another."

"No, things aren't always like this. In fact, sometimes, they're much worse. You should've seen what this station looked like fourteen years ago during the Unification Civil War. Anyone who supported Athinia here on the station was rounded up and, in some cases, publicly executed. Allied city-state loyalists were being murdered all over the main cylinder. Before my time, there was a terrible period when Civil Earth and the Colonial Accord were at war for the fifth time. Representatives skipped forum sessions, and citizens from both Free Worlds were killing each other daily throughout the station. Surprisingly the Federates and Dolrinions are more civilized with each other when at war. Have you ever heard of the Power-Ball Riots on Uropa?"

I shook my head, and Henry continued. "Every three years, the Free Worlds' Olympic games take place on a different Free Worlds home planet. Before the war, it was held on Uropa. During the final game between both teams, tensions started boiling over. Civil Earth and the Colonial team were both playing aggressively. The Colonial captain was tackled and airlifted off the field due to injury. Of course, the Accord fans believed the hit was excessive while the CE fans believed it was a valid strike. The game ended with Civil Earth winning. As one hundred thousand Civil Earth fans left the stadium cheering and celebrating, a segment from Uropa, looking to cause trouble, started fighting with fans. Scuffles occurred all over our capital city Warwick. Things spiraled out of control quickly. During the riots, hundreds of Civil Earth citizens were murdered in the streets. It was savage barbarism. CE Togas and Tier Two were dragged through the roadways and beaten to death by provokers of my world. The rioting went on for five nights before the city police were able to quell the disturbances. By the end, more than five hundred Civil Earth citizens were dead, and over five thousand hospitalized. Bodies with colorful togas hanging from their necks were hung from light posts near the stadium. The media had a field day, and Civil Earth Defense called their fleets. The war lasted nearly two years, nine million dead on our side alone. It was a disaster, all caused by a power-ball game."

Henry paused for a moment. "In a few more years, things will boil over again with two other Free Worlds governments going at it with each other because it's our society, my boy. Humanity's twisted. We play games that get innocents killed."

I tried to hold back a smile. "Good, at least I fit in then."

Henry smirked and said, "I wanted to ask earlier, but Juliet was in the room. Are the rabbits helping you with your anger?"

He gave me a dozen bunnies to help me cope, and so far, it had worked. "I need more."

Henry's surprise was evident. "You went through them all already? I just gave them to you two days ago."

I didn't respond because there was nothing to say. My urges got the best of me daily.

"It's no bother. I'll get you more and find you another way to help channel your emotions. The rabbits only worked for me when I was much younger than you."

My frustrations were more profound than just anger. I was sexually frustrated too. It had been so long since I felt the touch of someone. I slowly placed my hand over Henry's inner thigh and stared at him with desire. Henry peered back for a moment and carefully pushed my hand away in the nicest way he could.

"I'm sorry, lad. You have needs that I won't be able to help with, not in the way that you want. It's no issue. In the next few days, I'll bring someone here that can attend to your needs. That will help with your anger too. It does a world of wonder for me."

Because I was annoyed at his rejection, I spoke with a dismissive undertone. "How do you relieve yourself when you don't even sleep in the same bedroom as your wife?"

Henry glared at me for some time. What was he thinking about? He seemed to always be in deep thought.

"What's occurring between Alyssa and me is only a recent development. If it were one month ago, I'd already be upstairs, relieving my frustration inside of her two or three times."

Henry's rejection infuriated me. I looked back at the television as Henry told me to sleep well before leaving up the front staircase. He wasn't sleeping in his bedroom again.

The last sexual partner I had was Philip, who was several years younger than me. His family had been hiding us in their attic, and it only took a few days for me to realize he was interested. The first time we were together was soft, almost romantic. But as the days went on, and I was still trapped in that attic with only memories of my parents' abandonment of Juliet and me and the thought of the slaughter taking place in their name for company, my frustration grew. I became more aggressive and physical with him, forcing myself on him when I should have responded to his gentleness. He would ask me questions, trying to pry into my inner thoughts, and that bothered me too. I didn't want to open up to anyone and still don't. No one had ever understood me in any meaningful way, not Mom, Dad, Jules or anyone. It came to a point where he was trying to avoid me because he was bruised and in pain. Philip finally said that he had enough. I wouldn't accept that and overpowered him two or three more times against his will. After the fourth, he threatened to tell his parents and mine. That was when I snuck into his bedroom and smothered him with a pillow. I took him once more after. He had deserved better in life, but in death he wouldn't know how part of me was always aware of that. The other Adam always won. Anyway, it would be a while before I had another. Philip's parents didn't understand what happened. It was only after his death that they noticed the old bruising, and they couldn't figure it out. As far as everyone in that home was concerned, Juliet and I stayed in the attic and didn't interact with Philip much. My sister knew what transpired but never spoke.

About an hour passed and I still sat there, sulking in my anger. Alyssa came down the spiral stairs with an empty bottle of wine in her hands. She wore a revealing nightgown and stumbled off the last stair. One of her ample breasts popped out of the lingerie, revealing her pierced nipple. Alyssa slowly covered her chest and stared at me. She could see that I was watching her the entire time and smirked.

Alyssa slurred her words. "So, where's my husband now? Is he in the back bedroom with your sister?"

Observing the video on the television and without looking at Alyssa, I said, unconcerned, "No, Juliet's passed out drunk, snoring away. Your husband went up to the guest bedroom. It seems like he doesn't want to be near you tonight."

She rolled her eyes and went into the kitchen, but turned and snapped, "My husband isn't doing enough to find Benjamin."

It was strange how concerned Alyssa was for some random aide.

"Why do you care so much about a meaningless worker of your husband's?"

Alyssa sat on the couch, swaying slightly. "He does more for my husband than you would ever know. Things will get terrible here without Ben."

She stared at me strangely, and I said, "Can I help you with something?"

She smiled. "How much did you have to drink tonight?"

Enough that the room is still spinning for me even though the last drink I had was over an hour ago was what I wanted to say, but didn't.

"Enough."

Alyssa moved closer, and I could smell the wine on her breath.

"I saw you looking at me when I came down the stairs. Did you see anything that you liked?"

I was angry. People never understood my needs and desires. If I were someone else, my excitement at that half-naked woman would be uncontrollable. *I'm me, though.* She wasn't what I wanted in any way, shape, or form.

Alyssa pulled the same breast out of her nightgown, and the barbell piercing shone in the light of the television screen. She grabbed my hand and placed it over her. I felt the coldness of the metal over my palm. Henry's wife began to rub me between my legs over the top of my jeans, trying to stimulate me. I was entirely uninterested, and my lack of stiffness showed.

Alyssa begrudgingly took notice. She rubbed even faster, and I felt a burning sensation from the friction.

Alyssa slapped my hand away and spoke loudly. "What the fuck's wrong with you? Do you know how many men here would chop off one of their feet to be sitting next to me right now?"

I said without care, "Then you might want to go find one of them tonight."

Alyssa slapped me across the face and left to walk up the spiral staircase. That woman was a mess. I had a strange feeling like someone was watching me, so I turned, looking down the foyer hallway. Henry's security officer Pietro had observed everything.

Good, maybe he'll tell Henry how I turned down a sexual advance from his wife and gain me some favor. I really needed another dozen rabbits or a new Philip in my life so I could get over that hump.

CHAPTER 34

Searching the Highlands

Galma is a big planet (Askar)

Tears had been streaming from my eyes for at least an hour. I had a display screen on with Free Worlds' news highlights, so the noise concealed my sobs. This round of emotions came as I sharpened the Rite of Passage tip knife inside my quarters on our cruiser. Our tip knife was sacred to sentinels who completed the right successfully. It was the first badge of honor we earned to join our brother and sisterhood of warriors. No sentinel would ever willingly allow separation from their tip knife. It became part of a Dolrinion body from the moment we stepped through the archway after successful completion.

I was thinking of my Rite of Passage on my seventeenth birthday after BlackRock Command sent us to survive the elements on a rogue world for one year. Each command did things their own way for that duration.

Force Command War Dogs sent their recruits to the southern waste of Kora to survive the year with minimal gear. Fighting giant black-tailed scorpions with nothing more than a bladed weapon and battle armor was one way to make a sentinel hardy.

Force Command Red Legion sent its trainees to war on some of the furthest rogue worlds outlying occupied space. Each day of the year, new batches of recruit warriors committed to a hard drop onto the planet. Academy squad platoon leaders took control of battle efforts without senior sentinel guidance. The young ones managed planetary battles without assistance. At any given time, Red Legion recruits were fighting a war somewhere on at least two rogue worlds. One of the abandoned planets inside the DMZ was once a Rite World.

Other Force Commands had less invasive ways of committing recruits to the Rite. Commands like First Ones and Tacoma sent their young warriors to live in a rogue-world jungle or wasteland for a year and find dangerous predatory animals to hunt in order to survive. After the year, they'd walk through the archway and receive their tip knife.

Every ten years, Force Command Steel Talon sent their recruits to the Great-in-Between. The young ones took command of cruisers to hunt down an Androsian ship and assault it. After a successful stalker raid, the Rite ended, regardless of the timespan. Countless numbers of vessels and trainees perished during Decade Rites. Those ships that were successful typically came back with fewer than half of their recruits. Some could take an entire year to find Androsians because the Great-in-Between was vast.

Returning cruisers came with tales of other strange things happening in that enormous emptiness, especially near the Yalvon Nebula. Living leviathans floated through the beautiful illuminations of that great colorful cloudy display. Sentinels called them space whales because of their size. They could swallow our cruisers with ease, but thankfully they only ate the nebula gases and didn't bother with us. Inside the in-Between, close to the nebula, recruits during the Decade Rite reported stories that seemed fictional fabrications or works of horror—floating lights that took shapes resembling people, and some sentinels claimed to see wings flapping as they passed ships. The lights moved with rational thought as if they were playing with our vessels, and, of course, electrical systems and cameras malfunctioned when these entities appeared.

Other more frightening tales included ghost transports that followed warships for light-years before disappearing and then reappearing after FTL, strange noises that echoed through ships sounding like screams of terror, odd unknown radiation signatures with flashes of blue, red, and green lights, and random mysteriously caused infections of body worms that ate through victims' insides until they burst.

Sentinels of Steel Talon who completed the Decade Rite were among the strongest of that entire command. All five supreme generals of Force Command Steel Talon were survivors of one Decade Rite or another, and some of them had stories, intriguing stories of oddities happening in that blackness.

After completion of the Rite of Passage, recruits walked through the tunnel archway located at the center of the memory stone. The tunnel was created by years of water erosion and formed a perfect arch at both ends. The underpass was long and glowed yellow from the exposed interior stone. Once the recruit exited the other side of the tunnel, they were given a tip knife, blessed in the essential oils and became sentinels of the Offensive to their Force Commands.

Elder Tacoma caretakers believed that legendary sentinels from our past who resided in the stone halls of eternity would wash their presence over recruits giving them the strength to serve the Offensive with honor. The Rite happened every day of the year on the birthday of each sentinel. Tacoma elders always initiated the Rite for each command since the stone's care and safety was their responsibility. They said the same words that had been uttered for the last eighteen hundred and sixty years.

"You entered as a recruit without real purpose but exited the archway a true sentinel of the Dolrinion Offensive. Serve well, follow our principles as set down by the five founders: duty, valor, and glory to the Offensive, and you'll one day return to the memory stone in spirit to live forever."

BlackRock was the only Force Command to complete the Rite on capital ships in addition to the tunnel on Kora. Memories of my Rite on the homeworld and thoughts of my long-dead friends from growing up under the orange-yellow sky contributed to the tears and pain I felt often.

The emotions when I sharpened my tip knife came from thinking of my brother and sister sentinels who walked through the yellow glow with me ... and Belkin. *Oh, how I miss him.* Any time that memory came to mind, the aroma of that tunnel overwhelmed my senses. It smelled like a strange mix of garlic, peppermint, and sulfur but still slightly different. That was the best comparison I could ever come up with.

Our Rite was difficult, and more than half of my childhood friends died along with another two-thirds of the recruits. I couldn't bring myself to think about it now; those feelings were too much to bear, even forty-six years later. I was all that remained. The last of my Rite sentinels died more than ten years prior on some random rogue world defending a camp or enforcing our Dolrinion will. That was the legacy of a BlackRock sentinel.

There was a knock at my door. I regained my composure enough to speak. "What is it?"

Sentinel Mith's voice was muffled through the door. "Major Negal wants to see us on the bridge."

I wiped more tears away. Some fell into my mouth with the taste of salt, and I took a deep breath. "Give me five minutes, sentinel. I'll be there."

Sentinel Mith was a strange Dolrinion. She always looked at maps and played with computers. BlackRock sentinels were craftsmen in the art of war and occupation, not computer experts. She acted more like a Federate Corporation pencil pusher than a Dolrinion most of the time. Major Negal said she had a talent for computer-code cracking besides her expertise on Galma. Computers were silly to me, and that added skill was a waste of time. If we needed to get through an airlock door, nothing worked better than explosive cord charges.

I stood, feeling stiffness in my back and knees. The years had not been kind to me. After checking in the mirror to ensure my face didn't look like I had spent the last hour weeping, I left and went to command and control, located at our ship's center.

Cruisers didn't typically have Corin-steel plate covering for C&C, but

Third Grade General Addis had given us her personal cruiser with a few upgrades from engineers of First Ones and Overwatch overseeing the work. General Addis, the widowmaker, bragged that we'd stand up in single combat against battleships, which I thought was an overreach.

On the first few days of our trip, Sentinel Mith showed me some of the upgrades. My favorite part was the weapons systems because we had triple the armaments of standard cruisers of the same size.

Major Negal was near the center console table on a lower platform with screens above angled down. A hologram video played on the table, and Sentinel Mith gave a half-curled smirk when she saw me. They both looked strange wearing BlackRock battle armor. Having spent so much time thinking of the Rite and crying enough to fill a latrine, I wondered what these two did for theirs, since Overwatch's Rite of Passage was a guarded secret; no other command knew what they did. I'd seen recruits leave Kora for the year and return, never speaking of the deeds.

Negal spoke sharply. "Master gunny, thank you for making us wait five minutes. Force Command BlackRock's peculiar if they allow high-ranking officers to wait for sentinels called upon."

It angered me, hearing him speak that way. He was arrogant and young, not knowing the first thing about BlackRock.

I pulled my lips in tight and calmed myself before replying with a lie. "Meant no offense, sir. There was a need for repairs on my battle armor's leg joint. Otherwise, I'd be reporting to you naked."

Sentinels of the Offensive rarely got new battle armor. We wore the same war plate from our Rite since it could expand itself to the wearer's needs. My armor had had more overhauls and piecemeal repairs over the last four decades than all the rogue worlds combined. Our engineers worked tirelessly fixing damaged armor, but not shrapnel peppering, dents, or color fading. No one ever called the engineer's brigade artists. They worked as an assembly line, quickly, without care for appearance. Field sentinels always knew a veteran when they saw the armor, besides confirmed kills across chest plates.

The major smiled. "A naked Hero of Gliese would be interesting indeed. Sentinel Mith would appreciate that sight to be sure."

Mith laughed and said, "Even with his advanced age, a rock-hard sentinel veteran's always desirable to women of the Offensive."

Major Negal kept going with his torment. "He'd be rock hard if he saw you without your battle armor for sure. You've got a perfect warrior's body. Now, let's get back to our mission."

He waved his hand, displaying several videos of Mace Applegate plus one on Galma. One video had Applegate and his wife leaving a transport in the spaceport, another showed them inside the Stumble Inn, and the third displayed a firefight on the street including someone new with the pair.

"These are the recordings Overwatch was able to obtain from the Rogue Syndicate networks. We know that Mace and the wife went to the Stumble Inn after leaving the port. Then they left the inn, with a third person in tow. Facial recognition identified her as a dome security officer of the relations station that went missing. Zoey Walmer was formally assigned to guard Colonial Accord Center Seat Representative Henry McWright's wife. Now she's on Galma protecting the Applegates."

That was curious. "Are the other representatives trying to obtain Mace Applegate?"

"Our dome supreme generals aren't aware of any sanctioned actions. Given Representative McWright's recent history with circumventing capitol policies, he could be flying solo for reasons unknown to us."

"Who's the capitol officer protecting them from?"

Major Negal waved his hand again, changing the street camera angle. A MERC Guild agent and a mongrel that had damage to its rear auto guns were trying to box in the Applegates. The beast looked like it had seen bitter fighting.

"This agent has a head start on us to recover them. He failed when Syndicate enforcers engaged both agent and dome security officer. The Lamp District recording shows a hell of a good bout between the three groups. We'll start in the Lamp District and find the taxi driver who took them—

none of the cameras show where he brought the group. The taxi driver visits a local bar every night after his shift. We'll start there."

I shook my head in disbelief and said, "Something doesn't make sense here. Dome security and the Guild hold their allegiance to representatives under the dome. Why would these two be fighting each other?"

"We'll find out together, master gunnery sergeant."

Watching that firefight made me wish I was there. My death might have come gloriously in combat, so my name could finally go to the stone with honor. I felt my bottom lip quiver while liquid drowned my eyes. I turned away from the console and faked a cough. They couldn't see me wipe the tears away.

Mith asked, "Are you ok, sentinel?"

I took a moment to clean my face. "Yes. No concerns—reacting to the booster shots we received before going to a new world. Happens every time."

Major Negal tightened his lips and narrowed his eyes. "Sentinel Mith, go down to engineering and make sure engine power's down. We need to override basic entry protocols, so the ship doesn't commit to a hard drop into Galma. The Syndicate doesn't allow combat entries into their atmosphere. We don't want targets on us before landing."

She nodded and left the shell. I placed my hands on the console to catch my breath after the fake cough. Major Negal stared at me for some time before speaking.

"The Gray Boulder and I spoke at length about you, master gunny. I was concerned that your battle fatigue would jeopardize our mission on Galma. Your colonel told me that all sentinels who've seen as many years as you go through the symptoms. He advised that he went through it and that most times it passed after a few years. Will you be ok to conduct this assignment?"

My shock must have been clear from my expression. I had a sour sensation like I would be sick. Was that fear? It was a strange emotion, if so. How did Colonel Zilath and this Overwatch commander know what I was going through? I had kept my feelings in check whenever in public.

Only one word spewed from my mouth, and for me, it felt like the sound came out shrilly, though I believed that was my imagination. "How?"

Negal smirked and raised his chin. "How did we know? The cerebral connectors at the base of your neck that link you to your battle armor through the LENS. Key letter in that acronym is S for surveillance. It doesn't just feed you information, as you know. It allows your thoughts to transfer to command and control for each regiment. Overwatch keeps tabs on all sentinels' emotions. Only extreme feelings alert our monitors. Emotion monitoring's not something I'm familiar with—other divisions of Overwatch have that duty. You have no idea the number of sentinels from the Offensive who suffer from a form of battle fatigue. For advanced cases, we treat the symptoms without sentinels' knowledge."

I opened my eyes wide. Had these Overwatch sneaks tranquilized me before?

"Why so surprised, sentinel? You already knew your armor could provide medication through the connectors. Storage tubes contain antibiotics, painkillers, stimulants like erythroxylon neurocaine, and adrenaline. How do you think those Red Legionnaires can run kilometers and fight the way they do without tiring? Overwatch carefully monitors every battle and provides necessary help through sentinel armor when needed. What most of the Offensive doesn't know is that Overwatch can also, in extreme circumstances, provide antidepressants in cerebral connectors to assist battle fatigue."

I frowned and made a fist. Major Negal crossed his arms and looked at me as if he fully understood my thoughts.

"Don't worry, master gunny. We've never medicated you. Especially not now—the meds can make your brain foggy, and I need you at your best if a battle should break out." The major turned back to the hologram. "Our discussion's irrelevant to the mission. I need you ready and able to serve your Force Command and the Offensive."

I could barely keep the fury out of my voice. "My emotions don't matter, only following the commands of my superior officer to complete my mission. If death should take me, it will be with an empty rifle magazine and enemy blood staining my chest plate."

Major Negal smiled and tapped my pauldron. "Good, now that's how the Hero of Gliese should speak. We'll be landing shortly. Ensure you have everything you need—we won't be coming back until the completion of our objective."

I said sternly, "I'm yours to command, sir."

*

The Lamp District was strange. In a Dolrinion camp, everyone moved with purpose or an objective dictated by their commanding officers. Here the natives appeared to do things spontaneously with little reason. Some gave us strange looks because of our short stature, the way that we walked, and the grinding sounds from our battle armor. The air smelt moist, like rainfall might be near, and my knees could feel that pressure. We moved through the streets to the tavern our taxi driver lead visited often.

The architecture on Gliese was strange to me with roadways made from cobblestone bricks that weren't level and were frustrating to walk on because every block was of an independent height to the next. The buildings were timber-framed, with wooden overlapping planks cladding the walls. The roofs pitched high on a ninety-degree angle, set with slates, and endless chimneys puffed thick white smoke. Dusk had come and gone and faint stars punched through the dark gray sky.

We came to the location of the agent's and Capitol Security officer's firefight and observed the area for a few moments. I bent down and found a spent shell casing, MERC Guild pistol caliber, wedged between the uneven bricks. Black scuff marks of burn damage streaked across some of the blocks. I handed the casing to Major Negal, who shook it in his hand before placing the brass in an armored compartment.

Pedestrians on the sidewalks stared at us suspiciously and muttered with each other. Sentinel Mith was growing impatient with their stares.

Once we got outside the tavern, located on a corner street opposite an open field thick with mud that overflowed onto the walkway and cobblestones, we heard the faint sounds of music playing. Natives all over the area were making merry with each other. A committed sentinel didn't have time for such things.

The sun had finally set completely, and a large picture window next to the entryway of the tavern emitted bright yellow light onto the gray street. A hanging wooden sign swinging in gusts of wind on chain-link connectors had writing in numerous languages. The only recognizable lettering for me was the Language of Humanity. I couldn't read those words, only speak them.

Major Negal said the bar was called the Muddy Corner. We went inside, and locals near the front of the establishment grew quiet.

A bartender cleaning a pint glass asked, "Can I help you with something?"

We lifted our face shield covers at the same time, making sounds of pressure releasing, and the major said, "We're only here to have a drink. Our credits work the same as everyone else's."

The bartender seemed satisfied with that answer. "Find a seat. I'll send a waitress over."

I understood what Major Negal meant when he said that they didn't want a Red Legion Champion for the mission. Our small meaningless interaction would have ended in bloodshed if Red Death were in my place. The Reds always took everything personally, as an insult to their honor.

We had to walk with care in our bulky armor; the tables were close together, and natives sat everywhere. Thin strips of wood lined the floor, and it creaked, bending with each step as if our weight was too much for the weak structure. Thin walls punched out in different directions with hanging pictures. Even the tables and chairs came from trees. A better name for that establishment would be Tinderbox because if battle broke out, we'd all burn to death before collapsing through the weak flooring.

Sand particles sprinkled across the wood reminded me of powdered sugar on a cake, and my thick metal boots made a strange scratching sound with each step. We sat at a table in the back with a clear line to the front entrance. A waitress came, and we ordered dark draft beers, a preferred choice among Dolrinions. The thicker, the better.

Sentinel Mith said, "The driver isn't here yet, and his shift ended already.

He should be here by now." She surveyed the bar.

Major Negal stretched his neck and leaned back in his chair. "Be patient, he comes every night. We'll sit, be vigilant, and wait. Take small sips, so we don't draw unwanted attention."

The beers arrived, and some time passed without anything of real interest happening. There was an employee that I watched closely. He wasn't Dolrinion, yet he was much shorter than me by at least thirty centimeters. I'd never seen someone so small before. The major said he had a genetic anomaly not common on the Free Worlds.

That little man was quietly doing his job with honor. He cleaned the tables, put sand on the floor when people spilled their drinks, and cleaned up any mess made by customers without complaining. He followed the principles of duty, valor, and glory without realizing it. The small employee walked by me with a smile but kept to himself.

A group of men standing near the bar watched him do his duties. One of them, a big man, thick of shoulder, shorter than two meters but built like a warrior, spat slurs at the dwarf. My anger grew instantly, watching the taunts. The tiny worker ignored the drunk's antagonizing remarks and continued doing his job. It wasn't enough for the instigator, who threw things on the floor to make the small man clean up after him.

Major Negal could see my resentment flaring and tapped my arm, saying, "Don't get involved, sentinel. We have a mission to complete."

I held fast, but my patience was thin. Another minute of torment went by, and the big man tripped the dwarf to the ground and kicked him in his rear. The small man had sand on his face and didn't defend himself. The bartender yelled, but the group wasn't paying attention. I'd not watch that any longer. I stood. Major Negal tried to grab my arm, but I pulled away.

The well-built man saw me walk towards him and stopped laughing. I helped the dwarf to his feet and brushed off his pants and shirt. The drunk tried to belittle me with words to his friends. I quickly bumped the drunkard's chest, pinning him against the wooden bar.

"You want to pick on someone smaller than you? Try picking on me."

The drunk pushed me, but my armor and feet were firm.

He said, "You Dolrinions always talk tough from inside that armor. Man to man, you wouldn't last a minute against me."

He slapped hands with one of his friends like he had said something witty. They laughed and took sips of their drinks.

I sneered. "I see, you fear Dolrinion battle armor. No problem, fighter. I'll match you, skin to skin, like true ancient warriors of old."

I was speaking as I walked back around the table next to Major Negal and Sentinel Mith. I turned to the group of fools and gave a cold smile before pulling off my thick heavy helmet and slammed it on the table where our dark drafts spilled. The beer soaked into the sand and wood and the table creaked from the heavy helm.

Using my cerebral connectors and LENS, I focused for a moment to command the battle armor. With a grinding of gears, pressure valves released, and locked latches opened from the back, allowing me to step out. I shook my head to remove the lower connection cords from my neck, which controlled the LENS and armor. As I stepped ahead of the stationary armor, I rubbed its chest plate, where I felt the numerous rows of spirals. That feeling on my fingertips filled my heart with pride, a warrior's pride.

Straightening my back and gazing at the drunkard, who was much taller than me, came naturally and without fear. Even standing there in my dark-colored boxer briefs, I felt at peace, in my element, ready to battle. Anyone could see that my arms, chest, and legs were broader and stronger than that weakling.

Years of hard sentinel life were clear in the old scars across my body. Bites, stabs, bullets, and shrapnel marks littered my skin from head to toe. Gray curly hair covered my skin that didn't suffer from burn scarring. Negal and Mith stood to honor my individual combat.

The arrogant aggressor hesitated, staring at my body. "You're old. It wouldn't be right for me to beat you."

With a hard gaze, I said, "I may be old, but I have one good fight left in me." Then I raised my voice and pounded my chest. "Now, will you stand here all night making excuses, or do battle?"

His face turned red and he lifted his arms, squeezing those large hands into fists the size of melons. I took a breath of air and raised mine, ready to fight. If I was lucky, he might not be as weak as I believed. Maybe he could kill me so I could finally rest in the memory stone, but I had doubts.

The drunkard swung, connecting with my face. I was off in thought when he started. That wouldn't happen again. Quickly, I recovered and countered with two swift body blows. He cried out in pain. He swung wildly, punch after punch, and I blocked each throw until I found an opening. I brought my fist up to his jaw and made solid contact.

He fell against the bar and drinks spilled on the countertop. He recovered and came straight for me, swinging left, right, left again, and right. The drunk was clearly a trained fighter and had tremendous strength behind his fists, but it wasn't the power of Kora. Unfortunate for him. He hit my face, and I countered again with more body shots under his ribs. My next blow was accompanied by a cracking sound. He shrieked.

I closed in on him only centimeters from his chest. That made it harder for him to get me with full power shots. We kept fighting, swinging our arms, over and over, skin connecting with skin. He was growing tired, leaning against the bar. I was gaining the upper hand when another blow took my face from the side—one of his pathetic friends sucker punched me. I stumbled back towards the pub entrance as both men swung. It wasn't long before Sentinel Mith came from behind and threw one into the sidewall, pictures smashing against the wooden planks. The second friend tried to punch her, but she turned her head, and he broke his hand against her helmet. Mith smirked at the cracking of bone and his screams of pain. Sentinel Mith lifted him over her head and threw him behind the bar where he smashed against the glass wall. It shattered into a thousand pieces, with a clattering noise so loud patrons across the bar covered their ears.

She turned to me and smiled with such a fire it gave me a chill. I was wrong about her spending time with computers and maps. She was a Dolrinion sentinel through and through.

I yelled with delight, "A true sister of war!"

The tall drunkard stepped to the middle of the room, looking at me with a frown. He winced and grabbed his side before lifting his fists again.

I grunted. "Are you so weak you need friends to help you during single combat? I am old, remember? Fight me, you coward."

He screamed like a savage animal and barreled towards me. His face was so red—it appeared like red paint splashed on him.

I got low and timed my next blow perfectly. Just before he reached me, I swung an uppercut to his chin with so much power my feet lifted off the ground. He launched like a bottle rocket and fell on his back. Sand sprang up like it was on a trampoline. I got down and crawled on top of him, straddling his chest. It was time; punch after punch, my fist pounded his face repeatedly. At first, a soft yelp came from his mouth, but my grunts of fury at each hit overshadowed his noises of weakness. Bones crunched in his face, sounding like sticks breaking.

Major Negal and Sentinel Mith stomped their feet in unison. The noise of their sturdy armored feet hitting the wood, splashing sand into the air, encouraged me to punch harder. A few more hits, and he looked like a mangled slab of meat that had gone through a processing machine. Bones protruded from his skin, and my arms felt warm from blood up to my elbows. I dragged him across the sandy floor, then I picked him up over my head and screamed, "You're no longer welcome at this establishment, weakling."

He went through the window like a blade slicing through butter and slammed onto the uneven cobblestones. The entire bar was quiet, and the only sound was my feet across the sand. When I reached Major Negal, he puffed his chest out with a firm nod and gave me a half-smile as I stood there in my nakedness, breathing heavily.

He placed his hand on my shoulder and said, "The Hero of Gliese."

Sentinel Mith repeated his words, and both stared at me.

I glared at my blood-soaked arms and spoke softly, "Duty, valor and glory to the Offensive."

Both replied, "Duty, valor and glory."

I peered over my shoulder to observe my defeated foe and saw the taxi driver outside standing over the drunkard's pulverized near-dead body. I quickly stepped back into my armor and the latch locks closed one at a time.

"It's the driver," Sentinel Mith said and ran after him.

Major Negal followed. It only took me a moment to connect with the battle armor. The dwarf I fought for was already on the floor cleaning the mess I made during combat. He raised his head, looked at me and smiled. I nodded and ran, chasing after my commander and Mith.

The taxi driver jumped into his vehicle and tried to drive away. Mith showed great valor by leaping high and crashing down onto the car hood. Smoke came from the engine block. Major Negal ripped the driver's door off and pulled him out.

He shrieked, "Please no. Please. I come in peace. No trouble from me. Please."

The major slapped his frightened face and slammed him against the car. Negal looked up at the fat man and said, "The three who got into your taxi during the shootout. Where did you take them?"

The fat man tried to shield his face. "So much wildness in the Lamp District. I've got to leave this place for sure."

Sentinel Mith insisted. "Answer, now."

His voice cracked. "They went to the mid-crossing saying it was time to disappear. Best place to do that on Galma's down below."

Major Negal and I looked at Sentinel Mith in confusion. What a bizarre planet.

Mith said, "The Lowlands. They went into hiding down in the fog. We'll have trouble tracking them. Things are different there."

Major Negal replied, "The Lowlands it is then."

"The MERC man with his beast chased them down there too," the fat man squeaked. "He found me the night after I brought them to the crossing and made me tell him what I told you. The agent's already down there, making a mess of things for sure."

Sentinel Mith said, "Agents and mongrels attract attention. Natives there will all be talking about an agent in the fog lands. They've got a head start, but if we track the agent, that will lead us to the Applegates."

Finally, someone who might have the strength to take me in a fight. I grabbed my Corin-steel axe picturing the unmatched training Guild agents received for twenty years. They were among the best in occupied space. If he couldn't kill me, I feared I might die of old age like a coward.

CHAPTER 35

The Lowlands

Things were quite different down there (Mace)

The Lowlands of Galma were unlike the Highlands—they were like a different planet altogether because of the fog. It was constant and didn't let any sunlight through below three hundred meters, and had an odor that reminded me of cinnamon and rubber, which was strange.

No direct influence from the Highlands and the Rogue Syndicate trickled down. However, what happened on the mountains impacted the plains. If it rained up high, the Lowlands suffered from mudslides, rockfalls, and flooding. Visitors couldn't see well in the fog, it was so thick and unnatural to us, but Lowlanders' evolution had adapted well. They had huge dark pupils with greater sensitivity to the conditions.

Locals compensated for the lack of illumination with torches, flashlights, and an effective purple glow that reminded me of ultraviolet lights. Even with the artificial glow, there was no lack of natural lighting. A common orange flower with yellow spots and round petals called lumintansies grew in clusters everywhere. Locals nicknamed them luminous patches, for the brightness that radiated from the petals. Dragonflies on Dol'Arem were specks of salt compared to the cat-sized flies in the Lowlands. They were entirely harmless but menacing to watch because of their size and the blinding yellow balls of light bursting from rear sacs providing terrific radiance.

Mud huts varied in shape and size at each settlement we went through, but they all shared a similar theme, with domed and conical tops made of mud and bamboo. Jamie, Zoey, and I watched one under construction and were in awe of the speed and skills of the builders. They constantly mixed the wet mud with water because it dried so fast in the fog. Some of the larger huts could house hundreds and were several stories high, while other shelters were smaller, only having a few rooms. Candlelight was the best way to see indoors, and outside were caged dragonflies in addition to torches. Some settlements had gas generators, and a popular tourist settlement, Masgem, had a modified natural gas power plant that operated on noncomputerized analog systems.

Every settlement attracted caterpillars, butterflies, and moths. They glowed a blueish turquoise that shimmered through the fog. Near six o'clock every morning, hundreds of thousands of butterflies performed mating swarms high above for nearly an hour. In the Lowlands, it was the brightest light by far, and natives called the display a Lowlands sunrise.

At the mid-crossing, we met a local freelance guardian who specialized in escorting what he called White Eyes through distances in the fog. We paid him to take us to the spaceport nearly two hundred kilometers away. His name was Fellas, and he knew how to get through the settlements. Fellas was the only native local I saw that carried a firearm. He'd spent years working in the Highlands with the Rogue Syndicate.

There weren't any trees in the Lowlands; however, vegetation was in ample supply, like mosses and nightshade ferns. Although sunlight couldn't penetrate that far down, locals said the fog provided high nutrient levels for growth, including sulfur and other minerals in the mud. Giant hybrid spider plants resembling trees sprouted in clusters away from settlements, but Fellas told us to steer clear. The largest plants were breeding grounds for rattle spiders, which were bigger than dogs. Settlement guardians worked tirelessly to eradicate them since the spiders treated people as prey. Rattle spiders hunted their food in the fog and dragged them to breeding grounds where sticky webs injected nutrients into people's bodies so they wouldn't die from malnourishment. The webs imprisoned the victims—rattlers preferred their food alive during consumption. The spiders used the webbing to cover open wounds each day when their bellies were full. Limbs went first, and that thought terrified me.

Zoey promised to shoot us if that became our fate. Another predator we learned about were lurkers. They lived deep underground in caves in the lowest areas of the Lowlands near sea level. The only things that protected natives from lurkers were the mudslides and torrential rains through the year that flooded the caves. Fellas said lurkers were enormous lizards with thick brown spiked scales, claws large enough to strangle a rhinoceros and climb mountain walls quickly. Even if natives had guns, rifle rounds weren't strong enough to penetrate their armor. Lurkers killed more natives than any other threats to the Lowlands. Fellas said lurker encounters weren't frequent on pathways and that most of the deaths occurred when their normal food sources ran low outside of fog breeding seasons. It didn't stop Jamie from having nightmares about them. She'd wake at night breathing rapidly and covered in sweat. When I asked Jamie what she dreamed about, her answer was cold and short.

Native Lowlanders seemed ok to deal with, though they didn't trust anyone who had white in their eyes. None went out of their way to speak with us, but if we asked questions, answers would always be given but with brief pauses of suspicion. Free Worlds citizens heard hearsay of cannibal Lowlanders constantly, but those were fables. There was a small segment of the Lowlander population that despised all White Eyes. Settlement natives called this segment Scoffs, and they sharpened their teeth and had tattooed faces making them look like monsters. Scoffs didn't live near settlements and only caused trouble for travelers caught on pathways between communities, and their homes were off in the deep dark wilds.

Lowlanders had a strange appearance that would make anyone think they were aliens. They had gray skin that was nearly translucent with blue and red veins visible. Any bright lights disturbed their oversized sensitive pupils, and their hair was jet black.

In school, our education about Galma always said Lowlanders were wild primitives, and I saw for myself that this wasn't truly accurate. They had schools, local governance in the form of a council of elders, and herbal healers. I didn't find any coding programmers, scientists, or mechanical engineers, but Lowlanders wouldn't have use for those things down here anyway. Most technologies were useless in the fog. Even wireless communications didn't work. Ships that traveled through the spaceport had to ensure there was a combustion bypass because there was no computer guidance to land and take off.

Lowlanders never acted with haste, taking their time to complete tasks that would be quickly accomplished by Free Worlds citizens. Things happened slowly in the Lowlands if they happened at all. Natives down there simply didn't care for the things that most other people found important. Fellas acted more like someone from the Highlands because of the years he spent there.

It had been over a month since we signed on with Fellas as our escort and added security through one settlement to the next. He didn't know that we had a MERC Guild agent hunting us, and Zoey believed that information was better left unsaid.

Something I found interesting that we learned was no native Lowlanders suffered the affliction common across all occupied space. DNA degradation disease was unheard of in the fog, and I could only wonder why, because it was so prevalent across Humanity. Maybe the fog had something to do with it or something else entirely. The Titans never built any structures in the fog, which I found strange because any planet with people had some form of Old World remains.

Increased security and mistrust were everywhere in settlements because of numerous disappearances happening over the last year or so. Guardians didn't believe it was fog predators or Scoffs because of the strange circumstances surrounding the vanishings, and others blamed White Eyes. No one knew the cause, but Fellas said he was happy because his business was booming. Jamie jokingly thought he might be taking them to further his profits. Only Corporate employees would suggest something like that.

Artificial food was nonexistent in the Lowlands. Our meals mostly consisted of blind fish, mushrooms, and edible algae. Natives ate bugs daily too. Fellas told us a common saying with locals—green, black, brown, shove it on down. He said to stay away from any other-colored bugs, or we'd find ourselves laid up with the healers for days. We hadn't eaten any bugs to that point, thankfully.

Zoey believed the outer worlds would be the best place to disappear from the pursuing agent. If we could get to the spaceport before he caught up to us, there'd be no way for him to track us in space. We increased our speed through the settlements and passed Masgem altogether at Zoey's request. She said there were lots of eyes from the Free Worlds there because it was a popular tourist site. I was disappointed; we'd heard stories of the massive villas built there by wealthy independent families of the Free Worlds hundreds of years ago. In recent years, the upper class would rent them for vacation. Fellas protested that we should stop there, but Zoey won that argument.

Our only issue to that point while moving through the pathways with other groups was a close encounter with two Scoffs. The situation was tense for only a moment until Zoey and Fellas drew their firearms. Lowlanders used rudimentary weapons like poison-tipped bamboo spears, blow darts, and bows. Settlement guardians had flamethrowers for defense against fog predators too. The pathways ran from each settlement to the next and rarely went in different directions. Chunks of gravel covered six meters from side to side to allow carts, horses, and groups to travel with ease.

Pathways had scattered lighting, but it didn't help with visibility. Some areas on the path had nothing more than luminous patches on both sides of the roadway. Some locations had generators with light bulbs placed long ago, and caged dragonflies were the most frequent light source.

Lowlanders made do with the best things available to them in the fog. I was envious of their lifestyle in some ways. We were always so busy running miles per minute, never stopping long enough to breathe in the Free Worlds. Down there, apart from the stress of a pursuing Guild agent, life was like a time warp to a tranquil past. The settlement we were staying at had more frequent issues with fog predators, and the inhabitants had built a tall bamboo wall with guard towers and a moat loaded with poisoned spikes.

Jamie and Zoey had gone to do the normal rounds at the local market to buy blind fish. What Jamie didn't know was that I got a Free Worlds food recipe from Zoey and intended to try to cook real food for the first time in my life. We were eating blind fish constantly, but it was nearly flavorless and nothing like the delicacies from the Free Worlds. The recipe was breaded chicken with herbs and spices, green beans, and chopped garlic in olive oil, grated cheese, and seasoned rice. The aroma filled the room and smelled unbelievable, but I was nervous cooking over an open flame—grease sprayed me a few times, staining my clothes.

The food was nearly ready, and I could hear the ladies coming through the door. Zoey had loosened up over the past few weeks. She didn't drop her stern glare, but when sitting inside our rented mud hut, she would talk with us and even smiled a few times. She and Jamie were becoming fast friends.

The door creaked open. Jamie walked inside, taking a deep breath of the fogged air. Her eyes opened wide while Zoey stood in the doorway with a smirk. I'd already set up the silverware and plates made from bamboo and spread lumintansie petals across the table and floor with perfectly spaced-out candles giving the room a romantic feel.

Jamie looked around the kitchen. "What, wait, what is … this?"

Zoey went into her bedroom and closed the door. I took the bags from Jamie's hands and placed them on the counter. We could do without eating blind fish for one night.

"I wanted to surprise you, babes."

She took a long breath and made a sound of delight. "It smells amazing."

"Zoey gave me the recipe, and I wanted you to try real food that had more taste than blind fish."

Jamie kissed me with passion. "You're the greatest husband a woman could ever ask for, Mace. Everything going on, and you still found time to be romantic. I love you."

Her face glowed orange from the flower petals, and she had a sparkle in her eyes.

"I love you too."

We kissed again and sat at the table to eat that delicious food. Our lips shone with the chicken juices. Artificial food never had a taste or texture like that. It felt so satisfying eating real food with herbs and garlic, and was so different to eating from dispensers. Sure, artificial foods filled our stomachs, but there was always something missing and unsatisfying.

Jamie seemed deep in thought as she ate. She said, "I think the outer worlds would be a great place to raise our baby. The homeworld of the Nejem royal family has more technology than its other territories. I don't care where we go as long as we're together."

Looking at her, I had butterflies and goosebumps formed on my arms. After all these years, it felt like we were falling in love with each other all over again, like in school. Her face made me smile.

"Anywhere in occupied space, as long as we're together."

Jamie laughed uncontrollably, and it confused me. "What's so funny?"

She took a few more bites of the delicious food before speaking. "I was thinking of the first real date we went on in secondary school when you came to my house and asked my dad's permission to take me out, even though we had already been together for some time."

We had been friends for years before Jamie and I started dating. It was official when our mutual friend Jasper threw a party, and we hooked up for the first time.

Jamie continued, "You had this chivalrous thought that it was disrespectful for us to be together without you asking my father for permission."

I snorted. "Oh, I remember that. How dumb was I?"

"The next day after the party, you came to my house and knocked on the door. When my dad answered, he looked at you the same way a corporate-grade thirty-five would look at a grade twenty who showed up at their home."

I said, "Your father scared the crap out of me. He still does."

"I was standing behind him, smiling at you, and I remember what happened like it was yesterday. You said, 'Hello, sir, I'm Mace Applegate, here to take your daughter on a date.' He paused for a few seconds then said, 'No, you're not,' and closed the door in your face."

We both bellowed in laughter, and I said, "My heart sank into my feet when that happened. It was the worst feeling in the world."

Jamie nodded. "Dad was testing you. He looked back at me and said, 'Mace is a good kid, but he must show me how bad he wants to be with you. Life in the Corporation is hard, and things won't always work out the way an employee intends. Without real commitment, he'll fail. Let's see what he does out there.'"

"Yup. I sat on your front stoop for four hours, refusing to leave. The sun went down, and mosquitoes ate me alive."

"I kept looking through the window at you, yelling at my dad. Finally, he opened the door and said—"

I cut her off quickly, finishing her sentence. "'Mace Applegate, come in and have a drink. You and I should talk.'"

Jamie said, "We sat at the kitchen table for hours. After you left, Dad said that I would marry you someday. He could tell by the way we stared at each other."

"Your dad's a smart man. I knew that night that I wanted to spend the rest of my life with you. I thought on the car ride home that there was nothing in the world that would keep me from being with Jamie Kaska."

Music echoed through the kitchen window—drums, violins, guitars, and horns. Jamie peeked through the window and said, "Lowlanders next door are having a party. It looks like someone's birthday."

I stood, grabbed her hands, and attempted to move to the music. "Let's celebrate then."

We spun around the kitchen clumsily, and I bumped into everything. She laughed, knowing I was never a good dancer and moved with locked knees.

We kissed in a way that I had not experienced in years. I carefully guided her in the direction of our bedroom, trying not to bump into furniture along the way. We went inside and closed the door.

As we finished at the same time, Jamie opened her eyes and gave me a wide smile. She said, "I feel like we're teenagers again."

"I've been thinking about that since we started eating dinner."

We stayed in bed for an hour or so, holding each other and talking. Then Jamie's eyes opened wide, and she said, "Remember what Fellas told us about the settlement elders? Every night they gather and tell stories from the Lowlands' past. Let's go and hear some of those tales. It's like when we were kids and went to hear stories from the Years of Forgetting about giant Titans and disappearing stars."

"Well, I don't know anyone who ever got hurt going to hear a few ghost stories in the Lowlands."

We dressed and knocked on Zoey's door. When she opened the door and carefully inspected our red faces and messy hair that showed what we had been up to earlier, she raised an eyebrow and spoke. "I'm not joining you, if that's what you came to ask."

Jamie slapped her arm playfully. "Stop it, you're terrible. No, we want to hear one of those living memory stories from the elders. Mace thinks they're talking about ghosts."

Zoey said, "Settlement elders speak of the Lowlands' past. They don't keep written records of their history, only stories handed down from generation to generation. Much of what they say sounds fabricated."

A large bonfire blazed red hot, the flames moving in the wind like tall waves on an ocean, at the center of the settlement. The elder had the fire at her back and sat high on a bench. As visitors to the Lowlands, the flickering light didn't bother our eyes, but all the fog natives wore small round goggles for protection. We took a seat near the elder to listen.

"Tonight, we speak of the time before time, before the great destruction of our humanity, when things were different here and there across the worlds. We Dark Eyes lived in the fog long before humanity fell into its slumber. Our people were never touched by the gloom above because we already hid in the darkness below for thousands of years. Our blood is pure without corruption or taken, taken into the storm. Topsiders call them Titans, but that wasn't what they were, no, they were immoral of heart, body, and mind. The terrors of old."

A visitor sitting near me asked, "Who took people? Was it the Syndicate?"

The elder smiled and clicked her teeth together while shaking a ball of beads. "No, the Syndicate is new to Galma, so to speak, and the time we tell of is thousands of years into the past. At the end of the Old World, flashes of death from above went on for days, rays of light were so bright, it was as if the sun pierced through our fog with clarity and ease. Lowlanders went blind in great numbers, and that's why to this day, we keep goggles close, yes, close." She tapped her goggles, which rested on her head, for reassurance. "Back then, instead of rain and mudslides coming down the mountainside, buildings and death collapsed beneath the fog. We saved some Uplanders, and they became one with us, and others, others disappeared forever going into the void."

Another visitor who had a Colonial accent spoke. "The Titans were giants and gave us technology that we squandered. It was our fault. We drove ourselves into the Great Darkness. Cave paintings on Talbora from the Years of Forgetting show them standing two point seven meters tall, and people of the Old World worshipped them. The paintings always had radiant light with outlines of white and gold around displays of Titans."

I countered. "We found similar paintings on Dol'Arem, though ours displayed them with dark coloring and horns like demons. Humanity during the Great Darkness never saw a Titan and painted those pictures from stories handed down. Our scientists believe that the displays only signify the importance of Titans for their contributions to occupied space. They're not meant to be a representation of physical size, rather the scope of importance to our ancestors of the Old World."

The Colonial man frowned at me, and the elder said, "Would the two of you like to tell this story, or can I continue?" We sat in silence, and she made a sound halfway between a laugh and *tsk.* "The immoral of heart and their artificial, false unnaturalness spread through the stars like a plague, and when the time came, and fears overwhelmed those who wouldn't bow, death and degradation came. The degradation is key."

Another listener said, "We learned on my homeworld that a supernova from the core of our galaxy was the cause of Humanity's destruction."

"Is that what you learned?" The elder threw her head back with amusement and said, "Interesting, very interesting." She laughed in a deep voice, sounding nearly mad.

I asked, "What did you mean by degradation? Degradation from what?"

She clicked her teeth together again and said, "Blood, my boy, all the answers you seek are in your blood. Though for you," the elder paused, glancing at the spectators, "the answers would cause tremendous pain. Your blood holds the key. Blood, blood, blood. It's all in the blood." She giggled like a child.

Jamie covered her baby bump as the deranged woman spoke her last sentence, attempting to shield our baby from the crackpot words. The elder gazed at her belly as Jamie clutched it. Immoral of heart, the Titans, and destruction. She was crazy, and it disappointed me because the Years of Forgetting fascinated countless billions in the Free Worlds.

I wasn't prepared to give up on my questioning. "What do you know about the Great Darkness?"

The elder, with her pale grayish skin and visible blue and red veins, gave a wide smile and tilted her head to the side. "Truth Seers have all the stories from thousands of years into the past, and some of the future." She glanced at Jamie and Zoey once more before looking back at me. "Pain, nothing but pain. You want to hear of immoral ones from years past? Come back tomorrow night, and we'll share those stories."

I shook my head. "We called them Titans because of their technology. It was superior to our own, and in my opinion, it was that technology that killed them and most of our ancestors, not corruption of the heart. Every planet in occupied space has mass graves with billions of bones. None of those bones are from giants. I think most educated people from the Free Worlds are curious to know what happened."

She clattered her ball of beads again. "The bodies showered over us in the fog like torrential rains, but here the wet mud and predators consumed them: lies and pain, curious one, nothing but lies and pain. Come back tomorrow night. I'll share more that you seek and that which you don't know that you want to know."

The elder laughed maliciously again and narrowed her eyes. Jamie grabbed my arm and pulled me away from that craziness. Zoey was at our heels.

"She's mad, Mace. I can't believe she's an authority in this settlement," Jamie said.

Zoey glanced back at the blazing fire. "Lowlanders are superstitious people. They believe in strange things not based on reality. The Truth Seers she was talking about are nothing more than crazy old timers that believe they're wizards and witches. You'd make up these types of things too if you lived down here your whole life."

I was disappointed because the Years of the Great Darkness always fascinated me. What was she talking about, our blood, and why did she keep looking at Jamie and me so strangely? Maybe someone would have the answers about our past, but not tonight.

*

We woke to Fellas banging on our door. It took Jamie and me a few minutes to pull ourselves together. After getting dressed, we went into the living room, where Zoey had everything ready to go near the front door.

"Great, you're late again. The caravan's leaving in fifteen minutes, and the guardians won't wait for us. We need to move now." Fellas sounded agitated, bobbing his head up and down.

Zoey asked the same question every time we left a settlement. "What's the number of guardians and travelers?"

If Fellas's pupils hadn't covered both eyes entirely, it would have been easier to see him rolling them at Zoey. "Lady, you ask me every time we leave a settlement. Don't you get bored with that question?"

Zoey replied sternly, "The Applegates paid you well to answer my questions appropriately."

He sighed and shook his head. "Four spears, three flamethrowers, and fourteen travelers, including you three."

When we reached the departing group, they were already moving through the front gate. We made it just in time. Fellas had told us that White Eyes couldn't travel safely on pathways without guardian escort and protection. Truthfully, it seemed like a way to make money for the Lowlanders because everyone had to pay for safe travel. We passed numerous caravans on the road. Natives in the fog didn't pay for trips. The guardians all had padded leather armor made from hides that wouldn't stop bullets but served its purpose against fog predators.

We had been moving slowly on the path for nearly two hours. Zoey kept her eyes on the others traveling in our caravan, and she always watched Fellas with mistrust. Our caravan had two carted wagons pulled by horses with seating for those who couldn't walk great distances, and the back contained other supplies. Jamie was in the cart, and I walked next to her.

The guardian captain at the front stopped us, looking ahead. The fog was thicker in that location. It was dark where lighting should have been, and Fellas lifted his goggles, looking forward with his superior sight.

Zoey grabbed the handle of her pistol in its holster and turned to Fellas. "What's wrong?"

"The dragonfly cages ahead are open. That shouldn't happen on a pathway. These routes are checked every day by scouts to make sure the lighting is sufficient and no dangers are lurking about."

The captain came to our lead cart and pushed a button near Jamie. Purple lights, not bright, but powerful enough to give us good sight, emitted from under the wheels of both carts reflecting off the thick fog. Our guardians seemed concerned—they gripped their spears and flamethrowers tighter. Zoey and Fellas drew their weapons, glancing into the distance.

Our caravan captain waved his hand forward, and we moved off slowly.

A strange scurrying noise echoed on both sides of the pathway—followed by another odd clatter. That other sound was something I knew I'd never forget because the vibrations sent chills down my spine and reminded me of a rattlesnake, only much louder.

Fellas shouted, "Rattle spiders!"

All four spearmen took up defensive positions around the caravan, and the three guardian flamethrowers, one of whom was the captain, ignited their torches.

"Prepare to defend yourselves!" the captain screamed.

Travelers cried out in fear. There were extra bamboo spears attached to the wagon. I grabbed one and pulled it free, and others in our group did the same. Another rattling noise; it was terrifying, and more intense. My hands were sweating, and I felt my heart beating so rapidly it pulsated into my throat. Zoey and Fellas peered for targets through the fog.

Jamie wrapped her arms over her belly, which I realized was no longer a bump. Her abdomen seemed more rounded, and it shouldn't be that big yet. Another rattle from behind me. A flamethrower shot a bright hot flame across the foggy field like a firehose of red water. Fellas quickly pulled his goggles over his eyes, and for the first time, we saw them. Giant spiders on the moss-covered ground, dozens of them, and their sizes were unbelievable.

Two caught fire in the streams of flames. A terrible screeching noise of pain came from them as they ran through the field like fireballs. More spiders pushed closer to us. They shook their rattlers in unison, lifting their two front legs in our direction. More streaks of flame rang out in all directions, and more rattlers ignited.

One of the flaming spiders ran straight for me. I held the spear ahead and screamed with fear as the creature scurried at me. I could feel the heat from flames on my skin. Before it reached me, Zoey opened fire and killed it only centimeters away, and the two rattlers on its back slowly stopped pulsating. The spider's rattlers reminded me of branched murex seashells that washed up on tropical ocean shores of Dol'Arem. Even though flames engulfed the bug, I could see thick hair fibers covering each huge leg.

Another flaming spider crossed the pathway in front of our cart, from one side to the other, and Fellas shot into the blackness. We heard a scream from the carriage behind us. A traveler was on the ground sliding through the dirt and moss as a spider pulled on her legs, its rattles shaking. She disappeared into the fog, and her faint screams passed away. That poor woman would spend the next month being slowly eaten to death by those terrible things.

Zoey saw the chaos unfolding and turned to me. "Get in the cart with Jamie. You'll be the last line of defense for your wife if they get past me."

As she finished speaking, Zoey was violently jerked to the gravel, the spider's rattles shaking behind as arched legs move back, dragging her into the fog. Fellas looked back and saw Zoey but turned away without helping her.

I jumped high in the air with my poison-tipped spear in hand, landing on the bug's back, and drove the weapon through flesh. It screeched and lifted its front legs so I fell. Zoey turned and fired one bullet into the spider's head. The rattlers slowly stopped shaking.

The captain yelled, "Travelers, you need to get out of here. Spearmen, take them over the next hill—we'll stay behind and hold them back."

Spear carriers ran to the front of our caravan and pulled the horses. The flamethrowers took up the rear, holding back the rattle spiders. We passed over a small hill and down the other side where the next set of caged dragonfly lights were not disturbed. Behind us, over the hill, a red, yellow, and orange glow was overshadowed by thick fog. The shrieks of flaming bugs grew faint through the fog.

As we slowly trotted down the hill, a spearman walked alongside me, and I said, "There were no spider plants. Why were those bugs on the road? I thought they didn't do that?"

He was breathing heavily and shook his head. "They don't. I've never seen rattlers act like that before."

At the bottom of the hill, we stopped abruptly again. Two natives stood on the pathway, blocking us from continuing. They were barely wearing any clothing at all, and their bodies were tattooed from head to toe in shapes and symbols. One was a man and the other a woman. She held a bow with an arrow locked into place, and the other had a bamboo spear.

Fellas lifted his goggles and whispered, "Scoffs."

The man holding the spear smiled; his sharpened teeth resembling animal fangs were clear even in the fog.

"It was them. They led the spiders down to disorient us and separate the group," said the guardian standing next to me.

On both sides of the pathway were more Scoffs, armed with spears, bows, and blow darts.

Fellas took a step forward. "We're a caravan escort hosted by Lowlander blood. The same as you. Move aside and let us pass."

Another spearman said, "The travelers paid for safe passage through the pathway, move aside."

The native barbarian changed his smile to a frown. His eyes filled with hate. "You blind fools—the topside's to blame for our losses. We disappear too, not just you. The White Eyes need to go so we can live the way we did for thousands of years before the Syndicate came. You'll let us take a few. We're hungry."

Other Scoffs surrounding us made sounds of approval, and some in our caravan cried out at his words. I felt something new boiling inside of me. I wasn't afraid; it was anger, no, a rage I felt. I wasn't a violent man, but I remembered what the Rogue Ronin said to me. Experience had changed me. Gripping the spear, I took a few steps forward and pointed at the lead Scoff.

"You won't touch a single person in this caravan."

Something took over the rage, though. Before I could finish my last word, an unusually tight and painful sensation on my right shoulder overtook me. I had tunnel vision as I spoke to the Scoff leader on the pathway and didn't even realize what had happened to my side.

He was on me, with his head against my shoulder, those black pupils tinted purple in the undercarriage light. One of the barbarians had sunk his razor-sharp teeth through my shoulder, pushing past my shirt and skin with ease. He was trying to eat me! The feeling sent a chill through my body, and

Jamie screamed as she saw what was unfolding.

Fellas didn't hesitate and shot the Scoff in his head, but it was so close to me that the ringing sound echoed tumultuously in my ear, and I saw stars buzzing through the fog. I grabbed the side of my face in pain and dropped to one knee. Zoey, Fellas, and our guardians engaged. Zoey shot the lead Scoff on the road between his eyes, and then the bare-chested woman with her bow. Red blotches appeared on their gray skin as they fell, one after the other.

The guardian I was speaking to only moments earlier dropped next to me with several arrows embedded in his chest and neck. I put my back against the cart and felt Jamie's hand push onto the bite wound that was gushing with blood. She was speaking to me, but the ringing noise made it impossible to hear her.

Two Scoffs with spears charged right for Fellas and me. He was fighting others and didn't see them coming. We were going to die. There were lots of them, but then a flash of red and orange light came from the side and flames consumed both spears; their skin melted away as they screamed with pain. The captain had come over the hill in force, igniting streams of fire that overwhelmed the Scoffs. They faded away into the fog, retreating from our flamethrowers.

The battle was over as fast as it started. We took a count of the aftermath and paused to recover from the ordeal. One of the travelers with us was a Free Worlds doctor, on vacation with his family. They spent time in the Highlands and decided to travel the Lowlands since it was a once-in-a-lifetime journey. He'd regret that decision after this incident for sure. The doctor tended to the deep bites on my shoulder, and I glared at Fellas.

"Why did you not help Zoey when the spider was dragging her away?"

Zoey narrowed her eyes at Fellas as he said with a smile, "Remember when you hired me? Zoey said she didn't require my protection or guidance. She said she was only here to look out for you two. I said fine and gave you a thousand off the cost. What you paid me covers your wife, that baby, and you, nothing more. I'm a businessman, and this is a business deal. Give me another fifteen hundred, and next time I'll make sure Zoey isn't touched."

Zoey snapped back, "I don't need your assistance. Unlike you, I was protecting the family."

Fellas raised his head and said with a chuckle, "What do you mean? Did you not see me shoot the Scoff trying to eat Tasty Mace here? I saved him."

Zoey glanced at me. "You also blew out Mace's eardrum, shooting that gun right next to his head."

The guardian captain came to us. "Is everyone ok?"

Fellas said, "Yes, thank you for your protection, guardian. How many did we lose?"

"Two guardians, three travelers. The spiders got two, and the Scoffs made off with one. The other two died in the fight."

He moved on to check other travelers in our caravan.

"At least we didn't run into the lurkers," Jamie said with relief.

Fellas snorted to himself and said, "Darling, if even one lurker were on the pathway, we'd all be dead. No one here stands a chance against those lizards. I would've left you all high and dry in that situation. There are other fog predators out there too. We aren't near the coastline or any large lakes, but if we were, loptakus would take us faster than a lurker. Those things are three meters long, hundreds of legs, and claws powerful enough to snap a MERC mongrel in half. Their mouths have dozens of neurotoxin tentacles that can extend nearly a meter to grab their food. If those things touch your skin, you're paralyzed while the claws chop you up like sushi." The doctor stopped examining me to listen. "There are even worse terrors in the fog that do horrific things and would turn settlements into buffet lines if they wanted."

"Why don't they?" I asked.

Fellas shrugged. "The predators fight amongst themselves in the fog because they dwell close to each other in the deep places of the world. Others might not enjoy the taste of our flesh. Honestly, I can't say, but it's better for us because we won't be some nasty thing's next meal."

The doctor looked back at my wound and said, "There, you're all patched up." He turned to Jamie. "Are you ok? How's the baby?"

"Not sure, honestly. I'm only just out of the first trimester."

The doctor frowned and pulled his lip to the side. "Would you mind if I had a look?"

"Of course, you're a doctor, and the first one I've seen since getting pregnant."

He lifted her shirt to look at her belly and touched her stomach in several places.

"You're at least seven and a half months pregnant right now."

Jamie and Zoey were shocked, and I said, "That isn't possible, she can't be more than three months."

Jamie looked at her belly. "A little over four months." She turned to the doctor. "How? How's this possible?"

Fellas bellowed in laughter. "You're in the Lowlands of Galma, of course. I thought that's why you came here in the first place. That baby will be squirming itself out within two weeks as a healthy newborn."

Fellas continued to laugh while Jamie, Zoey, and I glared at each other, unsure what to say.

CHAPTER 36

The Fight

Fireheart of the Alliance (Isabel)

Our power-ball game ended only a few hours ago, and anxiety at the thought of fighting Ezra made me restless. Big Jack, Nina, Ethan, and I were in the shower room of our bunk, talking out the strange situation. I was confused by the pirate challenge.

"If Ezra can challenge me to a fight like this, why didn't Jack do the same when we first got here and put his miserable life to an end?"

Big Jack held his head up a little higher as if I said something that made him feel short.

Nina said, "Jack doesn't have rank to fight Ezra one on one. A pirate challenge can only come from someone equal or higher. A first mate can't take on a captain, the same way that a quartermaster can't challenge a first mate. During our brawls at the mines, Jack could kill Ezra if he could find him, but Ezra made sure to stay away."

Gideon chimed in, "There's also a nobility issue with challenging."

I laughed. "Nobility issue? Pirates aren't the most honorable among Humanity."

Nina said, "Challenges are a touchy subject. Depending on the situation, they're looked at by pirates as a move of desperation or a way to mock another ship. If captains or first mates can't overcome an equal rival through traditional means, the only thing left is a challenge. A high-ranking pirate challenging someone of lesser stature in a rival crew is a slight to that ship's captain. Ezra knows that Gideon cares for you, Isabel. He's doing this to mock our captain."

"A fight to the death?"

Jack shook his head. "No, the fight doesn't have to end in someone's death. The victor decides the loser's outcome. Live in shame or die. For pirates, either is the same. There's no reason to think Ezra will spare you."

"I should have challenged Ezra the first day we got here." Gideon's voice was filled with agitation. "But my tattoos wouldn't have helped me beat him, and even if I won, the Pirates of the Black here in camp would never have followed me after such an act. I would've needed to build the trust of these Draco Pirates before committing myself to a challenge. When I beat Naomi after she challenged me, it took her years to regain her stature as a captain of Draco."

"Who's Naomi?"

Nina and Big Jack appeared uncomfortable. After a moment of pause, Gideon answered, "That's a question for another time."

Nina said, "We should have foreseen this challenge. Ezra looked weak and powerless even with his superior numbers after we won the power-ball game. He had no choice. We're in a bad situation here."

I was angry. "You're all talking like I'm already dead. I was an officer conscript in the Athinia State Military for years. I've killed with my bare hands and will do it again tomorrow."

Gideon smiled at me. "The Fireheart in all her fury. I'll be placing a bet on her to win." He lowered his voice. "Ezra's a large brute. He'll overpower you with ease unless you keep moving. He'll charge, and swing his big arms slowly. You must be faster. Jack will help you with that."

Big Jack stepped forward. I looked at him and said, "Jack, the Giant."

He nodded. "Tomorrow morning, you and I will stay here in camp. Mathew's going to the mines for you."

Gideon said, "Aye, I'll fill Jack's quota. You two can train all day. If you can keep away from Jack while tiring him out, Ezra's going to have his work cut out for him."

I stared at Jack again, observing his massive arms and physique, which towered over Ezra and had him beat in kilograms by nearly twenty-seven. The following day would be interesting. One way or another, everything would change.

That evening while lying in bed, I had another nightmare. It wasn't of the civil war or what followed; that night's dream was a fictional forewarning of what was to come of me. Based on that dreadful nightmare my subconscious thought I couldn't win, because I saw Ezra naked and above me. He had my legs spread, and I couldn't get away. His breath was horrid, like the rotten stench of stale food, and the smell of sweat was everywhere. He had me pinned, holding my hands, and I was crying out. To the left and right were Pirates of the Brown staring at me. Geoff, the dead quartermaster, was there too with a mangled body after falling down the mountainside.

Ezra leaned down and whispered into my ear, "We can do this every night for the rest of your pathetic life. You can bear my children. Maybe they'll have green eyes with my strength."

He laughed, and I screamed again. My eyes opened. Nina and Gideon were on either side of me trying to comfort my nerves. They must have seen the uncertainty in my eyes, and Nina wiped my sweat-laced forehead.

Gideon held my hand tightly. "I believe in you, Isabel. You won't admit it, but you have much doubt in your head about tomorrow. Trust in yourself—you can win."

His words slowed my racing heart. I trusted Gideon with my life after everything that happened. I had to face Ezra alone, and that thought made me anxious.

"Thank you both for your concern. It was just another nightmare about my father and the war. Nothing else to worry about."

Both Gideon and Nina looked unconvinced and eyed each other wearily, but neither pressed me further. I fell back asleep until the morning.

Everyone left for camp inspection before going off to the mines. Jack moved the bunks away from the room's center. We had a wide-open space to train. I laughed.

Jack, in his slow speech, asked, "What's so funny?"

"This entire thing is silly to me. One long day of training isn't going to change the outcome for tonight."

Jack crinkled his nose and said, "I see, I see," but before finishing his sentence, he swung his heavy hand at me and slapped my face. It felt like being hit with a bat. I lowered myself and grabbed my throbbing cheek.

"First lesson of the day, always be ready for the unexpected." He smirked.

Before his confident expression diminished, I leaped into the air and punched his nose. He didn't even flinch as blood trickled from both nostrils.

"You won't be hitting Ezra like that. His head's as thick as mine. You need to tire him out first before striking."

Jack swung his arm again, but that time I ducked and spun behind him. Then I moved back, keeping my distance from his abnormally long reach.

Jack smiled. "Good. Every time Ezra takes a jab and misses, he'll exert energy. Make him chase you like a chicken that got out of its coop. His shouts of your cowardice will be endless. Ignore him."

Jack pursued me through the room, teasing me the whole time. "Those wonderful specialty moves you learned in conscript boot camp won't help against Ezra. Pirates of the three worlds fight dirty, like animals, to ensure victory. We taunt and try to distract our enemies into anger."

He lunged forward and wrapped his powerful arms around me. My feet dangled in the air.

"Don't let him get you like this or the fight's over in seconds."

I tried with all my strength to wriggle free in vain.

"Isabel." I stopped struggling and looked at Jack. "If he grabs you in this way, don't hesitate to bite his freaking nose off!"

When he released his massive arms, I dropped to the ground, and he

540

continued chasing me through our bunk for the next few hours. It felt like a strange game of cat and mouse, but my chasing cat was over two hundred kilograms of muscle.

We were sweating and needed a break. I sat on one of the pushed-away bunks, and Jack was on the floor nearby. We shared a bottle of water. I gazed at my feet, thinking of the chances for victory tonight and Jack noticed.

"The biggest thing I can say to help you is heart." He pointed his cucumber-sized finger at my chest.

I turned to him, confused, and repeated, "Heart?"

"Yes, without heart, you can't win. Believe in yourself here." He pointed again. "Most people that I fight lose before we even start. They take one look at me and already believe they have lost because of my size. I'll let you in on a secret that Gideon doesn't even know. His father and I would spar when we served on the *Viathon*. The famous Admiral Derwin, Dolrinion exile, only stands less than one hundred and fifty-two centimeters. I outweigh him by one hundred kilograms, at least, and stand over sixty centimeters taller, but the admiral always won our duels. That man has more heart and desire than every pirate on Draco combined. No matter the odds, he refused to lose. I would grow angry, trying to beat him, and he always won. I know you have heart, I've seen it myself. Before I even knew you were the Rebel Sideris. We all saw your strength on the refugee ship. You refused to give up or back down. The moment we came on board, you fought without fear." Jack took a sip of water. "I believe in you, Isabel Sideris. As Gideon says, you're the Fireheart of the Alliance. Use that fire tonight and believe in yourself."

Jack opening up was a first. He usually never said more than a sentence at a time. I always saw him as a slow, dumb oaf. I was wrong about him, the same way I was wrong about Gideon. I leaned in and wrapped my arms around him.

"Thank you, Jack."

He turned his eyes to the ground, appearing uncomfortable with affection, and it made me smile. He was a big teddy bear with those he trusted. I kissed his cheek, and the temporarily gentle giant stood and went to Gideon's trunk.

He opened it, reached inside, and came back with something in his hand.

"Gideon and I have a gift for you. Something you can use if everything else fails."

He opened his hand; lying in the palm were brass knuckles. "On Draco, we call this a roll of knuckles."

"They're brass knuckles in the Alliance."

"Yes, but brass is weak compared to this metal." He handed it to me. "It's Corin steel, and the knuckles have an internal power source to amplify the punches of the user. Titans' Belt is close to the three worlds, so most pirates have seen more of that metal than people of the Free Worlds. Some of our captains become rich by harvesting or stealing it from rock pickers working the belt."

I slid my fingers into the openings and gripped tightly, making a fist. Jack tapped the metal bar holding the bunk bed next to us and grunted. I lined myself up and lifted my hands. The punch was perfect, and when it connected to the metal, the entire bunk moved across the room and the metal bent with an imprint of the knuckles.

"During our intake process into camp, I noticed that the sentinels barely checked our belongings. Something like this, though …" I paused. "It would be hard to smuggle. How did you get it in?"

Jack grunted. "It was the previous captain's weapon and we found it here. Matthew hid it in the shower room. Gideon thinks the last captain brought it in through someone's butt or lady parts."

I frowned and dropped the knuckles to the floor, wiping my fingers.

Jack laughed in his deep proud voice and said, "Don't worry. Ethan had to clean it before we gave it to you. He wasn't happy, but the lowest man on the totem pole gets the shitty jobs. Do not use it at the beginning of your fight. If Ezra sees it, he'll take it from you. Only use it as a last resort."

I put the knuckles into my pocket and thanked Jack again. The day was winding down, and my heart was racing. Anticipation was the worst part. When committing to an action, whether it be jumping from a tremendous height into water below or charging a battle line through no-man's-land into enemy fire, it was best to do the deed without thought. The more time that passed, the more doubt spilled into my mind, like pouring milk into a bowl of toasted oats. Waiting was more dreadful than the fight.

*

The work crews came back for the night. As usual, they smelled of sweat and sulfur and were drenched in ash and soot. Gideon and Nina peered at Jack and me with a million questions on their faces.

Before they could speak, I said, "We trained all day, and I'm ready."

Nina smirked and turned to Gideon. He took a long breath. "Good. Let's roll it out."

Everyone concealed makeshift weapons of small shanks or sharpened wood under their clothes. Gideon wanted everyone to be ready for Brown treachery because that was their way. I believed Gideon was lying to the crew. If I were losing, he would attack. I could see it in his eye.

I was on the bunk, waiting, like I had been doing for hours. Gideon sat next to me and nudged my arm. He didn't speak and only stared at me for some time.

"There's something I feel guilty about."

Gideon narrowed his eye. "Guilt? For what?"

"I never really knew my kids. Not really. Before the Unification Civil War, I dedicated my time and energy into raising them. Once the war broke out, my focus changed completely." Tuddy's face was in my mind as I continued. "We spent years fighting New-Sparta. Every breath we took went into planning and carrying out attacks. Our kids were nothing but a shadow in the background. Sometimes we left them for days with whatever city-state loyalist family was hiding us at that time. If you asked me right now, I couldn't tell you their favorite food, music, or anything of real importance that I should know as their mother."

Gideon shook his head. "No, you were fighting a lost war against a society that wanted to destroy your family and kids. I believe you had enough justification for the way things played out."

Tears streamed from my left eye. "That was just an excuse that we, as parents, told ourselves to try and justify what we did. The truth was that we knew our children's faces and nothing else. I gave them nothing and didn't raise them the way a real mother would have." I sighed and shook my head. "For years, I lied to myself saying that I knew them, their thoughts, and what they wanted out of life, but that wasn't true at all." I turned to Gideon. "You want to know the truth? I haven't thought of them much since we got to camp. A mother should always think of her children, regardless of their age. A mother should always put their needs and goals ahead of her own. I never did those things, not even once. I might die tonight without ever really knowing them."

Gideon grabbed my hands and said, "Then don't let Ezra win. Beat him, and I promise you we'll leave this wretched world together, and I'll take you to your children. I give you my word."

I laughed under my breath. "Word of a pirate from Draco?"

Gideon ran his hands through his hair and looked into my eye. "Aye. Best you could hope for in a place like this. Besides, I'm a famous captain." He stood, slapped his leg, and screamed, "Alright, you scabs. Listen up." The members of our bunk circled us to listen to their captain. "Isabel might not be the Blood of Draco, but she's earned a place with our crew by doing more deeds of glory than most captains I have ever met. Free, outer and rogue worlds of occupied space know her by different names: the Rebel Sideris." Some yelled out in approval. "The Daughter of Athinia." More bunkmates screamed. "Lieutenant Colonel Sideris, or the city-state loyalist leader." More cheers from others standing nearby. "But me, I don't call her any of these names. She's fire made whole with her passion and heart that rival the Black Skull Admiral himself. Isabel's a survivor, unbreakable, and one who will not cower in defeat. Every Pirate of Draco will echo her name one day as we declare it on this day—Fireheart of the Alliance! The Fireheart's a true warrior that I would follow into hell if she asked me to." He turned to me, "Fireheart, we're with you to the end."

Every pirate inside our bunk screamed with thunderous approval, and the vibrations of their cries shook through my core like lightning. *I am the Fireheart, and Ezra will die by my hands.*

Gideon grabbed my arm, raised it and said, "Isabel Sideris, Draco is with you."

Everyone screamed back, including me, "Draco is with us all."

A chant broke out, "Fireheart! Fireheart! Fireheart!"

I felt my blood boiling with confidence, ready to take on that brown shit-stain pirate.

I looked at Gideon and said, "Banue Na'yah."

Gideon's eyes opened wide with a wild smile of support. "Freedom from tyranny."

All yelled even louder with cries of rage so loud that Dolrinion sentinels would fear the sound. I'd proudly storm a battlefield with those screams of fury. Big Jack raised his hands high and roared a wild cry that made those closest to him cover their ears. He turned and slammed through our bunk door so hard he ripped it right off the hinges. Everyone followed him into the opening like a line of ants running from water. We moved past rows of bunks, still echoing our shouts of pride and unity. Slaves from other bunks joined us doing the same. They all swarmed to me as I led our charge, and I had more confidence than I'd felt throughout my entire life. More slaves came to us on our march to the fighting ground, and I was ready for war.

Ezra was already there with his crew. They had used rocks to form a wide circle. That round area with sand beneath would be our combat ring. All the fear and doubt had left my body, and I stepped into the circle opposite the bearded captain.

Ezra laughed for all to hear and said, "Well, you came. I thought for sure you would try to hide and tremble with the rest of your bunk."

I didn't answer him and moved closer; an outer circle formed made up of the spectators around us. One side were the Pirates of the Brown, and the other, the Pirates of the Black. Above us were several sentinel guard towers with more eyes than usual looking down. The Dolrinions talked amongst themselves, placing bets on the fight.

"Don't worry, Isabel. I'm not going to kill you. I want you to live. When I win, you'll become my prize for the rest of your days. You're moving into my bunk. I'll take you whenever I feel like it. You won't have to watch, no, because I'm going to squeeze that head of yours like a pimple until your other eye pops out. It's a mercy. That way, you won't have to watch all the terrible things we Pirates of Martoosh plan on doing."

His crew laughed, and Ezra glared at me with wide eyes and a large grin. I turned back to Gideon, Big Jack, Nina, and Ethan, who had their chins up high. Gideon nodded.

I looked at Ezra and said, "Are we going to sit around all night talking or fight?"

His expression changed from a cocky smile to an agitated stare, and he moved around the perimeter of the rock circle, lifting his hands into the air, showing me his palms before making fists of them. His eyes became crazed, as they'd looked through most of the time in camp, and he spoke in a faint voice.

"Fresh meat for the grinder. Fresh meat for the grinder. Fresh meat in my bed tonight."

I was moving around the circle the same way he was, keeping my distance, then Ezra lashed in my direction, swinging his big arms, but he missed. I went to the other side of the circle away from him, the way Jack showed me. Ezra came several times, and I continued to dodge him, keeping space between us, and it was clear that the Brown captain was growing annoyed. He stopped at the other end of the circle, turned in the opposite direction and ran the perimeter, following the stone edge, and came right for me. That time he caught me and bashed his fist at my face. I put my arm up, attempting to block it, but it was like stopping a boulder falling down a mountainside. My entire body jerked hard from the force. I brought my leg from behind and kicked him in his stomach, at which he laughed mockingly.

I glanced at Gideon, who had his focus fixed in my direction. Ezra came again; I wasn't fast enough because I lost my footing in the sand. He punched me in the stomach, and I fell, winded. The ache of that hit jolted through my body, and I coughed. Ezra grabbed my arm and pulled me to my feet. Before standing up completely, I drove my knee between his legs. The crazed captain cried noisily in anguish and bent over to grab himself as if that would help. I brought my elbow up rapidly and connected to his mouth and nose. Ezra stumbled back with blood spewing from his mouth. He wiped the thick red liquid away with the back of his hand and became enraged.

Ezra got into a stance that reminded me of a guard from power-ball driving at a runner and charged. I tried to move, but he barreled through my side. I spun violently in the air and fell again. Coarse sand was on my face like sandpaper rubbing on skin. I tried to stand, getting into a prone position, but Ezra came and kicked me in the ribs. We'd switched roles, and I was crying out. Before he could grab me, I rolled and got to my feet putting some distance between us and held my side where a sharp pain jabbed with each breath.

Ezra smiled and said, "Stop resisting me so much. I don't want to tire you out completely. You'll need to be ready for tonight's fun."

His shit-stain pirates laughed again as I yelled, "You punch and kick like a little girl."

Ezra's face turned red, and veins bulged from his head. He charged me once more, and instead of following Jack's sound advice, this time I punched him in the face. He stumbled back, and I hit him again and again, two or three more times, but it was for nothing. Ezra wrapped his arms under me and grappled my body, lifting me off the ground the same way Jack did in the bunkhouse. My damn temper. Ezra had me locked in his arms, and he was squeezing and laughing.

I glanced over at Jack and remembered what he said. My face came down to Ezra's nose, and I sank my teeth deep. As hard as possible, I bit through flesh and bone. Ezra screamed out like a kid in agony, and I kept my jaw tight. He pulled on me and was finally able to throw me away from him. There was a tearing sound like dried leaves in someone's hands. A strangely shaped hole replaced his nose. Crimson blood bubbled as he breathed. Flaps of skin were on both sides of his cheeks where his nose once was. That fleshy knob was in my mouth, and I spat it to the sand and laughed viciously. Blood streamed everywhere on his face, and I felt some of its stickiness on my chin.

"You little bitch."

Ezra grabbed again and headbutted my face a few times; I lost count because the world spun with shooting stars everywhere. He threw me to the sand again. Blood was thick across my face. He came over and grabbed my hair, lifting me into the air, and I dangled for the third or fourth time that day. He used both hands to encircle my head and squeezed.

"Give me your other eye, Isabel."

There was so much pressure from his closing hands and images of Adam, Juliet, Tuddy, and Gideon streaked through my mind. I looked from the corner of my eye and saw Gideon trying to run into the fighting circle, but Jack and Nina held him back. Was this to be my end? The pressure was increasing, such pressure through my head like I was in a vice. Could he really squeeze my eye out as he claimed? No, I would write my own legacy and wouldn't let him beat me in that hellhole of a place. I reached into my pocket and slipped my fingers into the grips in the roll of knuckles.

Screaming with anger, I swung my fist and struck Ezra's face. There was a whizzing sound as the knuckles tripled the force. Ezra's mouth opened wide, and he gasped. I swung again, connecting with his eye socket, and he lost his grip and fell to one knee. There was an imprint of the Corin-steel knuckles on his skin, and his eye was puffy and swelled shut almost instantly. The other eye wandered in confusion; he was still in disbelief. I wrapped my other hand through his beard, gripping the matted hair tightly, then punched him with the knuckles, over and over. Every hit made his body buckle, he was weakening and threatened to fall, but my grip on his beard held him in place as I struck again and again. The rage was intoxicating, and my shouts came with absolute fury. Teeth fell from his mouth to the sand like snowflakes during a winter storm. On my last blow, his beard tore from the force as he collapsed to the sand.

I stared down at that mangled man, watching his struggles for breath, but the images of my horrible dream the night before were vivid, and I realized

I hadn't finished yet. I turned and grabbed the largest rock forming our fighting ring and slowly walked the heavy stone to Ezra. It was difficult to move, and I waddled like a Dolrinion. When I made it to his face and glared down at him, he opened his swollen eyes slowly. With every fiber of strength left in me, I lifted the rock high above. Ezra shouted fearfully just before the huge stone slammed over his face, pushing it down into the sand. His legs and arms twitched for a few seconds, then fell, lifeless. Ezra was dead.

It took me a few moments to realize where I even was, and when I remembered and looked at everyone outside the circle, their faces all told the same story. No one except for the Draco Pirates thought I'd win. The Martoosh Pirates appeared frightened and uncertain of their next move. A faint noise behind drew my attention to Gideon as it grew louder. The Pirates of the Black pounded their chests making a solid thumping sound.

Gideon and his crew chanted, "Fireheart. Fireheart. Fireheart."

Slaves from the Alliance, led by Sven Vlahoses, began another chant: "Banue Na'yah. Banue Na'yah." Bacon was there too, but he only had his mad smile.

I lifted my bloody arms into the air and shouted with pride, "Freedom from tyranny."

Slaves at the other end of the circle parted down the middle as a sentinel captain stormed onto the makeshift fighting grounds staining red around Ezra's squashed head. Sentinels swarmed us in all directions as the guard captain looked at Ezra's body and then me with narrowed eyes.

He spoke orders to the surrounding sentinels. "Take her. She's going to the oven."

Gideon said, "On what charge? She works every day, providing for the Offensive, and always follows your commands. A productive slave, the way you like it."

Bacon walked to my side before the sentinels got near me, and the Burning Star captain laughed.

"You want to go back to the oven again, dummy? Tenth time's the charm, is it?" He turned to Gideon and raised his voice. "No one asked you to speak, slave. Look there." He pointed to the Corin-steel roll of knuckles on the ground. "She has contraband. Slaves aren't permitted weapons in camp. Now, take her."

Bacon wrapped his arm through mine and held his head up high. The captain shook his head. "Fine, take him too, he'll go in the box next to hers."

Gideon said, "You lost money betting against her is what it looks like to me. What's the matter, you can't lose with honor?"

The Dolrinion captain slapped Gideon across his face as the sentinels dragged me away from the circle. I looked back at Ezra to make sure he was dead, then locked my eye on Gideon's single eye.

My Draco pirate had worry across his frowning face and slumped shoulders. His might be one of the last faces I'd ever see before my death came inside a dark, cramped box where thousands had perished before. Bacon smiled at me with a head nod. He was so loyal, and I didn't even know his real name. If Bacon had survived nine times in the oven, I could surely survive once.

CHAPTER 37

+1

You learn something new every day (Mace)

The doctor was looking over his computer scans, and a glow from the screen reflected off his glasses. He took notes from observations but I was becoming impatient. That doctor's office was hardly an office at all. There was a small wooden slab for Jamie to sit on and another bench for family. Doctor Redfrey stood away near the corner while performing his examinations. Any medical equipment used had to be brought in separately for whatever a patient required. He had a small generator providing light to the examination room. Although gloomy, it was the brightest area we'd seen since coming to the Lowlands.

We were lucky. A former Free Worlds doctor who lost his license for writing bad prescriptions to drug addicts lived in the settlement. He had come from Tautrus and moved to Galma to practice medicine. On any rogue planet frequently visited by the Free Worlds, this type of doctor was common.

"Doctor Redfrey, is the baby ok?"

He ignored me and kept writing.

Jamie sighed, and said aggressively, "Hey, you over there with the fancy pen." He stopped writing and glanced at her. "We aren't paying you to ignore our questions."

Doctor Redfrey tapped his pen on the clipboard a few times. "No, you're paying me to ensure that your baby's healthy. This scan was the first ever, and so late in the pregnancy. I must check everything carefully."

Zoey shifted her position in the other corner of the room, keeping a close eye on the doctor's movements.

He said, "Your baby's fine. Perfectly healthy and almost at full term. The head's already down, and the amniotic sac will be ready to rupture within the next week or so. That little baby's coming."

"This shouldn't be possible, and you still haven't answered our question. Jamie only got pregnant four months ago."

Doctor Redfrey chuckled. "You said you came from the mid-crossing near the Stumble Inn, correct?" We nodded. "Then you came through at least fourteen mud settlements to get here. Did you notice every settlement had at least one or two villas? Most settlements make those structures home to Truth Seers, but Masgem alone has at least twenty scattered throughout the settlement, built hundreds of years ago when the Syndicate first came here. Relations station wealthy, Tier One from Civil Earth, one-percenters from the six Colonial worlds, ultra-rich from the Human Alliance and grade-level thirty-two and up from your world Dol'Arem have been coming here for years. Those villas were built by the aforementioned elites so that they or their immediate family members could deliver babies quickly with no need for nearly ten-month pregnancies. In the Lowlands of Galma, it only requires three months for a full-term baby to come yelping into existence. You were already three months pregnant when you came down here. The process quickened."

Jamie was breathing a little faster. "But how?"

Redfrey exhaled extravagantly and said, "The fog. We don't fully understand it, and researchers have been coming down here for hundreds of years trying to determine the process. It's the reason the bugs, plants, and other interesting creatures can grow so large—nutrients in the fog cause it.

For whatever reason, human bodies aren't affected after birth ... that we know of. The Free Worlds Medical Corps believes it has something to do with our genetic makeup. Pregnant women, however, are different. The fog makes their body go into extreme overdrive producing all the hormones that the baby needs to form, happening in a quarter of the time."

Jamie and I looked at each other with excitement and fear. I said, "We learn something new every day down here."

"Could the baby be born right now and be perfectly healthy?" Zoey was blunt.

Doctor Redfrey narrowed his eyes over the display screen one more time and answered, "I don't see any reason why she couldn't be born tonight."

Jamie's eyes lit up and I was speechless and excited. She? He said she, right?

"She ... it's a girl?" Jamie's voice cracked with delight.

The doctor pursed his lips together and said, "Oh, did you not want to know the gender? One thousand apologies."

Jamie smiled, and her eyes were wet. "We have a little girl, Mace."

We kissed. A little girl, how thrilling and amazing; it was hard to handle these emotions. I had thought about this baby every day since Jamie told me she was pregnant. Now we knew—a girl. I hoped she'd look like Jamie.

I turned to Zoey. "Why'd you want to know if the baby could be born right now?"

Zoey hesitated and glanced at the doctor. "Fellas won't wait. Tomorrow morning, the caravan's leaving for the spaceport. The pathway's long with little cover for protection, and it'll take us three days with no other settlements between, and only a few shelters. It'll be hard enough without a baby. If Jamie were to go in labor on the road, her cries of birthing your girl would attract unwanted fog predators. As your security officer, I believe the best option is for the doctor to induce labor now before the morning. He can sell us any additional medication she might need for the healing process. We can't stay here past tomorrow, not with him still chasing us."

"Do you believe he's still after us?"

Jamie said, "They don't give up once the chase begins." She turned to Doctor Redfrey. "Can you accurately predict the delivery time?"

"Yes. With the medications, your baby can come within four hours. You'll spend the night here so we can complete all the necessary checks on both Mom and baby, and in the morning, leave with the caravan, though I would recommend you stay here a few more days. The choice is yours, of course."

"What do you think, Mace?" Jamie turned to me with her eyes wider.

"I think that only a few weeks ago you were still in your first trimester of pregnancy, and now we're deciding to induce labor. If you came to me six months ago and told me this is where I'd be standing today, I would have laughed at you and asked for a taste of whatever drugs you were taking."

Jamie raised an eyebrow and smirked. "Mace Applegate, don't start losing your nerve now. You've been so amazing the last few months and done so much to protect us. Tonight, we'll have our family. The three of us, and Zoey."

Zoey said sarcastically, "Wait a minute, do I get a say in this? I mean the two of you …" She paused. "Family? I'm good with the little nugget, but you two?"

Jamie threw one of the doctor's tools at Zoey, and they both laughed.

The doctor raised his voice. "Ladies, please, those tools are expensive, delicate instruments."

Jamie said, "Well, Doctor Redfrey, you better clean them all and get ready. Give me the meds. Let's bring this baby into the world."

The doctor nodded again and left the room.

I said, "Fellas should be back before the night ends with news of our ship."

Zoey's stern face returned. "Hopefully, he doesn't take your money and leave. You gave him so much and put trust in that weasel."

Jamie rubbed her belly and smiled then raised her head to Zoey. "No, he won't screw us over. He depends on his business down here, and we paid him extra money to find us a working ship."

I agreed with Zoey, but a fight with my wife before she gave birth to our daughter wasn't the way to go.

*

Doctor Redfrey said loudly, "Push! You're doing so well."

Jamie screamed. Her forehead was drenched in sweat and her face was red. I held her hand, and Zoey assisted the doctor using her paramedical skills as a Capitol Security officer. The entire situation felt surreal, like an out-of-body experience with me witnessing everything from above.

The doctor said, "Good, now take a breath and relax for a moment. The head's starting to appear. You're almost there."

Jamie cried out, and Doctor Redfrey said, "Now push."

Jamie's screams were even louder. She was having such a difficult time. Tears streamed from her eyes as she held her breath and pushed again.

Zoey said, "That's it. The head's out."

Doctor Redfrey smiled. "Yes, now time for the shoulders. Take a quick breath and do it again, push with all of your might."

"Ready? One, two, three, push."

Jamie cried out as she struggled. Our little one was out and crying, so beautiful and precious.

I kissed Jamie's forehead. "You did it, babes. You were amazing."

Jamie was crying with emotion, excitement, and adrenaline. She said, "Oh, my precious daughter."

Zoey handed me scissors after clamping the umbilical. "Dad, cut the cord."

I took the scissors in my hand and hesitated. My heart was racing—flashes of my life zipped into my mind like a fast-traveling river, and then this precious moment, what a significant and important event.

My daughter was alive. The Corporation didn't win; she wasn't aborted into oblivion like countless wanted pregnancies before her. We fought to have her and won. I had a child now and loved her so much within minutes. I cut the cord, and the doctor took her and placed that small, fragile body on the scanner. The computer spent a few seconds checking her over and cleaning any contaminants.

"A perfectly healthy baby girl, fifty-five and a half centimeters long, three kilograms. Congratulations, Mom and Dad."

Zoey took our baby and placed her on Jamie's chest. "This part's important. Let her feel your skin and hear your heart beating."

Our little one grabbed Jamie's finger with her small hand. Jamie looked down and then at me. "She's perfect, Mace. Our baby girl."

Doctor Redfrey said, "What's her name? I need it for the paperwork."

Jamie and I locked eyes and sat quietly for a few moments, and then we both looked at our daughter.

Jamie's smile widened as if a thought came to her. "Emma, her name's Emma Brook Applegate."

"Brook? After my mother?" I was surprised.

Jamie's eyes went back to Emma. "Yes, your mother was an amazing woman and raised a great man. She taught me so much before she died."

Smiles filled the room, and I hugged my wife and baby Emma. We held each other for a few moments before the doctor spoke.

"Dad, please take Emma, I need to stitch Mom up and then start the antibiotic and pain medication treatment." Doctor Redfrey turned to Jamie. "I'll give you enough medicine to hold you over for a week. After that, you'll need to find another doctor for further evaluations. The pain meds will make you a little loopy for tonight, and tomorrow you'll be fine."

Zoey said, "Formula. We'll need formula in case Jamie has trouble breastfeeding on the pathway. There won't be any other way to feed Emma out there in the fog."

The doctor said, "No problem. I'll supply a week's worth, but I recommend feeding her from your breast—we have enough artificial foods in the Free Worlds. Let the baby have something real. I do have sterilized pacifiers, too, for an extra fee, of course."

I spoke sharply. "No problem, Doctor, thank you."

That guy was only worried about getting paid.

Jamie looked up at me with tears of joy in her eyes and said, "Mace, I can't believe she's here. We have a baby girl."

Zoey grinned and got closer to us. "You both have blue eyes. Genetically your little girl has a ninety-nine percent chance of having that color if my memory from genetics class is right."

Emma's eyes were gray and would remain that neutral color for some time, but I couldn't wait to see them turn blue, and was slightly impatient to watch her grow up and be a part of our family. "As long as she looks like Jamie, everything will be fine."

Emma made a sucking noise while she chewed on her little fingers.

Jamie said, "I want her to have your temperament. That's important to me."

We stared at baby Emma and kissed. I took Emma in my arms and walked through the dismal doctor's office, talking to my daughter.

"Hello, little nugget. I'm your poppa. One day, when you get older, your mother and I will tell you all about the crazy things that happened to bring you into this world. Don't worry, we'll wait until you're old enough, it's a frightening tale. I'm not sure when that will be, because this story scares the crap out of me now, as an adult. But don't worry, you'll be stronger than both of us, Emma Brook Applegate."

Emma made funny noises taking puffs of air into her small chest as I continued. "Everything that happens does so with purpose. Life has a funny way of working itself out sometimes. One thing you can always know with certainty is that your mother and I love you more than words can describe, and we will always do everything in our power to protect you. I promise."

From the corner of my eye, I could see Jamie's lips shiver as she wiped tears of happiness away.

Doctor Redfrey finished his work and told us to stay there for the night. He would come in a few times periodically to make sure Jamie and the baby were ok. He gave Jamie drugs to help her sleep and something for the pain. After feeding Emma, Jamie fell fast asleep. I was holding Emma in my arms as she sucked on a pacifier with her eyes closed. Being born was hard work, it would seem, because that little nugget slept a lot.

Zoey was on a bench across from us with her back against the wall, and she was asleep too. I walked around the room for some time but then started nodding off myself with Emma in my arms. Before closing my eyes, I woke to Jamie making loud noises in her sleep. Zoey jumped to her feet and drew her firearm. Once she realized the sound was only Jamie, she re-holstered her weapon. As I stood next to Jamie with Emma, Zoey approached.

"The medication will give her strange dreams."

I said, "It sounds more like nightmares."

Jamie was in a deep trance, and her head moved from side to side. She mumbled out loud, "No, I'm not, no, we shouldn't, please, but, oh, oh. Help."

I held her hand, watching her eyes move under the lids. Jamie mumbled again, "Not my family, no. You can't."

Zoey placed a hand on Jamie's shoulder. "It sounds like she's dreaming of the Federate Corporation finding you three."

I felt uneasy. "I'd gladly sacrifice myself to the chamber so Jamie and Emma could live. I want you to promise me something, Zoey."

Our professional bodyguard raised her head with pride, listening. "If there's a chance that someone might try to take us, do everything in your power to protect Jamie and Emma. Don't worry about me. I come last in this group—first Emma, then Jamie."

Zoey looked at the baby, and Jamie, then to me.

"If something should happen that drastic, I'll sacrifice myself before allowing any harm to come to you. It's the job I signed up for when I took my oath of office under the dome inside the forum. I'm a Capitol Security officer for the relations station. I swear that oath of protection to you and your family."

I smiled and said, "The relations station lost its best security officer when they removed you. That much is clear."

Zoey's eyes went to the floor, filled with uncertainty. "If I could go back and do everything in my life all over again, I might have made different choices, I won't deny that. However, after you freed me and risked your safety to save me not once but twice, I realize that you, Jamie, and that little one, are the closest thing I've ever had to family in my life. The relations station can kiss my ass."

We both laughed as the door swung open, slamming against the back wall. Fellas came in, long-faced and breathing heavily.

Zoey was defensive. "Damn it, Fellas."

He didn't even react to her and glared at me. "Scouts just reported to guardians at the main gate. There's a MERC Guild agent and mongrel on the pathway. The agent had it out with the same Scoffs we did. He'll be here soon, and secondary scouts from the last settlement we came from said he's looking for three people, a pregnant woman, a man, and an angry short brunette. What the hell did you three do?"

Zoey replied, "Four, there are four of us now."

Fellas peered down at baby Emma and said, "Great, a crying baby on the path with Scoffs, fog predators, and now a MERC Guild agent. Nothing about this is good." He shook his head. "Nope, not happening. I know a bad gamble when I see one."

Fellas reached into his pocket and placed a PDD on the table.

"Here, you're now the owners of a transport junker. The PDD will direct you to your ship's dock at the port. The registration's good, so the ship will activate when you get inside with that device. You know where to go from here. I'm done with the lot of you. Take care, Tasty Mace."

I tried to protest, but before any words came from my mouth, Fellas left us. Zoey was already packing up the medical supplies left by Doctor Redfrey, and she gathered our bags.

"What are you doing?"

Zoey said quickly, "We're leaving. The agent's almost on us, and he knows where we're going." She pulled pistol magazines from her vest, staring at them. Three of the four were empty, and the other was only half full.

"I'm low on ammunition, Mace. We need to get to that ship and hope it can clear the atmosphere." Zoey picked up the PDD, scrolled through the screen, then handed it to me.

I glanced at the information on the screen. "Great, this transport's one hundred and thirty years old and hasn't had a maintenance checkup in ten years. We're in for an interesting ride."

Zoey said, "All we need to do is get past the planet's rings. Once we jump into FTL, all the technology in the Free Worlds won't help him to track us. He isn't a Frontiersman, so that's our play."

She pulled a wheelchair with thick mechanical wheels forward. I felt uncomfortable.

"The doctor won't mind if we borrow it. Give me the baby and put Jamie in the chair."

There was a display screen on the wheelchair that had a follow mode. I put Jamie in the wheelchair, Zoey gave Emma back to me, and we left the office. When we arrived at the southern settlement gate, several guardians blocked the entrance. All had hard stares and narrowed eyes.

The captain stepped closer. "What are you doing?"

Zoey said, "What does it look like? Open the gate."

"Not going to happen. You don't have an escort. The port's too far from here to go alone. We require escorts for White Eyes."

Zoey drew her firearm, and the guardians lifted their spears and bows.

I raised a hand to plead with them. "Captain, please, if we don't leave right now, we'll be dead before the morning. We're safer out there than we are in here."

He stared at me, Jamie, Zoey, and baby Emma, pondering his options. "That agent making his way here. He's coming for you?" I nodded, and the captain continued. "Open the gate. Let 'em through."

Zoey and I opened our eyes wide, and he said, "We do not like Free Worlds agents down here. They always make a mess of things when they're trying to hunt down bounties. I'd rather see you on a ship leaving the Lowlands than getting into a confrontation with him and his beast in my settlement."

Zoey holstered her pistol and we moved through the open gate.

I turned back to the gate. "Thank you, sir. We promise never to return to the Lowlands or this planet again."

We moved off on the pathway, and fear crept down my spine. One security officer with ten bullets, my wife unconscious and me holding a newborn baby walking for three days with a MERC Guild agent pursuing us, fog predators, and Scoffs everywhere. What could possibly go wrong?

CHAPTER 38

Shadows

A long night in the study (Henry)

My entire team was in my home office all day. We were preparing for the inquiry during closed session with my fellow representatives and the dome legal team. What a mess that situation had turned into. Distracted by my own arrogance and my cheating wife, I believed that the refugee dock incident would blow over like a feather in the wind. *Actions come with consequences.*

Malcolm said, "Someone will need to be held responsible for taking Adam and Juliet. Inquiries never conclude without someone taking the fall. The forum spends too much money stoking the fire and magistrates and lawyers salivate at a chance to prove their importance for all to see. It won't end without someone to blame. We can sit here throwing questions at Representative McWright to prepare him, but at the end of the day, someone's going down."

Stacy replied, "The senior agent who ordered the dock agents. Can't we place the blame on him?"

Stacy was naïve to the inner workings of what Malcolm, Ficco, and I did behind the curtain. It was true that Ficco went beyond my initial orders, but what had I really asked him to do? If he had come to me and said he saw them in the dock, but either the Pride or station security got them, my wrath would have broken this station into two pieces. Losing Ficco would be a tremendous blow. He did the right thing. Stacy didn't understand. She's not allowed behind closed doors with the likes of Oliver, Josue, Malcolm, and Ficco.

"That won't suffice. Senior Agent Ficco will be the next chief agent in the Guild. He has had an outstanding career thus far, and we need him for the future."

Three additional junior aides were in the room, taking notes and sitting quietly. They hadn't contributed to our discussion and seemed worthless. Was it fear or stupidity that kept them quiet, I wondered? Malcolm turned on the television screen and changed the channel to the relations station twenty-four-hour news. A newscaster was already speaking.

"Tomorrow's closed session inquiry will shed light on where Adam and Juliet Sideris are currently residing. There are endless accounts of their location. We won't speculate without proof. One fact we can report is that Center Seat Representative Henry McWright is responsible for this current fiasco taking shape under the dome. The five walls of the Capitol Forum will have their work cut out for them to ease rising tensions between the Free Worlds. In other news, leading charity organization from the Colonial Accord, Humanity's Hope, has had numerous transport ships disappear recently. Owners of the company, Paavo and Molly Duray, were asked to comment but refused. Our station has tried to obtain public records on how many ships returning from Galma disappeared but were unable to get an exact number. Estimates range from five to ten lost with all hands. The MERC Guild's investigating the cause, while senior leadership within the secretary of defense's office under Station Director Houlton blame the Frogmen of Gliese."

Malcolm turned off the screen and said, "Did you all hear that? Center Seat Representative Henry McWright is responsible for this current fiasco.

That's completely unacceptable. Every one of you is here to make sure what we just saw doesn't happen. Why are we paying you if you cannot perform your duties properly?"

An attractive young junior aide I had never seen before stood. She had youthful ebony skin and long straight hair. Her light eyes shone brightly, and she was beautiful, wearing Colonial business attire, but put together in a way that reminded me of myself. *Always dress in your suit of armor before stepping into the battlefield of station politics.* She was younger than Alyssa but older than Juliet—a perfect specimen.

Malcolm and Stacy watched her curiously. She held her shoulders high with confidence. "Representative McWright, the answer's here in this room."

Everyone wore some form of confused expression and looked around my office.

Before I could react, Malcolm said, "What are you talking about?"

She paced from one end to the other. "Who's missing right now? Someone involved with all the inner workings of your office who spent the last five years at your left side."

"Benjamin."

She smirked and nodded. "That's right. I've gone over all internal reports from the dock incident. If I'm not mistaken, your PDD was on call forwarding that day."

Malcolm raised his eyebrows with approval and glanced at me. I turned back to look at her perfect shape and asked, "What's your name?"

She stopped moving right in front of me. "Jordan, Jordan Corda, sir."

Stacy said, "Jordan started working for our office a few days after Benjamin's disappearance, sir. She's from Lars with a business and legal degree from the University of Uropa. Jordan previously served on the legal team in Chair Newfield's office on Lars."

Newfield was newer to the unions, working with Alliance of Mass Transit, for the Labor Party, and resided on the same planet as our Angry Tigress, Christine Keng. Newfield was once a Thorn with the Rose Party of Ardum, but after a misfortune with the flowers, he switched sides and became a dominant force with the unions against the Roses. Rose of Enduring, pathetic, all of them.

I stared at Jordan and she peered back through her lashes with a flirtatious smile.

"My favorite wine is from Lars."

Jordan snickered. "New Greta is everyone's favorite wine, sir."

I laughed. "Everyone who can afford it, that is."

Jordan tilted her head and raised one eyebrow. "The famous white and red of New Greta isn't the only wine made there. They also have New Greta blush for people of less privileged means. The wine is no less discerning."

She gained my interest rather fast. "Never heard of New Greta blush wine before."

Jordan stepped closer. "If you can afford to drink their vintage red, there wouldn't be a reason to try another."

I stood and said, "You have piqued my interest. I'll be following up with you regarding the wine." I turned. "Malcolm, investigate how we can use Benjamin as a fall for the inquiry. Everyone else, I bid you farewell. Get a good night's rest—tomorrow everyone needs to be at their best."

They filed out one at a time. Stacy cleared her throat. "Sir, do you truly want to use Benjamin as a pawn? What if he returns? He's been a loyal, hardworking aide for years."

The other two junior aides left, but Jordan kept her gaze at me, smiling. When our eyes locked, she rubbed her hands down her thighs before stepping out of the room. I'd need to spend more time with that one when I got a chance.

I turned back to Stacy. "We need to use any tool available. Fear not, I'd never do anything to endanger anyone working for me. Benjamin's the sixth aide to disappear in the last year. None of them have returned thus far. Based on that evidence, I don't believe we'll see him again. Speaking of which, will you please prepare a letter for me to send to his father. We grew up together, and I've not yet reached out."

Stacy hesitated and seemed uncomfortable. "Yes, Representative

McWright, I'll take care of the letter right away. Thank you, sir."

Malcolm remained with me, and he closed the door, waiting to ensure all had gone. Oliver was at the other corner standing firm. Malcolm took a seat and locked his eyes on the ceiling, something he always did when deep in thought.

"What are we going to do about your wife? She's emotional and dangerous."

I shook my head. "No, I always kept her at a distance from things that happen in rooms like these. She only knows what I want her to know."

Malcolm glanced at Oliver. "She needs to pay for what she did. It's open betrayal on a level greater than anything else."

"Ollie, what do you believe should be our course of action?"

"Nothing for now, sir. You already had one wife die. It would look suspicious for another to pass, even if by natural means."

Malcolm gave me an antagonistic smile. "Does being blown out of an airlock into space count as natural?"

"My only concern for Representative McWright is that Alyssa's actively looking for a way to get even with him. First, she was angry about him leaving on her birthday. Then she was angry because he brought a more attractive, younger woman into the residence, and Alyssa sees the way our center seat looks at her. Now Pietro tells us she's trying to sleep with the people in Representative McWright's life."

Malcolm furrowed his brow in my direction, and I said, "Alyssa tried to seduce Adam Sideris in my living room. I thought that was comical and would've loved to see her face when he turned her down."

Malcolm said, "I don't understand—how are you certain Adam would turn her down?"

"Adam came on to me only an hour earlier that night. He's gay." Malcolm leaned forward showing more interest. That was an idea—I should put those two in a private room together. I got up. "Don't worry about Alyssa trying to sleep with people in my life. There's no one close to me that would touch her, especially now that Benjamin's gone. Sex is Alyssa's biggest weapon. It's how she snared me all those years ago. Malcolm, speak to Ficco about the call forwarding from that day. See if there's something his Cyber Guild agents can do to assist. I need to eat and relax now."

"Yes, sir. I'll take care of it. Have a good night."

Malcolm left my office down the back staircase that led into the living room. I looked at Oliver.

"You've saved me time after time, and I've lost count. Good work, Ollie. Good work, indeed."

Oliver looked at me seriously and said, "It's been my life's honor to serve you, sir. You can always count on me."

We exited into the hallway from my upper office and walked down a second staircase that led to the utility room. There was a secret emergency exit that had a direct route down to the basement next to my laundry machines. Capitol Security Protection Services had installed the exit when I became a representative. In the basement where the lift doors opened was a small passenger train car that could transport me to a dome security outpost inside the main cylinder. I rarely used that staircase and only went down there to change my clothes in the utility room. I didn't feel like wearing a three-piece suit anymore that day. There was shouting in the kitchen and, after changing, I went out to see what the fuss was all about.

Alyssa and Juliet were at it again. They yelled at each other from across the raised island in the kitchen center. I only caught the tail end of that word game.

Alyssa shrieked with rage. "Listen here, you thief, don't touch what doesn't belong to you again. Do you understand?"

Juliet screamed, "Your stuff's slutty. I wouldn't touch it if you paid me."

Alyssa slammed her hand on the counter. "You little shit."

Juliet saw me and smiled, changing her demeanor completely, and spoke softly as if Alyssa wasn't even there. "Oh, hey, Henry. How was your day today?"

Alyssa's face turned beet red. She was in a dress cut low in the front, exposing her skin.

"Hello, ladies. What's going on here? Alyssa, are you going out?"

She gave me a grudging stare. "Your house guest here is stealing my clothes."

Juliet laughed. "Alyssa, two things: one, I can't fit into your clothes—you're heavier than me, and those tits are way bigger than mine. Two, even if I could fit into your outfits, I wouldn't be caught dead wearing something like, well, like that." Juliet curled her lip.

Alyssa's face puffed up in total rage. She grabbed a fork from the table and threw it at Juliet. The silverware struck her face and sliced her cheek. Slow dabs of blood lightly dripped down Juliet's face. For the first time since I met the young Sideris, her expression was completely dark. Alyssa stepped back looking shocked.

Juliet wiped the blood from her face and said, "You know, on Epsilon Prime, blood gets paid for with blood. When someone fights against another and fails, the victor will cut the pointer and middle finger from both the loser's hands so they can never take up arms against the winner again. There's a religious reason for leaving a few fingers. Did you know that, Alyssa?"

Alyssa's eyes opened wide, and she stepped back and turned to me but quickly turned away, realizing I wouldn't assist. Then she looked at Pietro and said, "Are you just going to stand there? You're my protection, and this little devil just threatened me."

Pietro stepped into the kitchen, observing the situation and the fresh cut on Juliet's face. "Ma'am, I've had years of training with Capitol Security, and I believe you're in no danger right now. Furthermore, it's my recommendation that we leave the residence as you initially intended before anything further happens."

I smirked at Pietro; he had proven himself to be precisely the kind of officer I needed in my service. Alyssa rolled her eyes and left with Pietro in tow.

"Where are you going tonight, my love?"

Alyssa said, "Oh, are you worried about your wife's safety now, Henry? I'm spending the night with people who truly care about me, and I won't be returning until the morning."

I spoke louder. "And where might that be?"

She turned back to me before leaving. "Hadlee's having a gathering at her house tonight with friends. I'll be spending the night there. You're welcome to join me if you'd like."

The door slammed closed, and my thoughts drifted to what Hadlee did at her gatherings. Alyssa knew I'd never go with her to one of those get-togethers because if I saw another man stick his prick anywhere near her, I'd … *No. Keep those thoughts tucked away.* Pietro's report the following day would be exciting, without a doubt.

Juliet ran to me and hugged me, pulling my arms around her body.

"You saved me, Henry. Thank you."

Her body felt perfectly fit, and she smelled fabulous. I needed to gain control because movement between my legs would be noticeable. I stepped back and went to the refrigerator for a cold drink. Adam came into the kitchen. He held a heavy-looking black garbage bag with thick bulges.

Juliet said, "Where were you? You didn't hear me getting into an argument with Alyssa?"

Adam's face was flush, and he replied, "I … I was busy."

He appeared uncomfortable, and I noticed fur on his shirtsleeve. Adam quickly opened the compactor and threw the bag inside. A crunching noise came from the trash compacting into its holder.

"Juliet," I said, "let me clean that cut, so it doesn't get infected."

Adam narrowed his eyes looking at Juliet's face. "Your wife did that to her?"

Juliet laughed and skipped closer. "Yes, but it was worth it." She looked at me. "Did you see her face when I said that stuff about the fingers on Epsilon Prime? It was priceless. I think she might have peed a little bit from fear."

I was curious. "Did you mean what you said? Would you have cut her fingers off?"

Juliet shrugged. "Maybe, maybe not. I didn't put much thought into it."

"And what about Alyssa's clothes? Did you take them?"

Juliet glanced at both Adam and me with a mischievous grin. "Well, Alyssa leaves her things all over the apartment. Every so often, I take something and bring it downstairs to some of the less fortunate living in your bubble. There's a donations bin in the lobby of this apartment building. Did you know that, Henry?"

"Now I do." I paused; a headache was starting to form. "Tomorrow will be a tough day on my brain. I'm going to take my food up to the study and remain there for the night. Will you two be ok for the evening?"

"We're fine. I'm going to spend the night in my room too. I'm exhausted today."

Something had Adam troubled. If things went well tomorrow, I planned on spending the night with him working on his issues. Through discreet inquiries, I'd found a night worker that would keep any relations quiet. That was important. No one could know, because the Green Eyes of Athinia were rebel royalty and marriage pacts were of the utmost importance on Epsilon Prime. It would be hard to form a marriage alliance if he was seen sleeping around.

Juliet said, "Well, it looks like it's a jammies night for me watching TV in bed."

She gave me a flirtatious smile. If I didn't know any better, I would think she was inviting me to her room, which interested me.

I grabbed some artificial food from the dispenser and took the spiral staircase to the master bedroom, which I had not slept in for a month. The room seemed disheveled. The jewelry bin on the dresser was open, and next to it was the priceless necklace I bought for her birthday. When I opened the box, the glowing blue light emanating from each gemstone sparkled and reflected off my shirt. The image of Benjamin choking Alyssa with that necklace appeared vividly in my mind. I took the necklace and placed it in my pocket. Alyssa didn't need it any longer. The damn thing was entirely too expensive to waste it on a cheating whore like her. Even though she said she was spending the night at Hadlee's home, I didn't fully believe her, so I decided to throw items on the bed and make it appear as if I was sleeping there. If she stumbled home drunk, she'd never come into bed with me already there, especially now.

I smiled, looking at the body outline under the covers and said to myself, "Small victories lead to positive results."

*

The hour grew late; it was after midnight. I'd been reviewing reports and trying to find leverage over my fellow representatives based on recent happenings through the Free Worlds and its outlying territories. The Dolrinions and Federates shouldn't be a concern. Civil Earth, the Alliance, and JJ were a different matter altogether.

While looking over numerous reports from the forum and the Colonial government, I saw an internal investigation into the missing Force Command Steel Talon expedition battle group. Colonial Accord intelligence services wrote that General Bonnavitte, Sharpeye of the DMZ, was commanding a battle group when it disappeared without a trace. The last location placed the vessels outside our satellite observation grid that connected every free, outer, and rogue world in occupied space. The observation grid was how we kept such accurate communications and ship locations. Millions of gifted engineers maintained the network daily. If I made it through the following day's dilemma, I wanted to investigate what happened and why that battle group disappeared. It troubled me that an entire military contingent loaded with destroyers, war barges, battleships, cruisers, frigates, light gunships, and a general's flagship could vanish. It happened before Gliese and it didn't make sense that the Corporation would attack so far away from the DMZ, and honestly, they couldn't remove an entire battle group with ease, and with no one escaping to speak of it. The Corporation wasn't that advanced. Who had the power to take on such a force?

There was a sound in the bedroom; someone was on the spiral staircase. Was Alyssa home after all? I wasn't sure I had it in me to watch her with another man, again. But the foyer door never opened. Was Juliet coming up? I would've enjoyed a late-night call from her.

I went to the railing and looked down into the bedroom to see two shadowy figures standing near the foot of the bed. After a moment, the entire room lit up with flashes of yellow light. Suppressed weapons fire. They shot into the outlined shape that was supposed to be me. One of them pulled the blanket down and saw that I wasn't there. Those assassins tried to kill me.

How did they get past the guards? Maybe the back terrace, or skylights?

I backed up slowly to my desk and reached inside the drawer where a small revolver lay. Dad taught me how to shoot when I was a young lad. My body shook as adrenaline coursed through my veins. Loud gunshots rang out downstairs. One of my security officers was engaged, and my heart sank into my guts. Everything to that point didn't feel real, but the explosions of weapons fire brought me back to reality. I turned and gasped at a shadow in the doorway. I was about to raise the pistol when the computer screen light showed me Oliver's face.

He brought his finger to his lips and showed me his wristwatch, which was flashing red. Ollie pointed to my arm, and I remembered. Each representative had a tracking chip embedded under their wrist. I pushed down three times, and my forearm blinked with red pulses of light under the skin. A notification had gone to Capitol Security Protection Services, Emergency Response Team. I wasn't sure how quickly they'd come.

We heard footsteps coming from the back staircase to the utility room. No one should come from there.

Oliver went to the entrance door and lowered himself closer to the floor. He peeked out to look down the staircase and fired his weapon. There was a thud as someone died on the stairs, and I felt relieved, but there were more flashes of light. The shadow assassins were numerous. Oliver pulled a grenade from his inner jacket, yanked on the pin, and tossed it down the stairs. He grabbed my arm and led me down the opposite staircase leading into the living room.

Additional gunshots, this time fainter, originated from the Green Eyes' rooms. I was concerned for their safety. We reached the hallway; the kitchen was on the opposite side.

I whispered to Oliver, "Adam and Juliet."

He kept his focus and quickly said, "Josue's defending them. We need to get you out of here, sir."

"No, these killers aren't here for me. I was secondary to them. They're here for the Sideris bloodline," I insisted defensively.

Zachery Laskaris speaking with me about the Lyons Twins seeking revenge because I took them in the dock blared in my mind. Maybe they were here for me after all. Oliver pulled my neck down and reached over, firing his pistol several times. More flashes through the dark rooms, and I heard bullets strike the wall above me. Ollie had saved me. Those rounds would've hit their mark if he hadn't pulled on my neck.

More gunfire from the hallway where Adam's and Juliet's rooms were. Every time the room brightened, I saw two shadows standing there, engaging Josue. They didn't notice Oliver and me on the other side of the living room. Ollie tapped my shoulder and pointed to the assassin on the left side. I brought my revolver up and closed one eye, aiming at the sneak's body. Oliver did the same with the other assassin. He held up three fingers, then two, and finally one. We fired our weapons several times. Oliver's target fell instantly. The one I shot at stumbled, and Ollie assisted in bringing him down.

My protector, who had spent years with me, grabbed another grenade and tossed it into the living room near the television. He told me to cover my eyes, and we ran as the entire room erupted into a flurry of blinding lights. We were now in the hallway that led to the Sideris bedrooms. Josue came with both Green Eyes, and I was grateful they weren't hurt. Adam had a knife in his hand and both arms were dark red as if he put his arms into huge cans of tomato sauce. It appeared he had taken out one of the killers in a grotesque manner.

"Josue, take Adam and Juliet to my emergency lift. Don't leave their side."

Josue appeared uncomfortable and glanced at Oliver, who nodded. They ran past the kitchen and into the back hallway leading into the utility room. The foyer area lit up, and rounds struck the wall behind Adam and Juliet. Oliver threw another grenade into the foyer, and more flashes came from other rooms nearby. I heard wisps pass my head, and a slight breeze from the bullets that barely missed me. Ollie pulled me into the kitchen behind the island.

He fought numerous assassins in different directions. Was it two or a dozen? It was too dark to tell. They were on all sides, and there seemed to be many of them judging by the numerous flashes. Oliver fired with such focus, a true craftsman in the art of war. It all seemed to go on for hours, but in truth, it was only a few brief moments. An object, round and dark, fell behind the island at my feet. What was that? Oliver saw it and shouted as he moved to cover me, but a bright flash blinded both of us. Everything turned white, I couldn't see anything other than a blur, and there was a deafening ring in my ears.

Someone grabbed my arm and dragged me away from the island. As my vision returned, I saw Oliver lying on the kitchen tile with blood coming from his eyes, mouth, and a hole in his head. Ollie was dead, and I could see his killers. They were in black from head to toe wearing tactical vests, pressurized suits resembling scuba gear, optical lenses, and compact rebreathing respirators. That gear was easily some of the most advanced technology available in the Free Worlds and it was impossible to know if they were young, old, male or female. I guessed that they must have space walked outside our embassy bubble and gained entry somehow.

They dragged me into the living room near my couch and slapped me to the floor like a piece of meat. One of them, shorter than the other by a few centimeters, had their lenses fixed on me, and I gazed back without fear. I spat, and the faceless body tilted its head to the side then punched my mouth. Blood pooled on my tongue and leaked from the sides of my mouth. Although I couldn't see their faces, I imagined them with smiles as they watched. They pulled me to my knees, and one stepped behind. My eyes adjusted to the lighting; other assassins were off to the sides in several different rooms. The shorter one walked circles around me in silence. The entire place was eerily quiet for what felt like an eternity. My faceless executioner stopped walking and raised a suppressed pistol to my head. This was it, the end of a long duty-bound life of service to the unions of the Labor Party, an accomplished representative to the relations station, and arguably the greatest politician in Colonial history, by my own standards. All of that was going to end in a dark room with killers I couldn't fully see—a bunch of pricks, all of them.

Enough waiting. "Well, do it already. What are you waiting for? I make my fate here. You have my permission to kill me, twat. It's my decision now, not yours."

The assassin's head tilted again, likely deciding if I had gone mad. A massive explosion went off above in the skylights and at the terrace sliding door. Streaks of bright hot light shot out in multiple directions like rain, no, it was like a Colonial Marine Hellfire on a smaller scale. One of the assassins jerked several times and blips of blood sprang like volcanoes from each round that penetrated armor and flesh. My executioner had disappeared into the shadows with others as more streaks flew in multiple directions.

Heavily armored tactical soldiers came from every entrance of the apartment. Capitol Security ERT was there, and at the sight of their pentagon emblem with its five stars crested across their chest plates I experienced the greatest relief I'd felt in recent memory. Oliver was one of them before taking a position with me. I glanced at his body and those cold, empty, dead eyes looking in my direction. His blood was making its way towards me. Even in death, Oliver tried to get by my side. He was the best protector and cleaner in my service since I started a career in politics.

A commanding officer came and held a scanner above my wrist. She spoke. "Representative McWright, are you injured?"

I shook my head, hearing gunfire upstairs and in the utility room.

"Come with us, sir. We'll keep you safe."

"Adam and Juliet Sideris went with Josue down to the train."

"We already have them in the main cylinder. Come with us. The area isn't secure yet."

*

The lights of my apartment were all on, and it looked like a war zone on a rogue world. Blast powder burns littered the floor and walls, bullet holes were everywhere, spent shell casings were sprinkled around like a broken piñata at a child's party, and shards of glass on the carpeting were stained with blood. A swarm of Capitol Security, Colonial investigators, representative officials, MERC Guild detectives with their mongrels, and Senior Agent Ficco were there conducting their business. Juliet and Adam were on the couch across from me.

Senior Agent Ficco asked, "Are you ok, sir?"

"Who were these shadow assassins, Lyons Pride?"

Ficco turned back at one of the bodies for a moment. "Facial recognition hasn't determined yet. They're not in our database. Technically, they could be from the Syndicate, pirates from the three worlds, Defender Corps from Civil Earth, Thorns from the Rose Party of Ardum, Human Alliance, or Frogmen from Gliese, for all we know. Hell, they might be one of the rival unions from the Labor Party."

I narrowed my eyes at him, and he swallowed deep.

"Not long ago, Zachery Laskaris warned me in my back office that a reckoning was coming. He said that I wasn't the only powerful person within the Free Worlds who could make things happen." My ears burned hot with rage as I raised my voice. "Isaac and Killian Lyons did this."

Ficco shrugged. "More than likely, it was, but without proof, we've got nothing but conjecture."

MERC Guild agents were with Adam and Juliet, interviewing them, and some of the other eyes in my apartment seemed taken back by Adam's blood-covered arms and splats of red on his shirt.

Ficco glanced over at the Green Eyes. "Adam did a number on one. Before Josue got to their hallway, one of these ninjas got into his bedroom. Adam was waiting for the bastard and stabbed him enough times that you wouldn't even have realized it was a person. Seriously, the soldier looks like roadkill. Adam had to have stabbed him one hundred times, and at least half were in his face. That fella has some demons in his closet."

"We all have demons, senior agent."

Adam stared coldly into the middle distance as if he wasn't here right now and off in a dream as the agent asked questions fruitlessly.

I pulled Ficco away from the ears that might be listening and said, "Did Malcolm reach out to you about tomorrow?"

"We're prepared, sir."

"Good. After tomorrow, we need to change our entire focus on how to move forward. Things under the dome will intensify."

Inspector-General Paula Nottage, the head of Capitol Security Protection Services, walked into the apartment with an entourage of personnel at her heels. She approached with her fake smile and bent over, taking a knee.

"Representative McWright. I'm so relieved you were unharmed. When the call came, I was fearful at the thought that something would befall the highest-ranking member inside the five walls."

"Your security officers performed admirably. Without Oliver, I'd be dead. He sacrificed himself for me. He deserves the highest merits of excellence for his deeds."

Paula stood and replied, "I'll see to it myself."

I looked around the battle-ridden apartment and sighed.

"It's time for me to retire for the evening. Tomorrow's inquiry will require my full focus."

Ficco responded sternly, "Absolutely not, sir. Some of these soldiers got away through your emergency exit in the laundry room."

Paula added, "He's correct. At least three retreated, rappelling down the elevator shaft. They fled through a maintenance hatch and killed a few engineers in the process when getting topside. You can't go to closed session tomorrow. We still don't know who these professionals were. We're doubling your security and placing you in protective custody under the dome."

"They weren't here for me. They wanted Adam and Juliet."

Ficco said in a low tone, "Henry." I stared at him. "It's the right move, especially for tomorrow."

Paula didn't know what the senior agent was referring to, but I understood his meaning.

"Ok, fine, where are we going?"

Inspector-General Nottage answered, "Under the golden road. We have a hidden apartment there and have used it over the last seven hundred and forty years for situations like this. From there, you'll have access to the entire station."

"That's fine. Alyssa won't be joining us. Take her to wherever you'd like, just not near me. Understood?"

Both made gestures of approval and left. I spoke with Adam and Juliet; each of us packed some things and left the apartment. I grabbed two high-end bottles of bourbon from the bar and the priceless necklace with its blue glow.

The hidden haven under the golden road was known to Capitol Security as the ruby refuge. Before last night I didn't even know the place existed. They nicknamed it after rare gems from Kora with a peculiar purple coloring like the memory stone. The rubies were spaced evenly along the walls in every room, reminding me of a chair rail. In the early days of the station, those gems were all the rage. Now they looked tacky. The entire shelter was like an ancient space station with three levels and no windows. Every door functioned like an airlock with a small window to see into the next room. All was metal—metal halls, grated flooring, and pipes running along the walls. I wondered if the Colonial Steel Workers union provided the materials for the structure, or perhaps Sadie Enama and her Federation of Iron Workers. Our unions made everything work properly.

Alyssa called my PDD numerous times throughout the night. I had yet to call her back. Including Josue, we had five new security officers. They all remained outside the only entrance to the fortress—one way in and one way out. I still believed the assassins were Lyons Pride Special Warfare conscripts but had no way to prove it.

I needed breakfast and left the bedroom. The bulkhead door made a whooshing sound, retracting into the wall, allowing me to pass through. I took the lift to the first floor. Adam and Juliet were already watching television and preparing food.

"Making some breakfast, are we?"

Adam smiled. That was strange. I hadn't seen him smile at all before.

"We wanted to surprise you and would have had it ready if Jules had quit messing around."

Adam seemed like a completely different person. He moved briskly and looked like a thousand kilograms were off his shoulders, a new lease on life.

Juliet ran over and hugged me. "They were Lyons Pride. I know it."

"You might be right, but without proof, it's all speculation."

Juliet puffed her lips and shrugged, then went to the restroom.

I could speak to Adam alone. "You seem different today. Agent Ficco told me what you did to the assassin in your room. How do you feel?"

He stared down at his hands, rotated his wrists and said, "It felt amazing driving that knife through flesh. I knew in the back of my mind they were sent by the Twins. Every push of the blade was revenge on a thousand sins against my family. As blood spewed all over his war gear, I felt my heart race. I felt alive. I tried to stop myself after I knew he was dead but couldn't."

Adam Sideris was more like me than I realized. After a moment observing his excitement, I said, "That worked better than the rabbits. You're renewed today. It appears we might have found a better way to channel your emotions. Let's see how long it lasts."

Before long, Juliet came back. "Henry, the inquiry already started. Adam and I were watching it for a while, but it was boring."

Adam added, "They were going over minute-by-minute reports of everything. A few witnesses went on the stand. That red-haired guy doesn't like you very much."

I turned the volume on the television up to watch the closed-circuit proceedings. It was a live feed of JJ questioning Senior Agent Ficco who sat in a chair at center stage. Nicolas Nomikos was in the Civil Earth guest seat, representing station command, and a few cathedral magistrates from the Hall of Justice were present.

"Senior Agent, on the day in question, you received orders from a specific representative to take Adam and Juliet Sideris, did you not?"

"Yes," answered Ficco.

"Who sent you the message? Be specific, please."

Ficco shuffled in his seat. "I received it from Center Seat Representative Henry McWright's PDD. The order was clear—take Adam and Juliet Sideris."

JJ raised his voice, pacing around center stage inside the pentagon. "So, you admit that it was, in fact, McWright who gave the order?"

Ficco hesitated and narrowed his eyes. "No."

JJ frowned and pulled his lips tight. "I don't understand. You just said the message came from Representative McWright's PDD."

Ficco gave a crooked half-smile. "I did, but as all respected representatives inside the forum will see, based on our cyber forensic investigation, we found that Center Seat Representative Henry McWright's personal display device was on call forwarding that entire day. It was his wife's birthday. His aide Benjamin Driverson was responding to all messages. For whatever reason, Benjamin ordered me to apprehend them. It's irrelevant now, anyway."

JJ's face changed to bright red, and he shouted back, "Irrelevant? A major violation under our Free Worlds' Relations Policy occurred, and you're calling it irrelevant?"

"Yes. Because Isabel, Adam, and Juliet have officially renounced their citizenship to Epsilon Prime. Our agents tracked down the ship they came to the station on. There was a corrupted file with the names of the refugees coming to the station, but we recovered most of the data. All three officially declared themselves refugees, and this station approved it. Mysteriously, that file disappeared from station records." Ficco looked at Nicolas Nomikos and the Silent Lion. "They were legal refugees that both sides, the Pride and station security, wanted to detain. Our agents made a tactical decision at my direction, regardless of any message received from Representative McWright's PDD, to bring Adam and Juliet to the cathedral. We did so legally so no harm came to them as we enforced the laws of the Capitol Forum."

A loud commotion erupted from each wall at that new fabricated information. Adam and Juliet were legally registered as refugees, but the bit about my PDD wasn't true. Malcolm, Stacy, Jordan, and members of our legal team sat at extra tables lining our Colonial wall.

Center Seat Representative Alexandra Onasis yelled, "What right do you have to sit there and tell us it was illegal to apprehend the Green Eyes of Athinia? They're openly rebelling against New-Sparta, which holds the prime regency of Epsilon Prime."

"Ma'am, it's my duty as a senior agent to advise you that article six Free Worlds' Relations Policy clearly states that any person who legally registers with the station as a refugee is no longer subject to the authority of their previous home planet. Refugees fall under the jurisdiction of the five walls. The Guild is exceedingly thorough at removing criminal applicants."

Zachery slammed his fist against the seat armrest. "Green eyes are illegal under the lawful orders of our governing regents and Prime Regent Isaac Lyons—"

Ficco cut in. "Under the Guild's principle operating procedures, we don't extradite over war crimes or issues regarding a civil war unless an official bill passes open convocation. It's not our place to intervene with internal squabbles. Adam and Juliet, as well as Isabel for that matter, are legal refugees to this station. Therefore, no one had a right to detain, arrest, or apprehend them in the refugee dock."

Shouts echoed everywhere, and in my absence, both Mia and our sergeant at arms tried to bring order back to the chamber; even the Iron Fist of Kora called out for order.

Mia raised her hands. "Silence at once—keep to the topic at hand. The rule of three only applied to Representative McWright giving an order to the Guild without two others' approval. If what this senior agent says is true, the Guild's action was legal. However legal that action was, Henry McWright's PDD message wasn't justified without two more walls. It was illegal under our articles, and if Benjamin Driverson sent the message, it's he who must be held accountable."

Alexandra gave Mia a dreadful stare for a tense moment, but everyone remained in their seats as JJ stood in center stage, looking like a noodle.

"The call-forwarding statements are troublesome. Where's Mr. Driverson now?"

Malcolm lifted his chin higher. "Representative Richmond, Senior Aide Benjamin Driverson went missing nearly a month ago. He's the latest in a growing list of staffers missing here under the dome and station command. We've petitioned the MERC Guild to investigate his disappearance. However, because of reluctance by the five walls, nothing has yet occurred."

JJ's skin was redder than his hair. He raised his voice. "Careful, Chief of Staff Booth, choose your words carefully when speaking of my fellow representatives."

Mia Stavish said, "A few months ago, I begged Representative McWright to work with me to dedicate resources for investigating the staff disappearances. The representative was less than interested at that time."

Malcolm replied, "That was then, and this is now. At that time, Henry McWright wasn't certain that the disappearances were anything more than chance. Since then, two more aides, including Benjamin, have vanished." Malcolm glared at JJ and spoke louder. "And frankly, Representative Richmond, I have chosen my words carefully. Maybe you should do the same."

Malcolm stood, walked over to JJ, and turned to look at the representatives who were watching carefully.

"Representative McWright had every intention of being here today, to answer questions and represent his constituents to the best of his ability. He was going to bring Adam and Juliet Sideris too. But, last night, without warning, his private residence was attacked by trained professional killers. All of you woke to the alerts across your PDDs. If not for the glorious deeds and sacrifices of Capitol Security Protection Services, Adam, Juliet, and the representative would be dead. Henry McWright has time and again looked out for the best interests of everyone on this station and the Free Worlds of Humanity. From refugees to the upper class, everyone receives fair treatment. This attack has vindicated our office's decision to keep the Sideris siblings under our care until further notice. No one in this sacred chamber will get them, no one will be able to harm them, and no one will speak with them without Center Seat Representative McWright's approval."

Malcolm was a political power himself. If he hadn't been born on Uropa or didn't belong to our union, the Twenty-Third Entente, he might be leading things, not me. Better him than Sadie Enama. He was far better at playing politics than JJ or his decrepit flower. I turned the television off and saw Adam's and Juliet's eyes opened wide with suspense and shock. Regardless of what happened last night, I was in a much stronger position that day.

Adam asked, "Now what?"

I hesitated. "Now, my boy, we move the chess pieces and get ready for our next move. Perception is reality on this station, and I create the perception."

CHAPTER 39

Colony World Nim

New places with new faces (Kathryn)

We arrived on Nim over a week ago, and it was amazing. The air was clear with a dark blue sky and beautiful puffy clouds. Grass was everywhere, leading to thick forests with wild animals inside. I never saw so much wildlife ever. Some of the Tiers One and Two colonists even had pet dogs. The colony city resembled megacities back home, but not nearly as large. We could walk outside without fear of surface gangs, yellow haze, or that squashing red wet mud—but I heard the sound in my head often. Streets had paved roads and walkways with grass on the opposite sides. Around the perimeter was a giant wall similar to our megacity walls on Civil Earth, which protected us from the native population and predatory animals.

Located at the colony center was our megastructure, the same size as normal tier buildings, and all the colonists lived there. Tobias said there were over ten thousand of us on Nim, and Renee told me it was the smallest colony of Civil Earth compared to a colony like Craylon, which had over five hundred million. The inner ring of buildings comprised the critical infrastructure, and the outer ring near the walls were things like entertainment and supply storage. Random streets had parks with swings, slides, and other areas that Renee said resembled public locations on the relations station and Colonial Accord worlds. I really enjoyed the water park and planned to go back.

Renee still made me spend several hours each day learning more about the free, outer, and rogue worlds. I enjoyed hearing about the three pirate planets and decided I would love to visit one day. Pirates were ferocious warriors who traveled occupied space attacking and raiding ships. The Black Skull Admiral, who was once a Dolrinion and abandoned his Force Command, forsaking the memory stone to live as a marauding pirate, was someone I wanted to meet.

I also learned more about the outer worlds. They didn't have a formal government like Civil Earth. The royal family controlled by the Exalted Ruler, King Sallu Nejem, and the thousand princes and princesses governed fifty worlds. The Colonials only had six planets, and some king near the edge of occupied space had fifty.

T told me the nearest natives were over one hundred and sixty kilometers away, and that they were hostile, but we didn't have to worry about them here.

I was walking along the sidewalk near our megastructure with the sun on my face and a light breeze pushing my hair. Tiers Three and Four were able to come outside, with restrictions. Most of the people I saw were from the Clouds or Upper Twenty-Three. Even on a colony world, the caste system ruled. Tin-suit defenders stood at roadway intersections guarding us against ourselves. Tier One had a few private botanical garden sanctuaries that we couldn't go near. What did they have in there, gold? But there was more freedom on Nim than the homeworld for sure.

I tried mingling with Tier Two teens at the water park, but they irritated me. My personality matched better with those who lived hard lives. Silver-spoon Upper Twenty-Three acted as if they'd seen everything life had to offer, which was silly.

A coughing fit took me. So far, I hadn't seen anyone else with a surface cough besides Tobias and me. When I was living with Daniel in the Lower

Forty, it was more common to hear the cough when walking through the second and third floors of our megastructure. I missed Daniel, Amber, and Lilly, especially Lilly. In my bedroom, I had a picture of us from Daniel's apartment taped to my mirror and looked at it often.

The destroyer we came to Nim on was huge, the largest thing I'd ever seen, and it was shaped like a beehive. It was bulky and odd-looking. Rehan said that warships needed substantial armor to withstand enemy bombardment, or everyone would suffocate from punctures in the hull. That strange beehive could take hits from several uranium missiles and keep fighting, which surprised me because vacuum uranium warheads were so powerful. Renee showed me videos of that too.

T questioned me repeatedly about living on the surface with Sadness. Something about my former protector affected the way Tobias spoke with me.

He had asked, "Do you remember what he said about his past? What did Sadness say about living inside?"

He never told me his real name, only that his life was full of sadness, and that was why he took the name. He told me he had a family once, and served in the Defender Corps until he didn't, whatever that meant. When he came to the surface, his child was left alone, like most in the lower tiers. Tiers Four and Three were hard-living, and parents dying or disappearing was common.

T pressed me when we were on the destroyer. "Did you ever notice any tattoos on his body or a small device on the left side of his belly button?" He took off his shirt and showed me a tattoo on his chest with numbers and letters, saying that it showed his core serial number, unit, rank, and last name. When T got his promotion, the Defender Corps lasered off his old rank and tattooed a new one. There was residue and mismatching skin coloring where the laser erased the old ink, and I noticed the same on his name, Norcross.

I told Tobias that I remembered Sadness changing a dirty shirt in front of me a few times. He had scars all over his body from old combat wounds and the same tattoo on his chest. I couldn't remember what it said, and he had that port on his stomach like all defenders to link to their battle armor.

Anyone who served with Civil Earth Defense had that small surgically attached port so they could interact with their suits and armor. Dolrinions had the same way of connecting at the back of their necks.

Those memories faded, and I kept walking outside the megastructure on Nim. It felt good to stretch my legs without looking over my shoulder, even though I kept my guard up and still glanced left to right often. A faint dripping sound echoed between two buildings, and the hairs on my arms raised at the sound. Like the squashing red mud, that drip was a constant on the surface. A leaking air handler had water striking a puddle on the concrete ground. I lifted my hand to catch the cloudy water falling steadily onto my fingertips. I had spent years drinking that contaminated liquid, and it was hard to believe that I lasted so long, even with Sadness's training.

Two teenage girls were headed in my direction; based on their clothing and the little yapping dog on the leash, they were Tier Two silver spoons. They curled their lips with disgust watching me catching the water. Was it the water that grossed them out, or my tactical clothing similar to defender gear that agitated them? The girls wore colorful dresses and jewelry from head to toe.

"Eww, what are you doing with that water?"

I told them without care, "None of your business."

The older girl snapped back, "Move out of our way. We're Tier Two, and you need to show us respect."

I smirked at those dummies. "You move for me, I'm Tier Two and will kick your asses if you don't get out of my way."

Both glared with disbelief, and the younger shouted, "Liar. You're not Upper Twenty-Three. No way."

I stepped closer, and both girls jumped back, raising their hands. I had my caste card hanging on my neck and pushed it towards their faces. They looked at it and opened their eyes wide, then stepped around me on the grass, moving away.

One of my hands clenched the pliers tightly in a pocket. I picked them up without T or Courtney noticing inside Orson Outler's apartment. The way those two girls talked made me angry and part of me wanted to pull their teeth out, the same way I would have on the surface. Another memory of Sadness stirred. Two people had come to us as we set up to sleep for the night. The man and woman were weak, scared, and hungry.

The man trembled as he tried to act strong, raising his voice to Sadness. "Please, just give … give us some food, or … or I'll kill you."

He had a small pocketknife in a shaking hand, and the woman behind had tears in her eyes. I had my spear, ready to attack, but Sadness shook his head and went to the man who almost fell over at his approach. The man closed his eyes, wincing at an expected pain that didn't come. My trainer only peered at him for a moment with his steadfast hazel eyes.

"How long have you two been out here?" Sadness stood with his legs apart, just in case.

The scared man opened one eye and said, "A week, only one week."

My protector turned away and went to his pack. He pulled out some dried city mole meat and gave two pieces to them, which they devoured quickly.

Sadness then offered more lessons. "Two blocks down from here on the right is an air handler. Go now and collect some water—you won't survive without it. Stay away from the gangs, hide when they're near you, or you're both dead. Find people like you trying to survive. It's the only way you won't be dead by next week."

The woman asked, "Can we stay with you?"

"No, now get out of here before I kill you both!"

They ran off into the yellow haze, and I was confused. "Why didn't you kill them and take their stuff?"

"Killing someone for no other reason than to kill them will make you no better than the surface gangs. We're not savages. When people want to harm us, we act. When those with fear come in desperation, we will try to use reason first. With the training I'm providing you, there will be few out here that can match your abilities. Always avoid killing people for no reason. If you start down that path, you'll be lost quickly. Kathryn, remember this when I'm gone."

I glanced back at the scared girls moving away and released my hold on the pliers. There was some clamminess on my palm from gripping so tight. Sadness always said that my fighting skills would be superior to everyone, but I never thought he literally meant what he said. Agamo Verk was a style from the Old World, and I was a master of it.

My PDD rang. I answered, and Tobias spoke. "Come back to the apartment. I have something for you before my shift starts."

"What do you have? I hate surprises."

"Shut up and come home, Kat."

We hung up, and I went to our megastructure. Our apartment was on the seventy-fifth floor, and Renee said that for Tiers One and Two, the lower your prestige, the lower the level people resided. That was why Orson Outler was on the ninety-fifth floor. He couldn't go any higher without being upgraded to Tier One. People who lived on the last level before the lower tier were close to tier demotions.

Before stepping into our megastructure, I had to pass outer airlocks where two warthogs stood guard. We still had to scan our cards to access any doors like back home. Before entering the second airlock door, I had to scan again with two railgun stations on both corners glaring down at me. Once inside, the main entrance was like the second floor of megastructures on Civil Earth with restaurants, hospitals, shopping, schools, and other government services. I liked the atmosphere there and preferred the people. The upper tiers never lingered, moving to the elevators with their Triple S security following closely at their sides; lower tiers were more social on the first floor.

I approached the Tier Two elevators, and the tin suits standing guard raised their rifles slightly at my presence. I scanned my card, and they relaxed their shoulders. I got back to the seventy-fifth floor and opened the apartment door. The lights were off, and I was suspicious. T should be there, so why were the lights off? I brought my hands up and stepped inside.

"Lights on," I said.

The lights came on, and I stepped back, seeing Tobias, Rehan, and Renee standing near the kitchen behind a table.

They said together, "Happy birthday, Kathryn."

I shook my head in confusion. "Huh?"

T said, "Today's your eighteenth birthday, and Renee made a cake."

Rehan rubbed his hands through my hair and said, "Happy birthday, Little Rascal."

My birthday? I had no memories of celebrating one of those and could hardly remember the taste of cake.

"I don't know what to say."

Renee grinned. "Don't say anything, dear. Now come here, take this knife and cut your cake. You must always take the first slice. It's for luck."

I took the knife, feeling its balanced weight in my hand. Faces of the dead flashed through my mind … pushing a blade just like that one through their soft skin, feeling resistance from muscle, bone, and organs as they cried in pain. The BreakNeck Boy who murdered Johnathan, his face was clear. My heart raced as I pushed the blade into the soft cake. Strange—blood was seeping from my slice, spilling onto the counter and dribbling on my boots. My hand shook as Renee took the handle and placed a hand on my back. The blood disappeared; there wasn't blood at all, and the interior of the cake was chocolate.

T whispered, "Breathe, Kat, just breathe. In through your nose and out through your mouth. Think of something pleasant and steady your breaths."

I did what he said and slowly calmed as Rehan said, "I've got your first gift. Tobias didn't want you to have it, but he's only my boss when we're on duty." He laughed and handed me a long pole wrapped in paper.

I narrowed my eyes. "What should I do with this?"

Renee rubbed her hand on my back. "Open the wrapping. What's inside is yours."

With excitement, I pulled away the wrapping. It was a long black metal pole with beautiful golden inlays slightly proud of the smooth metal. The designs were so detailed—flowers shaped into boxes and patterns all along the metal. Rehan smiled, and Tobias pursed his lips and frowned.

"What is it?"

Rehan stepped closer. "A ceremonial spear from a long-forgotten religion on Civil Earth from before the Years of Darkness. It's been with my family for countless generations, and my grandfather always bragged that blades like those were once used to slay demons. It's called a trishula. After seeing you using Agamo Verk in the simulation room, there's no doubt that you're the best person to have it. I don't have family, and when I die, the Benzo name dies with me. I'd rather the weapon go to someone who can use it properly. The blade makes it priceless by our standards." He twisted a raised brace near the top, and a thirty-centimeter blade sprang out with a slashing sound. Next to the larger sharp edge were two evenly spaced smaller points. I never saw metal like that before. It had black chips and glowing green lines.

"Why does it look like that?"

Renee's eyes were wide. "That's Corin steel."

"You taught me about that metal mined in Titans' Belt."

Rehan smiled and replied, "That's right, Little Rascal. That blade is strong enough to push through the thick battle armor of any Free World, even Dolrinion sentinel war plate."

Tobias interrupted. "There won't be a reason for you to use that while living in the colony. Please don't twist out that blade unless your life's in danger."

"Take it easy, T. I won't get us kicked out of Tier Two yet."

Rehan laughed, and Tobias lowered his head with an uneasy stare.

I turned to Rehan. "Thank you so much. I'll never let it out of my sight, I promise."

"Now, open mine," Renee said enthusiastically.

Her gift was in a smaller box, and it had a card attached. I started peeling the envelope back, and Renee said, "Open the gift box first."

I paused and did as she said, and after looking at what was inside, I instantly grew uneasy in my own skin. A pair of heeled red dress shoes that looked terribly uncomfortable. I pulled them out by the straps and spun them in my hand, frowning.

Renee cleared her throat. "You're a lady now, and every lady should have a pair of heels. One day someone will ask you out on a date, and when that day comes, it's important to wear something becoming of a strong woman."

"I'm strong enough with my boots." That was rude of me. I quickly countered, "Thank you, Renee. I'll wear them when that day comes."

Dating was the last thought on my mind. I opened the card, which contained a piece of paper with something written on it: "One week off tutoring studies."

That brought a smile to my face and I turned to Renee.

She said, "I knew you'd like that gift better than the heels."

Tobias handed me his gift. "This is for you."

I folded my arms and raised my voice. "You've already given me everything I could ever need. I'm not on the surface anymore, have clothes on my back, and haven't felt hungry in months."

He smirked and rubbed his hand through my hair. "Just open it, Kat."

I carefully unwrapped the paper and saw a framed picture Doctor Courtney took of T and me during his promotion ceremony. We looked great standing together. All dressed up. There was a small note attached. "When the world gets you down, don't frown, just look at this picture and remember that as long as we stick together, no one will have it better." Underneath that, it said, "Love you, Sis."

Of all the gifts that one was the best. Tears filled my eyes, and I hugged my brother. He was my family, my brother, and I loved him as any younger sister would. We spent some time together, talking and laughing. Rehan and T were complaining about Colonel Hanifin, their commanding officer who ran the colony. They said that she was arrogant and believed she knew better than the seasoned officers in her command. Tobias was worried that she wouldn't take any of his advice.

I ate a few more pieces of cake until my stomach hurt. We were distracted by Tobias's PDD ringing. T answered, and a woman appeared on the screen in a formal defender uniform. It was Colonel Hanifin.

"Major Norcross, our science team missed their second check-in from the survey mission. It's been twenty-four hours, and I sent out an aerial recovery squad to assess the situation. Base control just received this audio message."

She tapped something off-screen, and someone's scared voice played: "We need immediate assistance. Under attack from all sides." Gunshot and sounds of explosions were in the background as the voice shrieked.

Colonel Hanifin said, "They never returned, and we've lost vitals from their armor. Major, I want you to take a defender company to their last location. Engage and destroy the hostile native threat and try to recover anyone that survived."

Tobias tapped his fingers on his knees and appeared uncomfortable with her orders.

"Ma'am, might I suggest we send a half platoon? The attack and missing scientists could be a setup to lure more of our forces away from the colony. An entire company might be excessive."

Rehan spoke. "Ma'am, Captain Benzo here from the Fourteenth Armored Battery. I volunteer to take ground forces out to scout the area first."

Hanifin's face turned dark. "You're both out of line. Major Norcross, you'll take a full company of defenders as I commanded. Captain Benzo, you can bring your entire battery in support. Blast these primitives back into the Years of Forgetting and save who you can. I want you both ready to move in one hour." She sounded angry.

The call ended, and Tobias stood and rubbed his fingers on his chin.

"What's wrong, T?"

Rehan groaned. "That crazy woman's going to get us all killed is what's wrong." Rehan glanced at Renee, who pushed her lips together. "Sorry for my outburst, ma'am"

Tobias said, "Two hundred and fifty defenders are too many. It's a bad plan. Of the ten thousand colonists, only seventeen hundred are with the Defender Corps. Of that number, maybe nine hundred are frontline defenders. The rest are support personnel. At any given time, we have a quarter of that number outside the colony walls defending forward operations and scientists on the planet. After we leave with the armored group, the colony will only have a few hundred that can resist a hostile force. It's not enough protection."

Rehan replied, "We'll also be vulnerable without intelligence on what we're walking into. I've got a bad feeling. It'll take us over a day to get there on foot, and the same to come back, not counting the job. We could be out there for up to five days with our commanding officer sitting here with one thumb in her mouth and another in her ass while she plays switch."

"T, that colonel looks like a kid. If she doesn't know what she's doing, don't follow her orders and do what you think is right."

Tobias looked down at the floor like there was something interesting there. "Unfortunately, things in the Defender Corps don't work that way. No, she's given us an order, and we'll see it followed." He turned to Rehan. "Captain Benzo, call your column, have them ready to move out one hour from now. I'll do the same with the ground defenders."

"Yes, sir." Rehan walked to the door and spoke to me. "Take care of that blade and keep yourself out of trouble." He winked.

Tobias said, "Renee can look after you while I'm gone. Be careful and remember what I told you about fighting."

I nodded and hugged him. "I can't protect you when you're out of my reach."

He smiled and said, "It's my job to protect you, not the other way around. Keep your chin up. I'll see you in a few days."

T and Rehan left together, and I was filled with an emptiness that I hadn't felt since Johnathan died. I was powerless and could only hope that nothing would happen to them on their mission.

CHAPTER 40

Fleeing Galma

Confusion in many forms (Mace)

Jamie, baby Emma, Zoey, and I neared the Lowlands spaceport. Our three-day journey on the pathway went by with little issue other than guardian groups giving us curious stares. Most would continue without engaging with us, and a few captains asked why we were alone. Nothing further transpired. The mechanical wheelchair batteries died on the second day, forcing Jamie to walk. She constantly grimaced in pain, and that walk on the pathway showed how strong she was, having to trek so far on foot after delivering our daughter a few days earlier. We had to keep moving. The agent wasn't far behind. We left the last shelter a few hours prior, and an old native Lowlander fishing in a pond near the pathway told us that the spaceport was over the next hill. We did hear a ship, but the fog was too thick to see it.

Jamie was rocking Emma and said, "When we get on that ship, I want a hot shower and plan on lying in a bed for two days straight."

"You deserve it, babes. You did more than anyone else could have in your shoes." I glanced at Zoey, who also appeared tired. "Everyone deserves some time off their feet."

Outside the walls of the spaceport were guardians. The walls were tall, made from oak trees from the Highlands and staked side by side into the ground. Guardian watchtowers were spaced along the wall. We passed inside, and it was the dreariest port I'd ever seen. We couldn't go through to the hangars without clearance from the transfer station.

Zoey said, "You'll need to get travel papers, or they won't let us go to our hangar."

Jamie sat on a bench and sighed. "Can it wait? I need to relax for a few minutes."

"No, we need to get out of here now before it's too late," Zoey said in a stern voice.

"Ok, you two stay here with Emma. I'll go get our papers."

I kissed baby Emma and Jamie's forehead before walking inside. If we weren't in the fog, a computer could have taken care of our clearance, but the Lowlands did everything the slow way.

"Two thousand Free Worlds credits to get transfer documents," the employee said with a grin, knowing that the cost was robbery.

"That's a ridiculous price."

She shrugged with an expression I wanted to punch. "No problem. Enjoy living in our fog for the rest of your life. You aren't getting papers without paying that fee. Good luck going back to any port in occupied space without this."

I didn't have a choice and paid the fee. We had used nearly all our credits paying for that ship. The Lowlander laughed as I left the building. The women sat alone; no other travelers came or went.

Jamie saw me and stood. "How much do we have left?"

"Not enough."

Zoey said, "Don't worry. Free Worlds currency's worth triple the value on the outer planets." She snapped her head back, looking up, and grabbed for her sidearm.

I heard the sound of a motor, but it sputtered like something was wrong.

Jamie's eyes opened wide, and she shouted, "MERC gliders."

A small drone appeared through the fog, and when we saw it clearly, the machine stopped working and fell from the sky. *It must be the agent.* He was attempting to use his scout drones to track us, but the wireless tech wouldn't work in the fog.

Zoey pulled on Jamie's arm and said, "Run, now."

She opened fire near the main gate. The agent was there with his mongrel, and both took cover behind the oak wall. We cleared the transfer gate, and I heard cracks of gunfire behind us as the agent engaged the guardians at the gate. The mongrel tried to move in our direction, but Zoey's shooting kept it back.

I grabbed baby Emma and shouted, "Move your legs, Jamie, as fast as you can."

We ran, trying to navigate the thick fog. It was impossible to see anything, and all the mud huts and oak buildings looked the same. I pulled the PDD from my pocket and hit the directional controller. An arrow displayed where to go. Zoey was at our rear looking for the agent and his beast through the thick haze. A cracking buzz zipped past us and faint flashes lit the fog a short distance away. Zoey fired back.

We passed another building and turned the corner, but stopped dead in our tracks. The mongrel, complete with burned hair, stood with its chest puffed out a few meters away. Zoey came around the corner and reached over our shoulders, firing her pistol without hesitation. One round hit the beast as it dashed to cover. The slide on Zoey's gun racked back; she dropped the empty magazine and looked at me while loading another.

"It's my last mag, only half full."

We couldn't continue in the direction the PDD was advising because of the mongrel. Instead, we circled to the right following the perimeter oak wall. More gunshots sounded from our rear, and I felt the whizzing close to my head. Zoey took a knee and fired again into the blackness. An arrow just missed her shoulder, and two more impacted the mud beneath her feet. She turned and shot at a guardian in the tower above as he attempted to loose another arrow. The guardians fell back into the tower, and Zoey's pistol locked on an empty chamber with steam coming from the barrel.

"Mace, we need to get to the dock."

Tears were sliding down Jamie's face, and the only thought in my head was how important it was for our daughter to get out of there alive. I'd grab that mongrel myself so that Jamie and Emma could live. We'd gone too far and done too much to fail now. I wouldn't let anything happen to my family.

I clenched my hands into fists and shouted, "No! We aren't going to die here, ladies. Not like this, dammit. Come on, let's get off this planet."

They both raised their heads and shoulders a little higher in the face of my self-assured determination. We moved past a few more buildings and finally made it to our hangar. Zoey pulled open a sliding door that led us through a hallway to a second slider. I closed the door behind me and caught up to the women as they went through another sliding entry into our ship dock but stopped as I bumped into them. Why did they halt so abruptly? Emma was still in my arms with her eyes closed as she sucked on a pacifier.

Oh no. The agent was between us and our ship, which was a piece of crap junker. His face was flush, and he had clenched fists. The mongrel wasn't with him.

Zoey didn't have any more ammunition. She looked down at the slide, still locked back, and tossed it to the ground. The agent glanced down at his rifle and showed Zoey that it was also empty, and he dropped it. My heart pounded uncontrollably, and Jamie's breathing was heavy.

Zoey whispered, "Move to the back wall and make your way to the opposite side. If I can keep him busy, get on the ship, and leave."

From Jamie's face, I knew she wanted to protest, but before we could respond, Zoey pulled a small knife and an expandable baton and stepped towards the agent. He smirked, and pulled a bigger expanding stick with a small spiked ball on its end.

Another slider behind the agent opened, and the mongrel came inside. The agent glanced over his shoulder and closed his eyes. The mongrel did the same then sat. Both opened their eyes, and our fierce protector didn't waste any time. She ran for the agent, and they went into bloody and vicious battle.

Both the agent and Zoey moved so fast, swinging their weapons, it was like their arms blurred into the fog. They would attack and defend, moving in circles like a dance. Zoey landed a blow with her baton across his face and the goggles. For the first time since the train station in Lavlen, his deep brown eyes were visible.

Through the fog, his angry red face showed the level of frustration he felt. The agent closed his eyes for a moment, and the mongrel leaped up and rushed Jamie and me. The inner flooring was metal with grates to absorb exhaust from ships. I grabbed one of the grates, sticking my fingers through the individual holes, and held it up like a shield. Jamie helped me hold the heavy metal as the mongrel snapped at us, trying to bite through the divider with its powerful jaw. We had to retreat to the wall. The mongrel was too powerful. I hung on to Emma desperately with one arm while the other held the floor grating. The jaw was so large that the teeth couldn't bite our small fingers coming out of the metal holes. Saliva from the snapping teeth dripped onto my fingers, and I could smell the animal's breath.

The agent landed a powerful punch to Zoey's face, and she stumbled. Everything depended on our Capitol Security officer winning her battle. Emma began to cry at all the commotion, and the agent leaned his head to the side to observe our situation. Grief filled me. When the mongrel got past this metal barrier, we'd be dead. Emma was only a few days old, and Jamie hadn't had a chance to be a mom. How could that be our end?

Zoey fought on, striking, retreating, striking, and blocking. There was a flurry of blows from both warriors. The spiked baton landed on Zoey's arm, and she cried in pain but countered by stabbing his shoulder right next to the lining of his Corin-steel vest. He shouted and punched her with the other arm. Zoey stepped back, holding the fresh wound oozing with blood through her fingers. The agent took a knee and pulled the blade away, grunting from the force, and his blood mirrored Zoey's as it fell. Both combatants were exhausted.

He gave Zoey a hateful stare and then looked at our struggle with the mongrel. The agent closed his eyes, and his beast did the same with a slight twitch to the side before opening them and turning towards Zoey. It sprinted and bit her shoulder from behind. She screamed in a way I hadn't heard before as the animal shook her violently from side to side.

Jamie and I stood there dumbfounded, unsure what to do as we watched that enormous animal treat our protector and friend like food. The agent grinned, watching Zoey's fruitless struggle to resist. The beast slammed her to the grated metal flooring, and she groaned. It was biting and ripping at her back and body. Blood sprayed everywhere and random chunks of flesh, meat, and bone littered the area. We stood helplessly, watching the killer animal maul her. I looked over at the ramp to our ship, but couldn't pull Jamie that way because the agent was there blocking our escape.

Zoey still had the baton in her hand and lifted it aimlessly. The mongrel bit her at the elbow and took her arm off with a quick snap. She screamed louder as her body flailed on the floor like a fish out of water. How could one person have so much blood in their body? Emma screamed louder. More of Zoey's blood had stained the mongrel's fur, and it stepped back, pacing behind her, sniffing at her legs. She turned and saw us standing near the wall and struggled, trying to drag herself in our direction with the stump of her arm.

Jamie mumbled to herself as tears streamed from her eyes. She reached her hand out to the woman she had grown close to, but the mongrel growled and snapped down on Zoey's neck. Jamie recoiled her hand in fear and backed into me. A terrible gurgling sound came from Zoey as she attempted to breathe in shallow gasps. She stared at us with wide eyes until they closed. The mongrel released its grip, and she fell to the metal, motionless. It sniffed her head before walking back and stood behind the agent.

Jamie and I froze. What could we do? Zoey sacrificed herself for us, and Emma. If the agent didn't kill us here, the Corporation would when he brought us back. Emma would be in a chamber, and total grief absorbed me. No one spoke; we stared at each other until Emma cried again. The agent scowled, looking at my daughter with anger. He took two steps towards us and then his attention went to the sliding door that we came in only moments earlier.

It opened, and everyone in the hangar was wide-eyed with astonishment at what came inside—two short, stocky, black-armored Dolrinion sentinels with their faceplate covers raised. A man and a woman. Their smushed faces had prideful expressions. Another sliding door on the opposite wall opened and a third sentinel came inside. From his armor's appearance he must have been a veteran of countless battles, and the commanding poise on his face, even after seeing Zoey's distorted body, was amazing. He attempted a smile. Dolrinions didn't smile often. It was like he didn't want to be anywhere else in occupied space at that moment, as if he'd been waiting for that day his entire life. A master gunnery sergeant, honorary rank to any sentinel that survived so long without achieving an officer's promotion. I was never so happy to see Dolrinions in my life.

Jamie whispered, "BlackRock sentinels—why are they here?"

"No idea, but we have a buffer between us."

The younger male Dolrinion was a major, and he looked at me strangely before stepping into Zoey's blood. The three stood in front of Jamie and me, looking to challenge the agent and his mongrel.

The agent sighed and picked up Zoey's knife in his empty hand. He raised both arms, focusing on his hands to show that he didn't have a gun.

The battle-hardened master gunnery sergeant appeared pleased and placed his rifle over the locking device on his shoulder. He pulled a Corin-steel axe from his waist and spun the handle. Such a rare weapon. The other two sentinels looked at each other, then did the same with their rifles before pulling their tip knives.

Dolrinions and their damn pride. Those sentinels could have shot both agent and mongrel with ease. But their damn thickheaded belief in true combat to earn a place on the memory stone with honor. Fools. All of them.

The mongrel dashed at the master gunnery sergeant, and the other two sentinels ran for the agent. More battle broke out, and it gave us the chance we needed. I grabbed Jamie's arm and pulled her to our transport ramp. Before hitting the retract button and sealing the door, I observed the fight unfolding. The mongrel went for the battle-hardened sentinel, but he moved to the side and bellowed out a powerful grunt as he punched the beast's snout. Several teeth littered the grated metal and fell beneath. He followed this by spinning to the side and slashing with his axe, removing the animal's nubbed tail. It yelped at the quick cut.

That sentinel was a true professional without fear. The ramp door was nearly closed, and one of the two other sentinels was already dead with Zoey's knife embedded in her eye socket. The major was still slashing away at the agent who thwarted each attack. We made eye contact for a brief second as the door secured. Alarms blared in the vessel, and I went to the command deck. Jamie was powering up all systems to take off.

"Sit down and strap in," she yelled with authority.

I put the harnesses on and kept Emma tight in my arms. It wasn't long before we were airborne. A display screen near the center console showed our destination.

"We're going to a stop-off station before pushing through to the outer worlds."

Jamie glanced at the screen. "It's a junker and wouldn't make it any further."

Creaking sounds of metal echoed through the ship as if the frame was bending from the lift-off pressure. Would we even make it out of the atmosphere?

Emma's eyes opened, and I rocked her gently regardless of the shaking ship.

"We did it, babes, we made it off the planet."

Jamie lowered her head and seemed sad. She was thinking of Zoey.

I said, "Zoey and I talked in the doctor's office when you were sleeping. She told me she wouldn't hesitate to sacrifice herself for our family. Her death was already a guarantee at the Stumble Inn. Zoey spent her life protecting people she never really cared about, but when we freed her, it gave her something to live for, and she became part of our family. Zoey didn't die in vain. What she did was done with pride and acceptance of the consequences."

Jamie was crying uncontrollably but she nodded. The shaking subsided as we entered into the cold black of space. We could hear the FTL drives spooling up, moments away from jumping away from this terrible place, and I hoped that we were in the clear. Well, I didn't know anyone who got hurt traveling away from a rogue world.

*

An alarm had been going off for the last hour. Our FTL engines were overheating, and the ship wanted to drop out of the faster-than-light bubble to cool down. I told Jamie not to turn it off because we were nearly at the stop-off. If we exited too soon, we might be lost forever. Seconds in faster-than-light was hundreds of thousands of kilometers.

Jamie shouted over the alarms, "We need to power down."

"No, we're almost there, just a few more seconds."

Emma was crying, but the noise of our ship falling apart was louder as steam shot out of exhaust vents overhead under the tremendous strain and attempts to cool down critical systems.

"Ten more seconds."

A pulsating shriek of metal twisting rocked the walls, and I struggled to keep Emma in my grip. Jamie reached forward and hit the emergency override. The ship dropped out of FTL with the station directly in front. We were lucky; that sound was the spine of our ship breaking. Jamie looked at me and laughed.

I did the same and said, "If it's not one thing, it's another with us. When will our break come?"

"Who knows?"

After clearing the dock and landing, an engineer told us that we should be dead. The engine cooling system had failed, and there were fractures in the mainline support. The ship wouldn't fly again. Then he offered us two thousand credits to purchase it for parts, but Jamie negotiated with him to thirty-five hundred.

As we stepped out of the dock, the engineer said, "I hate negotiating with employees of the Corporation."

I said, "It had nothing to do with the Corporation. My wife never gives in and would haggle you out of your shoes if she wanted them."

The engineer chuckled to himself, and Jamie smiled. In the food court, ship commanders and captains were going about their business. Some reminded us of the captain who sold our fellow passengers as slaves, so we stayed clear of them. We found a captain who had registration with the relations station.

"Yes, I'm headed to the outer worlds, but first, I need to stop off at the station to deliver goods."

"We don't want to go anywhere near the relations station."

He raised an eyebrow and rubbed his beard before replying. "Don't worry, it's none of my business what your reasons are, there are other passengers on my ship too who feel the same way. When we dock, stay in your cabin. Station customs won't bother you."

Jamie said, "How much for travel?"

The captain smiled, looking at Emma and wiggling his fingers as she tried to grab them. "A thousand for each of you, the baby's free."

He was an honorable man and meant well, something rare in the Free Worlds. Within a few hours, we were in our cabin on his ship, traveling once again in FTL. It felt good to relax in a real bed. I massaged Jamie's shoulders while she played with Emma, making funny noises.

"It's probably good we got rid of that junker. The agent was in our hangar before us. He could have placed a tracking beacon without us knowing."

Jamie didn't respond. I could tell she was in deep thought.

Finally, she said, "You're right. He tracked us so far from Dol'Arem and might never give up."

"We won't give up either. We'll press on, and if the agent someday finds us on the outer worlds, we'll keep going as far as we must."

I was a gifted programmer, after all. The royal family on Helana might like upgraded Free Worlds defense programs for their planet. Maybe we could get a royal pardon and stay under their protection. Free Worlds law didn't apply to the outer planets.

After some time, we fell asleep for a much-needed rest.

A few days passed, and we spent time with other passengers; there were only six others, and they seemed friendly enough. The captain spent time with us too. He told us he had five children and sixteen grandchildren in the main cylinder of the relations station. He was going to retire a few years ago but decided to keep hauling to help his family. I appreciated the man more after hearing his story. Jamie did her best, but she was still coping with Zoey's death.

At night's end, we were back in our cabin, getting ready to sleep. Jamie was quieter, keeping to herself, and I was worried.

"Mace, when we get to the outer worlds, I want to have another baby."

I was surprised. "Emma's still a newborn, and you're thinking about having another?"

"You are already such a great father and deserve more children. You have so much love to give, and I see how happy you are with her. We should have a whole house full of kids. Little Applegates."

I laughed. "If we get there without any more issues, I'll have ten kids with you, babes. You know I can't stop myself from practicing under the sheets."

Jamie smirked but still seemed sad. "Once my body gets better from birthing our daughter, we can practice every day."

She fed baby Emma, and we fell asleep on the bed together. I loved that part most, snuggling with my wife and daughter. What more could I want? Within a short time, my eyes closed.

I woke with a racing heart and in total fear. Was this a dream? Why was I so scared? We weren't in the Lowlands anymore, there wasn't anything to worry about here on the ship. The ship ... we weren't in faster-than-light travel and must have stopped for a cooldown. Wait, Jamie wasn't in the room, but Emma was. *What the hell's going on?* I picked up my daughter and opened the cabin door, peeking my head down both sides of the hallway, scared someone would be there. Some passengers were in a common room talking.

"Have you seen Jamie, my wife?"

They seemed nervous, and one said at last, "No. But a MERC Guild agent scout ship just docked with ours. He's down in the loading dock. The first mate's waking up the captain to greet him."

I felt like I was falling off a cliff into a black emptiness, and my arms trembled. There wasn't anywhere to run, and Jamie was missing. The agent might already have her. Jamie wasn't weak, she was a strong woman, and if she knew he was here, she might do something to protect us. I had to act.

The elevator doors opened, and I ran down the hallway to the loading dock entry. Emma started crying in my arms. There was a small circular window at eye level, and I looked inside to see if the agent had gotten off his vessel yet.

Total panic and fear took me, and my mouth was so dry. Jamie was inside with her back to the door. Across the dock stood the agent with his bewildered mongrel. It appeared the Dolrinions lost their battle. The major and the other sentinel followed that old master gunnery sergeant's lead, and it caused their deaths. I was confused; what was happening in there? Jamie was talking to the agent, was she pleading with him? She was such a good talker, but how could her words work on him? The agent looked past my wife. Jamie turned back at me. Her face was red and tear-stained. She came to the glass and spoke, but I couldn't hear her, the door was too thick.

"Jamie," I screamed, "I can't hear you. Open the door. I can help."

Emma's cries were louder now, and Jamie was still talking. I was trying to read her lips, but all I could make out was: "I love you, and I'm sorry."

She turned to the side and hit the outer release door. Red lights flashed inside the dock, and emergency lights did the same in the hallway.

I shouted with fear, anger, and confusion, "No! What are you doing? No, Jamie, don't do it. There must be another way."

The mongrel bit on her and Jamie's mouth opened wide as her eyes squeezed shut. There was nothing I could do. The door wouldn't open. The beast ripped back, and a massive piece of my wife's neck was missing. Blood spooled from the sides of her mouth as more tears streamed down her cheeks. Jamie put her hand on the circle of glass, and I did the same.

I cried uncontrollably, "No, Jamie, no, please, no."

The agent tried running back to his ship, but it was too late; the dock doors opened, and he launched backward like a piece of lint being sucked into a vacuum. The mongrel followed, and then Jamie, my darling wife. We looked into each other's eyes one last time before she too went away into the blackness of space. I fell to the floor, leaning against the locked door with Emma crying hysterically on my chest. My face was wet from the liquid pouring out of my eyes, nose and mouth down my face and dripping onto Emma's head.

"My wife, no, my love, oh, Jamie, why?"

My vision became clouded from my tears, and in the distance, I saw light as the elevator door opened. The captain and first mate were over me, looking through the small window and down.

I whispered, "My love, my wife, my Jamie."

Things became a blur after that. Somehow, I was back in my cabin with Emma, but couldn't leave. Periodically the captain would come by to offer food and check on the baby, but days must have gone by. I did my best to look after Emma because she was all I had left, but depression took hold. Emma looked like her mother, and I missed her so much.

My baby cried again, and I rocked her in my arms saying, "It's ok, little nugget. Your mom will be back soon."

The cabin door opened again, and this time it wasn't just the captain. A new Guild agent was standing in the doorway, looking at Emma and me without sympathy.

"Mace, you have to go with the agent now. There's nothing more I can do for you."

"Where are we?"

The agent said, "Space dock of the cathedral on the relations station."

My heart sank into my gut and I looked down at Emma. Tears dropped onto her perfect baby skin. It was all for nothing. So much death so our family could hide, all for nothing. "I'm so sorry, my daughter, I failed you."

"Mr. Applegate, please follow me."

He led us off the dock and through several rooms. I felt hopeless.

"Are you turning me over to the Corporation? I'll go back willingly and let them take me to the chamber, but my daughter, please, can the Guild keep her safe?"

The agent didn't answer my desperate plea. There were agents and mongrels everywhere, and I couldn't escape. A door opened to a small white room. The walls, ceiling, and floor all looked like a continuous solid piece of white. At the center of the room was a table with chairs. He left me there alone with Emma. I sat and waited. There wasn't anything else I could do.

After some time, a Guild civilian employee came into the room and took two vials of blood, one from me and one from Emma.

"Why are you doing this? What's going on here?"

She gave a crooked half-smile with a glimpse at my daughter. "It's standard procedure. You both came from a rogue world—we can't let you onto the station with any pathogens."

She left, and after another hour of waiting, two MERC Guild agents entered the room with their mongrels. After the horrors I'd seen, those animals frightened me. They went into opposite corners and lay on the ground. The agents took seats on the other side of the table.

"Mr. Applegate, I'm Senior Agent Pawar of the internal investigations division here at the cathedral."

I glared and asked, "Are you taking me to the Federate Corporation bubble now?"

Both frowned and looked at each other. The senior agent glanced at Emma.

"Mr. Applegate, we want to first apologize for the unethical behavior of the agent that chased you."

What? What's he talking about? I shook my head and stared at my daughter. "What do you mean?"

"We at the Guild were already investigating this … situation months ago on Dol'Arem. After the attack in the Hollow Ward, we realized more was happening than we even knew. Guild leadership speculated on the circumstances further after the agent chased you to Galma. We sent a team to investigate but were unable to locate him or you. We needed proof to verify our suspicions. Proof finally obtained with your arrival."

I continued shaking my head. "Evidence? Proof? I don't understand—what suspicion? Please tell me what's going on here."

He studied Emma and me for a moment.

"The proof is that baby you're holding. Blood can't lie."

I looked at Emma in confusion and remembered the Truth Seer in the Lowlands. Her words blared through my head like a siren. "All the answers you seek are in your blood. Though for you, the answers would cause tremendous pain. Your blood holds the key. Blood, blood, blood. It's all in the blood."

My eyes locked on to Emma's face, and she slowly opened her eyes and looked at me.

Zoey's voice was in my head. "You both have blue eyes. Genetically your little girl has a ninety-nine percent chance of having that color if my memory from genetics class is right."

I stared at Emma closer, and in the bright lighting of the room, her eye color was clearer than ever before. Wasn't that strange—she had deep brown eyes. The agent who was chasing us had eyes like that too.

CHAPTER 41

Elevator to the Door of Life

What goes up must come down (Isabel)

I t was so hot inside that box. My lips were chapped and peeling, even though sweat trickled everywhere, creating terrible humidity, and the pain and stiffness in my crossed legs arched up under my chin was driving me insane. I lost sensation days ago below the waist. Was it days? Maybe it was only hours, but how could I know? The heat was making me hallucinate. Ezra stood there swinging his massive arms, but he was already dead, and how could he stand in such a small space? I was speaking in different languages but repeating the same words over and over.

"*Aho. Tha'tós eya. Banue Na'yah. Aho.* No. I will kill you. Freedom from tyranny. No."

Ezra disappeared, and Gideon, smiling, was clear as a summer day. Ezra was back, raping Gideon in the cave, but I was in the oven, not the cave. I wanted to lift my head from this balled-up position but couldn't. It was so tight in that box.

"Pirates of the Black, Draco is with you."

Both images faded away, and I was once again alone in the black nothingness of that box. Were my eyes even open? I couldn't tell. Bacon should be in the box next to me, but he didn't speak, so how could I know.

"Bacon, are you out there?"

My husband appeared. Tuddy, how were you there? His light brown hair, olive skin, and green eyes. What a handsome man he was.

"Tuddy? How did you come back from the dead?"

A forest emerged around me. Wait, I knew that forest. That was where we set up the ambush for Killian Lyons inside New-Sparta. We had intelligence that Killian was traveling to see his mistress at her home in the mountains to the east of their State capital city. From those mountains, I saw the outlines of buildings inside the city. The ambush took place on a dirt road with a single cabin at the top. Years before that time, hundreds of cabins sat on that mountain. Killian wanted privacy and had them removed.

"No, don't. It's a trap."

Tuddy rolled out spiked strips to trap the convoy as it passed. I saw myself laying out explosive charges near the sides of that road. There was a tree fall at the rear to block their retreat. City-state loyalist fighters lined the natural surroundings wearing ghillie suits and other camouflage. That forest was so dense and dark with thick tall trees. It was nearly impossible to see further than a few meters. Random boulders protruded from the dirt. Mountains were always rocky. We could hear the vehicles, three of them, black as night and rims shaped like lions' heads.

I turned to Tuddy. "If anything happens to me, tell the children—"

"You'll tell them yourself after we kill Killian Lyons and go home."

He always knew how to bring back my confidence. Gideon could do the same. Tires popped on the first truck, and Tuddy set off the bombs. Fire sprang like fountains of flame, consuming the first vehicle. Debris and metal fragments littered the dirt road. The tree-fall trap worked perfectly, crushing the rear truck like a pancake. Both hilltops opened up with a barrage of gunfire. Streaks of light with cracks and pops brightened the surroundings in a brilliant show. Fierce weapons fire pounded every square centimeter, and by the end, little solid material remained. The smell of gunpowder overwhelmed my nostrils, and the scent filled that small box. I called a ceasefire, and we slowly moved to the vehicle where Killian's body should have been waiting for us to claim victory.

I hollered again from inside that dark box, "Don't go—it's a trap, you fools."

Tuddy looked inside the smoking truck and quickly turned, but before any words left his mouth, an echo blared through the quiet forest. His body jolted back as a red hole appeared on his chest. The opening was massive, and I took cover behind a rock, but that cover was weak. I tried dragging him towards me, and he stared into my eyes. The wound was fatal; we both knew it. Loyalist fighters fell, cut down like animals by high-caliber machine-gun rounds.

Tuddy grabbed my face with his bloody hand to get my attention. I gazed at him again and felt my tears overflowing. Small puffs of dust jumped off the boulder from bullet strikes. Some of the rounds hit Tuddy's legs, and he didn't even flinch because his nerves were dying. Each new red mark on his legs appeared with no expression of pain on his face. Tuddy's body was failing him, and he knew it. All those years, fighting the Twins together, and in one blink of our eyes, it was over. He spoke, but I couldn't hear him over the loud battle, so I bent down.

"Protect Adam and Juliet. Keep our children safe, keep them ..."

His eyes closed. Colonel Tuddy Sideris, the Stonewall of the Allied States, died on a dirt road in foreign territory during a failed ambush on Killian Lyons. Brother to a usurper. The pretender to the prime regency that belonged to my father and killer of billions of innocents.

The hallucination from the past faded, and I screamed from inside the oven. "Damn you, Isaac and Killian Lyons! Damn you to oblivion. I'll take both your hands so the three acolytes look at you with pity when you get to the door of life and can't enter. Those Dark Priests won't be able to save you."

A banging smashed against the box, and someone outside said, "Shut up in there. You're driving me crazy. Random babbling, you weak woman. Die with honor. That's all you need to do in the oven."

"Cowardly sentinel! Open the box and fight me. I'll show you how to die with honor. It won't take long, and your soul can go to the memory stone as I smile down at your corpse."

He didn't reply, and after my outburst it was harder to breathe. That damn humidity got worse with each breath and every drop of sweat. There was a thud, and the box shook. What was that? Did he trip over my box?

"Hello? Is someone out there? Are you scared to answer me, sentinel?"

The box shook again, followed by a cranking sound, and the top opened. Everything was so blurry. The stars and night sky hurt my sensitive eye. Outlines of bodies were above, and someone picked me up, but I yelled from the pain of stretching out straight, and the same person covered my mouth.

My eye cleared—Gideon, Jack, Nina, and Ethan. The sentinel that yelled at me was dead next to the oven box. It looked like his soul would be going to Kora after all.

Gideon whispered, "Can you walk?"

Nina handed me a flask of water, and I drank long and hard. The liquid felt amazing going into my body, and I felt the coldness inside. More spilled from the sides onto the sand.

"No, I won't walk, but I can run."

All my comrades smiled, and Gideon said, "Good. Let's go."

"Wait, we need to get Bacon."

Ethan pried open the lock on Bacon's box and jumped back at the smell. Bacon had died, and his body released everything: stool, urine, and he threw up on himself. Poor Bacon; he survived nine times in the oven, and the tenth killed him. He died for me, and I felt guilty.

Gideon tapped my arm. "Come on, Isabel, we need to go."

Guard tower spotlights randomly streaked through the sand, and all the lights were off inside the command building to our rear. Nina and Ethan dragged the dead sentinel's body and pushed it under a random slave bunk as the rest of us kept a sharp eye on the surroundings. The slaves inside that bunk would all be executed in the morning for the Burning Star sentinel underneath their bunk.

Nina whispered, "There's a ship waiting for us in orbit. We're leaving."

"Where's the rendezvous?"

"The white peak mountains, south of camp," Ethan said.

Those mountains were so high, and frost covered the tops in the early hours of first light. It was eight kilometers away. So much could happen in that time. We cautiously moved from one slave bunk to the next, getting closer to the chain-link fencing where the spotlight guard towers loomed overhead. Gideon raised his hand, stopping us in our tracks. A sentinel sat in the sand around the next corner with her helmet off, trying to fix something inside. Gideon motioned with his hands, telling Jack to strangle her. I'd snuck behind Lyons Pride before, doing the same with piano wire. Jack walked slowly, trying his best not to make a sound. In the early hours of the morning, the slightest noise could seem like a shockwave. The sand made it easier to sneak up on someone. Jack wrapped his giant hand around her throat. She struggled for only a moment with her legs dangling in the air. That sentinel did her best, but Jack was too powerful.

It only took a few moments for Jack to drag her dead body to the bunkhouse; it seemed like an eternity because of the possibility of being seen by other sentinels. Was her soul off to the memory stone too? It didn't matter; we rolled her body under the bunk, and that was another group of slaves the Dolrinions would nail to the front of camp in the morning.

Another three rows down and the chain-link fencing was the greatest thing I'd seen in days. There were two different rows of fencing with a gap between and guard towers running along the inner row, and those damn spotlights randomly searching for slaves like us. Two sentinels were in the tower above, talking in the Dolrinion language.

Gideon looked up and smirked. "I'll go up there and push one down for you. The other is mine."

Nina said, "You'll only have a split second before the one in that tower you plan on fighting with could sound an alarm."

I shook my head at them. "Wait, what about the sentinel LENS? Technically they should already know we're out."

Gideon's smile was wider. "Our ship up high is jamming them. The night shift isn't as attentive as others who monitor the LENS for inconsistencies. These sentinels can cry all they want. No one's coming to help." He glanced up at the tower again and turned to me. "I'll be right back. Try not to miss me while I'm gone."

I rolled my eye. Draco captain—at least he was acting more like himself, and it didn't bother me as much. The tower rails were made from a composite material that didn't creak like wood, and Gideon slowly pulled himself up, one rail at a time. He stopped when one of the sentinels above laughed. They didn't turn, and he continued to climb like a professional assassin. Gideon would have done well working with the city-state loyalists after the war. His head was near the tower floor, waiting patiently, not moving a muscle. One of the guards looked out over the landscape past the fence, and Gideon pulled himself up slowly, but then had to drop back down, level with the floor, because that same sentinel turned and walked to the ladder, looking out over the camp. If he glanced at his feet, our entire attempt to leave would have been over. The guard turned, facing his fellow soldier to talk, and Gideon wasted no time jumping up and pulling on his beltline from behind. The guard fell, and Gideon lunged into the tower. Nina and Ethan made quick work of the fallen sentinel. The only area they could stab at was his face, and that turned into a savage mess. Jack grabbed the body and dragged it to another slave bunk. More for the wood out front of camp.

We all looked up at the tower for tense seconds. It was quiet up there; did Gideon die? Was he able to overwhelm the sentinel? My heart sank into my guts until Gideon poked his head out with an impudent smile. He climbed down, shoving a few grenades and other items into his pocket.

"Why so scared, Izzy? Worried that I died?"

Ignoring his words, I asked, "Bringing along a few mementos?"

"Aye, prepare for the worst, but hope for the best."

Ethan clipped at the fencing, and after removing enough links, we all climbed through the opening. We had to be careful because raised areas on the sand indicated mines. If we stepped on them a nice alarm would explode across camp. We reached the next fence and Ethan clipped the links.

I whispered to Gideon, "How long was I in the oven? It felt like days."

He handed me a flask of water and replied, "A little over a day. We got the signal this morning, and I knew we couldn't wait any longer. The timing was perfect because we would have been in trouble if the ship wasn't here."

"Why?"

Gideon smirked. "After everything that happened, did you really think I'd sit by and let you die inside that small box? No, Isabel, we would have freed you and got caught wandering the desert with nowhere to go."

Ethan cleared the fence away. Nina and Jack went through while Gideon and I stared at each other. My heart raced, looking at the Draco captain. We left through the fence opening and ran until we lost sight of the spotlights.

"So, what happened while I was inside?"

Nina said, "After you killed Ezra, everything went into chaos. The Martoosh Pirates got into a brawl in their bunk. Several fought for leadership, and after half died, one came out victorious."

"What was his name?"

Gideon laughed. "Her name was Max, Captain Max of the doesn't-matter-anymore. She won control for nothing."

"What do you mean, for nothing?"

Ethan turned to us. "When we marched to the mines this morning, all the other slaves attacked the Brown Pirates inside the mountain. It was a rage of fury led by Sven as payback for what happened to Finlay. They're all dead."

"Good. Camp can make their own rules now."

Big Jack bellowed, "Only because of you, Fireheart."

I smiled at Jack. "Without you, I would have died. You told me to bite his nose, and I listened."

Jack raised his head a little higher, and Ethan slapped his thigh in excitement. "That was great, you should've seen those asses when that rock smashed Ezra's face. They looked like Titans came back from the dead and were marching at them. Scared shitless."

Gideon smirked at whatever craziness was happening inside his head.

"So, Isabel, I must ask—how was it inside your box?"

I knew he was Gideon being Gideon in all his loathsome ways.

I said, "Warm, damp, and tight on space, prick."

He puffed some laughter and turned away. Strangely enough, my lip curled into a half-smile.

We heard a sound from behind. A hovercraft was traveling swiftly over the sand.

Gideon waved his hands. "Get down."

We dropped and tried to blend in with our surroundings. The craft passed by, moving into the distance; several sentinels were inside but didn't see us. Once it was far enough away, we got up and kept going.

Ethan peered into the distance watching the disturbed sand float back to the surface. "Was it looking for us?"

"No, it was a transit hovercraft, probably going to another camp. We should pick up the pace," Gideon said.

By the time we reached our destination, the sun was rising. A blurry object took shape the closer we got, and I couldn't believe what I saw. My mouth opened wide, and Gideon snickered at my face.

"Are you kidding me?"

Ethan and Nina laughed.

"A supply spool line? Breathing people aren't supposed to travel on those lifts, Gideon."

Gideon tapped my back and said, "Think outside of your box, Isabel."

"Very funny."

A sizeable square metal platform was resting on the sandy ground. At the center of the platform was a narrow circular spool of flexible aluminum and steel, the end of which shot up past the clouds. Around the spool were anchors for tying down supplies so they didn't fall off the platform. Colonies used spool lines as cheap ways to deliver supplies without burning fuel. The ship in orbit had an extensive cranking system to reel the metal rope up to their vessel. Under normal circumstances, provisions would be secured to the platform by the anchors and then lowered slowly to the destination.

Thrusters underneath kept the platform level. We stepped onto the metal square, and I shook my head.

"Wait. The spools take hours to reel up or down. We're short on time and we'll have little oxygen when we get up past the clouds."

Jack tilted his head and opened a crate fastened to one of the anchors. Inside were zero-g civilian suits that had to be two hundred years old by the look of them.

"It's better to breathe old air than no air at all."

Gideon nudged my shoulder. "That's the spirit, now put on your gear, and let's get rolling."

After gearing up, we attached ourselves to harnesses near the center. Sparks streaked on the rocky mountainside behind us and the platform near our feet. My attention went to the distance where hovercrafts cruised in our direction.

Gideon called out, "Looks like they found our gifts left at camp. Is everyone secure?"

We all indicated *yes* one way or another as cracking echoes from sentinel rifle fire ripped through the air.

"Gideon, you still didn't answer my question. How are we supposed to get up there before someone blows us out of the sky?"

He raised his eyebrows and pulled one side of his lip back. "Hold on tight, Fireheart. We're on an elevator trip to visit your door of life. May the acolyte of your choosing grant us entry!" He laughed.

Gideon pulled a lever, and I felt tremendous pressure and weight on my chest and my face was pulled towards the platform. It was worse than the most powerful roller-coaster ride, but Gideon screamed with laughter; he was having fun. Hard drops were easier than this, and everyone seemed to be struggling with the tension. Flames surrounded the platform edges—what the hell did Gideon do to us? He was still laughing. Even Jack hollered from the pressure. The thick metal flooring rattled viciously. We were already nearing the clouds.

Ethan shouted, and Jack reached out and grabbed his hand, holding on to it with all his strength. *Oh, no!* His harness had broken and he was dangling in the air like a flag blowing in a terrible wind. I could hear everything through my helmet speakers, which made it worse.

Nina yelled, "Ethan!"

Gideon tried unsuccessfully to use slack from his harness line to throw in Ethan's direction. Jack was losing his grip. He grunted and jerked his shoulders to hold on to the young man that he'd taken under his wing, but it was no use. Within a split second, Ethan disappeared into the clouds. That fall was at least nine kilometers.

Jack cried, "No, no, no," slamming his giant fist into the floor.

He had mentored Ethan and was proud when he earned his first tattoo, but that was it, the end of Ethan, born on Epsilon Prime to the twenty-one city-states and died a Shipmate of the Black on the slave world of Pomona.

The sky grew darker, and we jolted through the upper atmosphere. The higher we went, the easier the pressure was. Through the blackness, a ship came into focus and the spool drew closer, sparks streaking off the crank line spinning faster than it was ever meant to. The massive wheel grew bigger with each meter of line wheeled in. That ship was a pile of junk. The lower half was oval shaped, and at one end, a massive square shape pushed up, making the vessel disproportionate. Above the square the wheel crank was still spinning, and it was bigger than the entire ship.

We were on the landing area and walked into a small airlock next to an enormous docking door. Big Jack's shoulders moved up and down. Nina put her arms around the giant, trying to console him.

Air pressure equalized, and the inner airlock opened. We removed our helmets, clipped them to our belts and stepped inside. Hardened Draco Pirates moved through the ship purposefully. Each one of them had more tattoos than any of the slave pirates from camp. They were a bunch of seasoned shipmates.

Gideon grinned. "*Aah*, a real Draco crew hard at work. Look at all this ink—more to our liking, aye Jack?"

Jack nodded but tears still rolled down his face.

Inside the command center was a big man with a long thick mustache, bald head, and a huge fat belly. He was a few centimeters shorter than Jack, but still a giant. The pirates in command had the most tattoos besides Gideon and Jack.

The big man spoke in a boisterous voice. "Captain Gideon. Welcome aboard."

"Captain Kyson. What a pleasure."

They slapped arms together with wide, inviting smiles.

"When Admiral Derwin asked for someone to rescue his son from a slave world, I stepped up without hesitation. How could I not? Your first mate's my cousin."

Jack and Kyson gave each other a massive bear hug. "Cousin, what's wrong? You look troubled."

He struggled to speak, so Nina said, "We lost one on the ride up. Jack was training him. We'll need to honor the fallen."

Captain Kyson bobbed his head. "Aye. We lose the Blood of Draco all too often, Cousin, I know. We will pay tribute to your friend, I promise."

Jack raised his head, and they hugged once more.

Gideon shouted, "Pirates of the Black, Draco is with you!"

All yelled, "Draco is with us all!"

Gideon went to the navigation monitor and said, "We need to go. The Dolrinion fleet is coming around the planet."

Kyson stepped closer to the screen. "Aye, they picked up the heat signature from that damn spool reel—I was shocked it didn't melt. Another daring plan of the famous Captain Gideon." He raised his voice. "Ok, get my FTL engines online."

A pirate spoke up. "Captain, we have a problem."

We went to the computer screen she was looking at and saw a warship signature coming around the dark side of the planet's moon. It wasn't Dolrinion.

The captain shook his head. "Dolrinions from one side and another from their moon—who is it? Navigation, put video on the main screen."

An image appeared on a larger screen near the middle of command. It was a heavy carrier, nearly double the size of any Free Worlds destroyer. I knew right away who it was, from the beautifully intricate design at the front of an eagle head sparkling brightly with gold—the feathers shaped behind the head were carved into bulging pieces along the vessel hull before fading away into the ship design. The detail was a marvel. Gideon's face turned dark and angry. He knew who they were too—the same style of ship that took him prisoner fourteen years ago on his last relief mission to Athinia during the civil war. The city-state that left their neutrality and declared for New-Sparta, sealing the Allied States' fate. Those traitors circled their gigantic fleets above Epsilon Prime, preventing any further evacuations of civilians to safety. Any transport that refused to stop became nothing more than stardust, destroyed by screaming eagle missiles.

"The Chrysós Aetós," I said softly.

Gideon's face was red. "Golden Eagle bastards from Aetós." He lifted his hands, staring at his maimed fingers as he spoke.

Captain Kyson asked, "But why? Why are they here?"

Gideon, Jack and Nina turned to me as I said, "The Lyons Twins want their prize."

"They don't get to have you today. Captain Kyson, weapons?" Gideon's voice was furious.

The captain laughed. "It's a junker. We stole it to get you, nothing more. The plan was to jump away before anyone engaged us." The thick-mustached captain turned and puffed his lip. "Pilot, engine status?"

"Three minutes. Still warming up."

Gideon whispered, "We don't have three minutes."

The Chrysós Aetós heavy carrier opened fire and several screaming missiles shot out from forward tubes inside the golden eagle head. A dozen bright specks of flame appeared in the blackness coming right for us. Kyson ordered his pilot to perform evasive maneuvers, but that would be useless against such advanced weapons. They were tracking us the moment they left their tubes.

"Uhm, Captain? There's another problem."

No one needed to ask the navigator what that problem was—on the screen, distant bright flashes appeared everywhere. Ships were coming out of FTL.

Kyson crinkled his brow. "Who the hell's that?"

Gideon's eye opened wide. "Federate Corporation destroyers."

The screaming eagle missiles were nearly on us, and the shrieking vibrated on the walls, even inside command at the center of our vessel. Gideon narrowed his eye, looking at the screen, and I noticed too. The flaming blips were too high and passed above us. From behind, thousands of bright lines appeared, moving towards the heavy carrier. It was flak suppression fire. A Federate Corporation capital ship passed overhead on an intercept course for the carrier. It was larger and shaped oddly, similar to a shark fin, but bulkier with knots running along the sides. The Chrysós Aetós vessel opened up with salvo fire from tubes, guns, missiles and rail ports. But where were the carrier support ships? It should be able to launch a cruiser, three frigates, and five light gunships. With those extra support vessels, the odds of victory would be greater, but none were there.

The flak firewall streams of light discharging from the Corporation capital ship took out all the screaming missiles, and they returned fire with a direct spread. The Chrysós Aetós carrier launched its countermeasures. Both sides fired everything they had in a brilliant show of lights and explosions that created a smog of fire in front of the carrier.

Some of the rounds from both sides hit their marks, but most detonated in the streams of light from the flak wall. Even on the screen, it was bright like a meteor shower with millions of objects. All the Free Worlds militaries knew and feared seeing either a Federate capital ship or a Chrysós Aetós heavy carrier coming at them on a display screen. Neither had ever met in combat. We were witnessing history in the making. They were the pinnacles of all Free Worlds militaries.

In the distance, the Dolrinion battle group was heavily outnumbered by the Corporation fleet. They still engaged with little success. Destroyers, war barges, battleships, cruisers, frigates, and light gunships filled the screen, a full array of military power. Destroyers were the most favored ship because of their abilities, wielding at least one hundred and fifty primary batteries bulked together in groups of three, and over eight hundred secondary batteries, not including missile tubes, railguns, uranium spinners, and cluster charges. The primary cannons could fire every twenty seconds with three thousand seven-hundred-kilogram armor-piercing shells. From our position, those explosions looked like small sparkles, but in truth, that power could flatten a mountain in seconds.

The Dolrinion ships in the distance committed to barrage fire, launching their weapons in all directions. They didn't have a choice because they were heavily outnumbered. Their flak wall was falling apart, and the ships started breaking apart.

Gideon said, "The Dolrinion shield of flames is failing. They'll be dead in a few minutes."

They couldn't hope to win with such odds. The keepers of the memory stone would be busy etching new names after that battle. Even brighter flashes detonated where the primary fighting was happening. Nuclear weapons fire, the finishing touch on the beaten battle group. The Chrysós Aetós heavy carrier and capital ship were also starting to break apart in the overwhelming weapons fire. Hit after hit, they continued attacking. The level of damage on both behemoth vessels would have been enough to obliterate a handful of destroyers—what a rare sight.

Closer to Pomona, more flashes of light sparked. Federate missile starships jumped in and took attack positions away from the main fighting. They opened fire on the slave world with nukes, railguns, and kinetic projectile bombardment rods. In the Alliance, we called them rods from the gods, because of their destructive power. If those ships killed any Free Worlds citizens, they'd be violating the Free Worlds' Relations Policy.

Captain Kyson was still trying to maneuver our junker away from the fighting. "How much time until we can jump?"

The navigator said, "One minute."

"It's too late."

Several screaming missiles left the heavy carrier before the ship split into pieces. Both vessels had destroyed each other, and our time had come. The bright flaming balls grew larger as they drew near. Time seemed to slow down, and the echoing shriek started as just a whisper then grew into a deafening blast of noise.

I looked at Gideon and said, "I'm not done yet."

He didn't reply and only stared into my eye. A blinding light took over the display screen before it deactivated, the ship rumbled and we lost our balance in the shockwave. Fire appeared everywhere along the walls, consuming everything it touched. We were lost. Everything was lost. Nina, Jack, and Gideon had long faces. We were at our end. Strange that I wasn't scared. Gideon reached into his pocket, fumbling for something, and then a blinding bright flash of light overwhelmed me. Images of Adam and Juliet were clear in my mind before I closed my eye …

CHAPTER 42

Worlds Collide

Even playgrounds can be a dangerous place (Kathryn)

Tobias left only yesterday, but it felt like weeks. I woke up early and went to the command-and-control building near our megastructure. T told me that was where all Defender Corps leadership worked to protect us. Colonel Hanifin was in there, and I wanted to know if my brother was ok.

The entrance was guarded on both sides and set up with an outer and inner airlock to get inside. Armored warthogs stood guard with tin suits. They wouldn't let me in. I tried twice and wasn't giving up just yet.

A guard shook his head and said, "I told you the first two times, you're not getting inside. You don't have authorization, and the colonel is too busy to bother with the likes of you."

I frowned and made a fist. Another group of soldiers wearing dress uniforms walked by and went to the airlock door, sliding their cards and stepping inside. When the door opened, I saw the same setup as our megastructure airlock with elevated turret positions on both corners. The outer door closed.

"Did you ask her if she would see me, or are you telling me that she won't see me?"

The tin suit replied, "Both."

I paced from side to side because I was so annoyed, and the outer airlock door opened again. More officers walked out. Maybe one of them knew how T was doing.

"I want to know how my brother Major Tobias Norcross is doing on his mission. Why won't anyone tell me what's going on?"

"Get the hell out of here before I arrest you, girl."

A few of the officers leaving looked at me as they walked away.

I turned to the annoying tin suit and frowned. "Get real. You won't do anything to me." I stepped away and looked back. "I'll be back in one hour. Maybe you'll have a different answer for me then."

He shook his head as I left. They didn't even wonder what the beautifully intricate pole in my hands was. I was using the trishula blade as a walking stick, and no one seemed to care or take notice. Tobias wouldn't have approved, but I'd always kept a weapon close on the surface. There was a park nearby, and I sat on a bench, watching children laugh and play. One was on a swing with her mother pushing. I had no memories of doing anything like that. It was nice to see youthful innocence having fun.

A well-dressed officer stepped over to the bench and sat next to me. He didn't acknowledge that I was there and gazed at the children with a slight smile. He was older with gray hair, dark spots on his skin and overlapping creases on his jowls—a captain, from the bars on his shoulders. I stared at him but he ignored me, sitting in silence.

"Can I help you with something?"

He tilted his head slightly without looking at me and said, "No, you can't, but I can help you."

I turned back to watch the children, and he continued. "I've known Tobias since he was young. Knew his father too."

I snapped my head in his direction. "You knew T's dad?"

"That's what I said, wasn't it? He was a good man and cared for his family on a deep level. Tough choices when certain responsibilities linger on one's shoulders, especially someone like him. We were all sad when he disappeared."

I didn't understand what the old-timer was saying, but I listened.

"I'm not here about Major Norcross's father. I'm here to give you some information about the major. We lost contact with his detachment earlier today. Don't be alarmed by that development."

"Don't be alarmed? My brother's missing, and you're telling me not to worry?"

We locked eyes and the captain said, "He's not missing at all, simply not answering our calls. They disabled their transponders, and all forward operation defenders out in the field left their posts at his command and are moving quickly in this direction. Those detachments aren't answering either, and the colonel is furious. Major Norcross knows how to soldier, and every seasoned officer in the colony knew Colonel Hanifin's orders were wrong. It was dangerous and reckless to send out a whole company. There's something else going on out there that the major is aware of, and he would never make such a drastic decision without purpose. Some of the older officers wondered if he was doing something akin to what his father did, but I know the major better than most."

The captain stood. I did the same but was speechless.

"Fear not, Kathryn. Tobias Norcross is the smartest military mind I have ever seen. You will see him again."

"Wait, where are you going now?"

He turned and pursed his lips. "Disturbing reports are coming in from across the colony worlds. The Federate Corporation has launched a massive bombardment against every Dolrinion slave planet. We don't have any Fleet Branch support on Nim, only our defense grids in orbit. The colonel's nervous because war is afoot across occupied space, especially with the assassination attempt on Center Seat Representative McWright from the Colonial Accord. Their Labor Party unions are calling for war too. Things are starting to boil over the pot."

He left, and I was having trouble processing everything he told me. What did he mean about that stuff with T's father? That was too much information; I needed to stretch my legs and think about everything. Near the front entrance wall to our colony were several power-ball fields. As I got closer, I heard cheering. The stands were full of spectators watching teams play. I enjoyed the physical contact when players smashed against each other, fighting for possession of the ball. The grass was soft on my feet. To the left was a paved road large enough to fit several trucks side by side, leading to the main gate. Some of the spectators to my right watching the game sat on folding chairs. Across the field were seating stands, and behind that was the massive wall, not even half the size of our megacity walls of Civil Earth, but still sixty meters high.

Players were running up and down the field, throwing, kicking, and headbutting the ball as they tried to score and pass. Was that Renee sitting on the grass? I stepped over and looked closer. It was.

"Renee? You watch power-ball?"

She puffed her lips and said, "What? Am I not allowed to enjoy a full-contact sport because I'm your teacher?"

I shook my head. "It's not that … you're, well, you're old."

Renee laughed and said, "Dearie, I might be old now, but I'll have you know that when I was your age, I played for the Eatontown University power-ball team on the relations station. They gave me a partial scholarship because I was so good."

"Really? What position did you play?" I was shocked.

She turned her head back to the field, smirking. "I was a runner. My legs were faster than yours in their youth."

I sat on the grass next to Renee, placing my trishula under my legs, and replied with something she'd said to me countless times. "You really can't judge a book by its cover."

"No, you can't, dear."

We sat and watched the game for some time. At one point, I looked up at the towering wall. I didn't typically come this far away from the megastructure

… old habits from being on the surface. Building thirty-three was nowhere near our megacity wall back home.

Renee saw me looking up and did the same before saying, "Impressive, isn't it?"

"Yes. It's not as big as the one back home around our city."

"No, it's not," Renee said.

"But why is this one so much smaller? There are real threats outside the wall here. On Civil Earth, there's nothing past the megacities. A wasteland, not counting the south where they grow real food. Why did they build them so high on Earth?"

Renee hesitated and glanced at me. "Who told you there's nothing in the wastelands? When the Hawks created the tier system, not everyone conformed and came inside. A segment of the population stayed away. Tier One built the wall to keep them out and us in. Tobias would have to tell you about the military reasoning. That's beyond me. What I can say is that if a Free Worlds military wanted to attack a megacity, it would be difficult."

I continued watching the game, and Renee did the same.

"I do love this sport," she said.

Red lights spaced out evenly along the wall lit up and started spinning, followed by alarms pulsing in a repetitive beat. The power-ball game stopped, and everyone turned, watching the wall with uncertainty. Turrets made a powering up rotary sound, turning and spinning. Within seconds they opened fire over the wall. The barrels turned red from the heat as they spun in circles. Green lasers targeted the weapons from the other side, and within seconds the spinners erupted into flames. More explosions trickled from the top of the wall.

I grabbed Renee and pulled her to her feet with my spear in hand, and shouted, "We need to go."

It felt like I was out in the open on the surface of Civil Earth, and Rockland gang members were coming towards me. We ran, and even for her age, Renee could run pretty well. Spectators and players on the power-ball field didn't move. They were still gazing at the explosions on the wall.

Why didn't the base early-warning systems go off?

More bangs. Above, streams of smoke arched over the wall and massive detonations emitted near the entrance. Giant fireballs were everywhere and people who had been standing there only moments earlier were now dead on the ground. Tin suits ran for the front gate, and a warthog steamed towards us as we ran away.

A focused officer in the pilot seat gave us a quick look. She yelled, "Move to cover. Get back to the megastructure."

She pointed her short bot arms into the air, and a continuous barrage of thuds and popping sounds came from the cannon holes. Dozens of streaming rockets went into the air from her warthog leaving a blazing trail of smoke behind. The rockets went over the wall, and we kept running.

A discharge from a massive blast took us off our feet. My head was cloudy, and I couldn't hear anything but a strange humming. When I opened my eyes, Renee was above me. She was screaming, but I couldn't hear the words. My ears were muffled from the blast. It took me a moment to get to my feet, and I couldn't believe the devastation at the main gate. It was gone, obliterated from the blast, and a thick mist of ash and smoke was in its place.

Armored soldiers pushed through the thick plume, looking nothing like the tin suits from the Defender Corps. Their armor was gunmetal-colored with more sharp angles and edges cutting through instead of smooth like the tin suits. Their helmets were strangely molded with a flat front turning in and jetting back behind their head. Even their rifles were odd and different, banded and boxier than the expanding pistol, and with more ridges.

My hearing was coming back, and there was music playing, pipe music. Some of the new soldiers had added attachments with four pipes extending over their right shoulder and a long rod out front that the soldiers were carefully holding and pushing buttons. A blown-up bag was under their arms that they squeezed every few seconds.

Warthogs were engaging, firing their rockets, and the dark-armored soldiers fought back. Tanks came through the smoke, shooting bright streaks of light at the defenders. We kept moving away as rows of tin suits charged at the newcomers. Clinking sounds of empty rounds hit the street, and they were fighting hand to hand. There was a strange sound of crackling that reminded me of wood popping in a fire. Those noises overwhelmed my hearing. We got behind a brick building to catch our breath; my surface cough took me, and I spat out a gob of phlegm. Renee coughed as ash fell from above.

"Are those soldiers from the local population?"

"No. They're from one of the Free Worlds, but I haven't a clue which one. The technology is too advanced to be from the natives of Nim," Renee said.

The sounds of battle grew closer. We needed to move. I twisted the brace, and my trishula blade jetted out from the end. The Corin steel glistened in the sunlight, and those glowing green lines reminded me of the light display inside Obsessions. Renee's eyes opened wide, watching the spear extend.

I said, "Let's go."

There was so much smoke from destroyed buildings. More rockets streamed overhead, going for a target in the distance. The dust and debris reminded me of the yellow haze. The ground shook from explosions. We were back at the playground, where I spoke with the aged captain earlier in the day. Dead children with their parents replaced happy smiles and innocent giggles. One young girl was above her mom, looking down in tears, begging her to stand. The mother's entire abdomen was missing, her intestines dragged out along the concrete, reminding me of a snake baking in the sun. That little girl's mother wasn't coming back.

More whizzes behind us, with crackling sounds, and a missile struck the swing set ahead of us. We took cover behind the concrete wall outlining the park. Renee put her back against the wall and shook feverishly. I heard footsteps on the hard surface and peeked my head over the divider. The dark-armored soldiers shot their rifles at children trying to hide behind the recreational equipment in the playground—those scumbags. They had no hesitation shooting kids, and I wouldn't sit behind that wall and watch such savagery. The small child standing above her dead mom was down, and they kept firing their powerful rifles.

One of them ran out of ammo. He pulled on the front of his rifle, and the square-shaped latches around the barrel fell off. An identical square was in a pouch at his side, and he clipped it onto the barrel. As the soldier lifted his hand to rack the slide back so he could fire again, I jumped over the wall. He saw me and turned, but I was faster and more determined. With the back end of my trishula, I swatted the rifle away, spun the spear in my hands and brought the point into his chest. The glowing green lines of that fancy steel went through his armor like cutting into bread. The other soldier turned in my direction and opened fire. I flipped on the ground to get away from the incoming bullets, and got close enough to strike again. The amateur shot his friend who was already dead and falling from my work. Renee had to duck behind the concrete as bullets sprayed across the wall. I was too fast for that soldier as well and swept his legs out from under him. When he fell on his back, I drove the blade into his chest. The Corin steel passed the armor with ease and into his body, and my hands shook at the scraping that vibrated through my spear.

Renee stood and looked at me in disbelief. I guess she didn't know that I could fight like that, or maybe she thought everyone had exaggerated my abilities.

"We need to get to command and control."

She shook her head. "They told us to go back to the megastructure."

I grabbed her wrist and pulled her away with me. "There's more defenders at their command building. Our megastructure will be one big target for all those rockets in the air. The defenders won't care about that building, because critical infrastructure is inside command." T had taught me a lot about defender tactics.

We got to a quiet street, and it seemed like the fighting hadn't reached there yet. We still heard blasts and gunfire echoing in the distance, but that street was normal, aside from the ash falling from above. Halfway down, a tall wall of brick collapsed as something pushed through. We stopped and watched. A soldier wearing thicker dark armor than the others punched through the brick and mortar. The heavier war gear made him taller than he was, standing at least two hundred centimeters. On both shoulders were cannon holes similar to the warthog arms, and his fists had powerful thick bulging plates, which was what he used to punch through the wall. He wasn't as big as the warthog, but his gear seemed to be for a different purpose. His head turned and made a strange sound as he saw Renee and me in the middle of the street.

He punched his armored fists together, and I smiled, got low, and waved my hand, inviting him to try and come for me. My gesture made him angry. He shouted and got down in a position like the power-ball players before tackling. The soldier charged, and a strange cranking sound resonated through his armor with each step as he got closer and closer. I lowered myself and brought the trishula over my shoulder. Wait for him. The timing had to be perfect. Wait. Wait. *Now!* I threw the spear, and it landed just under his neck. He fell to his knees. Without hesitation, I pulled the blade out and quickly thrust it through his faceplate. Sadness's voice was telling me to wait, watch his shoulders, and make sure he wasn't breathing.

Renee grabbed my hand, and we continued running towards command. At the outer airlock, the same lieutenant I argued with earlier was there with a dozen other tin suits and numerous warthogs. As we approached, they raised their weapons in our direction.

"Don't shoot," Renee cried.

"Get back to the megastructure. It's the safest place," he commanded.

Before I could respond, whizzing sounds came overhead with fireballs and a trail of smoke behind. They detonated on the massive building floors where Tiers One and Two lived.

I turned to the officer and raised an eyebrow. "We aren't going to that dartboard. If you think it's so safe, you go there."

"No, I can't let you inside without authorization. Go back to the megastructure."

Well-dressed officers whose uniforms looked like they were cleaning out a supply warehouse based on the dust and debris that faded their sky-blue color came running to the airlock door.

The older captain from earlier was with that group, and he came to our side. "Let them in, Lieutenant. I'll take responsibility."

He moved and allowed us to follow the older captain through the first set of doors. They closed and secured. Then the next set opened slowly. The doors behind rumbled from a blast, and there was weapons fire outside. That annoying lieutenant was probably dead. The officers waiting for the inner airlock to open wasted no time and squeezed themselves through the doors as they parted, retracting into the wall. Soldiers up high behind the turrets were shouting out words of encouragement to each other, getting their minds ready for a fight. Renee and I followed the captain into command. One of the other officers squeezed through the door. He didn't wait for the inner door to open any further but pulled on a side lever inside command. A grinding sound rattled the walls and we covered our ears. Renee and I stepped through the inner door—we were the last ones scrambling to get inside. Smoke came from the cranking system opening and closing the inner airlock. The outer airlock started opening at the same time as the inner door was closing. That shouldn't have happened, but we all got inside command. Gunfire broke out with bright flashes from the turrets on the elevated platform. The inner airlock sealed, and the floor vibrated from whatever was happening inside the airlock tunnel between the doors. We were secure in the lobby of command and whatever terrible fighting was happening in the airlock there was a thick steel door blocking us from it. Colonel Hanifin was there yelling out orders to the officers standing around like dummies. That stupid woman should have never sent my brother off with all those fighters.

She gave me an irritated look and folded her arms. "What are these civilians doing here?"

The captain stepped over and said, "Ma'am, they're family of Major Norcross. I believed—"

"The major will be dealt with after we win." Hanifin cut him off with her sharp words.

That lady must have been watching a different battle because everything I'd seen to that point indicated that we were losing. Before the conversation could go any further, the inner airlock door creaked and pulled apart to open. Everyone turned, wide-eyed.

"Who opened the doors?" Colonel Dummy shouted.

"They're overriding our systems. They want to salvage the C&C," said the aged captain.

"Defenders, form a battle line and prepare for combat." She turned to a young captain standing near me. "Captain Opilio, get down to the computer room and destroy everything inside. They can't get any of our intel."

The nervous captain ran to an elevator and stepped inside. The inner door creaked open slowly, continuing to make a squeaking sound as gears rolled. It was pitch black inside the tunnel to the outer doors, and we couldn't see anything. A light mist blew into the lobby area, and it smelt like burned toast.

"Get behind the line. Those computer terminals are bulletproof—hide there," the captain said, pointing a meter away. Renee and I went behind the desks, and when the inner doors were nearly half open, all defenders shot their weapons, lighting up the lobby area with bright yellow and orange flashes. Nothing happened, no one shot back, and there weren't any sounds of death. I knew that sound well. The doors had nearly retracted fully into the wall, and Colonel Dummy ordered her defenders to stop shooting.

The room was so quiet I could hear Renee swallow deep. Tin suits turned weapon lights on, but the smoke was thick—nothing was visible. A thunderous thrashing sound hammered through the lobby and took me by surprise. Then quietness again for a few tense seconds. Again, another deafening bang, and silence. It happened again, and again.

Someone cried, "Thumpers!"

Thick and tall objects pushed through the smoke—shields, huge metal plates as tall as a man and stacked together, one after the other along the entire length of the entrance. A strange mechanical sound emitted as they lifted into the air, and all crashed down at the same time to the floor. That smash shook my feet. There were no gaps in the barricade, and they acted as a single unit, moving up and down while stepping closer in our direction. Music began to play, pipe music, the same as from the main gate; it was loud and shrieked through the lobby as if it played through speakers.

Again, they stepped closer. Some in the lobby covered their ears. The half-circle of metal grew larger. Defenders shot their weapons, but the bullets sparked on the thick metal and had no effect. At random locations in the massive wall of metal shields, heads popped over, followed by a few quick flashes of gunfire, and then retreated behind the wall as the shields lifted again and came crashing back down, stepping even closer towards us.

The battle line kept engaging, but defenders fell as they were fired on from above the wall. One or two of the aggressing soldiers' heads exploded after well-placed shots by the defenders in the lobby, but more of us were dying.

The same loud thump as the shield wall moved closer. Renee had tears in her eyes, looking at me with fear. I peeked over the terminal again and saw no way out. A tin suit nearby put a tube over his shoulder and dropped to one knee before pushing a button. A massively bright flash of light appeared and went through one of the shields, creating a red melted hole, and a dark-armored soldier dropped on top of his barrier. Another shield replaced that one quickly, and the tin suit was already dead by the time I looked back to him. The dead thumper was one of those dark-armored soldiers with a thick metal bar from the shield running up his arm and connected at his waist by moving joints hooked into a circular ring attached to his armor. The war gear was doing all the lifting. The pipe music still played, and even Colonel Hanifin seemed scared. Nearly half the battle line was no longer on their feet. Even with everything Sadness taught me, there was nothing I could do in that situation. We were more helpless than I was at the eastern square when that BreakNeck Boy was going to try and rape me. Renee closed her eyes and spoke out loud to herself, praying for help.

Even the veteran old captain who brought us in was dead, blood coming from his eyes and mouth. That made me sad; he knew more about Tobias and his father than anyone I'd met who was willing to share the information.

The thumping shields were nearly on us. Renee grabbed my hand, and her lip trembled. Our end had come, and my racing heart knew it. I hid behind the terminal desk as bright light and a blast of wind shook the entire building. My eyes took a moment to readjust from the beaming sunlight near the outer door. Gunfire and explosions echoed in the room of fighting on the other side of the shield wall. Someone had come. There were gaps in the wall like missing teeth when someone smiled. What remained of the battle line must have seen the same thing as me. They ran for the thumpers, following Colonel Hanifin into the gaps. The pipe music wasn't as loud as the shots, stabs, punches, and clatters of battle. I knew how to play that kind of music.

I ran to the nearest opening and engaged, slashing at anyone wearing dark armor. My instincts kicked in, and I moved as only I knew how, dropping three or four within seconds as if they weren't even wearing protective gear against my trishula. Sadness would be proud. Warthogs steamed towards the thumper line. One of the thumping soldiers tried to aim a pistol at my head. I countered and drove the spear point under her arm. She cried loudly and fell where my blade kissed her again.

Another warthog pushed into the line of shields from behind and cleared an even larger opening. It was Rehan. He screamed bloody rage and fire was in his eyes. He kicked the dark-armored soldiers and swung his small cannon arms at them. A music-playing piper stepped to Rehan's bot. He played his music and pushed on the long rods as if it were a weapon that would bring down his machine.

The attackers were strange people. Captain Benzo turned his head and saw the soldier playing his music, kicking his legs, and dancing to the notes. The warrior danced to the tune of his own death. Rehan kicked him square in his chest, and the music stopped abruptly as the soldier flew across the lobby.

Another dark-armored soldier had a tube similar to the one the tin suit used earlier and was aiming at Rehan's bot. I drove my trishula into the back of his neck before he could fire the powerful weapon.

Where was Tobias? I worked my way closer to Rehan's bot, swiping, stabbing and defending against the enemy soldiers. I felt my bottom lip tremble at the thought that something happened to him, but tried to keep my focus as tears swelled in my eyes.

Rehan saw me fighting and came closer, looking down from his elevated position.

"Where's my brother?"

Rehan's face was hard to read; he pulled his lips in and my heart sank.

No, I wouldn't believe it. Tobias couldn't die. I shook my head and looked down. But then, from the corner of my eye I saw someone that looked familiar. It was T. I exhaled a sigh of relief as if a thousand kilograms of weight had been lifted off me.

Tobias had come. T fought the same way he did in the simulation room, using his rifle, hands, and feet. After clearing a few of the soldiers from his path, Tobias came to me and took a deep breath. He dipped his chin seeing my spear embedded into the back of a soldier's neck and standing straight up like a flagpole. I pulled the blade back and rested it against my arm.

"I was so worried we wouldn't get back in time."

I looked back at the dead from the defender battle line and said, "You got here as fast as you could. Renee and I would be dead if you hadn't come."

Colonel Dummy came to us looking shocked. Defenders from T's company still fought around us. The colonel glanced around the room and it seemed like she had questions and thoughts going on in her little brain. She was about to speak when Captain Opilio ran to us and grabbed Tobias's hand, shaking it frantically.

The captain regained his composure and said, "Sir, sorry." He turned to Colonel Hanifin. "Ma'am, Major Norcross surprised them and we're gaining the upper hand."

Tobias looked around the room. "Troops don't fight well when they're facing the wrong way."

Hanifin was still speechless with her mouth open slightly.

I made a sound to get their attention and said, "It looks to me like the major saved everyone on this colony. If he hadn't changed his plans, we would all be dead right now."

The colonel gave me a dirty look before speaking to Tobias. "Major Norcross. I want a full report on what happened today. Secure the colony, and let's conduct a full post-battle assessment."

"Yes, ma'am."

I asked T, "Who are these soldiers?"

Tobias stared at one beneath us with holes punched through multiple spots on his armor and blood slowly dripping from the metal to the floor.

"The pipes and drummers give them away. It's been part of their culture since the Years of Forgetting when they fought with swords and bows. They believe that the music gives them power on the battlefield, and it needs to shower over battle lines as they fight." T stepped over the soldier and walked towards the airlock, and I pressed him.

"So, who are they?"

He turned to me and said, "Colonial Marines."

It took the tin suits nearly two hours to clear the colony. In the end, only six were captured alive. They refused to give up and fought almost to the last warrior. Tobias said he had never seen Colonials fight that way before, and something didn't seem right. Renee went back to her apartment to shower and rest. T went up to the seventy-fifth floor, and half our apartment was missing. One of the rockets had broken off a huge chunk of the megastructure, and numerous homes fell to the street. Luckily our rooms were still partially there, and T packed our things.

The six Colonial Marines sat near a curb on the street, their hands tied behind their backs. A defender attempted to interrogate them, but the soldiers wouldn't speak.

Colonel Hanifin said, "I reported to command back home. The generals believe it was retaliation for what happened to Representative McWright. Right Seat JJ Richmond's been on the news daily threatening our people with war, and the unions united behind their wielder of the Hammer of Labor, even though McWright has been radio silent. Their investigators claim it was our special operations that attempted the hit."

Tobias seemed unsure. "We wouldn't kill such a man in that fashion. It would be different, very different."

"I would need to have a star on my shoulder to know the truth of that statement. Regardless, the Colonial response here makes sense. They couldn't sit by and do nothing or they would look weak. The leaders of their six worlds had to do something. What better response than to attack the smallest and furthest colony from Earth? In the grand scheme of things across occupied space, this was a tiny pinprick, but loud enough to satisfy the thorns and hammers."

Tobias raised his chin and said, "The Accord didn't attack us."

Hanifin sighed and raised her voice. "You're supposed to be some genius military tactician, Major Tobias Norcross, the hero of the lower tiers. Tell me who those Colonial Marine armored soldiers are." She pointed to the prisoners still under interrogation. "Did you see the pipes playing their battle hymn? I don't know any other Free Worlds military who send musicians into battle besides those crazy marines."

"I'm not sure yet, ma'am. But I can tell you with one hundred percent clarity that those aren't marines of the Accord. These warriors fought without care. They were blood drunk. Eight hundred and ninety-three civilians died. No quarter given. Colonial Marines wouldn't do that."

She turned and looked at the interrogation off in the distance and spoke. "Your sister killed a paladin with a Corin-steel spear. Some of the officers are whispering that she was using Agamo Verk. I would love to know how a surface rat learned something so dangerous and illegal under our law."

"I have no idea what you're talking about, ma'am."

The colonel said, "Do you know why the Hawks sent you here, after your promotion to Tier Two?"

Tobias paused for a moment. "Nim was my next post. If my forty-five-kilo sister killed a Colonial paladin with her hands, she deserves respect on a level I can't even express with words."

Colonel Hanifin wasn't pleased with his response, and she talked as if T didn't say anything. "You started at the bottom—even worse, outside with the other lowlifes. The same as her." She looked at me. "Did you really think the generational elites from the Upper Twenty-Three wanted your stench defiling their floors in the megacities of Civil Earth? Your current classification is an insult to the caste system. There's a reason we keep eighty percent of the deadweight down in the Lower Forty, never elevating higher.

If our megastructures were top-heavy, they would all collapse. It was my job to try and turn you into something considered acceptable by Tier Two standards, and unfortunately, I failed. A forty-five-kilo Tier Two teenager shouldn't be able to kill a Colonial paladin."

T seemed even more uneasy as he looked down, but before he could say anything, a commotion interrupted his thoughts. One of the marines broke free from his restraints, and while tin suits tried to get control of him, he pushed something on his chest. An explosion rocked the immediate area. The colonel, T, and I were knocked off our feet by the blast and pushback of air. All the prisoners, interrogators, and anyone else standing near them were piles of mush, and there was a sizeable hole through the concrete road with smoke rising from beneath like a volcano top getting ready to blow—more death from that merciless attack.

Tobias jumped up and shoved a finger in his ear, but he came to me right away to make sure I was ok. After, he went to the colonel. She looked like a dummy again with an expression of confusion.

"They're acting like sentinels from Force Command War Dogs. Who does that?"

Tobias shouted, "You see, Colonel? Colonial Marines wouldn't fight this way. Something isn't right."

This was the first time I'd seen T act insubordinately to a superior, and she was dumbstruck. Hanifin turned and stared at the smoking leftovers of limbs, ash, and blood.

"You'll have a chance to explain your instincts to my fellow Hawks."

Tobias frowned. "Explain myself to leadership, ma'am?"

Colonel Hanifin rubbed her ear. "Yes. General Ebben wants you before a panel inside our embassy bubble. Stavish, Belitz, and Nasby demand to hear what you have to say, though, for them, it's more about the personas surrounding you and her." She glanced at me. "You're popular with the masses on Civil Earth because you've gone from the surface, and every tier up to the Upper Twenty-Three. Bottom feeders shout your names on common floors of buildings as if you were the second coming of the Titans. It'll be good for optics having Major Tobias Norcross with his adopted sister explaining what happened here. Anything to help top families in the clouds—they wouldn't pass up that chance. I always enjoyed Asbury Park right outside our bubble at the center of the main cylinder. It's near Waynetown." She paused in thought. "I failed to mold you. Now you're someone else's problem. Wheels up in thirty minutes, Major. Good luck, and farewell. I hope never to see you again."

The colonel walked away with a smirk, and Tobias looked like a confused child on the first day of school in a new building.

"T, what does this mean?"

He looked at me hesitantly and took a deep breath. "It means we're going to the relations station."

CHAPTER 43

Worlds Change

The Free Worlds of Humanity (Henry)

Listening to JJ babble on for the better part of fifteen minutes was all I could take at that moment. He and Christine came to my office for a meeting with the chairs of the six worlds in our Accord. On the back wall, there was a hologram to a live feed of Chair Enama of Uropa, Chair Newfield of Lars, Chair Abrams of Tautrus, Chair McGrellis of Pardalis, Chair Hitchner of Talbora, and Chair Perley Temme of Ardum, known to our Labor Unions as the Strangler. He always wore formal frock coat attire of Ardum, fitted well to his body with the Rose of Enduring woven into the lacing.

In living memory since our system war, Uropa, Lars, and Tautrus never had a chair elected from the Rose of Enduring. The same way Ardum, Pardalis, and Talbora never had a chair elected from our Hammer of Labor. Colonization Charter senate seats and mayoral positions changed hands across all the six worlds, but the top spots always remained loyal to their original banners. Behind Sadie Enama was a crested seal for her Federation of Iron Workers. It had a spark of flame in the middle with iron ingots pointing out of the blaze to form a wreath. The FIW had gained more influence over the last few years with unexpected key deaths of delegates from the Entente. The next Labor Union elections for leadership might not go well for me unless things changed soon. Chair Newfield's union crest of the Alliance of Mass Transit depicted all forms of public transit vehicles forming a circle and starting as normal size, but as they drew closer together, shrinking until they hit the center with all the other transports. His union and our Angry Tigress of Lars' union, the Fraternal Order of Operating Engineers, were always at each other's throats for control on their planet. Chair Abrams' seal was a circle with wheat stalks pushing up from a patch of dirt. FAA, the Farmers' Association of the Accord, was most wrath with me for my declaration in open session. One hundred million tons of food that went to the Corporation and Offensive primarily came from his union members. The officials from the Rose planets had their pathetic flower displayed in some way behind them. The Strangler had a single hybrid flower over his shoulder with petals nearly the same size as a person. Being the leader of his party, Perley enjoyed making himself stand out in any way possible.

When we created the relations station, key aspects from each of the Free Worlds went into its design and function. The idea of having three seats as the top elected officials under the dome came from the Human Alliance's religion, for the three acolytes, and the position declaration of left seat, right seat, and center seat came from our Colonial chairs of the Accord. The Dolrinions always bragged that we made five walls and accepted the Corporation into the Capitol Forum only because of our respect for them and the five original Force Commands, but that wasn't actually true. Anything to make them feel better about having their nemesis sitting at one of the walls.

JJ said, "There's no doubt that the attack on our center seat manifested itself from the top families of Civil Earth, or perhaps within their bubble here on the station. The Stavish family has gone to extremes lately, trying to gain influence over the Belitz family. The attempt was a way to show their capabilities as the top Hawk."

Sadie Enama pushed her lips together. "Representative Richmond, you need not try to convince us. The evidence is overwhelming, and all six chairs are in accord with each other."

Chair Temme could never let Sadie speak without adding his input. "Rose Party stands united with the Labor Party. We've identified some of the bodies as former special service soldiers from the Defender Corps, and the ship they came to the station on was registered to Lunar One."

I had to tune them out because from there, the other four chairs felt it necessary to add their two credits to the conversation. After the last breath wasted, I cleared my throat. "Why would Civil Earth want to kill Adam and Juliet Sideris? Their poor excuse for an attack had endless errors and using a ship registered to their moon. Really? That's insanity."

JJ rolled his eyes and exhaled loudly. "You're obsessed with this grand conspiracy that Isaac and Killian Lyons of New-Sparta are trying to undermine you and kill the Green Eyes."

Perley Temme added, "Henry, the Human Alliance is weak. The days of their city-states having the largest military of all the Free Worlds is long over."

Sadie said, "The Alliance doesn't have the power to conduct such an operation. You were the intended target of the attack. An aggressive attempt on the center seat representative of the Colonial Accord is an act of violence on all six worlds and both political parties."

I glared at Christine. "Will you not stand with me on this either?"

The Angry Tigress for once had nothing to say and only stared at her feet.

I'd get no help from her. "What you're all proposing is an open war with Civil Earth. Our delicate peace with them has lasted long years. These tensions are as high as they were after the Uropa Power-Ball Riots."

Sadie said, "Henry, secondary production facilities on Civil Earth turned their lights on. The Hawks are shipping throngs of workers up to Lunar One with one purpose. Our Chair Security Council meetings with the generals and admirals come with a level of nervousness from some, and confidence from others."

Perley once again couldn't sit idle. "Civil Earth technology is more advanced than ours, but our military outnumbers theirs dramatically. We'll need two ships for every one of theirs, and we must maintain supply lines."

"We've already voted. Shipsmen of the Colonial Navy are mobilizing in secret," Chair Newfield blurted, holding his head up high.

What the hell was wrong with these people? "Where are they mobilizing?"

JJ gave his clown grin. "They're in Titans' Belt. We found a giant open pocket where the meteors won't interfere with our ships. It's further away from the colonies, so they shouldn't find us."

JJ knew information before I did, which made me squint at him with agitation. Were the chairs so angry that they were excluding me from critical information?

Christine Keng said, "All building facilities are cranking out new warships for this effort. We're sending them to gather with the fleet in the belt."

Even Christine knew what was happening before I did. "That won't work." I raised my voice. "The mining colonies surely know the belt better than we do. They'll find us and report back to the other representatives. It's a serious violation of the Free Worlds' Relations Policy."

Sadie rolled her eyes. "Relax, Henry. No one will know. Appropriate measures will ensure the miners aren't able to report anything. Our Titans' Belt miners view themselves as independent of the Accord ... let them think that way, and our navy will treat them in kind."

I couldn't believe everyone was against me and I didn't want to say anything to alienate myself further, but I had to do something.

"And what of Macaroy Garner? I expect that the Roses in the belt would fall in line with whatever Chair Temme says, but the shop steward for the Twenty-Third and union leader inside the belt might have another opinion. They've been constructing what they call titan carriers for the better part of two years, and those ships are nearing completion. We've had enough rebellions in the belt to last ten generations. Do we want to provoke them and create another battlefront when the war comes?"

My words were affecting some of the chairs; it was clear from their expressions.

Chair Hitchner appeared annoyed by my comments. "Rock smashers creating war vessels isn't something to fear. They made them to stop pirates from the three worlds, not to use against us. Look how long it took them to create the damn things. You're wasting our time, Representative McWright. Our ships are already gathering."

Perley sat back in his chair. "We're calling it the Invincible Hammer and Everlasting Rose fleet of the Accord."

JJ smiled and whispered, "The shipsmen have a different name for the gathering. They call it Henry's Revenge. Catchy name, isn't it?"

Sadie said, "For our Golden Age, when the Hammer and Rose united as one. A present-day unified force to take on an evil tyrant Free World trying to end our existence." She seemed pleased with herself.

The name was pointless. Building a fleet for the sole purpose of war against Civil Earth wouldn't bring us into a Golden Age again. If anything, we'd shoot ourselves back into another Great Darkness. Henry's Revenge did have a nice ring to it. Maybe I should use that revenge on everyone in the meeting.

I stood and paced from one end of the room to the other while speaking. "We are secretly building warships, Civil Earth Defense is doing the same, and no one believes that they will find out what we're doing? How did we know that Civil Earth was ramping up production in their subterranean facilities on Lunar One? Does no one think spies from Earth wander through our ranks too? Let's get their representatives into a room and try to have a conversation like civilized Free Worlds."

Perley Temme laughed mockingly. "All you like to do is talk. The time for action has come."

If that pathetic rose only knew the kinds of things I was capable of, he'd take back those words and apologize.

Christine spoke in a soft tone, unusual behavior for her. "What choice do we have? The chairs already voted, Henry. Only they have the authority to send our troops to war."

I glanced at her and saw the defeat in her eyes. It appeared that they tamed the wild Tigress. Our control didn't extend to military decisions with the Colonial government. My ears heated up, and I felt my heart racing with anger. Six months ago, I was the one they would have been asking for advice from in those closed-door meetings. Now they all glared at me with contempt, for one reason or another. Had my decision-making been clouded by a beautiful green-eyed twenty-year-old and her insane brother? Maybe siding with the Sideris family was a slow trickling poison that I continued to ingest like a hot meal. Were they all correct? Did Civil Earth try to kill me?

Before I could think any further, Malcolm tapped my shoulder and showed me his PDD feed. JJ's and Christine's chiefs did the same. All six chairs appeared distracted in one way or another by the same thing I was reading. The headline was in bold lettering that read, "Civil Earth Colony World Nim Attacked by Colonial Marines."

I quickly glanced over the article that claimed our marines gave no quarter to civilians on the colony and that the death total so far was nine hundred and three civilians, and one hundred and ninety-six defenders. All Colonial Marine aggressors, numbering five hundred, died. There were pictures in the article of dead children in a playground. Sadie brought up a live video of Jaden Belitz, father to Right Seat Representative Olivia Belitz, speaking from a podium.

"We'll not stand by and do nothing after such an outrage. Not since the power-ball war with the Accord has an assault on the safety of our people been perpetrated in such a way. Tier One must protect the lower tiers."

Carmine Stavish went to Jaden's side and said, "Civil Earth's Administrative Authority, at our direction, has launched an official investigation into this act of terror. We've instructed Civil Earth Defense to elevate their alert status and take any forward-moving action by the Accord as an act of aggression. Our fleets are moving to protect all tiers across the occupied territories."

Everyone in our meeting wore genuine expressions that made it clear they had no idea about the attack. Sadie's and Perley's eyes were open wide with disbelief.

I said, "Given everyone's reaction to this new development, it seems pretty clear that the chairs didn't sanction an attack against a Civil Earth colony world."

Sadie tripped on her words. "We … no … I … nothing came from us. Chair Temme?"

He was flabbergasted. "Of course not, no, I mean, that's correct, we didn't authorize any attack. I think it's time to adjourn for now."

Chair Newfield said, "After speaking with leadership of the six planets, the chairs will reconvene in two hours. Representatives, anything we feel relevant to advise you on will come from the ambassador's office."

One at a time, each camera cut off, and Sadie was already yelling at her staff before powering down her camera. What an amateur.

JJ cleared his throat and said, "I don't understand. If we didn't attack Civil Earth, who did?"

Christine said, "And why did they make it appear like we committed that terrible act?"

I walked to the window of my office overlooking the flower gardens outside and looked down at the chessboard. Oliver and I would play during downtime. I pushed the queen over and spoke out loud. "Check. In the past, I wouldn't think twice about one of the Colonial chairs doing something like that because of each world's free-thinking structure. However, they couldn't have faked those expressions after hearing Jaden and Carmine speaking. It was real shock. Someone's trying to pit us against each other."

Christine stood, straightened out her shirt and came to me. She whispered in my ear. "We need stability with the unions. I'm going to set up a conference call with all the union leaders, and Macaroy. The Roses might try to use this against us in some way. After, I'll tell Macaroy what's going on in the belt, and ask him to keep the unions at bay there."

I turned to her. "I'll send him a message and advise that you're acting on my behalf. Keep them civilized. Some hardliners might see this as an opportunity to cause division and gain influence within our Labor Party."

She nodded and spoke aloud. "I'm going back to my office. Good day, gentlemen."

Christine left with her chief of staff in tow. JJ slouched in the chair, almost trying to make himself comfortable as if he had no intention of leaving.

"Our Rose of Enduring from Ardum predates your Labor Party. Did you know that, Henry?" JJ knew I was well aware of the history of his withering flower. "The Rose Party based itself on an ideology that predates the Years of Forgetting. Fossil records show our rose carved into finery from ancient kingdoms and weapons thousands of years before our Colonial Golden Age when we left the Darkness. We've endured so much longer than most, and the Rose of Ardum is a testament to that stamina and resilience."

I acted uninterested. "Yes, your weed survives difficult conditions. I know."

He grinned. "It's more than mere survival. We could plant our rose in a desert, middle of the Arctic, or wettest rainforest, and it will thrive. At first, there's only one flower, before long, a dozen, and given enough time, the flower spreads through every single crevice across the landscape, strangling everything that once stood. It doesn't matter if it's the strongest tree of the forest or thickest vines. The flower overwhelms the roots from within and snuffs them out. At first, native plants have no idea what's happening below eye level, but then, as flowers emerge from the dirt, it's already too late. Everything else dies from within, and the Rose of Enduring consumes and wins after a prolonged time. We spend millions of credits each year keeping wildflowers at bay, the same way we have for thousands of years."

"Why are you telling me all of this, JJ? What reason would you have at a time like this to egg me on in a fight?"

"You told me how precious the Uropa flower was and that all good things happen in time. Your Hammer of Labor always was about the moment. Do what's necessary to win votes, act as we must to ensure one union has power over the others, but the Labor Party never thinks about one hundred or one thousand years from now. Your mallet signifies power and strength, but over time, it rusts, cracks into pieces, and fails. The weakness comes from within, Henry. Our thorny stems keep finding ways to wrap around your hammer, and I believe with this new development across the occupied worlds, citizens of the Accord will see that Labor doesn't always have the best answers for major issues."

That pompous prick was picking a fight with me at a time like this, really?

"JJ, any other day of the week, I'd gladly get into a pissing contest with you to compare who has got the bigger hammer or rose. But today isn't that day. Going against Civil Earth while the Offensive and Corporation are at each other's throats isn't a good thing. It appears the only Free Worlds government missing from the equation is the Alliance. Convenient for them. There's never been a war between more than two Free Worlds at the same time. Our internal squabbles between the parties need to go on hold for the time being."

JJ still wore that grin. It was almost like throughout his entire speech he was trying to tell me something by beating around the bush, but what?

"Let's try to appear at least united even if we're not. Please stop going on camera and telling every news agency that Civil Earth tried to kill me."

JJ walked to the door with his chief and said, "You have endless enemies out there, Henry. Not just the Rose Party or Lyons Twins. That's all I'm saying. I won't stop speaking with the news until Perley tells me to. My poll numbers haven't been this good since I first ran for office."

The door closed, and Malcolm went to the liquor wall and poured two glasses of bourbon. We tapped and drank.

"That red-haired clown bastard wants to sit here and lecture me about his stupid plant."

Malcolm sat back in the chair and looked up at the ceiling. He was in deep thought for a moment. "Something he said stuck out to me. 'Weakness comes from within.' Do you think it's possible that one of the unions attacked you to make it look like Civil Earth?"

I took another sip, mulling that over. "Uropa's the financial powerhouse of the Colonial Accord, and that power comes from the unions of Labor. We've secretly battled each other for years, but those fights rarely turn into blatant assassination attempts where all eyes can see it happening, no. To do such a deed against the party leader and head of the Entente." I shook my head. "No, they wouldn't dare. When we kill each other, it always looks like an accident."

Was I trying to convince myself?

Malcolm raised an eyebrow and said, "You did piss them off with the declaration in open session."

650

"If the attempt on me had come after an attack on a Civil Earth colony world, I might agree with you that there was something suspicious at play. But two attacks, one blamed on Civil Earth and the other on us. No, I fear someone's playing everyone for fools."

Malcolm took a long gulp from his glass. "Federates attacking Dolrinion slave worlds adds more fuel to the fire. Where does the Human Alliance fit into all of this?"

I took another sip. "I've pondered that same question. They've thrived on misdirection and deception since the civil war. The Silent Lion is one of the most dangerous inside the five walls, in my opinion. He started all this by giving bad intel to the Dolrinions and Federates about Gliese, but why?"

"More dangerous than Mia or Jaxson?"

I smiled and raised my glass. "A different kind of dangerous. A poisonous spider, venomous snake, or toxic plant can kill you in different ways, some more painful than others. It doesn't change how treacherous each of the three can be."

Malcolm smirked and glanced at his PDD. "Center Seat Representative Stavish is downstairs in the lobby requesting permission to speak with you."

I went to the chessboard and lifted the queen, placing her back in her original location on the board.

"Don't keep Mia waiting. Entertain her aide outside in the hallway while we discuss the fate of Humanity."

I took another sip of the bourbon and felt a nice sting as it went down my throat. What did my predecessors do in these types of situations? Until that point, I always had a way of steering my Colonial government in the direction of my choosing, and most of the time, that path constantly went away from adverse conditions. The current climate hadn't been like this since before I was born. What did Center Seat Monica Kotarski do when she heard over five hundred Civil Earth Tiers One and Two were brutally cut down on Uropa during the Power-Ball Riots? Monica was with the Rose Party and had no real sway over Warwick and its mayor at the time, who were staunch union supporters. It was her job to try and negotiate peace with her hands tied. Did Kotarski suggest attacking first, knowing full well that Civil Earth Defense would retaliate? Did she recommend withdrawing into a shell and waiting them out, or did she not care one way or the other, sitting in her office drinking like me? Maybe she wanted the war. Why not? The blame was clearly Labor's, even though thorn agitators provoked the crowds too. Thorn agitators ... well, that was interesting. Malcolm might have been right. JJ was posturing in riddles, telling me that he and the thorns were responsible for the attack. But they'd have needed help. Only the extremist groups within their party could carry out such an attempt. Maybe I was overthinking it. The Strangler and JJ wouldn't conspire to kill me.

Mia entered the room, and in her hands was an amazingly beautiful Uropa flower inside a porcelain container. A perfect bloom at precisely the right time. It took three years for those petals to open for only a few days. The colors overwhelmed my eyes like a rainbow reflection off the sun.

"For you, Henry."

I smiled and took it, observing the incredible detail on the pot.

"The porcelain was hand-painted in the days when swordplay ruled the battle lines of old. It represents the six worlds of the Colonial Accord. The top rim patterns are from Uropa."

"Thoughtful, Mia. Thank you."

She took a seat and crossed her legs. Spiraling diamond jewelry ran from her calves down to her big toe, where a golden snakehead with red rubies shone in my direction, adding luster to her elegant sandals. Her thin silky toga was bright blue and black, and her nipples protruded through the fabric. It was a little chillier in my office than average.

"Henry, I'm sure you're fully aware of what Tier One leadership is threatening. We didn't try to kill you. I promise you this."

"And we didn't attack you on Nim—I promise you that. Our mutual issue is the fact that both governments are choosing to believe the lie. It seems memories are short. They all forget how terrible the last war was."

Mia frowned and glanced at her diamonds.

"My father and Jaden Belitz have their minds set, and all the other families are falling in line. It's hard to prove that one of the others didn't orchestrate the attempt on your life. They didn't need to go through Defender Corps channels to hire specialists. Regardless, I think it was someone else. It doesn't matter any longer that I'm center seat. The Hawks on Civil Earth are calling the shots now. They lost faith after open session when you humiliated me."

I took another sip of bourbon. "Remember our lunch at the Eatontown Avenue Café? We sat there confidently declaring how all occupied space and every major decision of the Free Worlds only happened over meals between the two of us."

"It appears we were wrong."

"We weren't wrong. For years, one push of a PDD and a few choice words to others and boom, the territories would be at peace or war. Sometimes we disagreed with each other and worked against one another, but on the real serious issues, we always found ways to coexist. We became too full of ourselves recently. You cut me, and I cut back. Sharks in the water smelled the blood and attacked us both. You and I can rebuild the trust in our governments together. We've been at odds for entirely too long."

She raised her chin and frowned. "That was JJ's fault."

"Yes, it was. We can ignore that clown for now. He's worthless as long as Christine works with me, and Xander Nasby sticks by you. Olivia won't help a Stavish, no matter how many billions might die if she doesn't. The Dolrinions and Corporation are officially at war with each other. Both sides declared it out front near the forum steps."

Mia said, "A third franchise war."

"If we aren't careful, it might become the Free Worlds' war. A conflict to end all others."

She stood and went to the window. Near the sill, I had a Frontiersmen ark ship figurine, and Mia carefully stroked the individual parts, tracing the outline from side to side.

"Do you think we will ever see them again? It's been what, nine years?"

I went to her and said, "There are a few constants we can depend on for the Free Worlds of Humanity: war, death, famine, pain, Androsians, and the Frontiersmen. We'll see them again."

Her eyes lowered with sorrow. "Speaking of death, I'm sorry for your loss."

"I don't understand, what loss? Who did I lose?"

She took a deep breath. "We had spy satellites in orbit over Pomona for reasons I can't discuss, but we confirmed that Isabel Sideris died trying to flee on a pirate ship."

How could that be? Guth gave me assurances, and we hadn't heard anything. My mouth was dry, and I was angry as Mia kept talking.

"It was terrible timing. The pirates entered the system on a drift and made it to the planet, using a supply spool line to get her. A Golden Eagle heavy carrier from Aetós was waiting on the dark side of the moon and attacked right as the Federates jumped into the system. Battles were happening everywhere. A Genesis Foundation capital ship went one on one with the carrier, and Isabel's rescue got caught between both. The fight between those two vessels worried our generals of Fleet Branch because they were so powerful. Both destroyed each other, but not before the carrier launched missiles and turned the pirate ship into dust. She's gone, Henry."

I sat in my chair and covered my eyes. There wasn't anything to say. We had no intelligence in that sector, and the Dolrinions assured me everything was fine. I gave them so much and received nothing. Why was Isabel fleeing Pomona with pirates? We'd set a deal.

Mia came to me and placed a hand on my shoulder. "Adam and Juliet Sideris are more important now than ever. They're last in an Athinian bloodline that stems back to the Old World, and those eyes, those beautiful glowing eyes. Keep them safe. We can use them in future challenges ahead." She lifted my chin so our eyes met. "You're important too. The Capitol Forum needs Henry McWright, especially at a time like this. The Free Worlds of Humanity don't realize." Mia shook her head. "They really don't."

Mia gently kissed my lips and went to the door.

I said, "Thank you, Mia. We shall see much of each other in the coming darkness."

With her departure, Malcolm came back. He saw my shoulders low. "Are you ok, sir?"

"I brushed off the attack on the slave worlds because Guth assured me Isabel was safe."

Malcolm said, "Why wouldn't she be safe? Slave camps weren't targeted because sentinels would die, and the Federates would violate the Relations Policy. They only targeted the mines and processing facilities from space. The Corporation's attempting to cripple Dolrinion production capabilities. What's wrong, sir?"

After a brief pause, I spoke softly. "I failed Liam. I failed my friend. The man who showed me how to see things differently."

Liam Sideris was the only person I ever truly trusted in my life. Malcolm exhaled deeply and sat low in a chair. He had worked hard, helping me secure Isabel's freedom.

"What can we do now?"

I finished my drink and slammed the glass on the table. "Nothing. It's time for me to leave and give this tragic news to Adam and Juliet. Get a good night's sleep. Tomorrow's a new day with new challenges to overcome."

We shook hands and departed.

*

Back at the ruby refuge, Adam and Juliet were relaxing inside watching the television, which was the only thing they could do there. Pietro was with us because I found it unnecessary to keep watching Alyssa any longer. As far as I was concerned, our time with each other was nearing its end. She still didn't know that I knew what she did. Alyssa was staying with Warrin, the ambassador to our bubble, and Beth, his wife. The governor of safety had told Alyssa that no other location in our Colonial bubble was safe.

When we eventually saw each other, Alyssa had hugged me with fake tears in her eyes, saying she'd feared the worst. She then asked if the Green Eyes were still with me, to which I gave the honest answer. Alyssa's demeanor changed once again, and that was it. I left and hadn't seen her since.

Adam and Juliet stared at me oddly when I came through the airlock door. They must have seen something wrong in my expression.

Juliet stepped closer. "Is everything ok?"

I ignored her and went to the top cabinet in the kitchen, grabbed one of the liquor bottles I brought from the apartment, and poured three glasses.

Adam came to the counter with his sister. "What happened?"

"Drink." I was blunt.

We tapped glasses and took sips, though mine was more of a gulp.

"Drink more."

I tipped their glasses up, so they consumed the contents. Both opened their mouths wide and squeezed their eyes shut at the burn. Juliet stuck her tongue out, too. I poured another for us.

"Sit, please."

The Green Eyes of Athinia looked at each other and sat on high-top chairs next to the counter.

"There's something important that you need to know." I hesitated. "Your mother tried to escape from the slave world Pomona. She got off the planet. The Federate Corporation attacked Pomona as a Golden Eagle heavy carrier ambushed her escape ship, where she met her end."

Adam grabbed his glass and finished it quickly, brown liquid falling from both sides of his mouth. Juliet aimed her eyes at the counter and didn't move. I handed her the glass and raised it to her mouth.

"Drink."

Adam gave me his empty glass, and I poured him another, this time filling it to the top.

"Things are going to get dicey on the station now that the Offensive and Corporation are officially at war. My government's blaming Civil Earth for the attempt on your lives, and a military force attacked the colony world Nim, belonging to the Hawks of Earth. The invaders wore Colonial Marine armor, but it wasn't us. We are inching closer to a total war not seen since before the Great Darkness."

Adam slammed the table and shouted, "It was Isaac and Killian Lyons who sent those killers to your apartment, not Civil Earth."

Juliet wiped a single tear away from her face and grew angry. She drank what remained in the glass and slammed it too. "New-Sparta will pay."

I topped off their glasses and said, "Everyone across the Free Worlds is only seeing what they want to see right now. Our peace was always nothing more than an illusion, but it was a cleverly concealed one that rarely poked its head out from behind the curtain. Every day we fought each other away from the view of our masses. Now things will be in the public light—citizens with no real issues will have deep anger and hate for the other worlds. That hate will push out like an infection consuming a host until death."

Adam finished his glass and walked towards the door.

"Where are you going, brother?"

"I need to go to my room for a few minutes. I'll be right back." He slurred his words.

After the door secured, Juliet turned to me and said, "I'm scared and angry."

I tapped her glass with mine, and we drank.

I said, "Put that fear in the back of your mind for now. Throw it in a box and lock it. Concentrate on your anger. Anger will produce results. Fear is nothing more than weakness. Feed off the anger, Juliet. The anger will make you strong. It always worked for me."

Her eyes grew dark and she frowned with rage.

"I am angry. The Lyons Twins will die by a Sideris hand."

With a smile, I said, "They will, my love."

She blushed and finished her glass.

Adam finally returned with a blank face of intoxication.

"Are you feeling better?"

He nodded. "Yes."

Juliet narrowed her eyes curiously. "What were you doing in there?"

It looked like Adam would answer, so I spoke. "Just blowing off steam on his own before returning. Nothing to worry about."

I filled Adam's glass, and he finished it quickly before sitting on the couch and falling asleep.

Juliet and I talked for a while, and it was fascinating to learn some of the things her mom did to keep them safe during their years in hiding after the war. Adam started making sounds and snoring with a wide-open mouth. Juliet giggled, and I picked him up and carried him to the airlock door.

"Juliet, be a darling and open the door, please. I'll take him up and return shortly."

I placed Adam in his bed and carefully moved his head to the side.

He mumbled, "I love you, Henry."

I placed my hand on his head and said, "Rest easy, lad."

Back downstairs, I poured another drink for Juliet and me.

"Henry, I think I might be drunk."

I tapped her glass to mine. "Good, remember what I told you? There are two perfectly good reasons to get intoxicated. One is for celebrating, which we did in the Colonial bubble, and the other is to mourn."

"I remember. You told me the last time you drank to mourn was for my grandfather."

"That's correct, love."

She blushed again, followed by a beautiful smirk. We drank.

"Juliet, I promise to do everything in my power to ensure those who killed your mother meet their end. I won't rest until they're in my hands."

Tears streamed down her cheeks, and the liquid inside her eyes glowed green. "The last thing Mom told me before the pirates came onto our ship was that I was stronger than I knew." She wiped away the tears, raised her shoulders, and pulled her lips tight. "I want to be there when you find them, to look in their eyes, and smile as they die."

The lighting was low, and I was mesmerized by the slight glow in her eyes. Her perfect skin and tight body. What an amazing young woman. Her posture reminded me of Keon, the Fighting Sideris.

"We will both look into their eyes as they beg us for death. No one knows my talent for inflicting pain on others. The real me is always behind the curtain, and I promise to bring you there and show you what I'm capable of. Together, we'll kill everyone."

Juliet smiled and leaned closer. My heart was racing with excitement after my admission. I couldn't resist any longer and brought my lips to hers. It was soft and fast. I pulled back and gazed at her. Juliet grabbed the back of my head and pulled me quickly to her. Our tongues met, massaging each other. She was only twenty, and I was fifty-nine. If anyone saw it happening, my career would be over. I always fantasized about her mother but never had an opportunity. When Isabel came with Liam seeking my help, I couldn't sleep that night. My mind couldn't stop thinking of crawling into Isabel's bed and taking her. Juliet was even more attractive.

Our clothes came off, and I ran my hands over her body, the body I had thought of repeatedly since she came here. Juliet wasn't new to that type of play. She wasted no time grabbing at me aggressively. Athinians were hardy people, strong, and forceful. Before long, our bodies were rubbing together the way I had done a thousand times with a thousand different women. Our age difference was entirely unacceptable by Free Worlds' standards, and I couldn't care less. Her shouts of approval were all that mattered in the moment.

I opened my mind and allowed the darkest thoughts to flow. Between the alcohol and that spectacularly shaped young woman, I couldn't resist allowing my brain to stream the deepest emotions and memories. Father wouldn't be happy, but fuck him, he was dead. I let the buried memories of my actions flow like photos on a PDD, swiping left to go back into time. The box was open. The day that JJ Richmond and Mia betrayed me and canceled my speech. I looked weak, and my anger boiled over. When I had left JJ's office, my PDD rang. On the other end of the call was Gabrielle Toro, the schoolteacher from earlier that day, with those snot-nosed brats in the main cylinder.

She called after hearing about my speech cancellation all those months ago, and we met for drinks near her apartment. I was screaming inside with complete rage while sitting there with a fake smile. It was only hours earlier that JJ gave me the news of my defeat. The emotions I bottled up during that meal with Gabby was the same fury I had as a child after smothering my baby brother to death in his crib. I was jealous of the attention he received and couldn't control the resentment for that little thing. I deserved the attention. That anger as a seven-year-old was the same when my first girlfriend broke up with me, and, near our usual hangout under a bridge just outside of Warwick where the stream ran into a sewer line, I beat her with a rotted tree branch lying near the river, crushing most of her face. Her body was there for a week before authorities found her.

Father taught me to keep my rage in check. It was important to keep my real emotions at bay, or people would see through me and know that I was a pure predator, a consumer of souls that viewed people like edible meat. Rage and anger were what always defined me my entire life, and that night with Gabrielle Toro, she received it in full. During dinner, I did as Father told me, *show one face on the outside, and keep the real one hidden.* Gabby took me back to her apartment, like countless others did because of my status as center seat. Her childhood crush on me became a nightmare.

Gabby tried to make love to me. I don't make love, I ravage women, the same way I was doing to Juliet, and that spitfire was enjoying it. People from the Alliance were more resilient than others. She screamed with pleasure as I pulled at her with such force. It brought my thoughts back to Gabby in her apartment, making the same sounds as Juliet ... until she wasn't. Besides being mad about my speech and getting sidestepped by JJ and Mia, I was also annoyed that Gabrielle's breasts were smaller than Alyssa's. Her pleasureful screams turned into shouts of dread, and I pictured JJ and Mia producing those sounds. As she told me to stop, I grew even angrier. Why would I stop? I was the most powerful man on the station. She had no right to tell me to do anything.

Gabby screeched in pain. "Please stop!"

I didn't listen. She tried to resist, but I was far more powerful. My mind came back to Juliet for a moment. Us naked together was all I'd thought of for such a long time.

Gabrielle Toro was a different matter. Without that relief after such defeat, I might have done something in the public eye that would damage the fake persona of me to citizens across the Free Worlds. The throat was always my favorite place to inflict pain. Father started buying me the baby rabbits when I was young, the same way I bought them for Adam. I would twist their necks and choke the life from them to satisfy my urges.

I was Gabrielle Toro's childhood crush, a hero, and that night I forever became her worst fear. Everything I did to Gabrielle Toro came with an image of JJ Richmond and Mia Stavish. After the thrashing had finished, I screamed out with such fury and rage, people across the street outside heard me. Oliver came into her room and saw the bloody mess I left in my wake. He and Josue cleaned everything up as they had for me countless times before, then we dropped her off at the local hospital. She survived. I paid for her medical expenses and reconstructive facial surgery, and the Syndicate visited her to ensure she would keep quiet about the incident. At that time, Gabby was the youngest woman I had ever had until Juliet. Under different circumstances, I might have developed a side relationship with the schoolteacher to satisfy my sexual appetite, but that night was unfortunate timing. Doing that with random women was the only way I could keep myself from hurting Alyssa, unlike my previous wife.

Father always knew what my rage was and did everything to help me channel it. I inherited it from him, but mine was much more dominant. One of my earliest memories of the man who raised me was in a damp, mildew-smelling basement somewhere in Warwick. He was beating a rival union delegate that he and my uncle kidnapped. Father was a powerful delegate with the Twenty-Third and taught me how to be a productive union member at face value and in the shadows. Uncle Dean was holding the rival as my father beat him until every tooth was on the concrete floor. A single hanging light bulb behind us cast huge shadows. There was more blood on that cold floor than in Gabrielle's bed. Father taught me a valuable lesson that day that stuck with me my entire life.

"Henry, you need always to appear as people would expect in public.

When I stand in front of the Entente, they see me as a standup guy who does everything to help others, and they consider me a family man. Behind closed doors, behind this curtain, the real me is what you see here in this basement. Never let anyone see the real you. Save it for your enemies. Everyone is your enemy. You're my son and have more anger than me. You'll need to find ways to channel it without anyone knowing. I'll help you, lad, and one day you'll be more successful and ruthless than I ever could be."

Slow drips of blood fell from his knuckles as he gave me that powerful life lesson. I received more lessons throughout my teenage years after he bypassed Colonial Communal Integration by intimidating or paying off the family I was supposed to live with six months out of the year. Father said it was for the best because I'd probably kill someone in every home the Colonial government made me live in until my eighteenth birthday.

That memory faded, and I flipped Juliet and took her from behind, the same way Benjamin was taking Alyssa.

Benjamin, that bloody pillock. That son of a bitch thought he was so smart working for me by day and sleeping with Alyssa at night. Malcolm and I talked at length after I removed him, and my chief of staff was right. Ben only wanted to stay and not return to Warwick because he was shagging my wife. It was Zoey's fault that it went on for so long, but that cunt was probably dead by now on Galma. The Twenty-Third Entente had a strong relationship with the Rogue Syndicate and their leadership through the years. Father especially worked closely with them and traveled to Galma a few times.

He would say, "One hand washes the other. If you use some soap, it works better." He was referring to payoffs with the bosses on Galma in their ancient castles of stone.

With the help of Senior Agent Ficco and the Syndicate, we smuggled Benjamin into the cathedral using an old docking port out of commission for years. In the lower storage areas seldomly visited by agents, there was another memory room device kept in a dark storage container. With Ficco, Malcolm, and an underboss from the Syndicate standing behind me, I beat Ben's face until he lost several teeth like the delegate in the basement with

Dad. Then Malcolm gave me a blade, and I cut the tip of his manhood off and placed it into a bag. At that time, I had the idea of giving it to my wife before I killed her, but Oliver dissuaded me. Benjamin pleaded for his life to no avail. Ficco turned on the machine, and within seconds, a flash of light removed Benjamin's memories from that moment back to his twentieth birthday. His dumbfounded face was similar to those of the failed recruits inside the Academy Hall memory room. We released the clamps on his wrists and told Ben that he'd be spending the next year abroad with the Dolrinions to help him understand politics with the Free Worlds better. Benjamin gave a stupid smile and said it would be a fun experience. As the underboss walked him from the storage container to smuggle him to the Dolrinion bubble for a modest fee, Ben grabbed at his crotch and complained of pain. He was on one of those slave worlds attacked by the Corporation, and with any luck, he too was dead.

As I finished inside Juliet, she squeezed my hands and turned to kiss me. We were both breathing heavily and covered in sweat. I sat on the couch to regain myself. Juliet grabbed water bottles from the kitchen and brought them over. We drank, and I poured some over my head.

"How do you feel?"

I smiled and said, "Amazing."

Juliet leaned closer and kissed my cheek. "Good, because you're coming to my room tonight so we can do that at least two more times."

For the first time in years, I felt like a young man with tremendous power coursing through my veins. The Hammer of Labor was between my legs that night, and I would wield it with precision. She was mine, from that day forward, no one would have Juliet but me. Alyssa was the past, and my future had lightly glowing green eyes and perfect young olive skin. As we walked away from that sex-smelling room, all that ran through my head was that neither she, nor the rest of our dark and twisted race, would ever know the murderous psychopath who inhabited my inner psyche, but it was he who enabled me to be the most powerful being in the Free Worlds of Humanity. *Lock the box, Henry. Lock it good and tight until the darkness is needed again..*

ABOUT THE AUTHOR

Anthony Almato doesn't think of himself as an author, and *Free Worlds of Humanity* began as a video game concept before taking its current form. Having survived nearly insurmountable challenges during childhood and adolescence, in addition to his former careers as a professional gamer and a corrections officer, Almato uses his personal experiences to breathe life into his stories. When he isn't writing, he can be found smoking a cigar, snowboarding and enjoying the company of his wife and children. Anthony has also lived with type one diabetes for over thirty years.

To discover more about Anthony and his writing, please visit his website:
anthonyalmato.com

You can also connect with him via social media:
facebook.com/AAlmato
instagram.com/anthonyalmato
twitter.com/AnthonyAlmato

FREE WORLDS OF HUMANITY REFERENCE GUIDE

(in alphabetical order):

Capitol Security – The law enforcement and protection arm for representatives of the Capitol Forum. Their jurisdiction resides solely under the dome and inside Capitol Forum, extending to anywhere the fifteen representatives travel in their daily routines to ensure their protection. Inspector-General Paula Nottage oversees a small but accommodating agency of uniformed officers, personal protection specialists, investigators, and numerous Emergency Response Teams. A common criticism from the main cylinder regarding Capitol Security is that they steal the best station security officers because the positions are the higher-paid under the dome.

Free Worlds – Five advanced societies that left the Years of Great Darkness/ Years of Forgetting, each having a seat inside the Capitol Forum on the relations station. These five societies span Occupied Space and control all the power of humanity.

Societies listed in order of leaving the Years of Forgetting:

Civil Earth: Left the Great Darkness twenty-one hundred years prior to the invasion of Gliese, and then entered their Age of Innovation, when the Watchful Hawks birthed the caste system and Earth became civilized again.

- *Homeworld:* Earth
- *Population:* Thirty-nine billion
- *Structure:* Set up into a caste system with the population segregated into tiers. Tier Four, placed in the Lower Forty, consists of eighty percent of the population living on the bottom forty floors of megastructures. Tier Three, placed in the Middle Thirty, consists of twelve percent of the population living on floors forty-three to seventy, forty-one and forty-two being common areas for the Middle Thirty. Tier Two, placed in the Upper Twenty-Three, consists of seven percent of the population living on floors seventy-four to ninety-five. Seventy-two is a buffer floor separating the tiers, and seventy-three is common space. Tier One, who live in the clouds (Cloud Walkers and Watchful Hawks), consists of one percent of the population and reside on floors ninety-seven and up, depending on the size of a megastructure. An administrator runs each megastructure to govern local building affairs. Powerful Tier One Hawk families govern society; the lower tiers are low-hanging branches of the tree above. Each Hawk family wants total control and attempts to gain influence and power over one another.
- *Representatives on the relations station:* Center Seat Mia Stavish, Right Seat Olivia Belitz, and Left Seat Xander Nasby

Colonial Accord: Left the Great Darkness nineteen hundred and thirty-two years prior to the invasion of Gliese, known as their Golden Age of the Accord, when all six worlds united under one flag after a massive war between the worlds.

- *Homeworlds:* Uropa (Capital world) Ardum, Tautrus, Lars, Pardalis, and Talbora

- *Population:* One hundred and forty-three billion
- *Structure:* Divided into two rival political factions: Labor Party, known as the Hammer of Labor, organizes unions that elect individual leaders to govern the party, and Rose Party, known as the Rose of Enduring, opposes everything Labor stands for and believes in strength through force. The Labor Party of Uropa organizes governance and leadership of elected officials to union presidents, district leaders, and shop stewards, while the Rose Party of Ardum strictly adheres to political leaders with backgrounds in law and local governance. The Accord is known as the breadbasket of Humanity for its rich food production abilities on all six worlds. Political disputes between Labor Party unions and issues between the Hammer of Labor and Rose of Enduring cause disputes within their planets' governance.
- *Powerful unions of Labor:* Twenty-Third Entente, Federation of Iron Workers, Alliance of Mass Transit, Fraternal Order of Operating Engineers, Colonial Steel Workers Association, Farmers Association of the Accord, and Fourth Union. The party leader wields the ceremonial Hammer of Labor to distinguish him/herself as the head member of all unions.
- *Representatives on the relations station:* Center Seat Henry McWright, Right Seat JJ Richmond, Left Seat Christine Keng (Angry Tigress of Lars)

Dolrinion Offensive: Left the Great Darkness eighteen hundred and sixty years prior to the invasion of Gliese, known as End of the Dark Age, when the first five Force Command founders, Maddox of First Ones, Constantine of Red Legion, Kace of Tacoma, Farah of Steel Talon, and Rayna of BlackRock, touched the memory stone on Kora and received visions on how to lead their people out of the Darkness.

- *Homeworld:* Kora
- *Population:* Forty-five billion estimated. Actual number unknown.
- *Structure:* A stratocracy broken into ten Force Commands of the Offensive. Five supreme generals run each Force Command. Lower-

ranking generals have titles from first-grade to fourth-grade in order of their power and authority. Each command is capable of sustaining itself, and they each focus on a specific area of expertise. Serving the Offensive is all that matters to a Dolrinion and falls in line with a religious belief that they must perform with honor and earn the right to have their name carved onto the memory stone, or their soul will be lost for eternity. The only way to enter the eternal stone halls is for caretakers to etch a name onto the stone. From galley cook to frontline battle sentinel, serving with honor is how their society survives. Sentinels learn from the time they can walk that duty, valor, and glory to the Offensive is all that matters in life. Commands are generally suspicious of each other and have made war with each other from time to time.

- *Ten commands:* First Ones, Red Legion, Tacoma, Steel Talon, BlackRock, Overwatch, Burning Star, War Dogs, Brim Fire, and Jackhammer
- *Representatives on the relations station:* Center Seat Supreme General Sharrar (Iron Fist of Kora,) Right Seat Supreme General Guth, Left Seat Supreme General Halku

Human Alliance: Left the Great Darkness seventeen hundred and ninety years prior to the invasion of Gliese, known as the Great Compromise, when all twenty-one city-states convened in the largest city-state, Athinia, to form a binding alliance between their leaders while keeping each city-state's traditional laws and customs intact. The summit to unite their world lasted for one year and one day.

- *Homeworld:* Epsilon Prime
- *Population:* Twenty-six billion
- *Structure:* The planet has twenty-one city-states that govern themselves by electing a state regent representing independent state territories. Regents come together every five years to elect a prime regent to hold the highest office and steer global policies for Epsilon

Prime. The compromise is a fragile balance for certain city-states that view each other with suspicion and spent generations at war during the Great Darkness. Even under the Alliance, some states fought at times, and it came to a tipping point during the Unification Civil War fourteen years before the current timeline. Epsilon Prime's global layout is interesting compared to other Free Worlds because every city-state only has one centralized state capital city, which acts as the governing region for each state. The surrounding massive landscape only has smaller villages and towns.

- *City-states of Epsilon Prime*: Athinia, Aetós, Rhódmore, Elpis, Macegia, Gelarhcret, Corinetus, Syrac, Delfa, Zacynth, Kythi, New-Sparta, Iskhoros, Photia, Knidonos, Thebos, Uranaea, Therisiám, Lémas, Bokós, Ampholpolis

- *Factions during the Unification Civil War*:

  ¤ *New-Sparta Pact (ten total, before Aetós declared)*: Iskhoros, Photia, Knidonos, Thebos, Uranaea, Therisiám, Lémas, Bokós, Ampholpolis

  ¤ *Athinia and the Allied States (nine total after Delfa joined)*: Elpis, Macegia, Gelarhcret, Corinetus, Syrac, Delfa, Zacynth, Kythi

  ¤ *Neutral states*: Aetós (before joining New-Sparta) and Rhódmore

- *Representatives on the relations station*: Center Seat Alexandra Onasis, Right Seat Christopher Floros (The Silent Lion), Left Seat Zachery Laskaris

Federate Corporation: The youngest recognized Free World which didn't exist during the Great Darkness. The Federate Corporation was a multi-planet conglomerate corporation with hundreds of companies under its umbrella that built a massive armada of six thousand ships in secret and took control of a depopulated air-breathing rogue world previously undiscovered within occupied space after the Frontiersmen revealed it. Chief Federate Officer

Allison Westbay of Tri-Co led the takeover of Dol'Arem, which started the first Franchise War against the Dolrinion Offensive. Once the Corporation secured the planet, they invited all employees to come to begin a new life, including civilians not previously a part of the Federate Corporation in any capacity.

- *Homeworld:* Dol'Arem
- *Population:* Fifty billion
- *Structure:* Designed into a Corporatocracy broken into four sister companies of the Corporation: Tri-Co, Genesis Foundation, Excalibur Industries, and Green Scrap Consumers. Under each sister company is a plethora of smaller businesses to which each citizen of Dol'Arem is an employee from birth. All four sister companies are run by a CFO, Chief Federate Officer, who sits on the board of directors for the Corporation alongside other high-value employees, like all three representatives to the relations station. The corporate motto, "If we work together, we win together," is a way of life forced on each employee who must maintain their micromanaged professionalism in everyday life while following the Corporate policy and procedures handbook.
- *Sister companies to the Corporation:*
  - ¤ Tri-Co: Oldest of the Four Sisters and commands the most board seats. They are the manufacturing arm for the Federate Corporation. Noted members past and present: CFO Allison Westbay and Representative Jaxson Boran.
  - ¤ Genesis Foundation: Second largest of the Four Sisters and utilizes top assets on planetary security, both cyber and physical. Human Resource employees are more often under Genesis Foundation than the other sisters. Lavlen is the capital city for Genesis Foundation on Dol'Arem. Noted members past and present: CFO Lavlen and Representative Michael Decelle.
  - ¤ Excalibur Industries: Third largest sister company commanding the largest ground armies for the Corporation,

with numerous secondary holdings of off-world drilling rights and exploration. Noted members past and present: Representative Cassandra Orwick.

¤ Green Scrap Consumers: The smallest sister company in terms of finance but has the largest employee rolls of any corporation. Green Scrap is the labor arm of the Corporation for construction, factory, farming, public services, and utilities. They hold the least number of board seats of all.

- *Representatives on the relations station:* Center Seat Jaxson Boran (the Man of Many Numbers), Right Seat Cassandra Orwick, Left Seat Michael Decelle (Huntsman of the Corporation).

Relations Station: Central location in the heart of occupied space where the Free Worlds of Humanity are unified to help govern humanity as a collective group. All five established Free Worlds built the station together in three separate parts; the Capitol Forum, Main Cylinder, and Cathedral. All three parts function independently, with five bubble embassies attached to the main cylinder for each Free Worlds' government. The Free Worlds created the station seven hundred and forty years prior, and it far exceeds its original intent by any stretch of the imagination of the founders, the first fifteen representatives. The station operates "between the lines," not being as a recognized Free, outer, or rogue world and independent within the pecking order. Upgrades and construction are ongoing for the station because its population grows with the regular arrival of refugees seeking asylum each day.

- Capitol Forum: Located under the dome at the top of the relations station where each Free Worlds' three representatives debate laws along their wall of the pentagon. The amphitheater above looks down to witness open session. All the Free Worlds have a back office to the capitol where representatives conduct business. The entire area under the dome is a popular tourist attraction. Spanning out from the forum is the famous golden road, which leads through a populated city and down the hillside to the founders' statue and other well-known locations under the dome. Civil Earth has the only straight wall in the pentagon, and then from right to left: Civil Earth, Dolrinion Offensive, Colonial Accord, Human Alliance, Federate Corporation. Each wall has three seats designed after the customs of each Free World government.

- *Three seat designs for each Free World government:*

  ¤ Civil Earth – extravagant in design and shaped like the ancient thrones of kings. All three are inlaid with gold trim lining the frame. A massive hawk's head encompasses the top rail, which peers across the pentagon. The wings travel down the side rails connecting to the armrests.

  ¤ Colonial Accord – hand-carved cherry oak; the upper portion has the Hammer of Labor on one side, and the Rose of Enduring on the other, signifying the two authorities of the Accord. Down the side rails of the oak are vines spiraling down to the Hammer of Labor and Rose of Enduring on either side of the wood framing supporting the armrests. The seats have dark leather cushions.

  ¤ Dolrinion Offensive – design of seats is cumbersome and thick in a solid mold of Corin steel and, given how much metal was needed to cast the shape, the seats are the most valuable in the pentagon.

  ¤ Human Alliance – seats made from cedar. Each armrest has a carved lion's head at the end with its mouth open as if roaring.

  ¤ Federate Corporation – like any corporation boardroom seats with tall splat backs and puffed-up cushions of generic leather. Bronze-headed round-top nails line the outer frame holding the leather to the pads. The Corporation's emblem, matching its flag, is in the center of the top rail.

  ¤ Main Cylinder: An O'Neil gravity cylinder home to seven hundred and eighty million souls spanning thirty-two hundred kilometers in length with a constant gravity rotation. People standing anywhere in the main cylinder can look up and see clouds in the artificial sky and then look past to see the ground again. Spaced out evenly across the cylinder are five embassy bubbles for each Free Worlds' society. Inside the embassies dwell roughly one million souls under the laws and governance of their respective Free World. The director's office governs the main cylinder under station command. Station command is independent of the Free Worlds and representatives under the dome. They're not considered a Free Worlds government yet have all Free Worlds privileges, including trade partnerships.

¤ Cathedral: Headquarters of the Monitoring Enforcement Regulations Chancery, MERC Guild, the chief law enforcement arm for occupied space. The large egg-shaped structure sits beneath the main cylinder and operates at the discretion of the Capitol Forum. The MERC Guild enforces all laws enacted by representatives in the pentagon and will assist local law enforcement when asked. The cathedral can sustain itself with its full production facilities. Famous locations inside the cathedral: Academy Hall, Kennel Hall, Justice Hall, Punishment Hall, and the Hall of Records.

Frontiersmen: The massive ark ships that travel through occupied space finding new air-breathing worlds. The Free Worlds tried early on, following the creation of the relations station, to contact the Frontiersmen. Their ships utilize lost Titan technology, and there's no way to locate their fleet as it randomly jumps into systems, sending powerful signal pings to give locations of new planets. Scientists from the Free Worlds believe no one resides on the ships since all forms of attempted communication go unanswered, and they seem to move in designated patterns as if a computer system controls jump algorithms. The Frontiersmen ark ships are all that remains from the Old World before technology fell into ruin.

Great Darkness/Years of Forgetting: A time-period labeled for each air-breathing world in occupied space when technology fell into ruin and some cataclysmic event that appears to be the same on each planet happened to usher humanity into a time of pre-technology to some capacity. The effect and byproduct of the Great Darkness is unique for each world. On Civil Earth and the Colonial Accord, humanity reverted to a mix of the Renaissance and Victorian-era technologies. In contrast, the Human Alliance and Dolrinion reverted to a combination of classical and early industrial revolutions, while rogue worlds reverted to Iron and Late Middle Age technologies. Some rogue worlds still view themselves as the center of the universe and haven't reinvented flight yet, and others are beginning to colonize their star systems. One constant for all occupied space is that their Years of Forgetting or Great Darkness was a harsh and unforgiving time with countless deaths and pain. Any planet that made it through the Great Darkness and survived is populated with strong-willed people because of what they had to endure. No one knows what could have had the power to cause all air-breathing planets to fall into their slumber near the same time throughout occupied space.

Great-in-Between: A vast emptiness without stars or life. At its center is the Androsian Singularity, an anomaly that causes the Androsian Effect, which alters the mental abilities of anyone who is near it for prolonged exposure. Years earlier, brilliant scientists spent too much time studying the singularity on a space station and became immune to pain and completely deranged cognitively. The Great-in-Between is a dangerous place. Because it is such a large area of space, some ship captains risk traveling through the in-Between rather than going the long way around. Other anomalies have been reported by traveling ships and Dolrinion Force Commands inside the in-Between, especially near the Yalvon Nebula. Some crews report floating lights that seem to take shapes resembling something familiar to the viewer. Other reports include ghost ships that pursue in and out from faster-than-light travel, odd radiation signatures, distress calls that sound like screams of terror, and body worm infections. The Great-in-Between is a difficult place to study because of its hostile nature.

Live-Emitting-Nano-Surveillance: LENS is a term for the cerebral connectors at the base of Dolrinion sentinel armor. The tubes connect to the brain stem of sentinels and allow their minds to function with the battle armor easily and allow for thoughts to project to command and control.

MERC Guild: Monitoring Enforcement Regulations Chancery, the chief law enforcement arm for occupied space, adheres to the Free Worlds' Relations Policy and reports directly to the fifteen representatives inside the Capitol Forum. The Guild has no justification or ability to enforce individual Free Worlds laws, nor do they need to explain their actions to anyone other than representatives of the pentagon. Agents of the Guild will act on behalf of a Free World when it comes to tracking down a criminal who fled an individual Free World's territories as long as official requests come through the Capitol Forum and its representatives. Their training takes twenty years to complete and is a closely guarded secret along with the breeding program for MERC mongrels.

Old World: A period before technology was lost across occupied space. The Free Worlds of Humanity look back into their histories with envy at the leftover relics that display how superior their ancestors were compared to current advancements. Something terrible caused the Old World to collapse, and the current technology level pales by comparison. Some rediscovered Old World tech was retrofitted to help advance the Free Worlds, though the population's ability to understand it is limited. Archaeologists have tried for countless years to unlock secrets from long-past times, but there is very little physical evidence remaining. There's no consensus on a start or end date for the Old World, and it varies slightly on each planet. The Free Worlds of Humanity came out of the Great Darkness sometime within the past two thousand years, and estimates that the Years of Forgetting lasted between three and ten thousand years; however, there isn't any agreement on that either. Best estimates suggest that the Old World ended sometime between five and fifteen thousand years prior to the invasion of Gliese. The distinction between ancestors of the Old World falls into two categories:

- Old World inhabitants – Common ancestors of the Old World who viewed Titans in two ways—seeing them as divine saviors or horrible oppressors. On each planet where digs or ancient markings come to light thanks to the investigating scientists, it appears that there is evidence of both views, which shows a divide between beliefs across each planet in occupied space.

- Titans – Mythical giants sometimes depicted as godly saints and other times shown as terrifying demons. All evidence suggests that Titans were human and had cognitive superiority to the Old World's general population. In ancient caves on Civil Earth, etchings in stone show a timeline of events spanning one thousand years. In that depiction, Titan figures, who stood centimeters higher than the people around them, had patterns drawn into their chest. Each design is unique and distinctive to a specific Titan. Going through the timeline, the same markings appear on those Titans as many as six hundred years before disappearing. Some scholars believe that Titans weren't giants. The drawings depict them so large because of their status or level of importance in the Old World. One clear understanding of anything recovered from the Old World is that Titans were not the same as humanity's ancestors, and their technology was superior.

Outer Worlds: A region in outermost occupied space where the United Union Royal Family controls fifty planets under Exalted Ruler, King Sallu Nejem. Their technology is not as advanced as the Free Worlds though they do possess faster-than-light travel and other relatively advanced technologies. The way the United Union governs their planets is considered inferior by the Free Worlds. Inner bulwark planetary systems of the Union have hot climates with constant red sandblasts surrounding Helana, home of the royal family. The thousand princes and princesses govern all territories and can trace their bloodlines to the first Exalted Ruler of the

Union, King Mathmür Shabwan, who took three wives and fathered thirty-three children.

The princes, princesses, and royal family are constantly undermining each other through conspiracy and betrayal. The Nejem Royal Family has only controlled Helana for two hundred years uncontested, having stolen the title by assaulting and conquering the Haffé family in a historical event known as the Night of Tears. Although the Union holds a guest seat inside the Capitol Forum, they are far from ever gaining a wall in the pentagon.

- *Homeworld:* Helana
- *Population:* Eighteen billion

Rogue Syndicate: An organized crime organization that controls the Highlands on the Rogue World Galma. Their leadership resides on Galma while thousands of cells operate across all occupied space owning illegal and legal businesses. Many of the organized illicit activities throughout the Free Worlds have some involvement with the diamond faces of Galma. The Highlands of Galma have multiple bosses who control their own outfits to earn profit and receive royalties from cells under their control. MERC Guild agents have a unique relationship with the Rogue Syndicate, where agents might go through great lengths to eradicate cells operating on the relations station or Free Worlds' territory but will largely ignore other operations and activities on multiple rogue worlds.

Rogue Worlds: One hundred and sixty-two air-breathing planets across occupied space that aren't considered Free Worlds or outer worlds. Some of these planets are deserted either through self-destruction, wars brought on by the Free Worlds, or a byproduct of whatever event caused the Great Darkness. The relations station estimates the total population across all rogue worlds to be around forty-eight billion. Rogue worlds are vastly different from one another. Some are still technically living in the Years of Forgetting with rudimentary technology, using swords to make war, while others have basic spaceflight abilities and a few are using recovered Old World technology to travel the stars.

Subcategory rogue worlds

Colony Worlds – Utilized by the Free Worlds and considered sovereign territories to one of the five governing societies. Colony worlds have different uses depending on which Free World claims them. The Dolrinions use most of their colonies as slave planets to harvest materials for each Force Command.

- Civil Earth colonies: Ten planets
- Colonial Accord colonies: Sixteen planets
- Dolrinion Offensive colonies: Twenty-three planets, including slave worlds
- Human Alliance colonies: Six planets
- Federate Corporation colonies: Eight planets
- Natural and Artificial Worlds – Planets that are naturally formed to sustain human life or were artificially created in their goldilocks zones by Titan technology known as world seed engines.
- Pirate Worlds – Another subcategory of rogue world for the three planets past Titans' Belt known as Draco, Martoosh, and Leo. Pirate worlds have some technological advancements while still following a primitive belief system in social terms. The pirate worlds cause constant issues for commercial and refugee transports throughout occupied space.

Station Security: Reports directly to station command and the director's office and is responsible for the relations station's main cylinder's safety. Station security officers play many roles such as law enforcement, military, customs enforcement, and peacekeepers. They command several small but well-equipped fleets that conduct diplomatic operations throughout occupied space.

Titans' Belt: Largest asteroid body in occupied space spanning several light-years that is the only known location of Corin steel ore. All five Free Worlds governing bodies have colonies inside the belt who view themselves as independent from their governments. Rebellions by miners frequently happen among Civil Earth and Colonial Accord colonies who want independence from the Free Worlds and relations station.

DISCOVER MORE

To learn more about the planets, cultures, tech and society of the
Free Worlds universe, visit the official website:

www.freeworldsofhumanity.com